THOMAS HARDY

THOMAS HARDY

TESS OF THE D'URBERVILLES

UNDER THE GREENWOOD TREE

THE WELL-BELOVED

CHANCELLOR
PRESS

Tess of the D'Urbervilles was first published in 1891
Under the Greenwood Tree was first published in 1872
The Well-Beloved was first published in 1897

An earlier version of *The Well-Beloved* was published in serial form in 1892 under
the title *The Pursuit of the Well-Beloved*

This collected volume first published in Great Britain in 1994 by
Chancellor Press an imprint of
Reed Consumer Books Ltd
Michelin House
81 Fulham Road
London sw3 6rb
and Auckland, Melbourne, Singapore and Toronto

Design and arrangement © 1994 Reed International Books Ltd

isbn 1 85152 498 3

A CIP catalogue record for this title is available at the British Library

Printed and bound in Great Britain by Cox and Wyman

Contents

TESS OF THE D'URBERVILLES

'... Poor wounded name! My bosom as a bed
Shall lodge thee.'

W. SHAKESPEARE

Author's Preface to the Fifth and Later Editions

THIS NOVEL BEING ONE WHEREIN the great campaign of the heroine begins after an event in her experience which has usually been treated as fatal to her part of protagonist, or at least as the virtual ending of her enterprises and hopes, it was quite contrary to avowed conventions that the public should welcome the book, and agree with me in holding that there was something more to be said in fiction than had been said about the shaded side of a well-known catastrophe. But the responsive spirit in which *Tess of the d'Urbervilles* has been received by the readers of England and America, would seem to prove that the plan of laying down a story on the lines of tacit opinion, instead of making it to square with the merely vocal formulae of society, is not altogether a wrong one, even when exemplified in so unequal and partial an achievement as the present. For this responsiveness I cannot refrain from expressing my thanks; and my regret is that, in a world where one so often hungers in vain for friendship, where even not to be wilfully misunderstood is felt as a kindness, I shall never meet in person these appreciative readers, male and female, and shake them by the hand.

I include amongst them the reviewers – by far the majority – who have so generously welcomed the tale. Their words show that they, like the others, have only too largely repaired my defects of narration by their own imaginative intuition.

Nevertheless, though the novel was intended to be neither didactic nor aggressive, but in the scenic parts to be representative simply, and in the contemplative to be oftener charged with impressions than with convictions, there have been objectors both to the matter and to the rendering.

The more austere of these maintain a conscientious difference of opinion concerning, among other things, subjects fit for art, and reveal an inability to associate the idea of the sub-title adjective with any but the artificial and derivative meaning which has resulted to it from the ordinances of civilization. They ignore the meaning of the word in Nature, together with all aesthetic claims upon it, not to mention the spiritual interpretation afforded by the finest side of their own Christianity. Others dissent on grounds which are intrinsically no more than

1

an assertion that the novel embodies the views of life prevalent at the end of the nineteenth century, and not those of an earlier and simpler generation – an assertion which I can only hope may be well founded. Let me repeat that a novel is an impression, not an argument; and there the matter must rest; as one is reminded by a passage which occurs in the letters of Schiller to Goethe on judges of this class: 'They are those who seek only their own ideas in a representation, and prize that which should be as higher than what is. The cause of the dispute, therefore, lies in the very first principles, and it would be utterly impossible to come to an understanding with them.' And again: 'As soon as I observe that any one, when judging of poetical representations, considers anything more important than the inner Necessity and Truth, I have done with him.'

In the introductory words to the first edition I suggested the possible advent of the genteel person who would not be able to endure something or other in these pages. That person duly appeared among the aforesaid objectors. In one case he felt upset that it was not possible for him to read the book through three times, owing to my not having made that critical effort which 'alone can prove the salvation of such an one'. In another, he objected to such vulgar articles as the Devil's pitchfork, a lodging-house carving-knife, and a shame-bought parasol, appearing in a respectable story. In another place he was a gentleman who turned Christian for half-an-hour the better to express his grief that a disrespectful phrase about the Immortals should have been used; though the same innate gentility compelled him to excuse the author in words of pity that one cannot be too thankful for: 'He does but give us of his best.' I can assure this great critic that to exclaim illogically against the gods, singular or plural, is not such an original sin of mine as he seems to imagine. True, it may have some local originality; though if Shakespeare were an authority on history, which perhaps he is not, I could show that the sin was introduced into Wessex as early as the Heptarchy itself. Says Glo'ster in *Lear*, otherwise Ina, king of that country:

> *As flies to wanton boys are we to the gods;*
> *They kill us for their sport.*

The remaining two or three manipulators of *Tess* were of the predetermined sort whom most writers and readers would gladly forget; professed literary boxers, who put on their convictions for the occasion; modern 'Hammers of Heretics'; sworn Discouragers, ever on the watch to prevent the tentative half-success from becoming the whole success later on; who pervert plain meanings, and grow personal under the name of practising the great historical method. However, they may have causes to advance, privileges to guard, traditions to keep going; some of which a mere tale-teller, who writes down how the things of the world strike him, without any ulterior intentions whatever, has overlooked, and may by pure inadvertence have run foul of when in the least aggressive mood. Perhaps some passing perception, the outcome of a dream hour, would, if generally acted on, cause such an assailant considerable inconvenience with respect to position, interests, family, servant, ox, ass, neighbour, or neighbour's wife. He therefore valiantly hides his personality behind a publisher's shutters, and cries 'Shame!' So densely is the world thronged that any shifting of positions, even the best warranted advance, galls somebody's kibe. Such shiftings often begin in sentiment, and such sentiment sometimes begins in a novel.

July 1892

The foregoing remarks were written during the early career of this story, when a spirited public and private criticism of its points was still fresh to the feelings. The pages are allowed to stand for what they are worth, as something once said; but probably they would not have been written now. Even in the short time which has elapsed since the book was first published, some of the critics who provoked the reply have 'gone down into silence', as if to remind one of the infinite unimportance of both their say and mine.

January 1895

The present edition of this novel contains a few pages that have never appeared in any previous edition. When the detached episodes were collected as stated in the preface of 1891, these pages were overlooked, though they were in the original manuscript. They occur in Chapter Ten.

Respecting the sub-title, to which allusion was made above, I may add that it was appended at the last moment, after reading the final proofs, as being the estimate left in a candid mind of the heroine's character – an estimate that nobody would be likely to dispute. It was disputed more than anything else in the book. *Melius fuerat non scribere.* But there it stands.

The novel was first published complete, in three volumes, in November 1891.

March 1912

T.H.

PHASE THE FIRST

The Maiden

♣ Chapter One ♣

ON AN EVENING IN THE latter part of May a middle-aged man was walking homeward from Shaston to the village of Marlott, in the adjoining Vale of Blakemore or Blackmoor. The pair of legs that carried him were rickety, and there was a bias in his gait which inclined him somewhat to the left of a straight line. He occasionally gave a smart nod, as if in confirmation of some opinion, though he was not thinking of anything in particular. An empty egg-basket was slung upon his arm, the nap of his hat was ruffled, a patch being quite worn away at its brim where his thumb came in taking it off. Presently he was met by an elderly parson astride on a gray mare, who, as he rode, hummed a wandering tune.

'Good night t'ee,' said the man with the basket.

'Good night, Sir John,' said the parson.

The pedestrian, after another pace or two, halted, and turned round.

'Now, sir, begging your pardon; we met last market-day on this road about this time, and I zaid "Good night", and you made reply "*Good night, Sir John*", as now.'

'I did,' said the parson.

'And once before that – near a month ago.'

'I may have.'

'Then what might your meaning be in calling me "Sir John" these different times, when I be plain Jack Durbeyfield, the haggler?'

The parson rode a step or two nearer.

'It was only my whim,' he said; and, after a moment's hesitation: 'It was on account of a discovery I made some little time ago, whilst I was hunting up pedigrees for the new county history. I am Parson Tringham, the antiquary, of Stagfoot Lane. Don't you really know, Durbeyfield, that you are the lineal representative of the ancient and knightly family of the d'Urbervilles, who derive their descent from Sir Pagan d'Urberville, that renowned knight who came from Normandy with William the Conqueror, as appears by Battle Abbey Roll?'

'Never heard it before, sir!'

'Well it's true. Throw up your chin a moment, so that I may catch the profile of your face better. Yes, that's the d'Urberville nose and chin – a little debased. Your ancestor was one of the twelve knights who assisted the Lord of Estremavilla in Normandy in his conquest of Glamorganshire. Branches of your family held manors over all this part of England; their names appear in the Pipe Rolls in the time of King Stephen. In the reign of King John one of them was rich enough to give a manor to the Knights Hospitallers; and in Edward the Second's time your forefather Brian was summoned to Westminster to attend the great Council there. You declined a little in Oliver Cromwell's time, but to no serious extent, and in Charles the Second's reign you were made Knights of the Royal Oak for your loyalty. Aye, there have been generations of Sir Johns among you, and if knighthood were hereditary, like a baronetcy, as it practically was in old times, when men were knighted from father to son, you would be Sir John now.'

'Ye don't say so!'

'In short,' concluded the parson, decisively smacking his leg with his switch, 'there's hardly such another family in England.'

'Daze my eyes, and isn't there?' said Durbeyfield. 'And here have I been knocking about, year after year, from pillar to post, as if I was no more than the commonest feller in the parish ... And how long hev this news about me been knowed, Pa'son Tringham?'

The clergyman explained that, as far as he was aware, it had quite died out of knowledge, and could hardly be said to be known at all. His own investigations had begun on a day in the preceding spring when, having been engaged in tracing the vicissitudes of the d'Urberville family, he had observed Durbeyfield's name on his waggon, and had thereupon been led to make enquiries about his father and grandfather till he had no doubt on the subject.

'At first I resolved not to disturb you with such a useless piece of information,' said he. 'However, our impulses are too strong for our judgment sometimes. I thought you might perhaps know something of it all the while.'

'Well, I have heard once or twice, 'tis true, that my family had seen better days afore they came to Blackmoor. But I took no notice o't, thinking it to mean that we had once kept two horses where we now keep only one. I've got a wold silver spoon, and a wold graven seal at home, too; but, Lord, what's a spoon and seal? ... And to think that I and these noble d'Urbervilles were one flesh all the time. 'Twas said that my gr't-grandfer had secrets, and didn't care to talk of where he came from ... And where do we raise our smoke, now, parson, if I may make so bold; I mean, where do we d'Urbervilles live?'

'You don't live anywhere. You are extinct – as a county family.'

'That's bad.'

'Yes – what the mendacious family chronicles call extinct in the male line – that is, gone down – gone under.'

'Then where do we lie?'

'At Kingsbere-sub-Greenhill: rows and rows of you in your vaults, with your effigies under Purbeck-marble canopies.'

'And where be our family mansions and estates?'

'You haven't any.'

'Oh? No lands neither?'

'None; though you once had 'em in abundance, as I said, for your family consisted of numerous branches. In this county there was a seat of yours at Kingsbere, and another at Sherton, and another at Millpond, and another at Lullstead, and another at Wellbridge.'

'And shall we ever come into our own again?'

'Ah – that I can't tell!'

'And what had I better do about it, sir?' asked Durbeyfield, after a pause.

'Oh – nothing, nothing; except chasten yourself with the thought of "how are the mighty fallen". It is a fact of some interest to the local historian and genealogist, nothing more. There are several families among the cottagers of this county of almost equal lustre. Good night.'

'But you'll turn back and have a quart of beer wi' me on the strength o't, Pa'son Tringham? There's a very pretty brew in tap at The Pure Drop – though, to be sure, not so good as at Rolliver's.'

'No, thank you – not this evening, Durbeyfield. You've had enough already.' Concluding thus the parson rode on his way, with doubts as to his discretion in retailing this curious bit of lore.

When he was gone Durbeyfield walked a few steps in a profound reverie, and then sat down upon the grassy bank by the roadside, depositing his basket before him. In a few minutes a youth appeared in the distance, walking in the same direction as that which had been pursued by Durbeyfield. The latter, on seeing him, held up his hand, and the lad quickened his pace and came near.

'Boy, take up that basket! I want 'ee to go on an errand for me.'

The lath-like stripling frowned. 'Who be you, then, John Durbeyfield, to order me about and call me "boy"? You know my name as well as I know yours!'

'Do you, do you? That's the secret – that's the secret! Now obey my orders, and take the message I'm going to charge 'ee wi' . . . Well, Fred, I don't mind telling you that the secret is that I'm one of a noble race – it has been just found out by me this present afternoon, P.M.' And as he made the announcement, Durbeyfield, declining from his sitting position, luxuriously stretched himself out upon the bank among the daisies.

9

The lad stood before Durbeyfield, and contemplated his length from crown to toe.

'Sir John d'Urberville – that's who I am,' continued the prostrate man. 'That is if knights were baronets – which they be. 'Tis recorded in history all about me. Dost know of such a place, lad, as Kingsbere-sub-Greenhill?'

'Ees. I've been there to Greenhill Fair.'

'Well, under the church of that city there lie – '

''Tisn't a city, the place I mean; leastwise 'twaddn' when I was there – 'twas a little one-eyed, blinking sort o' place.'

'Never you mind the place, boy, that's not the question before us. Under the church of that there parish lie my ancestors – hundreds of 'em – in coats of mail and jewels, in gr't lead coffins weighing tons and tons. There's not a man in the county o' South-Wessex that's got grander and nobler skillentons in his family than I.'

'Oh?'

'Now take up that basket, and goo on to Marlott, and when you've come to The Pure Drop Inn, tell 'em to send a horse and carriage to me immed'ately, to carry me hwome. And in the bottom o' the carriage they be to put a noggin o'rum in a small bottle, and chalk it up to my account. And when you've done that goo on to my house with the basket, and tell my wife to put away that washing, because she needn't finish it, and wait till I come hwome, as I've news to tell her.'

As the lad stood in a dubious attitude, Durbeyfield put his hand in his pocket, and produced a shilling, one of the chronically few that he possessed.

'Here's for your labour, lad.'

This made a difference in the young man's estimate of the position.

'Yes, Sir John. Thank 'ee. Anything else I can do for 'ee, Sir John?'

'Tell 'em at hwome that I should like for supper, – well, lamb's fry if they can get it; and if they can't, black-pot; and if they can't get that, well, chitterlings will do.'

'Yes, Sir John.'

The boy took up the basket, and as he set out the notes of a brass band were heard from the direction of the village.

'What's that?' said Durbeyfield. 'Not on account o' I?'

''Tis the women's club-walking, Sir John. Why, your da'ter is one o' the members.'

'To be sure – I'd quite forgot it in my thoughts of greater things! Well, vamp on to Marlott, will ye, and order that carriage, and maybe I'll drive round and inspect the club.'

The lad departed, and Durbeyfield lay waiting on the grass and daisies in the evening sun. Not a soul passed that way for a long while, and the faint notes of the band were the only human sounds audible within the rim of blue hills.

❦ Chapter Two ❧

THE VILLAGE OF MARLOTT lay amid the north-eastern undulations of the beautiful Vale of Blakemore or Blackmoor aforesaid, an engirdled and secluded region, for the most part untrodden as yet by tourist or land-scape-painter, though within a four hours' journey from London.

It is a vale whose acquaintance is best made by viewing it from the summits of the hills that surround it – except perhaps during the droughts of summer. An unguided ramble into its recesses in bad weather is apt to engender dissatisfaction with its narrow, tortuous, and miry ways.

This fertile and sheltered tract of country, in which the fields are never brown and the springs never dry, is bounded on the south by the bold chalk ridge that embraces the prominences of Hambledon Hill, Bulbar-row, Nettlecombe-Tout, Dogbury, High Stoy, and Bubb Down. The travel-ler from the coast, who, after plodding northward for a score of miles over calcareous downs and corn-lands, suddenly reaches the verge of one of these escarpments, is surprised and delighted to behold, extended like a map beneath him, a country differing absolutely from that which he has passed through. Behind him the hills are open, the sun blazes down upon fields so large as to give an unenclosed character to the landscape, the lanes are white, the hedges low and plashed, the atmos-phere colourless. Here, in the valley, the world seems to be constructed upon a smaller and more delicate scale; the fields are mere paddocks, so reduced that from this height their hedgerows appear a network of dark green threads overspreading the paler green of the grass. The atmosphere beneath is languorous, and is so tinged with azure that what artists call the middle distance partakes also of that hue, while the horizon beyond is of the deepest ultramarine. Arable lands are few and limited; with but slight exceptions the prospect is a broad rich mass of grass and trees, mantling minor hills and dales within the major. Such is the Vale of Blackmoor.

The district is of historic, no less than of topographical interest. The

Vale was known in former times as the Forest of White Hart, from a curious legend of King Henry III's reign, in which the killing by a certain Thomas de la Lynd of a beautiful white hart which the king had run down and spared, was made the occasion of a heavy fine. In those days, and till comparatively recent times, the country was densely wooded. Even now, traces of its earlier condition are to be found in the old oak copses and irregular belts of timber that yet survive upon its slopes, and the hollow-trunked trees that shade so many of its pastures.

The forests have departed, but some old customs of their shades remain. Many, however, linger only in a metamorphosed or disguised form. The May-Day dance, for instance, was to be discerned on the afternoon under notice, in the guise of the club revel, or 'club-walking', as it was there called.

It was an interesting event to the younger inhabitants of Marlott, though its real interest was not observed by the participators in the ceremony. Its singularity lay less in the retention of a custom of walking in procession and dancing on each anniversary than in the members being solely women. In men's clubs such celebrations were, though expiring, less uncommon; but either the natural shyness of the softer sex, or a sarcastic attitude on the part of male relatives, had denuded such women's clubs as remained (if any other did) of this their glory and consummation. The club of Marlott alone lived to uphold the local Cerealia. It had walked for hundreds of years, if not as benefit-club, as votive sisterhood of some sort; and it walked still.

The banded ones were all dressed in white gowns – a gay survival from Old Style days, when cheerfulness and May-time were synonyms – days before the habit of taking long views had reduced emotions to a monotonous average. Their first exhibition of themselves was in a processional march of two and two round the parish. Ideal and real clashed slightly as the sun lit up their figures against the green hedges and creeper-laced house-fronts; for, though the whole troop wore white garments, no two whites were alike among them. Some approached pure blanching; some had a bluish pallor; some worn by the older characters (which had possibly lain by folded for many a year) inclined to a cadaverous tint, and to a Georgian style.

In addition to the distinction of a white frock, every woman and girl carried in her right hand a peeled willow wand, and in her left a bunch of white flowers. The peeling of the former, and the selection of the latter, had been an operation of personal care.

There were a few middle-aged and even elderly women in the train, their silver-wiry hair and wrinkled faces, scourged by time and trouble, having almost a grotesque, certainly a pathetic, appearance in such a jaunty situation. In a true view, perhaps, there was more to be gathered and told of each anxious and experienced one, to whom the years were drawing nigh when she should say, 'I have no pleasure in them', than of her juvenile comrades. But let the elder be passed over here for those under whose bodices the life throbbed quick and warm.

The young girls formed, indeed, the majority of the band, and their heads of luxuriant hair reflected in the sunshine every tone of gold, and black, and brown. Some had beautiful eyes, others a beautiful nose, others a beautiful mouth and figure; few, if any, had all. A difficulty of arranging their lips in this crude exposure to public scrutiny, an inability to balance their heads, and to dissociate self-consciousness from their features, was apparent in them, and showed that they were genuine country girls, unaccustomed to many eyes.

And as each and all of them were warmed without by the sun, so each had a private little sun for her soul to bask in; some dream, some affection, some hobby, at least some remote and distant hope which, though perhaps starving to nothing, still lived on, as hopes will. Thus they were all cheerful, and many of them merry.

They came round by The Pure Drop Inn, and were turning out of the high road to pass through a wicket-gate into the meadows, when one of the women said

'The Lord-a-Lord! Why, Tess Durbeyfield, if there isn't thy father riding hwome in a carriage!'

A young member of the band turned her head at the exclamation. She was a fine and handsome girl – not handsomer than some others, possibly – but her mobile peony mouth and large innocent eyes added eloquence to colour and shape. She wore a red ribbon in her hair, and was the only one of the white company who could boast of such a pronounced adornment. As she looked round Durbeyfield was seen moving along the road in a chaise belonging to The Pure Drop, driven by a frizzle-headed brawny damsel with her gown-sleeves rolled above her elbows. This was the cheerful servant of that establishment, who, in her part of factotum, turned groom and ostler at times. Durbeyfield, leaning back, and with his eyes closed luxuriously, was waving his hand above his head, and singing in a slow recitative –

'I've-got-a-gr't-family-vault-at-Kingsbere – and knighted-forefathers-in-lead-coffins-there!'

The clubbists tittered, except the girl called Tess – in whom a slow heat seemed to rise at the sense that her father was making himself foolish in their eyes.

'He's tired, that's all,' she said hastily, 'and he has got a lift home, because our own horse has to rest to-day.'

'Bless thy simplicity, Tess,' said her companions. 'He's got his market-nitch. Haw-haw!'

'Look here; I don't walk another inch with you, if you say any jokes about him!' Tess cried, and the colour upon her cheeks spread over her face and neck. In a moment her eyes grew moist, and her glance drooped to the ground. Perceiving that they had really pained her they said no more, and order again prevailed. Tess's pride would not allow her to turn her head again, to learn what her father's meaning was, if he had any; and thus she moved on with the whole body to the enclosure where there was to be dancing on the green. By the time the spot was reached she had recovered her equanimity, and tapped her neighbour with her wand and talked as usual.

Tess Durbeyfield at this time of her life was a mere vessel of emotion untinctured by experience. The dialect was on her tongue to some extent, despite the village school: the characteristic intonation of that dialect for this district being the voicing approximately rendered by the syllable UR, probably as rich an utterance as any to be found in human speech. The pouted-up deep red mouth to which this syllable was native had hardly as yet settled into its definite shape, and her lower lip had a way of thrusting the middle of her top one upward, when they closed together after a word.

Phases of her childhood lurked in her aspect still. As she walked along to-day, for all her bouncing handsome womanliness, you could sometimes see her twelfth year in her cheeks, or her ninth sparkling from her eyes; and even her fifth would flit over the curves of her mouth now and then.

Yet few knew, and still fewer considered this. A small minority, mainly strangers, would look long at her in casually passing by, and grow momentarily fascinated by her freshness, and wonder if they would ever see her again: but to almost everybody she was a fine picturesque country girl, and no more.

Nothing was seen or heard further of Durbeyfield in his triumphal chariot under the conduct of the ostleress, and the club having entered the allotted space, dancing began. As there were no men in the company the girls danced at first with each other, but when the hour for the close of labour drew on, the masculine inhabitants of the village, together with other idlers and pedestrians, gathered round the spot, and appeared inclined to negotiate for a partner.

Among these on-lookers were three young men of a superior class, carrying small knapsacks strapped to their shoulders, and stout sticks in their hands. Their general likeness to each other, and their consecutive ages, would almost have suggested that they might be, what in fact they were, brothers. The eldest wore the white tie, high waistcoat, and thin-brimmed hat of the regulation curate; the second was the normal under-graduate; the appearance of the third and youngest would hardly have been sufficient to characterize him; there was an uncribbed, uncabined aspect in his eyes and attire, implying that he had hardly as yet found the entrance to his professional groove. That he was a desultory tentative student of something and everything might only have been predicted of him.

These three brethren told casual acquaintance that they were spending their Whitsun holidays in a walking tour through the Vale of Blackmoor, their course being south-westerly from the town of Shaston on the north-east.

They leant over the gate by the highway, and inquired as to the meaning of the dance and the white-frocked maids. The two elder of the brothers were plainly not intending to linger more than a moment, but the spectacle of a bevy of girls dancing without male partners seemed to amuse the third, and make him in no hurry to move on. He unstrapped his knapsack, put it, with his stick, on the hedge-bank, and opened the gate.

'What are you going to do, Angel?' asked the eldest.

'I am inclined to go and have a fling with them. Why not all of us – just for a minute or two – it will not detain us long?'

'No – no; nonsense!' said the first. 'Dancing in public with a troop of country hoydens – suppose we should be seen! Come along, or it will be dark before we get to Stourcastle, and there's no place we can sleep at nearer than that; besides, we must get through another chapter of *A Counterblast to Agnosticism* before we turn in, now I have taken the trouble to bring the book.'

'All right – I'll overtake you and Cuthbert in five minutes; don't stop; I give my word that I will, Felix.'

The two elder reluctantly left him and walked on, taking their brother's knapsack to relieve him in following, and the youngest entered the field.

'This is a thousand pities,' he said gallantly, to two or three of the girls nearest him, as soon as there was a pause in the dance. 'Where are your partners, my dears?'

'They've not left off work yet,' answered one of the boldest. 'They'll be here by and by. Till then, will you be one, sir?'

'Certainly. But what's one among so many!'

'Better than none. 'Tis melancholy work facing and footing it to one of your own sort, and no clipsing and colling at all. Now, pick and choose.'

''Ssh – don't be so for'ard!' said a shyer girl.

The young man, thus invited, glanced them over, and attempted some discrimination; but, as the group were all so new to him, he could not very well exercise it. He took almost the first that came to hand, which was not the speaker, as she had expected; nor did it happen to be

Tess Durbeyfield. Pedigree, ancestral skeletons, monumental record, the d'Urberville lineaments, did not help Tess in her life's battle as yet, even to the extent of attracting to her a dancing-partner over the heads of the commonest peasantry. So much for Norman blood unaided by Victorian lucre.

The name of the eclipsing girl, whatever it was, has not been handed down; but she was envied by all as the first who enjoyed the luxury of a masculine partner that evening. Yet such was the force of example that the village young men, who had not hastened to enter the gate while no intruder was in the way, now dropped in quickly, and soon the couples became leavened with rustic youth to a marked extent, till at length the plainest woman in the club was no longer compelled to foot it on the masculine side of the figure.

The church clock struck, when suddenly the student said that he must leave – he had been forgetting himself – he had to join his companions. As he fell out of the dance his eyes lighted on Tess Durbeyfield, whose own large orbs wore, to tell the truth, the faintest aspect of reproach that he had not chosen her. He, too, was sorry then that, owing to her backwardness, he had not observed her; and with that in his mind he left the pasture.

On account of his long delay he started in a flying-run down the lane westward, and had soon passed the hollow and mounted the next rise. He had not yet overtaken his brothers, but he paused to get breath, and looked back. He could see the white figures of the girls in the green enclosure whirling about as they had whirled when he was among them. They seemed to have quite forgotten him already.

All of them, except, perhaps, one. This white shape stood apart by the hedge alone. From her position he knew it to be the pretty maiden with whom he had not danced. Trifling as the matter was, he yet instinctively felt that she was hurt by his oversight. He wished that he had asked her; he wished that he had inquired her name. She was so modest, so expressive, she had looked so soft in her thin white gown that he felt he had acted stupidly.

However, it could not be helped, and turning, and bending himself to a rapid walk, he dismissed the subject from his mind.

❧ Chapter Three ❧

As FOR TESS DURBEYFIELD, she did not easily dislodge the incident from her consideration. She had no spirit to dance again for a long time, though she might have had plenty of partners; but, ah! they did not speak so nicely as the strange young man had done. It was not till the rays of the sun had absorbed the young stranger's retreating figure on the hill that she shook off her temporary sadness and answered her would-be partner in the affirmative.

She remained with her comrades till dusk, and participated with a certain zest in the dancing; though, being heart-whole as yet, she enjoyed treading a measure purely for its own sake; little divining when she saw 'the soft torments, the bitter sweets, the pleasing pains, and the agreeable distresses' of those girls who had been wooed and won, what she herself was capable of in that kind. The struggles and wrangles of the lads for her hand in a jig were an amusement to her – no more; and when they became fierce she rebuked them.

She might have stayed even later, but the incident of her father's odd appearance and manner returned upon the girl's mind to make her anxious, and wondering what had become of him she dropped away from the dancers and bent her steps towards the end of the village at which the parental cottage lay.

While yet many score yards off, other rhythmic sounds than those she had quitted became audible to her; sounds that she knew well – so well. They were a regular series of thumpings from the interior of the house, occasioned by the violent rocking of a cradle upon a stone floor, to which movement a feminine voice kept time by singing, in a vigorous gallopade, the favourite ditty of 'The Spotted Cow' –

> I saw her lie do'-own in yon'-der green gro'-ve;
> Come, love!' and I'll tell' you where!'

The cradle-rocking and the song would cease simultaneously for a moment, and an exclamation at highest vocal pitch would take the place of the melody.

'God bless thy diment eyes! And thy waxen cheeks! And thy cherry mouth! And thy Cubit's thighs! And every bit o' thy blessed body!'

After this invocation the rocking and the singing would recommence, and the 'Spotted Cow' proceed as before. So matters stood when Tess opened the door, and paused upon the mat within it surveying the scene.

The interior, in spite of the melody, struck upon the girl's senses with

17

an unspeakable dreariness. From the holiday gaieties of the field – the white gowns, the nosegays, the willow-wands, the whirling movements on the green, the flash of gentle sentiment towards the stranger – to the yellow melancholy of this one-cradled spectacle, what a step! Besides the jar of contrast there came to her a chill self-reproach that she had not returned sooner, to help her mother in these domesticities, instead of indulging herself out-of-doors.

There stood her mother amid the group of children, as Tess had left her, hanging over the Monday washing-tub, which had now, as always, lingered on to the end of the week. Out of that tub had come the day before – Tess felt it with a dreadful sting of remorse – the very white frock upon her back which she had so carelessly greened about the skirt on the damping grass – which had been wrung up and ironed by her mother's own hands.

As usual, Mrs Durbeyfield was balanced on one foot beside the tub, the other being engaged in the aforesaid business of rocking her youngest child. The cradle-rockers had done hard duty for so many years, under the weight of so many children, on that flagstone floor, that they were worn nearly flat, in consequence of which a huge jerk accompanied each swing of the cot, flinging the baby from side to side like a weaver's shuttle, as Mrs Durbeyfield, excited by her song, trod the rocker with all the spring that was left in her after a long day's seething in the suds.

Nick-knock, nick-knock, went the cradle; the candle-flame stretched itself tall, and began jigging up and down; the water dribbled from the matron's elbows, and the song galloped on to the end of the verse, Mrs Durbeyfield regarding her daughter the while. Even now, when burdened with a young family, Joan Durbeyfield was a passionate lover of tune. No ditty floated into Blackmoor Vale from the outer world but Tess's mother caught up its notation in a week.

There still faintly beamed from the woman's features something of the freshness, and even the prettiness, of her youth; rendering it probable that the personal charms which Tess could boast of were in main part her mother's gift, and therefore unknightly, unhistorical.

'I'll rock the cradle for 'ee, mother,' said the daughter gently. 'Or I'll take off my best frock and help you wring up? I thought you had finished long ago.'

Her mother bore Tess no ill-will for leaving the house-work to her singlehanded efforts for so long; indeed, Joan seldom upbraided her thereon at any time, feeling but slightly the lack of Tess's assistance whilst her instinctive plan for relieving herself of her labours lay in postponing them. To-night, however, she was even in a blither mood than usual. There was a dreaminess, a preoccupation, an exaltation, in the maternal look which the girl could not understand.

'Well, I'm glad you've come,' her mother said, as soon as the last note had passed out of her. 'I want to go and fetch your father; but what's more'n that, I want to tell 'ee what have happened. Y'll be fess enough, my poppet, when th'st know!' (Mrs Durbeyfield habitually spoke the dialect; her daughter who had passed the Sixth Standard in the National School under a London-trained mistress, spoke two languages; the dialect at home, more or less; ordinary English abroad and to persons of quality.)

'Since I've been away?' Tess asked.

'Ay!'

'Had it anything to do with father's making such a mommet of himself in thik carriage this afternoon? Why did 'er? I felt inclined to sink into the ground with shame!'

'That wer all a part of the larry! We've been found to be the greatest gentlefolk in the whole county – reaching all back long before Oliver Grumble's time – to the days of the Pagan Turks – with monuments, and vaults, and crests, and 'scutcheons, and the Lord knows what all. In Saint Charles's days we was made Knights o' the Royal Oak, our real name being d'Urberville! ... Don't that make your bosom plim? 'Twas on this account that your father rode home in the vlee; not because he'd been drinking, as people supposed.'

'I'm glad of that. Will it do us any good, mother?'

'O yes! 'Tis thoughted that great things may come o't. No doubt a mampus of volk of our own rank will be down here in their carriage as soon as 'tis known. Your father learnt it on his way hwome from Shaston and he has been telling me the whole pedigree of the matter.'

'Where is father now?' asked Tess suddenly.

Her mother gave irrelevant information by way of answer: 'He called to see the doctor to-day in Shaston. It is not consumption at all, it seems. It is fat round his heart, 'a says. There, it is like this.' Joan Durbeyfield, as she spoke, curved a sodden thumb and forefinger to the shape of the letter C, and used the other forefinger as a pointer. ' "At the present moment," he says to your father, "your heart is enclosed all round there, and all round there; this space is still open," 'a says. "As soon as it do meet, so," ' – Mrs Durbeyfield closed her fingers into a circle complete – ' "off you will go like a shadder, Mr Durbeyfield," 'a says.

'You mid last ten years; you mid go off in ten months, or ten days." '

Tess looked alarmed. Her father possibly to go behind the eternal cloud so soon, notwithstanding this sudden greatness!

'But where *is* father?' she asked again.

Her mother put on a deprecating look. 'Now don't you be bursting out angry! The poor man – he felt so rafted after his uplifting by the pa'son's news – that he went up to Rolliver's half an hour ago. He do want to get up his strength for his journey to-morrow with that load of beehives, which must be delivered, family or no. He'll have to start shortly after twelve to-night, as the distance is so long.'

'Get up his strength!' said Tess impetuously, the tears welling in her eyes. 'O my God! Go to a public-house to get up his strength! And you as well agreed as he, mother!'

Her rebuke and her mood seemed to fill the whole room, and to impart a cowed look to the furniture, and candle, and children playing about, and to her mother's face.

'No,' said the latter touchily, 'I be not agreed. I have been waiting for 'ee to bide and keep house while I go to fetch him.'

'I'll go.'

'O no, Tess. You see, it would be no use.'

Tess did not expostulate. She knew what her mother's objection meant. Mrs Durbeyfield's jacket and bonnet were already hanging slily upon a chair by her side, in readiness for this contemplated jaunt, the reason for which the matron deplored more than its necessity.

'And take the *Compleat Fortune-Teller* to the outhouse,' Joan continued, rapidly wiping her hands, and donning the garments.

The *Compleat Fortune-Teller* was an old thick volume, which lay on a table at her elbow, so worn by pocketing that the margins had reached the edge of the type. Tess took it up, and her mother started.

This going to hunt up her shiftless husband at the inn was one of Mrs Durbeyfield's still extant enjoyments in the muck and muddle of rearing children. To discover him at Rolliver's, to sit there for an hour or two by his side and dismiss all thought and care of the children during the interval, made her happy. A sort of halo, an occidental glow, came over life then. Troubles and other realities took on themselves a metaphysical impalpability, sinking to mere mental phenomena for serene contemplation, and no longer stood as pressing concretions which chafed body and soul. The youngsters, not immediately within sight, seemed rather bright and desirable appurtenances than otherwise; the incidents of daily life were not without humorousness and jollity in their aspect there. She felt a little as she had used to feel when she sat by her now wedded husband in the same spot during his wooing, shutting her eyes to his defects of character, and regarding him only in his ideal presentation as lover.

Tess, being left alone with the younger children, went first to the outhouse with the fortune-telling book, and stuffed it into the thatch. A curious fetichistic fear of this grimy volume on the part of her mother prevented her ever allowing it to stay in the house all night, and hither it was brought back whenever it had been consulted. Between the mother, with her fast-perishing lumber of superstitions, folk-lore, dialect, and orally transmitted ballads, and the daughter, with her trained National teachings and Standard knowledge under an infinitely Revised Code, there was a gap of two hundred years as ordinarily understood. When they were together the Jacobean and the Victorian ages were juxtaposed.

Returning along the garden path Tess mused on what the mother could have wished to ascertain from the book on this particular day. She guessed the recent ancestral discovery to bear upon it, but did not divine that it solely concerned herself. Dismissing this, however, she busied herself with sprinkling the linen dried during the daytime, in company with her nine-year-old brother Abraham, and her sister Eliza-Louisa of twelve and a half, called "Liza-Lu', the youngest ones being put to bed. There was an interval of four years and more between Tess and the next of the family, the two who had filled the gap having died in their infancy, and this lent her a deputy-maternal attitude when she was alone with her juniors. Next in juvenility to Abraham came two more girls, Hope and Modesty; then a boy of three, and then the baby, who had just completed his first year.

All these young souls were passengers in the Durbeyfield ship – entirely dependent on the judgment of the two Durbeyfield adults for their pleasures, their necessities, their health, even their existence. If the heads of the Durbeyfield household chose to sail into difficulty, disaster, starvation, disease, degradation, death, thither were these half-dozen little captives under hatches compelled to sail with them – six helpless creatures, who had never been asked if they wished for life on any terms, much less if they wished for it on such hard conditions as were involved in being of the shiftless house of Durbeyfield. Some people would like to know whence the poet whose philosophy is in these days deemed as profound and trustworthy as his song is breezy and pure, gets his authority for speaking of 'Nature's holy plan'.

It grew later, and neither father nor mother reappeared. Tess looked out of the door, and took a mental journey through Marlott. The village was shutting its eyes. Candles and lamps were being put out everywhere: she could inwardly behold the extinguisher and the extended hand.

Her mother's fetching simply meant one more to fetch. Tess began to perceive that a man in indifferent health, who proposed to start on a journey before one in the morning, ought not to be at an inn at this late hour celebrating his ancient blood.

'Abraham,' she said to her little brother, 'do you put on your hat – you bain't afraid? – and go up to Rolliver's, and see what has gone wi' father and mother.'

The boy jumped promptly from his seat, and opened the door, and the night swallowed him up. Half an hour passed yet again; neither man, woman, nor child returned. Abraham, like his parents, seemed to have been limed and caught by the ensnaring inn.

'I must go myself,' she said.

'Liza-Lu then went to bed, and Tess, locking them all in, started on her way up the dark and crooked lane or street not made for hasty progress; a street laid out before inches of land had value, and when one-handed clocks sufficiently subdivided the day.

❦ Chapter Four ❦

ROLLIVER'S INN, THE SINGLE alehouse at this end of the long and broken village, could only boast of an off-licence; hence, as nobody could legally drink on the premises, the amount of overt accommodation for consumers was strictly limited to a little board about six inches wide and two yards long, fixed to the garden palings by pieces of wire, so as to form a ledge. On this board thirsty strangers deposited their cups as they stood in the road and drank, and threw the dregs on the dusty ground to the pattern of Polynesia, and wished they could have a restful seat inside.

Thus the strangers. But there were also local customers who felt the same wish; and where there's a will there's a way.

In a large bedroom upstairs, the window of which was thickly curtained with a great woollen shawl lately discarded by the landlady Mrs Rolliver, were gathered on this evening nearly a dozen persons, all seeking beatitude; all old inhabitants of the nearer end of Marlott, and frequenters of this retreat. Not only did the distance to The Pure Drop, the fully-licensed tavern at the further part of the dispersed village, render its accommodation practically unavailable for dwellers at this end; but the far more serious question, the quality of the liquor, confirmed the prevalent opinion that it was better to drink with Rolliver in a corner of the housetop than with the other landlord in a wide house.

A gaunt four-post bedstead which stood in the room afforded sitting-space for several persons gathered round three of its sides; a couple more men had elevated themselves on a chest of drawers; another rested on the oak-carved 'cwoffer'; two on the wash-stand; another on the stool; and thus all were, somehow, seated at their ease. The stage of mental comfort to which they had arrived at this hour was one wherein their souls expanded beyond their skins, and spread their personalities warmly through the room. In this process the chamber and its furniture grew more and more dignified and luxurious; the shawl hanging at the window took upon itself the richness of tapestry; the brass handles of the chest of drawers were as golden knockers; and the carved bed-posts seemed to have some kinship with the magnificent pillars of Solomon's temple.

Mrs Durbeyfield, having quickly walked hitherward after parting from Tess, opened the front door, crossed the downstairs room, which was in deep gloom, and then unfastened the stair-door like one whose fingers knew the tricks of the latches well. Her ascent of the crooked staircase was a slower process, and her face, as it rose into the light above the last stair, encountered the gaze of all the party assembled in the bedroom.

' – Being a few private friends I've asked in to keep up club-walking at my own expense,' the landlady exclaimed at the sound of footsteps, as glibly as a child repeating the Catechism, while she peered over the stairs. 'Oh, 'tis you, Mrs Durbeyfield – Lard – how you frightened me! – I thought it might be some gaffer sent by Gover'ment.'

Mrs Durbeyfield was welcomed with glances and nods by the remainder of the conclave, and turned to where her husband sat. He was humming absently to himself, in a low tone: 'I be as good as some folks here and there! I've got a great family vault at Kingsbere-sub-Greenhill, and finer skillentons than any man in Wessex!'

'I've something to tell 'ee that's come into my head about that – a grand projick!' whispered his cheerful wife. 'Here, John, don't 'ee see me?' She nudged him, while he, looking through her as through a window-pane, went on with his recitative.

'Hush! Don't 'ee sing so loud, my good man,' said the landlady; 'in case any member of the Gover'ment should be passing, and take away my licends.'

'He's told 'ee what's happened to us, I suppose?' asked Mrs Durbeyfield.

'Yes – in a way. D'ye think there's any money hanging by it?'

'Ah, that's the secret,' said Joan Durbeyfield sagely. 'However, 'tis well to be kin to a coach, even if you don't ride in 'en.' She dropped her public voice, and continued in a low tone to her husband: 'I've been thinking since you brought the news that there's a great rich lady out by Trantridge, on the edge o' The Chase, of the name of d'Urberville.'

'Hey – what's that?' said Sir John.

She repeated the information. 'That lady must be our relation,' she said. 'And my projick is to send Tess to claim kin.'

'There is a lady of the name, now you mention it,' said Durbeyfield. 'Pa'son Tringham didn't think of that. But she's nothing beside we – a junior branch of us, no doubt, hailing along since King Norman's day.'

While this question was being discussed neither of the pair noticed, in their preoccupation, that little Abraham had crept into the room, and was awaiting an opportunity of asking them to return.

'She is rich, and she'd be sure to take notice o' the maid,' continued Mrs Durbeyfield; 'and 'twill be a very good thing. I don't see why two branches o' one family should not be on visiting terms.'

'Yes; and we'll all claim kin!' said Abraham brightly from under the bedstead. 'And we'll all go and see her when Tess has gone to live with her; and we'll ride in her coach and wear black clothes!'

'How do you come here, child? What nonsense be ye talking! Go away, and play on the stairs till father and mother be ready! ... Well, Tess ought to go to this other member of our family. She'd be sure to win the lady – Tess would; and likely enough 'twould lead to some noble gentleman marrying her. In short, I know it.'

'How?'

'I tried her fate in the *Fortune-Teller*, and it brought out that very thing! ... You should ha' seen how pretty she looked to-day; her skin is as sumple as a duchess's.'

'What says the maid herself to going?'

'I've not asked her. She don't know there is any such lady-relation yet. But it would certainly put her in the way of a grand marriage, and she won't say nay to going.'

'Tess is queer.'

'But she's tractable at bottom. Leave her to me.'

Though this conversation had been private, sufficient of its import reached the understandings of those around to suggest to them that the Durbeyfields had weightier concerns to talk of now than common folks had, and that Tess, their pretty eldest daughter, had fine prospects in store.

'Tess is a fine figure o'fun, as I said to myself to-day when I zeed her vamping round parish with the rest,' observed one of the elderly boozers in an undertone. 'But Joan Durbeyfield must mind that she don't get green malt in floor.' It was a local phrase which had a peculiar meaning, and there was no reply.

The conversation became inclusive, and presently other footsteps were heard crossing the room below.

' – Being a few private friends asked in to-night to keep up club-walking at my own expense.' The landlady had rapidly re-used the formula she kept on hand for intruders before she recognized that the newcomer was Tess.

Even to her mother's gaze the girl's young features looked sadly out of place amid the alcoholic vapours which floated here as no unsuitable medium for wrinkled middle-age; and hardly was a reproachful flash

from Tess's dark eyes needed to make her father and mother rise from
their seats, hastily finish their ale, and descend the stairs behind her,
Mrs Rolliver's caution following their footsteps.

'No noise, please, if ye'll be so good, my dears; or I mid lose my
licends, and be summons'd, and I don't know what all! 'Night t'ye!'

They went home together, Tess holding one arm of her father, and Mrs
Durbeyfield the other. He had, in truth, drunk very little – not a fourth
of the quantity which a systematic tippler could carry to church on a
Sunday afternoon without a hitch in his eastings or genuflections; but
the weakness of Sir John's constitution made mountains of his pretty
sins in this kind. On reaching the fresh air he was sufficiently unsteady
to incline the row of three at one moment as if they were marching to
London, and at another as if they were marching to Bath – which produced a comical effect, frequent enough in families on nocturnal homego-
ings; and, like most comical effects, not quite so comic after all. The two
women valiantly disguised these forced excursions and counter-marches
as well as they could from Durbeyfield their cause, and from Abraham,
and from themselves; and so they approached by degrees their own door,
the head of the family bursting suddenly into his former refrain as he
drew near, as if to fortify his soul at sight of the smallness of his present
residence –

'I've got a fam-ily vault at Kingsbere!'

'Hush – don't be so silly, Jacky,' said his wife. 'Yours is not the only
family that was of 'count in wold days. Look at the Anktells, and Horseys,
and the Tringhams themselves – gone to seed a'most as much as you –
though you was bigger folks than they, that's true. Thank God, I was
never of no family, and have nothing to be ashamed of in that way!'

'Don't you be so sure o'that. From your nater 'tis my belief you've
disgraced yourselves more than any o'us, and was kings and queens
outright at one time.'

Tess turned the subject by saying what was far more prominent in her
own mind at the moment than thoughts of her ancestry –

'I am afraid father won't be able to take the journey with the beehives
tomorrow so early.'

'I? I shall be all right in an hour or two,' said Durbeyfield.

It was eleven o'clock before the family were all in bed, and two o'clock
next morning was the latest hour for starting with the beehives if they
were to be delivered to the retailers in Casterbridge before the Saturday
market began, the way thither lying by bad roads over a distance of
between twenty and thirty miles, and the horse and waggon being of the
slowest. At half-past one Mrs Durbeyfield came into the large bedroom
where Tess and all her little brothers and sisters slept.

'The poor man can't go,' she said to her eldest daughter, whose great eyes had opened the moment her mother's hand touched the door.

Tess sat up in bed, lost in a vague interspace between a dream and this information.

'But somebody must go,' she replied. 'It is late for the hives already. Swarming will soon be over for the year; and if we put off taking'em till next week's market the call for'em will be past, and they'll be thrown on our hands.'

Mrs Durbeyfield looked unequal to the emergency. 'Some young feller, perhaps, would go? One of them who were so much after dancing with 'ee yesterday,' she presently suggested.

'O no – I wouldn't have it for the world!' declared Tess proudly. 'And letting everybody know the reasons – such a thing to be ashamed of! I think *I* could go if Abraham could go with me to kip me company.'

Her mother at length agreed to this arrangement. Little Abraham was aroused from his deep sleep in a corner of the same apartment, and made to put on his clothes while still mentally in the other world. Meanwhile Tess had hastily dressed herself; and the twain, lighting a lantern, went out to the stable. The rickety little waggon was already laden, and the girl led out the horse Prince, only a degree less rickety than the vehicle.

The poor creature looked wonderingly round at the night, at the lantern, at their two figures, as if he could not believe that at that hour, when every living thing was intended to be in shelter and at rest, he was called upon to go out and labour. They put a stock of candle-ends into the lantern, hung the latter to the off-side of the load, and directed the horse onward, walking at his shoulder at first during the uphill parts of the way, in order not to overload an animal of so little vigour. To cheer themselves as well as they could, they made an artificial morning with the lantern, some bread and butter, and their own conversation, the real morning being far from come. Abraham, as he more fully awoke (for he had moved in a sort of trance so far), began to talk of the strange shapes assumed by the various dark objects against the sky; of this tree that looked like a raging tiger springing from a lair; of that which resembled a giant's head.

When they had passed the little town of Stourcastle, dumbly somnolent under its thick brown thatch, they reached higher ground. Still higher, on their left, the elevation called Bulbarrow or Bealbarrow, well-nigh the highest in South Wessex, swelled into the sky; engirdled by its earthen trenches. From hereabout the long road was fairly level for some distance onward. They mounted in front of the waggon, and Abraham grew reflective.

'Tess!' he said in a preparatory tone, after a silence.

'Yes, Abraham.'

'Bain't you glad that we've become gentlefolk?'

'Not particular glad.'

'But you be glad that you 'm going to marry a gentleman?'

'What?' said Tess, lifting her face.

'That our great relation will help 'ee to marry a gentleman.'

'I? Our great relation? We have no such relation. What has put that into your head?'

'I heard 'em talking about it up at Rolliver's when I went to find father. There's a rich lady of our family out at Trantridge, and mother said that if you claimed kin with the lady, she'd put 'ee in the way of marrying a gentleman.'

His sister became abruptly still, and lapsed into a pondering silence. Abraham talked on, rather for the pleasure of utterance than for audition, so that his sister's abstraction was of no account. He leant back against the hives, and with upturned face made observations on the stars, whose cold pulses were beating amid the black hollows above, in serene dissociation from these two wisps of human life. He asked how far away those twinklers were, and whether God was on the other side of them. But ever and anon his childish prattle recurred to what impressed his imagination even more deeply than the wonders of creation. If Tess were made rich by marrying a gentleman, would she have money enough to buy a spy-glass so large that it would draw the stars as near to her as Nettlecombe-Tout?

The renewed subject, which seemed to have impregnated the whole family, filled Tess with impatience.

'Never mind that now!' she exclaimed.

'Did you say the stars were worlds, Tess?'

'Yes.'

'All like ours?'

'I don't know; but I think so. They sometimes seem to be like the apples on our stubbard-tree. Most of them splendid and sound – a few blighted.'

'Which do we live on – a splendid one or a blighted one?'

'A blighted one.'

''Tis very unlucky that we didn't pitch on a sound one, when there were so many more of 'em!'

'Yes.'

'Is it like that *really*, Tess?' said Abraham, turning to her much impressed, on reconsideration of this rare information. 'How would it have been if we had pitched on a sound one?'

'Well, father wouldn't have coughed and creeped about as he does,

27

and wouldn't have got too tipsy to go this journey; and mother wouldn't have been always washing, and never getting finished.'

'And you would have been a rich lady ready-made, and not have had to be made rich by marrying a gentleman?'

'O Aby, don't – don't talk of that any more!'

Left to his reflections Abraham soon grew drowsy. Tess was not skilful in the management of a horse, but she thought that she could take upon herself the entire conduct of the load for the present, and allow Abraham to go to sleep if he wished to do so. She made him a sort of nest in front of the hives, in such a manner that he could not fall, and taking the reins into her own hands, jogged on as before.

Prince required but slight attention, lacking energy for superfluous movements of any sort. With no longer a companion to distract her, Tess fell more deeply into reverie than ever, her back leaning against the hives. The mute procession past her shoulders of trees and hedges became attached to fantastic scenes outside reality, and the occasional heave of the wind became the sigh of some immense sad soul, conterminous with the universe in space, and with history in time.

Then, examining the mesh of events in her own life, she seemed to see the vanity of her father's pride; the gentlemanly suitor awaiting herself in her mother's fancy; to see him as a grimacing personage, laughing at her poverty, and her shrouded knightly ancestry. Everything grew more and more extravagant, and she no longer knew how time passed. A sudden jerk shook her in her seat, and Tess awoke from the sleep into which she, too, had fallen.

They were a long way further on than when she had lost consciousness, and the waggon had stopped. A hollow groan, unlike anything she had ever heard in her life, came from the front, followed by a shout of 'Hoi there!'

The lantern hanging at her waggon had gone out, but another was shining in her face – much brighter than her own had been. Something terrible had happened. The harness was entangled with an object which blocked the way.

In consternation Tess jumped down, and discovered the dreadful truth. The groan had proceeded from her father's poor horse Prince. The morning mail-cart, with its two noiseless wheels, speeding along these lanes like an arrow, as it always did, had driven into her slow and unlighted equipage. The pointed shaft of the cart had entered the breast of the unhappy Prince like a sword, and from the wound his life's blood was spouting in a stream, and falling with a hiss into the road.

In her despair Tess sprang forward and put her hand upon the hole, with the only result that she became splashed from face to skirt with the crimson drops. Then she stood helplessly looking on. Prince also stood firm and motionless as long as he could; till he suddenly sank down in a heap.

By this time the mail-cart man had joined her, and began dragging and unharnessing the hot form of Prince. But he was already dead, and, seeing that nothing more could be done immediately, the mail-cart man returned to his own animal, which was uninjured.

'You was on the wrong side.' he said. 'I am bound to go on with the mail-bags, so that the best thing for you to do is to bide here with your load. I'll send somebody to help you as soon as I can. It is getting daylight, and you have nothing to fear.'

He mounted and sped on his way; while Tess stood and waited. The atmosphere turned pale, the birds shook themselves in the hedges, arose, and twittered; the lane showed all its white features, and Tess showed hers, still whiter. The huge pool of blood in front of her was already assuming the iridescence of coagulation; and when the sun rose a hundred prismatic hues were reflected from it. Prince lay alongside still and stark; his eyes half open, the hole in his chest looking scarcely large enough to have let out all that had animated him.

''Tis all my doing – all mine!' the girl cried, gazing at the spectacle. 'No excuse for me – none. What will mother and father live on now? Aby, Aby!' She shook the child, who had slept soundly through the whole disaster. 'We can't go on with our load – Prince is killed!'

When Abraham realized all, the furrows of fifty years were extemporized on his young face.

'Why, I danced and laughed only yesterday!' she went on to herself. 'To think that I was such a fool!'

''Tis because we be on a blighted star, and not a sound one, isn't it, Tess?' murmured Abraham through his tears.

In silence they waited through an interval which seemed endless. At length a sound, and an approaching object, proved to them that the driver of the mail-cart had been as good as his word. A farmer's man from near Stourcastle came up, leading a strong cob. He was harnessed to the waggon of beehives in the place of Prince, and the load taken on towards Casterbridge.

The evening of the same day saw the empty waggon reach again the spot of the accident. Prince had lain there in the ditch since the morning; but the place of the blood-pool was still visible in the middle of the road, though scratched and scraped over by passing vehicles. All that was left of Prince was now hoisted into the waggon he had formerly hauled, and with his hoofs in the air, and his shoes shining in the setting sunlight he retraced the eight or nine miles to Marlott.

Tess had gone back earlier. How to break the news was more than she could think. It was a relief to her tongue to find from the faces of her

29

parents that they already knew of their loss, though this did not lessen the self-reproach which she continued to heap upon herself for her negligence.

But the very shiftlessness of the household rendered the misfortune a less terrifying one to them than it would have been to a striving family, though in the present case it meant ruin, and in the other it would only have meant inconvenience. In the Durbeyfield countenances there was nothing of the red wrath that would have burnt upon the girl from parents more ambitious for her welfare. Nobody blamed Tess as she blamed herself.

When it was discovered that the knacker and tanner would give only a very few shillings for Prince's carcase because of his decrepitude, Durbeyfield rose to the occasion.

'No,' said he stoically, 'I won't sell his old body. When we d'Urbervilles was knights in the land, we didn't sell our chargers for cat's meat. Let 'em keep their shillings! He've served me well in his lifetime, and I won't part from him now.'

He worked harder the next day in digging a grave for Prince in the garden than he had worked for months to grow a crop for his family. When the hole was ready, Durbeyfield and his wife tied a rope round the horse and dragged him up the path towards it, the children following in funeral train. Abraham and 'Liza-Lu sobbed, Hope and Modesty discharged their griefs in loud blares which echoed from the walls; and when Prince was tumbled in they gathered round the grave. The bread-winner had been taken away from them; what would they do?

'Is he gone to heaven?' asked Abraham, between the sobs.

Then Durbeyfield began to shovel in the earth, and the children cried anew. All except Tess. Her face was dry and pale, as though she regarded herself in the light of a murderess.

❧ Chapter Five ❧

THE HAGGLING BUSINESS, WHICH had mainly depended on the horse, became disorganized forthwith. Distress, if not penury, loomed in the distance. Durbeyfield was what was locally called a slack-twisted fellow; he had good strength to work at times; but the times could not be relied on to coincide with the hours of requirement; and, having been unaccustomed to the regular toil of the day-labourer, he was not particularly persistent when they did so coincide.

Tess, meanwhile, as the one who had dragged her parents into this quagmire, was silently wondering what she could do to help them out of it; and then her mother broached her scheme.

'We must take the ups wi' the downs, Tess,' said she; 'and never could your high blood have been found out at a more called-for moment. You must try your friends. Do ye know that there is a very rich Mrs d'Urberville living on the outskirts o' The Chase, who must be our relation? You must go to her and claim kin, and ask for some help in our trouble.'

'I shouldn't care to do that,' says Tess. 'If there is such a lady, 'twould be enough for us if she were friendly – not to expect her to give us help.'

'You could win her round to do anything, my dear. Besides, perhaps there's more in it than you know of. I've heard what I've heard, good-now.'

The oppressive sense of the harm she had done led Tess to be more deferential than she might otherwise have been to the maternal wish; but she could not understand why her mother should find such satisfaction in contemplating an enterprise of, to her, such doubtful profit. Her mother might have made inquiries, and have discovered that this Mrs d'Urberville was a lady of unequalled virtues and charity. But Tess's pride made the part of poor relation one of particular distaste to her.

'I'd rather try to get work,' she murmured.

'Durbeyfield, you can settle it,' said his wife, turning to where he sat in the background. 'If you say she ought to go, she will go.'

'I don't like my children going and making themselves beholden to strange kin,' murmured he. 'I'm the head of the noblest branch o' the family, and I ought to live up to it.'

His reasons for staying away were worse to Tess than her own objection to going. 'Well, as I killed the horse, mother,' she said mournfully, 'I suppose I ought to do something. I don't mind going and seeing her, but you must leave it to me about asking for help. And don't go thinking about her making a match for me – it is silly.'

'Very well said, Tess!' observed her father sententiously.

'Who said I had such a thought?' asked Joan.

'I fancy it is in your mind, mother. But I'll go.'

Rising early next day she walked to the hill-town called Shaston, and there took advantage of a van which twice in the week ran from Shaston eastward to Chaseborough, passing near Trantridge, the parish in which the vague and mysterious Mrs d'Urberville had her residence.

Tess Durbeyfield's route on this memorable morning lay amid the north-eastern undulations of the Vale in which she had been born, and in which her life had unfolded. The Vale of Blackmoor was to her the world, and its inhabitants the races thereof. From the gates and stiles of Marlott she had looked down its length in the wondering days of infancy, and what had been mystery to her then was not much less than mystery to her now. She had seen daily from her chamber-window towers, villages, faint white mansions; above all the town of Shaston standing majestically on its height; its windows shining like lamps in the evening sun. She had hardly ever visited the place, only a small tract even of the Vale and its environs being known to her by close inspection. Much less had she been far outside the valley. Every contour of the surrounding hills was as personal to her as that of her relatives' faces; but for what lay beyond her judgment was dependent on the teaching of the village school, where she had held a leading place at the time of her leaving, a year or two before this date.

In those early days she had been much loved by others of her own sex and age, and had used to be seen about the village as one of three – all nearly of the same year – walking home from school side by side; Tess the middle one – in a pink print pinafore, of a finely reticulated pattern, worn over a stuff frock that had lost its original colour for a nondescript tertiary – marching on upon long stalky legs, in tight stockings which had little ladder-like holes at the knees, torn by kneeling in the roads and banks in search of vegetable and mineral treasures; her then earth-coloured hair hanging like pot-hooks; the arms of the two outside girls resting round the waist of Tess; her arms on the shoulders of the two supporters.

As Tess grew older, and began to see how matters stood, she felt quite a Malthusian towards her mother for thoughtlessly giving her so many little sisters and brothers, when it was such a trouble to nurse and provide for them. Her mother's intelligence was that of a happy child: Joan Durbeyfield was simply an additional one, and that not the eldest, to her own long family of waiters on Providence.

However, Tess became humanely beneficent towards the small ones, and to help them as much as possible she used, as soon as she left school, to lend a hand at haymaking or harvesting on neighbouring farms; or, by preference, at milking or butter-making processes, which she had learnt when her father had owned cows; and being deft-fingered it was a kind of work in which she excelled.

Every day seemed to throw upon her young shoulders more of the family burdens, and that Tess should be the representative of the Durbeyfields at the d'Urberville mansion came as a thing of course. In this instance it must be admitted that the Durbeyfields were putting their fairest side outward.

She alighted from the van at Trantridge Cross, and ascended on foot a hill in the direction of the district known as The Chase, on the borders of which, as she had been informed, Mrs d'Urberville's seat, The Slopes, would be found. It was not a manorial home in the ordinary sense, with fields, and pastures, and a grumbling farmer, out of whom the owner had to squeeze an income for himself and his family by hook or by crook. It was more, far more; a country-house built for enjoyment pure and simple, with not an acre of troublesome land attached to it beyond what was required for residential purposes, and for a little fancy farm kept in hand by the owner, and tended by a bailiff.

The crimson brick lodge came first in sight, up to its eaves in dense evergreens. Tess thought this was the mansion itself till, passing through the side wicket with some trepidation, and onward to a point at which the drive took a turn, the house proper stood in full view. It was of recent erection – indeed almost new – and of the same rich red colour that formed such a contrast with the evergreens of the lodge. Far behind the corner of the house – which rose like a geranium bloom against the subdued colours around – stretched the soft azure landscape of The Chase – a truly venerable tract of forest land, one of the few remaining woodlands in England of undoubted primaeval date, wherein Druidical mistletoe was still found on aged oaks, and where enormous yew-trees, not planted by the hand of man, grew as they had grown when they were pollarded for bows. All this sylvan antiquity, however, though visible from The Slopes, was outside the immediate boundaries of the estate.

Everything on this snug property was bright, thriving, and well kept; acres of glass-houses stretched down the inclines to the copses at their feet. Everything looked like money – like the last coin issued from the Mint. The stables, partly screened by Austrian pines and evergreen oaks, and fitted with every late appliance, were as dignified as Chapels-of-Ease. On the extensive lawn stood an ornamental tent, its door being towards her.

Simple Tess Durbeyfield stood at gaze, in a half-alarmed attitude, on the edge of the gravel sweep. Her feet had brought her onward to this point before she had quite realized where she was; and now all was contrary to her expectation.

'I thought we were an old family; but this is all new!' she said, in her artlessness. She wished that she had not fallen in so readily with her mother's plans for 'claiming kin', and had endeavoured to gain assistance nearer home.

The d'Urbervilles – or Stoke-d'Urbervilles, as they at first called themselves – who owned all this, were a somewhat unusual family to find in such an old-fashioned part of the country. Parson Tringham had spoken truly when he said that our shambling John Durbeyfield was the only really lineal representative of the old d'Urberville family existing in the county, or near it; he might have added, what he knew very well, that the Stoke-d'Urbervilles were no more d'Urbervilles of the true tree than he was himself. Yet it must be admitted that this family formed a very good stock whereon to regraft a name which sadly wanted such renovation.

When old Mr Simon Stoke, latterly deceased, had made his fortune as an honest merchant (some said money-lender) in the North, he decided to settle as a county man in the South of England, out of hail of his business district; and in doing this he felt the necessity of recommencing with a name that would not too readily identify him with the smart tradesman of the past, and that would be less commonplace than the original bald stark words. Conning for an hour in the British Museum the pages of works devoted to extinct, half-extinct, obscured, and ruined families appertaining to the quarter of England in which he proposed to settle, he considered that *d'Urberville* looked and sounded as well as any of them: and d'Urberville accordingly was annexed to his own name for himself and his heirs eternally. Yet he was not an extravagant-minded man in this, and in constructing his family tree on the new basis was duly reasonable in framing his intermarriages and aristocratic links, never inserting a single title above a rank of strict moderation.

Of this work of imagination poor Tess and her parents were naturally in ignorance – much to their discomfiture: indeed, the very possibility of such annexations was unknown to them; who supposed that, though to be well-flavoured might be the gift of fortune, a family name came by nature.

Tess still stood hesitating like a bather about to make his plunge, hardly knowing whether to retreat or to persevere, when a figure came forth from the dark triangular door of the tent. It was that of a tall young man, smoking.

He had an almost swarthy complexion, with full lips, badly moulded, though red and smooth, above which was a well-groomed black moustache with curled points, though his age could not be more than three-or four-and-twenty. Despite the touches of barbarism in his contours, there was a singular force in the gentleman's face, and in his bold rolling eye.

'Well, my beauty, what can I do for you?' said he, coming forward. And perceiving that she stood quite confounded: 'Never mind me. I am Mr d'Urberville. Have you come to see me or my mother?'

This embodiment of a d'Urberville and a namesake differed even more from what Tess had expected than the house and grounds had differed. She had dreamed of an aged and dignified face, the sublimation of all the d'Urberville lineaments, furrowed with incarnate memories representing in hierogylphic the centuries of her family's and England's history. But she screwed herself up to the work in hand, since she could not get out of it, and answered –

'I came to see your mother, sir.'

'I am afraid you cannot see her – she is an invalid.' replied the present representative of the spurious house; for this was Mr Alec, the only son of the lately deceased gentleman. 'Cannot I answer your purpose? What is the business you wish to see her about?'

'It isn't business – it is – I can hardly say what!'

'Pleasure?'

'Oh no. Why, sir, if I tell you, it will seem – '

Tess's sense of a certain ludicrousness in her errand was now so strong that, notwithstanding her awe of him, and her general discomfort at being here, her rosy lips curved towards a smile, much to the attraction of the swarthy Alexander.

'It is so very foolish,' she stammered; 'Fear I can't tell you!'

'Never mind; I like foolish things. Try again, my dear,' said he kindly.

'Mother asked me to come,' Tess continued: 'and, indeed, I was in the mind to do so myself likewise. But I did not think it would be like this. I came, sir, to tell you that we are of the same family as you.'

'Ho! Poor relations?'

'Yes.'

'Stokes?'

'No; d'Urbervilles.'

'Ay, ay; I mean d'Urbervilles.'

'Our names are worn away to Durbeyfield; but we have several proofs that we are d'Urbervilles. Antiquarians hold we are, – and – and we have an old seal, marked with a ramping lion on a shield, and a castle over him. And we have a very old silver spoon, round in the bowl like a little ladle, and marked with the same castle. But it is so worn that mother uses it to stir the pea-soup.'

'A castle argent is certainly my crest,' said he blandly. 'And my arms a lion rampant.'

'And so mother said we ought to make ourselves beknown to you – as we've lost our horse by a bad accident, and are the oldest branch o' the family.'

'Very kind of your mother, I'm sure. And I, for one, don't regret her step.' Alec looked at Tess as he spoke, in a way that made her blush a little. 'And so, my pretty girl, you've come on a friendly visit to us, as relations?'

'I suppose I have,' faltered Tess, looking uncomfortable again.

'Well – there's no harm in it. Where do you live? What are you?'

She gave him brief particulars; and responding to further inquiries told him that she was intending to go back by the same carrier who had brought her.

'It is a long while before he returns past Trantridge Cross. Supposing we walk round the grounds to pass the time, my pretty Coz?'

Tess wished to abridge her visit as much as possible; but the young man was pressing, and she consented to accompany him. He conducted her about the lawns, and flower-beds, and conservatories; and thence to the fruit-garden and green-houses, where he asked her if she liked strawberries.

'Yes,' said Tess, 'when they come.'

'They are already here.' D'Urberville began gathering specimens of the fruit for her, handing them back to her as he stooped; and, presently, selecting a specially fine product of the 'British Queen' variety, he stood up and held it by the stem to her mouth.

'No – no! she said quickly, putting her fingers between his hand and her lips. 'I would rather take it in my own hand.'

'Nonsense!' he insisted; and in a slight distress she parted her lips and took it in.

They had spent some time wandering desultorily thus. Tess eating in a half-pleased, half-reluctant state whatever d'Urberville offered her. When she could consume no more of the strawberries he filled her little basket with them; and then the two passed round to the rose trees, whence he gathered blossoms and gave her to put in her bosom. She obeyed like one in a dream, and when she could affix no more he himself tucked a bud or two into her hat, and heaped her basket with others in the prodigality of his bounty. At last, looking at his watch, he said, 'Now, by the time you have had something to eat, it will be time for you to leave, if you want to catch the carrier to Shaston. Come here, and I'll see what grub I can find.'

Stoke-d'Urberville took her back to the lawn and into the tent, where he left her, soon reappearing with a basket of light luncheon, which he put before her himself. It was evidently the gentleman's wish not to be disturbed in this pleasant *tête-à-tête* by the servantry.

'Do you mind my smoking?' he asked.

'Oh, not at all, sir.'

He watched her pretty and unconscious munching through the skeins of smoke that pervaded the tent, and Tess Durbeyfield did not divine, as she innocently looked down at the roses in her bosom, that there behind the blue narcotic haze was potentially the 'tragic mischief' of her drama – one who stood fair to be the blood-red ray in the spectrum of her young life. She had an attribute which amounted to a disadvantage just now; and it was this that caused Alec d'Urberville's eyes to rivet themselves upon her. It was a luxuriance of aspect, a fulness of growth, which made her appear more of a woman than she really was. She had inherited the feature from her mother without the quality it denoted. It had troubled her mind occasionally, till her companions had said that it was a fault which time would cure.

She soon had finished her lunch. 'Now I am going home, sir,' she said, rising.

'And what do they call you?' he asked, as he accompanied her along the drive till they were out of sight of the house.

'Tess Durbeyfield, down at Marlott.'

'And you say your people have lost their horse?'

'I – killed him!' she answered, her eyes filling with tears as she gave particulars of Prince's death. 'And I don't know what to do for father on account of it!'

'I must think if I cannot do something. My mother must find a berth for you. But, Tess, no nonsense about "d'Urberville"; – "Durbeyfield" only, you know – quite another name.'

'I wish for no better, sir,' said she with something of dignity.

For a moment – only for a moment – when they were in the turning of the drive, between the tall rhododendrons and conifers, before the lodge became visible, he inclined his face towards her as if – but no: he thought better of it, and let her go.

Thus the thing began. Had she perceived this meeting's import she might have asked why she was doomed to be seen and coveted that day by the wrong man, and not by some other man, the right and desired one in all respects – as nearly as humanity can supply the right and desired; yet to him who amongst her acquaintance might have approximated to this kind, she was but a transient impression, half forgotten.

In the ill-judged execution of the well-judged plan of things the call seldom produces the comer, the man to love rarely coincides with the hour of loving. Nature does not often say 'see!' to her poor creature at a time when seeing can lead to happy doing; or reply 'Here!' to a body's cry of 'Where?' till the hide-and-seek has become an irksome, outworn game. We may wonder whether at the acme and summit of the human progress these anachronisms will be corrected by a finer intuition, a closer interaction of the social machinery than that which now jolts us round and along; but such completeness is not to be prophesied, or even conceived as possible. Enough that in the present case, as in millions, it was not the two halves of a perfect whole that confronted each other at the perfect moment; a missing counterpart wandered independently about the earth waiting in crass obtuseness till the late time came. Out of which maladroit delay sprang anxieties, disappointments, shocks, catastrophes, and passing-strange destinies.

When d'Urberville got back to the tent he sat down astride on a chair reflecting, with a pleased gleam in his face. Then he broke into a loud laugh.

'Well, I'm damned! What a funny thing! Ha-ha-ha! And what a crumby girl!'

❧ Chapter Six ❧

TESS WENT DOWN THE HILL to Trantridge Cross, and inattentively waited to take her seat in the van returning from Chaseborough to Shaston. She did not know what the other occupants said to her as she entered, though she answered them; and when they had started anew she rode along with an inward and not an outward eye.

One among her fellow-travellers addressed her more pointedly than any had spoken before: 'Why, you be quite a posy! And such roses in early June!'

Then she became aware of the spectacle she presented to their surprised vision: roses at her breast; roses in her hat; roses and strawberries in her basket to the brim. She blushed, and said confusedly that the flowers had been given to her. When the passengers were not looking she stealthily removed the more prominent blooms from her hat and placed them in the basket, where she covered them with her handkerchief. Then she fell to reflecting again, and in looking downwards a thorn of the rose remaining in her breast accidentally pricked her chin. Like all the cottagers in Blackmoor Vale, Tess was steeped in fancies and prefigurative superstitions; she thought this an ill omen – the first she had noticed that day.

The van travelled only so far as Shaston, and there were several miles of pedestrian descent from that mountain-town into the vale to Marlott. Her mother had advised her to stay here for the night, at the house of a cottage-woman they knew, if she should feel too tired to come on; and this Tess did, not descending to her home till the following afternoon.

When she entered the house she perceived in a moment from her mother's triumphant manner that something had occurred in the interim.

'Oh yes; I know all about it! I told 'ee it would be all right, and now 'tis proved!'

'Since I've been away? What has?' said Tess rather wearily.

Her mother surveyed the girl up and down with arch approval, and went on banteringly: 'So you've brought 'em round!'

'How do you know, mother?'

'I've had a letter.'

Tess then remembered that there would have been time for this.

'They say – Mrs d'Urberville says – that she wants you to look after a little fowl-farm which is her hobby. But this is only her artful way of getting 'ee there without raising your hopes. She's going to own 'ee as kin – that's the meaning o't.'

'But I didn't see her.'

'You zid somebody, I suppose?'

'I saw her son.'

'And did he own 'ee?'

'Well – he called me Coz.'

'An' I knew it! Jacky – he called her Coz!' cried Joan to her husband. 'Well, he spoke to his mother, of course, and she do want 'ee there.'

'But I don't know that I am apt at tending fowls,' said the dubious Tess.

'Then I don't know who is apt. You've be'n born in the business, and brought up in it. They that be born in a business always know more about it than any 'prentice. Besides, that's only just a show of something for you to do, that you midn't feel beholden.'

'I don't altogether think I ought to go,' said Tess thoughtfully. 'Who wrote the letter? Will you let me look at it?'

'Mrs d'Urberville wrote it. Here it is.'

The letter was in the third person, and briefly informed Mrs Durbeyfield that her daughter's services would be useful to that lady in the management of her poultry-farm, that a comfortable room would be provided for her if she could come, and that the wages would be on a liberal scale if they liked her.

'Oh – that's all!' said Tess.

'You couldn't expect her to throw her arms round 'ee, an' to kiss and to coll 'ee all at once.'

Tess looked out of the window.

'I would rather stay here with father and you,' she said.

'But why?'

'I'd rather not tell you why, mother; indeed, I don't quite know why.'

A week afterwards she came in one evening from an unavailing search for some light occupation in the immediate neighbourhood. Her idea had been to get together sufficient money during the summer to purchase another horse. Hardly had she crossed the threshold before one of the children danced across the room, saying, 'The gentleman's been here!'

Her mother hastened to explain, smiles breaking from every inch of her person. Mrs d'Urberville's son had called on horseback, having been riding by chance in the direction of Marlott. He had wished to know, finally, in the name of his mother, if Tess could really come to manage the old lady's fowl-farm or not; the lad who had hitherto super-intended the birds having proved untrustworthy. 'Mr d'Urberville says you must be a good girl if you are at all as you appear; he knows you must be worth your weight in gold. He is very much interested in 'ee – truth to tell.'

Tess seemed for the moment really pleased to hear that she had won such high opinion from a stranger when, in her own esteem, she had sunk so low.

'It is very good of him to think that.' she murmured; 'and if I was quite sure how it would be living there, I would go any-when.'

'He is a mighty handsome man!'

'I don't think so,' said Tess coldly.

'Well, there's your chance, whether or no; and I'm sure he wears a beautiful diamond ring!'

'Yes,' said little Abraham, brightly, from the window-bench; 'and I seed it! and it did twinkle when he put his hand up to his mistarshers. Mother, why did our grand relation keep on putting his hand up to his mistarshers?'

'Hark at that child!' cried Mrs Durbeyfield, with parenthetic admiration.

'Perhaps to show his diamond ring,' murmured Sir John, dreamily, from his chair.

'I'll think it over,' said Tess, leaving the room.

'Well, she's made a conquest o' the younger branch of us, straight off,' continued the matron to her husband, 'and she's a fool if she don't follow it up.'

'I don't quite like my children going away from home,' said the haggler. 'As the head of the family, the rest ought to come to me.'

'But do let her go, Jacky,' coaxed his poor witless wife. 'He's struck wi' her – you can see that. He called her Coz! He'll marry her, most likely, and make a lady of her; and then she'll be what her forefathers was.'

John Durbeyfield had more conceit than energy or health, and this supposition was pleasant to him.

'Well, perhaps, that's what young Mr d'Urberville means,' he admitted; 'and sure enough he mid have serious thoughts about improving his blood by linking on to the old line. Tess, the little rogue! And have she really paid 'em a visit to such an end as this?'

Meanwhile Tess was walking thoughtfully among the gooseberrybushes in the garden, and over Prince's grave. When she came in her mother pursued her advantage.

'Well, what be you going to do?' She asked.

'I wish I had seen Mrs d'Urberville,' said Tess.

'I think you mid as well settle it. Then you'll see her soon enough.'

Her father coughed in his chair.

'I don't know what to say!' answered the girl restlessly. 'It is for you to decide. I killed the old horse, and I suppose I ought to do something to get ye a new one. But – but – I don't quite like Mr d'Urberville being there!'

The children, who had made use of this idea of Tess being taken up by their wealthy kinsfolk (which they imagined the other family to be) as a species of dolorifuge after the death of the horse, began to cry at Tess's reluctance, and teased and reproached her for hesitating.

'Tess won't go – o – o and be made a la – a – dy of! – no, she says she wo – o – on't!' they wailed, with square mouths. 'And we shan't have a nice new horse, and lots o' golden money to buy fairlings! And Tess won't look pretty in her best cloze no mo – o – ore!'

Her mother chimed in to the same tune: a certain way she had of making her labours in the house seem heavier than they were by prolonging them indefinitely, also weighed in the argument. Her father alone preserved an attitude of neutrality.

'I will go,' said Tess at last.

Her mother could not repress her consciousness of the nuptial Vision conjured up by the girl's consent.

'That's right! For such a pretty maid as 'tis, this is a fine chance!'

Tess smiled crossly.

'I hope it is a chance for earning money. It is no other kind of chance. You had better say nothing of that silly sort about parish.'

Mrs Durbeyfield did not promise. She was not quite sure that she did not feel proud enough, after the visitor's remarks, to say a good deal.

Thus it was arranged; and the young girl wrote, agreeing to be ready to set out on any day on which she might be required. She was duly informed that Mrs d'Urberville was glad of her decision, and that a spring-cart should be sent to meet her and her luggage at the top of the Vale on the day after the morrow, when she must hold herself prepared to start. Mrs d'Urberville's handwriting seemed rather masculine.

'A cart?' murmured Joan Durbeyfield doubtingly. 'It might have been a carriage for her own kin!'

Having at last taken her course Tess was less restless and abstracted, going about her business with some self-assurance in the thought of acquiring another horse for her father by an occupation which would not be onerous. She had hoped to be a teacher at the school, but the fates seemed to decide otherwise. Being mentally older than her mother she did not regard Mrs Durbeyfield's matrimonial hopes for her in a serious aspect for a moment. The light-minded woman had been discovering good matches for her daughter almost from the year of her birth.

Chapter Seven

ON THE MORNING APPOINTED for her departure Tess was awake before dawn – at the marginal minute of the dark when the grove is still mute, save for one prophetic bird who sings with a clear-voiced conviction that he at least knows the correct time of day, the rest preserving silence as if equally convinced that he is mistaken. She remained upstairs packing till breakfast-time, and then came down in her ordinary week-day clothes, her Sunday apparel being carefully folded in her box.

Her mother expostulated. 'You will never set out to see your folks without dressing up more the dand than that?'

'But I am going to work!' said Tess.

'Well, yes,' said Mrs Durbeyfield; and in a private tone, 'at first there mid be a little pretence o't . . . But I think it will be wiser of 'ee to put your best side outward,' she added.

'Very well; I suppose you know best,' replied Tess with calm abandonment.

And to please her parent the girl put herself quite in Joan's hands, saying serenely – 'Do what you like with me, mother.'

Mrs Durbeyfield was only too delighted at this tractability. First she fetched a great basin, and washed Tess's hair with such thoroughness that when dried and brushed it looked twice as much as at other times. She tied it with a broader pink ribbon than usual. Then she put upon her the white frock that Tess had worn at the club-walking, the airy fulness of which, supplementing her enlarged *coiffure*, imparted to her developing figure an amplitude which belied her age, and might cause her to be estimated as a woman when she was not much more than a child.

'I declare there's a hole in my stocking-heel!' said Tess.

'Never mind holes in your stockings – they don't speak! When I was a maid, so long as I had a pretty bonnet the devil might ha' found me in heels.'

Her mother's pride in the girl's appearance led her to step back, like a painter from his easel, and survey her work as a whole.

'You must zee yourself!' she cried. 'It is much better than you was t'other day.'

As the looking-glass was only large enough to reflect a very small portion of Tess's person at one time, Mrs Durbeyfield hung a black cloak outside the casement, and so made a large reflector of the panes, as it is the wont of bedecking cottagers to do. After this she went downstairs to her husband, who was sitting in the lower room.

'I'll tell 'ee what 'tis, Durbeyfield,' said she exultingly; 'he'll never have the heart not to love her. But whatever you do, don't zay too much to Tess of his fancy for her, and this chance she has got. She is such an odd maid that it mid zet her against him, or against going there, even now. If all goes well, I shall certainly be for making some return to that pa'son at Stagfoot Lane for telling us – dear, good man!'

However, as the moment for the girl's setting out drew nigh, when the first excitement of the dressing had passed off, a slight misgiving found place in Joan Durbeyfield's mind. It prompted the matron to say that she would walk a little way – as far as to the point where the acclivity from the valley began its first steep ascent to the outer world. At the top Tess was going to be met with the spring-cart sent by the Stoke-d'Urbervilles, and her box had already been wheeled ahead towards this summit by a lad with trucks, to be in readiness.

Seeing their mother put on her bonnet the younger children clamoured to go with her.

'I do want to walk a little-ways wi' Sissy, now she's going to marry our gentleman-cousin, and wear fine cloze!'

'No,' said Tess, flushing and turning quickly, 'I'll hear no more o' that! Mother, how could you ever put such stuff into their heads?'

'Going to work, my dears, for our rich relation, and help get enough money for a new horse,' said Mrs Durbeyfield pacifically.

'Good-bye, father,' said Tess, with a lumpy throat.

'Good-bye, my maid,' said Sir John, raising his head from his breast as he suspended his nap, induced by a slight excess this morning in honour of the occasion. 'Well, I hope my young friend will like such a comely sample of his own blood. And tell'n, Tess, that being sunk, quite, from our former grandeur, I'll sell him the title – yes, sell it – and at no onreasonable figure.'

'Not for less than a thousand pound!' cried Lady Durbeyfield.

'Tell'n – I'll take a thousand pound. Well, I'll take less, when I come to think o't. He'll adorn it better than a poor lammicken feller like myself can. Tell'n he shall hae it for a hundred. But I won't stand upon trifles – tell'n he shall hae it for fifty – for twenty pound! Yes, twenty pound – that's the lowest. Dammy, family honour is family honour, and I won't take a penny less!'

Tess's eyes were too full and her voice too choked to utter the sentiments that were in her. She turned quickly, and went out.

So the girls and their mother all walked together, a child on each side of Tess, holding her hand, and looking at her meditatively from time to time, as at one who was about to do great things; her mother just behind with the smallest; the group forming a picture of honest beauty flanked by innocence, and backed by simple-souled vanity. They followed the way till they reached the beginning of the ascent, on the crest of which the vehicle from Trantridge was to receive her, this limit having been fixed to save the horse the labour of the last slope. Far away behind the first hills the cliff-like dwellings of Shaston broke the line of the ridge. Nobody was visible in the elevated road which skirted the ascent save the lad whom they had sent on before them, sitting on the handle of the barrow that contained all Tess's worldly possessions.

'Bide here a bit, and the cart will soon come, no doubt,' said Mrs Durbeyfield. 'Yes, I see it yonder!'

It had come – appearing suddenly from behind the forehead of the nearest upland, and stopping beside the boy with the barrow. Her mother and the children thereupon decided to go no farther, and bidding them a hasty good-bye Tess bent her steps up the hill.

They saw her white shape draw near to the spring-cart, on which her box was already placed. But before she had quite reached it another vehicle shot out from a clump of trees on the summit, came round the bend of the road there, passed the luggage-cart, and halted beside Tess, who looked up as if in great surprise.

Her mother perceived, for the first time, that the second vehicle was not a humble conveyance like the first, but a spick-and-span gig or dog-cart, highly varnished and equipped. The driver was a young man of three- or four-and-twenty, with a cigar between his teeth; wearing a dandy cap, drab jacket, breeches of the same hue, white neckcloth, stick-up collar, and brown driving-gloves – in short, he was the handsome, horsey young buck who had visited Joan a week or two before to get her answer about Tess.

Mrs Durbeyfield clapped her hands like a child. Then she looked down, then stared again. Could she be deceived as to the meaning of this?

'Is dat the gentleman-kinsman who'll make Sissy a lady?' asked the youngest child.

Meanwhile the muslined form of Tess could be seen standing still, undecided, beside this turn-out, whose owner was talking to her. Her seeming indecision was, in fact, more than indecision: it was misgiving. She would have preferred the humble cart. The young man dismounted, and appeared to urge her to ascend. She turned her face down the hill to her relatives, and regarded the little group. Something seemed to quicken her to a determination: possibly the thought that she had killed Prince. She suddenly stepped up; he mounted beside her, and immediately whipped on the horse. In a moment they had passed the slow cart with the box, and disappeared behind the shoulder of the hill.

Directly Tess was out of sight, and the interest of the matter as a drama was at an end, the little ones' eyes filled with tears. The youngest child said, 'I wish poor, poor Tess wasn't gone away to be a lady!' and, lowering the corners of his lips, burst out crying. The new point of view was infectious, and the next child did likewise, and then the next, till the whole three of them wailed loud.

There were tears also in Joan Durbeyfield's eyes as she turned to go home. But by the time she had got back to the village she was passively trusting to the favour of accident. However, in bed that night she sighed, and her husband asked her what was the matter.

'Oh, I don't know exactly,' she said. 'I was thinking that perhaps it would ha' been better if Tess had not gone.'

'Oughtn't ye to have thought of that before?'

'Well, 'tis a chance for the maid – Still, if 'twere the doing again, I wouldn't let her go till I had found out whether the gentleman is really a good-hearted young man and choice over her as his kinswoman.'

'Yes, you ought, perhaps, to ha' done that,' snored Sir John.

Joan Durbeyfield always managed to find consolation somewhere: 'Well, as one of the genuine stock, she ought to make her way with 'en, if she plays her trump card aright. And if he don't marry her afore he will after. For that he's all afire wi' love for her any eye can see.'

'What's her trump card? Her d'Urberville blood, you mean?'

'No, stupid; her face – as 'twas mine.'

❧ Chapter Eight ❦

HAVING MOUNTED BESIDE HER, Alec d'Urberville drove rapidly along the crest of the first hill, chatting compliments to Tess as they went, the cart with her box being left far behind. Rising still, an immense landscape stretched around them on every side; behind, the green valley of her birth, before, a gray country of which she knew nothing except from her first brief visit to Trantridge. Thus they reached the verge of an incline down which the road stretched in a long straight descent of nearly a mile.

Ever since the accident with her father's horse Tess Durbeyfield, courageous as she naturally was, had been exceedingly timid on wheels; the least irregularity of motion startled her. She began to get uneasy at a certain recklessness in her conductor's driving.

'You will go down slow, sir, I suppose?' she said with attempted unconcern.

D'Urberville looked round upon her, nipped his cigar with the tips of his large white centre-teeth, and allowed his lips to smile slowly of themselves.

'Why, Tess,' he answered, after another whiff or two, 'it isn't a brave bouncing girl like you who asks that? Why, I always go down at full gallop. There's nothing like it for raising your spirits.'

'But perhaps you need not now?'

'Ah,' he said, shaking his head, 'there are two to be reckoned with. It is not me alone. Tib has to be considered, and she has a very queer temper.'

'Who?'

'Why, this mare. I fancy she looked round at me in a very grim way just then. Didn't you notice it?'

'Don't try to frighten me, sir,' said Tess stiffly.

'Well, I don't. If any living man can manage this horse I can: – I won't say any living man can do it – but if such has the power, I am he.'

'Why do you have such a horse?'

'Ah, well may you ask it! It was my fate, I suppose. Tib has killed one chap; and just after I bought her she nearly killed me. And then, take my word for it, I nearly killed her. But she's touchy still, very touchy; and one's life is hardly safe behind her sometimes.'

They were just beginning to descend; and it was evident that the horse, whether of her own will or of his (the latter being the more likely), knew so well the reckless performance expected of her that she hardly required a hint from behind.

Down, down, they sped, the wheels humming like a top, the dog-cart rocking right and left, its axis acquiring a slightly oblique set in relation to the line of progress; the figure of the horse rising and falling in undulations before them. Sometimes a wheel was off the ground, it seemed, for many yards; sometimes a stone was sent spinning over the hedge, and flinty sparks from the horse's hoofs outshone the daylight. The aspect of the straight road enlarged with their advance, the two banks dividing like a splitting stick; one rushing past at each shoulder.

The wind blew through Tess's white muslin to her very skin, and her washed hair flew out behind. She was determined to show no open fear, but she clutched d'Urberville's rein-arm.

'Don't touch my arm! We shall be thrown out if you do! Hold on round my waist!'

She grasped his waist, and so they reached the bottom.

'Safe, thank God, in spite of your fooling!' said she, her face on fire.

'Tess – fie! that's temper!' said d'Urberville.

'"Tis truth.'

'Well, you need not let go your hold of me so thanklessly the moment you feel yourself out of danger.'

She had not considered what she had been doing; whether he were man or woman, stick or stone, in her involuntary hold on him. Recovering her reserve she sat without replying, and thus they reached the summit of another declivity.

'Now then, again!' said d'Urberville.

'No, no!' said Tess. 'Show more sense, do, please.'

'But when people find themselves on one of the highest points in the county, they must get down again,' he retorted.

He loosened rein, and away they went a second time. D'Urberville turned his face to her as they rocked, and said, in playful raillery: 'Now then, put your arms round my waist again, as you did before, my Beauty.'

'Never!' said Tess independently, holding on as well as she could without touching him.

'Let me put one little kiss on those holmberry lips, Tess, or even on that warmed cheek, and I'll stop – on my honour, I will!'

Tess, surprised beyond measure, slid farther back still on her seat, at which he urged the horse anew, and rocked her the more.

'Will nothing else do?' she cried at length, in desperation, her large eyes staring at him like those of a wild animal. This dressing her up so prettily by her mother had apparently been to lamentable purpose.

'Nothing, dear Tess,' he replied.

'Oh, I don't know – very well; I don't mind!' she panted miserably.

He drew rein, and as they slowed he was on the point of imprinting the desired salute, when, as if hardly yet aware of her own modesty, she dodged aside. His arms being occupied with the reins there was left him no power to prevent her manoeuvre.

'Now, damn it – I'll break both our necks!' swore her capriciously passionate companion. 'So you can go from your word like that, you young witch, can you?'

'Very well,' said Tess, 'I'll not move since you be so determined! But I – thought you would be kind to me, and protect me, as my kinsman!'

'Kinsman be hanged! Now!'

'But I don't want anybody to kiss me, sir!' she implored, a big tear beginning to roll down her face, and the corners of her mouth trembling in her attempts not to cry. 'And I wouldn't ha' come if I had known!'

He was inexorable, and she sat still, and d'Urberville gave her the kiss of mastery. No sooner had he done so than she flushed with shame, took out her handkerchief, and wiped the spot on her cheek that had been touched by his lips. His ardour was nettled at the sight, for the act on her part had been unconsciously done.

'You are mighty sensitive for a cottage girl!' said the young man.

Tess made no reply to this remark, of which, indeed, she did not quite comprehend the drift, unheeding the snub she had administered by her instinctive rub upon her cheek. She had, in fact, undone the kiss, as far as such a thing was physically possible. With a dim sense that he was vexed she looked steadily ahead as they trotted on near Melbury Down and Wingreen, till she saw, to her consternation, that there was yet another descent to be undergone.

'You shall be made sorry for that!' he resumed, his injured tone still remaining, as he flourished the whip anew. 'Unless, that is, you agree willingly to let me do it again, and no handkerchief.'

She sighed. 'Very well, sir!' she said. 'Oh – let me get my hat!'

At the moment of speaking her hat had blown off into the road, their present speed on the upland being by no means slow. D'Urberville pulled up, and said he would get it for her, but Tess was down on the other side.

She turned back and picked up the article.

'You look prettier with it off, upon my soul, if that's possible,' he said, contemplating her over the back of the vehicle. 'Now then, up again! What's the matter?'

The hat was in place and tied, but Tess had not stepped forward.

'No, sir,' she said, revealing the red and ivory of her mouth as her eye lit in defiant triumph; 'not again, if I know it!'

'What – you won't get up beside me?'

'No; I shall walk.'

''Tis five or six miles yet to Trantridge.'

'I don't care if 'tis dozens. Besides, the cart is behind.'

'You artful hussy! Now, tell me – didn't you make that hat blow off on purpose? I'll swear you did!'

Her strategic silence confirmed his suspicion.

Then d'Urberville cursed and swore at her, and called her everything he could think of for the trick. Turning the horse suddenly he tried to drive back upon her, and so hem her in between the gig and the hedge. But he could not do this short of injuring her.

'You ought to be ashamed of yourself for using such wicked words!' cried Tess with spirit, from the top of the hedge into which she had scrambled. 'I don't like 'ee at all! I hate and detest you! I'll go back to mother, I will!'

D'Urberville's bad temper cleared up at sight of hers; and he laughed heartily.

'Well, I like you all the better,' he said. 'Come, let there be peace. I'll never do it any more against your will. My life upon it now!'

Still Tess could not be induced to remount. She did not, however, object to his keeping his gig alongside her; and in this manner, at a slow pace, they advanced towards the village of Trantridge. From time to time d'Urberville exhibited a sort of fierce distress at the sight of the tramping he had driven her to undertake by his misdemeanour. She might in truth have safely trusted him now; but he had forfeited her confidence for the time, and she kept on the ground, progressing thoughtfully, as if wondering whether it would be wiser to return home. Her resolve, however, had been taken, and it seemed vacillating even to childishness to abandon it now, unless for graver reasons. How could she face her parents, get back on her box, and disconcert the whole scheme for the rehabilitation of her family on such sentimental grounds?

A few minutes later the chimneys of The Slopes appeared in view, and in a snug nook to the right the poultry-farm and cottage of Tess's destination.

❧ Chapter Nine ❧

THE COMMUNITY OF FOWLS to which Tess had been appointed as supervisor, purveyor, nurse, surgeon, and friend, made its headquarters in an old thatched cottage standing in an enclosure that had once been a garden, but was now a trampled and sanded square. The house was overrun with ivy, its chimney being enlarged by the boughs of the parasite to the aspect of a ruined tower. The lower rooms were entirely given over to the birds, who walked about them with a proprietary air, as though the place had been built by themselves, and not by certain dusty copyholders who now lay east and west in the churchyard. The descendants of these bygone owners felt it almost as a slight to their family when the house which had so much of their affection, had cost so much of their forefathers' money, and had been in their possession for several generations before the d'Urbervilles came and built here, was indifferently turned into a fowlhouse by Mrs Stoke-d'Urberville as soon as the property fell into hand according to law. ''Twas good enough for Christians in grandfather's time,' they said.

The rooms wherein dozens of infants had wailed at their nursing now resounded with the tapping of nascent chicks. Distracted hens in coops occupied spots where formerly stood chairs supporting sedate agriculturists. The chimney-corner and once blazing hearth was now filled with inverted beehives, in which the hens laid their eggs; while out of doors the plots that each succeeding householder had carefully shaped with his spade were torn by the cocks in wildest fashion.

The garden in which the cottage stood was surrounded by a wall, and could only be entered through a door.

When Tess had occupied herself about an hour the next morning in altering and improving the arrangements, according to her skilled ideas as the daughter of a professed poulterer, the door in the wall opened and a servant in white cap and apron entered. She had come from the manor-house.

'Mrs d'Urberville wants the fowls as usual,' she said; but perceiving that Tess did not quite understand, she explained, 'Mis'ess is a old lady, and blind.'

'Blind!' said Tess.

Almost before her misgiving at the news could find some time to shape itself she took, under her companion's direction, two of the most beautiful of the Hamburgh's in her arms, and followed the maid-servant, who had likewise taken two, to the adjacent mansion, which, though ornate and imposing, showed traces everywhere on this side that some occupant of its chambers could bend to the love of dumb creatures – feathers floating within view of the front, and hencoops standing on the grass.

In a sitting-room on the ground-floor, ensconced in an armchair with her back to the light, was the owner and mistress of the estate, a white-haired woman of not more than sixty, or even less, wearing a large cap. She had the mobile face frequent in those whose sight has decayed by stages, has been laboriously striven after, and reluctantly let go, rather than the stagnant mien apparent in persons long sightless or born blind. Tess walked up to this lady with her feathered charges – one sitting on each arm.

'Ah, you are the young woman come to look after my birds?' said Mrs d'Urberville, recognizing a new footstep. 'I hope you will be kind to them. My bailiff tells me you are quite the proper person. Well, where are they? Ah, this is Strut! But he is hardly so lively to-day, is he? He is alarmed at being handled by a stranger, I suppose. And Phena too – yes, they are a little frightened – aren't you, dears? But they will soon get used to you.'

While the old lady had been speaking Tess and the other maid, in obedience to her gestures, had placed the fowls severally in her lap, and she had felt them over from head to tail, examining their beaks, their combs, the manes of the cocks, their wings, and their claws. Her touch enabled her to recognize them in a moment, and to discover if a single feather were crippled or draggled. She handled their crops, and knew what they had eaten, and if too little or too much; her face enacting a vivid pantomime of the criticisms passing in her mind.

The birds that the two girls had brought in were duly returned to the yard, and the process was repeated till all the pet cocks and hens had been submitted to the old woman – Hamburghs, Bantams, Cochins, Brahmas, Dorkings, and such other sorts as were in fashion just then – her perception of each visitor being seldom at fault as she received the bird upon her knees.

It reminded Tess of a Confirmation, in which Mrs d'Urberville was the bishop, the fowls the young people presented, and herself and the maid-servant the parson and curate of the parish bringing them up. At the end of the ceremony Mrs d'Urberville abruptly asked Tess, wrinkling and twitching her face into undulations, 'Can you whistle?'

'Whistle, Ma'am?'

'Yes, whistle tunes.'

Tess could whistle like most other country girls though the accomplishment was one which she did not care to profess in genteel company. However, she blandly admitted that such was the fact.

'Then you will have to practise it every day. I had a lad who did it very well, but he has left. I want you to whistle to my bullfinches; as I cannot see them I like to hear them, and we teach 'em airs that way. Tell her where the cages are, Elizabeth. You must begin to-morrow, or they will go back in their piping. They have been neglected these several days.'

'Mr d'Urberville whistled to 'em this morning, ma'am,' said Elizabeth.

'He! Pooh!'

51

The old lady's face creased into furrows of repugnance, and she made no further reply.

Thus the reception of Tess by her fancied kinswoman terminated, and the birds were taken back to their quarters. The girl's surprise at Mrs d'Urberville's manner was not great; for since seeing the size of the house she had expected no more. But she was far from being aware that the old lady had never heard a word of the so-called kinship. She gathered that no great affection flowed between the blind woman and her son. But in that, too, she was mistaken. Mrs d'Urberville was not the first mother compelled to love her offspring resentfully, and to be bitterly fond.

In spite of the unpleasant initiation of the day before, Tess inclined to the freedom and novelty of her new position in the morning when the sun shone, now that she was once installed there; and she was curious to test her powers in the unexpected direction asked of her, so as to ascertain her chance of retaining her post. As soon as she was alone within the walled garden she sat herself down on a coop, and seriously screwed up her mouth for the long-neglected practice. She found her former ability to have degenerated to the production of a hollow rush of wind through the lips, and no clear note at all.

She remained fruitlessly blowing and blowing, wondering how she could have so grown out of the art which had come by nature, till she became aware of a movement among the ivy-boughs which cloaked the garden-wall no less than the cottage. Looking that way she beheld a form springing from the coping to the plot. It was Alec d'Urberville, whom she had not set eyes on since he had conducted her the day before to the door of the gardener's cottage where she had lodgings.

'Upon my honour!' cried he, 'there was never before such a beautiful thing in Nature or Art as you look, "Cousin" Tess ["Cousin" had a faint ring of mockery]. I have been watching you from over the wall – sitting like *im*-patience on a monument, and pouting up that pretty red mouth to whistling shape, and whooing and whooing, and privately swearing, and never being able to produce a note. Why, you are quite cross because you can't do it.'

'I may be cross, but I didn't swear.'

'Ah! I understand why you are trying – those bullies! My mother wants you to carry on their musical education. How selfish of her! As if attending to these curst cocks and hens here were not enough work for any girl. I would flatly refuse, if I were you.'

'But she wants me particularly to do it, and to be ready by to-morrow morning.'

'Does she? Well then – I'll give you a lesson or two.'

'Oh no, you won't!' said Tess, withdrawing towards the door.

'Nonsense; I don't want to touch you. See – I'll stand on this side of the wire-netting, and you can keep on the other; so you may feel quite safe. Now, look here; you screw up your lips too harshly. There 'tis – so.'

He suited the action to the word, and whistled a line of 'Take, O take those lips away.' But the allusion was lost upon Tess.

'Now try,' said d'Urberville.

She attempted to look reserved; her face put on a sculptural severity. But he persisted in his demand, and at last, to get rid of him, she did put up her lips as directed for producing a clear note; laughing distressfully, however, and then blushing with vexation that she had laughed.

He encouraged her with 'Try again!'

Tess was quite serious, painfully serious by this time; and she tried – ultimately and unexpectedly emitting a real round sound. The momentary pleasure of success got the better of her; her eyes enlarged, and she involuntarily smiled in his face.

'That's it! Now I have started you – you'll go on beautifully. There – I said I would not come near you; and, in spite of such temptation as never before fell to mortal man, I'll keep my word . . . Tess, do you think my mother a queer old soul?'

'I don't know much of her yet, sir.'

'You'll find her so; she must be, to make you learn to whistle to her bullfinches. I am rather out of her books just now, but you will be quite in favour if you treat her live-stock well. Good morning. If you meet with any difficulties and want help here, don't go to the bailiff, come to me.'

It was in the economy of this *régime* that Tess Durbeyfield had undertaken to fill a place. Her first day's experiences were fairly typical of those which followed through many succeeding days. A familiarity with Alec d'Urberville's presence – which that young man carefully cultivated in her by playful dialogue, and by jestingly calling her his cousin when they were alone – removed much of her original shyness of him, without, however, implanting any feeling which could engender shyness of a new and tenderer kind. But she was more pliable under his hands than a mere companionship would have made her, owing to her unavoidable dependence upon his mother, and, through that lady's comparative helplessness, upon him.

She soon found that whistling to the bullfinches in Mrs d'Urberville's room was no such onerous business when she had regained the art, for she had caught from her musical mother numerous airs that suited those songsters admirably. A far more satisfactory time than when she practised in the garden was this whistling by the cages each morning. Unrestrained by the young man's presence she threw up her mouth, put her lips near the bars, and piped away in easeful grace to the attentive listeners.

Mrs d'Urberville slept in a large four-post bedstead hung with heavy damask curtains, and the bullfinches occupied the same apartment, where they flitted about freely at certain hours, and made little white spots on the furniture and upholstery. Once while Tess was at the window where the cages were ranged, giving her lesson as usual, she thought she heard a rustling behind the bed. The old lady was not present, and turning round the girl had an impression that the toes of a pair of boots were visible below the fringe of the curtains. Thereupon her whistling became so disjointed that the listener, if such there were, must have discovered her suspicion of his presence. She searched the curtains every morning after that, but never found anybody within them. Alec d'Urberville had evidently thought better of his freak to terrify her by an ambush of that kind.

❧ Chapter Ten ❧

EVERY VILLAGE HAS ITS idiosyncrasy, its constitution, often its own code of morality. The levity of some of the younger women in and about Trantridge was marked, and was perhaps symptomatic of the choice spirit who ruled The Slopes in that vicinity. The place had also a more abiding defect; it drank hard. The staple conversation on the farms around was on the uselessness of saving money; and smockfrocked arithmeticians, leaning on their ploughs or hoes, would enter into calculations of great nicety to prove that parish relief was a fuller provision for a man in his old age than any which could result from savings out of their wages during a whole lifetime.

The chief pleasure of these philosophers lay in going every Saturday night, when work was done, to Chaseborough, a decayed market-town two or three miles distant; and, returning in the small hours of the next morning, to spend Sunday in sleeping off the dyspeptic effects of the curious compounds sold to them as beer by the monopolizers of the once independent inns.

For a long time Tess did not join in the weekly pilgrimages. But under pressure from matrons not much older than herself – for a field-man's wages being as high at twenty-one as at forty, marriage was early here – Tess at length consented to go. Her first experience of the journey afforded her more enjoyment that she had expected, the hilariousness of the others being quite contagious after her monotonous attention to the poultry-farm all the week. She went again and again. Being graceful and interesting, standing moreover on the momentary threshold of womanhood, her appearance drew down upon her some sly regards from loungers in the streets of Chaseborough; hence, though sometimes her journey to the town was made independently, she always searched for her fellows at nightfall, to have the protection of their companionship homeward.

This had gone on for a month or two when there came a Saturday in September, on which a fair and a market coincided; and the pilgrims from Trantridge sought double delights at the inns on that account. Tess's occupations made her late in setting out, so that her comrades reached the town long before her. It was a fine September evening, just before sunset, when yellow lights struggle with blue shades in hair-like lines, and the atmosphere itself forms a prospect without aid from more solid objects, except the innumerable winged insects that dance in it. Through this low-lit mistiness Tess walked leisurely along.

She did not discover the coincidence of the market with the fair till she had reached the place, by which time it was close upon dusk. Her limited marketing was soon completed; and then as usual she began to look about for some of the Trantridge cottagers.

At first she could not find them, and she was informed that most of them had gone to what they called a private little jig at the house of a hay-trusser and peat-dealer who had transactions with their farm. He lived in an out-of-the-way nook of the townlet, and in trying to find her course thither her eyes fell upon Mr d'Urberville standing at a street corner.

'What – my Beauty? You here so late?' he said.

She told him that she was simply waiting for company homeward.

'I'll see you again,' said he over her shoulder as she went on down the back lane.

Approaching the hay-trussers she could hear the fiddled notes of a reel proceeding from some building in the rear; but no sound of dancing was audible – an exceptional state of things for these parts, where as a rule the stamping drowned the music. The front door being open she could see straight through the house into the garden at the back as far as the shades of night would allow; and nobody appearing to her knock she traversed the dwelling and went up the path to the outhouse whence the sound had attracted her.

It was a windowless erection used for storage, and from the open door there floated into the obscurity a mist of yellow radiance, which at first

Tess thought to be illuminated smoke. But on drawing nearer she perceived that it was a cloud of dust, lit by candles within the outhouse, whose beams upon the haze carried forward the outline of the doorway into the wide night of the garden.

When she came close and looked in she beheld indistinct forms racing up and down to the figure of the dance, the silence of their footfalls arising from their being overshoe in 'scroff' – that is to say, the powdery residuum from the storage of peat and other products, the stirring of which by their turbulent feet created the nebulosity that involved the scene. Through this floating, fusty *débris* of peat and hay, mixed with the perspirations and warmth of the dancers, and forming together a sort of vegeto-human pollen, the muted fiddles feebly pushed their notes, in marked contrast to the spirit with which the measure was trodden out. They coughed as they danced, and laughed as they coughed. Of the rushing couples there could barely be discerned more than the high lights – the indistinctness shaping them to satyrs clasping nymphs – a multiplicity of Pans whirling a multiplicity of Syrinxes; Lotis attempting to elude Priapus, and always failing.

At intervals a couple would approach the doorway for air, and the haze no longer veiling their features, the demigods resolved themselves into the homely personalities of her own next-door neighbours. Could Trantridge in two or three short hours have metamorphosed itself thus madly!

Some Sileni of the throng sat on benches and hay-trusses by the wall; and one of them recognized her.

'The maids don't think it respectable to dance at "The Flower-de-Luce",' he explained. 'They don't like to let everybody see which be their fancy-men. Besides, the house sometimes shuts up just when their jints begin to get greased. So we come here and send out for liquor.'

'But when be any of you going home?' asked Tess with some anxiety.

'Now – a'most directly. This is all but the last jig.'

She waited. The reel drew to a close, and some of the party were in the mind for starting. But others would not, and another dance was formed. This surely would end it, thought Tess. But it merged in yet another. She became restless and uneasy; yet, having waited so long, it was necessary to wait longer; on account of the fair the roads were dotted with roving characters of possibly ill intent; and, though not fearful of measurable dangers, she feared the unknown. Had she been near Marlott she would have had less dread.

'Don't ye be nervous, my dear good soul,' expostulated, between his coughs, a young man with a wet face, and his straw hat so far back upon his head that the brim encircled it like the nimbus of a saint. 'What's yer hurry? To-morrow is Sunday, thank God, and we can sleep it off in church-time. Now, have a turn with me?'

She did not abhor dancing, but she was not going to dance here. The movement grew more passionate: the fiddlers behind the luminous pillar of cloud now and then varied the air by playing on the wrong side of the bridge or with the back of the bow. But it did not matter; the panting shapes spun onwards.

They did not vary their partners if their inclination were to stick to previous ones. Changing partners simply meant that a satisfactory choice had not as yet been arrived at by one or other of the pair, and by this time every couple had been suitably matched. It was then that the ecstasy and the dream began, in which emotion was the matter of the universe, and matter but an adventitious intrusion likely to hinder you from spinning where you wanted to spin.

Suddenly there was a dull thump on the ground: a couple had fallen, and lay in a mixed heap. The next couple, unable to check its progress, came toppling over the obstacle. An inner cloud of dust rose around the prostrate figures amid the general one of the room, in which a twitching entanglement of arms and legs was discernible.

'You shall catch it for this, my gentleman, when you get home!' burst in female accents from the human heap – those of the unhappy partner of the man whose clumsiness had caused the mishap; she happened also to be his recently married wife, in which assortment there was nothing unusual at Trantridge as long as any affection remained between wedded couples; and, indeed, it was not uncustomary in their later lives, to avoid making odd lots of the single people between whom there might be a warm understanding.

A loud laugh from behind Tess's back, in the shade of the garden, united with the titter within the room. She looked round, and saw the red coal of a cigar: Alec d'Urberville was standing there alone. He beckoned to her, and she reluctantly retreated towards him.

'Well, my Beauty, what are you doing here?'

She was so tired after her long day and her walk that she confided her trouble to him – that she had been waiting ever since he saw her to have their company home, because the road at night was strange to her. 'But it seems they will never leave off, and I really think I will wait no longer.'

'Certainly do not. I have only a saddle-horse here to-day; but come to "The Flower-de-Luce", and I'll hire a trap, and drive you home with me.'

Tess, though flattered, had never quite got over her original mistrust of him, and, despite their tardiness, she preferred to walk home with the work-folk. So she answered that she was much obliged to him, but would not trouble him. 'I have said that I will wait for 'em, and they will expect me to now.'

'Very well, Miss Independence. Please yourself ... Then I shall not hurry ... My good Lord, what a kick-up they are having there!'

He had not put himself forward into the light, but some of them had perceived him, and his presence led to a slight pause and a consideration of how the time was flying. As soon as he had re-lit a cigar and walked away the Trantridge people began to collect themselves from amid those who had come in from other farms, and prepared to leave in a body. Their bundles and baskets were gathered up, and half an hour later, when the clock-chime sounded a quarter past eleven, they were straggling along the lane which led up the hill towards their homes.

It was a three-mile walk, along a dry white road, made whiter to-night by the light of the moon.

Tess soon perceived as she walked in the flock, sometimes with this one, sometimes with that, that the fresh night air was producing staggerings and serpentine courses among the men who had partaken too freely; some of the more careless women also were wandering in their gait – to wit, a dark virago, Car Darch, dubbed Queen of Spades, till lately a favourite of d'Urberville's; Nancy, her sister, nick-named the Queen of Diamonds; and the young married woman who had already tumbled down. Yet however terrestrial and lumpy their appearance just now to the mean unglamoured eye, to themselves the case was different. They followed the road with a sensation that they were soaring along in a supporting medium, possessed of original and profound thoughts, themselves and surrounding nature forming an organism of which all the parts harmoniously and joyously interpenetrated each other. They were as sublime as the moon and stars above them, and the moon and stars were as ardent as they.

Tess, however, had undergone such painful experiences of this kind in her father's house, that the discovery of their condition spoilt the pleasure she was beginning to feel in the moonlight journey. Yet she stuck in the party, for reasons above given.

In the open highway they had progressed in scattered order; but now their route was through a field-gate, and the foremost finding a difficulty in opening it they closed up together.

This leading pedestrian was Car the Queen of Spades, who carried a wicker-basket containing her mother's groceries, her own draperies, and other purchases for the week. The basket being large and heavy, Car had placed it for convenience of porterage on the top of her head, where it rode on in jeopardized balance as she walked with arms akimbo.

'Well – whatever is that a-creeping down thy back, Car Darch?' said one of the group suddenly.

All looked at Car. Her gown was a light cotton print, and from the back of her head a kind of rope could be seen descending to some distance below her waist, like a Chinaman's queue. ''Tis her hair falling down,' said another.

No; it was not her hair: it was a black stream of something oozing from her basket, and it glistened like a slimy snake in the cold still rays of the moon.

''Tis treacle,' said an observant matron.

Treacle it was. Car's poor old grandmother had a weakness for the sweet stuff. Honey she had in plenty out of her own hives, but treacle was what her soul desired, and Car had been about to give her a treat of surprise. Hastily lowering the basket the dark girl found that the vessel containing the syrup had been smashed within.

By this time there had arisen a shout of laughter at the extraordinary appearance of Car's back, which irritated the dark queen into getting rid of the disfigurement by the first sudden means available, and independently of the help of the scoffers. She rushed excitedly into the field they were about to cross, and flinging herself flat on her back upon the grass, began to wipe her gown as well as she could by spinning horizontally on the herbage and dragging herself over it up upon her elbows.

The laughter rang louder; they clung to the gate, to the posts, rested on their staves, in the weakness engendered by their convulsions at the spectacle of Car. Our heroine, who had hitherto held her peace, at this wild moment could not help joining in with the rest.

It was a misfortune – in more ways than one. No sooner did the dark queen hear the soberer richer note of Tess among those of the other work-people than a long smouldering sense of rivalry inflamed her to madness. She sprang to her feet and closely faced the object of her dislike.

'How darest th'laugh at me, hussy!' she cried.

'I couldn't really help it when t'others did,' apologized Tess, still tittering.

'Ah, th'st think th'beest everybody, dostn't, because th'beest first favourite with He just now! But stop a bit, my lady, stop a bit! I'm as good as two of such! Look here – here's at 'ee!'

To Tess's horror the dark queen began stripping off the bodice of her gown – which for the added reason of its ridiculed condition she was only too glad to be free of – till she had bared her plump neck, shoulders, and arms to the moonshine, under which they looked as luminous and beautiful as some Praxitelean creation, in their possession of the faultless rotundities of a lusty country girl. She closed her fists and squared up at Tess.

'Indeed, then, I shall not fight!' said the latter majestically; 'and if I had known you was of that sort, I wouldn't have so let myself down as to come with such a whorage as this is!'

The rather too inclusive speech brought down a torrent of vituperation from other quarters upon fair Tess's unlucky head, particularly from the Queen of Diamonds, who having stood in the relations to d'Urberville that Car had also been suspected of, united with the latter against the common enemy. Several other women also chimed in, with an animus which none of them would have been so fatuous as to show but for the rollicking evening they had passed. Thereupon, finding Tess unfairly browbeaten, the husbands and lovers tried to make peace by defending her; but the result of that attempt was directly to increase the war.

Tess was indignant and ashamed. She no longer minded the loneliness of the way and the lateness of the hour; her one object was to get away from the whole crew as soon as possible. She knew well enough that the better among them would repent of their passion next day. They were all now inside the field, and she was edging back to rush off alone when a horseman emerged almost silently from the corner of the hedge that screened the road, and Alec d'Urberville looked round upon them.

'What the devil is all this row about, work-folk?' he asked.

The explanation was not readily forthcoming; and, in truth, he did not require any. Having heard their voices while yet some way off he had ridden creepingly forward, and learnt enough to satisfy himself.

Tess was standing apart from the rest, near the gate. He bent over towards her. 'Jump up behind me,' he whispered, 'and we'll get shot of the screaming cats in a jiffy!'

She felt almost ready to faint, so vivid was her sense of the crisis. At almost any other moment of her life she would have refused such proffered aid and company, as she had refused them several times before; and now the loneliness would not of itself have forced her to do otherwise. But coming as the invitation did at the particular juncture when fear and indignation at these adversaries could be transformed by a spring of the foot into a triumph over them, she abandoned herself to her impulse, climbed the gate, put her toe upon his instep, and scrambled into the saddle behind him. The pair were speeding away into the distant gray by the time that the contentious revellers became aware of what had happened.

The Queen of Spades forgot the stain on her bodice, and stood beside the Queen of Diamonds and the new-married, staggering young woman – all with a gaze of fixity in the direction in which the horse's tramp was diminishing into silence on the road.

'What be ye looking at?' asked a man who had not observed the incident.

'Ho-ho-ho!' laughed dark Car.

'Hee-hee-hee!' laughed the tippling bride, as she steadied herself on the arm of her fond husband.

'Heu-heu-heu!' laughed dark Car's mother, stroking her moustache as she explained laconically: 'Out of the frying-pan into the fire!'

Then these children of the open air, whom even excess of alcohol could scarce injure permanently, betook themselves to the field-path; and as they went there moved onward with them, around the shadow of each one's head, a circle of opalized light, formed by the moon's rays upon the glistening sheet of dew. Each pedestrian could see no halo but his or her own, which never deserted the head-shadow, whatever its vulgar unsteadiness might be; but adhered to it, and persistently beautified it; till the erratic motions seemed an inherent part of the irradiation, and the fumes of their breathing a component of the night's mist; and the spirit of the scene, and of the moonlight, and of Nature, seemed harmoniously to mingle with the spirit of wine.

❦ Chapter Eleven ❧

THE TWAIN CANTERED ALONG for some time without speech, Tess as she clung to him still panting in her triumph, yet in other respects dubious. She had perceived that the horse was not the spirited one he sometimes rode, and felt no alarm on that score, though her seat was precarious enough despite her tight hold of him. She begged him to slow the animal to a walk, which Alec accordingly did.

'Neatly done, was it not, dear Tess?' he said by and by.

'Yes!' said she. 'I am sure I ought to be much obliged to you.'

'And are you?'

She did not reply.

'Tess, why do you always dislike my kissing you?'

'I suppose – because I don't love you.'

'You are quite sure?'

'I am angry with you sometimes!'

'Ah, I half feared as much.' Nevertheless, Alec did not object to that confession. He knew that anything was better than frigidity. 'Why haven't you told me when I have made you angry?'

'You know very well why. Because I cannot help myself here.'

'I haven't offended you often by love-making?'

'You have sometimes.'

'How many times?'

'You know as well as I – too many times.'

'Every time I have tried?'

She was silent, and the horse ambled along for a considerable distance, till a faint luminous fog, which had hung in the hollows all the evening, became general and enveloped them. It seemed to hold the moonlight in suspension, rendering it more pervasive than in clear air. Whether on this account, or from absent-mindedness, or from sleepiness, she did not perceive that they had long ago passed the point at which the lane to Trantridge branched from the highway, and that her conductor had not taken the Trantridge track.

She was inexpressibly weary. She had risen at five o'clock every morning of that week, had been on foot the whole of each day, and on this evening had in addition walked the three miles to Chaseborough, waited three hours for her neighbours without eating or drinking, her impatience to start them preventing either; she had walked a mile of the way home, and had undergone the excitement of the quarrel, till, with the slow progress of their steed, it was now nearly one o'clock. Only once, however, was she overcome by actual drowsiness. In that moment of oblivion her head sank gently against him.

D'Urberville stopped the horse, withdrew his feet from the stirrups, turned sideways on the saddle, and enclosed her waist with his arm to support her.

This immediately put her on the defensive, and with one of those sudden impulses of reprisal to which she was liable she gave him a little push from her. In his ticklish position he nearly lost his balance and only just avoided rolling over into the road, the horse, though a powerful one, being fortunately the quietest he rode.

'That is devilish unkind!' he said. 'I mean no harm – only to keep you from falling.'

She pondered suspiciously; till, thinking that this might after all be true, she relented, and said quite humbly, 'I beg your pardon, sir.'

'I won't pardon you unless you show some confidence in me. Good God!' he burst out, 'what am I, to be repulsed so by a mere chit like you? For near three mortal months have you trifled with my feelings, eluded me, and snubbed me; and I won't stand it!'

'I'll leave you to-morrow, sir.'

'No, you will not leave me to-morrow! Will you, I ask once more, show your belief in me by letting me clasp you with my arm? Come, between us two and nobody else, now. We know each other well; and you know that I love you, and think you the prettiest girl in the world, which you are. Mayn't I treat you as a lover?'

She drew a quick pettish breath of objection, writhing uneasily on her seat, looked far ahead, and murmured, 'I don't know – I wish – how can I say yes or no when – '

He settled the matter by clasping his arm round her as he desired, and Tess expressed no further negative. Thus they sidled slowly onward till it struck her they had been advancing for an unconscionable time – far longer than was usually occupied by the short journey from Chaseborough, even at this walking pace, and that they were no longer on hard road, but in a mere trackway.

'Why, where be we?' she exclaimed.

'Passing by a wood.'

'A wood – what wood? Surely we are quite out of the road?'

'A bit of The Chase – the oldest wood in England. It is a lovely night, and why should we not prolong our ride a little?'

'How could you be so treacherous!' said Tess, between archness and real dismay, and getting rid of his arm by pulling open his fingers one by one, though at the risk of slipping off herself. 'Just when I've been putting such trust in you, and obliging you to please you, because I thought I had wronged you by that push! Please set me down, and let me walk home.'

'You cannot walk home, darling, even if the air were clear. We are miles away from Trantridge, if I must tell you, and in this growing fog you might wander for hours among these trees.'

'Never mind that,' she coaxed. 'Put me down, I beg you. I don't mind where it is; only let me get down, sir, please!'

'Very well, then, I will – on one condition. Having brought you here to this out-of-the-way place, I feel myself responsible for your safe-conduct home, whatever you may yourself feel about it. As to your getting to Trantridge without assistance, it is quite impossible; for, to tell the truth, dear, owing to this fog, which so disguises everything, I don't quite know where we are myself. Now, if you will promise to wait beside the horse while I walk through the bushes till I come to some road or house, and ascertain exactly our whereabouts, I'll deposit you here willingly. When I come back I'll give you full directions, and if you insist upon walking you may; or you may ride – at your pleasure.'

She accepted these terms, and slid off on the near side, though not till he had stolen a cursory kiss. He sprang down on the other side.

'I suppose I must hold the horse?' said she.

'Oh no; it's not necessary,' replied Alec, patting the panting creature. 'He's had enough of it for to-night.'

He turned the horse's head into the bushes, hitched him on to a bough, and made a sort of couch or nest for her in the deep mass of dead leaves.

'Now, you sit there,' he said. 'The leaves have not got damp as yet. Just give an eye to the horse – it will be quite sufficient.'

He took a few steps away from her, but, returning, said, 'Bye the bye, Tess, your father has a new cob to-day. Somebody gave it to him.'

'Somebody? You!'

D'Urberville nodded.

'O how very good of you that is!' she exclaimed, with a painful sense of the awkwardness of having to thank him just then.

'And the children have some toys.'

'I didn't know – you ever sent them anything!' she murmured, much moved. 'I almost wish you had not – yet, I almost wish it!'

'Why, dear?'

'It – hampers me so.'

'Tessy – don't you love me ever so little now?'

'I'm grateful,' she reluctantly admitted. 'But I fear I do not – ' The sudden vision of his passion for herself as a factor in this result so distressed her that, beginning with one slow tear, and then following with another, she wept outright.

'Don't cry, dear, dear one! Now sit down here, and wait till I come.' She passively sat down amid the leaves he had heaped, and shivered slightly. 'Are you cold?' he asked.

'Not very – a little.'

He touched her with his fingers, which sank into her as into down. 'You have only that puffy muslin dress on – how's that?'

'It's my best summer one. 'Twas very warm when I started, and I didn't know I was going to ride, and that it would be night.'

'Nights grow chilly in September. Let me see.' He pulled off a light overcoat that he had worn, and put it round her tenderly. 'That's it – now you'll feel warmer,' he continued. 'Now, my pretty, rest there; I shall soon be back again.'

Having buttoned the overcoat round her shoulders he plunged into the webs of vapour which by this time formed veils between the trees. She could hear the rustling of the branches as he ascended the adjoining slope, till his movements were no louder than the hopping of a bird, and finally died away. With the setting of the moon the pale light lessened, and Tess became invisible as she felt into reverie upon the leaves where he had left her.

In the meantime Alec d'Urberville had pushed on up the slope to clear his genuine doubt as to the quarter of The Chase they were in. He had, in fact, ridden quite at random for over an hour, taking any turning that came to hand in order to prolong companionship with her, and giving far more attention to Tess's moonlit person than to any wayside object. A little rest for the jaded animal being desirable, he did not hasten his search for landmarks. A clamber over the hill into the adjoining vale brought him to the fence of a highway whose contours he recognized, which settled the question of their whereabouts. D'Urberville thereupon turned back; but by this time the moon had quite gone down, and partly on account of the fog The Chase was wrapped in thick darkness, although morning was not far off. He was obliged to advance with outstretched hands to avoid contact with the boughs, and discovered that to hit the exact spot from which he had started was at first entirely beyond him. Roaming up and down, round and round, he at length heard a slight movement of the horse close at hand; and the sleeve of his overcoat unexpectedly caught his foot.

'Tess!' said d'Urberville.

There was no answer. The obscurity was now so great that he could see absolutely nothing but a pale nebulousness at his feet, which represented the white muslin figure he had left upon the dead leaves. Everything else was blackness alike. D'Urberville stooped; and heard a gentle regular breathing. He knelt and bent lower, till her breath warmed his face, and in a moment his cheek was in contact with hers. She was sleeping soundly, and upon her eyelashes there lingered tears.

Darkness and silence ruled everywhere around. Above them rose the primeval yews and oaks of The Chase, in which were poised gentle roosting birds in their last nap; and about them stole the hopping rabbits and hares. But, might some say, where was Tess's guardian angel? where was the providence of her simple faith? Perhaps, like that other god of whom the ironical Tishbite spoke, he was talking, or he was pursuing, or he was in a journey, or he was sleeping and not to be awaked.

Why it was that upon this beautiful feminine tissue, sensitive as gossamer, and practically blank as snow as yet, there should have been traced such a coarse pattern as it was doomed to receive; why so often the coarse appropriates the finer thus, the wrong man the woman, the wrong woman the man, many thousand years of analytical philosophy have failed to explain to our sense of order. One may, indeed, admit the possibility of a retribution lurking in the present catastrophe. Doubtless some of Tess d'Urberville's mailed ancestors rollicking home from a fray had dealt the same measure even more ruthlessly towards peasant girls of their time. But though to visit the sins of the fathers upon the children may be a morality good enough for divinities, it is scorned by average human nature; and it therefore does not mend the matter.

As Tess's own people down in those retreats are never tired of saying among each other in their fatalistic way: 'It was to be.' There lay the pity of it. An immeasurable social chasm was to divide our heroine's personality thereafter from that previous self of hers who stepped from her mother's door to try her fortune at Trantridge poultry-farm.

PHASE THE SECOND

Maiden no more

❦ Chapter Twelve ❦

THE BASKET WAS HEAVY and the bundle was large, but she lugged them along like a person who did not find her especial burden in material things. Occasionally she stopped to rest in a mechanical way by some gate or post; and then, giving the baggage another hitch upon her full round arm, went steadily on again.

It was a Sunday morning in late October, about four months after Tess Durbeyfield's arrival at Trantridge, and some few weeks subsequent to the night ride in the The Chase. The time was not long past daybreak, and the yellow luminosity upon the horizon behind her back lighted the ridge towards which her face was set – the barrier of the vale wherein she had of late been a stranger – which she would have to climb over to reach her birthplace. The ascent was gradual on this side, and the soil and scenery differed much from those within Blakemore Vale. Even the character and accent of the two peoples had shades of difference, despite the amalgamating effects of a roundabout railway; so that, though less than twenty miles from the place of her sojourn at Trantridge, her native village had seemed a far-away spot. The field-folk shut in there traded northward and westward, travelled, courted, and married northward and westward, thought northward and westward; those on this side mainly directed their energies and attention to the east and south.

The incline was the same down which d'Urberville had driven with her so wildly on that day in June. Tess went up the remainder of its length without stopping, and on reaching the edge of the escarpment gazed over the familiar green world beyond, now half-veiled in mist. It was always beautiful from here; it was terribly beautiful to Tess to-day, for since her eyes last fell upon it she had learnt that the serpent hisses where the sweet birds sing, and her views of life had been totally changed for her by the lesson. Verily another girl than the simple one she had been at home was she who, bowed by thought, stood still here, and turned to look behind her. She could not bear to look forward into the Vale.

Ascending by the long white road that Tess herself had just laboured up, she saw a two-wheeled vehicle, beside which walked a man, who held up his hand to attract her attention.

She obeyed the signal to wait for him with unspeculative repose, and in a few minutes man and horse stopped beside her.

'Why did you slip away by stealth like this?' said d'Urberville, with upbraiding breathlessness; 'on a Sunday morning, too, when people were all in bed! I only discovered it by accident, and I have been driving like the deuce to overtake you. Just look at the mare. Why go off like this? You know that no-body wished to hinder your going. And how unnecessary it has been for you to toil along on foot, and encumber yourself with this heavy load! I have followed like a madman, simply to drive you the rest of the distance, if you won't come back.'

'I shan't come back,' said she.

'I thought you wouldn't – I said so! Well, then, put up your baskets, and let me help you on.'

She listlessly placed her basket and bundle within the dog-cart, and stepped up, and they sat side by side. She had no fear of him now, and in the cause of her confidence her sorrow lay.

D'Urberville mechanically lit a cigar, and the journey was continued with broken unemotional conversation on the commonplace objects by the wayside. He had quite forgotten his struggle to kiss her when, in the early summer, they had driven in the opposite direction along the same road. But she had not, and she sat now, like a puppet, replying to his remarks in monosyllables. After some miles they came in view of the clump of trees beyond which the village of Marlott stood. It was only then that her still face showed the least emotion, a tear or two beginning to trickle down.

'What are you crying for?' he coldly asked.

'I was thinking that I was born over there,' murmured Tess.

'Well – we must all be born somewhere.'

'I wish I had never been born – there or anywhere else!'

'Pooh! Well, if you didn't wish to come to Trantridge why did you come?'

She did not reply.

'You didn't come for love of me, that I'll swear.'

''Tis quite true. If I had gone for love o' you, if I had ever sincerely loved you, if I loved you still, I should not so loathe and hate myself for my weakness as I do now! ... My eyes were dazed by you for a little, and that was all.'

He shrugged his shoulders. She resumed –

'I didn't understand your meaning till it was too late.'

'That's what every woman says.'

'How can you dare to use such words!' she cried, turning impetuously upon him, her eyes flashing as the latent spirit (of which he was to see more some day) awoke in her. 'My God! I could knock you out of the gig! Did it never strike your mind that what every woman says some women may feel?'

'Very well,' he said, laughing; 'I am sorry to wound you. I did wrong – I admit it.' He dropped into some little bitterness as he continued: 'Only you needn't be so everlastingly flinging it in my face. I am ready to pay to the uttermost farthing. You know you may not work in the fields or the dairies again. You know you may clothe yourself with the best, instead of in the bald plain way you have lately affected, as if you couldn't get a ribbon more than you earn.'

Her lip lifted slightly, though there was little scorn, as a rule, in her large and impulsive nature.

'I have said I will not take anything more from you, and I will not – I cannot! I *should* be your creature to go on doing that, and I won't!'

'One would think you were a princess from your manner, in addition to a true and original d'Urberville – ha! ha! Well, Tess, dear, I can say no more. I suppose I am a bad fellow – a damn bad fellow. I was born bad, and I have lived bad, and I shall die bad in all probability. But, upon my lost soul, I won't be bad towards you again, Tess. And if certain circumstances should arise – you understand – in which you are in the least need, the least difficulty, send me one line, and you shall have by return whatever you require. I may not be at Trantridge – I am going to London for a time – I can't stand the old woman. But all letters will be forwarded.'

She said that she did not wish him to drive her further, and they stopped just under the clump of trees. D'Urberville alighted, and lifted her down bodily in his arms, afterwards placing her articles on the ground beside her. She bowed to him slightly, her eye just lingering in his; and then she turned to take the parcels for departure.

Alec d'Urberville removed his cigar, bent towards her, and said –

'You are not going to turn away like that, dear? Come!'

'If you wish,' she answered indifferently. 'See how you've mastered me!'

She thereupon turned round and lifted her face to his, and remained like a marble term while he imprinted a kiss upon her cheek – half perfunctorily, half as if zest had not yet quite died out. Her eyes vaguely rested upon the remotest trees in the lane while the kiss was given, as though she were nearly unconscious of what he did.

'Now the other side, for old acquaintance' sake.'

She turned her head in the same passive way, as one might turn at the request of a sketcher or hairdresser, and he kissed the other side, his lips touching cheeks that were damp and smoothly chill as the skin of the mushrooms in the fields around.

'You don't give me your mouth and kiss me back. You never willingly do that – you'll never love me, I fear.'

'I have said so, often. It is true. I have never really and truly loved you, and I think I never can.' She added mournfully, 'Perhaps, of all things, a lie on this thing would do the most good to me now; but I have honour enough left, little as 'tis, not to tell that lie. If I did love you I may have the best o' causes for letting you know it. But I don't.'

He emitted a laboured breath, as if the scene were getting rather oppressive to his heart, or to his conscience, or to his gentility.

'Well, you are absurdly melancholy, Tess. I have no reason for flattering you now, and I can say plainly that you need not be so sad. You can hold your own for beauty against any woman of these parts, gentle or simple; I say it to you as a practical man and well-wisher. If you are wise you will show it to the world more than you do before it fades . . . And yet, Tess, will you come back to me? Upon my soul I don't like to let you go like this!'

'Never, never! I made up my mind as soon as I saw – what I ought to have seen sooner; and I won't come.'

'Then good morning, my four months' cousin – good-bye!'

He leapt up lightly, arranged the reins, and was gone between the tall redberried hedges.

Tess did not look after him, but slowly wound along the crooked lane. It was still early, and though the sun's lower limb was just free of the hill, his rays, ungenial and peering, addressed the eye rather than the touch as yet. There was not a human soul near. Sad October and her sadder self seemed the only two existences haunting that lane.

As she walked however, some footsteps approached behind her, the footsteps of a man; and owing to the briskness of his advance he was close at her heels and had said 'Good morning' before she had been long aware of his propinquity. He appeared to be an artisan of some sort, and carried a tin pot of red paint in his hand. He asked in a business-like manner if he should take her basket, which she permitted him to do, walking beside him.

'It is early to be astir this Sabbath morn!' he said cheerfully.

'Yes,' said Tess.

'When most people are at rest from their week's work.'

She also assented to this.

'Though I do more real work to-day than all the week besides.'

'Do you?'

'All the week I work for the glory of man, and on Sunday for the glory of God. That's more real than the other – hey? I have a little to do here at this stile.' The man turned as he spoke to an opening at the roadside leading into a pasture. 'If you'll wait a moment,' he added, 'I shall not be long.'

As he had her basket she could not well do otherwise; and she waited, observing him. He set down her basket and the tin pot, and stirring the paint with the brush that was in it began painting large square letters on the middle board of the three composing the stile, placing a comma after each word, as if to give pause while that word was driven well home to the reader's heart –

THY, DAMNATION, SLUMBERETH, NOT.

2 PET. II. 3.

Against the peaceful landscape, the pale, decaying tints of the copses, the blue air of the horizon, and the lichened stileboards, these staring vermilion words shone forth. They seemed to shout themselves out and make the atmosphere ring. Some people might have cried 'Alas, poor Theology!' at the hideous defacement – the last grotesque phase of a creed which had served mankind well in its time. But the words entered Tess with accusatory horror. It was as if this man had known her recent history; yet he was a total stranger.

Having finished his text he picked up her basket, and she mechanically resumed her walk beside him.

'Do you believe what you paint?' she asked in low tones.

'Believe that tex? Do I believe in my own existence!'

'But,' said she tremulously, 'suppose your sin was not of your own seeking?'

He shook his head.

'I cannot split hairs on that burning query,' he said. 'I have walked hundreds of miles this past summer, painting these texes on every wall, gate, and stile in the length and breadth of this district. I leave their application to the hearts of the people who read 'em.'

'I think they are horrible,' said Tess. 'Crushing! killing!'

'That's what they are meant to be!' he replied in a trade voice. 'But you should read my hottest ones – them I kips for slums and seaports. They'd make ye wriggle! Not but what this is a very good tex for rural districts . . . Ah – there's a nice bit of blank wall up by that barn standing to waste. I must put one there – one that it will be good for dangerous young females like yerself to heed. Will ye wait, missy?'

'No,' said she; and taking her basket Tess trudged on. A little way forward she turned her head. The old gray wall began to advertise a similar fiery lettering to the first, with a strange and unwonted mien, as if distressed at duties it had never before been called upon to perform.

It was with a sudden flush that she read and realized what was to be the inscription he was now half-way through –

THOU, SHALT, NOT, COMMIT –

Her cheerful friend saw her looking, stopped his brush, and shouted –
'If you want to ask for edification on these things of moment, there's a very earnest good man going to preach a charity-sermon to-day in the parish you are going to – Mr Clare of Emminster. I'm not of his persuasion now, but he's a good man, and he'll expound as well as any parson I know. 'Twas he began the work in me.'

But Tess did not answer; she throbbingly resumed her walk, her eyes fixed on the ground. 'Pooh – I don't believe God said such things!' she murmured contemptuously when her flush had died away.

A plume of smoke soared up suddenly from her father's chimney, the sight of which made her heart ache. The aspect of the interior, when she reached it, made her heart ache more. Her mother, who had just come down stairs, turned to greet her from the fireplace, where she was kindling barked-oak twigs under the breakfast kettle. The young children were still above, as was also her father, it being Sunday morning, when he felt justified in lying an additional half-hour.

'Well! – my dear Tess!' exclaimed her surprised mother, jumping up and kissing the girl. 'How be ye? I didn't see you till you was in upon me! Have you come home to be married?'

'No, I have not come for that, mother.'

'Then for a holiday?'

'Yes – for a holiday; for a long holiday,' said Tess.

'What, isn't your cousin going to do the handsome thing?'

'He's not my cousin, and he's not going to marry me.'

Her mother eyed her narrowly.

'Come, you have not told me all,' she said.

Then Tess went up to her mother, put her face upon Joan's neck, and told.

'And yet th'st not got him to marry 'ee!' reiterated her mother. 'Any woman would have done it but you, after that!'

'Perhaps any woman would except me.'

'It would have been something like a story to come back with, if you had!' continued Mrs Durbeyfield, ready to burst into tears of vexation. 'After all the talk about you and him which has reached us here, who would have expected it to end like this! Why didn't ye think of doing some good for your family instead o' thinking only of yourself? See how I've got to teave and slave, and your poor weak father with his heart clogged like a dripping-pan. I did hope for something to come out o' this! To see what a pretty pair you and he made that day when you drove away together four months ago! See what he has given us – all, as we thought, because we were his kin. But if he's not, it must have been done because of his love for 'ee. And yet you've not got him to marry!'

Get Alec d'Urberville in the mind to marry her! He marry *her*! On matrimony he had never once said a word. And what if he had? How a convulsive snatching at social salvation might have impelled her to answer him she could not say. But her poor foolish mother little knew her present feeling towards this man. Perhaps it was unusual in the circumstances, unlucky, unaccountable; but there it was; and this, as she had said, was what made her detest herself. She had never wholly cared for him, she did not at all care for him now. She had dreaded him, winced before him, succumbed to adroit advantages he took of her helplessness; then, temporarily blinded by his ardent manners, had been stirred to confused surrender awhile: had suddenly despised and disliked him, and had run away. That was all. Hate him she did not quite; but he was dust and ashes to her, and even for her name's sake she scarcely wished to marry him.

'You ought to have been more careful if you didn't mean to get him to make you his wife!'

'O mother, my mother!' cried the agonized girl, turning passionately upon her parent as if her poor heart would break. 'How could I be expected to know? I was a child when I left this house four months ago. Why didn't you tell me there was danger in men-folk? Why didn't you warn me? Ladies know what to fend hands against, because they read novels that tell them of these tricks; but I never had the chance o' learning in that way, and you did not help me!'

Her mother was subdued.

'I thought if I spoke of his fond feelings and what they might lead to, you would be hontish wi' him and lose your chance,' she murmured, wiping her eyes with her apron. 'Well, we must make the best of it, I suppose. 'Tis nater, after all, and what do please God!'

❧ Chapter Thirteen ❧

THE EVENT OF TESS DURBEYFIELD'S return from the manor of her bogus kinsfolk was rumoured abroad, if rumour be not too large a word for a space of a square mile. In the afternoon several young girls of Marlott, former schoolfellows and acquaintances of Tess, called to see her, arriving dressed in their best starched and ironed, as became visitors to a person who had made a transcendent conquest (as they supposed), and sat round the room looking at her with great curiosity. For the fact that it was this said thirty-first cousin, Mr d'Urberville, who had fallen in love with her, a gentleman not altogether local, whose reputation as a reckless gallant and heart-breaker was beginning to spread beyond the immediate boundaries of Trantridge, lent Tess's supposed position, by its fearsomeness, a far higher fascination that it would have exercised if unhazardous.

Their interest was so deep that the younger ones whispered when her back was turned –

'How pretty she is; and how that best frock do set her off! I believe it cost an immense deal, and that it was a gift from him.'

Tess, who was reaching up to get the tea-things from the corner-cupboard, did not hear these commentaries. If she had heard them, she might soon have set her friends right on the matter. But her mother heard, and Joan's simple vanity, having been denied the hope of a dashing marriage, fed itself as well as it could upon the sensation of a dashing flirtation. Upon the whole she felt gratified, even though such a limited and evanescent triumph should involve her daughter's reputation; it might end in marriage yet, and in the warmth of her responsiveness to their admiration she invited her visitors to stay to tea.

Their chatter, their laughter, their good-humoured innuendoes, above all, their flashes and flickerings of envy, revived Tess's spirits also; and, as the evening wore on, she caught the infection of their excitement, and grew almost gay. The marble hardness left her face, she moved with something of her old bounding step, and flushed in all her young beauty.

At moments, in spite of thought, she would reply to their inquiries with a manner of superiority, as if recognizing that her experiences in the field of courtship had, indeed, been slightly enviable. But so far was she from being, in the words of Robert South, 'in love with her own ruin,' that the illusion was transient as lightning; cold reason came back to mock her spasmodic weakness; the ghastliness of her momentary pride would convict her, and recall her to reserved listlessness again.

And the despondency of the next morning's dawn, when it was no longer Sunday, but Monday; and no best clothes; and the laughing

75

visitors were gone, and she awoke alone in her old bed, the innocent younger children breathing softly around her. In place of the excitement of her return, and the interest it had inspired, she saw before her a long and stony highway which she had to tread, without aid, and with little sympathy. Her depression was then terrible, and she could have hidden herself in a tomb.

In the course of a few weeks Tess revived sufficiently to show herself so far as was necessary to get to church one Sunday morning. She liked to hear the chanting – such as it was – and the old Psalms, and to join in the Morning Hymn. That innate love of melody, which she had inherited from her ballad-singing mother, gave the simplest music a power over her which could well-nigh drag her heart out of her bosom at times.

To be as much out of observation as possible for reasons of her own, and to escape the gallantries of the young men, she set out before the chiming began, and took a back seat under the gallery, close to the lumber, where only old men and women came, and where the bier stood on end among the churchyard tools.

Parishioners dropped in by twos and threes, deposited themselves in rows before her, rested three-quarters of a minute on their foreheads as if they were praying, through they were not; then sat up, and looked around. When the chants came on one of her favourites happened to be chosen among the rest – the old double chant 'Langdon' – but she did not know what it was called, though she would much have liked to know. She thought, without exactly wording the thought, how strange and godlike was a composer's power, who from the grave could lead through sequences of emotion, which he alone had felt at first, a girl like her who had never heard of his name, and never would have a clue to his personality.

The people who had turned their heads turned them again as the service proceeded; and at last observing her they whispered to each other. She knew what their whispers were about, grew sick at heart, and felt that she could come to church no more.

The bedroom which she shared with some of the children formed her retreat more continually than ever. Here, under her few square yards of thatch, she watched winds, and snows, and rains, gorgeous sunsets, and successive moons at their full. So close kept she that at length almost everybody thought she had gone away.

The only exercise that Tess took at this time was after dark; and it was then, when out in the woods, that she seemed least solitary. She knew how to hit to a hair's-breadth that moment of evening when the light and the darkness are so evenly balanced that the constraint of day and the suspense of night neutralize each other, leaving absolute mental liberty. It is then that the plight of being alive becomes attenuated to its least possible dimensions. She had no fear of the shadows; her sole idea seemed to be to shun mankind – or rather that cold accretion called the world, which, so terrible in the mass, is so unformidable, even pitiable, in its units.

On these lonely hills and dales her quiescent glide was of a piece with the element she moved in. Her flexuous and stealthy figure became an integral part of the scene. At times her whimsical fancy would intensify natural processes around her till they seemed a part of her own story. Rather they became a part of it; for the world is only a psychological phenomenon, and what they seemed they were. The midnight airs and gusts, moaning amongst the tightly-wrapped buds and bark of the winter twigs, were formulae of bitter reproach. A wet day was the expression of irremediable grief at her weakness in the mind of some vague ethical being whom she could not class definitely as the God of her childhood, and could not comprehend as any other.

But this encompassment of her own characterization, based on shreds of convention, peopled by phantoms and voices anti-pathetic to her, was a sorry and mistaken creation of Tess's fancy – a cloud of moral hobgoblins by which she was terrified without reason. It was they that were out of harmony with the actual world, not she. Walking among the sleeping birds in the hedges, watching the skipping rabbits on a moonlit warren, or standing under a pheasant-laden bough, she looked upon herself as a figure of Guilt intruding into the haunts of Innocence. But all the while she was making a distinction where there was no difference. Feeling herself in antagonism she was quite in accord. She had been made to break an accepted social law, but no law known to the environment in which she fancied herself such an anomaly.

Chapter Fourteen

IT WAS A HAZY SUNRISE IN August. The denser nocturnal vapours, attacked by the warm beams, were dividing and shrinking into isolated fleeces within hollows and coverts, where they waited till they should be dried away to nothing.

The sun, on account of the mist, had a curious sentient, personal look, demanding the masculine pronoun for its adequate expression. His present aspect, coupled with the lack of all human forms in the scene, explained the old-time heliolatries in a moment. One could feel that a saner religion had never prevailed under the sky. The luminary was a golden-haired, beaming, mild-eyed, God-like creature, gazing down in the vigour and intentness of youth upon an earth that was brimming with interest for him.

His light, a little later, broke through chinks of cottage shutters, throwing stripes like red-hot pokers upon cupboards, chests of drawers, and other furniture within; and awakening harvesters who were not already astir.

But of all ruddy things that morning the brightest were two broad arms of painted wood, which rose from the margin of a yellow cornfield hard by Marlott village. They, with two others below, formed the revolving Maltese cross of the reaping-machine, which had been brought to the field on the previous evening to be ready for operations this day. The paint with which they were smeared, intensified in hue by the sunlight, imparted to them a look of having been dipped in liquid fire.

The field had already been 'opened'; that is to say, a lane a few feet wide had been hand-cut through the wheat along the whole circumference of the field, for the first passage of the horses and machine.

Two groups, one of men and lads, the other of women, had come down the lane just at the hour when the shadows of the eastern hedge-top struck the west hedge midway, so that the heads of the groups were enjoying sunrise while their feet were still in the dawn. They disappeared from the lane between the two stone posts which flanked the nearest field-gate.

Presently there arose from within a ticking like the love-making of the grasshopper. The machine had begun, and a moving concatenation of three horses and the aforesaid long rickety machine was visible over the gate, a driver sitting upon one of the hauling horses, and an attendant on the seat of the implement. Along one side of the field the whole wain went, the arms of the mechanical reaper revolving slowly, till it passed down the hill quite out of sight. In a minute it came up on the other side of the field at the same equable pace; the glistening brass star in the forehead of the fore horse first catching the eye as it rose into view over the stubble, then the bright arms, and then the whole machine.

The narrow lane of stubble encompassing the field grew wider with each circuit, and the standing corn was reduced to smaller area as the morning wore on. Rabbits, hares, snakes, rats, mice, retreated inwards as into a fastness, unaware of the ephemeral nature of their refuge, and of the doom that awaited them later in the day when, their covert shrinking to a more and more horrible narrowness, they were huddled together, friends and foes, till the last few yards of upright wheat fell also under the teeth of the unerring reaper, and they were every one put to death by the sticks and stones of the harvesters.

The reaping-machine left the fallen corn behind it in little heaps, each heap being of the quantity for a sheaf; and upon these the active binders in the rear laid their hands – mainly women, but some of them men in print shirts, and trousers supported round their waists by leather straps, rendering useless the two buttons behind, which twinkled and bristled with sunbeams at every movement of each wearer, as if they were a pair of eyes in the small of his back.

But those of the other sex were the most interesting of this company of binders, by reason of the charm which is acquired by woman when she becomes part and parcel of outdoor nature, and is not merely an object set down therein as at ordinary times. A field-man is a personality afield; a field-woman is a portion of the field; she has somehow lost her own margin, imbibed the essence of her surrounding, and assimilated herself with it.

The women – or rather girls, for they were mostly young – wore drawn cotton bonnets with great flapping curtains to keep off the sun, and gloves to prevent their hands being wounded by the stubble. There was one wearing a pale pink jacket, another in a cream-coloured tight-sleeved gown, another in a petticoat as red as the arms of the reaping-machine; and others, older, in the brown-rough 'wropper' or over-all – the old-established and most appropriate dress of the field-woman, which the young ones were abandoning. This morning the eye returns involuntarily to the girl in the pink cotton jacket, she being the most flexuous and finely-drawn figure of them all. But her bonnet is pulled so far over her brow that none of her face is disclosed while she binds, though her complexion may be guessed from a stray twine or two of dark brown hair which extends below the curtain of her bonnet. Perhaps one reason why she seduces casual attention is that she never courts it, though the other women often gaze around them.

Her binding proceeds with clock-like monotony. From the sheaf last finished she draws a handful of ears, patting their tips with her left palm to bring them even. Then stooping low she moves forward, gathering the corn with both hands against her knees, and pushing her left gloved hand under the bundle to meet the right on the other side, holding the corn in an embrace like that of a lover. She brings the ends of the bond together, and kneels on the sheaf while she ties it, beating back her skirts now and then when lifted by the breeze. A bit of her naked arm is visible between the buff leather of the gauntlet and the sleeve of her gown; and as the day wears on its feminine smoothness becomes scarified by the stubble, and bleeds.

At intervals, she stands up to rest, and to retie her disarranged apron, or to pull her bonnet straight. Then one can see the oval face of a handsome young woman with deep dark eyes and long heavy clinging tresses, which seem to clasp in a beseeching way anything they fall against. The cheeks are paler, the teeth more regular, the red lips thinner than is usual in a country-bred girl.

It is Tess Durbeyfield, otherwise d'Urberville, somewhat changed – the same, but not the same; at the present stage of her existence living as a stranger and an alien here, though it was no strange land that she was in. After a long seclusion she had come to a resolve to undertake outdoor work in her native village, the busiest season of the year in the agricultural world having arrived, and nothing that she could do within the house being so remunerative for the time as harvesting in the fields.

The movements of the other women were more or less similar to Tess's, the whole bevy of them drawing together like dancers in a quadrille at the completion of a sheaf by each, every one placing her sheaf on end against those of the rest, till a shock, or 'stitch' as it was here called, of ten or a dozen was formed.

They went to breakfast, and came again, and the work proceeded as before. As the hour of eleven drew near a person watching her might have noticed that every now and then Tess's glance flitted wistfully to the brow of the hill, though she did not pause in her sheafing. On the verge of the hour the heads of a group of children, of ages ranging from six to fourteen, rose above the stubbly convexity of the hill.

The face of Tess flushed slightly, but still she did not pause.

The eldest of the comers, a girl who wore a triangular shawl, its corner draggling on the stubble, carried in her arms what at first sight seemed to be a doll, but proved to be an infant in long clothes. Another brought some lunch. The harvesters ceased working, took their provisions, and sat down against one of the shocks. Here they fell to, the men plying a stone jar freely, and passing round a cup.

Tess Durbeyfield had been one of the last to suspend her labours. She sat down at the end of the shock, her face turned somewhat away from her companions. When she had deposited herself a man in a rabbit-skin cap and with a red handkerchief tucked into his belt, held the cup of ale over the top of the shock for her to drink. But she did not accept his offer. As soon as her lunch was spread she called up the big girl her sister, and took the baby off her, who, glad to be relieved of the burden, went away to the next shock and joined the other children playing there. Tess, with a curiously stealthy yet courageous movement, and with a still rising colour, unfastened her frock and began suckling the child.

The men who sat nearest considerately turned their faces towards the other end of the field, some of them beginning to smoke; one, with absent-minded fondness, regretfully stroking the jar that would no longer yield a stream. All the women but Tess fell into animated talk, and adjusted the disarranged knots of their hair.

When the infant had taken its fill the young mother sat it upright in her lap, and looking into the far distance dandled it with a gloomy indifference that was almost dislike; then all of a sudden she fell to violently kissing it some dozens of times, as if she could never leave off, the child crying at the vehemence of an onset which strangely combined passionateness with contempt.

'She's fond of that there child, though she mid pretend to hate en, and say she wishes the baby and her too were in the churchyard,' observed the woman in the red petticoat.

'She'll soon leave off saying that,' replied the one in buff. 'Lord, 'tis wonderful what a body can get used to o' that sort in time!'

'A little more than persuading had to do wi' the coming o't, I reckon. There were they that heard a sobbing one night last year in The Chase; and it mid ha' gone hard wi' a certain party if folks had come along.'

'Well, a little more, or a little less, 'twas a thousand pities that it should have happened to she, of all others. But 'tis always the comeliest! The plain ones be as safe as churches – hey, Jenny?' The speaker turned to one of the group who certainly was not ill-defined as plain.

It was a thousand pities, indeed; it was impossible for even an enemy to feel otherwise on looking at Tess as she sat there, with her flower-like mouth and large tender eyes, neither black nor blue nor gray nor violet; rather all those shades together, and a hundred others, which could be seen if one looked into their irises – shade behind shade – tint beyond tint – around pupils that had no bottom; an almost standard woman, but for the slight incautiousness of character inherited from her race.

A resolution which had surprised herself had brought her into the fields this week for the first time during many months. After wearing and wasting her palpitating heart with every engine of regret that lonely inexperience could devise, commonsense had illumined her. She felt that she would do well to be useful again – to taste anew sweet independence at any price. The past was past; whatever it had been it was no more at hand. Whatever its consequences, time would close over them; they would all in a few years be as if they had never been, and she herself grassed down and forgotten. Meanwhile the trees were just as green as before; the birds sang and the sun shone as clearly now as ever. The familiar surroundings had not darkened because of her grief, nor sickened because of her pain.

She might have seen that what had bowed her head so profoundly – the thought of the world's concern at her situation – was founded on an illusion. She was not an existence, an experience, a passion, a structure

81

of sensations, to anybody but herself. To all humankind besides Tess was only a passing thought. Even to friends she was no more than a frequently passing thought. If she made herself miserable the livelong night and day it was only this much to them – 'Ah, she makes herself unhappy.' If she tried to be cheerful, to dismiss all care, to take pleasure in the daylight, the flowers, the baby, she could only be this idea to them – 'Ah, she bears it very well.' Moreover, alone in a desert island would she have been wretched at what had happened to her? Not greatly. If she could have been but just created, to discover herself as a spouseless mother, with no experience of life except as the parent of a nameless child, would the position have caused her to despair? No, she would have taken it calmly, and found pleasures therein. Most of the misery had been generated by her conventional aspect, and not by her innate sensations.

Whatever Tess's reasoning, some spirit had induced her to dress herself up neatly as she had formerly done, and come out into the fields, harvest-hands being greatly in demand just then. This was why she had borne herself with dignity, and had looked people calmly in the face at times, even when holding the baby in her arms.

The harvest-men rose from the shock of corn, and stretched their limbs, and extinguished their pipes. The horses, which had been unharnessed and fed, were again attached to the scarlet machine. Tess, having quickly eaten her own meal, beckoned to her eldest sister to come and take away the baby, fastened her dress, put on the buff gloves again, and stooped anew to draw a bond from the last completed sheaf for the tying of the next.

In the afternoon and evening the proceedings of the morning were continued, Tess staying on till dusk with the body of harvesters. Then they all rode home in one of the largest waggons, in the company of a broad tarnished moon that had risen from the ground to the eastwards, its face resembling the outworn gold-leaf halo of some worm-eaten Tuscan saint. Tess's female companions sang songs, and showed themselves very sympathetic and glad at her reappearance out of doors, though they could not refrain from mischievously throwing in a few verses of the ballad about the maid who went to the merry green wood and came back a changed state. There are counterpoises and compensations in life; and the event which had made of her a social warning had also for the moment made her the most interesting personage in the village to many. Their friendliness won her still farther away from herself, their lively spirits were contagious, and she became almost gay.

But now that her moral sorrows were passing away a fresh one arose on the natural side of her which knew no social law. When she reached home it was to learn to her grief that the baby had been suddenly taken ill since the afternoon. Some such collapse had been probable, so tender and puny was its frame; but the event came as a shock nevertheless.

The baby's offence against society in coming into the world was forgotten by the girl-mother; her soul's desire was to continue that offence by preserving the life of the child. However, it soon grew clear that the hour of emancipation for that little prisoner of the flesh was to arrive earlier than her worst misgivings had conjectured. And when she had discovered this she was plunged into a misery which transcended that of the child's simple loss. Her baby had not been baptized.

Tess had drifted into a frame of mind which accepted passively the consideration that if she should have to burn for what she had done, burn she must, and there was an end of it. Like all village girls she was well grounded in the Holy Scriptures, and had dutifully studied the histories of Aholah and Aholibah, and knew the inferences to be drawn therefrom. But when the same question arose with regard to the baby, it had a very different colour. Her darling was about to die, and no salvation.

It was nearly bedtime, but she rushed downstairs and asked if she might send for the parson. The moment happened to be one at which her father's sense of the antique nobility of his family was highest, and his sensitiveness to the smudge which Tess had set upon that nobility most pronounced, for he had just returned from his weekly booze at Rolliver's Inn. No parson should come inside his door, he declared, prying into his affairs, just then, when, by her shame, it had become more necessary than ever to hide them. He locked the door and put the key in his pocket.

The household went to bed, and, distressed beyond measure, Tess retired also. She was continually waking as she lay, and in the middle of the night found that the baby was still worse. It was obviously dying – quietly and painlessly, but none the less surely.

In her misery she rocked herself upon the bed. The clock struck the solemn hour of one, that hour when fancy stalks outside reason, and malignant possibilities stand rock-firm as facts. She thought of the child consigned to the nethermost corner of hell, as its double doom for lack of baptism and lack of legitimacy; saw the arch-fiend tossing it with his three-pronged fork, like the one they used for heating the oven on baking days; to which picture she added many other quaint and curious details of torment sometimes taught the young in this Christian country. The lurid presentment so powerfully affected her imagination in the silence of the sleeping house that her nightgown became damp with perspiration, and the bedstead shook with each throb of her heart.

The infant's breathing grew more difficult, and the mother's mental tension increased. It was useless to devour the little thing with kisses; she could stay in bed no longer, and walked feverishly about the room.

'O merciful God, have pity; have pity upon my poor baby!' she cried. 'Heap as much anger as you want to upon me, and welcome; but pity the child!'

She leant against the chest of drawers, and murmured incoherent supplications for a long while, till she suddenly started up.

'Ah! perhaps baby can be saved! Perhaps it will be just the same!'

She spoke so brightly that it seemed as though her face might have shone in the gloom surrounding her.

She lit a candle, and went to a second and a third bed under the wall, where she awoke her young sisters and brothers, all of whom occupied the same room. Pulling out the washingstand so that she could get behind it, she poured some water from a jug, and made them kneel around, putting their hands together with fingers exactly vertical. While the children, scarcely awake, awe-stricken at her manner, their eyes growing larger and larger, remained in this position, she took the baby from her bed – a child's child – so immature as scarce to seem a sufficient personality to endow its producer with the maternal title. Tess then stood erect with the infant on her arm beside the basin, the next sister held the Prayer-Book open before her, as the clerk at church held it before the parson; and thus the girl set about baptizing her child.

Her figure looked singularly tall and imposing as she stood in her long white nightgown, a thick cable of twisted dark hair hanging straight down her back to her waist. The kindly dimness of the weak candle abstracted from her form and features the little blemishes which sunlight might have revealed – the stubble scratches upon her wrists, and the weariness of her eyes – her high enthusiasm having a transfiguring effect upon the face which had been her undoing, showing it as a thing of immaculate beauty, with a touch of dignity which was almost regal. The little ones kneeling round, their sleepy eyes blinking and red, awaited her preparations full of a suspended wonder which their physical heaviness at that hour would not allow to become active.

The most impressed of them said:

'Be you really going to christen him, Tess?'

The girl-mother replied in a grave affirmative.

'What's his name going to be?'

She had not thought of that, but a name suggested by a phrase in the book of Genesis came into her head as she proceeded with the baptismal service, and now she pronounced it:

'SORROW, I baptize thee in the name of the Father, and of the Son, and of the Holy Ghost.'

She sprinkled the water, and there was silence.

84

'Say "Amen", children.'

The tiny voices piped in obedient response 'Amen!'

Tess went on:

'We receive this child' – and so forth – 'and do sign him with the sign of the Cross.'

Here she dipped her hand into the basin, and fervently drew an immense cross upon the baby with her forefinger, continuing with the customary sentences as to his manfully fighting against sin, the world, and the devil, and being a faithful soldier and servant unto his life's end. She duly went on with the Lord's Prayer, the children lisping it after her in a thin gnat-like wail, till, at the conclusion, raising their voices to clerk's pitch, they again piped into the silence, 'Amen!'

Then their sister, with much augmented confidence in the efficacy of this sacrament, poured forth from the bottom of her heart the thanksgiving that follows, uttering it boldly and triumphantly in the stopt-diapason note which her voice acquired when her heart was in her speech, and which will never be forgotten by those who knew her. The ecstasy of faith almost apotheosized her; it set upon her face a glowing irradiation, and brought a red spot into the middle of each cheek; while the miniature candle-flame inverted in her eye-pupils shone like a diamond. The children gazed up at her with more and more reverence, and no longer had a will for questioning. She did not look like Sissy to them now, but as a being large, towering, and awful – a divine personage with whom they had nothing in common.

Poor Sorrow's campaign against sin, the world, and the devil was doomed to be of limited brilliancy – luckily perhaps for himself, considering his beginnings. In the blue of the morning that fragile soldier and servant breathed his last, and when the other children awoke they cried bitterly, and begged Sissy to have another pretty baby.

The calmness which had possessed Tess since the christening remained with her in the infant's loss. In the daylight, indeed, she felt her terrors about his soul to have been somewhat exaggerated; whether well founded or not she had no uneasiness now, reasoning that if Providence would not ratify such an act of approximation she, for one, did not value the kind of heaven lost by the irregularity – either for herself or for her child.

So passed away Sorrow the Undesired – that intrusive creature, that bastard gift of shameless Nature who respects not the social law; a waif to whom eternal Time had been a matter of days merely, who knew not that such things as years and centuries ever were; to whom the cottage interior was the universe, the week's weather climate, new-born babyhood human existence, and the instinct to suck human knowledge.

Tess, who mused on the christening a good deal, wondered if it were doctrinally sufficient to secure a Christian burial for the child. Nobody could tell this but the parson of the parish, and he was a new-comer, and did not know her. She went to his house after dusk, and stood by the gate, but could not summon courage to go in. The enterprise would have been abandoned if she had not by accident met him coming homeward as she turned away. In the gloom she did not mind speaking freely.

'I should like to ask you something, sir.'

He expressed his willingness to listen, and she told the story of the baby's illness and the extemporized ordinance.

'And now, sir,' she added earnestly, 'can you tell me this – will it be just the same for him as if you had baptized him?'

Having the natural feelings of a tradesman at finding that a job he should have been called in for had been unskilfully botched by his customers among themselves, he was disposed to say no. Yet the dignity of the girl, the strange tenderness in her voice, combined to affect his nobler impulses – or rather those that he had left in him after ten years of endeavour to graft technical belief on actual scepticism. The man and the ecclesiastic fought within him, and the victory fell to the man.

'My dear girl,' he said, 'it will be just the same.'

'Then will you give him a Christian burial?' she asked quickly.

The vicar felt himself cornered. Hearing of the baby's illness, he had conscientiously gone to the house after nightfall to perform the rite, and, unaware that the refusal to admit him had come from Tess's father and not from Tess, he could not allow the plea of necessity for its irregular administration.

'Ah – that's another matter,' he said.

'Another matter – why?' asked Tess, rather warmly.

'Well – I would willingly do so if only we two were concerned. But I must not – for certain reasons.'

'Just for once, sir!'

'Really I must not.'

'O sir!' She seized his hand as she spoke.

He withdrew it, shaking his head.

'Then I don't like you!' she burst out, 'and I'll never come to your church no more!'

'Don't talk so rashly.'

'Perhaps it will be just the same to him if you don't? . . . Will it be just the same? Don't for God's sake speak as saint to sinner, but as you yourself to me myself – poor me!'

How the Vicar reconciled his answer with the strict notions he supposed himself to hold on these subjects it is beyond a layman's power to tell, though not to excuse. Somewhat moved, he said in this case also –

'It will be just the same.'

So the baby was carried in a small deal box, under an ancient woman's shawl, to the churchyard that night, and buried by lantern-light, at the cost of a shilling and a pint of beer to the sexton, in that shabby corner of God's allotment where He lets the nettles grow, and where all unbaptized infants, notorious drunkards, suicides, and others of the conjecturally damned are laid. In spite of the untoward surroundings, however, Tess bravely made a little cross of two laths and a piece of string, and having bound it with flowers, she stuck it up at the head of the grave one evening when she could enter the churchyard without being seen, putting at the foot also a bunch of the same flowers in a little jar of water to keep them alive. What matter was it that on the outside of the jar the eye of mere observation noted the words 'Keelwell's Marmalade'? The eye of maternal affection did not see them in its vision of higher things.

❧ Chapter Fifteen ❧

'BY EXPERIENCE,' SAYS ROGER Ascham, 'we find out a short way by a long wandering.' Not seldom that long wandering unfits us for further travel, and of what use is our experience to us then? Tess Durbeyfield's experience was of this incapacitating kind. At last she had learned what to do; but who would now accept her doing?

If before going to the d'Urbervilles' she had vigorously moved under the guidance of sundry gnomic texts and phrases known to her and to the world in general, no doubt she would never have been imposed on. But it had not been in Tess's power – nor is it in anybody's power – to feel the whole truth of golden opinions while it is possible to profit by them. She – and how many more – might have ironically said to God with Saint Augustine: 'Thou hast counselled a better course than Thou hast permitted.'

She remained in her father's house during the winter months, plucking fowls, or cramming turkeys and geese, or making clothes for her sisters and brothers out of some finery which d'Urberville had given her, and she had put by with contempt. Apply to him she would not. But she would often clasp her hands behind her head and muse when she was supposed to be working hard.

She philosophically noted dates as they came past in the revolution of the year; the disastrous night of her undoing at Trantridge with its dark background of The Chase; also the dates of the baby's birth and death; also her own birthday; and every other day individualized by incidents in which she had taken some share. She suddenly thought one afternoon, when looking in the glass at her fairness, that there was yet another date, of greater importance to her than those; that of her own death, when all these charms would have disappeared; a day which lay sly and unseen and among all the other days of the year, giving no sign or sound when she annually passed over it; but not the less surely there. When was it? Why did she not feel the chill of each yearly encounter with such a cold relation? She had Jeremy Taylor's thought that some time in the future those who had known her would say? 'It is the -th, the day that poor Tess Durbeyfield died'; and there would be nothing singular to their minds in the statement. Of that day, doomed to be her terminus in time through all the ages, she did not know the place in month, week, season, or year.

Almost at a leap Tess thus changed from simple girl to complex woman. Symbols of reflectiveness passed into her face, and a note of tragedy at times into her voice. Her eyes grew larger and more eloquent. She became what would have been called a fine creature; her aspect was fair and arresting; her soul that of a woman whom the turbulent experiences of the last year or two had quite failed to demoralize. But for the world's opinion those experiences would have been simply a liberal education.

She had held so aloof of late that her trouble, never generally known, was nearly forgotten in Marlott. But it became evident to her that she could never be really comfortable again in a place which had seen the collapse of her family's attempt to 'claim kin' – and, through her, even closer union – with the rich d'Urbervilles. At least she could not be comfortable there till long years should have obliterated her keen consciousness of it. Yet even now Tess felt the pulse of hopeful life still warm within her; she might be happy in some nook which had no memories. To escape the past and all that appertained thereto was to annihilate it, and to do that she would have to get away.

Was once lost always lost really true of chastity? she would ask herself. She might prove it false if she could veil bygones. The recuperative power which pervaded organic nature was surely not denied to maidenhood alone.

She waited a long time without finding opportunity for a new departure. A particularly fine spring came round, and the stir of germination was almost audible in the buds; it moved her, as it moved the wild animals, and made her passionate to go. At last, one day in early May, a letter reached her from a former friend of her mother's, to whom she had addressed inquiries long before – a person whom she had never seen – that a skilful milkmaid was required at a dairy-house many miles to the southward, and that the dairyman would be glad to have her for the summer months.

It was not quite so far off as could have been wished; but it was probably far enough, her radius of movement and repute having been so small. To persons of limited spheres, miles are as geographical degrees, parishes as counties, counties as provinces and kingdoms.

On one point she was resolved: there should be no more d'Urberville air-castles in the dreams and deeds of her new life. She would be the dairymaid Tess, and nothing more. Her mother knew Tess's feeling on this point so well, though no words had passed between them on the subject, that she never alluded to the knightly ancestry now.

Yet such is human inconsistency that one of the interests of the new place to her was the accidental virtue of its lying near her forefathers' country (for they were not Blakemore men, though her mother was Blakemore to the bone). The dairy called Talbothays, for which she was bound, stood not remotely from some of the former estates of the d'Urbervilles, near the great family vaults of her granddames and their powerful husbands. She would be able to look at them, and think not only that d'Urberville, like Babylon, had fallen, but that the individual innocence of a humble descendant could lapse as silently. All the while she wondered if any strange good thing might come to her being in her ancestral land; and some spirit within her rose automatically as the sap in the twigs. It was unexpended youth, surging up anew after its temporary check, and bringing with it hope, and the invincible instinct towards self-delight.

PHASE THE THIRD

The Rally

❧ Chapter Sixteen ❧

ON A THYME-SCENTED, BIRD-HATCHING morning in May, between two and three years after the return from Trantridge – silent reconstructive years for Tess Durbeyfield – she left her home for the second time.

Having packed up her luggage so that it could be sent to her later, she started in a hired trap for the little town of Stourcastle, through which it was necessary to pass on her journey, now in a direction almost opposite to that of her first adventuring. On the curve of the nearest hill she looked back regretfully at Marlott and her father's house, although she had been so anxious to get away.

Her kindred dwelling there would probably continue their daily lives as heretofore, with no great diminution of pleasure in their consciousness, although she would be far off, and they deprived of her smile. In a few days the children would engage in their games as merrily as ever without the sense of any gap left by her departure. This leaving of the younger children she had decided to be for the best; were she to remain they would probably gain less good by her precepts than harm by her example.

She went through Stourcastle without pausing, and onward to a junction of highways, where she could await a carrier's van that ran to the south-west; for the railways which engirdled this interior tract of country had never yet struck across it. While waiting, however, there came along a farmer in his spring-cart, driving approximately in the direction that she wished to pursue. Though he was a stranger to her she accepted his offer of a seat beside him, ignoring that its motive was a mere tribute to her countenance. He was going to Weatherbury, and by accompanying him thither she could walk the remainder of the distance instead of travelling in the van by way of Casterbridge.

Tess did not stop at Weatherbury, after this long drive, further than to make a slight nondescript meal at noon at a cottage to which the farmer recommended her. Thence she started on foot, basket in hand, to reach the wide upland of heath dividing this district from the low-lying meads of a further valley in which the dairy stood that was the aim and end of her day's pilgrimage.

Tess had never before visited this part of the country, and yet she felt akin to the landscape. Not so very far to the left of her she could discern a dark patch in the scenery, which inquiry confirmed her in supposing to be trees marking the environs of Kingsbere – in the church of which parish the bones of her ancestors – her useless ancestors – lay entombed.

She had no admiration for them now; she almost hated them for the dance they had led her; not a thing of all that had been theirs did she retain but the old seal and spoon. 'Pooh – I have as much of mother as father in me!' she said. 'All my prettiness comes from her, and she was only a dairymaid.'

The journey over the intervening uplands and lowlands of Egdon, when she reached them, was a more troublesome walk than she had anticipated, the distance being actually but a few miles. It was two hours, owing to sundry wrong turnings, ere she found herself on a summit commanding the long-sought-for vale, the Valley of the Great Dairies, the valley in which milk and butter grew to rankness, and were produced more profusely, if less delicately, than at her home – the verdant plain so well watered by the river Var or Froom.

It was intrinsically different from the Vale of Little Dairies, Blackmoor Vale, which, save during her disastrous sojourn at Trantridge, she had exclusively known till now. The world was drawn to a larger pattern here. The enclosures numbered fifty acres instead of ten, the farmsteads were more extended, the groups of cattle formed tribes hereabout; there only families. These myriads of cows stretching under her eyes from the far east to the far west outnumbered any she had ever seen at one glance before. The green lea was speckled as thickly with them as a canvas by Van Alsloot or Sallaert with burghers. The ripe hue of the red and dun kine absorbed the evening sunlight, which the white-coated animals returned to the eye in rays almost dazzling, even at the distant elevation on which she stood.

The bird's-eye perspective before her was not so luxuriantly beautiful, perhaps, as that other one which she knew so well; yet it was more cheering. It lacked the intensely blue atmosphere of the rival vale, and its heavy soils and scents; the new air was clear, bracing, ethereal. The river itself, which nourished the grass and cows of these renowned dairies, flowed not like the streams in Blackmoor. Those were slow, silent, often turbid; flowing over beds of mud into which the incautious wader might sink and vanish unawares. The Froom waters were clear as the pure River of Life shown to the Evangelist, rapid as the shadow of a cloud, with pebbly shallows that prattled to the sky all day long. There the water-flower was the lily; the crowfoot here.

Either the change in the quality of the air from heavy to light, or the sense of being amid new scenes where there were no invidious eyes upon her, sent up her spirits wonderfully. Her hopes mingled with the sunshine in an ideal photosphere which surrounded her as she bounded along against the soft south wind. She heard a pleasant voice in every breeze, and in every bird's note seemed to lurk a joy.

Her face had latterly changed with changing states of mind, continually fluctuating between beauty and ordinariness, according as the thoughts were gay or grave. One day she was pink and flawless; another pale and tragical. When she was pink she was feeling less than when pale; her more perfect beauty accorded with her less elevated mood; her more intense mood with her less perfect beauty. It was her best face physically that was now set against the south wind.

The irresistible, universal, automatic tendency to find sweet pleasure somewhere, which pervades all life, from the meanest to the highest, had at length mastered Tess. Being even now only a young woman of twenty, one who mentally and sentimentally had not finished growing, it was impossible that any event should have left upon her an impression that was not in time capable of transmutation.

And thus her spirits, and her thankfulness, and her hopes, rose higher and higher. She tried several ballads, but found them inadequate; till, recollecting the psalter that her eyes had so often wandered over of a Sunday morning before she had eaten of the tree of knowledge, she chanted: 'O ye Sun and Moon . . . O ye Stars . . . ye Green Things upon the Earth . . . ye Fowls of the Air . . . Beasts and Cattle . . . Children of Men . . . bless ye the Lord, praise Him and magnify Him for ever!'

She suddenly stopped and murmured: 'But perhaps I don't quite know the Lord as yet.'

And probably the half-unconscious rhapsody was a Fetichistic utterance in a Monotheistic setting; women whose chief companions are the forms and forces of outdoor Nature retain in their souls far more of the Pagan fantasy of their remote forefathers than of the systematized religion taught their race at later date. However, Tess found at least approximate expression for her feelings in the old *Benedicite* that she had lisped from infancy; and it was enough. Such high contentment with such a slight initial performance as that of having started towards a means of independent living was a part of the Durbeyfield temperament. Tess really wished to walk uprightly, while her father did nothing of the kind; but she resembled him in being content with immediate and small achievements, and in having no mind for laborious effort towards such petty social advancement as could alone be effected by a family so heavily handicapped as the once powerful d'Urbervilles were now.

There was, it might be said, the energy of her mother's unexpended family, as well as the natural energy of Tess's years, rekindled after the experience which had so overwhelmed her for the time. Let the truth be told – women do as a rule live through such humiliations, and regain their spirits, and again look about them with an interested eye. While there's life there's hope is a conviction not so entirely unknown to the 'betrayed' as some amiable theorists would have us believe.

Tess Durbeyfield, then, in good heart, and full of zest for life, descended the Egdon slopes lower and lower towards the dairy of her pilgrimage.

The marked difference, in the final particular, between the rival vales now showed itself. The secret of Blackmoor was best discovered from the heights around; to read aright the valley before her it was necessary to descend into its midst. When Tess had accomplished this feat she found herself to be standing on a carpeted level, which stretched to the east and west as far as the eye could reach.

The river had stolen from the higher tracts and brought in particles to the vale all this horizontal land; and now, exhausted, aged, and attenuated, lay serpentining along through the midst of its former spoils.

Not quite sure of her direction Tess stood still upon the hemmed expanse of verdant flatness, like a fly on a billiard-table of indefinite length, and of no more consequence to the surroundings than that fly. The sole effect of her presence upon the placid valley so far had been to excite the mind of a solitary heron, which, after descending to the ground not far from her path, stood with neck erect, looking at her.

Suddenly there arose from all parts of the lowland a prolonged and repeated call –

'Waow! waow! waow!'

From the furthest east to the furthest west the cries spread as if by contagion, accompanied in some cases by the barking of a dog. It was not the expression of the valley's consciousness that beautiful Tess had arrived, but the ordinary announcement of milking-time – half-past four o'clock, when the dairymen set about getting in the cows.

The red and white herd nearest at hand, which had been phlegmatically waiting for the call, now trooped towards the steading in the background, their great bags of milk swinging under them as they walked. Tess followed slowly in their rear, and entered the barton by the open gate through which they had entered before her. Long thatched sheds stretched round the enclosure, their slopes encrusted with vivid green moss, and their eaves supported by wooden posts rubbed to a glossy smoothness by the flanks of infinite cows and calves of bygone years, now passed to an oblivion almost inconceivable in its profundity. Between the posts were ranged the milchers, each exhibiting herself at the present moment to a whimsical eye in the rear as a circle on two stalks, down the centre of which a switch moved pendulum-wise; while the sun, lowering itself behind this patient row, threw their shadows accurately inwards upon the wall. Thus it threw shadows of these obscure and homely figures every evening with as much care over each contour as if it had been the profile of a Court beauty on a palace wall; copied them as diligently as it had copied Olympian shapes on marble *façades* long ago, or the outline of Alexander, Caesar, and the Pharaohs.

They were the less restful cows that were stalled. Those that would stand still of their own will were milked in the middle of the yard, where many of such better behaved ones stood waiting now – all prime milchers, such as were seldom seen out of this valley, and not always within it; nourished by the succulent feed which the water-meads supplied at this prime season of the year. Those of them that were spotted with white reflected the sunshine in dazzling brilliancy, and the polished brass knobs on their horns glittered with something of military display. Their large-veined udders hung ponderous as sandbags, the teats sticking out like the legs of a gipsy's crock; and as each animal lingered for her turn to arrive the milk oozed forth and fell in drops to the ground.

❧ Chapter Seventeen ❦

THE DAIRYMAIDS AND MEN had flocked down from their cottages and out of the dairy-house with the arrival of the cows from the meads; the maids walking in pattens, not on account of the weather, but to keep their shoes above the mulch of the barton. Each girl sat down on her three-legged stool, her face sideways, her right cheek resting against the cow; and looked musingly along the animal's flank at Tess as she approached. The male milkers, with hat-brims turned down, resting flat on their foreheads and gazing on the ground, did not observe her.

One of these was a sturdy middle-aged man – whose long white 'pinner' was somewhat finer and cleaner than the wraps of the others, and whose jacket underneath had a presentable marketing aspect – the master-dairyman, of whom she was in quest, his double character as a working milker and buttermaker here during six days, and on the seventh as a man in shining broad-cloth in his family pew at church, being so marked as to have inspired a rhyme –

> *Dairyman Dick*
> *All the week:*
> *On Sundays Mister Richard Crick.*

Seeing Tess standing at gaze he went across to her.

The majority of dairymen have a cross manner at milking-time, but it happened that Mr Crick was glad to get a new hand – for the days were busy ones now – and he received her warmly; inquiring for her mother and the rest of the family – (though this as a matter of form merely, for in reality he had not been aware of Mrs Durbeyfield's existence till apprised of the fact by a brief business-letter about Tess).

'Oh – ay, as a lad I knowed your part o' the country very well,' he said terminatively. 'Though I've never been there since. And a aged woman of ninety that used to live nigh here, but is dead and gone long ago, told me that a family of some such name as yours in Blackmoor Vale came originally from these parts, and that 'twere a old ancient race that had all but perished off the earth – though the new generations didn't know it. But, Lord, I took no notice of the old woman's ramblings, not I.'

'Oh no – it is nothing,' said Tess.

Then the talk was of business only.

'You can milk 'em clean, my maidy? I don't want my cows going azew at this time o' year.'

She reassured him on that point, and he surveyed her up and down. She had been staying indoors a good deal, and her complexion had grown delicate.

'Quite sure you can stand it? 'Tis comfortable enough here for rough folk; but we don't live in a cowcumber frame.'

She declared that she could stand it, and her zest and willingness seemed to win him over.

'Well, I suppose you'll want a dish o' tay, or victuals of some sort, hey? Not yet? Well, do as ye like about it. But faith, if 'twas I, I should be as dry as a kex wi' travelling so far.'

'I'll begin milking now, to get my hand in,' said Tess.

She drank a little milk as temporary refreshment – to the surprise – indeed, slighty contempt – of Dairyman Crick, to whose mind it had apparently never occurred that milk was good as a beverage.

'Oh, if ye can swaller that, be it so,' he said indifferently, while one held up the pail that she sipped from. ''Tis what I hain't touched for years – not I. Rot the stuff; it would lie in my innerds like lead. You can try your hand upon she,' he pursued, nodding to the nearest cow. 'Not but what she do milk rather hard. We've hard ones and we've easy ones, like other folks. However, you'll find out that soon enough.'

When Tess had changed her bonnet for a hood, and was really on her stool under the cow, and the milk was squirting from her fists into the pail, she appeared to feel that she really had laid a new foundation for her future. The conviction bred serenity, her pulse slowed, and she was able to look about her.

The milkers formed quite a little batallion of men and maids, the men operating on the hard-teated animals, the maids on the kindlier natures. It was a large dairy. There were nearly a hundred milchers under Crick's management, all told; and of the herd the master-dairyman milked six or eight with his own hands, unless away from home. These were the cows that milked hardest of all; for his journey-milkmen being more or less casually hired, he would not entrust this half-dozen to their treatment, lest, from indifference, they should not milk them fully; nor to the maids, lest they should fail in the same way for lack of finger-grip; with the result that in course of time the cows would 'go azew' – that is, dry up. It was not the loss for the moment that made slack milking so serious, but that with the decline of demand there came decline, and ultimately cessation, of supply.

After Tess had settled down to her cow there was for a time no talk in the barton, and not a sound interfered with the purr of the milk-jets into the numerous pails, except a momentary exclamation to one or other of the beasts requesting her to turn round or stand still. The only movements were those of the milkers' hands up and down, and the swing of the cows' tails. Thus they all worked on, encompassed by the vast flat mead which extended to either slope of the valley – a level landscape compounded of old landscapes long forgotten, and, no doubt, differing in character very greatly from the landscape they composed now.

'To my thinking,' said the dairyman, rising suddenly from a cow he had just finished off, snatching up his three-legged stool in one hand and the pail in the other, and moving on to the next hard-yielder in his vicinity; 'to my thinking, the cows don't gie down their milk to-day as usual. Upon my life, if Winker do begin keeping back like this, she'll not be worth going under by midsummer.'

''Tis because there's a new hand come among us,' said Jonathan Kail. 'I've noticed such things afore.'

'To be sure. It may be so. I didn't think o't.'

'I've been told that it goes up into their horns at such times,' said a dairymaid.

'Well, as to going up into their horns,' replied Dairyman Crick dubiously, as though even witchcraft might be limited by anatomical possibilities, 'I couldn't say; I certainly could not. But as nott cows will keep it back as well as the horned ones, I don't quite agree to it. Do ye know that riddle about the nott cows, Jonathan? Why do nott cows give less milk in a year than horned?'

'I don't!' interposed the milkmaid. 'Why do they?'

'Because there bain't so many of 'em,' said the dairyman. 'Howsom-ever, these gam'sters do certainly keep back their milk to-day. Folks, we must lift up a stave or two – that's the only cure for't.'

Songs were often resorted to in dairies hereabout as an enticement to the cows when they showed signs of withholding their usual yield; and the band of milkers at this request burst into melody – in purely business-like tones, it is true, and with no great spontaneity; the result, according to their own belief, being a decided improvement during the song's continuance. When they had gone through fourteen or fifteen verses of a cheerful ballad about a murderer who was afraid to go to bed in the dark because he saw certain brimstone flames around him, one of the male milkers said –

'I wish singing on the stoop didn't use up so much of a man's wind! You should get your harp, sir; not but what a fiddle is best.'

Tess, who had given ear to this, thought the words were addressed to the dairyman, but she was wrong. A reply, in the shape of 'Why?' came as it were out of the belly of a dun cow in the stalls; it had been spoken by a milker behind the animal, whom she had not hitherto perceived.

'Oh yes; there's nothing like a fiddle,' said the dairyman. 'Though I do think that bulls are more moved by a tune than cows – at least that's my experience. Once there was a old aged man over at Mellstock – William Dewy by name – one of the family that used to do a good deal of business as tranters over there, Jonathan, do ye mind? – I knowed the man by sight as well as I know my own brother, in a manner of speaking. Well, this man was a coming home-along from a wedding where he had been playing his fiddle, one fine moonlight night, and for shortness' sake he took a cut across Forty-acres, a field lying that way, where a bull was out to grass. The bull seed William, and took after him, horns aground, begad; and though William runned his best, and hadn't *much* drink in him (considering 'twas a wedding, and the folks well off), he found he'd never reach the fence and get over in time to save himself. Well, as a last thought, he pulled out his fiddle as he runned, and struck up a jig, turning to the bull, and backing towards the corner. The bull softened down, and stood still, looking hard at William Dewy, who fiddled on and on; till a sort of a smile stole over the bull's face. But no sooner did William stop his playing and turn to get over hedge than the bull would stop his smiling and lower his horns towards the seat of William's breeches. Well, William had to turn about and play on, willy-nilly; and 'twas only three o'clock in the world, and 'a knowed that nobody would come that way for hours, and he so leery and tired that 'a didn't know what to do. When he had scraped till about four o'clock he felt that he verily would have to give over soon, and he said to himself, "There's only this last tune between me and eternal welfare! Heaven save me, or

I'm a done man." Well, then he called to mind how he'd seen the cattle kneel o' Christmas Eves in the dead o' night. It was not Christmas Eve then, but it came into his head to play a trick upon the bull. So he broke into the 'Tivity Hymn, just as at Christmas carol-singing; when, lo and behold, down went the bull on his bended knees, in his ignorance, just as if 'twere the true 'Tivity night and hour. As soon as his horned friend were down, William turned, clinked off like a long-dog, and jumped safe over hedge, before the praying bull had got on his feet again to take after him. William used to say that he'd seen a man look a fool a good many times, but never such a fool as that bull looked when he found his pious feelings had been played upon, and 'twas not Christmas Eve . . . Yes, William Dewy, that was the man's name; and I can tell you to a foot where's he a-lying in Mellstock Churchyard at this very moment – just between the second yew-tree and the north aisle.'

'It's a curious story; it carries us back to mediaeval times, when faith was a living thing!'

The remark, singular for a dairy-yard, was murmured by the voice behind the dun cow; but as nobody understood the reference no notice was taken, except that the narrator seemed to think it might imply scepticism as to his tale.

'Well, 'tis quite true, sir, whether or no. I knowed the man well.'

'Oh yes; I have no doubt of it,' said the person behind the dun cow.

Tess's attention was thus attracted to the dairyman's interlocutor, of whom she could see but the merest patch, owing to his burying his head so persistently in the flank of the milcher. She could not understand why he should be addressed as 'sir' even by the dairyman himself. But no explanation was discernible; he remained under the cow long enough to have milked three, uttering a private ejaculation now and then, as if he could not get on.

'Take it gentle, sir; take it gentle,' said the dairyman. ''Tis knack, not strength that does it.'

'So I find,' said the other, standing up at last and stretching his arms. 'I think I have finished her, however, though she made my fingers ache.'

Tess could then see him at full length. He wore the ordinary white pinner and leather leggings of a dairy-farmer when milking, and his boots were clogged with the mulch of the yard; but this was all his local livery. Beneath it was something educated, reserved, subtle, sad, differing.

But the details of his aspect were temporarily thrust aside by the discovery that he was one whom she had seen before. Such vicissitudes had Tess passed through since that time that for a moment she could not remember where she had met him; and then it flashed upon her that he was the pedestrian who had joined in the club-dance at Marlott – the passing stranger who had come she knew not whence, had danced with others but not with her, had slightingly left her, and gone on his way with his friends.

The flood of memories brought back by this revival of an incident anterior to her troubles produced a momentary dismay lest, recognizing her also, he should by some means discover her story. But it passed away when she found no sign of remembrance in him. She saw by degrees that since their first and only encounter his mobile face had grown more thoughtful, and had acquired a young man's shapely moustache and beard – the latter of the palest straw colour where it began upon his cheeks, and deepening to a warm brown farther from its root. Under his linen milking-pinner he wore a dark velveteen jacket, cord breeches and gaiters, and a starched white shirt. Without the milking-gear nobody could have guessed what he was. He might with equal probability have been an eccentric landowner or a gentlemanly ploughman. That he was but a novice at dairywork she had realized in a moment, from the time he had spent upon the milking of one cow.

Meanwhile many of the milkmaids had said to one another of the new-comer, 'How pretty she is!' with something of real generosity and admiration, though with a half hope that the auditors would qualify the assertion – which, strictly speaking, they might have done, prettiness being an inexact definition of what struck the eye in Tess. When the milking was finished for the evening they straggled indoors, where Mrs Crick, the dairyman's wife – who was too respectable to go out milking herself, and wore a hot stuff gown in warm weather because the dairymaids wore prints – was giving an eye to the leads and things.

Only two or three of the maids, Tess learnt, slept in the dairy-house besides herself; most of the helpers going to their homes. She saw nothing at supper-time of the superior milker who had commented on the story, and asked no questions about him, the remainder of the evening being occupied in arranging her place in the bed-chamber. It was a large room over the milk-house, some thirty feet long; the sleeping-cots of the other three indoor milkmaids being in the same apartment. They were blooming young women, and, except one, rather older than herself. By bedtime Tess was thoroughly tired, and fell asleep immediately.

But one of the girls who occupied an adjoining bed was more wakeful than Tess, and would insist upon relating to the latter various particulars of the homestead into which she had just entered. The girl's whispered words mingled with the shades, and, to Tess's drowsy mind, they seemed to be generated by the darkness in which they floated.

'Mr Angel Clare – he that is learning milking, and that plays the harp – never says much to us. He is a pa'son's son, and is too much taken up wi' his own thoughts to notice girls. He is the dairyman's pupil – learning farming in all its branches. He has learnt sheep-farming at another place, and he's now mastering dairy-work ... Yes, he is quite the gentleman-born. His father is the Reverent Mr Clare at Emminster – a good many miles from here.'

'Oh – I have heard of him,' said her companion, now awake. 'A very earnest clergyman, is he not?'

'Yes – that he is – the earnestest man in all Wessex, they say – the last of the old Low Church sort, they tell me – for all about here be what they call High. All his sons, except our Mr Clare, be made pa'sons too.'

Tess had not at this hour the curiosity to ask why the present Mr Clare was not made a parson like his brethren, and gradually fell asleep again, the words of her informant coming to her along with the smell of the cheeses in the adjoining cheese-loft, and the measured dripping of the whey from the wrings downstairs.

❧ Chapter Eighteen ❧

ANGEL CLARE RISES OUT of the past not altogether as a distinct figure, but as an appreciative voice, a long regard of fixed, abstracted eyes, and a mobility of mouth somewhat too small and delicately lined for a man's, though with an unexpectedly firm close of the lower lip now and then; enough to do away with any inference of indecision. Nevertheless, some-thing nebulous, preoccupied, vague, in his bearing and regard, marked him as one who probably had no very definite aim or concern about his material future. Yet as a lad people had said of him that he was one who might do anything if he tried.

He was the youngest son of his father, a poor parson at the other end of the county, and had arrived at Talbothays Dairy as a six months' pupil, after going the round of some other farms, his object being to acquire a practical skill in the various processes of farming, with a view either to the Colonies, or the tenure of a home-farm, as circumstances might decide.

His entry into the ranks of the agriculturists and breeders was a step in the young man's career which had been anticipated neither by himself nor by others.

Mr Clare the elder, whose first wife had died and left him a daughter, married a second late in life. This lady had somewhat unexpectedly brought him three sons, so that between Angel, the youngest, and his father the vicar there seemed to be almost a missing generation. Of these boys the aforesaid Angel, the child of his old age, was the only son who had not taken a University degree, though he was the single one of them whose early promise might have done full justice to an academical training.

Some two or three years before Angel's appearance at the Marlott dance, on a day when he had left school and was pursuing his studies at home, a parcel came to the vicarage from the local bookseller's, directed to the Reverend James Clare. The vicar having opened it and found it to contain a book, read a few pages; whereupon he jumped up from his seat and went straight to the shop with the book under his arm.

'Why has this been sent to my house?' he asked peremptorily, holding up the volume.

'It was ordered, sir.'

'Not by me, or any one belonging to me, I am happy to say.'

The shopkeeper looked into his order-book.

'Oh, it has been misdirected, sir,' he said. 'It was ordered by Mr Angel Clare, and should have been sent to him.'

Mr Clare winced as if he had been struck. He went home pale and dejected, and called Angel into his study.

'Look into this book, my boy,' he said. 'What do you know about it?'

'I ordered it,' said Angel simply.

'What for?'

'To read.'

'How can you think of reading it?'

'How can I? Why – it is a system of philosophy. There is no more moral, or even religious, work published.'

'Yes – moral enough; I don't deny that. But religious! – and for *you*, who intend to be a minister of the Gospel!'

'Since you have alluded to the matter, father,' said the son, with anxious thought upon his face, 'I should like to say, once for all, that I should prefer not to take Orders. I fear I could not conscientiously do so. I love the Church as one loves a parent. I shall always have the warmest affection for her. There is no institution for whose history I have a deeper admiration; but I cannot honestly be ordained her minister, as my brothers are, while she refuses to liberate her mind from an untenable redemptive theolatry.'

It had never occurred to the straightforward and simple-minded Vicar that one of his own flesh and blood could come to this! He was stultified, shocked, paralyzed. And if Angel were not going to enter the Church, what was the use of sending him to Cambridge? The University as a step to anything but ordination seemed, to this man of fixed ideas, a preface without a volume. He was a man not merely religious, but devout; a firm believer – not as the phrase is now elusively construed by theological thimble-riggers in the Church and out of it, but in the old and ardent sense of the Evangelical school: one who could

> Indeed opine
> That the Eternal and Divine
> Did, eighteen centuries ago
> In very truth . . .

Angel's father tried argument, persuasion, entreaty.

'No, father; I cannot underwrite Article Four (leave alone the rest), taking it "in the literal and grammatical sense" as required by the Declaration; and, therefore, I can't be a parson in the present state of affairs,' said Angel. 'My whole instinct in matters of religion is towards reconstruction: to quote your favourite Epistle to the Hebrews, "the removing of those things that are shaken, as of things that are made, that those things which cannot be shaken may remain".'

His father grieved so deeply that it made Angel quite ill to see him.

'What is the good of your mother and me economizing and stinting ourselves to give you a University education, if it is not to be used for the honour and glory of God?' his father repeated.

'Why, that it may be used for the honour and glory of man, father.'

Perhaps if Angel had persevered he might have gone to Cambridge like his brothers. But the Vicar's view of that seat of learning as a stepping-stone to Orders alone was quite a family tradition; and so rooted was the idea in his mind that perseverance began to appear to the sensitive son akin to an intent to misappropriate a trust, and wrong the pious heads of the household, who had been and were, as his father had hinted, compelled to exercise much thrift to carry out this uniform plan of education for the three young men.

'I will do without Cambridge,' said Angel at last. 'I feel that I have no right to go there in the circumstances.'

The effects of this decisive debate were not long in showing themselves. He spent years and years in desultory studies, undertakings, and meditations; he began to evince considerable indifference to social forms and observances. The material distinctions of rank and wealth he increasingly despised. Even the 'good old family' (to use a favourite phrase of a late local worthy) had no aroma for him unless there were good new resolutions in its representatives. As a balance to these austerities, when he went to live in London to see what the world was like, and with a view to practising a profession or business there, he was carried off his head, and nearly entrapped by a woman much older than himself, though luckily he escaped not greatly the worse for the experience.

Early association with country solitudes had bred in him an unconquerable, and almost unreasonable, aversion to modern town life, and shut him out from such success as he might have aspired to by following a mundane calling in the impracticability of the spiritual one. But something had to be done; he had wasted many valuable years; and having an acquaintance who was starting on a thriving life as a Colonial farmer, it occurred to Angel that this might be a lead in the right direction. Farming, either in the Colonies, America, or at home – farming at any rate, after becoming well qualified for the business by a careful apprenticeship – that was a vocation which would probably afford an independence without the sacrifice of what he valued even more than a competency – intellectual liberty.

So we find Angel Clare at six-and-twenty here at Talbothays as a student of kine, and, as there were no houses near at hand in which he could get a comfortable lodging, a boarder at the dairyman's.

His room was an immense attic which ran the whole length of the dairy-house. It could only be reached by a ladder from the cheese-loft, and had been closed up for a long time till he arrived and selected it as his retreat. Here Clare had plenty of space, and could often be heard by the dairy-folk pacing up and down when the household had gone to rest. A portion was divided off at one end by a curtain, behind which was his bed, the outer part being furnished as a homely sitting-room.

At first he lived up above entirely, reading a good deal, and strumming upon an old harp which he had bought at a sale, saying when in a bitter humour that he might have to get his living by it in the streets some day. But he soon preferred to read human nature by taking his meals downstairs in the general dining-kitchen, with the dairyman and his wife, and the maids and men, who all together formed a lively assembly; for though but few milking hands slept in the house, several joined the family at meals. The longer Clare resided here the less objection had he to his company, and the more did he like to share quarters with them in common.

Much to his surprise he took, indeed, a real delight in their companionship. The conventional farm-folk of his imagination – personified by the pitiable dummy known as Hodge – were obliterated after a few days' residence. At close quarters no Hodge was to be seen. At first, it is true, when Clare's intelligence was fresh from a contrasting society, these friends with whom he now hobnobbed seemed a little strange. Sitting down as a level member of the dairyman's household seemed at the outset an undignified proceeding. The ideas, the modes, the surroundings, appeared retrogressive and unmeaning. But with living on there, day after day, the acute sojourner became conscious of a new aspect in the spectacle. Without any objective change whatever, variety had taken the place of monotonousness. His host and his host's household, his men and his maids, as they became intimately known to Clare, began to differentiate themselves as in a chemical process. The thought of Pascal's was brought home to him: 'A mesure qu'on a plus d'esprit, on trouve qu'il y a plus d'hommes originaux. Les gens du commun ne trouvent pas de différence entre les hommes.' The typical and unvarying Hodge ceased to exist. He had been disintegrated into a number of varied-fellow-creatures – beings of many minds, beings infinite in difference; some happy, many serene, a few depressed, one here and there bright even to genius, some stupid, others wanton, others austere; some mutely Miltonic, some potentially Cromwellian; into men who had private views of each other, as he had of his friends; who could applaud or condemn each other, amuse or sadden themselves by the contemplation of each other's foibles or vices; men every one of whom walked in his own individual way the road to dusty death.

Unexpectedly he began to like the outdoor life for its own sake, and for what it brought, apart from its bearing on his own proposed career. Considering his position he became wonderfully free from the chronic melancholy which is taking hold of the civilized races with the decline of belief in a beneficent Power. For the first time of late years he could read as his musings inclined him, without any eye to cramming for a profession, since the few farming handbooks which he deemed it desirable to master occupied him but little time.

He grew away from old associations, and saw something new in life and humanity. Secondarily, he made close acquaintance with phenomena which he had before known but darkly – the seasons in their moods, morning and evening, night and noon, winds in their different tempers, trees, waters and mists, shades and silences, and the voices of inanimate things.

The early mornings were still sufficiently cool to render a fire acceptable in the large room wherein they breakfasted; and, by Mrs Crick's orders, who held that he was too genteel to mess at their table, it was Angel Clare's custom to sit in the yawning chimney-corner during the meal, his cup-and-saucer and plate being placed on a hinged flap at his elbow. The light from the long, wide, mullioned window opposite shone in upon his nook, and, assisted by a secondary light of cold blue quality which shone down the chimney, enabled him to read there easily whenever disposed to do so. Between Clare and the window was the table at which his companions sat, their munching profiles rising sharp against the panes; while to the side was the milk-house door, through which were visible the rectangular leads in rows, full to the brim with the morning's milk. At the further end the great churn could be seen revolving, and its slip-slopping heard – the moving power being discernible through the window in the form of a spiritless horse walking in a circle and driven by a boy.

For several days after Tess's arrival Clare, sitting abstractedly reading from some book, periodical, or piece of music just come by post, hardly noticed that she was present at table. She talked so little, and the other maids talked so much, that the babble did not strike him as possessing a new note, and he was ever in the habit of neglecting the particulars of an outward scene for the general impression. One day, however, when he had been conning one of his music-scores, and by force of imagination was hearing the tune in his head, he lapsed into listlessness, and the music-sheet rolled to the hearth. He looked at the fire of logs, with its one flame pirouetting on the top in a dying dance after the breakfast-cooking and boiling, and it seemed to jig to his inward tune; also at the two chimney crooks dangling down from the cotterel or cross-bar, plumed with soot which quivered to the same melody; also at the half-empty kettle whining an accompaniment. The conversation at the table mixed in with his phantasmal orchestra till he thought: 'What a fluty voice one of those milkmaids has! I suppose it is the new one.'

Clare looked round upon her, seated with the others.

She was not looking towards him. Indeed, owing to his long silence, his presence in the room was almost forgotten.

'I don't know about ghosts,' she was saying; 'but I do know that our souls can be made to go outside our bodies when we are alive.'

The dairyman turned to her with his mouth full, his eyes charged with serious inquiry, and his great knife and fork (breakfasts were breakfasts here) planted erect on the table, like the beginning of a gallows.

'What – really now? And is it so, maidy?' he said.

'A very easy way to feel 'em go,' continued Tess, 'is to lie on the grass at night and look straight up at some big bright star; and, by fixing your mind upon it, you will soon find that you are hundreds and hundreds o' miles away from your body, which you don't seem to want at all.'

The dairyman removed his hard gaze from Tess, and fixed it on his wife.

'Now that's a rum thing, Christianner – hey? To think o' the miles I've vamped o' starlight nights these last thirty year, courting, or trading, or for doctor, or for nurse, and yet never had the least notion o' that till now, or feeled my soul rise so much as an inch above my shirt-collar.'

The general attention being drawn to her, including that of the dairyman's pupil, Tess flushed and remarking evasively that it was only a fancy, resumed her breakfast.

Clare continued to observe her. She soon finished her eating, and having a consciousness that Clare was regarding her, began to trace imaginary patterns on the tablecloth with her forefinger with the constraint of a domestic animal that perceives itself to be watched.

'What a fresh and virginal daughter of Nature that milkmaid is!' he said to himself.

And then he seemed to discern in her something that was familiar, something which carried him back into a joyous and unforeseeing past, before the necessity of taking thought had made the heavens gray. He concluded that he had beheld her before; where he could not tell. A casual encounter during some country ramble it certainly had been, and he was not greatly curious about it. But the circumstance was sufficient to lead him to select Tess in preference to the other pretty milkmaids when he wished to contemplate contiguous womankind.

❧ Chapter Nineteen ❧

IN GENERAL THE COWS WERE milked as they presented themselves, without fancy or choice. But certain cows will show a fondness for a particular pair of hands, sometimes carrying this predilection so far as to refuse to stand at all except to their favourite, the pail of a stranger being unceremoniously kicked over.

It was Dairyman Crick's rule to insist on breaking down these partialities and aversions by constant interchange, since otherwise, in the event of a milkman or maid going away from the dairy, he was placed in a difficulty. The maids' private aims, however, were the reverse of the dairyman's rule, the daily selection by each damsel of the eight or ten cows to which she had grown accustomed rendering the operation on their willing udders surprisingly easy and effortless.

Tess, like her compeers, soon discovered which of the cows had a preference for her style of manipulation, and her fingers having become delicate from the long domiciliary imprisonments to which she had subjected herself at intervals during the last two or three years, she would have been glad to meet the milchers' views in this respect. Out of the whole ninety-five there were eight in particular – Dumpling, Fancy, Lofty, Mist, Old Pretty, Young Pretty, Tidy, and Loud – who, though the teats of one or two were as hard as carrots, gave down to her with a readiness that made her work on them a mere touch of the fingers. Knowing, however, the dairyman's wish, she endeavoured conscientiously to take the animals just as they came, excepting the very hard yielders which she could not yet manage.

But she soon found a curious correspondence between the ostensibly chance position of the cows and her wishes in this matter, till she felt that their order could not be the result of accident. The dairyman's pupil had lent a hand in getting the cows together of late, and at the fifth or sixth time she turned her eyes, as she rested against the cow, full of sly inquiry upon him.

'Mr Clare, you have ranged the cows!' she said, blushing; and in making the accusation symptoms of a smile gently lifted her upper lip in spite of her, so as to show the tips of her teeth, the lower lip remaining severely still.

'Well, it makes no difference,' said he. 'You will always be here to milk them.'

'Do you think so? I *hope* I shall! But I don't *know*.'

She was angry with herself afterwards, thinking that he, unaware of her grave reasons for liking this seclusion, might have mistaken her meaning. She had spoken so earnestly to him, as if his presence were somehow a factor in her wish. Her misgiving was such that at dusk, when the milking was over, she walked in the garden alone, to continue her regrets that she had disclosed to him her discovery of his considerateness.

It was a typical summer evening in June, the atmosphere being in such delicate equilibrium and so transmissive that inanimate objects seemed endowed with two or three senses, if not five. There was no distinction between the near and the far, and an auditor felt close to everything within the horizon. The soundlessness impressed her as a positive entity rather than as the mere negation of noise. It was broken by the strumming of strings.

Tess had heard those notes in the attic above her head. Dim, flattened, constrained by their confinement, they had never appealed to her as now, when they wandered in the still air with a stark quality like that of nudity. To speak absolutely, both instrument and execution were poor; but the relative is all, and as she listened Tess, like a fascinated bird, could not leave the spot. Far from leaving she drew up towards the performer, keeping behind the hedge that he might not guess her presence.

The outskirt of the garden in which Tess found herself had been left uncultivated for some years, and was now damp and rank with juicy grass which sent up mists of pollen at a touch; and with tall blooming weeds emitting offensive smells – weeds whose red and yellow and purple hues formed a polychrome as dazzling as that of cultivated flowers. She went stealthily as a cat through this profusion of growth, gathering cuckoo-spittle on her skirts, cracking snails that were underfoot, staining her hands with thistle-milk and slug-slime, and rubbing off upon her naked arms sticky blights which, though snow-white on the apple-tree trunks, made madder stains on her skin; thus she drew quite near to Clare, still unobserved of him.

Tess was conscious of neither time nor space. The exaltation which she had described as being producible at will by gazing at a star, came now without any determination of hers; she undulated upon the thin notes of the second-hand harp, and their harmonies passed like breezes through her, bringing tears into her eyes. The floating pollen seemed to be his notes made visible, and the dampness of the garden the weeping of the garden's sensibility. Though near nightfall, the rank-smelling weed-flowers glowed as if they would not close for intentness, and the waves of colour mixed with the waves of sound.

The light which still shone was derived mainly from a large hole in the western bank of cloud; it was like a piece of day left behind by accident, dusk having closed in elsewhere. He concluded his plaintive melody, a very simple performance, demanding no great skill; and she waited, thinking another might be begun. But, tired of playing, he had desultorily come round the fence, and was rambling up behind her. Tess, her cheeks on fire, moved away furtively, as if hardly moving at all.

Angel, however, saw her light summer gown, and he spoke; his low tones reaching her, though he was some distance off.

'What makes you draw off in that way, Tess?' said he. 'Are you afraid?'

'Oh no, sir ... not of outdoor things; especially just now when the appleblooth is falling, and everything so green.'

'But you have your indoor fears – eh?'

'Well – yes, sir.'

'What of?'

'I couldn't quite say.'

'The milk turning sour?'

'No.'

'Life in general?'

'Yes, sir.'

'Ah – so have I, very often. This hobble of being alive is rather serious, don't you think so?'

'It is – now you put it that way.'

'All the same, I shouldn't have expected a young girl like you to see it so just yet. How is it you do?'

She maintained a hesitating silence.

'Come, Tess, tell me in confidence.'

She thought that he meant what were the aspects of things to her, and replied shyly –

'The trees have inquisitive eyes, haven't they? – that is, seem as if they had. And the river says, – "Why do ye trouble me with your looks?" And you seem to see numbers of tomorrows just all in a line, the first of them the biggest and clearest, the others getting smaller and smaller as they stand farther away; but they all seem very fierce and cruel and as if they said, "I'm coming! Beware of me! Beware of me!" ... But *you*, sir, can raise up dreams with your music, and drive all such horrid fancies away!'

He was surprised to find this young woman – who though but a milkmaid had just that touch of rarity about her which might make her the envied of her housemates – shaping such sad imaginings. She was expressing in her own native phrases – assisted a little by her Sixth Standard training – feelings which might almost have been called those of the age – the ache of modernism. The perception arrested him less when he reflected that what are called advanced ideas are really in great part but the latest fashion in definition – a more accurate expression, by words in *logy* and *ism*, of sensations which men and women have vaguely grasped for centuries.

Still, it was strange that they should have come to her while yet so young; more than strange; it was impressive, interesting, pathetic. Not guessing the cause, there was nothing to remind him that experience is as to intensity, and not as to duration. Tess's passing corporeal blight had been her mental harvest.

Tess, on her part, could not understand why a man of clerical family and good education, and above physical want, should look upon it as a mishap to be alive. For the unhappy pilgrim herself there was very good reason. But how could this admirable and poetic man ever have descended into the Valley of Humiliation, have felt with the man of Uz – as she herself had felt two or three years ago – 'My soul chooseth strangling and death rather than my life. I loathe it; I would not live alway.'

It was true that he was at present out of his class. But she knew that was only because, like Peter the Great in a shipwright's yard, he was studying what he wanted to know. He did not milk cows because he was obliged to milk cows, but because he was learning how to be a rich and prosperous dairyman, landowner, agriculturist, and breeder of cattle. He would become an American or Australian Abraham, commanding like a monarch his flocks and his herds, his spotted and his ring-straked, his men-servants and his maids. At times, nevertheless, it did seem unaccountable to her that a decidedly bookish, musical, thinking young

111

man should have chosen deliberately to be a farmer, and not a clergyman, like his father and brothers.

Thus, neither having the clue to the other's secret, they were respectively puzzled at what each revealed, and awaited new knowledge of each other's character and moods without attempting to pry into each other's history.

Every day, every hour, brought to him one more little stroke of her nature, and to her one more of his. Tess was trying to lead a repressed life, but she little divined the strength of her own vitality.

At first Tess seemed to regard Angel Clare as an intelligence rather than as a man. As such she compared him with herself; and at every discovery of the abundance of his illuminations, of the distance between her own modest mental standpoint and the unmeasurable, Andean altitude of his, she became quite dejected, disheartened from all further effort on her own part whatever.

He observed her dejection one day, when he had casually mentioned something to her about pastoral life in ancient Greece. She was gathering the buds called 'lords and ladies' from the bank while he spoke.

'Why do you look so woebegone all of a sudden?' he asked.

'Oh 'tis only – about my own self,' she said, with a frail laugh of sadness, fitfully beginning to peel 'a lady' meanwhile. 'Just a sense of what might have been with me! My life looks as if it had been wasted for want of changes! When I see what you know, what you have read, and seen, and thought, I feel what a nothing I am! I'm like the poor Queen of Sheba who lived in the Bible. There is no more spirit in me.'

'Bless my soul, don't go troubling about that! Why,' he said with some enthusiasm, 'I should be only too glad, my dear Tess, to help you do anything in the way of history, or any line of reading you would like to take up –'

'It is a lady again,' interrupted she, holding out the bud she had peeled.

'What?'

'I meant that there are always more ladies than lords when you come to peel them.'

'Never mind about the lords and ladies. Would you like to take up any course of study – history, for example?'

'Sometimes I feel I don't want to know anything more about it than I know already.'

'Why not?'

'Because what's the use of learning that I am one of a long row only – finding out that there is set down in some old book somebody just like me, and to know that I shall only act her part; making me sad, that's all. The best is not to remember that your nature and past doings have been

112

just like thousands' and thousands', and that your coming life and doing
'll be like thousands' and thousands'.'

'What, really, then, you don't want to learn anything?'

'I shouldn't mind learning why – why the sun do shine on the just
and the unjust alike,' she answered, with a slight quaver in her voice.
'But that's what books will not tell me.'

'Tess, fie for such bitterness!' Of course he spoke with a conventional
sense of duty only, for that sort of wondering had not been unknown to
himself in bygone days. And as he looked at the unpractised mouth and
lips, he thought that such a daughter of the soil could only have caught
up the sentiment by rote. She went on peeling the lords and ladies till
Clare, regarding for a moment the wave-like curl of her lashes as they
drooped with her bent gaze on her soft cheek, lingeringly went away.
When he was gone she stood awhile, thoughtfully peeling the last bud;
and then, awakening from her reverie, flung it and all the crowd of floral
nobility impatiently on the ground, in an ebullition of displeasure with
herself for her *niaiseries*, and with a quickening warmth in her heart of
hearts.

How stupid he must think her! In an access of hunger for his good
opinion she bethought herself of what she had latterly endeavoured to
forget, so unpleasant had been its issues – the identity of her family with
that of the knightly d'Urbervilles. Barren attribute as it was, disastrous
as its discovery had been in many ways to her, perhaps Mr Clare, as a
gentleman and a student of history, would respect her sufficiently to
forget her childish conduct with the lords and ladies if he knew that
those Purbeck-marble and alabaster people in Kingsbere Church really
represented her own lineal forefathers; that she was no spurious d'Urberville, compounded of money and ambition like those at Trantridge, but
true d'Urberville to the bone.

But, before venturing to make the revelation, dubious Tess indirectly
sounded the dairyman as to its possible effect upon Mr Clare, by asking
the former if Mr Clare had any great respect for old county families
when they had lost all their money and land.

'Mr Clare,' said the dairyman emphatically, 'is one of the most rebellest
rozums you ever knowed – not a bit like the rest of his family; and if
there's one thing that he do hate more than another 'tis the notion of
what's called a' old family. He says that it stands to reason that old
families have done their spurt of work in past days, and can't have
anything left in 'em now. There's the Billetts and the Drenkhards and
the Greys and the St Quintins and the Hardys and the Goulds, who used
to own the lands for miles down this valley; you could buy 'em all up
now for an old song a'most. Why, our little Retty Priddle here, you know,
is one of the Paridelles – the old family that used to own lots o' the lands

out by King's-Hintock now owned by the Earl o' Wessex, afore even he or his was heard of. Well, Mr Clare found this out, and spoke quite scornful to the poor girl for days. "Ah!" he says to her, "you'll never make a good dairymaid! All your skill was used up ages ago in Palestine, and you must lie fallow for a thousand years to git strength for more deeds!" A boy came here t'other day asking for a job, and said his name was Matt, and when we asked him his surname he said he'd never heard that 'a had any surname, and when we asked why, he said he supposed his folks hadn't been 'stablished long enough. "Ah! you're the very boy I want!" says Mr Clare, jumping up and shaking hands wi'en; "I've great hopes of you"; and gave him half-a-crown. O no! he can't stomach old families!'

After hearing this caricature of Clare's opinions poor Tess was glad that she had not said a word in a weak moment about her family – even though it was so unusually old as almost to have gone round the circle and become a new one. Besides, another dairy-girl was as good as she, it seemed, in that respect. She held her tongue about the d'Urberville vault, and the Knight of the Conqueror whose name she bore. The insight afforded into Clare's character suggested to her that it was largely owing to her supposed untraditional newness that she had won interest in his eyes.

❧ Chapter Twenty ❧

THE SEASON DEVELOPED AND matured. Another year's instalment of flowers, leaves, nightingales, thrushes, finches, and such ephemeral creatures, took up their positions where only a year ago others had stood in their place when these were nothing more than germs and inorganic particles. Rays from the sunrise drew forth the buds and stretched them into long stalks, lifted up sap in noiseless streams, opened petals, and sucked out scents in invisible jets and breathings.

Dairyman Crick's household of maids and men lived on comfortably, placidly, even merrily. Their position was perhaps the happiest of all positions in the social scale, being above the line at which neediness ends, and below the line at which the *convenances* begin to cramp natural feeling, and the stress of threadbare modishness makes too little of enough.

Thus passed the leafy time when arborescence seems to be the one thing aimed at out of doors. Tess and Clare unconsciously studied each other, ever balanced on the edge of a passion, yet apparently keeping out of it. All the while they were converging, under an irresistible law, as surely as two streams in one vale.

Tess had never in her recent life been so happy as she was now, possibly never would be so happy again. She was, for one thing, physically and mentally suited among these new surroundings. The sapling which had rooted down to a poisonous stratum on the spot of its sowing had been transplanted to a deeper soil. Moreover she, and Clare also, stood as yet on the debatable land between predilection and love; where no profundities have been reached; no reflections have set in, awkwardly inquiring, 'Whither does this new current tend to carry me? What does it mean to my future? How does it stand towards my past?'

Tess was the merest stray phenomenon to Angel Clare as yet – a rosy warming apparition which had only just acquired the attribute of persistence in his consciousness. So he allowed his mind to be occupied with her, deeming his preoccupation to be no more than a philosopher's regard of an exceedingly novel, fresh, and interesting specimen of womankind.

They met continually; they could not help it. They met daily in that strange and solemn interval, the twilight of the morning, in the violet or pink dawn; for it was necessary to rise early, so very early, here. Milking was done betimes; and before the milking came the skimming, which began at a little past three. It usually fell to the lot of some one or other of them to wake the rest, the first being aroused by an alarm-clock; and, as Tess was the latest arrival, and they soon discovered that she could be depended upon not to sleep through the alarm as the others did, this task was thrust most frequently upon her. No sooner had the hour of three struck and whizzed, than she left her room and ran to the dairyman's door; then up the ladder to Angel's, calling him in a loud whisper; then woke her fellow-milkmaids. By the time that Tess was dressed Clare was downstairs and out in the humid air. The remaining maids and the dairyman usually gave themselves another turn on the pillow, and did not appear till a quarter of an hour later.

The gray half-tones of daybreak are not the gray half-tones of the day's close, though the degree of their shade may be the same. In the twilight of the morning light seems active, darkness passive; in the twilight of evening it is the darkness which is active and crescent, and the light which is the drowsy reverse.

Being so often – possibly not always by chance – the first two persons to get up at the dairy-house, they seemed to themselves the first persons up of all the world. In these early days of her residence here Tess did not skim, but went out of doors at once after rising, where he was generally awaiting her. The spectral, half-compounded, aqueous light which pervaded the open mead, impressed them with a feeling of isolation, as if they were Adam and Eve. At this dim inceptive stage of the day Tess seemed to Clare to exhibit a dignified largeness both of disposition and physique, an almost regnant power, possibly because he knew that at that preternatural time hardly any woman so well endowed in person as she was likely to be walking in the open air within the boundaries of his horizon; very few in all England. Fair women are usually asleep at midsummer dawns. She was close at hand, and the rest were nowhere.

The mixed, singular, luminous gloom in which they walked along together to the spot where the cows lay, often made him think of the Resurrection hour. He little thought that the Magdalen might be at his side. Whilst all the landscape was in neutral shade his companion's face, which was the focus of his eyes, rising above the mist stratum, seemed to have a sort of phosphorescence upon it. She looked ghostly, as if she were merely a soul at large. In reality her face, without appearing to do so, had caught the cold gleam of day from the north-east; his own face, though he did not think of it, wore the same aspect to her.

It was then, as has been said, that she impressed him most deeply. She was no longer the milkmaid, but a visionary essence of woman – a whole sex condensed into one typical form. He called her Artemis, Demeter, and other fanciful names half teasingly, which she did not like because she did not understand them.

'Call me Tess,' she would say askance; and he did.

Then it would grow lighter, and her features would become simply feminine; they had changed from those of a divinity who could confer bliss to those of a being who craved it.

At these non-human hours they could get quite close to the waterfowl. Herons came, with a great bold noise as of opening doors and shutters, out of the boughs of a plantation which they frequented at the side of the mead; or, if already on the spot, hardily maintained their standing in the water as the pair walked by, watching them by moving their heads round in a slow, horizontal, passionless wheel, like the turn of puppets by clockwork.

They could then see the faint summer fogs in layers, woolly, level, and apparently no thicker than counterpanes, spread about the meadows in detached remnants of small extent. On the gray moisture of the grass were marks where the cows had lain through the night – dark-green islands of dry herbage the size of their carcases, in the general sea of dew. From each island proceeded a serpentine trail, by which the cow had rambled away to feed after getting up, at the end of which trail they found her; the snoring puff from her nostrils, when she recognized them, making an intenser little fog of her own amid the prevailing one. Then they drove the animals back to the barton, or sat down to milk them on the spot, as the case might require.

Or perhaps the summer fog was more general, and the meadows lay like a white sea, out of which the scattered trees rose like dangerous rocks. Birds would soar through it into the upper radiance, and hang on the wing sunning themselves, or alight on the wet rails subdividing the mead, which now shone like glass rods. Minute diamonds of moisture from the mist hung, too, upon Tess's eyelashes, and drops upon her hair, like seed pearls. When the day grew quite strong and commonplace these dried off her; moreover, Tess then lost her strange and ethereal beauty; her teeth, lips, and eyes scintillated in the sunbeams, and she was again the dazzlingly fair dairymaid only, who had to hold her own against the other women of the world.

About this time they would hear Dairyman Crick's voice, lecturing the non-resident milkers for arriving late, and speaking sharply to old Deborah Fyander for not washing her hands.

'For Heaven's sake, pop thy hands under the pump, Deb! Upon my soul, if the London folk only knowed of thee and thy slovenly ways, they'd swaller their milk and butter more mincing than they do a'ready; and that's saying a good deal.'

The milking progressed, till towards the end Tess and Clare, in common with the rest, could hear the heavy breakfast table dragged out from the wall in the kitchen by Mrs Crick, this being the invariable preliminary to each meal; the same horrible scrape accompanying its return journey when the table had been cleared.

❧ Chapter Twenty-One ❧

THERE WAS A GREAT STIR in the milk-house just after breakfast. The churn revolved as usual, but the butter would not come. Whenever this happened the dairy was paralyzed. Squish, squash, echoed the milk in the great cylinder, but never arose the sound they waited for.

Dairyman Crick and his wife, the milkmaids Tess, Marian, Retty Priddle, Izz Huett, and the married ones from the cottages; also Mr Clare, Jonathan Kail, old Deborah, and the rest, stood gazing hopelessly at the churn; and the boy who kept the horse going outside put on moon-like eyes to show his sense of the situation. Even the melancholy horse himself seemed to look in at the window in inquiring despair at each walk round.

"Tis years since I went to Conjuror Trendle's son in Egdon – years!' said the dairyman bitterly. 'And he was nothing to what his father had been. I have said fifty times, if I have said once, that I don't believe in en. And I *don't* believe in en. But I shall have to go to 'n if he's alive. O yes, I shall have to go to 'n, if this sort of thing continnys!'

Even Mr Clare began to feel tragical at the dairyman's desperation.

'Conjuror Fall, t'other side of Casterbridge, that they used to call "Wide-O", was a very good man when I was a boy,' said Jonathan Kail. 'But he's rotten as touchwood by now.'

'My grandfather used to go to Conjuror Mynterne, out at Owlscombe, and a clever man a' were, so I've heard grandf'er say,' continued Mr Crick. 'But there's no such genuine folk about nowadays!'

Mrs Crick's mind kept nearer to the matter in hand.

'Perhaps somebody in the house is in love,' she said tentatively. 'I've heard tell in my younger days that that will cause it. Why, Crick – that maid we had years ago, do ye mind, and how the butter didn't come then – '

'Ah yes, yes! – but that isn't the rights o't. It had nothing to do with the lovemaking. I can mind all about it – 'twas the damage to the churn.'

He turned to Clare.

'Jack Dollop, a 'hore's-bird of a fellow we had here as milker at one time, sir, courted a young woman over at Mellstock, and deceived her as he had deceived many afore. But he had another sort o' woman to reckon wi' this time, and it was not the girl herself. One Holy Thursday, of all days in the almanack, we was here as we mid be now, only there was no churning in hand, when we zid the girl's mother coming up to the door, wi' a great brass-mounted umbrella in her hand that would ha' felled an ox, and saying "Do Jack Dollop work here? – because I want him! I have a big bone to pick with he, I can assure 'n!" And some way behind her mother walked Jack's young woman, crying bitterly into her handkercher. "O Lard, here's a time!" said Jack, looking out o' winder at 'em. "She'll murder me! Where shall I get – where shall I – ? Don't tell her where I be!" And with that he scrambled into the churn through the trap-door, and shut himself inside, just as the young woman's mother busted into the milk-house. 'The villain – where is he?' says she, 'I'll claw his face for'n, let me only catch him!' Well, she hunted about everywhere, ballyragging Jack by side and by seam, Jack lying a'most stifled inside the churn, and the poor maid – or young woman rather – standing at the door crying her eyes out. I shall never forget it, never! 'Twould have melted a marble stone! But she couldn't find him nowhere at all.'

The dairyman paused, and one or two words of comment came from the listeners.

Dairyman Crick's stories often seemed to be ended when they were not really so, and strangers were betrayed into premature interjections of finality; though old friends knew better. The narrator went on –

'Well, how the old woman should have had the wit to guess it I could never tell, but she found out that he was inside that there churn. Without saying a word she took hold of the winch (it was turned by handpower then), and round she swung him, and Jack began to flop about inside. "O Lard! stop the churn! let me out!" says he, popping out his head, "I shall be churned into a pummy!" (he was a cowardly chap in his heart, as such men mostly be). "Not till ye make amends for ravaging her virgin innocence!" says the old woman. "Stop the churn, you old witch!" screams he. "You call me old witch, do ye, you deceiver!" says she, "when ye ought to ha' been calling me mother-law these last five months!" And on went the churn, and Jack's bones rattled round again. Well, none of us ventured to interfere; and at last 'a promised to make it right wi' her. "Yes – I'll be as good as my word!" he said. And so it ended that day.'

While the listeners were smiling their comments there was a quick movement behind their backs, and they looked round. Tess, pale-faced, had gone to the door.

'How warm 'tis to-day!' she said, almost inaudibly.

It was warm, and none of them connected her withdrawal with the reminiscences of the dairyman. He went forward, and opened the door for her, saying with tender raillery –

'Why, maidy' (he frequently, with unconscious irony, gave her this pet name), 'the prettiest milker I've got in my dairy; you mustn't get so fagged as this at the first breath of summer weather, or we shall be finely put to for want of 'ee by dogdays, shan't we, Mr Clare?'

'I was faint – and – I think I am better out o' doors,' she said mechanically; and disappeared outside.

Fortunately for her the milk in the revolving churn at that moment changed its squashing for a decided flick-flack.

''Tis coming!' cried Mrs Crick, and the attention of all was called off from Tess.

That fair sufferer soon recovered herself externally; but she remained much depressed all the afternoon. When the evening milking was done she did not care to be with the rest of them, and went out of doors wandering along she knew not whither. She was wretched – O so wretched – at the perception that to her companions the dairyman's story had been rather a humorous narration than otherwise; none of them but herself seemed to see the sorrow of it; to a certainty, not one knew how cruelly it touched the tender place in her experience. The evening sun was now ugly to her, like a great inflamed wound in the sky. Only a solitary cracked-voiced reed-sparrow greeted her from the bushes by the river, in a sad, machine-made tone, resembling that of a past friend whose friendship she had outworn.

In these long June days the milkmaids, and, indeed, most of the household, went to bed at sunset or sooner, the morning work before milking being so early and heavy at a time of full pails. Tess usually accompanied her fellows upstairs. To-night, however, she was the first to go to their common chamber; and she had dozed when the other girls came in. She saw them undressing in the orange light of the vanished sun, which flushed their forms with its colour; she dozed again, but she was reawakened by their voices, and quietly turned her eyes towards them.

Neither of her three chamber-companions had got into bed. They were standing in a group, in their nightgowns, barefooted, at the window, the last red rays of the west still warming their faces and necks, and the walls around them. All were watching somebody in the garden with deep interest, their three faces close together: a jovial and round one, a pale one with dark hair, and a fair one whose tresses were auburn.

'Don't push! You can see as well as I,' said Retty, the auburn-haired and youngest girl, without removing her eyes from the window.

''Tis no use for you to be in love with him any more than me, Retty Priddle,' said jolly-faced Marian, the eldest, slily. 'His thoughts be of other cheeks than thine!'

Retty Priddle still looked, and the others looked again.

'There he is again!' cried Izz Huett, the pale girl with dark damp hair and keenly cut lips.

'You needn't say anything, Izz,' answered Retty. 'For I zid you kissing his shade.'

'*What* did you see her doing?' asked Marian.

'Why – he was standing over the whey-tub to let off the whey, and the shade of his face came upon the wall behind, close to Izz, who was standing there filling a vat. She put her mouth against the wall and kissed the shade of his mouth; I zid her, though he didn't.'

'O Izz Huett!' said Marian.

A rosy spot came into the middle of Izz Huett's cheek.

'Well, there was no harm in it,' she declared, with attempted coolness.

'And if I be in love wi'en, so is Retty, too; and so be you, Marian, come to that.'

Marian's full face could not blush past its chronic pinkness.

'I!' she said. 'What a tale! Ah, there he is again! Dear eyes – dear face – dear Mr Clare!'

'There – you've owned it!'

'So have you – so have we all,' said Marian, with the dry frankness of complete indifference to opinion. 'It is silly to pretend otherwise amongst ourselves, though we need not own it to other folks. I would just marry 'n tomorrow!'

'So would I – and more,' murmoured Izz Huett.

'And I too,' whispered the more timid Retty.

The listener grew warm.

'We can't all marry him,' said Izz.

'We shan't, either of us; which is worse still,' said the eldest. 'There he is again!'

They all three blew him a silent kiss.

'Why?' asked Retty quickly.

'Because he likes Tess Durbeyfield best,' said Marian, lowering her voice. 'I have watched him every day, and have found it out.'

There was a reflective silence.

'But she don't care anything for 'n?' at length breathed Retty.

'Well – I sometimes think that too.'

'But how silly all this is!' said Izz Huett impatiently. 'Of course he won't marry any one of us, or Tess either – a gentleman's son, who's going to be a great landowner and farmer abroad! More likely to ask us to come wi'en as farm-hands at so much a year!'

One sighed, and another sighed, and Marian's plump figure sighed biggest of all. Somebody in bed hard by sighed too. Tears came into the eyes of Retty Priddle, the pretty red-haired youngest – the last bud of the Paridelles, so important in the county annals. They watched silently a little longer, their three faces still close together as before, and the triple hues of their hair mingling. But the unconscious Mr Clare had gone indoors, and they saw him no more; and, the shades beginning to deepen, they crept into their beds. In a few minutes they heard him ascend the ladder to his own room. Marian was soon snoring, but Izz did not drop into forgetfulness for a long time. Retty Priddle cried herself to sleep.

The deeper-passioned Tess was very far from sleeping even then. This conversation was another of the bitter pills she had been obliged to swallow that day. Scarce the least feeling of jealousy arose in her breast. For that matter she knew herself to have the preference. Being more finely formed, better educated, and, though the youngest except Retty, more woman than either, she perceived that only the slightest ordinary

121

care was necessary for holding her own in Angel Clare's heart against these her candid friends. But the grave question was, ought she to do this? There was, to be sure, hardly a ghost of a chance for either of them, in a serious sense; but there was, or had been, a chance of one or the other inspiring him with a passing fancy for her, and enjoying the pleasure of his attentions while he stayed here. Such unequal attachments had led to marriage; and she had heard from Mrs Crick that Mr Clare had one day asked, in a laughing way, what would be the use of his marrying a fine lady, and all the while ten thousand acres of Colonial pasture to feed, and cattle to rear, and corn to reap. A farm-woman would be the only sensible kind of wife for him. But whether Mr Clare had spoken seriously or not, why should she, who could never conscientiously allow any man to marry her now, and who had religiously determined that she never would be tempted to do so, draw off Mr Clare's attention from other women, for the brief happiness of sunning herself in his eyes while he remained at Talbothays?

❧ Chapter Twenty-Two ❧

THEY CAME DOWNSTAIRS YAWNING next morning; but skimming and milking were proceeded with as usual, and they went indoors to breakfast. Dairyman Crick was discovered stamping about the house. He had received a letter, in which a customer had complained that the butter had a twang.

'And begad, so 't have!' said the dairyman, who held in his left hand a wooden slice on which a lump of butter was stuck. 'Yes – taste for yourself!'

Several of them gathered round him; and Mr Clare tasted, Tess tasted, also the other indoor milkmaids, one or two of the milking-men, and last of all Mrs Crick, who came out from the waiting breakfast-table. There certainly was a twang.

The dairyman, who had thrown himself into abstraction to better realize the taste, and so divine the particular species of noxious weed to which it appertained, suddenly exclaimed –

"'Tis garlic! and I thought there wasn't a blade left in that mead!'

Then all the old hands remembered that a certain dry mead, into which a few of the cows had been admitted of late, had, in years gone by, spoilt the butter in the same way. The dairyman had not recognized the taste at that time, and thought the butter bewitched.

'We must overhaul that mead,' he resumed; 'this mustn't continny!'

All having armed themselves with old pointed knives they went out together. As the inimical plant could only be present in very microscopic dimensions to have escaped ordinary observation, to find it seemed rather a hopeless attempt in the stretch of rich grass before them. However, they formed themselves into line, all assisting, owing to the importance of the search; the dairyman at the upper end with Mr Clare, who had volunteered to help; then Tess, Marian, Izz Huett, and Retty; then Bill Lewell, Jonathan, and the married dairywomen – Beck Knibbs, with her woolly black hair and rolling eyes; and flaxen Frances, consumptive from the winter damps of the watermeads – who lived in their respective cottages.

With eyes fixed upon the ground they crept slowly across a strip of the field, returning a little further down in such a manner that, when they should have finished, not a single inch of pasture but would have fallen under the eye of some one of them. It was a most tedious business, not more than half a dozen shoots of garlic being discoverable in the whole field; yet such was the herb's pungency that probably one bite of it by one cow had been sufficient to season the whole dairy's produce for the day.

Differing one from another in natures and mood so greatly as they did, they yet formed, bending, a curiously uniform row – automatic, noiseless; and an alien observer passing down the neighbouring lane might well have been excused for massing them as 'Hodge'. As they crept along, stooping low to discern the plant, a soft yellow gleam was reflected from the buttercups into their shaded faces, giving them an elfish, moonlit aspect, though the sun was pouring upon their backs in all the strength of noon.

Angel Clare, who communistically stuck to his rule of taking part with the rest in everything, glanced up now and then. It was not, of course, by accident that he walked next to Tess.

'Well, how are you?' he murmured.

'Very well, thank you, sir' she replied demurely.

As they had been discussing a score of personal matters only half-an-hour before, the introductory style seemed a little superfluous. But they got no further in speech just then. They crept and crept, the hem of her petticoat just touching his gaiter, and his elbow sometimes brushing hers. At last the dairyman, who came next, could stand it no longer.

'Upon my soul and body, this here stooping do fairly make my back open and shut!' he exclaimed, straightening himself slowly with an excruciated look till quite upright. 'And you, maidy Tess, you wasn't well a day or two ago – this will make your head ache finely! Don't do any more, if you feel fainty; leave the rest to finish it.'

Dairyman Crick withdrew, and Tess dropped behind. Mr Clare also stepped out of line, and began privateering about for the weed. When she found him near her, her very tension at what she had heard the night before made her the first to speak.

'Don't they look pretty?' she said.

'Who?'

'Izzy Huett and Retty.'

Tess had moodily decided that either of these maidens would make a good farmer's wife, and that she ought to recommend them, and obscure her own wretched charms.

'Pretty? Well, yes – they are pretty girls – fresh looking. I have often thought so.'

'Though, poor dears, prettiness won't last long!'

'O no, unfortunately.'

'They are excellent dairywomen.'

'Yes: though not better than you.'

'They skim better than I.'

'Do they?'

Clare remained observing them – not without their observing him.

'She is colouring up,' continued Tess heroically.

'Who?'

'Retty Priddle.'

'Oh! Why is that?'

'Because you are looking at her.'

Self-sacrificing as her mood might be Tess could not well go further and cry, 'Marry one of them, if you really do want a dairywoman and not a lady; and don't think of marrying me!' She followed Dairyman Crick, and had the mournful satisfaction of seeing that Clare remained behind.

From this day she forced herself to take pains to avoid him – never allowing herself, as formerly, to remain long in his company, even if their juxtaposition were purely accidental. She gave the other three every chance.

Tess was woman enough to realize from their avowals to herself that Angel Clare had the honour of all the dairymaids in his keeping, and her perception of his care to avoid compromising the happiness of either in the least degree bred a tender respect in Tess for what she deemed, rightly or wrongly, the self-controlling sense of duty shown by him, a quality which she had never expected to find in one of the opposite sex, and in the absence of which more than one of the simple hearts who were his housemates might have gone weeping on her pilgrimage.

❧ Chapter Twenty-Three ❧

THE HOT WEATHER OF JULY had crept upon them unawares, and the atmosphere of the flat vale hung heavy as an opiate over the dairy-folk, the cows, and the trees. Hot steaming rains fell frequently, making the grass where the cows fed yet more rank, and hindering the late hay-making in the other meads.

It was Sunday morning; the milking was done; the outdoor milkers had gone home. Tess and the other three were dressing themselves rapidly, the whole bevy having agreed to go together to Mellstock Church, which lay some three or four miles distant from the dairy-house. She had now been two months at Talbothays, and this was her first excursion.

All the preceding afternoon and night heavy thunderstorms had hissed down upon the meads, and washed some of the hay into the river; but this morning the sun shone out all the more brilliantly for the deluge, and the air was balmy and clear.

The crooked lane leading from their own parish to Mellstock ran along the lowest levels in a portion of its length, and when the girls reached the most depressed spot they found that the result of the rain had been to flood the lane over-shoe to a distance of some fifty yards. This would have been no serious hindrance on a week-day; they would have clicked through it in their high pattens and boots quite unconcerned; but on this day of vanity, this Sun's-day, when flesh went forth to coquet with flesh while hypocritically affecting business with spiritual things; on this occasion for wearing their white stockings and thin shoes, and their pink, white, and lilac gowns, on which every mud spot would be visible, the pool was an awkward impediment. They could hear the churchbell calling – as yet nearly a mile off.

'Who would have expected such a rise in the river in summertime!' said Marian, from the top of the roadside-bank on which they had climbed, and were maintaining a precarious footing in the hope of creeping along its slope till they were past the pool.

'We can't get there anyhow, without walking right through it, or else going round the Turnpike way; and that would make us so very late!' said Retty, pausing hopelessly.

'And I do colour up so hot, walking into church late, and all the people staring round,' said Marian, 'that I hardly cool down again till we get into the That-it-may-please-Thees.'

While they stood clinging to the bank they heard a splashing round the bend of the road, and presently appeared Angel Clare, advancing along the lane towards them through the water.

Four hearts gave a big throb simultaneously.

His aspect was probably as un-Sabbatarian a one as a dogmatic parson's son often presented; his attire being his dairy clothes, long wading boots, a cabbage-leaf inside his hat to keep his head cool, with a thistlespud to finish him off.

'He's not going to church,' said Marian.

'No – I wish he was!' murmured Tess.

Angel, in fact, rightly or wrongly (to adopt the safe phrase of evasive controversialists), preferred sermons in stones to sermons in churches and chapels on fine summer days. This morning, moreover, he had gone out to see if the damage to the hay by the flood was considerable or not. On his walk he observed the girls from a long distance, though they had been so occupied with their difficulties of passage as not to notice him. He knew that the water had risen at that spot, and that it would quite check their progress. So he had hastened on, with a dim idea of how he could help them – one of them in particular.

The rosy-cheeked, bright-eyed, quartet looked so charming in their light summer attire, clinging to the roadside bank like pigeons on a roof-slope, that he stopped a moment to regard them before coming close. Their gauzy skirts had brushed up from the grass innumerable flies and butterflies which, unable to escape, remained caged in the transparent tissue as in an aviary. Angel's eye at last fell upon Tess, the hindmost of the four; she, being full of suppressed laughter at their dilemma, could not help meeting his glance radiantly.

He came beneath them in the water, which did not rise over his long boots; and stood looking at the entrapped flies and butterflies.

'Are you trying to get to church?' he said to Marian, who was in front, including the next two in his remark, but avoiding Tess.

'Yes, sir; and 'tis getting late; and my colour do come up so – '

'I'll carry you through the pool – every Jill of you.'

The whole four flushed as if one heart beat through them.

'I think you can't, sir,' said Marian.

'It is the only way for you to get past. Stand still. Nonsense – you are not too heavy! I'd carry you all four together. Now, Marian, attend,' he continued, 'and put your arms round my shoulders, so. Now! Hold on. That's well done.'

Marian had lowered herself upon his arm and shoulder as directed, and Angel strode off with her, his slim figure, as viewed from behind, looking like the mere stem to the great nosegay suggested by hers. They disappeared round the curve of the road, and only his sousing footsteps and the top ribbon of Marian's bonnet told where they were. In a few minutes he reappeared. Izz Huett was the next in order upon the bank.

'Here he comes,' she murmured, and they could hear that her lips were dry with emotion. 'And I have to put my arms round his neck and look into his face as Marian did.'

'There's nothing in that,' said Tess quickly.

'There's a time for everything,' continued Izz, unheeding. 'A time to embrace, and a time to refrain from embracing; the first is now going to be mine.'

'Fie – it is Scripture, Izz!'

'Yes,' said Izz, 'I've always a' ear at church for pretty verses.'

Angel Clare, to whom three-quarters of this performance was a commonplace act of kindness, now approached Izz. She quietly and dreamily lowered herself into his arms, and Angel methodically marched off with her. When he was heard returning for the third time Retty's throbbing heart could be almost seen to shake her. He went up to the red-haired girl, and while he was seizing her he glanced at Tess. His lips could not have pronounced more plainly, 'It will soon be you and I.' Her comprehension appeared in her face; she could not help it. There was an understanding between them.

Poor little Retty, though by far the lightest weight, was the most troublesome of Clare's burdens. Marian had been like a sack of meal, a dead weight of plumpness under which he had literally staggered. Izz had ridden sensibly and calmly. Retty was a bunch of hysterics.

However, he got through with the disquieted creature, deposited her, and returned. Tess could see over the hedge the distant three in a group, standing as he had placed them on the next rising ground. It was now her turn. She was embarrassed to discover that excitement at the proximity of Mr Clare's breath and eyes, which she had condemned in her companions, was intensified in herself; and as if fearful of betraying her secret she paltered with him at the last moment.

'I may be able to clim' along the bank perhaps – I can clim' better than they. You must be so tired, Mr Clare!'

'No, no, Tess,' said he quickly. And almost before she was aware she was seated in his arms and resting against his shoulder.

'Three Leahs to get one Rachel,' he whispered.

127

'They are better women than I,' she replied, magnanimously sticking to her resolve.

'Not to me,' said Angel.

He saw her grow warm at this; and they went some steps in silence.

'I hope I am not too heavy?' she said timidly.

'O no. You should lift Marian! Such a lump. You are like an undulating billow warmed by the sun. And all this fluff of muslin about you is the froth.'

'It is very pretty – if I seem like that to you.'

'Do you know that I have undergone three-quarters of this labour entirely for the sake of the fourth quarter?'

'No.'

'I did not expect such an event to-day.'

'Nor I . . . The water came up so sudden.'

That the rise in the water was what she understood him to refer to, the state of her breathing belied. Clare stood still and inclined his face towards hers.

'O Tessy!' he exclaimed.

The girl's cheeks burned to the breeze, and she could not look into his eyes for her emotion. It reminded Angel that he was somewhat unfairly taking advantage of an accidental position; and he went no further with it. No definite words of love had crossed their lips as yet, and suspension at this point was desirable now. However, he walked slowly, to make the remainder of the distance as long as possible; but at last they came to the bend, and the rest of their progress was in full view of the other three. The dry land was reached, and he set her down.

Her friends were looking with round thoughtful eyes at her and him, and she could see that they had been talking of her. He hastily bade them farewell, and splashed back along the stretch of submerged road.

The four moved on together as before, till Marian broke the silence by saying –

'No – in all truth; we have no chance against her!' She looked joylessly at Tess.

'What do you mean?' asked the latter.

'He likes 'ee best – the very best! We could see it as he brought 'ee. He would have kissed 'ee, if you had encouraged him to do it, ever so little.'

'No, no,' said she.

The gaiety with which they had set out had somehow vanished; and yet there was no enmity or malice between them. They were generous young souls; they had been reared in the lonely country nooks where fatalism is a strong sentiment, and they did not blame her. Such supplanting was to be.

Tess's heart ached. There was no concealing from herself the fact that she loved Angel Clare, perhaps all the more passionately from knowing that the others had also lost their hearts to him. There is contagion in this sentiment, especially among women. And yet that same hungry heart of hers compassionated her friends. Tess's honest nature had fought against this, but too feebly, and the natural result had followed.

'I will never stand in your way, nor in the way of either of you!' she declared to Retty that night in the bedroom (her tears running down). 'I can't help this, my dear! I don't think marrying is in his mind at all; but if he were even to ask me I should refuse him, as I should refuse any man.'

'Oh! would you? Why?' said wondering Retty.

'It cannot be! But I will be plain. Putting myself quite on one side, I don't think he will choose either of you.'

'I have never expected it – thought of it!' moaned Retty. 'But O! I wish I was dead!'

The poor child, torn by a feeling which she hardly understood, turned to the other two girls who came upstairs just then.

'We be friends with her again,' she said to them. 'She thinks no more of his choosing her than we do.'

So the reserve went off, and they were confiding and warm.

'I don't seem to care what I do now,' said Marian, whose mood was tuned to its lowest bass. 'I was going to marry a dairyman at Stickleford, who's asked me twice; but – my soul – I would put an end to myself rather'n be his wife now! Why don't ye speak, Izz?'

'To confess, then,' murmured Izz, 'I made sure to-day that he was going to kiss me as he held me; and I lay still against his breast, hoping the hoping, and never moved at all. But he did not. I don't like biding here at Talbothays any longer! I shall go hwome.'

The air of the sleeping-chamber seemed to palpitate with the hopeless passion of the girls. They writhed feverishly under the oppressiveness of an emotion thrust on them by cruel Nature's law – an emotion which they had neither expected nor desired. The incident of the day had fanned the flame that was burning the inside of their hearts out, and the torture was almost more than they could endure. The differences which distinguished them as individuals were abstracted by this passion, and each was but portion of one organism called sex. There was much frankness and so little jealousy because there was no hope. Each one was a girl of fair common sense, and she did not delude herself with any vain conceits, or deny her love, or give herself airs, in the idea of outshining the others. The full recognition of the futility of their infatuation, from a social point of view; its purposeless beginning; its self-bounded outlook; its lack of everything to justify its existence in the eye of civilization (while lacking nothing in the eye of Nature); the one fact that it did exist, ecstasizing them to a killing joy; all this imparted to them a resignation, a dignity, which a practical and sordid expectation of winning him as a husband would have destroyed.

They tossed and turned on their little beds, and the cheese-wring dripped monotonously downstairs.

'B' you awake, Tess?' whispered one, half-an-hour later.

It was Izz Huett's voice.

Tess replied in the affirmative, whereupon also Retty and Marian suddenly flung the bedclothes off them, and sighed –

'So be we!'

'I wonder what she is like – the lady they say his family have looked out for.'

'I wonder,' said Izz.

'Some lady looked out for him?' gasped Tess, starting. 'I have never heard o' that!'

'O yes – 'tis whispered; a young lady of his own rank, chosen by his family; a Doctor of Divinity's daughter near his father's parish of Emminster; he don't care for her, they say. But he is sure to marry her.'

They had heard so very little of this; yet it was enough to build up wretched dolorous dreams upon, there in the shade of the night. They pictured all the details of his being won round to consent, of the wedding preparations, of the bride's happiness, of her dress and veil, of her blissful home with him, when oblivion would have fallen upon themselves as far as he and their love were concerned. Thus they talked, and ached, and wept till sleep charmed their sorrow away.

After this disclosure Tess nourished no further foolish thought that there lurked any grave and deliberate import in Clare's attentions to her. It was a passing summer love of her face, for love's own temporary sake – nothing more. And the thorny crown of this sad conception was that she whom he really did prefer in a cursory way to the rest, she who knew herself to be more impassioned in nature, cleverer, more beautiful than they, was in the eyes of propriety far less worthy of him than the homelier ones whom he ignored.

❧ Chapter Twenty-Four ❧

AMID THE OOZING FATNESS and warm ferments of the Var Vale, at a season when the rush of juices could almost be heard below the hiss of fertilization, it was impossible that the most fanciful love should not grow passionate. The ready bosoms existing there were impregnated by their surroundings.

July passed over their heads, and the Thermidorean weather which came in its wake seemed an effort on the part of Nature to match the state of hearts at Talbothays Dairy. The air of the place, so fresh in the spring and early summer, was stagnant and enervating now. Its heavy scents weighed upon them, and at mid-day the landscape seemed lying in a swoon. Ethiopic scorchings browned the upper slopes of the pastures, but there was still bright green herbage here where the watercourses purled. And as Clare was oppressed by the outward heats, so was he burdened inwardly by waxing fervour of passion for the soft and silent Tess.

The rains having passed the uplands were dry. The wheels of the dairyman's spring cart, as he sped home from market, licked up the pulverized surface of the highway, and were followed by white ribands of dust, as if they had set a thin powder-train on fire. The cows jumped wildly over the five-barred barton-gate, maddened by the gadfly; Dairyman Crick kept his shirt-sleeves permanently rolled up from Monday to Saturday: open windows had no effect in ventilation without open doors, and in the dairy-garden the blackbirds and thrushes crept about under the current-bushes, rather in the manner of quadrupeds than of winged creatures. The flies in the kitchen were lazy, teasing, and familiar, crawling about in unwonted places, on the floor, into drawers, and over the backs of the milkmaids' hands. Conversations were concerning sunstroke; while butter-making, and still more butter-keeping, was a despair.

They milked entirely in the meads for coolness and convenience, without driving in the cows. During the day the animals obsequiously followed the shadow of the smallest tree as it moved round the stem with the diurnal roll; and when the milkers came they could hardly stand still for the flies.

On one of these afternoons four or five unmilked cows chanced to stand apart from the general herd, behind the corner of a hedge, among them being Dumpling and Old Pretty, who loved Tess's hands above those of any other maid. When she rose from her stool under a finished cow Angel Clare, who had been observing her for some time, asked her if she would take the aforesaid creatures next. She silently assented, and with her stool at arm's length, and the pail against her knee, went round to where they stood. Soon the sound of Old Pretty's milk fizzing into the pail came through the hedge, and then Angel felt inclined to go round the corner also, to finish off a hard-yielding milcher who had strayed there, he being now as capable of this as the dairyman himself.

All the men, and some of the women, when milking, dug their fore-heads into the cows and gazed into the pail. But a few – mainly the younger ones – rested their heads sideways. This was Tess Durbeyfield's habit, her temple pressing the milcher's flank, her eyes fixed on the far end of the meadow with the quiet of one lost in meditation. She was milking Old Pretty thus, and the sun chancing to be on the milking-side it shone flat upon her pink-gowned form and her white curtain-bonnet, and upon her profile, rendering it keen as a cameo cut from the dun background of the cow.

She did not know that Clare had followed her round, and that he sat under his cow watching her. The stillness of her head and features was remarkable: she might have been in a trance, her eyes open, yet unseeing. Nothing in the picture moved but Old Pretty's tail and Tess's pink hands, the latter so gently as to be a rhythmic pulsation only, as if they were obeying a reflex stimulus, like a beating heart.

How very lovable her face was to him. Yet there was nothing ethereal about it; all was real vitality, real warmth, real incarnation. And it was in her mouth that this culminated. Eyes almost as deep and speaking he had seen before, and cheeks perhaps as fair; brows as arched, a chin and throat almost as shapely; her mouth he had seen nothing to equal on the face of the earth. To a young man with the least fire in him that little upward lift in the middle of her red top lip was distracting, infatuating, maddening. He had never before seen a woman's lips and teeth which forced upon his mind with such persistent iteration the old Elizabethan simile of roses filled with snow. Perfect, he, as a lover, might have called them off-hand. But no – they were not perfect. And it was the touch of the imperfect upon the would-be perfect that gave the sweetness, because it was that which gave the humanity.

Clare had studied the curves of those lips so many times that he could reproduce them mentally with ease: and now, as they again confronted him, clothed with colour and life, they sent an *aura* over his flesh, a breeze through his nerves, which wellnigh produced a qualm; and actu-ally produced, by some mysterious physiological process, a prosaic sneeze.

She then became conscious that he was observing her; but she would not show it by any change in position, though the curious dream-like fixity disappeared, and a close eye might easily have discerned that the rosiness of her face deepened, and then faded till only a tinge of it was left.

The influence that had passed into Clare like an excitation from the sky did not die down. Resolutions, reticences, prudences, fears, fell back like a defeated battalion. He jumped up from his seat, and, leaving his pail to be kicked over if the milcher had such a mind, went quickly towards the desire of his eyes, and, kneeling down beside her, clasped her in his arms.

Tess was taken completely by surprise, and she yielded to his embrace with unreflecting inevitableness. Having seen that it was really her lover who had advanced, and no one else, lips parted, and she sank upon him in her momentary joy, with something very like an ecstatic cry.

He had been on the point of kissing that too tempting mouth, but he checked himself, for tender conscience' sake.

'Forgive me, Tess dear!' he whispered. 'I ought to have asked. I – did not know what I was doing. I do not mean it as a liberty. I am devoted to you, Tessy, dearest, in all sincerity!'

Old Pretty by this time had looked round, puzzled; and seeing two people crouching under her where, by immemorial custom, there should have been only one, lifted her hind leg crossly.

'She is angry – she doesn't know what we mean – she'll kick over the milk!' cried Tess, gently striving to free herself, her eyes concerned with the quadruped's actions, her heart more deeply concerned with herself and Clare.

She slipped up from her seat, and they stood together, his arm still encircling her. Tess's eyes, fixed on distance, began to fill.

'Why do you cry, my darling?' he said.

'O – I don't know!' she murmured.

As she saw and felt more clearly the position she was in she became agitated and tried to withdraw.

'Well, I have betrayed my feeling, Tess, at last,' said he, with a curious sigh of desperation, signifying unconsciously that his heart had outrun his judgment. 'That I – love you dearly and truly I need not say. But I – it shall go no further now – it distresses you – I am as surprised as you are. You will not think I have presumed upon your defencelessness – been too quick and unreflecting, will you?

'N' – I can't tell.'

He had allowed her to free herself; and in a minute or two the milking of each was resumed. Nobody had beheld the gravitation of the two into one; and when the dairyman came round by that screened nook a few minutes later there was not a sign to reveal that the markedly sundered pair were more to each other than mere acquaintance. Yet in the interval since Crick's last view of them something had occurred which changed the pivot of the universe for their two natures, something which, had he known its quality, the dairyman would have despised, as a practical man; yet which was based upon a more stubborn and resistless tendency than a whole heap of so-called practicalities. A veil had been whisked aside; the tract of each one's outlook was to have a new horizon thenceforward – for a short time or for a long.

PHASE THE FOURTH

The Consequence

❧ Chapter Twenty-Five ❧

CLARE, RESTLESS, WENT OUT into the dusk when evening drew on, she who had won him having retired to her chamber.

The night was as sultry as the day. There was no coolness after dark unless on the grass. Roads, garden-paths, the house-fronts, the barton-walls were warm as hearths, and reflected the noontide temperature into the noctambulist's face.

He sat on the east gate of the dairy-yard, and knew not what to think of himself. Feeling had indeed smothered judgement that day.

Since the sudden embrace, three hours before, the twain had kept apart. She seemed stilled, almost alarmed, at what had occurred, while the novelty, unpremeditation, mastery of circumstance disquieted him – palpitating, contemplative being that he was. He could hardly realize their true relations to each other as yet, and what their mutual bearing should be before third parties thenceforward.

Angel had come as pupil to this dairy in the idea that his temporary existence here was to be the merest episode in his life, soon passed through and early forgotten; he had come as to a place from which as from a screened alcove he could calmly view the absorbing world without, and, apostrophizing it with Walt Whitman –

> *Crowds of men and women attired in the usual costumes,*
> *How curious you are to me! –*

resolve upon a plan for plunging into that world anew. But, behold, the absorbing scene had been imported hither. What had been the engrossing world had dissolved into an uninteresting outer dumb-show; while here, in this apparently dim and unimpassioned place, novelty had volcanic-ally started up, as it had never, for him, started up elsewhere.

Every window of the house being open Clare could hear across the yard each trivial sound of the retiring household. That dairy-house, so humble, so insignificant, so purely to him a place of constrained sojourn that he had never hitherto deemed it of sufficient importance to be reconnoitred as an object of any quality whatever in the landscape; what was it now? The aged and lichened brick gables breathed forth 'Stay!'

The windows smiled, the door coaxed and beckoned, the creeper blushed confederacy. A personality within it was so far-reaching in her influence as to spread into and make the bricks, mortar, and whole overhanging sky throb with a burning sensibility. Whose was this mighty personality? A milk-maid's.

It was amazing, indeed, to find how great a matter the life of the obscure dairy had become to him. And though new love was to be held partly responsible for this it was not solely so. Many besides Angel have learnt that the magnitude of lives is not as to their external displacements, but as to their subjective experiences. The impressionable peasant leads a larger, fuller, more dramatic life than the pachydermatous king. Looking at it thus he found that life was to be seen of the same magnitude here as elsewhere.

Despite his heterodoxy, faults, and weaknesses, Clare was a man with a conscience. Tess was no insignificant creature to toy with and dismiss; but a woman living her precious life – a life which, to herself who endured or enjoyed it, possessed as great a dimension as the life of the mightiest to himself. Upon her sensations the whole world depended to Tess; through her existence all her fellow-creatures existed, to her. The universe itself only came into being for Tess on the particular day in the particular year in which she was born.

This consciousness upon which he had intruded was the single opportunity of existence ever vouchsafed to Tess by an unsympathetic First Cause – her all; her every and only chance. How then should he look upon her as of less consequence than himself; as a pretty trifle to caress and grow weary of; and not deal in the greatest seriousness with the affection which he knew that he had awakened in her – so fervid and so impressionable as she was under her reserve, in order that it might not agonize and wreck her?

To encounter her daily in the accustomed manner would be to develop what had begun. Living in such close relations, to meet meant to fall into endearment; flesh and blood could not resist it; and, having arrived at no conclusion as to the issue of such a tendency, he decided to hold aloof for the present from occupations in which they would be mutually engaged. As yet the harm done was small.

But it was not easy to carry out the resolution never to approach her. He was driven towards her by every heave of his pulse.

He thought he would go and see his friends. It might be possible to sound them upon this. In less than five months his term here would have ended, and after a few additional months spent upon other farms he would be fully equipped in agricultural knowledge, and in a position to start on his own account. Would not a farmer want a wife, and should a farmer's wife be a drawing-room wax-figure, or a woman who understood farming? Notwithstanding the pleasing answer returned to him by the silence he resolved to go his journey.

One morning when they sat down to breakfast at Talbothays Dairy some maid observed that she had not seen anything of Mr Clare that day.

'O no,' said Dairyman Crick. 'Mr Clare has gone hwome to Emminster to spend a few days wi' his kinsfolk.'

For four impassioned ones around the table the sunshine of the morning went out at a stroke, and the birds muffled their song. But neither girl by word or gesture revealed her blankness.

'He's getting on towards the end of his time wi' me,' added the dairyman, with a phlegm which unconsciously was brutal; 'and so I suppose he is beginning to see about his plans elsewhere.'

'How much longer is he to bide here?' asked Izz Huett, the only one of the gloom-stricken bevy who could trust her voice with the question.

The others waited for the dairyman's answer as if their lives hung upon it; Retty, with parted lips, gazing on the table-cloth, Marian with heat added to her redness, Tess throbbing and looking out at the meads.

'Well, I can't mind the exact day without looking at my memorandum-book,' replied Crick, with the same intolerable unconcern. 'And even that may be altered a bit. He'll bide to get a little practice in the calving out at the strawyard, for certain. He'll hang on till the end of the year I should say.'

Four months or so of torturing ecstacy in his society – of 'pleasure girdled about with pain'. After that the blackness of unutterable night.

At this moment of the morning Angel Clare was riding along a narrow lane ten miles distant from the breakfasters, in the direction of his father's vicarage at Emminster, carrying, as well as he could, a little basket which contained some black-puddings and a bottle of mead, sent by Mrs Crick, with her kind respects, to his parents. The white lane stretched before him, and his eyes were upon it; but they were staring into next year, and not at the lane. He loved her; ought he to marry her? Dared he to marry her? What would his mother and his brothers say? What would he himself say a couple of years after the event? That would depend upon whether the germs of staunch comradeship underlay the temporary emotion, or whether it were a sensuous joy in her form only, with no substratum of everlastingness.

His father's hill-surrounded little town, the Tudor church-tower of red stone, the clump of trees near the vicarage, came at last into view beneath him, and he rode down towards the well-known gate. Casting a glance in the direction of the church before entering his home, he beheld standing by the vestry-door a group of girls, of ages between twelve and sixteen, apparently awaiting the arrival of some other one, who in a moment became visible; a figure somewhat older than the school-girls, wearing a broad-brimmed hat and highly-starched cambric morning-gown, with a couple of books in her hand.

Clare knew her well. He could not be sure that she observed him; he hoped she did not, so as to render it unnecessary that he should go and speak to her, blameless creature that she was. An overpowering reluctance to greet her made him decide that she had not seen him. The young lady was Miss Mercy Chant, the only daughter of his father's neighbour and friend, whom it was his parents' quiet hope that he might wed some day. She was great at Antinomianism and Bible-classes, and was plainly going to hold a class now. Clare's mind flew to the impassioned, summer-steeped heathens in the Var Vale, their rosy faces court-patched with cow-droppings; and to one the most impassioned of them all.

It was on the impulse of the moment that he had resolved to trot over to Emminster, and hence had not written to apprise his mother and father, aiming, however, to arrive about the breakfast hour, before they should have gone out to their parish duties. He was a little late, and they had already sat down to the morning meal. The group at table jumped up to welcome him as soon as he entered. They were his father and mother, his brother the Reverend Felix – curate at a town in the adjoining county, home for the inside of a fortnight – and his other brother, the Reverend Cuthbert, the classical scholar, and Fellow and Dean of his College, down from Cambridge for the long vacation. His mother appeared in a cap and silver spectacles, and his father looked what in fact he was – an earnest, God-fearing man, somewhat gaunt, in years about sixty-five, his pale face lined with thought and purpose. Over their heads hung the picture of Angel's sister, the eldest of the family, sixteen years his senior, who had married a missionary and gone out to Africa.

Old Mr Clare was a clergyman of a type which, within the last twenty years, has wellnigh dropped out of contemporary life. A spiritual descendant in the direct line of Wycliff, Huss, Luther, Calvin; an Evangelical of the Evangelicals, a Conversionist, a man of Apostolic simplicity in life and thought, he had in his raw youth made up his mind once for all on the deeper questions of existence, and admitted no further reasoning on them thenceforward. He was regarded even by those of his own date and school of thinking as extreme; while, on the other hand, those totally opposed to him were unwillingly won to admiration for his thoroughness, and for the remarkable power he showed in dismissing all question as to principles in his energy for applying them. He loved Paul of Tarsus, liked St John, hated St James as much as he dared, and regarded with mixed feelings Timothy, Titus, and Philemon. The New

Testament was less a Christiad than a Pauliad to his intelligence – less an argument than an intoxication. His creed of determinism was such that it almost amounted to a vice, and quite amounted, on its negative side, to a renunciative philosophy which had cousinship with that of Schopenhauer and Leopardi. He despised the Canons and Rubric, swore by the Articles, and deemed himself consistent through the whole category – which in a way he might have been. One thing he certainly was – sincere.

To the aesthetic, sensuous, pagan pleasure in natural life and lush womanhood which his son Angel had lately been experiencing in Var Vale, his temper would have been antipathetic in a high degree, had he either by inquiry or imagination been able to apprehend it. Once upon a time Angel had been so unlucky as to say to his father, in a moment of irritation, that it might have resulted far better for mankind if Greece had been the source of the religion of modern civilization, and not Palestine; and his father's grief was of that blank description which could not realize that there might lurk a thousandth part of a truth, much less a half truth or a whole truth, in such a proposition. He had simply preached austerely at Angel for some time after. But the kindness of his heart was such that he never resented anything for long, and welcomed his son to-day with a smile which was as candidly sweet as a child's.

Angel sat down, and the place felt like home; yet he did not so much as formerly feel himself one of the family gathered there. Every time that he returned hither he was conscious of this divergence, and since he had last shared in the Vicarage life it had grown even more distinctly foreign to his own than usual. Its transcendental aspirations – still unconsciously based on the geocentric view of things, a zenithal paradise, a nadiral hell – were as foreign to his own as if they had been the dreams of people on another planet. Latterly he had seen only Life, felt only the great passionate pulse of existence, unwarped, uncontorted, untrammelled by those creeds which futilely attempt to check what wisdom would be content to regulate.

On their part they saw a great difference in him, a growing divergence from the Angel Clare of former times. It was chiefly a difference in his manner that they noticed just now, particularly his brothers. He was getting to behave like a farmer; he flung his legs about; the muscles of his face had grown more expressive; his eyes looked as much information as his tongue spoke, and more. The manner of the scholar had nearly disappeared; still more the manner of the drawing-room young man. A prig would have said that he had lost culture, and a prude that he had become coarse. Such was the contagion of domiciliary fellowship with the Talbothays nymphs and swains.

After breakfast he walked with his two brothers, non-evangelical, well-educated, hall-marked young men, correct to their remotest fibre; such unimpeachable models as are turned out yearly by the lathe of a systematic tuition. They were both somewhat short-sighted, and when it was the custom to wear a single eyeglass and string they wore a single eyeglass and string; when it was the custom to wear a double glass they wore a double glass; when it was the custom to wear spectacles they wore spectacles straightway, all without reference to the particular variety of defect in their own vision. When Wordsworth was enthroned they carried pocket copies; and when Shelly was belittled they allowed him to grow dusty on their shelves. When Correggio's Holy Families were admired, they admired Correggio's Holy Families; when he was decried in favour of Velasquez, they sedulously followed suit without any personal objection.

If these two noticed Angel's growing social ineptness, he noticed their growing mental limitations. Felix seemed to him all Church; Cuthbert all College. His Diocesan Synod and Visitations were the mainsprings of the world to the one; Cambridge to the other. Each brother candidly recognized that there were a few unimportant scores of millions of outsiders in civilized society, persons who were neither University men nor churchmen; but they were to be tolerated rather than reckoned with and respected.

They were both dutiful and attentive sons, and were regular in their visits to their parents. Felix, though an offshoot from a far more recent point in the devolution of theology than his father, was less self-sacrificing and disinterested. More tolerant than his father of a contradictory opinion, in its aspect as a danger to its holder, he was less ready than his father to pardon it as a slight to his own teaching. Cuthbert was, upon the whole, the more liberal-minded, though, with greater subtlety, he had not so much heart.

As they walked along the hillside Angel's former feeling revived in him – that whatever their advantages by comparison with himself, neither saw or set forth life as it really was lived. Perhaps, as with many men, their opportunities of observation were not so good as their opportunities of expression. Neither had an adequate conception of the complicated forces at work outside the smooth and gentle current in which they and their associates floated. Neither saw the difference between local truth and universal truth; that what the inner world said in their clerical and academic hearing was quite a different thing from what the outer world was thinking.

'I suppose it is farming or nothing for you now, my dear fellow,' Felix was saying, among other things, to his youngest brother, as he looked through his spectacles at the distant fields with sad austerity. 'And, therefore, we must make the best of it. But I do entreat you to endeavour to keep as much as possible in touch with moral ideals. Farming, of course, means roughing it externally; but high thinking may go with plain living, nevertheless.'

'Of course it may,' said Angel. 'Was it not proved nineteen hundred years ago – if I may trespass upon your domain a little? Why should you think, Felix, that I am likely to drop my high thinking and my moral ideals?'

'Well, I fancied, from the tone of your letters and our conversation – it may be fancy only – that you were somehow losing intellectual grasp. Hasn't it struck you, Cuthbert?'

'Now, Felix,' said Angel drily, 'we are very good friends, you know; each of us treading our allotted circles; but if it comes to intellectual grasp, I think you, as a contented dogmatist, had better leave mine alone, and inquire what has become of yours.'

They returned down the hill to dinner, which was fixed at any time at which their father's and mother's morning work in the parish usually concluded. Convenience as regarded afternoon callers was the last thing to enter into the consideration of unselfish Mr and Mrs Clare; though the three sons were sufficiently in unison on this matter to wish that their parents would conform a little to modern notions.

The walk had made them hungry, Angel in particular, who was now an outdoor man, accustomed to the profuse *dapes inemptae* of the dairyman's somewhat coarsely-laden table. But neither of the old people had arrived, and it was not till the sons were almost tired of waiting that their parents entered. The self-denying pair had been occupied in coaxing the appetites of some of their sick parishioners, whom they, somewhat inconsistently, tried to keep imprisoned in the flesh, their own appetites being quite forgotten.

The family sat down to table, and a frugal meal of cold viands was deposited before them. Angel looked round for Mrs Crick's black-puddings, which he had directed to be nicely grilled, as they did them at the dairy, and of which he wished his father and mother to appreciate the marvellous herbal savours as highly as he did himself.

'Ah! you are looking for the black-puddings, my dear boy,' observed Clare's mother. 'But I am sure you will not mind doing without them, as I am sure your father and I shall not, when you know the reason. I suggested to him that we should take Mrs Crick's kind present to the children of the man who can earn nothing just now because of his attacks of delirium tremens; and he agreed that it would be a great pleasure to them; so we did.'

'Of course,' said Angel cheerfully, looking round for the mead.

'I found the mead so extremely alcoholic,' continued his mother, 'that it was quite unfit for use as a beverage, but as valuable as rum or brandy in an emergency; so I have put it in my medicine-closet.'

'We never drink spirits at this table, on principle,' added his father.

'But what shall I tell the dairyman's wife?' said Angel.

'The truth, of course,' said his father.

'I rather wanted to say we enjoyed the mead and the black-puddings very much. She is a kind, jolly sort of body, and is sure to ask me directly I return.'

'You cannot, if we did not,' Mr Clare answered lucidly.

'Ah – no; though the mead was a drop of pretty tipple.'

'A what?' said Cuthbert and Felix both.

'Oh – 'tis an expression they use down at Talbothays,' replied Angel, blushing. He felt that his parents were right in their practice if wrong in their want of sentiment, and said no more.

❧ Chapter Twenty-Six ❧

IT WAS NOT TILL THE EVENING, after family prayers, that Angel found opportunity of broaching to his father one or two subjects near his heart. He had strung himself up to the purpose while kneeling behind his brothers on the carpet, studying the little nails in the heels of their walking boots. When the service was over they went out of the room with their mother, and Mr Clare and himself were left alone.

The young man first discussed with the elder his plans for the attainment of his position as a farmer on an extensive scale – either in England or in the Colonies. His father then told him that, as he had not been put to the expense of sending Angel up to Cambridge, he had felt it his duty to set by a sum of money every year towards the purchase or lease of land for him some day, that he might not feel himself unduly slighted.

'As far as wordly wealth goes,' continued his father, 'you will no doubt stand far superior to your brothers in a few years.'

This considerateness on old Mr Clare's part led Angel onward to the other and dearer subject. He observed to his father that he was then six-and-twenty, and that when he should start in the farming business he would require eyes in the back of his head to see to all matters – some one would be necessary to superintend the domestic labours of his establishment whilst he was afield. Would it not be well, therefore, for him to marry?

His father seemed to think this idea not unreasonable; and then Angel put the question –

'What kind of wife do you think would be best for me as a thrifty hard-working farmer?'

'A truly Christian woman, who will be a help and a comfort to you in your goings-out and your comings-in. Beyond that, it really matters little. Such an one can be found; indeed, my earnest-minded friend and neighbour, Dr Chant – '

'But ought she not primarily to be able to milk cows, churn good butter, make immense cheeses; know how to sit hens and turkeys, and rear chickens, to direct a field of labourers in an emergency, and estimate the value of sheep and calves?'

'Yes; a farmer's wife; yes, certainly. It would be desirable.' Mr Clare, the elder, had plainly never thought of these points before. 'I was going to add,' he said, 'that for a pure and saintly woman you will not find one more to your true advantage, and certainly not more to your mother's mind and my own, than your friend Mercy, whom you used to show a certain interest in. It is true that my neighbour Chant's daughter has lately caught up the fashion of the younger clergy round about us for decorating the Communion-table – altar, as I was shocked to hear her call it one day – with flowers and other stuff on festival occasions. But her father, who is quite as opposed to such flummery as I, says that can be cured. It is a mere girlish outbreak which, I am sure, will not be permanent.'

'Yes, yes; Mercy is good and devout, I know. But, father, don't you think that a young woman equally pure and virtuous as Miss Chant, but one who, in place of that lady's ecclesiastical accomplishments, under-stands the duties of farm life as well as a farmer himself, would suit me infinitely better?'

His father persisted in his conviction that a knowledge of a farmer's wife's duties came second to a Pauline view of humanity; and the impul-sive Angel, wishing to honour his father's feelings and to advance the cause of his heart at the same time, grew specious. He said that fate or Providence had thrown in his way a woman who possessed every qualification to be the helpmate of an agriculturist, and was decidedly of a serious turn of mind. He would not say whether or not she had attached herself to the sound Low Church School of his father; but she would probably be open to conviction on that point; she was a regular church-goer of simple faith; honest-hearted, receptive, intelligent, grace-ful to a degree, chaste as a vestal, and, in personal appearance, exception-ally beautiful.

'Is she of a family such as you would care to marry into – a lady, in short?' asked his startled mother, who had come softly into the study during the conversation.

'She is not what in common parlance is called a lady,' said Angel, unflinchingly, 'for she is a cottager's daughter, as I am proud to say. But she *is* a lady, nevertheless – in feeling and nature.'

'Mercy Chant is of a very good family.'

'Pooh! – what's the advantage of that, mother?' said Angel quickly. 'How is family to avail the wife of a man who has to rough it as I have, and shall have to do?'

'Mercy is accomplished. And accomplishments have their charm,' returned his mother, looking at him through her silver spectacles.

'As to external accomplishments, what will be the use of them in the life I am going to lead? – while as to her reading, I can take that in hand. She'll be apt pupil enough, as you would say if you knew her. She's brim full of poetry – actualized poetry, if I may use the expression. She *lives* what paper-poets only write ... And she is an unimpeachable Christian, I am sure; perhaps of the very tribe, genus, and species you desire to propagate.'

'O Angel, you are mocking!'

'Mother, I beg pardon. But as she really does attend Church almost every Sunday morning, and is a good Christian girl, I am sure you will tolerate any social shortcomings for the sake of that quality, and feel that I may do worse than choose her.' Angel waxed quite earnest on that rather automatic orthodoxy in his beloved Tess which (never dreaming that it might stand him in such good stead) he had been prone to slight when observing it practised by her and the other milkmaids, because of its obvious unreality amid beliefs essentially naturalistic.

In their sad doubts as to whether their son had himself any right whatever to the title he claimed for the unknown young woman, Mr and Mrs Clare began to feel it as an advantage not to be overlooked that she at least was sound in her views; especially as the conjunction of the pair must have arisen by an act of Providence; for Angel never would have made orthodoxy a condition of his choice. They said finally that it was better not to act in a hurry, but that they would not object to see her.

Angel therefore refrained from declaring more particulars now. He felt that, single-minded and self-sacrificing as his parents were, there yet existed certain latent prejudices of theirs, as middle-class people, which it would require some tact to overcome. For though legally at liberty to do as he chose, and though their daughter-in-law's qualifications could make no practical difference to their lives, in the probability of her living far away from them, he wished for affection's sake not to wound their sentiment in the most important decision of his life.

He observed his own inconsistencies in dwelling upon accidents in Tess's life as if they were vital features. It was for herself that he loved Tess; her soul, her heart, her substance – not for her skill in the dairy, her aptness as his scholar, and certainly not for her simple formal faith-professions. Her unsophisticated open-air existence required no varnish of conventionality to make it palatable to him. He held that education had as yet but little affected the beats of emotion and impulse on which domestic happiness depends. It was probable that, in the lapse of ages, improved systems of moral and intellectual training would appreciably, perhaps considerably, elevate the involuntary and even the unconscious instincts of human nature; but up to the present day culture, as far as he could see, might be said to have affected only the mental epiderm of those lives which had been brought under its influence. This belief was confirmed by his experience of women, which, having latterly been extended from the cultivated middle-class into the rural community, had taught him how much less was the intrinsic difference between the good and wise woman of one social stratum and the good and wise woman of another social stratum, than between the good and bad, the wise and the foolish, of the same stratum or class.

It was the morning of his departure. His brothers had already left the vicarage to proceed on a walking tour in the north, whence one was to return to his college, and the other to his curacy. Angel might have accompanied them, but preferred to rejoin his sweetheart at Talbothays. He would have been an awkward member of the party; for, though the most appreciative humanist, the most ideal religionist, even the best-versed Christologist of the three, there was alienation in the standing consciousness that his squareness would not fit the round hole that had been prepared for him. To neither Felix nor Cuthbert had he ventured to mention Tess.

His mother made him sandwiches, and his father accompanied him, on his own mare, a little way along the road. Having fairly well advanced his own affairs Angel listened in a willing silence, as they jogged on together through the shady lanes, to his father's account of his parish difficulties, and the coldness of brother clergymen whom he loved, because of his strict interpretations of the New Testament by the light of what they deemed a pernicious Calvinistic doctrine.

'Pernicious!' said Mr Clare, with genial scorn; and he proceeded to recount experiences which would show the absurdity of that idea. He told of wondrous conversions of evil livers of which he had been the instrument, not only amongst the poor, but amongst the rich and well-to-do; and he also candidly admitted many failures.

As an instance of the latter, he mentioned the case of a young upstart squire named d'Urberville, living some forty miles off, in the neighbour-hood of Trantridge.

'Not one of the ancient d'Urbervilles of Kingsbere and other places?' asked his son. 'That curiously historic worn-out family with its ghostly legend of the coach-and-four?'

'O no. The original d'Urbervilles decayed and disappeared sixty or eighty years ago – at least, I believe so. This seems to be a new family which has taken the name; for the credit of the former knightly line I hope they are spurious, I'm sure. But it is odd to hear you express interest in old families. I thought you set less store by them even than I.'

'You misapprehend me, father; you often do,' said Angel with a little impatience. 'Politically I am sceptical as to the virtue of their being old. Some of the wise even among themselves "exclaim against their own succession", as Hamlet puts it, but lyrically, dramatically, and even his-torically, I am tenderly attached to them.'

This distinction, though by no means a subtle one, was yet too subtle for Mr Clare the elder, and he went on with the story he had been about to relate; which was that after the death of the senior so-called d'Urberville the young man developed the most culpable passions, though he had a blind mother, whose condition should have made him know better. A knowledge of his career having come to the ears of Mr Clare, when he was in that part of the country preaching missionary sermons, he boldly took occasion to speak to the delinquent on his spiritual state. Though he was a stranger, occupying another's pulpit, he had felt this to be his duty, and took for his text the words from St Luke: 'Thou fool, this night thy soul shall be required of thee!' The young man much resented this directness of attack, and in the war of words which followed when they met he did not scruple publicly to insult Mr Clare, without respect for his gray hairs.

Angel flushed with distress.

'Dear father,' he said sadly, 'I wish you would not expose yourself to such gratuitous pain from scoundrels!'

'Pain?' said his father, his rugged face shining in the ardour of self-abnegation. 'The only pain to me was pain on his account, poor, foolish young man. Do you suppose his incensed words could give me any pain, or even his blows? "Being reviled we bless; being persecuted we suffer it; being defamed we entreat; we are made as the filth of the world, and as the off-scouring of all things unto this day." Those ancient and noble words to the Corinthians are strictly true at this present hour.'

'Not blows, father? He did not proceed to blows?'

'No, he did not. Though I have borne blows from men in a mad state of intoxication.'

'No!'

'A dozen times, my boy. What then? I have saved them from the guilt of murdering their own flesh and blood thereby; and they have lived to thank me, and praise God.'

'May this young man do the same!' said Angel fervently. 'But I fear otherwise, from what you say.'

'We'll hope, nevertheless,' said Mr Clare. 'And I continue to pray for him, though on this side of the grave we shall probably never meet again. But, after all, one of those poor words of mine may spring up in his heart as a good seed some day.'

Now, as always, Clare's father was sanguine as a child; and though the younger could not accept his parent's narrow dogma he revered his practice, and recognized the hero under the pietist. Perhaps he revered his father's practice even more now than ever, seeing that, in the question of making Tessy his wife, his father had not once thought of inquiring whether she were well provided or penniless. The same unworldliness was what had necessitated Angel's getting a living as a farmer, and would probably keep his brothers in the position of poor parsons for the term of their activities; yet Angel admired it none the less. Indeed, despite his own heterodoxy, Angel often felt that he was nearer to his father on the human side than was either of his brethren.

❧ Chapter Twenty-Seven ❧

AN UP-HILL AND DOWN-DALE ride of twenty-odd miles through a garish mid-day atmosphere brought him in the afternoon to a detached knoll a mile or two west of Talbothays, whence he again looked into that green trough of sappiness and humidity, the valley of the Var or Froom. Immediately he began to descend from the upland to the fat alluvial soil below, the atmosphere grew heavier; the languid perfume of the summer fruits, the mists, the hay, the flowers, formed therein a vast pool of odour which at this hour seemed to make the animals, the very bees and butterflies, drowsy. Clare was now so familiar with the spot that he knew the individual cows by their names when, a long distance off, he saw them dotted about the meads. It was with a sense of luxury that he recognized his power of viewing life here from its inner side, in a way that had been quite foreign to him in his student-days; and, much as he loved his parents, he could not help being aware that to come here, as now, after an experience of homelife, affected him like throwing off splints and bandages; even the one customary curb on the humours of English rural societies being absent in this place, Talbothays having no resident landlord.

Not a human being was out of doors at the dairy. The denizens were all enjoying the usual afternoon nap of an hour or so which the exceedingly early hours kept in summer-time rendered a necessity. At the door the wood-hooped pails, sodden and bleached by infinite scrubbings, hung like hats on a stand upon the forked and peeled limb of an oak fixed there for that purpose; all of them ready and dry for the evening milking. Angel entered, and went through the silent passages of the house to the back quarters, where he listened for a moment. Sustained snores came from the cart-house, where some of the men were lying down; the grunt and squeal of sweltering pigs arose from the still further distance. The large-leaved rhubarb and cabbage plants slept too, their broad limp surfaces hanging in the sun like half-closed umbrellas.

He unbridled and fed his horse, and as he re-entered the house the clock struck three. Three was the afternoon skimming-hour; and, with the stroke, Clare heard the creaking of the floor-boards above, and then the touch of a descending foot on the stairs. It was Tess's, who in another moment came down before his eyes.

She had not heard him enter, and hardly realized his presence there. She was yawning, and he saw the red interior of her mouth as if it had been a snake's. She had stretched one arm so high above her coiled-up cable of hair that he could see its satin delicacy above the sunburn; her face was flushed with sleep, and her eyelids hung heavy over their pupils. The brimfulness of her nature breathed from her. It was a moment when a woman's soul is more incarnate than at any other time; when the most spiritual beauty bespeaks itself flesh; and sex takes the outside place in the presentation.

Then those eyes flashed brightly through their filmy heaviness, before the remainder of her face was well awake. With an oddly compounded look of gladness, shyness, and surprise, she exclaimed –

'O Mr Clare! How you frightened me – I – '

There had not at first been time for her to think of the changed relations which his declaration had introduced; but the full sense of the matter rose up in her face when she encountered Clare's tender look as he stepped forward to the bottom stair.

'Dear, darling Tessy!' he whispered, putting his arm round her, and his face to her flushed cheek. 'Don't, for Heaven's sake, Mister me any more. I have hastened back so soon because of you!'

Tess's excitable heart beat against his by way of reply; and there they stood upon the red-brick floor of the entry, the sun slanting in by the window upon his back, as he held her tightly to his breast; upon her inclining face, upon the blue veins of her temple, upon her naked arm, and her neck, and into the depths of her hair. Having been lying down in her clothes she was warm as a sunned cat. At first she would not look straight up at him, but her eyes soon lifted, and his plumbed the deepness of the ever-varying pupils, with their radiating fibrils of blue, and black, and gray, and violet, while she regarded him as Eve at her second waking might have regarded Adam.

'I've got to go a-skimming,' she pleaded, 'and I have on'y old Deb to help me to-day. Mrs Crick is gone to market with Mr Crick, and Retty is not well, and the others are gone out somewhere, and won't be home till milking.'

As they retreated to the milk-house Deborah Fyander appeared on the stairs.

'I have come back, Deborah,' said Mr Clare, upwards. 'So I can help Tess with the skimming; and, as you are very tired, I am sure, you needn't come down till milking-time.'

Possibly the Talbothays milk was not very thoroughly skimmed that afternoon. Tess was in a dream wherein familiar objects appeared as having light and shade and position, but no particular outline. Every time she held the skimmer under the pump to cool it for the work her hand trembled, the ardour of his affection being so palpable that she seemed to flinch under it like a plant in too burning a sun.

Then he pressed her again to his side, and when she had done running her forefinger round the leads to cut off the cream-edge, he cleaned it in nature's way; for the unconstrained manners of Talbothays dairy came convenient now.

'I may as well say it now as later, dearest,' he resumed gently. 'I wish to ask you something of a very practical nature, which I have been thinking of ever since that day last week in the meads. I shall soon want to marry, and, being a farmer, you see I shall require for my wife a woman who knows all about the management of farms. Will you be that woman, Tessy?'

He put it in that way that she might not think he had yielded to an impulse of which his head would disapprove.

She turned quite careworn. She had bowed to the inevitable result of proximity, the necessity of loving him; but she had not calculated upon this sudden corollary, which, indeed, Clare had put before her without quite meaning himself to do it so soon. With pain that was like the bitterness of dissolution she murmured the words of her indispensable and sworn answer as an honourable woman.

'O Mr Clare – I cannot be your wife – I cannot be!'

The sound of her own decision seemed to break Tess's very heart, and she bowed her face in her grief.

'But, Tess!' he said, amazed at her reply, and holding her still more greedily close. 'Do you say no? Surely you love me?'

'O yes, yes! And I would rather be yours than anybody's in the world,' returned the sweet and honest voice of the distressed girl. 'But I *cannot* marry you!'

'Tess,' he said, holding her at arm's length, 'you are engaged to marry some one else!'

'No, no!'

'Then why do you refuse me?'

'I don't want to marry! I have not thought of doing it. I cannot! I only want to love you.'

'But why?'

Driven to subterfuge, she stammered –

'Your father is a parson, and your mother wouldn't like you to marry such as me. She will want you to marry a lady.'

'Nonsense – I have spoken to them both. That was partly why I went home.'

'I feel I cannot – never, never!' she echoed.

'Is it too sudden to be asked thus, my Pretty?'

'Yes – I did not expect it.'

'If you will let it pass, please, Tessy, I will give you time,' he said. 'It was very abrupt to come home and speak to you all at once. I'll not allude to it again for a while.'

She again took up the shining skimmer, held it beneath the pump, and began anew. But she could not, as at other times, hit the exact under-surface of the cream with the delicate dexterity required, try as she might: sometimes she was cutting down into the milk, sometimes in the air. She could hardly see, her eyes having filled with two blurring tears drawn forth by a grief which, to this her best friend and dear advocate, she could never explain.

'I can't skim – I can't!' she said, turning away from him.

Not to agitate and hinder her longer the considerate Clare began talking in a more general way:

'You quite misapprehend my parents. They are the most simple-man-nered people alive, and quite unambitious. They are two of the few remaining Evangelical school. Tessy, are you an Evangelical?'

'I don't know.'

'You go to church very regularly, and our parson here is not very High, they tell me.'

Tess's ideas on the views of the parish clergyman, whom she heard every week, seemed to be rather more vague than Clare's, who had never heard him at all.

'I wish I could fix my mind on what I hear there more firmly than I do,' she remarked as a safe generality. 'It is often a great sorrow to me.'

She spoke so unaffected that Angel was sure in his heart that his father could not object to her on religious grounds, even though she did not know whether her principles were High, Low, or Broad. He himself knew that, in reality, the confused beliefs which she held, apparently imbibed in childhood, were, if any thing, Tractarian as to phraseology, and Pantheistic as to essence. Confused or otherwise, to disturb them was his last desire:

> Leave thou thy sister, when she prays,
> Her early Heaven, her happy views;
> Nor thou with shadow'd hint confuse
> A life that leads melodious days.

He had occasionally thought the counsel less honest than musical; but he gladly conformed to it now.

He spoke further of the incidents of his visit, of his father's mode of life, of his zeal for his principles; she grew serener, and the undulations disappeared from her skimming; as she finished one lead after another he followed her, and drew the plugs for letting down the milk.

'I fancied you looked a little downcast when you came in,' she ventured to observe, anxious to keep away from the subject of herself.

'Yes – well, my father has been talking a good deal to me of his troubles and difficulties, and the subject always tends to depress me. He is so zealous that he gets many snubs and buffetings from people of a different way of thinking from himself, and I don't like to hear of such humiliations to a man of his age, the more particularly as I don't think earnestness does any good when carried so far. He has been telling me of a very unpleasant scene in which he took part quite recently. He went as the deputy of some missionary society to preach in the neighbourhood of Trantridge, a place forty miles from here, and made it his business to expostulate with a lax young cynic he met somewhere about there – son of some landowner up that way – and who has a mother afflicted with blindness. My father addressed himself to the gentleman pointblank, and there was quite a disturbance. It was very foolish of my father, I must say, to intrude his conversation upon a stranger when the probabilities were so obvious that it would be useless. But whatever he thinks to be his duty, that he'll do, in season or out of season; and, of course, he makes many enemies, not only among the absolutely vicious, but among the easy-going, who hate being bothered. He says he glories in what happened, and that good may be done indirectly; but I wish he would not so wear himself out now he is getting old, and would leave such pigs to their wallowing.'

Tess's look had grown hard and worn, and her ripe mouth tragical; but she no longer showed any tremulousness. Clare's revived thoughts of his father prevented his noticing her particularly; and so they went on down the white row of liquid rectangles till they had finished and drained them off, when the other maids returned, and took their pails, and Deb came to scald out the leads for the new milk. As Tess withdrew to go afield to the cows he said to her softly –

'And my question, Tessy?'

'O no – no!' replied she with grave hopelessness, as one who had heard anew the turmoil of her own past in the allusion to Alec d'Urberville. 'It *can't* be!'

She went out towards the mead, joining the other milkmaids with a bound, as if trying to make the open air drive away her sad constraint. All the girls drew onward to the spot where the cows were grazing in the farther mead, the bevy advancing with the bold grace of wild animals – the reckless unchastened motion of women accustomed to unlimited space – in which they abandoned themselves to the air as a swimmer to the wave. It seemed natural enough to him now that Tess was again in sight to choose a mate from unconstrained Nature, and not from the abodes of Art.

❧ Chapter Twenty-Eight ❧

HER REFUSAL, THOUGH UNEXPECTED, did not permanently daunt Clare. His experience of women was great enough for him to be aware that the negative often meant nothing more than the preface to the affirmative; and it was little enough for him not to know that in the manner of the present negative there lay a great exception to the dallyings of coyness. That she had already permitted him to make love to her he read as an additional assurance, not fully trowing that in the fields and pastures to 'sigh gratis' is by no means deemed waste; love-making being here more often accepted inconsiderately and for its own sweet sake than in the carking anxious homes of the ambitious, where a girl's craving for an establishment paralyzes her healthy thought of a passion as an end.

'Tess, why did you say "no" in such a positive way?' he asked her in the course of a few days.

She started.

'Don't ask me. I told you why – partly. I am not good enough – not worthy enough.'

'How? Not fine lady enough?'

'Yes – something like that,' murmured she. 'Your friends would scorn me.'

'Indeed, you mistake them – my father and mother. As for my brothers, I don't care – ' He clasped his fingers behind her back to keep her from slipping away. 'Now – you did not mean it, sweet? – I am sure you did not! You have made me so restless that I cannot read, or play, or do anything. I am in no hurry, Tess, but I want to know – to hear from your own warm lips – that you will some day be mine – any time you may choose; but some day?'

She could only shake her head and look away from him.

Clare regarded her attentively, conned the characters of her face as if they had been hieroglyphics. The denial seemed real.

'Then I ought not to hold you in this way – ought I? I have no right to you – no right to seek out where you are, or to walk with you! Honestly, Tess, do you love any other man?'

'How can you ask?' she said, with continued self-suppression.

'I almost know that you do not. But then, why do you repulse me?'

'I don't repulse you. I like you to – tell me you love me; and you may always tell me so as you go about with me – and never offend me.'

'But you will not accept me as a husband?'

'Ah – that's different – it is for your good, indeed my dearest! O, believe me, it is only for your sake! I don't like to give myself the great happiness o' promising to be yours in that way – because – because I am *sure* I ought not to do it.'

'But you will make me happy!'

'Ah – you think so, but you don't know!'

At such times as this, apprehending the grounds of her refusal to be her modest sense of incompetence in matters social and polite, he would say that she was wonderfully well-informed and versatile – which was certainly true, her natural quickness, and her admiration for him, having led her to pick up his vocabulary, his accent, and fragments of his knowledge, to a surprising extent. After these tender contests and her victory she would go away by herself under the remotest cow, if at milking-time, or into the sedge, or into her room, if at a leisure interval, and mourn silently, not a minute after an apparently phlegmatic negative.

The struggle was so fearful; her own heart was so strongly on the side of his – two ardent hearts against one poor little conscience – that she tried to fortify her resolution by every means in her power. She had come to Talbothays with a made-up mind. On no account could she agree to a step which might afterwards cause bitter rueing to her husband for his blindness in wedding her. And she held that what her conscience had decided for her when her mind was unbiassed ought not to be overruled now.

'Why don't somebody tell him all about me?' she said. 'It was only forty miles off – why hasn't it reached here? Somebody must know!'

Yet nobody seemed to know; nobody told him.

For two or three days no more was said. She guessed from the sad countenances of her chamber companions that they regarded her not only as the favourite, but as the chosen; but they could see for themselves that she did not put herself in his way.

Tess had never before known a time in which the thread of her life was so distinctly twisted of two strands, positive pleasure and positive pain. At the next cheese-making the pair were again left alone together. The dairyman himself had been lending a hand; but Mr Crick, as well as his wife, seemed latterly to have acquired a suspicion of mutual interest between these two; though they walked so circumspectly that suspicion was but of the faintest. Anyhow, the dairyman left them to themselves.

They were breaking up the masses of curd before putting them into the vats. The operation resembled the act of crumbling bread on a large scale; and amid the immaculate whiteness of the curds Tess Durbeyfield's hands showed themselves of the pinkness of the rose. Angel, who was filling the vats with his handfuls, suddenly ceased, and laid his hands flat upon hers. Her sleeves were rolled far above the elbow, and bending lower he kissed the inside vein of her soft arm.

Although the early September weather was sultry, her arm, from her dabbling in the curds, was as cold and damp to his mouth as a new-gathered mushroom, and tasted of the whey. But she was such a sheaf of susceptibilities that her pulse was accelerated by the touch, her blood driven to her finger-ends, and the cool arms flushed hot. Then, as though her heart had said, 'Is coyness longer necessary? Truth is truth between man and woman, as between man and man.' she lifted her eyes, and they beamed devotedly into his, as her lip rose in a tender half-smile.

'Do you know why I did that, Tess?' he said.

'Because you love me very much!'

'Yes, and as a preliminary to a new entreaty.'

'Not *again*!'

She looked a sudden fear that her resistance might break down under her own desire.

'O, Tessy!' he went on, 'I *cannot* think why you are so tantalizing. Why do you disappoint me so? You seem almost like a coquette, upon my life you do – a coquette of the first urban water! They blow hot and blow cold, just as you do; and it is the very last sort of thing to expect to find in a retreat like Talbothays ... And yet, dearest,' he quickly added, observing how the remark had cut her, 'I know you to be the most honest, spotless creature that ever lived. So how can I suppose you a flirt? Tess, why don't you like the idea of being my wife, if you love me as you seem to do?'

'I have never said I don't like the idea, and I never could say it; because – it isn't true!'

The stress now getting beyond endurance her lip quivered, and she was obliged to go away. Clare was so pained and perplexed that he ran after and caught her in the passage.

'Tell me, tell me!' he said, passionately clasping her, in forgetfulness of his curdy hands: 'do tell me that you won't belong to anybody but me!'

'I will, I will tell you!' she exclaimed. 'And I will give you a complete answer, if you will let me go now. I will tell you my experiences – all about myself – all!'

'Your experiences, dear; yes, certainly; any number.' He expressed assent in loving satire, looking into her face. 'My Tess has, no doubt, almost as many experiences as that wild convolvulus out there on the garden hedge, that opened itself this morning for the first time. Tell me anything, but don't use that wretched expression any more about not being worthy of me.'

'I will try – not! And I'll give you my reasons to-morrow – next week.'

'Say on Sunday?'

'Yes, on Sunday.'

At last she got away, and did not stop in her retreat till she was in the thicket of pollard willows at the lower side of the barton, where she could be quite unseen. Here Tess flung herself down upon the rustling undergrowth of speargrass, as upon a bed, and remained crouching in palpitating misery broken by momentary shoots of joy, which her fears about the ending could not altogether suppress.

In reality, she was drifting into acquiescence. Every see-saw of her breath, every wave of her blood, every pulse singing in her ears, was a voice that joined with nature in revolt against her scrupulousness. Reckless, inconsiderate acceptance of him; to close with him at the altar, revealing nothing, and chancing discovery; to snatch ripe pleasure before the iron teeth of pain could have time to shut upon her: that was what love counselled; and in almost a terror of ecstasy Tess divined that, despite her many months of lonely self-chastisement, wrestlings, communings, schemes to lead a future of austere isolation, love's counsel would prevail.

The afternoon advanced, and still she remained among the willows. She heard the rattle of taking down the pails from the forked stands; the 'waow-waow!' which accompanied the getting together of the cows. But she did not go to the milking. They would see her agitation; and the dairyman, thinking the cause to be love alone, would good-naturedly tease her; and that harassment could not be borne.

Her lover must have guessed her overwrought state, and invented some excuse for her non-appearance, for no inquiries were made or calls given. At half-past six the sun settled down upon the levels, with the aspect of a great forge in the heavens, and presently a monstrous pumpkin-like moon arose on the other hand. The pollard willows, tortured out of their natural shape by incessant choppings, became spiny-haired monsters as they stood up against it. She went in, and upstairs without a light.

It was now Wednesday. Thursday came, and Angel looked thoughtfully at her from a distance, but intruded in no way upon her. The indoor milkmaids, Marian and the rest, seemed to guess that something definite was afoot, for they did not force any remarks upon her in the bedchamber. Friday passed; Saturday. To-morrow was the day.

'I shall give way – I shall say yes – I shall let myself marry him – I cannot help it!' she jealously panted, with her hot face to the pillow that night, on hearing one of the other girls sigh his name in her sleep. 'I can't bear to let anybody have him but me! Yet it is a wrong to him, and may kill him when he knows! O my heart – O – O – O!'

❧ Chapter Twenty-Nine ❧

'Now, WHO MID YE THINK I've heard news o' this morning?' said Dairyman Crick, as he sat down to breakfast next day, with a riddling gaze round upon the munching men and maids. 'Now just who mid ye think?'

One guessed, and another guessed. Mrs Crick did not guess, because she knew already.

'Well,' said the dairyman, "tis that slack-twisted 'hore's-bird of a fellar, Jack Dollop. He's lately got married to a widow-woman.'

'Not Jack Dollop? A villain – to think o' that!' said a milker.

The name entered quickly into Tess Durbeyfield's consciousness, for it was the name of the lover who had wronged his sweetheart, and had afterwards been so roughly used by the young woman's mother in the butter-churn.

'And has he married the valiant matron's daughter, as he promised?' asked Angel Clare absently, as he turned over the newspaper he was reading at the little table to which he was always banished by Mrs Crick, in her sense of his gentility.

'Not he, sir. Never meant to,' replied the dairyman. 'As I say, 'tis a widow-woman, and she had money, it seems – fifty poun' a year or so; and that was all he was after. They were married in a great hurry; and then she told him that by marrying she had lost her fifty poun' a year. Just fancy the state o' my gentleman's mind at that news! Never such a cat-and-dog life as they've been leading ever since! Serves him well beright. But onluckily the poor woman gets the worst o't.'

'Well, the silly body should have told en sooner that the ghost of her first man would trouble him,' said Mrs Crick.

'Ay; ay,' responded the dairyman indecisively. 'Still, you can see exactly how t'was. She wanted a home, and didn't like to run the risk of losing him. Don't ye think that was something like it, maidens?'

He glanced towards the row of girls.

'She ought to ha' told him just before they went to church, when he could hardly have backed out,' exclaimed Marian.

'Yes, she ought,' agreed Izz.

'She must have seen what he was after, and should ha' refused him,' cried Retty spasmodically.

'And what do you say, my dear?' asked the dairyman of Tess.

'I think she ought – to have told him the true state of things – or else refused him – I don't know,' replied Tess, the bread-and-butter choking her.

'But cust if I'd have done either o't,' said Beck Knibbs, a married helper from one of the cottages. 'All's fair in love and war. I'd ha' married en just as she did, and if he'd said two words to me about not telling him beforehand anything whatsomdever about my first chap that I hadn't chose to tell, I'd ha' knocked him down wi' the rolling-pin – a scram little feller like he! Any woman could do it.'

The laughter which followed this sally was supplemented only by a sorry smile, for form's sake, from Tess. What was comedy to them was tragedy to her; and she could hardly bear their mirth. She soon rose from table, and, with an impression that Clare would follow her, went along

a little wriggling path, now stepping to one side of the irrigating chan-
nels, and now to the other, till she stood by the main stream of the Var.
Men had been cutting the water-weeds higher up the river, and masses
of them were floating past her – moving islands of green crow-foot,
whereon she might almost have ridden; long locks of which weed had
lodged against the piles driven to keep the cows from crossing.

Yes, there was the pain of it. This question of a woman telling her
story – the heaviest of crosses to herself – seemed but amusement to
others. It was as if people should laugh at martyrdom.

'Tessy!' came from behind her, and Clare sprang across the gully,
alighting beside her feet. 'My wife – soon!'

'No, no; I cannot. For your sake, O Mr Clare; for your sake, I say no!'

'Tess!'

'Still I say no!' she repeated.

Not expecting this he had put his arm lightly round her waist the
moment after speaking, beneath her hanging tail of hair. (The younger
dairymaids, including Tess, breakfasted with their hair loose on Sunday
mornings before building it up extra high for attending church, a style
they could not adopt when milking with their heads against the cows.)
If she had said 'Yes' instead of 'No' he would have kissed her; it had
evidently been his intention; but her determined negative deterred his
scrupulous heart. Their condition of domiciliary comradeship put her, as
the woman, to such disadvantage by its enforced intercourse, that he felt
it unfair to her to exercise any pressure of blandishment which he might
have honestly employed had she been better able to avoid him. He
released her momentarily-imprisoned waist, and withheld the kiss.

It all turned on that release. What had given her strength to refuse
him this time was solely the tale of the widow told by the dairyman;
and that would have been overcome in another moment. But Angel said
no more; his face was perplexed; he went away.

Day after day they met – somewhat less constantly than before; and
thus two or three weeks went by. The end of September drew near,
and she could see in his eye that he might ask her again.

His plan of procedure was different now – as though he had made up
his mind that her negatives were, after all, only coyness and youth
startled by the novelty of the proposal. The fitful evasiveness of her
manner when the subject was under discussion countenanced the idea.
So he played a more coaxing game; and while never going beyond words,
or attempting the renewal of caresses, he did his utmost orally.

In this way Clare persistently wooed her in undertones like that of the
purling milk – at the cow's side, at skimmings, at butter-makings, at
cheese-makings, among broody poultry, and among farrowing pigs – as
no milkmaid was ever wooed before by such a man.

Tess knew that she must break down. Neither a religious sense of a certain moral validity in the previous union nor a conscientious wish for candour could hold out against it much longer. She loved him so passionately, and he was so godlike in her eyes; and being, though untrained, instinctively refined, her nature cried for his tutelary guidance. And thus, though Tess kept repeating to herself, 'I can never be his wife', the words were vain. A proof of her weakness lay in the very utterance of what calm strength would not have taken the trouble to formulate. Every sound of his voice beginning on the old subject stirred her with a terrifying bliss, and she coveted the recantation she feared.

His manner was – what man's is not? – so much that of one who would love and cherish and defend her under any conditions, changes, charges, or revelations, that her gloom lessened as she basked in it. The season meanwhile was drawing onward to the equinox, and though it was still fine, the days were much shorter. The dairy had again worked by morning candle-light for a long time; and a fresh renewal of Clare's pleading occurred one morning between three and four.

She had run up in her bedgown to his door to call him as usual; then had gone back to dress and call the others; and in ten minutes was walking to the head of the stairs with the candle in her hand. At the same moment he came down his steps from above in his shirt-sleeves and put his arm across the stairway.

'Now, Miss Flirt, before you go down,' he said peremptorily. 'It is a fortnight since I spoke, and this won't do any longer. You *must* tell me what you mean, or I shall have to leave this house. My door was ajar just now, and I saw you. For your own safety I must go. You don't know. Well? Is it to be yes at last?'

'I am only just up, Mr Clare, and it is too early to take me to task!' she pouted. 'You need not call me Flirt. 'Tis cruel and untrue. Wait till by and by. Please wait till by and by! I will really think seriously about it between now and then. Let me go downstairs!'

She looked a little like what he said she was as, holding the candle sideways, she tried to smile away the seriousness of her words.

'Call me Angel, then, and not Mr Clare.'

'Angel.'

'Angel dearest – why not?'

''Twould mean that I agree, wouldn't it?'

'It would only mean that you love me, even if you cannot marry me; and you were so good as to own that long ago.'

'Very well, then, "Angel dearest", if I *must*,' she murmured, looking at her candle, a roguish curl coming upon her mouth, notwithstanding her suspense.

Clare had resolved never to kiss her until he had obtained her promise;

160

but somehow, as Tess stood there in her prettily tucked-up milking gown, her hair carelessly heaped upon her head till there should be leisure to arrange it when skimming and milking were done, he broke his resolve, and brought his lips to her cheek for one moment. She passed downstairs very quickly, never looking back at him or saying another word. The other maids were already down, and the subject was not pursued. Except Marian they all looked wistfully and suspiciously at the pair, in the sad yellow rays which the morning candles emitted in contrast with the first cold signals of the dawn without.

When skimming was done – which, as the milk diminished with the approach of autumn, was a lessening process day by day – Retty and the rest went out. The lovers followed them.

'Our tremulous lives are so different from theirs, are they not?' he musingly observed to her, as he regarded the three figures tripping before him through the frigid pallor of opening day.

'Not so very different, I think,' she said.

'Why do you think that?'

'There are very few women's lives that are not – tremulous,' Tess replied, pausing over the new word as if it impressed her. 'There's more in those three than you think.'

'What is in them?'

'Almost either of 'em,' she began, 'would make – perhaps would make – a properer wife than I. And perhaps they love you as well as I – almost.'

'O, Tessy!'

There were signs that it was an exquisite relief to her to hear the impatient exclamation, though she had resolved so intrepidly to let generosity make one bid against herself. That was now done, and she had not the power to attempt self-immolation a second time then. They were joined by a milker from one of the cottages, and no more was said on that which concerned them so deeply. But Tess knew that this day would decide it.

In the afternoon several of the dairyman's household and assistants went down to the meads as usual, a long way from the dairy, where many of the cows were milked without being driven home. The supply was getting less as the animals advanced in calf, and the supernumerary milkers of the lush green season had been dismissed.

The work progressed leisurely. Each pailful was poured into tall cans that stood in a large spring-waggon which had been brought upon the scene; and when they were milked the cows trailed away.

Dairyman Crick, who was there with the rest, his wrapper gleaming miraculously white against a leaden evening sky, suddenly looked at his heavy watch.

'Why, 'tis later than I thought,' he said. 'Begad! We shan't be soon enough with this milk at the station, if we don't mind. There's no time to-day to take it home and mix it with the bulk afore sending off. It must go to station straight from here. Who'll drive it across?'

Mr Clare volunteered to do so, though it was none of his business, asking Tess to accompany him. The evening, though sunless, had been warm and muggy for the season, and Tess had come out with her milking-hood only, naked-armed and jacketless; certainly not dressed for a drive. She therefore replied by glancing over her scant habiliments; but Clare gently urged her. She assented by relinquishing her pail and stool to the dairyman to take home; and mounted the spring-waggon beside Clare.

₰ Chapter Thirty ₰

IN THE DIMINISHING DAYLIGHT they went along the level roadway through the meads, which stretched away into gray miles, and were backed in the extreme edge of distance by the swarthy and abrupt slopes of Edgon Heath. On its summit stood clumps and stretches of fir-trees, whose notched tips appeared like battlemented towers crowning black-fronted castles of enchantment.

They were so absorbed in the sense of being close to each other that they did not begin talking for a long while, the silence being broken only by the clucking of the milk in the tall cans behind them. The lane they followed was so solitary that the hazel nuts had remained on the boughs till they slipped from their shells, and the blackberries hung in heavy clusters. Every now and then Angel would fling the lash of his whip round one of these, pluck it off, and give it to his companion.

The dull sky soon began to tell its meaning by sending down herald-drops of rain, and the stagnant air of the day changed into a fitful breeze which played about their faces. The quick-silvery glaze on the rivers and pools vanished; from broad mirrors of light they changed to lustreless sheets of lead, with a surface like a rasp. But that spectacle did not affect her preoccupation. Her countenance, a natural carnation slightly embrowned by the season, had deepened its tinge with the beating of the rain-drops; and her hair, which the pressure of the cows' flanks had, as usual, caused to tumble down from its fastenings and stray beyond the curtain of her calico bonnet, was made clammy by the moisture, till it hardly was better than seaweed.

'I ought not to have come, I suppose,' she murmured, looking at the sky.

'I am sorry for the rain,' said he. 'But how glad I am to have you here!'

Remote Egdon disappeared by degrees behind the liquid gauze. The evening grew darker, and the roads being crossed by gates it was not safe to drive faster than at a walking pace. The air was rather chill.

'I am so afraid you will get cold, with nothing upon your arms and shoulders,' he said. 'Creep close to me, and perhaps the drizzle won't hurt you much. I should be sorrier still if I did not think that the rain might be helping me.'

She imperceptibly crept closer, and he wrapped round them both a large piece of sail-cloth, which was sometimes used to keep the sun off the milk-cans. Tess held it from slipping off him as well as herself, Clare's hands being occupied.

'Now we are all right again. Ah – no we are not! It runs down into my neck a little, and it must still more into yours. That's better. Your arms are like wet marble, Tess. Wipe them in the cloth. Now, if you stay quiet, you will not get another drop. Well, dear – about that question of mine – that long-standing question?'

The only reply that he could hear for a little while was the smack of the horse's hoofs on the moistening road, and the cluck of the milk in the cans behind them.

'Do you remember what you said?'

'I do,' she replied.

'Before we get home, mind.'

'I'll try.'

He said no more then. As they drove on the fragment of an old manor house of Caroline date rose against the sky, and was in due course passed and left behind.

'That,' he observed, to entertain her, 'is an interesting old place – one of the several seats which belonged to an ancient Norman family formerly of great influence in this county, the d'Urbervilles. I never pass one of their residences without thinking of them. There is something very sad in the extinction of a family of renown, even if it was fierce, domineering, feudal renown.'

'Yes,' said Tess.

They crept along towards a point in the expanse of shade just at hand at which a feeble light was beginning to assert its presence, a spot where, by day, a fitful white streak of steam at intervals upon the dark green background denoted intermittent moments of contact between their secluded world and modern life. Modern life stretched out its steam feeler to this point three or four times a day, touched the native existences, and quickly withdrew its feeler again, as if what it touched had been uncongenial.

They reached the feeble light, which came from the smoky lamp of a little railway station; a poor enough terrestrial star, yet in one sense of more importance to Talbothays Dairy and mankind than the celestial ones to which it stood in such humiliating contrast. The cans of new milk were unladen in the rain, Tess getting a little shelter from a neighbouring holly tree.

Then there was the hissing of a train, which drew up almost silently upon the wet rails, and the milk was rapidly swung can by can into the truck. The light of the engine flashed for a second upon Tess Durbeyfield's figure, motionless under the great holly tree. No object could have looked more foreign to the gleaming cranks and wheels than this unsophisticated girl, with the round bare arms, the rainy face and hair, the suspended attitude of a friendly leopard at pause, the print gown of no date or fashion, and the cotton bonnet drooping on her brow.

She mounted again beside her lover, with a mute obedience characteristic of impassioned natures at times, and when they had wrapped themselves up over head and ears in the sail-cloth again, they plunged back into the now thick night. Tess was so receptive that the few minutes of contact with the whirl of material progress lingered in her thought.

'Londoners will drink it at their breakfasts to-morrow, won't they?' she asked. 'Strange people that we have never seen.'

'Yes – I suppose they will. Though not as we send it. When its strength has been lowered, so that it may not get up into their heads.'

'Noble men and noble women, ambassadors and centurions, ladies and tradeswomen, and babies who have never seen a cow.'

'Well, yes; perhaps; particularly centurions.'

'Who don't know anything of us, and where it comes from; or think how we two drove miles across the moor to-night in the rain that it might reach 'em in time?'

'We did not drive entirely on account of these precious Londoners; we drove a little on our own – on account of that anxious matter which you will, I am sure, set at rest, dear Tess. Now, permit me to put it in this way. You belong to me already, you know; your heart, I mean. Does it not?'

'You know as well as I. O yes – yes!'

'Then, if your heart does, why not your hand?'

'My only reason was on account of you – on account of a question. I have something to tell you –'

'But suppose it to be entirely for my happiness, and my worldly convenience also?'

'O yes; if it is for your happiness and worldly convenience. But my life before I came here – I want –'

'Well, it is for my convenience as well as my happiness. If I have a very large farm, either English or colonial, you will be invaluable as a wife to me; better than a woman out of the largest mansion in the country. So please – please, dear Tessy, disabuse your mind of the feeling that you will stand in my way.'

'But my history. I want you to know it – you must let me tell you – you will not like me so well!'

'Tell it if you wish to, dearest. This previous history then. Yes, I was born at so and so, Anno Domini –'

'I was born at Marlott,' she said, catching at his words as a help, lightly as they were spoken. 'And I grew up there. And I was in the Sixth Standard when I left school, and they said I had great aptness, and should make a good teacher, so it was settled that I should be one. But there was trouble in my family; father was not very industrious, and he drank a little.'

'Yes, yes. Poor child! Nothing new.' He pressed her more closely to his side.

'And then – there is something very unusual about it – about me. I – I was – ' Tess's breath quickened.

'Yes, dearest. Never mind.'

'I – I am not a Durbeyfield, but a d'Urberville – a descendant of the same family as those that owned the old house we passed. And – we are all gone to nothing!'

'A d'Urberville! – Indeed! And is that all the trouble, dear Tess?'

'Yes,' she answered faintly.

'Well – why should I love you less after knowing this?'

'I was told by the dairyman that you hated old families.'

He laughed.

'Well, it is true, in one sense. I do hate the aristocratic principle of blood before everything, and do think that as reasoners the only pedigrees we ought to respect are those spiritual ones of the wise and virtuous, without regard to corporeal paternity. But I am extremely interested in this news – you can have no idea how interested I am! Are not you interested yourself in being one of that well-known line?'

'No. I have thought it sad – especially since coming here, and knowing that many of the hills and fields I see once belonged to my father's people. But other hills and fields belonged to Retty's people, and perhaps others to Marian's, so that I don't value it particularly.'

'Yes – it is surprising how many of the present tillers of the soil were once owners of it, and I sometimes wonder that a certain school of politicians don't make capital of the circumstance; but they don't seem to know it ... I wonder that I did not see the resemblance of your name to d'Urberville, and trace the manifest corruption. And this was the carking secret!'

She had not told. At the last moment her courage had failed her, she feared his blame for not telling him sooner; and her instinct of self-preservation was stronger than her candour.

'Of course,' continued the unwitting Clare, 'I should have been glad to know you to be descended exclusively from the long-suffering, dumb, unrecorded rank and file of the English nation, and not from the self-seeking few who made themselves powerful at the expense of the rest. But I am corrupted away from that by my affection for you, Tess [he laughed as he spoke], and made selfish likewise. For your own sake I rejoice in your descent. Society is hopelessly snobbish, and this fact of your extraction may make an appreciable difference to its acceptance of you as my wife, after I have made you the well-read woman that I mean to make you. My mother too, poor soul, will think so much better of you on account of it. Tess, you must spell your name correctly – d'Urberville – from this very day.'

'I like the other way rather best.'

'But you *must*, dearest! Good heavens, why dozens of mushroom millionaires would jump at such a possession! By the bye, there's one of that kidney who has taken the name – where have I heard of him? – Up in the neighbourhood of The Chase, I think. Why, he is the very man who had that rumpus with my father I told you of. What an odd coincidence!'

'Angel, I think I would rather not take the name! It is unlucky, perhaps!' She was agitated.

'Now then, Mistress Teresa d'Urberville, I have you. Take my name, and so you will escape yours! The secret is out, so why should you any longer refuse me?'

'If it is *sure* to make you happy to have me as your wife, and you feel that you do wish to marry me, *very, very* much –'

'I do, dearest, of course!'

'I mean, that it is only your wanting me very much, and being hardly able to keep alive without me, whatever my offences, that would make me feel I ought to say I will.'

'You will – you do say it, I know! You will be mine for ever and ever.' He clasped her close and kissed her.

'Yes!'

She had no sooner said it than she burst into a dry hard sobbing, so violent that it seemed to rend her. Tess was not a hysterical girl by any means, and he was surprised.

'Why do you cry, dearest?'

'I can't tell – quite! – I am so glad to think – of being yours, and making you happy!'

'But this does not seem very much like gladness, my Tessy!'

'I mean – I cry because I have broken down in my vow! I said I would die unmarried!'

'But, if you love me you would like me to be your husband?'

'Yes, yes, yes! But O, I sometimes wish I had never been born!'

'Now, my dear Tess, if I did not know that you are very much excited, and very inexperienced, I should say that remark was not very complimentary. How came you to wish that if you care for me? Do you care for me? I wish you would prove it in some way.'

'How can I prove it more than I have done?' she cried, in a distraction of tenderness. 'Will this prove it more?'

She clasped his neck, and for the first time Clare learnt what an impassioned woman's kisses were like upon the lips of one whom she loved with all her heart and soul, as Tess loved him.

'There – now do you believe?' she asked, flushed, and wiping her eyes.

'Yes. I never really doubted – never, never!'

So they drove on through the gloom, forming one bundle inside the sail-cloth, the horse going as he would, and the rain driving against them. She had consented. She might as well have agreed at first. The 'appetite for joy' which pervades all creation, that tremendous force which sways humanity to its purpose, as the tide sways the helpless weed, was not to be controlled by vague lucubrations over the social rubric.

'I must write to my mother,' she said. 'You don't mind my doing that?'

'Of course not, dear child. You are a child to me, Tess, not to know how very proper it is to write to your mother at such a time, and how wrong it would be in me to object. Where does she live?'

'At the same place – Marlott. On the further side of Blackmoor Vale.'

'Ah, then I *have* seen you before this summer – '

'Yes; at that dance on the green; but you would not dance with me. O, I hope that is of no ill-omen for us now!'

❧ Chapter Thirty-One ❧

TESS WROTE A MOST TOUCHING and urgent letter to her mother the very next day, and by the end of the week a response to her communication had arrived in Joan Durbeyfield's wandering last-century hand.

> DEAR TESS, – J write these few lines Hoping they will find you well, as they leave me at Present, thank God for it. Dear Tess, we are all glad to Hear that you are going really to be married soon. But with respect to your question, Tess, J say between ourselves, quite private but very strong, that on no account do you say a word of your Bygone Trouble to him. J did not tell everything to your Father, he being so Proud on account of his Respectability, which, perhaps, your Intended is the same. Many a woman – some of the Highest in the Land – have had a Trouble in their time; and why should you Trumpet yours when others don't Trumpet theirs? No girl would be such a Fool, specially as it is so long ago, and not your Fault at all. J shall answer the same if you ask me fifty times. Besides, you must bear in mind that, knowing it to be your Childish Nature to tell all that's in your heart – so simple! – J made you promise me never to let it out by Word or Deed, having your Welfare in my Mind; and you most solemnly did promise it going from this Door. J have not named either that Question or your coming marriage to your Father, as he would blab it everywhere, poor Simple Man.
>
> Dear Tess, keep up your Spirits, and we mean to send you a Hogshead of Cyder for your Wedding, knowing there is not much in your parts, and thin Sour Stuff what there is. So no more at present, and with kind love to your Young Man. – From your affectte. Mother,
>
> J. DURBEYFIELD

'O mother, mother!' murmured Tess.

She was recognizing how light was the touch of events the most oppressive upon Mrs Durbeyfield's elastic spirit. Her mother did not see life as Tess saw it. That haunting episode of bygone days was to her mother but a passing accident. But perhaps her mother was right as to the course to be followed, whatever she might be in her reasons. Silence seemed, on the face of it, best for her adored one's happiness: silence it should be.

Thus steadied by a command from the only person in the world who had any shadow of right to control her action, Tess grew calmer. The responsibility was shifted, and her heart was lighter than it had been for weeks. The days of declining autumn which followed her assent, beginning with the month of October, formed a season through which she lived in spiritual altitudes more nearly approaching ecstasy than any other period of her life.

There was hardly a touch of earth in her love for Clare. To her sublime trustfulness he was all that goodness could be – knew all that a guide, philosopher, and friend should know. She thought every line in the contour of his person the perfection of masculine beauty, his soul the soul of a saint, his intellect that of a seer. The wisdom of her love for him, as love, sustained her dignity; she seemed to be wearing a crown. The compassion of his love for her, as she saw it, made her lift up her heart to him in devotion. He would sometimes catch her large, worshipful eyes, that had no bottom to them, looking at him from their depths, as if she saw something immortal before her.

She dismissed the past – trod upon it and put it out, as one treads on a coal that is smouldering and dangerous.

She had not known that men could be so disinterested, chivalrous, protective, in their love for women as he. Angel Clare was far from all that she thought him in this respect; absurdly far, indeed; but he was, in truth, more spiritual than animal; he had himself well in hand, and was singularly free from grossness. Though not cold-natured, he was rather bright than hot – less Byronic than Shelleyan; could love desperately, but with a love more especially inclined to the imaginative and ethereal; it was a fastidious emotion which could jealously guard the loved one against his very self. This amazed and enraptured Tess, whose slight experiences had been so infelicitous till now; and in her reaction from indignation against the male sex she swerved to excess of honour for Clare.

They unaffectedly sought each other's company; in her honest faith she did not disguise her desire to be with him. The sum of her instincts on this matter, if clearly stated, would have been that the elusive quality in her sex which attracts men in general might be distasteful to so perfect a man after an avowal of love, since it must in its very nature carry with it a suspicion of art.

The country custom of unreserved comradeship out of doors during betrothal was the only custom she knew, and to her it had no strangeness; though it seemed oddly anticipative to Clare till he saw how normal a thing she, in common with all the other dairy-folk, regarded it. Thus, during this October month of wonderful afternoons they roved along the meads by creeping paths which followed the brinks of trickling tributary brooks, hopping across by little wooden bridges to the other side, and back again. They were never out of the sound of some purling weir, whose buzz accompanied their own murmuring, while the beams of the sun, almost as horizontal as the mead itself, formed a pollen of radiance over the landscape. They saw tiny blue fogs in the shadows of trees and hedges, all the time that there was bright sunshine elsewhere. The sun was so near the ground, and the sward so flat, that the shadows of Clare and Tess would stretch a quarter of a mile ahead of them, like two long fingers pointing afar to where the green alluvial reaches abutted against the sloping sides of the vale.

Men were at work here and there – for it was the season for 'taking up' the meadows, or digging the little waterways clear for the winter irrigation, and mending their banks where trodden down by the cows. The shovelfuls of loam, black as jet, brought there by the river when it was as wide as the whole valley, were an essence of soils, pounded champaigns of the past, steeped, refined, and subtilized to extraordinary richness, out of which came all the fertility of the mead, and of the cattle grazing there.

Clare hardily kept his arm round her waist in sight of these watermen, with the air of a man who was accustomed to public dalliance, though actually as shy as she who, with lips parted and eyes askance on the labourers, wore the look of a wary animal the while.

'You are not ashamed of owning me as yours before them!' she said gladly.

'O no!'

'But if it should reach the ears of your friends at Emminster that you are walking about like this with me, a milkmaid – '

'The most bewitching milkmaid ever seen.'

'They might feel it a hurt to their dignity.'

'My dear girl – a d'Urberville hurt the dignity of a Clare! It is a grand card to play – that of your belonging to such a family, and I am reserving it for a grand effect when we are married, and have the proofs of your descent from Parson Tringham. Apart from that, my future is to be totally foreign to my family – it will not affect even the surface of their lives. We shall leave this part of England – perhaps England itself – and what does it matter how people regard us here? You will like going, will you not?'

She could answer no more than a bare affirmative, so great was the emotion aroused in her at the thought of going through the world with him as his own familiar friend. Her feelings almost filled her ears like a babble of waves, and surged up to her eyes. She put her hand in his, and thus they went on, to a place where the reflected sun glared up from the river, under a bridge, with a molten-metallic glow that dazzled their eyes, though the sun itself was hidden by the bridge. They stood still, whereupon little furred and feathered heads popped up from the smooth surface of the water; but, finding that the disturbing presences had paused, and not passed by, they disappeared again. Upon this river-brink they lingered till the fog began to close round them – which was very early in the evening at this time of the year – settling on the lashes of her eyes, where it rested like crystals, and on his brows and hair.

They walked later on Sundays, when it was quite dark. Some of the dairy-people, who were also out of doors on the first Sunday evening after their engagement, heard her impulsive speeches, ecstasized to frag-ments, though they were too far off to hear the words discoursed; noted the spasmodic catch in her remarks, broken into syllables by the leapings of her heart, as she walked leaning on his arm; her contented pauses, the occasional little laugh upon which her soul seemed to ride – the laugh of a woman in company with the man she loves and has won from all other women – unlike anything else in nature. They marked the buoyancy of her tread, like the skim of a bird which has not quite alighted.

Her affection for him was now the breath and life of Tess's being; it enveloped her as a photosphere, irradiated her into forgetfulness of her past sorrows, keeping back the gloomy spectres that would persist in their attempts to touch her – doubt, fear, moodiness, care, shame. She knew that they were waiting like wolves just outside the circumscribing light, but she had long spells of power to keep them in hungry subjection there.

A spiritual forgetfulness co-existed with an intellectual remembrance. She walked in brightness, but she knew that in the background those shapes of darkness were always spread. They might be receding, or they might be approaching, one or the other, a little every day.

One evening Tess and Clare were obliged to sit indoors keeping house, all the other occupants of the domicile being away. As they talked she looked thoughtfully up at him, and met his two appreciative eyes.

'I am not worthy of you – no, I am not!' she burst out, jumping up from her low stool as though appalled at his homage, and the fulness of her own joy thereat.

Clare, deeming the whole basis of her excitement to be that which was only the smaller part of it, said –

'I won't have you speak like it, dear Tess! Distinction does not consist in the facile use of a contemptible set of conventions, but in being numbered among those who are true, and honest, and just, and pure, and lovely, and of good report – as you are, my Tess.'

She struggled with the sob in her throat. How often had that string of excellences made her young heart ache in church of late years, and how strange that he should have cited them now.

'Why didn't you stay and love me when I – was sixteen; living with my little sisters and brothers, and you danced on the green? O, why didn't you, why didn't you!' she said, impetuously clasping her hands.

Angel began to comfort and reassure her, thinking to himself, truly enough, what a creature of moods she was, and how careful he would have to be of her when she depended for her happiness entirely on him.

'Ah – why didn't I stay!' he said. 'That is just what I feel. If I had only known! But you must not be so bitter in your regret – why should you be?'

With the woman's instinct to hide she diverged hastily –

'I should have had four years more of your heart than I can ever have now. Then I should not have wasted my time as I have done – I should have had so much longer happiness!'

It was no mature woman with a long dark vista of intrigue behind her who was tormented thus; but a girl of simple life, not yet one-and-twenty, who had been caught during her days of immaturity like a bird in a springe. To calm herself the more completely she rose from her little stool and left the room, overturning the stool with her skirts as she went.

He sat on by the cheerful firelight thrown from a bundle of green ash-sticks laid across the dogs; the sticks snapped pleasantly, and hissed out bubbles of sap from their ends. When she came back she was herself again.

'Do you not think you are just a wee bit capricious, fitful, Tess?' he said, good humouredly, as he spread a cushion for her on the stool, and seated himself in the settle beside her. 'I wanted to ask you something, and just then you ran away.'

'Yes, perhaps I am capricious,' she murmured. She suddenly approached him, and put a hand upon each of his arms. 'No, Angel, I am not really so – by Nature, I mean!' The more particularly to assure him that she was not, she placed herself close to him in the settle, and allowed her head to find a restingplace against Clare's shoulder. 'What did you want to ask me – I am sure I will answer it,' she continued humbly.

'Well, you love me, and have agreed to marry me, and hence there follows a thirdly, "When shall the day be?"'

'I like living like this.'

'But I must think of starting in business on my own hook with the new year, or a little later. And before I get involved in the multifarious details of my new position, I should like to have secured my partner.'

'But,' she timidly answered, 'to talk quite practically, wouldn't it be best not to marry till after all that? – Though I can't bear the thought o' your going away and leaving me here!'

'Of course you cannot – and it is not best in this case. I want you to

172

help me in many ways in making my start. When shall it be? Why not a fortnight from now?'

'No,' she said, becoming grave; 'I have so many things to think of first.'

'But – '

He drew her gently nearer to him.

The reality of marriage was startling when it loomed so near. Before discussion of the question had proceeded further there walked round the corner of the settle into the full firelight of the apartment Mr Dairy-man Crick, Mrs Crick, and two of the milkmaids.

Tess sprang like an elastic ball from his side to her feet, while her face flushed and her eyes shone in the firelight.

'I knew how it would be if I sat so close to him!' she cried, with vexation. 'I said to myself, they are sure to come and catch us! But I wasn't really sitting on his knee, though it might ha' seemed as if I was almost!'

'Well – if so be you hadn't told us, I am sure we shouldn't ha' noticed that ye had been sitting anywhere at all in this light,' replied the dairy-man. He continued to his wife, with the stolid mien of a man who understood nothing of the emotions relating to matrimony – 'Now, Christianer, that shows that folks should never fancy other folks be supposing things when they bain't. O no, I should never ha' thought a word of where she was a sitting to, if she hadn't told me – not I.'

'We are going to be married soon,' said Clare, with improvised phlegm.

'Ah – and be ye! Well, I am truly glad to hear it, sir. I've thought you mid do such a thing for some time. She's too good for a dairymaid – I said so the very first day I *zid* her – and a prize for any man; and what's more, a wonderful woman for a gentleman-farmer's wife; he won't be at the mercy of his baily wi'her at his side.'

Somehow Tess disappeared. She had been even more struck with the look of the girls who followed Crick than abashed by Crick's blunt praise.

After supper, when she reached her bedroom, they were all present. A light was burning, and each damsel was sitting up whitely in her bed, awaiting Tess, the whole like a row of avenging ghosts.

But she saw in a few moments that there was no malice in their mood. They could scarcely feel as a loss what they had never expected to have. Their condition was objective, contemplative.

'He's going to marry her!' murmured Retty, never taking eyes off Tess. 'How her face do show it!'

'You *be* going to marry him?' asked Marian.

'Yes,' said Tess.

'When?'

'Some day.'

They thought that this was evasiveness only.

'*Yes* – going to *marry* him – a gentleman!' repeated *Izz Huett*.

And by a sort of fascination the three girls, one after another, crept out of their beds, and came and stood barefooted round Tess. Retty put her hands upon Tess's shoulders, as if to realize her friend's corporeality after such a miracle, and the other two laid their arms round her waist, all looking into her face.

'How it do seem! Almost more than I can think of!' said *Izz* Huett.

Marian kissed Tess. 'Yes,' she murmured as she withdrew her lips.

'Was that because of love for her, or because other lips have touched there by now?' continued Izz drily to Marian.

'I wasn't thinking o' that,' said Marian simply. 'I was on'y feeling all the strangeness o't – that she is to be his wife, and nobody else. I don't say nay to it, nor either of us, because we did not think of it – only loved him. Still, nobody else is to marry'n in the world – no fine lady, nobody in silks and satins; but she who do live like we.'

'Are you sure you don't dislike me for it?' said Tess in a low voice.

They hung about her in their white nightgowns before replying, as if they considered their answer might lie in her look.

'I don't know – I don't know,' murmured Retty Priddle. 'I want to hate 'ee; but I cannot!'

'That's how I feel,' echoed Izz and Marian. 'I can't hate her. Somehow she hinders me!'

'He ought to marry one of you,' murmured Tess.

'Why?'

'You are all better than I.'

'We better than you?' said the girls in a low, slow whisper. 'No, no, dear Tess!'

'You are!' she contradicted impetuously. And suddenly tearing away from their clinging arms she burst into a hysterical fit of tears, bowing herself on the chest of drawers and repeating incessantly, 'O yes, yes, yes!'

Having once given way she could not stop her weeping.

'He ought to have had one of you!' she cried. 'I think I ought to make him even now! You would be better for him than – I don't know what I'm saying! O! O!'

They went up to her and clasped her round, but still her sobs tore her.

'Get some water,' said Marian. 'She's upset by us, poor thing, poor thing!'

They gently led her back to the side of her bed, where they kissed her warmly.

'You are best for'n,' said Marian. 'More ladylike, and a better scholar

174

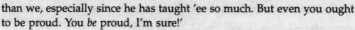

than we, especially since he has taught 'ee so much. But even you ought
to be proud. You *be* proud, I'm sure!'

'Yes, I am,' said she; 'and I am ashamed at so breaking down!'

When they were all in bed, and the light was out, Marian whispered
across to her –

'You will think of us when you be his wife, Tess, and of how we told
'ee that we loved him, and how we tried not to hate you, and did not
hate you, and could not hate you, because you were his choice, and we
never hoped to be chose by him.'

They were not aware that, at these words, salt, stinging tears trickled
down upon Tess's pillow anew, and how she resolved, with a bursting
heart, to tell all her history to Angel Clare, despite her mother's command
– to let him for whom she lived and breathed despise her if he would,
and her mother regard her as a fool, rather than preserve a silence which
might be deemed a treachery to him, and which somehow seemed a
wrong to these.

❧ Chapter Thirty-Two ❦

THIS PENITENTIAL MOOD KEPT her from naming the wedding-day. The
beginning of November found its date still in abeyance, though he asked
her at the most tempting times. But Tess's desire seemed to be for a
perpetual betrothal in which everything should remain as it was then.

The meads were changing now; but it was still warm enough in early
afternoons before milking to idle there awhile, and the state of dairy-
work at this time of year allowed a spare hour for idling. Looking over
the damp sod in the direction of the sun, a glistening ripple of gossamer
webs was visible to their eyes under the luminary, like the track of
moonlight on the sea. Gnats, knowing nothing of their brief glorification,
wandered across the shimmer of this pathway, irradiated as if they bore
fire within them, then passed out of its line, and were quite extinct. In
the presence of these things he would remind her that the date was
still the question.

Or he would ask her at night, when he accompanied her on some
mission invented by Mrs Crick to give him the opportunity. This was
mostly a journey to the farmhouse on the slopes above the vale, to

inquire how the advanced cows were getting on in the straw-barton to which they were relegated. For it was a time of the year that brought great changes to the world of kine. Batches of the animals were sent away daily to their lying-in hospital, where they lived on straw till their calves were born, after which event, and as soon as the calf could walk, mother and offspring were driven back to the dairy. In the interval which elapsed before the calves were sold there was, of course, little milking to be done, but as soon as the calf had been taken away the milkmaids would have to set to work as usual.

Returning from one of these dark walks they reached a great gravel-cliff immediately over the levels, where they stood still and listened. The water was now high in the streams, squirting through the weirs, and tinkling under culverts; the smallest gullies were all full; there was no taking short cuts anywhere, and foot-passengers were compelled to follow the permanent ways. From the whole extent of the invisible vale came a multitudinous intonation; it forced upon their fancy that a great city lay below them, and that the murmur was the vociferation of its populace.

'It seems like tens of thousands of them,' said Tess; 'holding public-meetings in their market-places, arguing, preaching, quarrelling, sobbing, groaning, praying, and cursing.'

Clare was not particularly heeding.

'Did Crick speak to you to-day, dear, about his not wanting much assistance during the winter months?'

'No.'

'The cows are going dry rapidly.'

'Yes. Six or seven went to the straw-barton yesterday, and three the day before, making nearly twenty in the straw already. Ah – is it that the farmer don't want my help for the calving? O, I am not wanted here any more! And I have tried so hard to –'

'Crick didn't exactly say that he would no longer require you. But, knowing what our relations were, he said in the most good-natured and respectful manner possible that he supposed on my leaving at Christmas I should take you with me, and on my asking what he would do without you he merely observed that, as a matter of fact, it was a time of year when he could do with a very little female help. I am afraid I was sinner enough to feel rather glad that he was in this way forcing your hand.'

'I don't think you ought to have felt glad, Angel. Because 'tis always mournful not to be wanted, even if at the same time 'tis convenient.'

'Well, it is convenient – you have admitted that.' He put his finger upon her cheek. 'Ah!' he said.

'What?'

176

'I feel the red rising up at her having been caught! But why should I trifle so! We will not trifle – life is too serious.'

'It is. Perhaps I saw that before you did.'

She was seeing it then. To decline to marry him after all – in obedience to her emotion of last night – and leave the dairy, meant to go to some strange place, not a dairy; for milkmaids were not in request now calving-time was coming on; to go to some arable farm where no divine being like Angel Clare was. She hated the thought, and she hated more the thought of going home.

'So that, seriously, dearest Tess,' he continued, 'since you will probably have to leave at Christmas, it is in every way desirable and convenient that I should carry you off then as my property. Besides, if you were not the most uncalculating girl in the world you would know that we could not go on like this for ever.'

'I wish we could. That it would always be summer and autumn, and you always courting me, and always thinking as much of me as you have done through the past summer-time!'

'I always shall.'

'O, I know you will!' she cried, with a sudden fervour of faith in him. 'Angel, I will fix the day when I will become yours for always!'

Thus at last it was arranged between them, during that dark walk home, amid the myriads of liquid voices on the right and left.

When they reached the dairy Mr and Mrs Crick were promptly told – with injunctions to secrecy; for each of the lovers was desirous that the marriage should be kept as private as possible. The dairyman, though he had thought of dismissing her soon, now made a great concern about losing her. What should he do about his skimming? Who would make the ornamental butter-pats for the Anglebury and Sandbourne ladies? Mrs Crick congratulated Tess on the shilly-shallying having at last come to an end, and said that directly she set eyes on Tess she divined that she was to be the chosen one of somebody who was no common outdoor man; Tess had looked so superior as she walked across the barton on that afternoon of her arrival; that she was of a good family she could have sworn. In point of fact Mrs Crick did remember thinking that Tess was graceful and good-looking as she approached; but the superiority might have been a growth of the imagination aided by subsequent knowledge.

Tess was now carried along upon the wings of the hours, without the sense of a will. The word had been given; the number of the day written down. Her naturally bright intelligence had begun to admit the fatalistic convictions common to field-folk and those who associate more exten-sively with natural phenomena than with their fellow-creatures; and she accordingly drifted into that passive responsiveness to all things her lover suggested, characteristic of the frame of mind.

But she wrote anew to her mother, ostensibly to notify the wedding-day; really to again implore her advice. It was a gentleman who had chosen her, which perhaps her mother had not sufficiently considered. A post-nuptial explanation, which might be accepted with a light heart by a rougher man, might not be received with the same feeling by him. But this communication brought no reply from Mrs Durbeyfield.

Despite Angel Clare's plausible representations to himself and to Tess of the practical need for their immediate marriage, there was in truth an element of precipitancy in the step, as became apparent at a later date. He loved her dearly, though perhaps rather ideally and fancifully than with the impassioned thoroughness of her feeling for him. He had entertained no notion, when doomed as he had thought to an unintellectual bucolic life, that such charms as he beheld in this idyllic creature would be found behind the scenes. Unsophistication was a thing to talk of; but he had not known how it really struck one until he came here. Yet he was very far from seeing his future track clearly, and it might be a year or two before he would be able to consider himself fairly started in life. The secret lay in the tinge of recklessness imparted to his career and character by the sense that he had been made to miss his true destiny through the prejudices of his family.

'Don't you think 'twould have been better for us to wait till you were quite settled in your midland farm?' she once asked timidly. (A midland farm was the idea just then.)

'To tell the truth, my Tess, I don't like you to be left anywhere away from my protection and sympathy.'

The reason was a good one, so far as it went. His influence over her had been so marked that she had caught his manner and habits, his speech and phrases, his likings and his aversions. And to leave her in farmland would be to let her slip back again out of accord with him. He wished to have her under his charge for another reason. His parents had naturally desired to see her once at least before he carried her off to a distant settlement, English or colonial; and as no opinion of theirs was to be allowed to change his intention, he judged that a couple of months' life with him in lodgings whilst seeking for an advantageous opening would be of some social assistance to her at what she might feel to be a trying ordeal – her presentation to his mother at the Vicarage.

Next, he wished to see a little of the working of a flour-mill, having an idea that he might combine the use of one with corn-growing. The proprietor of a large old water-mill at Wellbridge – once the mill of an Abbey – had offered him the inspection of his time-honoured mode of procedure, and a hand in the operations for a few days, whenever he should choose to come. Clare paid a visit to the place, some few miles distant, one day at this time, to inquire particulars, and returned to Talbothays in the evening. She found him determined to spend a short time at the Wellbridge flour-mills. And what had determined him? Less the opportunity of an insight into grinding and bolting than the casual fact that lodgings were to be obtained in that very farmhouse which, before its mutilation, had been the mansion of a branch of the d'Urberville family. This was always how Clare settled practical questions; by a sentiment which had nothing to do with them. They decided to go immediately after the wedding, and remain for a fortnight, instead of journeying to towns and inns.

'Then we will start off to examine some farms on the other side of London that I have heard of,' he said, 'and by March or April we will pay a visit to my father and mother.'

Questions of procedure such as these arose and passed, and the day, the incredible day, on which she was to become his, loomed large in the near future. The thirty-first of December, New Year's Eve, was the date. His wife, she said to herself. Could it ever be? Their two selves together, nothing to divide them, every incident shared by them; why not? And yet why?

One Sunday morning Izz Huett returned from church, and spoke privately to Tess.

'You was not called home* this morning.'

'What?'

'It should ha' been the first time of asking to-day,' she answered, looking quietly at Tess. 'You meant to be married New Year's Eve, deary?'

The other returned a quick affirmative.

'And there must be three times of asking. And now there be only two Sundays left between.'

Tess felt her cheek paling; Izz was right; of course there must be three. Perhaps he had forgotten! If so, there must be a week's postponement, and that was unlucky. How could she remind her lover? She who had been so backward, was suddenly fired with impatience and alarm lest she should lose her dear prize.

A natural incident relieved her anxiety. Izz mentioned the omission of the banns to Mrs Crick, and Mrs Crick assumed a matron's privilege of speaking to Angel on the point.

'Have ye forgot 'em, Mr Clare? The banns, I mean.'

'No, I have not forgot 'em,' says Clare.

As soon as he caught Tess alone he assured her:

'Don't let them tease you about the banns. A licence will be quieter

* 'Called home' – local phrase for publication of banns.

179

for us, and I have decided on a licence without consulting you. So if you go to church on Sunday morning you will not hear your own name, if you wished to.'

'I didn't wish to hear it, dearest,' she said proudly.

But to know that things were in train was an immense relief to Tess notwithstanding, who had well-nigh feared that somebody would stand up and forbid the banns on the ground of her history. How events were favouring her!

'I don't quite feel easy,' she said to herself. 'All this good fortune may be scourged out of me afterwards by a lot of ill. That's how Heaven mostly does. I wish I could have had common banns!'

But everything went smoothly. She wondered whether he would like her to be married in her present best white frock, or if she ought to buy a new one. The question was set at rest by his forethought, disclosed by the arrival of some large packages addressed to her. Inside them she found a whole stock of clothing, from bonnet to shoes, including a perfect morning costume, such as would well suit the simple wedding they planned. He entered the house shortly after the arrival of the packages, and heard her upstairs undoing them.

A minute later she came down with a flush on her face and tears in her eyes.

'How thoughtful you've been!' she murmured, her cheek upon his shoulder. 'Even to the gloves and handkerchief! My own love – how good, how kind!'

'No, no, Tess; just an order to a tradeswoman in London – nothing more.'

And to divert her from thinking too highly of him he told her to go upstairs, and take her time, and see if it all fitted; and, if not, to get the village sempstress to make a few alterations.

She did return upstairs, and put on the gown. Alone, she stood for a moment before the glass looking at the effect of her silk attire; and then there came into her head her mother's ballad of the mystic robe –

> *That never would become that wife*
> *That had once done amiss,*

which Mrs Durbeyfield had used to sing to her as a child, so blithely and so archly, her foot on the cradle, which she rocked to the tune. Suppose this robe should betray her by changing colour, as her robe had betrayed Queen Guénever. Since she had been at the dairy she had not thought of the lines till now.

❧ Chapter Thirty-Three ❧

ANGEL FELT THAT HE WOULD like to spend a day with her before the wedding, somewhere away from the dairy, as a last jaunt in her company while they were yet mere lover and mistress; a romantic day, in circumstances that would never be repeated; with that other and greater day beaming close ahead of them. During the preceding week, therefore, he suggested making a few purchases in the nearest town, and they started together.

Clare's life at the dairy had been that of a recluse in respect to the world of his own class. For months he had never gone near a town, and, requiring no vehicle, had never kept one, hiring the dairyman's cob or gig if he rode or drove. They went in the gig that day.

And then for the first time in their lives they shopped as partners in one concern. It was Christmas Eve, with its loads of holly and mistletoe, and the town was very full of strangers who had come in from all parts of the country on account of the day. Tess paid the penalty of walking about with happiness superadded to beauty on her countenance by being much stared at as she moved amid them on his arm.

In the evening they returned to the inn at which they had put up, and Tess waited in the entry while Angel went to see the horse and gig brought to the door. The general sitting-room was full of guests, who were continually going in and out. As the door opened and shut each time for the passage of these, the light within the parlour fell full upon Tess's face. Two men came out and passed by her among the rest. One of them had stared her up and down in surprise, and she fancied he was a Trantridge man, though that village lay so many miles off that Trantridge folk were rarities here.

'A comely maid that,' said the other.

'True, comely enough. But unless I make a great mistake – ' And he negatived the remainder of the definition forthwith.

Clare had just returned from the stable-yard, and, confronting the man on the threshold, heard the words, and saw the shrinking of Tess. The insult to her stung him to the quick, and before he had considered anything at all he struck the man on the chin with the full force of his fist, sending him staggering backwards into the passage.

The man recovered himself, and seemed inclined to come on, and Clare, stepping outside the door, put himself in a posture of defence. But his opponent began to think better of the matter. He looked anew at Tess as he passed her, and said to Clare –

181

'I beg pardon, sir; 'twas a complete mistake. I thought she was another woman, forty miles from here.'

Clare, feeling then that he had been too hasty, and that he was, moreover, to blame for leaving her standing in an inn-passage, did what he usually did in such cases, gave the man five shillings to plaster the blow; and thus they parted, bidding each other a pacific good-night. As soon as Clare had taken the reins from the ostler, and the young couple had driven off, the two men went in the other direction.

'And was it a mistake?' said the second one.

'Not a bit of it. But I didn't want to hurt the gentleman's feelings – not I.'

In the meantime the lovers were driving onward.

'Could we put off our wedding till a little later?' Tess asked in a dry dull voice. 'I mean if we wished?'

'No, my love. Calm yourself. Do you mean that the fellow may have time to summon me for assault?' he asked good-humouredly.

'No – I only meant – if it should have to be put off.'

What she meant was not very clear, and he directed her to dismiss such fancies from her mind, which she obediently did as well as she could. But she was grave, very grave, all the way home; till she thought, 'We shall go away, a very long distance, hundreds of miles from these parts, and such as this can never happen again, and no ghost of the past reach there.'

They parted tenderly that night on the landing, and Clare ascended to his attic. Tess sat up getting on with some little requisites, lest the few remaining days should not afford sufficient time. While she sat she heard a noise in Angel's room overhead, a sound of thumping and struggling. Everybody else in the house was asleep, and in her anxiety lest Clare should be ill she ran up and knocked at his door, and asked him what was the matter.

'Oh, nothing dear,' he said from within. 'I am so sorry I disturbed you! But the reason is rather an amusing one: I fell asleep and dreamt that I was fighting that fellow again who insulted you and the noise you heard was my pummelling away with my fists at my portmanteau, which I pulled out to-day for packing. I am occasionally liable to these freaks in my sleep. Go to bed and think of it no more.'

This was the last drachm required to turn the scale of her indecision. Declare the past to him by word of mouth she could not; but there was another way. She sat down and wrote on the four pages of a note-sheet a succinct narrative of those events of three or four years ago, put it into an envelope, and directed it to Clare. Then, lest the flesh should again be weak, she crept upstairs without any shoes and slipped the note under his door.

Her night was a broken one, as it well might be, and she listened for the first faint noise overhead. It came, as usual; he descended, as usual. She descended. He met her at the bottom of the stairs and kissed her. Surely it was as warmly as ever!

He looked a little disturbed and worn, she thought. But he said not a word to her about her revelation, even when they were alone. Could he have had it? Unless he began the subject she felt that she could say nothing. So the day passed, and it was evident that whatever he thought he meant to keep to himself. Yet he was frank and affectionate as before. Could it be that her doubts were childish? that he forgave her; that he loved her for what she was, just as she was, and smiled at her disquiet as at a foolish nightmare? Had he really received her note? She glanced into his room, and could see nothing of it. It might be that he forgave her. But even if he had not received it she had a sudden enthusiastic trust that he surely would forgive her.

Every morning and night he was the same, and thus New Year's Eve broke – the wedding-day.

The lovers did not rise at milking-time, having through the whole of this last week of their sojourn at the dairy been accorded something of the position of guests, Tess being honoured with a room of her own. When they arrived downstairs at breakfast-time they were surprised to see what effects had been produced in the large kitchen for their glory since they had last beheld it. At some unnatural hour of the morning the dairyman has caused the yawning chimney-corner to be whitened, and the brick hearth reddened, and a blazing yellow damask blower to be hung across the arch in place of the old grimy blue cotton one with a black sprig pattern which had formerly done duty here. This renovated aspect of what was the focus indeed of the room on a dull winter morning, threw a smiling demeanour over the whole apartment.

'I was determined to do summat in honour o't,' said the dairyman. 'And as you wouldn't hear of my gieing a rattling good randy wi' fiddles and bass-viols complete, as we should ha' done in old times, this was all I could think o' as a noiseless thing.'

Tess's friends lived so far off that none could conveniently have been present at the ceremony, even had any been asked; but as a fact nobody was invited from Marlott. As for Angel's family, he had written and duly informed them of the time, and assured them that he would be glad to see one at least of them there for the day if he would like to come. His brothers had not replied at all, seeming to be indignant with him; while his father and mother had written a rather sad letter, deploring his precipitancy in rushing into marriage, but making the best of the matter by saying that, though a dairywoman was the last daughter-in-law they

183

could have expected, their son had arrived at an age at which he might be supposed to be the best judge.

This coolness in his relations distressed Clare less than it would have done had he been without the grand card with which he meant to surprise them ere long. To produce Tess, fresh from the dairy, as a d'Urberville and a lady, he had felt to be temerarious and risky; hence he had concealed her lineage till such time as, familiarized with wordly ways by a few months' travel and reading with him, he could take her on a visit to his parents, and impart the knowledge while triumphantly producing her as worthy of such an ancient line. It was a pretty lover's dream, if no more. Perhaps Tess's lineage had more value for himself than for anybody in the world besides.

Her perception that Angel's bearing towards her still remained in no whit altered by her own communication rendered Tess guiltily doubtful if he could have received it. She rose from breakfast before he had finished, and hastened upstairs. It had occurred to her to look once more into the queer gaunt room which had been Clare's den, or rather eyrie, for so long, and climbing the ladder she stood at the open door of the apartment, regarding and pondering. She stooped to the threshold of the doorway, where she had pushed in the note two or three days earlier in such excitement. The carpet reached close to the sill, and under the edge of the carpet she discerned the faint white margin of the envelope containing her letter to him, which he obviously had never seen, owing to her having in her haste thrust it beneath the carpet as well as beneath the door.

With a feeling of faintness she withdrew the letter. There it was – sealed up, just as it had left her hands. The mountain had not yet been removed. She could not let him read it now, the house being in full bustle of preparation; and descending to her own room she destroyed the letter there.

She was so pale when he saw her again that he felt quite anxious. The incident of the misplaced letter she had jumped at as if it prevented a confession; but she knew in her conscience that it need not; there was still time. Yet everything was in a stir; there was coming and going; all had to dress, the dairyman and Mrs Crick having been asked to accompany them as witnesses; and reflection or deliberate talk was well-nigh impossible. The only minute Tess could get to be alone with Clare was when they met upon the landing.

'I am so anxious to talk to you – I want to confess all my faults and blunders!' she said with attempted lightness.

'No, no – we can't have faults talked of – you must be deemed perfect to-day at least, my Sweet!' he cried. 'We shall have plenty of time, hereafter, I hope, to talk over our failings. I will confess mine at the same time.'

'But it would be better for me to do it now, I think, so that you could not say – '

'Well, my quixotic one, you shall tell me anything – say, as soon as we are settled in our lodging; now now. I, too, will tell you my faults then. But do not let us spoil the day with them; they will be excellent matter for a dull time.'

'Then you don't wish me to, dearest?'

'I do not, Tessy, really,'

The hurry of dressing and starting left no time for more than this. Those words of his seemed to reassure her on further reflection. She was whirled onward through the next couple of critical hours by the mastering tide of her devotion to him, which closed up further meditation. Her one desire, so long resisted, to make herself his, to call him her lord, her own – then, if necessary, to die – had at last lifted her up from her plodding reflective pathway. In dressing, she moved about in a mental cloud of many-coloured idealities, which eclipsed all sinister contingencies by its brightness.

The church was a long way off, and they were obliged to drive, particularly as it was winter. A close carriage was ordered from a roadside inn, a vehicle which had been kept there ever since the old days of post-chaise travelling. It had stout wheel-spokes, and heavy felloes, a great curved bed, immense straps and springs, and a pole like a battering-ram. The postilion was a venerable 'boy' of sixty – a martyr to rheumatic gout, the result of excessive exposure in youth, counteracted by strong liquors – who had stood at inn-doors doing nothing for the whole five-and-twenty years that had elapsed since he had no longer been required to ride professionally, as if expecting the old times to come back again. He had a permanent running wound on the outside of his right leg, originated by the constant bruisings of aristocratic carriage-poles during the many years that he had been in regular employ at the King's Arms, Casterbridge.

Inside this cumbrous and creaking structure, and behind this decayed conductor, the *partie carrée* took their seats – the bride and bridegroom and Mr and Mrs Crick. Angel would have liked one at least of his brothers to be present as groomsman, but their silence after his gentle hint to that effect by letter had signified that they did not care to come. They disapproved of the marriage, and could not be expected to counten-ance it. Perhaps it was as well that they could not be present. They were not worldly young fellow, but fraternizing with dairy-folk would have struck unpleasantly upon their biassed niceness, apart from their views of the match.

185

Upheld by the momentum of the time Tess knew nothing of this; did not see anything; did not know the road they were taking to the church. She knew that Angel was close to her; all the rest was a luminous mist. She was a sort of celestial person, who owed her being to poetry – one of those classical divinities Clare was accustomed to talk to her about when they took their walks together.

The marriage being by licence there were only a dozen or so of people in the church; had there been a thousand they would have produced no more effect upon her. They were at stellar distances from her present world. In the ecstatic solemnity with which she swore her faith to him the ordinary sensibilities of sex seemed a flippancy. At a pause in the service, while they were kneeling together, she unconsciously inclined herself towards him, so that her shoulder touched his arm; she had been frightened by a passing thought, and the movement had been automatic, to assure herself that he was really there, and to fortify her belief that his fidelity would be proof against all things.

Clare knew that she loved him – every curve of her form showed that – but he did not know at that time the full depth of her devotion, its single-mindedness, its meekness; what long-suffering it guaranteed, what honesty, what endurance, what good faith.

As they came out of church the ringers swung the bells off their rests, and a modest peal of three notes broke forth – that limited amount of expression having been deemed sufficient by the church builders for the joys of such a small parish. Passing by the tower with her husband on the path to the gate she could feel the vibrant air humming round them from the louvred belfry in a circle of sound, and it matched the highly-charged mental atmosphere in which she was living.

This condition of mind, wherein she felt glorified by an irradiation not her own, like the angel whom St John saw in the sun, lasted till the sound of the church bells had died away, and the emotions of the wedding-service had calmed down. Her eyes could dwell upon details more clearly now, and Mr and Mrs Crick having directed their own gig to be sent for them, to leave the carriage to the young couple, she observed the build and character of that conveyance for the first time. Sitting in silence she regarded it long.

'I fancy you seem oppressed, Tessy,' said Clare.

'Yes,' she answered, putting her hand to her brow. 'I tremble at many things. It is all so serious, Angel. Among other things I seem to have seen this carriage before, to be very well acquainted with it. It is very odd – I must have seen it in a dream.'

'Oh – you have heard the legend of the d'Urberville Coach – that well-known superstition of this county about your family when they were very popular here; and this lumbering old thing reminds you of it.'

'I have never heard of it to my knowledge,' said she. 'What is the legend – may I know it?'

'Well – I would rather not tell it in detail just now. A certain d'Urberville of the sixteenth or seventeenth century committed a dreadful crime in his family coach; and since that time members of the family see or hear the old coach whenever – But I'll tell you another day – it is rather gloomy. Evidently some dim knowledge of it has been brought back to your mind by the sight of this venerable caravan.'

'I don't remember hearing it before,' she murmured. 'Is it when we are going to die, Angel, that members of my family see it, or is it when we have committed a crime?'

'Now, Tess!'

He silenced her by a kiss.

By the time they reached home she was contrite and spiritless. She was Mrs Angel Clare, indeed, but had she any moral right to the name? Was she not more truly Mrs Alexander d'Urberville? Could intensity of love justify what might be considered in upright souls as culpable reticence? She knew not what was expected of women in such cases; and she had no counsellor.

However, when she found herself alone in her room for a few minutes – the last day this on which she was ever to enter it – she knelt down and prayed. She tried to pray to God, but it was her husband who really had her supplication. Her idolatry of this man was such that she herself almost feared it to be ill-omened. She was conscious of the notion expressed by Friar Laurence: 'These violent delights have violent ends.' It might be too desperate for human conditions – too rank, too wild, too deadly.

'O my love, my love, why do I love you so!' she whispered there alone; 'for she you love is not my real self, but one in my image; the one I might have been!'

Afternoon came, and with it the hour for departure. They had decided to fulfil the plan of going for a few days to the lodgings in the old farmhouse near Wellbridge Mill, at which he meant to reside during his investigation of flour processes. At two o'clock there was nothing left to do but to start. All the servantry of the dairy were standing in the red-brick entry to see them go out, the dairyman and his wife following to the door. Tess saw her three chamber mates in a row against the wall, pensively inclining their heads. She had much questioned if they would appear at the parting moment; but there they were, stoical and staunch to the last. She knew why the delicate Retty looked so fragile, and Izz so tragically sorrowful, and Marian so blank; and she forgot her own dogging shadow for a moment in contemplating theirs.

She impulsively whispered to him –

'Will you kiss 'em all, once, poor things, for the first and last time?'

Clare had not the least objection to such a farewell formality – which was all that it was to him – and as he passed them he kissed them in succession where they stood, saying 'Goodbye' to each as he did so. When they reached the door Tess femininely glanced back to discern the effect of that kiss of charity; there was no triumph in her glance, as there might have been. If there had it would have disappeared when she saw how moved the girls all were. The kiss had obviously done harm by awakening feelings they were trying to subdue.

Of all this Clare was unconscious. Passing on to the wicket-gate he shook hands with the dairyman and his wife, and expressed his last thanks to them for their attentions; after which there was a moment of silence before they had moved off. It was interrupted by the crowing of a cock. The white one with the rose comb had come and settled on the palings in front of the house, within a few yards of them, and his notes thrilled their ears through, dwindling away like echoes down a valley of rocks.

'Oh?' said Mrs Crick. 'An afternoon crow!'

Two men were standing by the yard gate, holding it open.

'That's bad,' one murmured to the other, not thinking that the words could be heard by the group at the door-wicket.

The cock crew again – straight towards Clare.

'Well!' said the dairyman.

'I don't like to hear him!' said Tess to her husband. 'Tell the man to drive on. Good-bye, good-bye!'

The cock crew again.

'Hoosh! Just you be off, sir, or I'll twist your neck!' said the dairyman with some irritation, turning to the bird and driving him away. And to his wife as they went indoors: 'Now, to think o' that just to-day! I've not heard his crow of an afternoon all the year afore.'

'It only means a change in the weather,' said she; 'not what you think: 'tis impossible!'

♣ Chapter Thirty-Four ♣

THEY DROVE BY THE LEVEL road along the valley to a distance of a few miles, and, reaching Wellbridge, turned away from the village to the left, and over the great Elizabethan bridge which gives the place half its name. Immediately behind it stood the house wherein they had engaged lodgings, whose exterior features are so well known to all travellers through the Froom Valley; once portion of a fine manorial residence, and the property and seat of a d'Urberville, but since its partial demolition a farm-house.

'Welcome to one of your ancestral mansions!' said Clare as he handed her down. But he regretted the pleasantry; it was too near a satire.

On entering they found that, though they had only engaged a couple of rooms, the farmer had taken advantage of their proposed presence during the coming days to pay a New Year's visit to some friends, leaving a woman from a neighbouring cottage to minister to their few wants. The absoluteness of possession pleased them, and they realized it as the first moment of their experience under their own exclusive rooftree.

But he found that the mouldy old habitation somewhat depressed his bride. When the carriage was gone they ascended the stairs to wash their hands, the charwoman showing the way. On the landing Tess stopped and started.

'What's the matter?' said he.

'Those horrid women!' she answered, with a smile. 'How they frightened me.'

He looked up, and perceived two life-size portraits on panels built into the masonry. As all visitors to the mansion are aware, these paintings represent women of middle age, of a date some two hundred years ago, whose lineaments once seen can never be forgotten. The long pointed features, narrow eye, and smirk of the one, so suggestive of merciless treachery; the bill-hook nose, large teeth, and bold eye of the other, suggesting arrogance to the point of ferocity, haunt the beholder afterwards in his dreams.

'Whose portraits are those?' asked Clare of the charwoman.

'I have been told by old folk that they were ladies of the d'Urberville family, the ancient lords of this manor,' she said. 'Owing to their being builded into the wall they can't be moved away.'

The unpleasantness of the matter was that, in addition to their effect upon Tess, her fine features were unquestionably traceable in these exaggerated forms. He said nothing of this, however, and, regretting that he had gone out of his way to choose the house for their bridal time, went on into the adjoining room. The place having been rather hastily prepared for them they washed their hands in one basin. Clare touched hers under the water.

'Which are my fingers and which are yours?' he said, looking up. 'They are very much mixed.'

'They are all yours,' said she, very prettily, and endeavoured to be gayer than she was. He had not been displeased with her thoughtfulness on such an occasion; it was what every sensible woman would show: but Tess knew that she had been thoughtful to excess, and struggled against it.

The sun was so low on that short last afternoon of the year that it shone in through a small opening and formed a golden staff which stretched across to her skirt, where it made a spot like a paint-mark set upon her. They went into the ancient parlour to tea, and here they shared their first common meal alone. Such was their childishness, or rather his, that he found it interesting to use the same bread-and-butter plate as herself, and to brush crumbs from her lips with his own. He wondered a little that she did not enter into these frivolities with his own zest.

Looking at her silently for a long time; 'She is a dear dear Tess,' he thought to himself, as one deciding on the true construction of a difficult passage. 'Do I realize solemnly enough how utterly and irretrievably this little womanly thing is the creature of my good or bad faith and fortune? I think not. I think I could not, unless I were a woman myself. What I am in wordly estate, she is. What I become, she must become. What I cannot be, she cannot be. And shall I ever neglect her, or hurt her, or even forget to consider her? God forbid such a crime!'

They sat on over the tea-table waiting for their luggage, which the dairyman had promised to send before it grew dark. But evening began to close in, and the luggage did not arrive, and they had brought nothing more than they stood in. With the departure of the sun the calm mood of the winter day changed. Out of doors there began noises as of silk smartly rubbed; the restful dead leaves of the preceding autumn were stirred to irritated resurrection, and whirled about unwillingly, and tapped against the shutters. It soon began to rain.

'That cock knew the weather was going to change,' said Clare.

The woman who had attended upon them had gone home for the night, but she had placed candles upon the table, and now they lit them. Each candle-flame drew towards the fireplace.

'These old houses are so draughty,' continued Angel, looking at the flames, and at the grease guttering down the sides. 'I wonder where that luggage is. We haven't even a brush and comb.'

'I don't know,' she answered, absent-minded.

'Tess, you are not a bit cheerful this evening – not at all as you used to be. Those harridans on the panels upstairs have unsettled you. I am sorry I brought you here. I wonder if you really love me, after all?'

He knew that she did, and the words had no serious intent; but she was surcharged with emotion, and winced like a wounded animal. Though she tried not to shed tears she could not help showing one or two.

'I did not mean it!' said he, sorry. 'You are worried at not having your things, I know. I cannot think why old Jonathan has not come with them. Why, it is seven o'clock? Ah, there he is!'

A knock had come to the door, and, there being nobody else to answer it, Clare went out. He returned to the room with a small package in his hand.

'It is not Jonathan, after all,' he said.

'How vexing!' said Tess.

The packet had been brought by a special messenger, who had arrived at Talbothays from Emminster Vicarage immediately after the departure of the married couple, and had followed them hither, being under injunction to deliver it into nobody's hands but theirs. Clare brought it to the light. It was less than a foot long, sewed up in canvas, sealed in red wax with his father's seal, and directed in his father's hand to 'Mrs Angel Clare.'

'It is a little wedding-present for you, Tess,' said he, handing it to her. 'How thoughtful they are!'

Tess looked a little flustered as she took it.

'I think I would rather have you open it, dearest,' said she, turning over the parcel. 'I don't like to break those great seals; they look so serious. Please open it for me!'

He undid the parcel. Inside was a case of morocco leather, on the top of which lay a note and a key.

The note was for Clare, in the following words:

MY DEAR SON, – possibly you have forgotten that on the death of your godmother, Mrs Pitney, when you were a lad, she – vain kind woman that she was – left to me a portion of the contents of her jewel-case in trust for your wife, if you should ever have one, as a mark of her affection for you and whomsoever you should choose. This trust I have fulfilled, and the diamonds have been locked up at my banker's ever since. Though I feel it to be a somewhat incongruous act in the circumstances, I am, as you will see, bound to hand over the articles to the woman to whom the use of them for her lifetime will now rightly belong, and they are therefore promptly sent. They become, I believe, heirlooms, strictly

191

speaking, according to the terms of your godmother's will. The precise words of the clause that refers to this matter are enclosed.'

'I do remember,' said Clare; 'but I had quite forgotten.'

Unlocking the case, they found it to contain a necklace, with pendant, bracelets, and ear-rings; and also some other small ornaments.

Tess seemed afraid to touch them at first, but her eyes sparkled for a moment as much as the stones when Clare spread out the set.

'Are they mine?' she asked incredulously.

'They are, certainly,' said he.

He looked into the fire. He remembered how, when he was a lad of fifteen, his godmother, the Squire's wife – the only rich person with whom he had ever come in contact – had pinned her faith to his success; had prophesied a wondrous career for him. There had seemed nothing at all out of keeping with such a conjectured career in the storing up of these showy ornaments for his wife and the wives of her descendants. They gleamed somewhat ironically now. 'Yet why?' he asked himself. It was but a question of vanity throughout; and if that were admitted into one side of the equation it should be admitted into the other. His wife was a d'Urberville: whom could they become better than her?

Suddenly he said with enthusiasm –

'Tess, put them on – put them on!' And he turned from the fire to help her.

But as if by magic she had already donned them – necklace, ear-rings, bracelets, and all.

'But the gown isn't right, Tess,' said Clare. 'It ought to be a low one for a set of brilliants like that.'

'Ought it?' said Tess.

'Yes,' said he.

He suggested to her how to tuck in the upper edge of her bodice, so as to make it roughly approximate to the cut for evening wear; and when she had done this, and the pendant to the necklace hung isolated amid the whiteness of her throat, as it was designed to do, he stepped back to survey her.

'My heavens,' said Clare, 'how beautiful you are!'

As everybody knows, fine feathers make fine birds; a peasant girl but very moderately prepossessing to the casual observer in her simple condition and attire, will bloom as an amazing beauty if clothed as a woman of fashion with the aids that Art can render; while the beauty of the midnight crush would often cut but a sorry figure if placed inside the fieldwoman's wrapper upon a monotonous acreage of turnips on a dull day. He had never till now estimated the artistic excellence of Tess's limbs and features.

'If you were only to appear in a ball-room!' he said. 'But no – no,

dearest; I think I love you best in the wing-bonnet and cotton-frock –
yes, better than in this, well as you support these dignities.'

Tess's sense of her striking appearance had given her a flush of
excitement, which was yet not happiness.

'I'll take them off,' she said, 'in case Jonathan should see me. They are
not fit for me, are they? They must be sold, I suppose?'

'Let them stay a few minutes longer. Sell them? Never. It would be a
breach of faith.'

Influenced by a second thought she readily obeyed. She had something
to tell, and there might be help in these. She sat down with the jewels
upon her; and they again indulged in conjectures as to where Jonathan
could possibly be with their baggage. The ale they had poured out for
his consumption when he came had gone flat with long standing.

Shortly after this they began supper, which was already laid on a side-
table. Ere they had finished there was a jerk in the fire-smoke, the rising
skein of which bulged out into the room, as if some giant had laid his
hand on the chimney-top for a moment. It had been caused by the
opening of the outer door. A heavy step was now heard in the passage,
and Angel went out.

'I couldn' make nobody hear at all by knocking,' apologized Jonathan
Kail, for it was he at last; 'and as't was raining out I opened the door.
I've brought the things, sir.'

'I am very glad to see them. But you are very late.'

'Well, yes, sir.'

There was something subdued in Jonathan Kail's tone which had not
been there in the day, and lines of concern were ploughed upon his
forehead in addition to the lines of years. He continued –

'We've all been gallied at the dairy at what might ha' been a most
terrible affliction since you and your Mis'ess – so to name her now – left
us this a'ternoon. Perhaps you ha'nt forgot the cock's afternoon crow?'

'Dear me; – what – '

'Well, some says it do mane one thing, and some another; but what's
happened is that poor little Retty Priddle hev tried to drown herself.'

'No! Really! Why, she bade us good-bye with the rest – '

'Yes. Well, sir, when you and your Mis'ess – so to name what she
lawful is – when you two drove away, as I say, Retty and Marian put on
their bonnets and went out; and as there is not much doing now, being
New Year's Eve, and folks mops and brooms from what's inside 'em,
nobody took much notice. They went on to Lew-Everard, where they
had summut to drink, and then on they vamped to Dree-armed Cross,
and there they seemed to have parted, Retty striking across the water-
meads as if for home, and Marian going on to the next village, where
there's another public-house. Nothing more was zeed or heard o' Retty

till the waterman, on his way home, noticed something by the Great Pool; 'twas her bonnet and shawl packed up. In the water he found her. He and another man brought her home, thinking 'a was dead; but she fetched round by degrees.'

Angel, suddenly recollecting that Tess was overhearing this gloomy tale, went to shut the door between the passage and the ante-room to the inner parlour where she was; but his wife, flinging a shawl round her, had come to the outer room and was listening to the man's narrative, her eyes resting absently on the luggage and the drops of rain glistening upon it.

'And, more than this, there's Marian; she's been found dead drunk by the withy-bed – a girl who hev never been known to touch anything before except shilling ale; though, to be sure, 'a was always a good trencher-woman, as her face showed. It seems as if the maids had all gone out o' their minds!'

'And Izz?' asked Tess.

'Izz is about house as usual; but 'a do say 'a can guess how it happened; and she seems to be very low in mind about it, poor maid, as well she mid be. And so you see, sir, as all this happened just when we was packing your few traps and your Mis'ess's night-rail and dressing things into the cart, why, it belated me.'

'Yes. Well, Jonathan, will you get the trunks upstairs, and drink a cup of ale, and hasten back as soon as you can, in case you should be wanted?'

Tess had gone back to the inner parlour, and sat down by the fire, looking wistfully into it. She heard Jonathan Kail's heavy footsteps up and down the stairs till he had done placing the luggage, and heard him express his thanks for the ale her husband took out to him, and for the gratuity he received. Jonathan's footsteps then died from the door, and his cart creaked away.

Angel slid forward the massive oak bar which secured the door, and coming in to where she sat over the hearth, pressed her cheeks between his hands from behind. He expected her to jump up gaily and unpack the toilet-gear that she had been so anxious about, but as she did not rise he sat down with her in the firelight, the candles on the supper-table being too thin and glimmering to interfere with its glow.

'I am so sorry you should have heard this sad story about the girls,' he said. 'Still, don't let it depress you. Retty was naturally morbid, you know.'

'Without the least cause,' said Tess. 'While they who have cause to be, hide it, and pretend they are not.'

This incident had turned the scale for her. They were simple and innocent girls on whom the unhappiness of unrequited love had fallen;

194

they had deserved better at the hands of Fate. She had deserved worse – yet she was the chosen one. It was wicked of her to take all without paying. She would pay to the uttermost farthing; she would tell, there and then. This final determination she came to when she looked into the fire, he holding her hand.

A steady glare from the now flameless embers painted the sides and back of the fireplace with its colour, and the well-polished andirons, and the old brass tongs that would not meet. The underside of the mantel-shelf was flushed with the high-coloured light, and the legs of the table nearest the fire. Tess's face and neck reflected the same warmth, which each gem turned into an Aldebaran or a Sirius – a constellation of white, red and green flashes, that interchanged their hues with her every pulsation.

'Do you remember what we said to each other this morning about telling our faults?' he asked abruptly, finding that she still remained immovable. 'We spoke lightly perhaps, and you may well have done so. But for me it was no light promise. I want to make a confession to you, Love.'

This, from him, so unexpectedly apposite, had the effect upon her of a Providential interposition.

'You have to confess something?' she said quickly, and even with gladness and relief.

'You did not expect it? Ah – you thought too highly of me. Now listen. Put your head there, because I want you to forgive me, and not to be indignant with me for not telling you before, as perhaps I ought to have done.'

How strange it was! He seemed to be her double. She did not speak, and Clare went on –

'I did not mention it because I was afraid of endangering my chance of you, darling, the great prize of my life – my Fellowship I call you. My brother's Fellowship was won at his college, mine at Talbothays Dairy. Well, I would not risk it. I was going to tell you a month ago – at the time you agreed to be mine, but I could not; I thought it might frighten you away from me. I put it off; then I thought I would tell you yesterday, to give you a chance at least of escaping me. But I did not. And I did not this morning, when you proposed our confessing our faults on the landing – the sinner that I was! But I must, now I see you sitting there so solemnly. I wonder if you will forgive me?'

'O yes! I am sure that – '

'Well, I hope so. But wait a minute. You don't know. To begin at the beginning. Though I imagine my poor father fears that I am one of the eternally lost for my doctrines, I am of course, a believer in good morals, Tess, as much as you. I used to wish to be a teacher of men, and it was a great disappointment to me when I found I could not enter the Church. I admired spotlessness, even though I could lay no claim to it, and hated impurity, as I hope I do now. Whatever one may think of plenary inspiration, one must heartily subscribe to these words of Paul: "Be thou an example – in word, in conversation, in charity, in spirit, in faith, in purity." It is the only safeguard for us poor human beings. "Integar vitae", says a Roman poet, who is strange company for St Paul –

> *The man of upright life, from frailties free,*
> *Stands not in need of Moorish spear or bow.*

Well, a certain place is paved with good intentions, and having felt all that so strongly, you will see what a terrible remorse it bred in me when, in the midst of my fine aims for other people, I myself fell.'

He then told her of that time of his life to which allusion has been made when, tossed about by doubts and difficulties in London, like a cork on the waves, he plunged into eight-and-forty hours' dissipation with a stranger.

'Happily I awoke almost immediately to a sense of my folly,' he continued. 'I would have no more to say to her, and I came home. I have never repeated the offence. But I felt I should like to treat you with perfect frankness and honour, and I could not do so without telling this. Do you forgive me?'

She pressed his hand tightly for an answer.

'Then we will dismiss it at once and for ever! – too painful as it is for the occasion – and talk of something lighter.'

'O, Angel – I am almost glad – because now *you* can forgive *me*! I have not made my confession. I have a confession, too – remember, I said so.'

'Ah, to be sure! Now then for it, wicked little one.'

'Perhaps, although you smile, it is as serious as yours, or more so.'

'It can hardly be more serious, dearest.'

'It cannot – O no, it cannot!' She jumped up joyfully at the hope. 'No, it cannot be more serious, certainly,' she cried, 'because 'tis just the same! I will tell you now.'

She sat down again.

Their hands were still joined. The ashes under the grate were lit by the fire vertically, like a torrid waste. Imagination might have beheld a Last Day luridness in this red-coaled glow, which fell on his face and hand, and on hers, peering into the loose hair about her brow, and firing the delicate skin underneath. A large shadow of her shape rose upon the wall and ceiling. She bent forward, at which each diamond on her neck gave a sinister wink like a toad's; and pressing her forehead against his temple she entered on her story of her acquaintance with Alec d'Urberville and its results, murmuring the words without flinching, and with her eyelids drooping down.

PHASE THE FIFTH

The Woman Pays

❦ Chapter Thirty-Five ❧

HER NARRATIVE ENDED; EVEN its re-assertions and secondary explanations were done. Tess's voice throughout had hardly risen higher than its opening tone; there had been no exculpatory phrase of any kind, and she had not wept.

But the complexion even of external things seemed to suffer transmutation as her announcement progressed. The fire in the grate looked impish – demoniacally funny, as if it did not care in the least about her strait. The fender grinned idly, as if it too did not care. The light from the water-bottle was merely engaged in a chromatic problem. All material objects around announced their irresponsibility with terrible iteration. And yet nothing had changed since the moments when he had been kissing her; or rather, nothing in the substance of things. But the essence of things had changed.

When she ceased the auricular impressions from their previous endearments seemed to hustle away into the corners of their brains, repeating themselves as echoes from a time of supremely purblind foolishness.

Clare performed the irrelevant act of stirring the fire; the intelligence had not even yet got to the bottom of him. After stirring the embers he rose to his feet; all the force of her disclosure had imparted itself now. His face had withered. In the strenuousness of his concentration he treadled fitfully on the floor. He could not, by any contrivance, think closely enough; that was the meaning of his vague movement. When he spoke it was in the most inadequate, commonplace voice of the many varied tones she had heard from him.

'Tess!'

'Yes, dearest.'

'Am I to believe this? From your manner I am to take it as true. O you cannot be out of your mind! You ought to be! Yet you are not ... My wife, my Tess – nothing in you warrants such a supposition as that?'

'I am not out of my mind,' she said.

'And yet – ' He looked vacantly at her, to resume with dazed senses: 'Why didn't you tell me before? Ah, yes, you would have told me, in a way – but I hindered you, I remember!'

These and other of his words were nothing but the perfunctory babble of the surface while the depths remained paralyzed. He turned away, and bent over a chair. Tess followed him to the middle of the room where he was, and stood there staring at him with eyes that did not weep. Presently she slid down upon her knees beside his foot, and from this position she crouched in a heap.

'In the name of our love, forgive me!' she whispered with a dry mouth. 'I have forgiven you for the same!'

And, as he did not answer, she said again –

'Forgive me as you are forgiven! I forgive *you*, Angel.'

'You – yes, you do.'

'But you do not forgive me?'

'O Tess, forgiveness does not apply to the case. You were one person; now you are another. My God – how can forgiveness meet such a grotesque – prestidigitation as that!'

He paused, contemplating this definition; then suddenly broke into horrible laughter – as unnatural and ghastly as a laugh in hell.

'Don't – don't! It kills me quite, that!' she shrieked. 'O have mercy upon me – have mercy!'

He did not answer; and, sickly white, she jumped up.

'Angel, Angel! what do you mean by that laugh?' she cried out. 'Do you know what this is to me?'

He shook his head.

'I have been hoping, longing, praying, to make you happy! I have thought what joy it will be to do it, what an unworthy wife I shall be if I do not! That's what I have felt, Angel!'

'I know that.'

'I thought, Angel, that you loved me – me, my very self! If it is I you do love, O how can it be that you look and speak so? It frightens me! Having begun to love you, I love you for ever – in all changes, in all disgraces, because you are yourself. I ask no more. Then how can you, O my own husband, stop loving me?'

'I repeat, the woman I have been loving is not you.'

'But who?'

'Another woman in your shape.'

She perceived in his words the realization of her own apprehensive foreboding in former times. He looked upon her as a species of impostor; a guilty woman in the guise of an innocent one. Terror was upon her white face as she saw it; her cheek was flaccid, and her mouth had almost the aspect of a round little hole. The horrible sense of his view of her so deadened her that she staggered; and he stepped forward, thinking she was going to fall.

'Sit down, sit down,' he said gently. 'You are ill; and it is natural that you should be.'

She did sit down, without knowing where she was, that strained look still upon her face, and her eyes such as to make his flesh creep.

'I don't belong to you any more, then; do I, Angel?' she asked helplessly. 'It is not me, but another woman like me that he loved, he says.'

The image raised caused her to take pity upon herself as one who was ill-used. Her eyes filled as she regarded her position further; she turned round and burst into a flood of self-sympathetic tears.

Clare was relieved at this change, for the effect on her of what had happened was beginning to be a trouble to him only less than the woe of the disclosure itself. He waited patiently, apathetically, till the violence of her grief had worn itself out, and her rush of weeping had lessened to a catching gasp at intervals.

'Angel,' she said suddenly, in her natural tones, the insane, dry voice of terror having left her now. 'Angel, am I too wicked for you and me to live together?'

'I have not been able to think what we can do.'

'I shan't ask you to let me live with you, Angel, because I have no right to! I shall not write to mother and sisters to say we be married, as I said I would do; and I shan't finish the good hussif I cut out and meant to make while we were in lodgings.

'Shan't you?'

'No, I shan't do anything, unless you order me to; and if you go away from me I shall not follow 'ee; and if you never speak to me any more I shall not ask why, unless you tell me I may.'

'And if I do order you to do anything?'

'I will obey you like your wretched slave, even if it is to lie down and die.'

'You are very good. But it strikes me that there is a want of harmony between your present mood of self-sacrifice and your past mood of self-preservation.'

These were the first words of antagonism. To fling elaborate sarcasms at Tess, however, was much like flinging them at a dog or cat. The charms of their subtlety passed by her unappreciated, and she only received them as inimical sounds which meant that anger ruled. She remained mute, not knowing that he was smothering his affection for her. She hardly observed that a tear descended slowly upon his cheek, a tear so large that it magnified the pores of the skin over which it rolled, like the object lens of a microscope. Meanwhile reillumination as to the terrible and total change that her confession had wrought in his life, in his universe, returned to him, and he tried desperately to advance among the new conditions in which he stood. Some consequent action was necessary; yet what?

'Tess,' he said, as gently as he could speak, 'I cannot stay – in this room – just now. I will walk out a little way.'

He quietly left the room, and the two glasses of wine that he had poured out for their supper – one for her, one for him – remained on the table untasted. This was what their *Agape* had come to. At tea, two or three hours earlier, they had, in the freakishness of affection, drunk from one cup.

The closing of the door behind him, gently as it had been pulled to, roused Tess from her stupor. He was gone; she could not stay. Hastily flinging her cloak around her she opened the door and followed, putting out the candles as if she were never coming back. The rain was over and the night was now clear.

She was soon close at his heels, for Clare walked slowly and without purpose. His form beside her light gray figure looked black, sinister, and forbidding, and she felt as sarcasm the touch of the jewels of which she had been momentarily so proud. Clare turned at hearing her footsteps, but his recognition of her presence seemed to make no difference in him, and he went on over the five yawning arches of the great bridge in front of the house.

The cow and horse tracks in the road were full of water, the rain having been enough to charge them, but not enough to wash them away. Across these minute pools the reflected stars flitted in a quick transit as she passed; she would not have known they were shining overhead if she had not seen them there – the vastest things of the universe imaged in objects so mean.

The place to which they had travelled to-day was in the same valley as Talbothays, but some miles lower down the river; and the surroundings being open she kept easily in sight of him. Away from the house the road wound through the meads, and along these she followed Clare without any attempt to come up with him or to attract him, but with dumb and vacant fidelity.

At last, however, her listless walk brought her up alongside him, and still he said nothing. The cruelty of fooled honesty is often great after enlightenment, and it was mighty in Clare now. The outdoor air had apparently taken away from him all tendency to act on impulse; she knew that he saw her without irradiation – in all her bareness; that Time was chanting his satiric psalm at her then –

> *Behold, when thy face is made bare, he that loved thee shall hate;*
> *Thy face shall be no more fair at the fall of thy fate.*
> *For thy life shall fall as a leaf and be shed as the rain;*
> *And the veil of thine head shall be grief, and the crown shall be pain.*

He was still intently thinking, and her companionship had now insufficient power to break or divert the strain of thought. What a weak thing her presence must have become to him! She could not help addressing Clare.

'What have I done – what *have* I done! I have not told of anything that interferes with or belies my love for you. You don't think I planned it, do you? It is in your own mind what you are angry at, Angel: it is not in me. O, it is not in me, and I am not that deceitful woman you think me!'

'H'm – well. Not deceitful, my wife; but not the same. No, not the same. But do not make me reproach you. I have sworn that I will not; and I will do everything to avoid it.'

But she went on pleading in her distraction; and perhaps said things that would have been better left to silence.

'Angel! – Angel! I was a child – a child when it happened! I knew nothing of men.'

'You were more sinned against than sinning, that I admit.'

'Then you will not forgive me?'

'I do forgive you, but forgiveness is not all.'

'And love me?'

To this question he did not answer.

'O Angel – my mother says that it sometimes happens so! – she knows several cases where they were worse than I, and the husband has not minded it much – has got over it at least. And yet the woman has not loved him as I do you!'

'Don't, Tess; don't argue. Different societies, different manners. You almost make me say you are an unapprehending peasant woman, who have never been initiated into the proportions of social things. You don't know what you say.'

'I am only a peasant by position, not by nature!'

She spoke with an impulse to anger, but it went as it came.

'So much the worse for you. I think that parson who unearthed your pedigree would have done better if he had held his tongue. I cannot help associating your decline as a family with this other fact – of your want of firmness. Decrepit families imply decrepit wills, decrepit conduct. Heaven, why did you give me a handle for despising you more by informing me of your descent! Here was I thinking you a new-sprung child of nature; there were you, the belated seedling of an effete aristocracy!'

'Lots of families are as bad as mine in that! Retty's family were once large landowners, and so were Dairyman Billett's. And the Debbyhouses, who now are carters, were once the De Bayeux family. You find such as I everywhere; 'tis a feature of our county, and I can't help it.'

'So much the worse for the county.'

She took these reproaches in their bulk simply, not in their particulars; he did not love her as he had loved her hitherto, and to all else she was indifferent.

They wandered on again in silence. It was said afterwards that a cottager of Wellbridge, who went out late that night for a doctor, met two lovers in the pastures, walking very slowly, without converse, one behind the other, as in a funeral procession, and the glimpse that he obtained of their faces seemed to denote that they were anxious and sad. Returning later, he passed them again in the same field, progressing just as slowly, and as regardless of the hour and of the cheerless night as before. It was only on account of his preoccupation with his own affairs, and the illness in his house, that he did not bear in mind the curious incident, which, however, he recalled a long while after.

During the interval of the cottager's going and coming, she had said to her husband –

'I don't see how I can help being the cause of much misery to you all your life. The river is down there. I can put an end to myself in it. I am not afraid.'

'I don't wish to add murder to my other follies,' he said.

'I will leave something to show that I did it myself – on account of my shame. They will not blame you then.'

'Don't speak so absurdly – I wish not to hear it. It is nonsense to have such thoughts in this kind of case, which is rather one for satirical laughter than for tragedy. You don't in the least understand the quality of the mishap. It would be viewed in the light of a joke by nine-tenths of the world if it were known. Please oblige me by returning to the house, and going to bed.'

'I will,' said she dutifully.

They had rambled round by a road which led to the well-known ruins of the Cistercian abbey behind the mill, the latter having, in centuries past, been attached to the monastic establishment. The mill still worked on, food being a perennial necessity; the abbey had perished, creeds being transient. One continually sees the ministration of the temporary outlasting the ministration of the eternal. Their walk having been circuitous they were still not far from the house, and in obeying his direction she only had to reach the large stone bridge across the main river, and follow the road for a few yards. When she got back everything remained as she had left it, the fire being still burning. She did not stay downstairs for more than a minute, but proceeded to her chamber, whither the luggage had been taken. Here she sat down on the edge of the bed, looking blankly around, and presently began to undress. In removing the light towards the bedstead its rays fell upon the tester of white dimity; something was hanging beneath it, and she lifted the candle to see what it was. A bough of mistletoe. Angel had put it there; she knew that in an instant. This was the explanation of that mysterious parcel which it had been so difficult to pack and bring; whose contents he would not explain to her, saying that time would soon show her the purpose thereof. In his zest and his gaiety he had hung it there. How foolish and inopportune that mistletoe looked now.

Having nothing more to fear, having scarce anything to hope, for that he would relent there seemed no promise whatever, she lay down dully. When sorrow ceases to be speculative sleep sees her opportunity. Among so many happier moods which forbid repose this was a mood which welcomed it, and in a few minutes the lonely Tess forgot existence, surrounded by the aromatic stillness of the chamber that had once, possibly, been the bride-chamber of her own ancestry.

Later on that night Clare also retraced his steps to the house. Entering softly to the sitting-room he obtained a light, and with the manner of one who had considered his course he spread his rugs upon the old horse-hair sofa which stood there, and roughly shaped it to a sleeping-couch. Before lying down he crept shoeless upstairs, and listened at the door of her apartment. Her measured breathing told that she was sleeping profoundly.

'Thank God!' murmured Clare; and yet he was conscious of a pang of bitterness at the thought – approximately true, though not wholly so – that having shifted the burden of her life to his shoulders she was now reposing without care.

He turned away to descend; then, irresolute, faced round to her door again. In the act he caught sight of one of the d'Urberville dames, whose portrait was immediately over the entrance to Tess's bedchamber. In the candlelight the painting was more than unpleasant. Sinister design lurked in the woman's features, a concentrated purpose of revenge on the other sex – so it seemed to him then. The Caroline bodice of the portrait was low – precisely as Tess's had been when he tucked it in to show the necklace; and again he experienced the distressing sensation of a resemblance between them.

The check was sufficient. He resumed his retreat and descended.

His air remained calm and cold, his small compressed mouth indexing his powers of self-control, his face wearing still that terribly sterile expression which had spread thereon since her disclosure. It was the face of a man who was no longer passion's slave, yet who found no advantage in his enfranchisement. He was simply regarding the harrowing contingencies of human experience, the unexpectedness of things. Nothing so pure, so sweet, so virginal as Tess had seemed possible all the long while that he had adored her, up to an hour ago; but

The little less, and what worlds away!

He argued erroneously when he said to himself that her heart was not indexed in the honest freshness of her face; but Tess had no advocate to set him right. Could it be possible, he continued, that eyes which as they gazed never expressed any divergence from what the tongue was telling, were yet ever seeing another world behind her ostensible one, discordant and contrasting.

He reclined on his couch in the sitting-room, and extinguished the light. The night came in, and took up its place there, unconcerned and indifferent; the night which had already swallowed up his happiness, and was now digesting it listlessly; and was ready to swallow up the happiness of a thousand other people with as little disturbance or change of mien.

❧ Chapter Thirty-Six ❧

CLARE AROSE IN THE LIGHT of a dawn that was ashy and furtive, as though associated with crime. The fireplace confronted him with its extinct embers; the spread supper-table, whereon stood the two full glasses of untasted wine, now flat and filmy; her vacated seat and his own; the other articles of furniture, with their eternal look of not being able to help it, their intolerable inquiry what was to be done? From above there was no sound; but in a few minutes there came a knock at the door. He remembered that it would be the neighbouring cottager's wife, who was to minister to their wants while they remained here.

The presence of a third person in the house would be extremely awkward just now, and, being already dressed, he opened the window and informed her that they could manage to shift for themselves that morning. She had a milk-can in her hand, which he told her to leave at the door. When the dame had gone away he searched in the back quarters of the house for fuel, and speedily lit a fire. There was plenty of eggs, butter, bread, and so on in the larder, and Clare soon had breakfast laid, his experiences at the dairy having rendered him facile in domestic preparations. The smoke of the kindled wood rose from the chimney without like a lotus-headed column; local people who were passing by saw it, and thought of the newly-married couple, and envied their happiness.

Angel cast a final glance round, and then going to the foot of the stairs, called in a conventional voice –

'Breakfast is ready!'

He opened the front door, and took a few steps in the morning air. When, after a short space, he came back she was already in the sitting-room, mechanically readjusting the breakfast things. As she was fully attired, and the interval since his calling her had been but two or three minutes, she must have been dressed or nearly so before he went to summon her. Her hair was twisted up in a large round mass at the back of her head, and she had put on one of the new frocks – a pale blue woollen garment with neck-frillings of white. Her hands and face appeared to be cold, and she had possibly been sitting dressed in the bedroom a long time without any fire. The marked civility of Clare's tone in calling her seemed to have inspired her, for the moment, with a new glimmer of hope. But it soon died when she looked at him.

The pair were, in truth, but the ashes of their former fires. To the hot sorrow of the previous night had succeeded heaviness; it seemed as if nothing could kindle either of them to fervour of sensation any more.

He spoke gently to her, and she replied with a like undemonstrativeness. At last she came up to him, looking in his sharply-defined face as one who had no consciousness that her own formed a visible object also.

'Angel!' she said, and paused, touching him with her fingers lightly as a breeze, as though she could hardly believe to be there in the flesh the man who was once her lover. Her eyes were bright, her pale cheek still showed its wonted roundness, though half-dried tears had left glistening traces thereon; and the usually ripe red mouth was almost as pale as her cheek. Throbbingly alive as she was still, under the stress of her mental grief the life beat so brokenly, that a little further pull upon it would cause real illness, dull her characteristic eyes, and make her mouth thin.

She looked absolutely pure. Nature, in her fantastic trickery, had set such a seal of maidenhood upon Tess's countenance that he gazed at her with a stupefied air.

'Tess! Say it is not true! No, it is not true!'

'It is true.'

'Every word?'

'Every word.'

He looked at her imploringly, as if he would willingly have taken a lie from her lips, knowing it to be one, and have made of it, by some sort of sophistry, a valid denial. However, she only repeated –

'It is true.'

'Is he living?' Angel then asked.

'The baby died.'

'But the man?'

'He is alive.'

A last despair passed over Clare's face.

'Is he in England?'

'Yes.'

He took a few vague steps.

'My position – is this,' he said abruptly. 'I thought – any man would have thought – that by giving up all ambition to win a wife with social standing, with fortune, with knowledge of the world, I should secure rustic innocence as surely as I should secure pink cheeks; but – However, I am no man to reproach you, and I will not.'

Tess felt his position so entirely that the remainder had not been needed. Therein lay just the distress of it; she saw that he had lost all round.

'Angel – I should not have let it go on to marriage with you if I had not known that, after all, there was a last way out of it for you; though I hoped you would never – '

Her voice grew husky.

'A last way?'

'I mean, to get rid of me. You *can* get rid of me.'

'How?'

'By divorcing me.'

'Good heavens – how can you be so simple! How can I divorce you?'

'Can't you – now I have told you? I thought my confession would give you grounds for that.'

'O Tess – you are too, too – childish – unformed – crude, I suppose! I don't know what you are. You don't understand the law – you don't understand!'

'What – you cannot?'

'Indeed I cannot.'

A quick shame mixed with the misery upon his listener's face.

'I thought – I thought,' she whispered. 'O, now I see how wicked I seem to you! Believe me – believe me, on my soul, I never thought but that you could! I hoped you would not; yet I believed, without a doubt, that you could cast me off if you were determined, and didn't love me at – at – all!'

'You were mistaken,' he said.

'O, then I ought to have done it, to have done it last night! But I hadn't the courage. That's just like me!'

'The courage to do what?'

As she did not answer he took her by the hand.

'What were you thinking of doing?' he inquired.

'Of putting an end to myself.'

'When?'

She writhed under this inquisitorial manner of his. 'Last night,' she answered.

'Where?'

'Under your mistletoe.'

'My good – ! How?' he asked sternly.

'I'll tell you, if you won't be angry with me!' she said, shrinking. 'It was with the cord of my box. But I could not – do the last thing! I was afraid that it might cause a scandal to your name.'

The unexpected quality of this confession, wrung from her, and not volunteered, shook him perceptibly. But he still held her, and, letting his glance fall from her face downwards, he said,

'Now, listen to this. You must not dare to think of such a horrible thing! How could you! You will promise me as your husband to attempt that no more.'

'I am ready to promise. I saw how wicked it was.'

'Wicked! The idea was unworthy of you beyond description.'

'But, Angel,' she pleaded, enlarging her eyes in calm unconcern upon him, 'it was thought of entirely on your account – to set you free without the scandal of the divorce that I thought you would have to get. I should never have dreamt of doing it on mine. However, to do it with my own hand is too good for me, after all. It is you, my ruined husband, who ought to strike the blow. I think I should love you more, if that were possible, if you could bring yourself to do it, since there's no other way of escape for 'ee. I feel I am so utterly worthless! So very greatly in the way!'

'Ssh!'

'Well, since you say no, I won't. I have no wish opposed to yours.'

He knew this to be true enough. Since the desperation of the night her activities had dropped to zero, and there was no further rashness to be feared.

Tess tried to busy herself again over the breakfast-table with more or less success, and they sat down both on the same side, so that their glances did not meet. There was at first something awkward in hearing each other eat and drink, but this could not be escaped; moreover, the amount of eating done was small on both sides. Breakfast over he rose, and telling her the hour at which he might be expected to dinner, went off to the miller's in a mechanical pursuance of the plan of studying that business, which had been his only practical reason for coming here.

When he was gone Tess stood at the window, and presently saw his form crossing the great stone bridge which conducted to the mill premises. He sank behind it, crossed the railway beyond, and disappeared.

Then, without a sigh, she turned her attention to the room, and began clearing the table and setting it in order.

The charwoman soon came. Her presence was at first a strain upon Tess, but afterwards an alleviation. At half-past twelve she left her assistant alone in the kitchen, and, returning to the sitting-room, waited for the reappearance of Angel's form behind the bridge.

About one he showed himself. Her face flushed, although he was a quarter of a mile off. She ran to the kitchen to get the dinner served by the time he should enter. He went first to the room where they had washed their hands together the day before, and as he entered the sitting-room the dish-covers rose from the dishes as if by his own motion.

'How punctual!' he said.

'Yes. I saw you coming over the bridge,' said she.

The meal was passed in commonplace talk of what he had been doing during the morning at the Abbey Mill, of the methods of bolting and the old-fashioned machinery, which he feared would not enlighten him greatly on modern improved methods, some of it seeming to have been in use ever since the days it ground for the monks in the adjoining conventual buildings – now a heap of ruins. He left the house again in the course of an hour, coming home at dusk, and occupying himself through the evening with his papers. She feared she was in the way, and, when the old woman was gone, retired to the kitchen, where she made herself busy as well as she could for more than an hour.

Clare's shape appeared at the door.

'You must not work like this,' he said. 'You are not my servant; you are my wife.'

She raised her eyes, and brightened somewhat. 'I may think myself that – indeed?' she murmured, in piteous raillery. 'You mean in name! Well, I don't want to be anything more.'

'You *may* think so, Tess! You are. What do you mean?'

'I don't know,' she said hastily, with tears in her accents. 'I thought I – because I am not respectable, I mean. I told you I thought I was not respectable enough long ago – and on that account I didn't want to marry you, only – only you urged me!'

She broke into sobs, and turned her back to him. It would almost have won round any man but Angel Clare. Within the remote depths of his constitution, so gentle and affectionate as he was in general, there lay hidden a hard logical deposit, like a vein of metal in a soft loam, which turned the edge of everything that attempted to traverse it. It had blocked his acceptance of the Church; it blocked his acceptance of Tess. Moreover, his affection itself was less fire than radiance, and, with regard to the other sex, when he ceased to believe he ceased to follow: contrasting in this with many impressionable natures, who remain sensuously infatuated with what they intellectually despise. He waited till her sobbing ceased.

'I wish half the women in England were as respectable as you,' he said, in an ebullition of bitterness against womankind in general. 'It isn't a question of respectability, but one of principle!'

He spoke such things as these and more of a kindred sort to her, being still swayed by the antipathetic wave which warps direct souls with such persistence when once their vision finds itself mocked by appearances. There was, it is true, underneath, a back current of sympathy through which a woman of the world might have conquered him. But Tess did not think of this; she took everything as her deserts, and hardly opened her mouth. The firmness of her devotion to him was indeed almost pitiful; quick-tempered as she naturally was, nothing that he could say made her unseemly; she sought not her own; was not provoked; thought no evil of his treatment of her. She might just now have been Apostolic Charity herself returned to a self-seeking modern world.

This evening, night, and morning were passed precisely as the preceding ones had been passed. On one, and only one, occasion did she – the formerly free and independent Tess – venture to make any advances. It was on the third occasion of his starting after a meal to go out to the flour-mill. As he was leaving the table he said 'Good-bye', and she replied in the same words, at the same time inclining her mouth in the way of his. He did not avail himself of the invitation, saying, as he turned hastily aside –

'I shall be home punctually.'

Tess shrank into herself as if she had been struck. Often enough had he tried to reach those lips against her consent – often had he said gaily that her mouth and breath tasted of the butter and eggs and milk and honey on which she mainly lived, that he drew sustenance from them, and other follies of that sort. But he did not care for them now. He observed her sudden shrinking, and said gently –

'You know, I have to think of a course. It was imperative that we should stay together a little while, to avoid the scandal to you that would have resulted from our immediate parting. But you must see it is only for form's sake.'

'Yes,' said Tess absently.

He went out, and on his way to the mill stood still, and wished for a moment that he had responded yet more kindly, and kissed her once at least.

Thus they lived through this despairing day or two; in the same house, truly; but more widely apart than before they were lovers. It was evident to her that he was, as he had said, living with paralyzed activities, in his endeavour to think of a plan of procedure. She was awe-stricken to

212

discover such determination under such apparent flexibility. His consistency was, indeed, too cruel. She no longer expected forgiveness now. More than once she thought of going away from him during his absence at the mill; but she feared that this, instead of benefiting him, might be the means of hampering and humiliating him yet more if it should become known.

Meanwhile Clare was meditating, verily. His thought had been unsuspended; he was becoming ill with thinking; eaten out with thinking, withered by thinking; scourged out of all his former pulsating flexuous domesticity. He walked about saying to himself, 'What's to be done – what's to be done?' and by chance she overheard him. It caused her to break the reserve about their future which had hitherto prevailed.

'I suppose – you are not going to live with me – long, are you, Angel?' she asked, the sunk corners of her mouth betraying how purely mechanical were the means by which she retained that expression of chastened calm upon her face.

'I cannot,' he said, 'without despising myself, and what is worse, perhaps, despising you. I mean, of course, cannot live with you in the ordinary sense. At present, whatever I feel, I do not despise you. And, let me speak plainly, or you may not see all my difficulties. How can we live together while that man lives? – he being your husband in Nature, and not I. If he were dead it might be different ... Besides, that's not all the difficulty; it lies in another consideration – one bearing upon the future of other people than ourselves. Think of years to come and children being born to us, and this past matter getting known – for it must get known. There is not an uttermost part of the earth but somebody comes from it or goes to it from elsewhere. Well, think of wretches of our flesh and blood growing up under a taunt which they will gradually get to feel the full force of with their expanding years. What an awakening for them! What a prospect! Can you honestly say Remain, after contemplating this contingency? Don't you think we had better endure the ills we have than fly to others?'

Her eyelids, weighted with trouble, continued drooping as before.

'I cannot say Remain,' she answered. 'I cannot; I had not thought so far.'

Tess's feminine hope – shall we confess it – had been so obstinately recuperative as to revive in her surreptitious visions of a domiciliary intimacy continued long enough to break down his coldness even against his judgment. Though unsophisticated in the usual sense, she was not incomplete; and it would have denoted deficiency of womanhood if she had not instinctively known what an argument lies in propinquity. Nothing else would serve her, she knew, if this failed. It was wrong to hope in what was of the nature of strategy, she said to herself: yet that sort of hope she could not extinguish. His last representation had now been made, and it was, as she said, a new view. She had truly never thought so far as that, and his lucid picture of possible offspring who would scorn her was one that brought deadly conviction to an honest heart which was humanitarian to its centre. Sheer experience had already taught her that, in some circumstances, there was one thing better than to lead a good life, and that was to be saved from leading any life whatever. Like all who have been previsioned by suffering, she could, in the words of M. Sully-Prudhomme, hear a penal sentence in the fiat, 'You shall be born,' particularly if addressed to potential issue of hers.

Yet such is the vulpine slyness of Dame Nature, that, till now, Tess had been hoodwinked by her love for Clare into forgetting it might result in vitalizations that would inflict upon others what she had bewailed as a misfortune to herself.

She therefore could not withstand his argument. But with the self-combating proclivity of the super-sensitive, an answer thereto arose in Clare's own mind, and he almost feared it. It was based on her exceptional physical nature; and she might have used it promisingly. She might have added besides: 'On an Australian upland or Texan plain, who is to know or care about my misfortunes, or to reproach me or you?' Yet, like the majority of women, she accepted the momentary presentment as if it were the inevitable. And she may have been right. The intuitive heart of woman knoweth not only its own bitterness, but its husband's, and even if these assumed reproaches were not likely to be addressed to him or to his by strangers, they might have reached his ears from his own fastidious brain.

It was the third day of the estrangement. Some might risk the odd paradox that with more animalism he would have been the nobler man. We do not say it. Yet Clare's love was doubtless ethereal to a fault, imaginative to impracticability. With these natures, corporeal presence is sometimes less appealing than corporeal absence; the latter creating an ideal presence that conveniently drops the defects of the real. She found that her personality did not plead her cause so forcibly as she had anticipated. The figurative phrase was true: she was another woman than the one who had excited his desire.

'I have thought over what you say,' she remarked to him, moving her forefinger over the tablecloth, her other hand, which bore the ring that mocked them both, supporting her forehead. 'It is quite true all of it; it must be. You must go away from me.'

'But what can you do?'

'I can go home.'

Clare had not thought of that.

'Are you sure?' he inquired.

214

'Quite sure. We ought to part, and we may as well get it past and done. You once said that I was apt to win men against their better judgment; and if I am constantly before your eyes I may cause you to change your plans in opposition to your reason and wish; and afterwards your repentance and my sorrow will be terrible.'

'And you would like to go home?' he asked.

'I want to leave you, and go home.'

'Then it shall be so.'

Though she did not look up at him, she started. There was a difference between the proposition and the covenant, which she had felt only too quickly.

'I feared it would come to this,' she murmured, her countenance meekly fixed. 'I don't complain, Angel. I – I think it best. What you said has quite convinced me. Yes, though nobody else should reproach me if we should stay together, yet somewhen, years hence, you might get angry with me for any ordinary matter, and knowing what you do of my bygones you yourself might be tempted to say words, and they might be overheard, perhaps by my own children. O, what only hurts me now would torture and kill me then! I will go – to-morrow.'

'And I shall not stay here. Though I didn't like to initiate it, I have seen that it was advisable we should part – at least for a while, till I can better see the shape that things have taken, and can write to you.'

Tess stole a glance at her husband. He was pale, even tremulous; but, as before, she was appalled by the determination revealed in the depths of this gentle being she had married – the will to subdue the grosser to the subtler emotion, the substance to the conception, the flesh to the spirit. Propensities, tendencies, habits, were as dead as leaves upon the tyrannous wind of his imaginative ascendency.

He may have observed her look, for he explained –

'I think of people more kindly when I am away from them;' adding cynically, 'God knows; perhaps we shall shake down together some day, for weariness; thousands have done it!'

That day he began to pack up, and she went upstairs and began to pack also. Both knew that it was in their two minds that they might part the next morning for ever, despite the gloss of assuaging conjectures thrown over their proceeding because they were of the sort to whom any parting which has an air of finality is a torture. He knew, and she knew, that, though the fascination which each had exercised over the other – on her part independently of accomplishments – would probably in the first days of their separation be even more potent than ever, time must attenuate that effect; the practical arguments against accepting her as a housemate might pronounce themselves more strongly in the boreal light of a remoter view. Moreover, when two people are once parted –

have abandoned a common domicile and a common environment – new growths insensibly bud upward to fill each vacated place; unforseen accidents hinder intentions, and old plans are forgotten.

❧ Chapter Thirty-Seven ❧

MIDNIGHT CAME AND PASSED silently, for there was nothing to announce it in the Valley of the Froom.

Not long after one o'clock there was a slight creak in the darkened farmhouse once the mansion of the d'Urbervilles. Tess, who used the upper chamber, heard it and awoke. It had come from the corner step of the staircase, which, as usual, was loosely nailed. She saw the door of her bedroom open, and the figure of her husband crossed the stream of moonlight with a curiously careful tread. He was in his shirt and trousers only, and her first flush of joy died when she perceived that his eyes were fixed in an unnatural stare on vacancy. When he reached the middle of the room he stood still and murmured, in tones of undescribable sadness –

'Dead! dead! dead!'

Under the influence of any strongly-disturbing force Clare would occasionally walk in his sleep, and even perform strange feats, such as he had done on the night of their return from market just before their marriage, when he re-enacted in his bedroom his combat with the man who had insulted her. Tess saw that continued mental distress had wrought him into that somnambulistic state now.

Her loyal confidence in him lay so deep down in her heart that, awake or asleep, he inspired her with no sort of personal fear. If he had entered with a pistol in his hand he would scarcely have disturbed her trust in his protectiveness.

Clare came close, and bent over her. 'Dead, dead, dead!' he murmured.

After fixedly regarding her for some moments with the same gaze of unmeasurable woe he bent lower, enclosed her in his arms, and rolled her in the sheet as in a shroud. Then lifting her from the bed with as much respect as one would show to a dead body, he carried her across the room, murmuring –

'My poor, poor Tess – my dearest, darling Tess! So sweet, so good, so true!'

The words of endearment, withheld so severely in his waking hours, were inexpressibly sweet to her forlorn and hungry heart. If it had been to save her weary life she would not, by moving or struggling, have put an end to the position she found herself in. Thus she lay in absolute stillness, scarcely venturing to breathe, and, wondering what he was going to do with her, suffered herself to be borne out upon the landing.

'My wife – dead, dead!' he said.

He paused in his labours for a moment to lean with her against the banister. Was he going to throw her down? Self-solicitude was near extinction in her, and in the knowledge that he had planned to depart on the morrow, possibly for always, she lay in his arms in this precarious position with a sense rather of luxury than of terror. If they could only fall together, and both be dashed to pieces, how fit, how desirable.

However, he did not let her fall, but took advantage of the support of the handrail to imprint a kiss upon her lips – lips in the daytime scorned. Then he clasped her with a renewed firmness of hold, and descended the staircase. The creak of the loose stair did not awaken him, and they reached the ground-floor safely. Freeing one of his hands from his grasp of her for a moment, he slid back the door-bar and passed out, slightly striking his stockinged toe against the edge of the door. But this he seemed not to mind, and, having room for extension in the open air, he lifted her against his shoulder, so that he could carry her with ease, the absence of clothes taking much from his burden. Thus he bore her off the premises in the direction of the river a few yards distant.

His ultimate intention, if he had any, she had not yet devined; and she found herself conjecturing on the matter as a third person might have done. So easefully had she delivered her whole being up to him that it pleased her to think he was regarding her as his absolute possession, to dispose of as he should choose. It was consoling, under the hovering terror of to-morrow's separation, to feel that he really recognized her now as his wife Tess, and did not cast her off, even if in that recognition he went so far as to arrogate to himself the right of harming her.

Ah! now she knew what he was dreaming of – that Sunday morning when he had borne her along through the water with the other dairymaids, who had loved him nearly as much as she, if that were possible, which Tess could hardly admit. Clare did not cross the bridge with her, but proceeding several paces on the same side towards the adjoining mill, at length stood still on the brink of the river.

Its waters, in creeping down these miles of meadowland, frequently divided, serpentining in purposeless curves, looping themselves around little islands that had no name, returning and re-embodying themselves as a broad main stream further on. Opposite the spot to which he had brought her was such a general confluence, and the river was proportionately voluminous and deep. Across it was a narrow foot-bridge; but now the autumn flood had washed the handrail away, leaving the bare plank only, which, lying a few inches above the speeding current, formed a giddy pathway for even steady heads; and Tess had noticed from the window of the house in the daytime young men walking across upon it as a feat in balancing. Her husband had possibly observed the same performance; anyhow, he now mounted the plank, and sliding one foot forward, advanced along it.

Was he going to drown her? Probably he was. The spot was lonely, the river deep and wide enough to make such a purpose easy of accomplishment. He might drown her if he would; it would be better than parting to-morrow to lead severed lives.

The swift stream raced and gyrated under them, tossing, distorting, and splitting the moon's reflected face. Spots of froth travelled past, and intercepted weeds waved behind the piles. If they could both fall together into the current now, their arms would be so tightly clasped together that they could not be saved; they would go out of the world almost painlessly, and there would be no more reproach to her, or to him for marrying her. His last half-hour with her would have been a loving one, while if they lived till he awoke his daytime aversion would return, and this hour would remain to be contemplated only as a transient dream.

The impulse stirred in her, yet she dared not indulge it, to make a movement that would have precipitated them both into the gulf. How she valued her own life had been proved; but his – she had no right to tamper with it. He reached the other side with her in safety.

Here they were within a plantation which formed the Abbey grounds, and taking a new hold of her he went onward a few steps till they reached the ruined choir of the Abbey-church. Against the north wall was the empty stone coffin of an abbot, in which every tourist with a turn for grim humour was accustomed to stretch himself. In this Clare carefully laid Tess. Having kissed her lips a second time he breathed deeply, as if a greatly desired end were attained. Clare then lay down on the ground alongside, when he immediately fell into the deep dead slumber of exhaustion, and remained motionless as a log. The spurt of mental excitement which had produced the effort was now over.

Tess sat up in the coffin. The night, though dry and mild for the season, was more than sufficiently cold to make it dangerous for him to remain here long, in his half-clothed state. If he were left to himself he would in all probability stay there till the morning, and be chilled to certain death. She had heard of such deaths after sleep-walking. But how could she dare to awaken him, and let him know what he had been doing, when it would mortify him to discover his folly in respect of her? Tess, however, stepping out of her stone confine, shook him slightly, but was unable to arouse him without being violent. It was indispensable to do something, for she was beginning to shiver, the sheet being but a poor protection. Her excitement had in a measure kept her warm during the few minutes' adventure; but that beatific interval was over.

It suddenly occurred to her to try persuasion; and accordingly she whispered in his ear, with as much firmness and decision as she could summon –

'Let us walk on, darling,' at the same time taking him suggestively by the arm. To her relief, he unresistingly acquiesced; her words had apparently thrown him back into his dream, which thenceforward seemed to enter on a new phase, wherein he fancied she had risen as a spirit, and was leading him to Heaven. Thus she conducted him by the arm to the stone bridge in front of their residence, crossing which they stood at the manor-house door. Tess's feet were quite bare, and the stones hurt her, and chilled her to the bone; but Clare was in his woollen stockings, and appeared to feel no discomfort.

There was no further difficulty. She induced him to lie down on his own sofa bed, and covered him up warmly, lighting a temporary fire of wood, to dry any dampness out of him. The noise of these attentions she thought might awaken him, and secretly wished that they might. But the exhaustion of his mind and body was such that he remained undisturbed.

As soon as they met the next morning Tess divined that Angel knew little or nothing of how far she had been concerned in the night's excursion, though, as regarded himself he may have been aware that he had not lain still. In truth, he had awakened that morning from a sleep deep as annihilation; and during those first few moments in which the brain, like a Samson shaking himself, is trying its strength, he had some dim notion of an unusual nocturnal proceeding. But the realities of his situation soon displaced conjecture on the other subject.

He waited in expectancy to discern some mental pointing; he knew that if any intention of his, concluded over-night, did not vanish in the light of morning, it stood on a basis approximating to one of pure reason, even if initiated by impulse of feeling, that it was so far, therefore, to be trusted. He thus beheld in the pale morning light the resolve to separate from her; not as a hot and indignant instinct, but denuded of the passionateness which had made it scorch and burn; standing in its bones; nothing but a skeleton, but none the less there. Clare no longer hesitated.

At breakfast, and while they were packing the few remaining articles, he showed his weariness from the night's effort so unmistakably that Tess was on the point of revealing all that had happened; but the reflection that it would anger him, grieve him, stultify him, to know that he had instinctively manifested a fondness for her of which his common-sense did not approve; that his inclination had compromised his dignity when reason slept, again deterred her. It was too much like laughing at a man when sober for his erratic deeds during intoxication.

It just crossed her mind, too, that he might have a faint recollection of his tender vagary, and was disinclined to allude to it from a conviction that she would take amatory advantage of the opportunity it gave her of appealing to him anew not to go.

He had ordered by letter a vehicle from the nearest town, and soon after breakfast it arrived. She saw in it the beginning of the end – the temporary end, at least, for the revelation of his tenderness by the incident of the night raised dreams of a possible future with him. The luggage was put on the top, and the man drove them off, the miller and the old waiting-woman expressing some surprise at their precipitate departure, which Clare attributed to his discovery that the mill-work was not of the modern kind which he wished to investigate, a statement that was true so far as it went. Beyond this there was nothing in the manner of their leaving to suggest a *fiasco*, or that they were not going together to visit friends.

Their route lay near the dairy from which they had started with such solemn joy in each other a few days back, and, as Clare wished to wind up his business with Mr Crick, Tess could hardly avoid paying Mrs Crick a call at the same time, unless she would excite suspicion of their unhappy state.

To make the call as unobtrusive as possible they left the carriage by the wicket leading down from the high road to the dairy-house, and descended the track on foot, side by side. The withy-bed had been cut, and they could see over the stumps the spot to which Clare had followed her when he pressed her to be his wife; to the left the enclosure in which she had been fascinated by his harp; and far away behind the cowstalls the mead which had been the scene of their first embrace. The gold of the summer picture was now gray, the colours mean, the rich soil mud, and the river cold.

Over the barton-gate the dairyman saw them, and came forward, throwing into his face the kind of jocularity deemed appropriate in Talbothays and its vicinity on the re-appearance of the newly-married. Then Mrs Crick emerged from the house, and several others of their old acquaintance, though Marian and Retty did not seem to be there.

Tess valiantly bore their sly attacks and friendly humours, which affected her far otherwise than they supposed. In the tacit agreement of husband and wife to keep their estrangement a secret they behaved as would have been ordinary. And then, although she would rather there had been no word spoken on the subject, Tess had to hear in detail the story of Marian and Retty. The latter had gone home to her father's, and Marian had left to look for employment elsewhere. They feared she would come to no good.

To dissipate the sadness of this recital Tess went and bade all her favourite cows good-bye, touching each of them with her hand, and as she and Clare stood side by side at leaving, as if united body and soul, there would have been something peculiarly sorry in their aspect to one who should have seen it truly; two limbs of one life, as they outwardly were, his arm touching hers, her skirts touching him, facing one way, as against all the dairy facing the other, speaking in their adieux as 'we', and yet sundered like the poles. Perhaps something unusually stiff and embarrassed in their attitude, some awkwardness in acting up to their profession of unity, different from the natural shyness of young couples, may have been apparent, for when they were gone Mrs Crick said to her husband –

'How unnatural the brightness of her eyes did seem, and how they stood like waxen images and talked as if they were in a dream! Didn't it strike 'ee that 'twas so? Tess had always sommat strange in her, and she's not now quite like the proud young bride of a well-be-doing man.'

They re-entered the vehicle, and were driven along the roads towards Weatherbury and Stagfoot Lane, till they reached the Lane inn, where Clare dismissed the fly and man. They rested here a while, and entering the Vale were next driven onward towards her home by a stranger who did not know their relations. At a midway point, when Nuttlebury had been passed, and where there were cross-roads, Clare stopped the conveyance and said to Tess that if she meant to return to her mother's house it was here that he would leave her. As they could not talk with freedom in the driver's presence he asked her to accompany him for a few steps on foot along one of the branch roads; she assented, and directing the man to wait a few minutes they strolled away.

'Now, let us understand each other,' he said gently. 'There is no anger between us, though there is that which I cannot endure at present. I will try to bring myself to endure it. I will let you know where I go to as soon as I know myself. And if I can bring myself to bear it – if it is desirable, possible – I will come to you. But until I come to you it will be better that you should not try to come to me.'

The severity of the decree seemed deadly to Tess; she saw his view of her clearly enough; he could regard her in no other light than that of one who had practised gross deceit upon him. Yet could a woman who had done even what she had done deserve all this? But she could contest the point with him no further. She simply repeated after him his own words.

'Until you come to me I must not try to come to you?'

'Just so.'

'May I write to you?'

'O yes – if you are ill, or want anything at all. I hope that will not be the case; so that it may happen that I write first to you.'

'I agree to the conditions, Angel; because you know best what my punishment ought to be; only – only – don't make it more than I can bear!'

That was all she said on the matter. If Tess had been artful, had she made a scene, fainted, wept hysterically, in that lonely lane, notwithstanding the fury of fastidiousness with which he was possessed, he would probably not have withstood her. But her mood of long-suffering made his way easy for him, and she herself was his best advocate. Pride, too, entered into her submission – which perhaps was a symptom of that reckless acquiescence in chance too apparent in the whole d'Urberville family – and the many effective chords which she could have stirred by an appeal were left untouched.

The remainder of their discourse was on practical matters only. He now handed her a packet containing a fairly good sum of money, which he had obtained from his bankers for the purpose. The brilliants, the interest in which seemed to be Tess's for her life only (if he understood the wording of the will), he advised her to let him send to a bank for safety; and to this she readily agreed.

These things arranged he walked with Tess back to the carriage, and handed her in. The coachman was paid and told where to drive her. Taking next his own bag and umbrella – the sole articles he had brought with him hitherwards – he bade her good-bye, and they parted there and then.

The fly moved creepingly up a hill, and Clare watched it go with an unpremeditated hope that Tess would look out of the window for one moment. But that she never thought of doing, would not have ventured to do, lying in a half-dead faint inside. Thus he beheld her recede, and in the anguish of his heart quoted a line from a poet, with peculiar emendations of his own –

God's *not* in his heaven: all's *wrong* with the world!

When Tess had passed over the crest of the hill he turned to go his own way, and hardly knew that he loved her still.

♣ Chapter Thirty-Eight ♣

As she drove on through Blackmoor Vale, and the landscape of her youth began to open around her, Tess aroused herself from her stupor. Her first thought was how would she be able to face her parents?

She reached a turnpike-gate which stood upon the highway to the village. It was thrown open by a stranger, not by the old man who had kept it for many years, and to whom she had been known; he had probably left on New Year's Day, the date when such changes were made. Having received no intelligence lately from her home, she asked the turnpike-keeper for news.

'Oh – nothing, miss,' he answered. 'Marlott is Marlott still. Folks have died and that. John Durbeyfield, too, hev had a daughter married this week to a gentleman-farmer; not from John's own house, you know; they was married elsewhere; the gentleman being of that high standing that John's own folk was not considered well-be-doing enough to have any part in it, the bridegroom seeming not to know how't have been discovered that John is a old and ancient nobleman himself by blood, with family skillentons in their own vaults to this day, but done out of his property in the time o' the Romans. However, Sir John, as we call 'n now, kept up the wedding-day as well as he could, and stood treat to everybody in the parish; and John's wife sung songs at The Pure Drop till past eleven o'clock.'

Hearing this, Tess felt so sick at heart that she could not decide to go home publicly in the fly with her luggage and belongings. She asked the turnpike-keeper if she might deposit her things at his house for a while, and, on his offering no objection, she dismissed her carriage, and went on to the village alone by a back lane.

At sight of her father's chimney she asked herself how she could possibly enter the house? Inside that cottage her relations were calmly supposing her far away on a wedding-tour with a comparatively rich man, who was to conduct her to bouncing prosperity; while here she was, friendless, creeping up to the old door quite by herself, with no better place to go to in the world.

She did not reach the house unobserved. Just by the garden-hedge she was met by a girl who knew her – one of the two or three with whom she had been intimate at school. After making a few inquiries as to how Tess came there, her friend, unheeding her tragic look, interrupted with –

'But where's thy gentleman, Tess?'

Tess hastily explained that he had been called away on business, and, leaving her interlocutor, clambered over the garden-hedge, and thus made her way to the house.

As she went up the garden-path she heard her mother singing by the back door, coming in sight of which she perceived Mrs Durbeyfield on the doorstep in the act of wringing a sheet. Having performed this without observing Tess, she went indoors, and her daughter followed her.

The washing-tub stood in the same old place on the same old quarter-hogshead, and her mother, having thrown the sheet aside, was about to plunge her arms in anew.

'Why – Tess! – my chil' – I thought you was married! – married really and truly this time – we sent the cider – '

'Yes, mother; so I am.'

'Going to be?'

'No – I am married.'

'Married! Then where's thy husband?'

'Oh, he's gone away for a time.'

'Gone away! When was you married, then? The day you said?'

'Yes, Tuesday, mother.'

'And now 'tis on'y Saturday, and he gone away?'

'Yes; he's gone.'

'What's the meaning o' that? 'Nation seize such husbands as you seem to get, say I!'

'Mother!' Tess went across to Joan Durbeyfield, laid her face upon the matron's bosom, and burst into sobs. 'I don't know how to tell 'ee, mother! You said to me, and wrote to me, that I was not to tell him. But I did tell him – I couldn't help it – and he went away!'

'O you little fool – you little fool!' burst out Mrs Durbeyfield, splashing Tess and herself in her agitation. 'My good God! that ever I should ha' lived to say it, but I say it again, you little fool!'

Tess was convulsed with weeping, the tension of so many days having relaxed at last.

'I know it – I know – I know!' she gasped through her sobs. 'But, O my mother, I could not help it! He was so good – and I felt the wickedness of trying to blind him as to what had happened! If – if – it were to be done again – I should do the same. I could not – I dared not – so sin – against him!'

'But you sinned enough to marry him first!'

'Yes, yes; that's where my misery do lie! But I thought he could get rid o' me by law if he were determined not to overlook it. And O, if you knew – if you could only half know how I loved him – how anxious I was to have him – and how wrung I was between caring so much for him and my wish to be fair to him!'

224

Tess was so shaken that she could get no further, and sank a helpless thing into a chair.

'Well, well; what's done can't be undone! I'm sure I don't know why children o' my bringing forth should all be bigger simpletons than other people's – not to know better than to blab such a thing as that, when he couldn't ha' found it out till too late!' Here Mrs Durbeyfield began shedding tears on her own account as a mother to be pitied. 'What your father will say I don't know,' she continued; 'for he's been talking about the wedding up at Rolliver's and The Pure Drop every day since, and about his family getting back to their rightful position through you – poor silly man! – and now you've made this mess of it! The Lord-a-Lord!'

As if to bring matters to a focus, Tess's father was heard approaching at that moment. He did not, however, enter immediately, and Mrs Durbeyfield said that she would break the bad news to him herself, Tess keeping out of sight for the present. After her first burst of disappointment Joan began to take the mishap as she had taken Tess's original trouble, as she would have taken a wet holiday or failure in the potato-crop; as a thing which had come upon them irrespective of desert or folly; a chance external impingement to be borne with; not a lesson.

Tess retreated upstairs, and beheld casually that the beds had been shifted, and new arrangements made. Her old bed had been adapted for two younger children. There was no place here for her now.

The room below being unceiled she could hear most of what went on there. Presently her father entered, apparently carrying a live hen. He was a foothaggler now, having been obliged to sell his second horse, and he travelled with his basket on his arm. The hen had been carried about this morning as it was often carried, to show people that he was in his work, though it had lain, with its legs tied, under the table at Rolliver's for more than an hour.

'We've just had up a story about – ' Durbeyfield began, and thereupon related in detail to his wife a discussion which had arisen at the inn about the clergy, originated by the fact of his daughter having married into a clerical family. 'They was formerly styled "sir", like my own ancestry,' he said, 'though nowadays their true style, strictly speaking, is "clerk" only.' As Tess had wished that no great publicity should be given to the event, he had mentioned no particulars. He hoped she would remove that prohibition soon. He proposed that the couple should take Tess's own name, d'Urberville, as uncorrupted. It was better than her husband's. He asked if any letter had come from her that day.

Then Mrs Durbeyfield informed him that no letter had come, but Tess unfortunately had come herself.

When at length the collapse was explained to him a sullen

225

mortification, not usual with Durbeyfield, overpowered the influence of the cheering glass. Yet the intrinsic quality of the event moved his touchy sensitiveness less than its conjectured effect upon the minds of others.

'To think, now, that this was to be the end o't!' said Sir John. 'And I with a family vault under that there church of Kingsbere as big as Squire Jollard's alecellar, and my folk lying there in sixes and sevens, as genuine county bones and marrow as any recorded in history. And now to be sure what they fellers at Rolliver's and The Pure Drop will say to me! How they'll squint and glane, and say, "This is yer mighty match is it; this is yer getting back to the true level of yer forefathers in King Norman's time!" I feel this is too much, Joan; I shall put an end to myself, title and all – I can bear it no longer! . . . But she can make him keep her if he's married her?'

'Why, yes. But she won't think o' doing that.'

'D'ye think he really have married her? – or is it like the first – '

Poor Tess, who had heard as far as this, could not bear to hear more. The perception that her word could be doubted even here, in her own parental house, set her mind against the spot as nothing else could have done. How unexpected were the attacks of destiny! And if her father doubted her a little, would not neighbours and acquaintance doubt her much? O, she could not live long at home!

A few days, accordingly, were all that she allowed herself here, at the end of which time she received a short note from Clare, informing her that he had gone to the North of England to look at a farm. In her craving for the lustre of her true position as his wife, and to hide from her parents the vast extent of the division between them, she made use of this letter as her reason for again departing, leaving them under the impression that she was setting out to join him. Still further to screen her husband from any imputation of unkindness to her, she took twenty-five pounds of the fifty pounds Clare had given her, and handed the sum over to her mother, as if the wife of a man like Angel Clare could well afford it, saying that it was a slight return for the trouble and humiliation she had brought upon them in years past. With this assertion of her dignity she bade them farewell; and after that there were lively doings in the Durbeyfield household for some time on the strength of Tess's bounty, her mother saying, and, indeed, believing, that the rupture which had arisen between the young husband and wife had adjusted itself under their strong feeling that they could not live apart from each other.

❧ Chapter Thirty-Nine ❧

IT WAS THREE WEEKS AFTER the marriage that Clare found himself descending the hill which led to the well-known parsonage of his father. With his downward course the tower of the church rose into the evening sky in a manner of inquiry as to why he had come; and no living person in the twilighted town seemed to notice him, still less to expect him. He was arriving like a ghost, and the sound of his own footsteps was almost an encumbrance to be got rid of.

The picture of life had changed for him. Before this time he had known it but speculatively; now he thought he knew it as a practical man; though perhaps he did not, even yet. Nevertheless humanity stood before him no longer in the pensive sweetness of Italian art, but in the staring and ghastly attitudes of a Wiertz Museum, and with the leer of a study by Van Beers.

His conduct during these first weeks had been desultory beyond description. After mechanically attempting to pursue his agricultural plans as though nothing unusual had happened, in the manner recommended by the great and wise men of all ages, he concluded that very few of those great and wise men had ever gone so far outside themselves as to test the feasibility of their counsel. 'This is the chief thing: be not perturbed,' said the Pagan moralist. That was just Clare's own opinion. But he was perturbed. 'Let not your heart be troubled, neither let it be afraid,' said the Nazarene. Clare chimed in cordially; but his heart was troubled all the same. How he would have liked to confront those two great thinkers, and earnestly appeal to them as fellow-man to fellow-men, and ask them to tell him their method!

His mood transmuted itself into a dogged indifference till at length he fancied he was looking on his own existence with the passive interest of an outsider.

He was embittered by the conviction that all this desolation had been brought about by the accident of her being a d'Urberville. When he found that Tess came of that exhausted ancient line, and was not of the new tribes from below, as he had fondly dreamed, why had he not stoically abandoned her, in fidelity to his principles? This was what he had got by apostasy, and his punishment was deserved.

Then he became weary and anxious, and his anxiety increased. He wondered if he had treated her unfairly. He ate without knowing that he ate, and drank without tasting. As the hours dropped past, as the motive of each act in the long series of bygone days presented itself to his view, he perceived how intimately the notion of having Tess as a dear possession was mixed up with all his schemes and words and ways.

In going hither and thither he observed in the outskirts of a small town a red-and-blue placard setting forth the great advantages of the Empire of Brazil as a field for the emigrating agriculturalist. Land was offered there on exceptionally advantageous terms. Brazil somewhat attracted him as a new idea. Tess could eventually join him there, and perhaps in that country of contrasting scenes and notions and habits the conventions would not be so operative which made life with her seem impracticable to him here. In brief he was strongly inclined to try Brazil, especially as the season for going thither was just at hand.

With this view he was returning to Emminster to disclose his plan to his parents, and to make the best explanation he could make of arriving without Tess, short of revealing what had actually separated them. As he reached the door the new moon shone upon his face, just as the old one had done in the small hours of that morning when he had carried his wife in his arms across the river to the graveyard of the monks; but his face was thinner now.

Clare had given his parents no warning of his visit, and his arrival stirred the atmosphere of the Vicarage as the dive of the kingfisher stirs a quiet pool. His father and mother were both in the drawing-room, but neither of his brothers was now at home. Angel entered, and closed the door quietly behind him.

'But – where's your wife, dear Angel?' cried his mother. 'How you surprise us!'

'She is at her mother's – temporarily. I have come home rather in a hurry because I've decided to go to Brazil.'

'Brazil! Why they are all Roman Catholics there surely!'

'Are they? I hadn't thought of that.'

But even the novelty and painfulness of his going to a Papistical land could not displace for long Mr and Mrs Clare's natural interest in their son's marriage.

'We had your brief note three weeks ago announcing that it had taken place,' said Mrs Clare, 'and your father sent your godmother's gift to her, as you know. Of course it was best that none of us should be present, especially as you preferred to marry her from the dairy, and not at her home, wherever that may be. It would have embarrassed you, and given us no pleasure. Your brothers felt that very strongly. Now it is done we do not complain, particularly if she suits you for the business you have chosen to follow instead of the ministry of the Gospel ... Yet I wish I could have seen her first, Angel, or have known a little more about her. We sent her no present of our own, not knowing what would best give her pleasure, but you must suppose it only delayed. Angel, there is no irritation in my mind or your father's against you for this marriage; but we have thought it much better to reserve our liking for your wife till we could see her. And now you have not brought her. It seems strange. What has happened?'

He replied that it had been thought best by them that she should go to her parents' home for the present, whilst he came there.

'I don't mind telling you, dear mother,' he said, 'that I always meant to keep her away from this house till I should feel she could come with credit to you. But this idea of Brazil is quite a recent one. If I do go it will be unadvisable for me to take her on this my first journey. She will remain at her mother's till I come back.'

'And I shall not see her before you start?'

He was afraid they would not. His original plan had been, as he had said, to refrain from bringing her there for some little while – not to wound their prejudices – feelings – in any way; and for other reasons he had adhered to it. He would have to visit home in the course of a year, if he went out at once; and it would be possible for them to see her before he started a second time – with her.

A hastily prepared supper was brought in, and Clare made further exposition of his plans. His mother's disappointment at not seeing the bride still remained with her. Clare's late enthusiasm for Tess had infected her through her maternal sympathies, till she had almost fancied that a good thing could come out of Nazareth – a charming woman out of Talbothays Dairy. She watched her son as he ate.

'Cannot you describe her? I am sure she is very pretty, Angel.'

'Of that there can be no question!' he said, with a zest which covered its bitterness.

'And that she is pure and virtuous goes without question?'

'Pure and virtuous, of course, she is.'

'I can see her quite distinctly. You said the other day that she was fine in figure; roundly built; had deep red lips like Cupid's bow; dark eye-lashes and brows, an immense rope of hair like a ship's cable; and large eyes violety-bluey-blackish.'

'I did, mother.'

'I quite see her. And living in such seclusion she naturally had scarce ever seen any young man from the world without till she saw you.'

'Scarcely.'

'You were her first love?'

'Of course.'

'There are worse wives than these simple, rosy-mouthed, robust girls of the farm. Certainly I could have wished – well, since my son is to be an agriculturist, it is perhaps but proper that his wife should have been accustomed to an outdoor life.'

His father was less inquisitive; but when the time came for the chapter from the Bible which was always read before evening prayers, the Vicar observed to Mrs Clare –

'I think, since Angel has come, that it will be more appropriate to read the thirty-first of Proverbs than the chapter which we should have had in the usual course of our reading?'

'Yes, certainly,' said Mrs Clare. 'The words of King Lemuel' (she could cite chapter and verse as well as her husband). 'My dear son, your father has decided to read us the chapter in Proverbs in praise of a virtuous wife. We shall not need to be reminded to apply the words to the absent one. May Heaven shield her in all her ways!'

A lump rose in Clare's throat. The portable lectern was taken out from the corner and set in the middle of the fireplace, the two old servants came in, and Angel's father began to read at the tenth verse of the aforesaid chapter – ' "Who can find a virtuous woman? for her price is far above rubies. She riseth while it is yet night, and giveth meat to her household. She girdeth her loins with strength and strengtheneth her arms. She perceiveth that her merchandise is good; her candle goeth not out by night. She looketh well to the ways of her household, and eateth not the bread of idleness. Her children arise up and call her blessed; her husband also, and he praiseth her. Many daughters have done virtuously, but thou excellest them all." '

When prayers were over, his mother said –

'I could not help thinking how very aptly that chapter your dear father read applied, in some of its particulars, to the woman you have chosen. The perfect woman, you see, was a working woman; not an idler; not a fine lady; but one who used her hands and her head and her heart for the good of others. "Her children arise up and call her blessed; her husband also, and he praiseth her. Many daughters have done virtuously, but she excelleth them all." Well, I wish I could have seen her, Angel. Since she is pure and chaste she would have been refined enough for me.'

Clare could bear this no longer. His eyes were full of tears, which seemed like drops of molten lead. He bade a quick good-night to these sincere simple souls whom he loved so well; who knew neither the world, the flesh, nor the devil in their own hearts; only as something vague and external to themselves. He went to his own chamber.

His mother followed him, and tapped at his door. Clare opened it to discover her standing without, with anxious eyes.

'Angel,' she asked, 'is there something wrong that you go away so soon? I am quite sure you are not yourself.'

'I am not, quite, mother,' he said.

'About her? Now, my son, I know it is that – I know it is about her! Have you quarrelled in these three weeks?

'We have not exactly quarrelled,' he said. 'But we have had a difference – '

'Angel – is she a young woman whose history will bear investigation?'

With a mother's instinct Mrs Clare had put her finger on the kind of trouble that would cause such a disquiet as seemed to agitate her son.

'She is spotless!' he replied; and felt that if it had sent him to eternal hell there and then he would have told that lie.

'Then never mind the rest. After all, there are few purer things in nature than an unsullied country maid. Any crudeness of manner which may offend your more educated sense at first, will, I am sure, disappear under the influence of your companionship and tuition.'

Such terrible sarcasm of blind magnanimity brought home to Clare the secondary perception that he had utterly wrecked his career by his marriage, which had not been among his early thoughts after the disclosure. True, on his own account he cared very little about his career; but he had wished to make it at least a respectable one on account of his parents and brothers. And now as he looked into the candle its flame dumbly expressed to him that it was made to shine on sensible people, and that it abhorred lighting the face of a dupe and a failure.

When his agitation had cooled he would be at moments incensed with his poor wife for causing a situation in which he was obliged to practise deception on his parents. He almost talked to her in his anger, as if she had been in the room. And then her cooing voice, plaintive in expostulation, disturbed the darkness, the velvet touch of her lips passed over his brow, and he could distinguish in the air the warmth of her breath.

This night the woman of his belittling deprecations was thinking how great and good her husband was. But over them both there hung a deeper shade than the shade which Angel Clare perceived, namely, the shade of his own limitations. With all his attempted independence of judgment this advanced and well-meaning young man, a sample product of the last five-and-twenty years, was yet the slave to custom and conventionality when surprised back into his early teachings. No prophet had told him, and he was not prophet enough to tell himself, that essentially this young wife of his was as deserving of the praise of King Lemuel as any other woman endowed with the same dislike of evil, her moral value having to be reckoned not by achievement but by tendency. Moreover, the figure near at hand suffers on such occasions, because it shows up its sorriness without shade; while vague figures afar off are honoured, in that their distance makes artistic virtues of their stains. In considering what Tess was not, he overlooked what she was, and forgot that the defective can be more than the entire.

❧ Chapter Forty ❧

AT BREAKFAST BRAZIL WAS the topic, and all endeavoured to take a hopeful view of Clare's proposed experiment with that country's soil, notwithstanding the discouraging reports of some farm-labourers who had emigrated thither and returned home within the twelve months. After breakfast Clare went into the little town to wind up such trifling matters as he was concerned with there, and to get from the local bank all the money he possessed. On his way back he encountered Miss Mercy Chant by the church, from whose walls she seemed to be a sort of emanation. She was carrying an armful of Bibles for her class, and such was her view of life that events which produced heartache in others wrought beatific smiles upon her – an enviable result, although, in the opinion of Angel, it was obtained by a curiously unnatural sacrifice of humanity to mysticism.

She had learnt that he was about to leave England, and observed what an excellent and promising scheme it seemed to be.

'Yes; it is a likely scheme enough in a commercial sense, no doubt,' he replied. 'But, my dear Mercy, it snaps the continuity of existence. Perhaps a cloister would be preferable.'

'A cloister! O, Angel Clare!'

'Well.'

'Why, you wicked man, a cloister implies a monk, and a monk Roman Catholicism.'

'And Roman Catholicism sin, and sin damnation. Thou art in a parlous state, Angel Clare.'

'*I* glory in my Protestantism!' she said severely.

Then Clare, thrown by sheer misery into one of the demoniacal moods in which a man does despite to his true principles, called her close to him, and fiendishly whispered in her ear the most heterodox ideas he could think of. His momentary laughter at the horror which appeared on her fair face ceased when it merged in pain and anxiety for his welfare.

'Dear Mercy,' he said, 'you must forgive me. I think I am going crazy!'

She thought that he was; and thus the interview ended, and Clare re-entered the Vicarage. With the local banker he deposited the jewels till happier days should arise. He also paid into the bank thirty pounds – to be sent to Tess in a few months, as she might require; and wrote to her at her parents' home in Blackmoor Vale to inform her of what he had done. This amount, with the sum he had already placed in her hands – about fifty pounds – he hoped would be amply sufficient for her wants just at present, particularly as in an emergency she had been directed to apply to his father.

He deemed it best not to put his parents into communication with her by informing them of her address; and, being unaware of what had really happened to estrange the two, neither his father nor his mother suggested that he should do so. During the day he left the parsonage, for what he had to complete he wished to get done quickly.

As the last duty before leaving this part of England it was necessary for him to call at the Wellbridge farmhouse, in which he had spent with Tess the first three days of their marriage, the trifle of rent having to be paid, the key given up of the rooms they had occupied, and two or three small articles fetched away that they had left behind. It was under this roof that the deepest shadow ever thrown upon his life had stretched its gloom over him. Yet when he had unlocked the door of the sitting-room and looked into it, the memory which returned first upon him was that of their happy arrival on a similar afternoon, the first fresh sense of sharing a habitation conjointly, the first meal together, the chatting by the fire with joined hands.

The farmer and his wife were in the fields at the moment of his visit, and Clare was in the rooms alone for some time. Inwardly swollen with a renewal of sentiments that he had not quite reckoned with, he went upstairs to her chamber, which had never been his. The bed was smooth as she had made it with her own hands on the morning of leaving. The mistletoe hung under the tester just as he had placed it. Having been there three or four weeks it was turning colour, and the leaves and berries were wrinkled. Angel took it down and crushed it into the grate. Standing there he for the first time doubted whether his course in this conjuncture had been a wise, much less a generous, one. But had he not been cruelly blinded? In the incoherent multitude of his emotions he knelt down at the bedside wet-eyed. 'O Tess! If you had only told me sooner, I would have forgiven you!' he mourned.

Hearing a footstep below he rose and went to the top of the stairs. At the bottom of the flight he saw a woman standing, and on her turning up her face recognized the pale, dark-eyed Izz Huett.

'Mr Clare,' she said, 'I've called to see you and Mrs Clare, and to inquire if ye be well. I thought you might be back here again.'

This was a girl whose secret he had guessed, but who had not yet guessed his; an honest girl who loved him – one who would have made as good, or nearly as good, a practical farmer's wife as Tess.

'I am here alone,' he said; 'we are not living here now.' Explaining why he had come, he asked, 'Which way are you going home, Izz?'

'I have no home at Talbothays Dairy now, sir,' she said.

'Why is that?'

Izz looked down.

'It was so dismal there that I left! I am staying out this way.' She pointed in a contrary direction, the direction in which he was journeying.

'Well – are you going there now? I can take you if you wish for a lift.'

Her olive complexion grew richer in hue.

'Thank 'ee, Mr Clare,' she said.

He soon found the farmer, and settled the account for his rent and the few other items which had to be considered by reason of the sudden abandonment of the lodgings. On Clare's return to his horse and gig Izz jumped up beside him.

'I am going to leave England, Izz,' he said, as they drove on. 'Going to Brazil.'

'And do Mrs Clare like the notion of such a journey?' she asked.

'She is not going at present – say for a year or so. I am going out to reconnoitre – to see what life there is like.'

They sped along eastward for some considerable distance, Izz making no observation.

'How are the others?' he inquired. 'How is Retty?'

'She was in a sort of nervous state when I zid her last; and so thin and hollow-cheeked that 'a do seem in a decline. Nobody will ever fall in love wi' her any more,' said Izz absently.

'And Marian?'

Izz lowered her voice.

'Marian drinks.'

'Indeed!'

'Yes. The dairyman has got rid of her.'

'And you!'

'I don't drink, and I bain't in a decline. But – I am no great things at singing afore breakfast now!'

'How is that? Do you remember how neatly you used to turn " 'Twas down in Cupid's Gardens" and "The Tailor's Breeches" at morning milking?'

'Ah, yes! When you first came, sir, that was. Not when you had been there a bit.'

'Why was that falling-off?'

Her black eyes flashed up to his face for one moment by way of answer.

'Izz! – how weak of you – for such as I!' he said, and fell into reverie. 'Then – suppose I had asked *you* to marry me?'

'If you had I should have said "Yes", and you would have married a woman who loved 'ee!'

'Really!'

'Down to the ground!' she whispered vehemently. 'O my God! did you never guess it till now!'

By-and-by they reached a branch road to a village.

'I must get down. I live out there,' said Izz abruptly, never having spoken since her avowal.

Clare slowed the horse. He was incensed against his fate, bitterly disposed towards social ordinances; for they had cooped him up in a corner, out of which there was no legitimate pathway. Why not be revenged on society by shaping his future domesticities loosely, instead of kissing the pedagogic rod of convention in this ensnaring manner.

'I am going to Brazil alone, Izz,' said he. 'I have separated from my wife for personal, not voyaging, reasons. I may never live with her again. I may not be able to love you; but – will you go with me instead of her?'

'You truly wish me to go?'

'I do. I have been badly used enough to wish for relief. And you at least love me disinterestedly.'

'Yes – I will go,' said Izz, after a pause.

'You will? You know what it means, Izz?'

'It means that I shall live with you for the time you are over there – that's good enough for me.'

'Remember, you are not to trust me in morals now. But I ought to remind you that it will be wrong-doing in the eyes of civilization – Western civilization, that is to say.'

'I don't mind that; no woman do when it comes to agony-point, and there's no other way!'

'Then don't get down, but sit where you are.'

He drove past the cross-roads, one mile, two miles, without showing any signs of affection.

'You love me very, very much, Izz?' he suddenly asked.

'I do – I have said I do! I loved you all the time we was at the dairy together!'

'More than Tess?'

She shook her head.

'No,' she murmured, 'not more than she.'

'How's that?'

'Because nobody could love'ee more than Tess did! . . . She would have laid down her life for 'ee. I could do no more.'

Like the prophet on the top of Peor Izz Huett would fain have spoken perversely at such a moment, but the fascination exercised over her rougher nature by Tess's character compelled her to grace.

Clare was silent; his heart had risen at these straightforward words from such an unexpected unimpeachable quarter. In his throat was something as if a sob had solidified there. His ears repeated. '*She would have laid down her life for 'ee. I could do no more!*'

'Forget our idle talk, Izz,' he said, turning the horse's head suddenly. 'I don't know what I've been saying! I will now drive you back to where your lane branches off.'

'So much for honesty towards 'ee! O – how can I bear it – how can I – how can I!'

Izz Huett burst into wild tears, and beat her forehead as she saw what she had done.

'Do you regret that poor little act of justice to an absent one? O, Izz, don't spoil it by regret!'

She stilled herself by degrees.

'Very well, sir. Perhaps I didn't know what I was saying, either, wh – when I agreed to go! I wish – what cannot be!'

'Because I have a loving wife already.'

'Yes, yes! You have.'

They reached the corner of the lane which they had passed half an hour earlier, and she hopped down.

'Izz – please, please forget my momentary levity!' he cried. 'It was so ill-considered, so ill-advised!'

'Forget it? Never, never! O, it was no levity to me!'

He felt how richly he deserved the reproach that the wounded cry conveyed, and, in a sorrow that was inexpressible, leapt down and took her hand.

'Well, but, Izz, we'll part friends, anyhow? You don't know what I've had to bear!'

She was a really generous girl, and allowed no further bitterness to mar their adieux.

'I forgive 'ee, sir!' she said.

'Now Izz,' he said, while she stood beside him there, forcing himself to the mentor's part he was far from feeling; I want you to tell Marian when you see her that she is to be a good woman, and not to give way to folly. Promise that, and tell Retty that there are more worthy men than I in the world, that for my sake she is to act wisely and well – remember the words – wisely and well – for my sake. I send this message to them as a dying man to the dying; for I shall never see them again. And you, Izzy, you have saved me by your honest words about my wife from an incredible impulse towards folly and treachery. Women may be bad, but they are not so bad as men in these things! On that one account I can never forget you. Be always the good and sincere girl you have hitherto been; and think of me as a worthless lover, but a faithful friend. Promise.'

She gave the promise.

'Heaven bless and keep you, sir. Good-bye!'

He drove on; but no sooner had Izz turned into the lane, and Clare was out of sight, than she flung herself down on the bank in a fit of racking anguish; and it was with a strained unnatural face that she entered her mother's cottage late that night. Nobody ever was told how Izz spent the dark hours that intervened between Angel Clare's parting from her and her arrival home.

Clare, too, after bidding the girl farewell, was wrought to aching thoughts and quivering lips. But his sorrow was not for Izz. That evening he was within a feather-weight's turn of abandoning his road to the nearest station, and driving across that elevated dorsal line of South Wessex which divided him from his Tess's home. It was neither a contempt for her nature, nor the probable state of her heart, which deterred him.

No; it was a sense that, despite her love, as corroborated by Izz's admission, the facts had not changed. If he was right at first, he was right now. And the momentum of the course on which he had embarked tended to keep him going in it, unless diverted by a stronger, more sustained force than had played upon him this afternoon. He could soon come back to her. He took the train that night for London, and five days after shook hands in farewell of his brothers at the port of embarkation.

❦ Chapter Forty-One ❦

FROM THE FOREGOING EVENTS of the winter-time let us press on to an October day, more than eight months subsequent to the parting of Clare and Tess. We discover the latter in changed conditions; instead of a bride with boxes and trunks which others bore, we see her a lonely woman with a basket and a bundle in her own porterage, as at an earlier time when she was no bride; instead of the ample means that were projected by her husband for her comfort through this probationary period, she can produce only a flattened purse.

After again leaving Marlott, her home, she had got through the spring and summer without any great stress upon her physical powers, the time being mainly spent in rendering light irregular service at dairy-work near Port-Bredy to the west of the Blackmoor Valley, equally remote from her native place and from Talbothays. She preferred this to living on his allowance. Mentally she remained in utter stagnation, a condition which the mechanical occupation rather fostered than checked. Her consciousness was at that other dairy, at that other season, in the presence of the tender lover who had confronted her there – he who, the moment she had grasped him to keep for her own, had disappeared like a shape in a vision.

The dairy-work lasted only till the milk began to lessen, for she had not met with a second regular engagement as at Talbothays, but had done duty as a supernumerary only. However, as harvest was now beginning, she had simply to remove from the pasture to the stubble to find plenty of further occupation, and this continued till harvest was done.

Of the five-and-twenty pounds which had remained to her of Clare's allowance, after deducting the other half of the fifty as a contribution to her parents for the trouble and expense to which she had put them, she had as yet spent but little. But there now followed an unfortunate interval of wet weather, during which she was obliged to fall back upon her sovereigns.

She could not bear to let them go. Angel had put them into her hand, had obtained them bright and new from his bank for her; his touch had consecrated them to souvenirs of himself – they appeared to have had as yet no other history than such as was created by his and her own experiences – and to disperse them was like giving away relics. But she had to do it, and one by one they left her hands.

She had been compelled to send her mother her address from time to time, but she concealed her circumstances. When her money had almost gone a letter from her mother reached her. Joan stated that they were in dreadful difficulty; the autumn rains had gone through the thatch of the house, which required entire renewal; but this could not be done because the previous thatching had never been paid for. New rafters and a new ceiling upstairs also were required, which, with the previous bill, would amount to a sum of twenty pounds. As her husband was a man of means, and had doubtless returned by this time, could she not send them the money?

Tess had thirty pounds coming to her almost immediately from Angel's bankers, and, the case being so deplorable, as soon as the sum was received she sent the twenty as requested. Part of the remainder she was obliged to expend in winter clothing, leaving only a nominal sum for the whole inclement season at hand. When the last pound had gone, a remark of Angel's that whenever she required further resources she was to apply to his father, remained to be considered.

But the more Tess thought of the step the more reluctant was she to take it. The same delicacy, pride, false shame, whatever it may be called, on Clare's account, which had led her to hide from her own parents the prolongation of the estrangement, hindered her in owning to his that she was in want after the fair allowance he had left her. They probably despised her already; how much more they would despise her in the character of a mendicant! The consequence was that by no effort could the parson's daughter-in-law bring herself to let him know her state.

Her reluctance to communicate with her husband's parents might, she thought, lessen with the lapse of time; but with her own the reverse obtained. On her leaving their house after the short visit subsequent to her marriage they were under the impression that she was ultimately going to join her husband; and from that time to the present she had done nothing to disturb their belief that she was awaiting his return in comfort, hoping against hope that his journey to Brazil would result in a short stay only, after which he would come to fetch her, or that he would write for her to join him; in any case that they would soon present a united front to their families and the world. This hope she still fostered. To let her parents know that she was a deserted wife, dependent, now that she had relieved their necessities, on her own hands for a living, after the *éclat* of a marriage which was to nullify the collapse of the first attempt, would be too much indeed.

The set of brilliants returned to her mind. Where Clare had deposited them she did not know, and it mattered little, if it were true that she could only use and not sell them. Even were they absolutely hers it would be passing mean to enrich herself by a legal title to them which was not essentially hers at all.

Meanwhile her husband's days had been by no means free from trial. At this moment he was lying ill of fever in the clay lands near Curitiba in Brazil, having been drenched with thunder-storms and persecuted by other hardships, in common with all the English farmers and farm-labourers who, just at this time, were deluded into going thither by the promises of the Brazilian Government, and by the baseless assumption that those frames which, ploughing and sowing on English uplands, had resisted all the weathers to whose moods they had been born, could resist equally well all the weathers by which they were surprised on Brazilian plains.

To return. Thus it happened that when the last of Tess's sovereigns had been spent she was unprovided with others to take their place, while on account of the season she found it increasingly difficult to get employment. Not being aware of the rarity of intelligence, energy, health, and willingness in any sphere of life, she refrained from seeking an indoor occupation; fearing towns, large houses, people of means and social sophistication, and of manners other than rural. From that direction of gentility Black Care had come. Society might be better than she supposed from her slight experience of it. But she had no proof of this, and her instinct in the circumstances was to avoid its purlieus.

The small dairies to the west, beyond Port-Bredy, in which she had served as supernumerary milkmaid during the spring and summer required no further aid. Room would probably have been made for her at Talbothays, if only out of sheer compassion; but comfortable as her life had been there she could not go back. The anti-climax would be too intolerable; and her return might bring reproach upon her idolized husband. She could not have borne their pity, and their whispered remarks to one another upon her strange situation; though she would almost have faced a knowledge of her circumstances by every individual there, so long as her story had remained isolated in the mind of each. It was the interchange of ideas about her that made her sensitiveness wince. Tess could not account for this distinction; she simply knew that she felt it.

She was on her way to an upland farm in the centre of the county, to which she had been recommended by a wandering letter which had reached her from Marian. Marian has somehow heard that Tess was separated from her husband – probably through Izz Huett – and the good-natured and now tippling girl, deeming Tess in trouble, had hastened to notify to her former friend that she herself had gone to this upland spot after leaving the dairy, and would like to see her there, where there was room for other hands, if it was really true that she worked again as of old.

With the shortening of the days all hope of obtaining her husband's forgiveness began to leave her; and there was something of the habitude of the wild animal in the unreflecting instinct with which she rambled on – disconnecting herself by littles from her eventful past at every step, obliterating her identity, giving no thought to accidents or contingencies which might make a quick discovery of her whereabouts by others of importance to her own happiness, if not to theirs.

Among the difficulties of her lonely position not the least was the attention she excited by her appearance, a certain bearing of distinction, which she had caught from Clare, being superadded to her natural attractiveness. Whilst the clothes lasted which had been prepared for her marriage, these casual glances of interest caused her no inconvenience, but as soon as she was compelled to don the wrapper of a fieldwoman, rude words were addressed to her more than once; but nothing occurred to cause her bodily fear till a particular November afternoon.

She had preferred the country west of the River Brit to the upland farm for which she was now bound, because, for one thing, it was nearer to the home of her husband's father; and to hover about that region unrecognized, with the notion that she might decide to call at the

Vicarage some day, gave her pleasure. But having once decided to try the higher and drier levels, she pressed back eastward, marching afoot towards the village of Chalk-Newton, where she meant to pass the night.

The lane was long and unvaried, and, owing to the rapid shortening of the days, dusk came upon her before she was aware. She had reached the top of a hill down which the lane stretched its serpentine length in glimpses, when she heard footsteps behind her back, and in a few moments she was overtaken by a man. He stepped up alongside Tess and said –

'Good-night, my pretty maid': to which she civilly replied.

The light still remaining in the sky lit up her face, though the landscape was nearly dark. The man turned and stared hard at her.

'Why, surely, it is the young wench who was at Trantridge awhile – young Squire d'Urberville's friend? I was there at that time, though I don't live there now.'

She recognized in him the well-to-do boor whom Angel had knocked down at the inn for addressing her coarsely. A spasm of anguish shot through her, and she returned him no answer.

'Be honest enough to own it, and that what I said in the town was true, though your fancy-man was so up about it – hey, my sly one? You ought to beg my pardon for that blow of his, considering.'

Still no answer came from Tess. There seemed only one escape for her hunted soul. She suddenly took to her heels with the speed of the wind, and, without looking behind her, ran along the road till she came to a gate which opened directly into a plantation. Into this she plunged, and did not pause till she was deep enough in its shade to be safe against any possibility of discovery.

Under foot the leaves were dry, and the foliage of some holly bushes which grew among the deciduous trees was dense enough to keep off draughts. She scraped together the dead leaves till she had formed them into a large heap, making a sort of nest in the middle. Into this Tess crept.

Such sleep as she got was naturally fitful; she fancied she heard strange noises, but persuaded herself that they were caused by the breeze. She thought of her husband in some vague warm clime on the other side of the globe, while she was here in the cold. Was there another such a wretched being as she in the world? Tess asked herself; and, thinking of her wasted life, said, 'All is vanity.' She repeated the words mechanically, till she reflected that this was a most inadequate thought for modern days. Solomon had thought as far as that more than two thousand years ago; she herself, though not in the van of thinkers, had got much further. If all were only vanity, who would mind it? All was, alas, worse than vanity – injustice, punishment, exaction, death. The wife of Angel Clare put her hand to her brow, and felt its curve, and the edges of her eye-sockets perceptible under the soft skin, and thought as she did so that a time would come when that bone would be bare. 'I wish it were now,' she said.

In the midst of these whimsical fancies she heard a new strange sound among the leaves. It might be the wind; yet there was scarcely any wind. Sometimes it was a palpitation, sometimes a flutter; sometimes it was a sort of gasp or gurgle. Soon she was certain that the noises came from wild creatures of some kind, the more so when, originating in the boughs overhead, they were followed by the fall of a heavy body upon the ground. Had she been ensconced here under other and more pleasant conditions she would have become alarmed; but, outside humanity, she had at present no fear.

Day at length broke in the sky. When it had been day aloft for some little while it became day in the wood.

Directly the assuring and prosaic light of the world's active hours had grown strong she crept from under her hillock of leaves, and looked around boldly. Then she perceived what had been going on to disturb her. The plantation wherein she had taken shelter ran down at this spot into a peak, which ended it hitherward, outside the hedge being arable ground. Under the trees several pheasants lay about, their rich plumage dabbled with blood; some were dead, some feebly twitching a wing, some staring up at the sky, some pulsating quickly, some contorted, some stretched out – all of them writhing in agony, except the fortunate ones whose tortures had ended during the night by the inability of nature to bear more.

Tess guessed at once the meaning of this. The birds had been driven down into this corner the day before by some shooting-party; and while those that had dropped dead under the shot, or had died before nightfall, had been searched for and carried off, many badly wounded birds had escaped and hidden themselves away, or risen among the thick boughs, where they had maintained their position till they grew weaker with loss of blood in the night-time, when they had fallen one by one as she had heard them.

She had occasionally caught glimpses of these men in girlhood, looking over hedges, or peering through bushes, and pointing their guns, strangely accoutred, a bloodthirsty light in their eyes. She had been told that, rough and brutal as they seemed just then, they were not like this all the year round, but were, in fact, quite civil persons save during certain weeks of autumn and winter, when, like the inhabitants of the Malay Peninsula, they ran amuck, and made it their purpose to destroy life – in this case harmless feathered creatures, brought into being by artificial means solely to gratify these propensities – at once so unmannerly and so unchivalrous towards their weaker fellows in Nature's teeming family.

With the impulse of a soul who could feel for kindred sufferers as much as for herself, Tess's first thought was to put the still living birds out of their torture, and to this end with her own hands she broke the necks of as many as she could find, leaving them to lie where she had found them till the gamekeepers should come – as they probably would come – to look for them a second time.

'Poor darlings – to suppose myself the most miserable being on earth in the sight o' such misery as yours!' she exclaimed, her tears running down as she killed the birds tenderly. 'And not a twinge of bodily pain about me! I be not mangled, and I be not bleeding; and I have two hands to feed and clothe me.' She was ashamed of herself for her gloom of the night, based on nothing more tangible than a sense of condemnation under an arbitrary law of society which had no foundation in Nature.

❧ Chapter Forty-Two ❧

IT WAS NOW BROAD DAY, and she started again, emerging cautiously upon the highway. But there was no need for caution; not a soul was at hand, and Tess went onward with fortitude, her recollection of the birds' silent endurance of their night of agony impressing upon her the relativity of sorrows and the tolerable nature of her own, if she could once rise high enough to despise opinion. But that she could not do so long as it was held by Clare.

She reached Chalk-Newton, and breakfasted at an inn, where several young men were troublesomely complimentary to her good looks. Somehow she felt hopeful, for was it not possible that her husband also might say these same things to her even yet? She was bound to take care of herself on the chance of it, and keep off these casual lovers. To this end Tess resolved to run no further risks from her appearance. As soon as she got out of the village she entered a thicket and took from her basket one of the oldest field-gowns, which she had never put on even at the dairy – never since she had worked among the stubble at Marlott. She also, by a felicitous thought, took a handkerchief from her bundle and tied it round her face under her bonnet, covering her chin and half her cheeks and temples, as if she were suffering from toothache. Then with her little scissors, by the aid of a pocket looking-glass, she mercilessly nipped her eyebrows off, and thus insured against aggressive admiration she went on her uneven way.

'What a mommet of a maid!' said the next man who met her to a companion.

Tears came into her eyes for very pity of herself as she heard him.

'But I don't care!' she said. 'O no – I don't care! I'll always be ugly now, because Angel is not here, and I have nobody to take care of me. My husband that was is gone away, and never will love me any more; but I love him just the same, and hate all other men, and like to make 'em think scornfully of me!'

Thus Tess walks on; a figure which is part of the landscape; a field-woman pure and simple, in winter guise; a gray serge cape, a red woollen cravat, a stuff skirt covered by a whitey-brown rough wrapper, and buff-leather gloves. Every thread of that old attire has become faded and thin under the stroke of raindrops, the burn of sunbeams, and the stress of winds. There is no sign of young passion in her now –

> *The maiden's mouth is cold*
> . . . . .
> *Fold over simple fold*
> *Binding her head.*

Inside this exterior, over which the eye might have roved as over a thing scarcely percipient, almost inorganic, there was the record of a pulsing life which had learnt too well, for its years, of the dust and ashes of things, of the cruelty of lust and the fragility of love.

Next day the weather was bad, but she trudged on, the honesty, directness, and impartiality of elemental enmity disconcerting her but little. Her object being a winter's occupation and a winter's home, there was no time to lose. Her experience of short hirings had been such that she was determined to accept no more.

Thus she went forward from farm to farm in the direction of the place whence Marian had written to her, which she determined to make use of as a last shift only, its rumoured stringencies being the reverse of tempting. First she inquired for the lighter kinds of employment, and, as acceptance in any variety of these grew hopeless, applied next for the less light, till, beginning with the dairy and poultry tendance that she liked best, she ended with the heavy and coarse pursuits which she liked least – work on arable land: work of such roughness, indeed, as she would never have deliberately volunteered for.

Towards the second evening she reached the irregular chalk table-land or plateau, bosomed with semi-globular tumuli – as if Cybele the Many-breasted were supinely extended there – which stretched between the valley of her birth and the valley of her love.

Here the air was dry and cold, and the long cart-roads were blown white and dusty within a few hours after rain. There were few trees, or none, those that would have grown in the hedges being mercilessly plashed down with the quickset by the tenant-farmers, the natural enemies of tree, bush, and brake. In the middle distance ahead of her she could see the summits of Bulbarrow and of Nettlecombe Tout, and they seemed friendly. They had a low and unassuming aspect from this upland, though as approached on the other side from Blackmoor in her childhood they were as lofty bastions against the sky. Southerly, at many miles' distance, and over the hills and ridges coastward, she could discern a surface like polished steel: it was the English Channel at a point far out towards France.

Before her, in a slight depression, were the remains of a village. She had, in fact, reached Flintcomb-Ash, the place of Marian's sojourn. There seemed to be no help for it; hither she was doomed to come. The stubborn soil around her showed plainly enough that the kind of labour in demand here was of the roughest kind; but it was time to rest from searching, and she resolved to stay, particularly as it began to rain. At the entrance to the village was a cottage whose gable jutted into the road, and before applying for a lodging she stood under its shelter, and watched the evening close in.

'Who would think I was Mrs Angel Clare!' she said.

The wall felt warm to her back and shoulders, and she found that immediately within the gable was the cottage fireplace, the heat of which came through the bricks. She warmed her hands upon them, and also put her cheek – red and moist with the drizzle – against their comforting surface. The wall seemed to be the only friend she had. She had so little wish to leave it that she could have stayed there all night.

Tess could hear the occupants of the cottage – gathered together after their day's labour – talking to each other within, and the rattle of their supper-plates was also audible. But in the village-street she had seen no soul as yet. The solitude was at last broken by the approach of one feminine figure, who, though the evening was cold, wore the print gown and the tilt-bonnet of summer time. Tess instinctively thought it might be Marian, and when she came near enough to be distinguishable in the gloom surely enough it was she. Marian was even stouter and redder in the face than formerly, and decidedly shabbier in attire. At any previous period of her existence Tess would hardly have cared to renew the acquaintance in such conditions; but her loneliness was excessive, and she responded readily to Marian's greeting.

Marian was quite respectful in her inquiries, but seemed much moved by the fact that Tess should still continue in no better condition than at first; though she had dimly heard of the separation.

'Tess – Mrs Clare – the dear wife of dear he! And is it really so bad as this, my child? Why is your cwomely face tied up in such a way? Anybody been beating 'ee? Not *he*?'

'No, no, no! I merely did it not to be clipsed or colled, Marian.'

She pulled off in disgust a bandage which could suggest such wild thoughts.

'And you've got no collar on' (Tess had been accustomed to wear a little white collar at the dairy).

'I know it, Marian.'

'You've lost it travelling.'

'I've not lost it. The truth is, I don't care anything about my looks; and so I didn't put it on.'

'And you don't wear your wedding-ring?'

'Yes, I do; but not in public. I wear it round my neck on a ribbon. I don't wish people to think who I am by marriage, or that I am married at all; it would be so awkward while I lead my present life.'

Marian paused.

'But you *be* a gentleman's wife; and it seems hardly fair that you should live like this!'

'O yes it is, quite fair; though I am very unhappy.'

'Well, well. *He* married you – and you can be unhappy!'

'Wives are unhappy sometimes; from no fault of their husbands – from their own.'

'You've no faults, deary; that I'm sure of. And he's none. So it must be something outside ye both.'

'Marian, dear Marian, will you do me a good turn without asking questions? My husband has gone abroad, and somehow I have overrun my allowance, so that I have to fall back upon my old work for a time. Do not call me Mrs Clare, but Tess, as before. Do they want a hand here?'

'O yes; they'll take one always, because few care to come. 'Tis a starve-acre place. Corn and swedes are all they grow. Though I be here myself, I feel 'tis a pity for such as you to come.'

'But you used to be as good a dairywoman as I.'

'Yes; but I've got out o' that since I took to drink. Lord, that's the only comfort I've got now! If you engage, you'll be set swede-hacking. That's what I be doing; but you won't like it.'

'O – anything! Will you speak for me?'

'You will do better by speaking for yourself.'

'Very well. Now, Marian, remember – nothing about *him*, if I get the place. I don't wish to bring his name down to the dirt.'

246

Marian, who was really a trustworthy girl though of coarser grain than Tess, promised anything she asked.

'This pay-night,' she said, 'and if you were to come with me you would know at once. I be real sorry that you are not happy; but 'tis because he's away, I know. You couldn't be unhappy if he were here, even if he gie'd ye no money – even if he used you like a drudge.'

'That's true; I could not!'

They walked on together, and soon reached the farmhouse, which was almost sublime in its dreariness. There was not a tree within sight; there was not, at this season, a green pasture – nothing but fallow and turnips everywhere; in large fields divided by hedges plashed to unrelieved levels.

Tess waited outside the door of the farmhouse till the group of work-folk had received their wages, and then Marian introduced her. The farmer himself, it appeared, was not at home, but his wife, who represented him this evening, made no objection to hiring Tess, on her agreeing to remain till Old Lady-Day. Female field-labour was seldom offered now, and its cheapness made it profitable for tasks which women could perform as readily as men.

Having signed the agreement, there was nothing more for Tess to do at present than to get a lodging, and she found one in the house at whose gable-wall she had warmed herself. It was a poor subsistence that she had ensured, but it would afford a shelter for the winter at any rate.

That night she wrote to inform her parents of her new address, in case a letter should arrive at Marlott from her husband. But she did not tell them of the sorriness of her situation: it might have brought reproach upon him.

◆ Chapter Forty-Three ◆

THERE WAS NO EXAGGERATION in Marian's definition of Flintcomb-Ash farm as a starve-acre place. The single fat thing on the soil was Marian herself; and she was an importation. Of the three classes of village, the village cared for by its lord, the village cared for by itself, and the village uncared for either by itself or by its lord (in other words, the village of a resident squire's tenantry, the village of free or copy-holders, and the absentee-owner's village, farmed with the land) this place, Flintcomb-Ash, was the third.

But Tess set to work. Patience, that blending of moral courage with physical timidity, was now no longer a minor feature in Mrs Angel Clare; and it sustained her.

The swede-field in which she and her companion were set hacking was a stretch of a hundred odd acres, in one patch, on the highest ground of the farm, rising above stony lanchets or lynchets – the outcrop of siliceous veins in the chalk formation, composed of myriads of loose white flints in bulbous, cusped, and phallic shapes. The upper half of each turnip had been eaten off by the livestock, and it was the business of the two women to grub up the lower or earthy half of the root with a hooked fork called a hacker, that it might be eaten also. Each leaf of the vegetable having already been consumed, the whole field was in colour a desolate drab; it was a complexion without features, as if a face, from chin to brow, should be only an expanse of skin. The sky wore, in another colour, the same likeness; a white vacuity of countenance with the lineaments gone. So these two upper and nether visages confronted each other all day long, the white face looking down on the brown face, and the brown face looking up at the white face, without anything standing between them but the two girls crawling over the surface of the former like flies.

Nobody came near them, and their movements showed a mechanical regularity; their forms standing enshrouded in Hessian 'wroppers' – sleeved brown pinafores, tied behind to the bottom, to keep their gowns from blowing about – scant skirts revealing boots that reached high up the ankles, and yellow sheepskin gloves with gauntlets. The pensive character which the curtained hood lent to their bent heads would have reminded the observer of some early Italian conception of the two Marys.

They worked on hour after hour, unconscious of the forlorn aspect they bore in the landscape, not thinking of the justice or injustice of their lot. Even in such a position as theirs it was possible to exist in a dream. In the afternoon the rain came on again, and Marian said that they need not work any more. But if they did not work they would not be paid; so they worked on. It was so high a situation, this field, that the rain had no occasion to fall, but raced along horizontally upon the yelling wind, sticking into them like glass splinters till they were wet through. Tess had not known till now what was really meant by that. There are degrees of dampness, and a very little is called being wet through in common talk. But to stand working slowly in a field, and feel the creep of rain-water, first in legs and shoulders, then on hips and head, then at back, front, and sides, and yet to work on till the leaden light diminishes

248

and marks that the sun is down, demands a distinct modicum of stoicism, even of valour.

Yet they did not feel the wetness so much as might be supposed. They were both young, and they were talking of the time when they lived and loved together at Talbothays Dairy, that happy green tract of land where summer had been liberal in her gifts; in substance to all, emotionally to these. Tess would fain not have conversed with Marian of the man who was legally, if not actually, her husband; but the irresistible fascination of the subject betrayed her into reciprocating Marian's remarks. And thus, as has been said, though the damp curtains of their bonnets flapped smartly into their faces, and their wrappers clung about them to weari-someness, they lived all this afternoon in memories of green, sunny, romantic Talbothays.

'You can see a gleam of a hill within a few miles o' Froom Valley from here when 'tis fine,' said Marian.

'Ah! Can you?' said Tess, awake to the new value of this locality.

So the two forces were at work here as everywhere, the inherent will to enjoy, and the circumstantial will against enjoyment. Marian's will had a method of assisting itself by taking from her pocket as the afternoon wore on a pint bottle corked with white rag, from which she invited Tess to drink. Tess's unassisted power of dreaming, however, being enough for her sublimation at present, she declined except the merest sip, and then Marian took a pull herself from the spirits.

'I've got used to it,' she said, 'and can't leave it off now. 'Tis my only comfort – You see I lost him: you didn't; and you can do without it perhaps.'

Tess thought her loss as great as Marian's, but upheld by the dignity of being Angel's wife, in the letter at least, she accepted Marian's differen-tiation.

Amid this scene Tess slaved in the morning frosts and in the afternoon rains. When it was not swede-grubbing it was swede-trimming, in which process they sliced off the earth and the fibres with a bill-hook before storing the roots for future use. At this occupation they could shelter themselves by a thatched hurdle if it rained; but if it was frosty even their thick leather gloves could not prevent the frozen masses they handled from biting their fingers. Still Tess hoped. She had a conviction that sooner or later the magnanimity which she persisted in reckoning as a chief ingredient of Clare's character would lead him to rejoin her.

Marian, primed to a humorous mood, would discover the queer-shaped flints aforesaid, and shriek with laughter, Tess remaining severely obtuse. They often looked across the country to where the Var or Froom was known to stretch, even though they might not be able to see it; and, fixing their eyes on the cloaking gray mist, imagined the old times they had spent out there.

'Ah,' said Marian, 'how I should like another or two of our old set to come here! Then we could bring up Talbothays every day here afield, and talk of he, and of what nice times we had there, and o' the old things we used to know, and make it all come back again a'most, in seeming!' Marian's eyes softened, and her voice grew vague as the visions returned. 'I'll write to Izz Huett,' she said. 'She's biding at home doing nothing now, I know, and I'll tell her we be here, and ask her to come; and perhaps Retty is well enough now.'

Tess had nothing to say against the proposal, and the next she heard of this plan for importing old Talbothay's joys was two or three days later, when Marian informed her that Izz had replied to her inquiry, and had promised to come if she could.

There had not been such a winter for years. It came on in stealthy and measured glides, like the moves of a chess-player. One morning the few lonely trees and the thorns of the hedgerows appeared as if they had put off a vegetable for an animal integument. Every twig was covered with a white nap as of fur grown from the rind during the night, giving it four times its usual stoutness; the whole bush or tree forming a staring sketch in white lines on the mournful gray of the sky and horizon. Cobwebs revealed their presence on sheds and walls where none had ever been observed till brought out into visibility by the crystallizing atmosphere, hanging like loops of white worsted from salient points of the out-houses, posts, and gates.

After this season of congealed dampness came a spell of dry frost, when strange birds from behind the North Pole began to arrive silently on the upland of Flintcomb-Ash; gaunt spectral creatures with tragical eyes – eyes which had witnessed scenes of cataclysmal horror in inaccessible polar regions of a magnitude such as no human being had ever conceived, in curdling temperatures that no man could endure; which had beheld the crash of icebergs and the slide of snow-hills by the shooting light of the Aurora; been half blinded by the whirl of colossal storms and terraqueous distortions; and retained the expression of feature that such scenes had engendered. These nameless birds came quite near to Tess and Marian, but of all they had seen which humanity would never see, they brought no account. The traveller's ambition to tell was not theirs, and, with dumb impassivity, they dismissed experiences which they did not value for the immediate incidents of this homely upland – the trivial movements of the two girls in disturbing the clods with their hackers so as to uncover something or other that these visitants relished as food.

Then one day a peculiar quality invaded the air of this open country.

There came a moisture which was not of rain, and a cold which was not of frost. It chilled the eyeballs of the twain, made their brows ache, penetrated to their skeletons, affecting the surface of the body less than its core. They knew that it meant snow, and in the night the snow came. Tess, who continued to live at the cottage with the warm gable that cheered any lonely pedestrian who paused beside it, awoke in the night, and heard above the thatch noises which seemed to signify that the roof had turned itself into a gymnasium of all the winds. When she lit her lamp to get up in the morning she found that the snow had blown through a chink in the casement, forming a white cone of the finest powder against the inside, and had also come down the chimney, so that it lay sole-deep upon the floor, on which her shoes left tracks when she moved about. Without, the storm drove so fast as to create a snow-mist in the kitchen; but as yet it was too dark out-of-doors to see anything.

Tess knew that it was impossible to go on with the swedes; and by the time she had finished breakfast beside the solitary little lamp, Marian arrived to tell her that they were to join the rest of the women at reed-drawing in the barn till the weather changed. As soon, therefore, as the uniform cloak of darkness without began to turn to a disordered medley of grays, they blew out the lamp, wrapped themselves up in their thickest pinners, tied their woollen cravats round their necks and across their chests, and started for the barn. The snow had followed the birds from the polar basin as a white pillar of a cloud, and individual flakes could not be seen. The blast smelt of icebergs, arctic seas, whales, and white bears, carrying the snow so that it licked the land but did not deepen on it. They trudged onwards with slanted bodies through the flossy fields, keeping as well as they could in the shelter of hedges, which, however, acted as strainers rather than screens. The air, afflicted to pallor with the hoary multitudes that infested it, twisted and spun them eccentrically, suggesting an achromatic chaos of things. But both the young women were fairly cheerful; such weather on a dry upland is not in itself dispiriting.

'Ha-ha! the cunning northern birds knew this was coming,' said Marian. 'Depend upon't, they keep just in front o't all the way from the North Star. Your husband, my dear, is, I make no doubt, having scorching weather all this time. Lord, if he could only see his pretty wife now! Not that this weather hurts your beauty at all – in fact, it rather does it good.'

'You mustn't talk about him to me, Marian,' said Tess severely.

'Well, but – surely you care for 'n! Do you?'

Instead of answering, Tess, with tears in her eyes, impulsively faced in the direction in which she imagined South America to lie, and, putting up her lips, blew out a passionate kiss upon the snowy wind.

'Well, well, I know you do. But 'pon my body, it is a rum life for a married couple! There – I won't say another word! Well, as for the weather, it won't hurt us in the wheat-barn; but reed-drawing is fearful hard work – worse than swedehacking. I can stand it because I'm stout; but you be slimmer than I. I can't think why maister should have set 'ee at it.'

They reached the wheat-barn and entered it. One end of the long structure was full of corn; the middle was where the reed-drawing was carried on, and there had already been placed in the reed-press the evening before as many sheaves of wheat as would be sufficient for the women to draw from during the day.

'Why, here's Izz!' said Marian.

Izz it was, and she came forward. She had walked all the way from her mother's home on the previous afternoon, and, not deeming the distance so great, had been belated, arriving, however, just before the snow began, and sleeping at the ale-house. The farmer had agreed with her mother at market to take her on if she came to-day, and she had been afraid to disappoint him by delay.

In addition to Tess, Marian, and Izz, there were two women from a neighbouring village; two Amazonian sisters, whom Tess with a start remembered as Dark Car the Queen of Spades and her junior the Queen of Diamonds – those who had tried to fight with her in the midnight quarrel at Trantridge. They showed no recognition of her, and possibly had none, for they had been under the influence of liquor on that occasion, and were only temporary sojourners there as here. They did all kinds of men's work by preference, including well-sinking, hedging, ditching, and excavating, without any sense of fatigue. Noted reed-drawers were they too, and looked round upon the other three with some superciliousness.

Putting on their gloves all set to work in a row in front of the press, an erection formed of two posts connected by a cross-beam, under which the sheaves to be drawn from were laid ears outward, the beam being pegged down by pins in the uprights, and lowered as the sheaves diminished.

The day hardened in colour, the light coming in at the barn-door upwards from the snow instead of downwards from the sky. The girls pulled handful after handful from the press; but by reason of the presence of the strange women, who were recounting scandals, Marian and Izz could not at first talk of old times as they wished to do. Presently they heard the muffled tread of a horse, and the farmer rode up to the barn-door. When he had dismounted he came close to Tess, and remained looking musingly at the side of her face. She had not turned at first, but his fixed attitude led her to look round, when she perceived that her employer was the native of Trantridge from whom she had taken flight on the high-road because of his allusion to her history.

He waited till she had carried the drawn bundles to the pile outside, when he said, 'So you be the young woman who took my civility in such ill part? Be drowned if I didn't think you might be as soon as I heard of your being hired! Well, you thought you had got the better of me the first time at the inn with your fancy-man, and the second time on the road, when you bolted; but now I think I've got the better of you.' He concluded with a hard laugh.

Tess, between the Amazons and the farmer like a bird caught in a clap-net, returned no answer, continuing to pull the straw. She could read character sufficiently well to know by this time that she had nothing to fear from her employer's gallantry; it was rather the tyranny induced by his mortification at Clare's treatment of him. Upon the whole she preferred that sentiment in man and felt brave enough to endure it.

'You thought I was in love with 'ee I suppose? Some women are such fools, to take every look as serious earnest. But there's nothing like a winter afield for taking that nonsense out o' young wenches' heads; and you've signed and agreed till Lady-Day. Now, are you going to beg my pardon?'

'I think you ought to beg mine.'

'Very well – as you like. But we'll see which is master here. Be they all the sheaves you've done to-day?'

'Yes, sir.'

''Tis a very poor show. Just see what they've done over there' (pointing to the two stalwart women). 'The rest, too, have done better than you.'

'They've all practised it before, and I have not. And I thought it made no difference to you as it is task work, and we are only paid for what we do.'

'Oh, but it does. I want the barn cleared.'

'I am going to work all the afternoon instead of leaving at two as the others will do.'

He looked sullenly at her and went away. Tess felt that she could not have come to a much worse place; but anything was better than gallantry. When two o'clock arrived the professional reed-drawers tossed off the last half-pint in their flagon, put down their hooks, tied their last sheaves, and went away. Marian and Izz would have done likewise, but on hearing that Tess meant to stay, to make up by longer hours for her lack of skill, they would not leave her. Looking out at the snow, which still fell, Marian exclaimed, 'Now we've got it all to ourselves.' And so at last the conversation turned to their old experiences at the dairy; and, of course, the incidents of their affection for Angel Clare.

'Izz and Marian,' said Mrs Angel Clare, with a dignity which was extremely touching, seeing how very little of a wife she was: 'I can't join in talk with you now, as I used to do, about Mr Clare; you will see that I cannot; because, although he is gone away from me for the present, he is my husband.'

Izz was by nature the sauciest and most caustic of all the four girls who had loved Clare. 'He was a very splendid lover, no doubt,' she said; 'but I don't think he is a too fond husband to go away from you so soon.'

'He had to go – he was obliged to go, to see about the land over there!' pleaded Tess.

'He might have tided 'ee over the winter.'

'Ah – that's owing to an accident – a misunderstanding; and we won't argue it,' Tess answered, with tearfulness in her words. 'Perhaps there's a good deal to be said for him! He did not go away, like some husbands, without telling me; and I can always find out where he is.'

After this they continued for some long time in a reverie, as they went on seizing the ears of corn, drawing out the straw, gathering it under their arms, and cutting off the ears with their bill-hooks, nothing sounding in the barn but the swish of the straw and the crunch of the hook. Then Tess suddenly flagged, and sank down upon the heap of wheat-ears at her feet.

'I knew you wouldn't be able to stand it!' cried Marian. 'It wants harder flesh than yours for this work.'

Just then the farmer entered. 'Oh, that's how you get on when I am away,' he said to her.

'But it is my own loss,' she pleaded. 'Not yours.'

'I want it finished.' he said doggedly, as he crossed the barn and went out at the other door.

'Don't 'ee mind him, there's a dear,' said Marian. 'I've worked here before. Now you go and lie down there, and Izz and I will make up your number.'

'I don't like to let you do that. I'm taller than you, too.'

However, she was so overcome that she consented to lie down awhile, and reclined on a heap of pull-tails – the refuse after the straight straw had been drawn – thrown up at the further side of the barn. Her succumbing had been as largely owing to agitation at re-opening the subject of her separation from her husband as to the hard work. She lay in a state of percipience without volition, and the rustle of the straw and the cutting of the ears by the others had the weight of bodily touches.

She could hear from her corner, in addition to these noises, the murmur of their voices. She felt certain that they were continuing the subject already broached, but their voices were so low that she could not catch the words. At last Tess grew more and more anxious to know what they were saying, and, persuading herself that she felt better, she got up and resumed work.

Then Izz Huett broke down. She had walked more than a dozen miles the previous evening, had gone to bed at midnight, and had risen again at five o'clock. Marian alone, thanks to her bottle of liquor and her stoutness of build, stood the strain upon back and arms without suffering. Tess urged Izz to leave off, agreeing, as she felt better, to finish the day without her, and make equal division of the number of sheaves.

Izz accepted the offer gratefully, and disappeared through the great door into the snowy track to her lodging. Marian, as was the case every afternoon at this time on account of the bottle, began to feel in a romantic vein.

'I should not have thought it of him – never!' she said in a dreamy tone. 'And I loved him so! I didn't mind his having *you*. But this about Izz is too bad!'

Tess, in her start at the words, narrowly missed cutting off a finger with the bill-hook.

'Is it about my husband?' she stammered.

'Well, yes. Izz said, "Don't 'ee tell her;" but I am sure I can't help it! It was what he wanted Izz to do. He wanted her to go off to Brazil with him.'

Tess's face faded as white as the scene without, and its curves straight-ened. 'And did Izz refuse to go?' she asked.

'I don't know. Anyhow he changed his mind.'

'Pooh – then he didn't mean it! 'Twas just a man's jest!'

'Yes he did; for he drove her a good-ways towards the station.'

'He didn't take her!'

They pulled on in silence till Tess, without any premonitory symptoms, burst out crying.

'There!' said Marian. 'Now I wish I hadn't told 'ee!'

'No. It is a very good thing that you have done! I have been living on in a thirtover, lackaday way, and have not seen what it may lead to! I ought to have sent him a letter oftener. He said I could not go to him, but he didn't say I was not to write as often as I liked. I won't dally like this any longer! I have been very wrong and neglectful in leaving everything to be done by him!'

The dim light in the barn grew dimmer, and they could see to work no longer. When Tess had reached home that evening, and had entered into the privacy of her little white-washed chamber, she began impetu-ously writing a letter to Clare. But falling into doubt she could not finish it. Afterwards she took the ring from the ribbon on which she wore it next her heart, and retained it on her finger all night, as if to fortify herself in the sensation that she was really the wife of this elusive lover of hers; who could propose that Izz should go with him abroad, so shortly after he had left her. Knowing that, how could she write entreaties to him, or show that she cared for him any more?

❧ Chapter Forty-Four ❧

By the disclosure in the barn her thoughts were led anew in the direction which they had taken more than once of late – to the distant Emminster Vicarage. It was through her husband's parents that she had been charged to send a letter to Clare if she desired; and to write to them direct if in difficulty. But that sense of her having morally no claim upon him had always led Tess to suspend her impulse to send these notes; and to the family at the Vicarage, therefore, as to her own parents since her marriage, she was virtually non-existent. This self-effacement in both directions had been quite in consonance with her independent character of desiring nothing by way of favour or pity to which she was not entitled on a fair consideration of her deserts. She had set herself to stand or fall by her qualities, and to waive such merely technical claims upon a strange family as had been established for her by the flimsy fact of a member of that family, in a season of impulse, writing his name in a church-book beside hers.

But now that she was stung to a fever by Izz's tale there was a limit to her powers of renunciation. Why had her husband not written to her? He had distinctly implied that he would at least let her know of the locality to which he had journeyed; but he had not sent a line to notify his address. Was he really indifferent? But was he ill? Was it for her to make some advance? Surely she might summon the courage of solicitude, call at the Vicarage for intelligence, and express her grief at his silence. If Angel's father were the good man she had heard him represented to be, he would be able to enter into her heart-starved situation. Her social hardships she could conceal.

To leave the farm on a week-day was not in her power; Sunday was the only possible opportunity. Flintcomb-Ash being in the middle of the cretaceous tableland over which no railway had climbed as yet, it would be necessary to walk. And the distance being fifteen miles each way she would have to allow herself a long day for the undertaking by rising early.

A fortnight later, when the snow had gone, and had been followed by a hard black frost, she took advantage of the state of the roads to try the experiment. At four o'clock that Sunday morning she came downstairs and stepped out into the starlight. The weather was still favourable, the ground ringing under her feet like an anvil.

Marian and Izz were much interested in her excursion, knowing that the journey concerned her husband. Their lodgings were in a cottage a little further along the lane, but they came and assisted Tess in her departure, and argued that she should dress up in her very prettiest guise to captivate the hearts of her parents-in-law; though she, knowing of the austere and Calvinistic tenets of old Mr Clare, was indifferent, and even doubtful. A year had now elapsed since her sad marriage, but she had preserved sufficient draperies from the wreck of her then full wardrobe to clothe her very charmingly as a simple country girl with no pretensions to recent fashion; a soft gray woollen gown, with white crape quilling against the pink skin of her face and neck, and a black velvet jacket and hat.

'Tis a thousand pities your husband can't see 'ee now – you do look a real beauty!' said Izz Huett, regarding Tess as she stood on the threshold between the steely starlight without and the yellow candlelight within. Izz spoke with a magnanimous abandonment of herself to the situation; she could not be – no woman with a heart bigger than a hazel-nut could be – antagonistic to Tess in her presence, the influence which she exercised over those of her own sex being of a warmth and strength quite unusual, curiously overpowering the less worthy feminine feelings of spite and rivalry.

With a final tug and touch here, and a slight brush there, they let her go; and she was absorbed into the pearly air of the fore-dawn. They heard her footsteps tap along the hard road as she stepped out to her full pace. Even Izz hoped she would win, and, though without any particular respect for her own virtue, felt glad that she had been prevented wronging her friend when momentarily tempted by Clare.

It was a year ago, all but a day, that Clare had married Tess, and only a few days less than a year that he had been absent from her. Still, to start on a brisk walk, and on such an errand as hers, on a dry clear wintry morning, through the rarefied air of these chalky hogs'-backs, was not depressing; and there is no doubt that her dream at starting was to win the heart of her mother-in-law, tell her whole history to that lady, enlist her on her side, and so gain back the truant.

In time she reached the edge of the vast escarpment below which stretched the loamy Vale of Blackmoor, now lying misty and still in the dawn. Instead of the colourless air of the uplands the atmosphere down there was a deep blue. Instead of the great enclosures of a hundred acres in which she was now accustomed to toil there were little fields below her of less than half-a-dozen acres, so numerous that they looked from this height like the meshes of a net. Here the landscape was whitey-brown; down there, as in Froom Valley, it was always green. Yet it was in that vale that her sorrow had taken shape, and she did not love it as formerly. Beauty to her, as to all who have felt, lay not in the thing, but in what the thing symbolized.

Keeping the Vale on her right she steered steadily westward; passing above the Hintocks, crossing at right-angles the high-road from Sherton-Abbas to Casterbridge, and skirting Dogbury Hill and High-Stoy, with the dell between them called 'The Devil's Kitchen'. Still following the elevated way she reached Cross-in-Hand, where the stone pillar stands desolate and silent, to mark the site of a miracle, or murder, or both. Three miles further she cut across the straight and deserted Roman road called Long-Ash Lane; leaving which as soon as she reached it she dipped down a hill by a transverse lane into the small town or village of Evershead, being now about half-way over the distance. She made a halt here, and breakfasted a second time, heartily enough – not at the Sow-and-Acorn, for she avoided inns, but at a cottage by the church.

The second half of her journey was through a more gentle country, by way of Benvill Lane. But as the mileage lessened between her and the spot of her pilgrimage, so did Tess's confidence decrease, and her enterprise loom out more formidably. She saw her purpose in such staring lines, and the landscape so faintly, that she was sometimes in danger of losing her way. However, about noon she paused by a gate on the edge of the basin in which Emminster and its Vicarage lay.

The square tower, beneath which she knew that at that moment the Vicar and his congregation were gathered, had a severe look in her eyes. She wished that she had somehow contrived to come on a week-day. Such a good man might be prejudiced against a woman who had chosen Sunday, never realizing the necessities of her case. But it was incumbent upon her to go on now. She took off the thick boots in which she had walked thus far, put on her pretty thin ones of patent leather, and, stuffing the former into the hedge by the gate-post where she might readily find them again, descended the hill; the freshness of colour she had derived from the keen air thinning away in spite of her as she drew near the parsonage.

Tess hoped for some accident that might favour her, but nothing favoured her. The shrubs on the Vicarage lawn rustled uncomfortably in the frosty breeze; she could not feel by any stretch of imagination, dressed to her highest as she was, that the house was the residence of near relations; and yet nothing essential, in nature or emotion, divided her from them: in pains, pleasures, thoughts, birth, death, and after-death, they were the same.

She nerved herself by an effort, entered the swing-gate, and rang the door-bell. The thing was done; there could be no retreat. No; the thing was not done. Nobody answered to her ringing. The effort had to be risen to and made again. She rang a second time, and the agitation of the act, coupled with her weariness after the fifteen miles' walk, led her to support herself while she waited by resting her hand on her hip, and her elbow against the wall of the porch. The wind was so nipping that the ivy-leaves had become wizened and gray, each tapping incessantly upon its neighbour with a disquieting stir of her nerves. A piece of blood-stained paper, caught up from some meatbuyer's dust-heap, beat up and down the road without the gate; too flimsy to rest, too heavy to fly away; and a few straws kept it company.

The second peal had been louder, and still nobody came. Then she walked out of the porch, opened the gate, and passed through. And though she looked dubiously at the house-front as if inclined to return, it was with a breath of relief that she closed the gate. A feeling haunted her that she might have been recognized (though how she could not tell), and orders been given not to admit her.

Tess went as far as the corner. She had done all she could do; but determined not to escape present trepidation at the expense of future distress, she walked back again quite past the house, looking up at all the windows.

Ah – the explanation was that they were all at church, every one. She remembered her husband saying that his father always insisted upon the household, servants included, going to morning-service, and, as a consequence, eating cold food when they came home. It was, therefore, only necessary to wait till the service was over. She would not make herself conspicuous by waiting on the spot, and she started to get past the church into the lane. But as she reached the churchyard-gate the people began pouring out, and Tess found herself in the midst of them.

The Emminster congregation looked at her as only a congregation of small country-townsfolk walking home at its leisure can look at a woman out of the common whom it perceives to be a stranger. She quickened her pace, and ascended the road by which she had come, to find a retreat between its hedges till the Vicar's family should have lunched, and it might be convenient for them to receive her. She soon distanced the churchgoers, except two youngish men, who, linked arm-in-arm, were beating up behind her at a quick step.

As they drew nearer she could hear their voices engaged in earnest discourse, and, with the natural quickness of a woman in her situation, did not fail to recognize in those voices the quality of her husband's tones. The pedestrians were his two brothers. Forgetting all her plans, Tess's one dread was lest they should overtake her now, in her disorganized condition, before she was prepared to confront them; for though she felt that they could not identify her she instinctively dreaded their scrutiny. The more briskly they walked the more briskly walked she. They were plainly bent upon taking a short quick stroll before going indoors to lunch or dinner, to restore warmth to limbs chilled with sitting through a long service.

Only one person had preceded Tess up the hill – a ladylike young woman, somewhat interesting, though, perhaps, a trifle *guindée* and prudish. Tess had nearly overtaken her when the speed of her brothers-in-law brought them so nearly behind her back that she could hear every word of their conversation. They said nothing, however, which particularly interested her till, observing the young lady still further in front, one of them remarked, 'There is Mercy Chant. Let us overtake her.'

Tess knew the name. It was the woman who had been destined for Angel's life-companion by his and her parents, and whom he probably would have married but for her intrusive self. She would have known as much without previous information if she had waited a moment, for one of the brothers proceeded to say: 'Ah! poor Angel, poor Angel! I never see that nice girl without more and more regretting his precipitancy in throwing himself away upon a dairymaid, or whatever she may be. It is a queer business, apparently. Whether she has joined him yet or not I don't know; but she had not done so some months ago when I heard from him.'

'I can't say. He never tells me anything nowadays. His ill-considered marriage seems to have completed that estrangement from me which was begun by his extraordinary opinions.'

Tess beat up the long hill still faster; but she could not outwalk them without exciting notice. At last they outsped her altogether, and passed her by. The young lady still further ahead heard their footsteps and turned. Then there was a greeting and a shaking of hands, and the three went on together.

They soon reached the summit of the hill, and, evidently intending this point to be the limit of their promenade, slackened pace and turned all three aside to the gate whereat Tess had paused an hour before that time to reconnoitre the town before descending into it. During their discourse one of the clerical brothers probed the hedge carefully with his umbrella, and dragged something to light.

'Here's a pair of old boots,' he said. 'Thrown away, I suppose, by some tramp or other.'

'Some impostor who wished to come into the town barefoot, perhaps, and so excite our sympathies,' said Miss Chant. 'Yes, it must have been, for they are excellent walking-boots – by no means worn out. What a wicked thing to do! I'll carry them home for some poor person.'

Cuthbert Clare, who had been the one to find them, picked them up for her with the crook of his stick; and Tess's boots were appropriated.

She, who had heard this, walked past under the screen of her woollen veil, till, presently looking back, she perceived that the church party had left the gate with her boots and retreated down the hill.

Thereupon our heroine resumed her walk. Tears, blinding tears, were running down her face. She knew that it was all sentiment, all baseless impressibility, which had caused her to read the scene as her own condemnation; nevertheless she could not get over it; she could not contravene in her own defenceless person all these untoward omens. It was impossible to think of returning to the Vicarage. Angel's wife felt almost as if she had been hounded up that hill like a scorned thing by those – to her – super-fine clerics. Innocently as the slight had been inflicted, it was somewhat unfortunate that she had encountered the son and not the father, who, despite his narrowness, was far less starched and ironed than they, and had to the full the gift of charity. As she again thought of her dusty boots she almost pitied those habiliments for the quizzing to which they had been subjected, and felt how hopeless life was for their owner.

'Ah!' she said, still sighing in pity of herself, '*they* didn't know that I wore those over the roughest part of the road to save these pretty ones *he* bought for me – no – they did not know it! And they didn't think that *he* chose the colour o' my pretty frock – no – how could they? If they had known perhaps they would not have cared, for they don't care much for him, poor thing!'

Then she grieved for the beloved man whose conventional standard of judgment had caused her all these latter sorrows; and she went her way without knowing that the greatest misfortune of her life was this feminine loss of courage at the last and critical moment through her estimating her father-in-law by his sons. Her present condition was precisely one which would have enlisted the sympathies of old Mr and Mrs Clare. Their hearts went out of them at a bound towards extreme cases, when the subtle mental troubles of the less desperate among mankind failed to win their interest or regard. In jumping at Publicans and Sinners they would forget that a word might be said for the worries of Scribes and Pharisees; and this defect or limitation might have recommended their own daughter-in-law to them at this moment as a fairly choice sort of lost person for their love.

Thereupon she began to plod back along the road by which she had come not altogether full of hope, but full of a conviction that a crisis in her life was approaching. No crisis, apparently, had supervened; and there was nothing left for her to do but to continue upon that starve-acre farm till she could again summon courage to face the vicarage. She did, indeed, take sufficient interest in herself to throw up her veil on this return journey, as if to let the world see that she could at least exhibit a face such as Mercy Chant could not show. But it was done with a sorry shake of the head. 'It is nothing – it is nothing!' she said. 'Nobody loves it; nobody sees it. Who cares about the looks of a castaway like me!'

Her journey back was rather a meander than a march. It had no sprightliness, no purpose; only a tendency. Along the tedious length of Benvill Lane she began to grow tired, and she leant upon gates and paused by milestones.

She did not enter any house till, at the seventh or eight mile, she descended the steep long hill below which lay the village or townlet of Evershead, where in the morning she had breakfasted with such contrasting expectations. The cottage by the church, in which she again sat down, was almost the first at that end of the village, and while the woman fetched her some milk from the pantry, Tess, looking down the street, perceived that the place seemed quite deserted.

'The people are gone to afternoon service, I suppose?' she said.

'No, my dear,' said the old woman. ''Tis too soon for that; the bells hain't strook out yet. They be all gone to hear the preaching in yonder barn. A ranter preaches there between the services – an excellent, fiery, Christian man, they say. But, Lord, I don't go to hear'n! What comes in the regular way over the pulpit is hot enough for I.'

Tess soon went onward into the village, her footsteps echoing against the houses as though it were a place of the dead. Nearing the central part her echoes were intruded on by other sounds; and seeing the barn not far off the road, she guessed these to be the utterances of the preacher.

His voice became so distinct in the still clear air that she could soon catch his sentences, though she was on the closed side of the barn. The sermon, as might be expected, was of the extremest antinomian type; on justification by faith, as expounded in the theology of St Paul. This fixed idea of the rhapsodist was delivered with animated enthusiasm, in a manner entirely declamatory, for he had plainly no skill as a dialectician. Although Tess had not heard the beginning of the address, she learnt what the text had been from its constant iteration –

'O foolish Galatians, who hath bewitched you, that ye should not obey the truth, before whose eyes Jesus Christ hath been evidently set forth, crucified among you?'

Tess was all the more interested, as she stood listening behind, in finding that the preacher's doctrine was a vehement form of the views of Angel's father, and her interest intensified when the speaker began to detail his own spiritual experiences of how he had come by those views. He had, he said, been the greatest of sinners. He had scoffed; he had wantonly associated with the reckless and the lewd. But a day of awakening had come, and, in a human sense, it had been brought about mainly by the influence of a certain clergyman, whom he had at first grossly insulted; but whose parting words had sunk into his heart, and had remained there, till by the grace of Heaven they had worked this change in him, and made him what they saw him.

But more startling to Tess than the doctrine had been the voice, which, impossible as it seemed, was precisely that of Alec d'Urberville. Her face fixed in painful suspense she came round to the front of the barn, and passed before it. The low winter sun beamed directly upon the great double-doored entrance on this side; one of the doors being open, so that the rays stretched far in over the threshing-floor to the preacher and his audience, all snugly sheltered from the northern breeze. The listeners were entirely villagers, among them being the man whom she had seen carrying the red paint-pot on a former memorable occasion. But her attention was given to the central figure, who stood upon some sacks of corn, facing the people and the door. The three o'clock sun shone full upon him, and the strange enervating conviction that her seducer confronted her, which had been gaining ground in Tess ever since she had heard his words distinctly, was at last established as a fact indeed.

PHASE THE SIXTH

The Convert

❧ Chapter Forty-Five ❧

TILL THIS MOMENT SHE HAD never seen or heard from d'Urberville since her departure from Trantridge.

The encounter came at a heavy moment, one of all moments calculated to permit its impact with the least emotional shock. But such was unreasoning memory that, though he stood there openly and palpably a converted man, who was sorrowing for his past irregularities, a fear overcame her, paralyzing her movement so that she neither retreated nor advanced.

To think of what emanated from that countenance when she saw it last, and to behold it now! . . . There was the same handsome unpleasantness of mien, but now he wore neatly trimmed, old-fashioned whiskers, the sable moustache having disappeared; and his dress was half-clerical, a modification which had changed his expression sufficiently to abstract the dandyism from his features, and to hinder for a second her belief in his identity.

To Tess's sense there was, just at first, a ghastly *bizarrerie*, a grim incongruity, in the march of these solemn words of Scripture out of such a mouth. This too familiar intonation, less than four years earlier, had brought to her ears expressions of such divergent purpose that her heart became quite sick at the irony of the contrast.

It was less a reform than a transfiguration. The former curves of sensuousness were now modulated to lines of devotional passion. The lip-shapes that had meant seductiveness were now made to express supplication; the glow on the cheek that yesterday could be translated as riotousness was evangelized to-day into the splendour of pious rhetoric; animalism had become fanaticism; Paganism Paulinism; the bold rolling eye that had flashed upon her form in the old time with such mastery now beamed with the rude energy of a theolatry that was almost ferocious. Those black angularities which his face had used to put on when his wishes were thwarted now did duty in picturing the incorrigible backslider who would insist upon turning again to his wallowing in the mire.

The lineaments, as such, seemed to complain. They had been diverted from their hereditary connotation to signify impressions for which nature did not intend them. Strange that their very elevation was a misapplication, that to raise seemed to falsify.

Yet could it be so? She would admit the ungenerous sentiment no longer. D'Urberville was not the first wicked man who had turned away from his wickedness to save his soul alive, and why should she deem it unnatural in him? It was but the usage of thought which had been jarred in her at hearing good new words in bad old notes. The greater the sinner the greater the saint; it was not necessary to dive far into Christian history to discover that.

Such impressions as these moved her vaguely, and without strict definiteness. As soon as the nerveless pause of her surprise would allow her to stir, her impulse was to pass on out of his sight. He had obviously not discerned her yet in her position against the sun.

But the moment that she moved again he recognized her. The effect upon her old lover was electric, far stronger than the effect of his presence upon her. His fire, the tumultuous ring of his eloquence, seemed to go out of him. His lip struggled and trembled under the words that lay upon it; but deliver them it could not as long as she faced him. His eyes, after their first glance upon her face, hung confusedly in every other direction but hers, but came back in a desperate leap every few seconds. This paralysis lasted, however, but a short time; for Tess's energies returned with the atrophy of his, and she walked as fast as she was able past the barn and onward.

As soon as she could reflect it appalled her, this change in their relative platforms. He who had wrought her undoing was now on the side of the Spirit, while she remained unregenerate. And, as in the legend, it had resulted that her Cyprian image had suddenly appeared upon his altar, whereby the fire of the priest has been wellnigh extinguished.

She went on without turning her head. Her back seemed to be endowed with a sensitiveness to ocular beams – even her clothing – so alive was she to a fancied gaze which might be resting upon her from the outside of that barn. All the way along to this point her heart had been heavy with an inactive sorrow; now there was a change in the quality of its trouble. That hunger for affection too long withheld was for the time displaced by an almost physical sense of an implacable past which still engirdled her. It intensified her consciousness of error to a practical despair; the break of continuity between her earlier and present existence, which she had hoped for, had not, after all, taken place. Bygones would never be complete bygones till she was a bygone herself.

Thus absorbed she recrossed the northern part of Long-Ash Lane at right angles, and presently saw before her the road ascending whitely to the upland along whose margin the remainder of her journey lay. Its dry pale surface stretched severely onward, unbroken by a single figure, vehicle, or mark, save some occasional brown horse-droppings which dotted its cold aridity here and there. While slowly breasting this ascent Tess became conscious of footsteps behind her, and turning she saw approaching that well-known form – so strangely accoutred as the Methodist – the one personage in all the world she wished not to encounter alone on this side of the grave.

There was not much time, however, for thought or elusion, and she yielded as calmly as she could to the necessity of letting him overtake her. She saw that he was excited, less by the speed of his walk than by the feelings within him.

'Tess!' he said.

She slackened speed without looking round.

'Tess!' he repeated. 'It is I – Alec d'Urberville.'

She then looked back at him, and he came up.

'I see it is,' she answered coldly.

'Well – is that all? Yet I deserve no more! Of course,' he added, with a slight laugh, 'there is something of the ridiculous to your eyes in seeing me like this. But – I must put up with that ... I heard you had gone away, nobody knew where. Tess, you wonder why I have followed you?'

'I do, rather; and I would that you had not, with all my heart!'

'Yes – you may well say it,' he returned grimly, as they moved onward together, she with unwilling tread. 'But don't mistake me; I beg this because you may have been led to do so in noticing – if you did notice it – how your sudden appearance unnerved me down there. It was but a momentary faltering; and considering what you had been to me, it was natural enough. But will helped me through it – though perhaps you think me a humbug for saying it – and immediately afterwards I felt that, of all persons in the world whom it was my duty and desire to save from the wrath to come – sneer if you like – the woman whom I had so grievously wronged was that person. I have come with that sole purpose in view – nothing more.'

There was the smallest vein of scorn in her words of rejoinder: 'Have you saved yourself? Charity begins at home, they say.'

'I have done nothing!' said he indifferently. 'Heaven, as I have been telling my hearers, has done all. No amount of contempt that you can pour on me, Tess, will equal what I have poured upon myself – the old Adam of my former years! Well, it is a strange story; believe it or not; but I can tell you the means by which my conversion was brought about, and I hope you will be interested enough at least to listen. Have you ever heard the name of the parson of Emminster – you must have done so? – old Mr Clare; one of the most earnest of his school; one of the few intense men left in the Church; not so intense as the extreme wing of Christian believers with which I have thrown in my lot, but quite an

268

exception among the Established clergy, the younger of whom are gradually attenuating the true doctrines by their sophistries, till they are but the shadow of what they were. I only differ from him on the question of Church and State – the interpretation of the text, "Come out from among them and be ye separate, saith the Lord" – that's all. He is one who, I firmly believe, has been the humble means of saving more souls in this country than any other man you can name. You have heard of him?'

'I have,' she said.

'He came to Trantridge two or three years ago to preach on behalf of some missionary society; and I, wretched fellow that I was, insulted him when, in his disinterestedness, he tried to reason with me and show me the way. He did not resent my conduct, he simply said that some day I should receive the first-fruits of the Spirit – that those who came to scoff sometimes remained to pray. There was a strange magic in his words. They sank into my mind. But the loss of my mother hit me most; and by degrees I was brought to see daylight. Since then my one desire has been to hand on the true view to others, and that is what I was trying to do to-day; though it is only lately that I have preached hereabout. The first months of my ministry have been spent in the North of England among strangers, where I preferred to make my earliest clumsy attempts, so as to acquire courage before undergoing that severest of all tests of one's sincerity, addressing those who have known one, and have been one's companions in the days of darkness. If you could only know, Tess, the pleasure of having a good slap at yourself, I am sure – '

'Don't go on with it!' she cried passionately, as she turned away from him to a stile by the wayside, on which she bent herself. 'I can't believe in such sudden things! I feel indignant with you for talking to me like this, when you know – when you know what harm you've done me! You, and those like you, take your fill of pleasure on earth by making the life of such as me bitter and black with sorrow; and then it is a fine thing, when you have had enough of that, to think of securing your pleasure in heaven by becoming converted! Out upon such – I don't believe in you – I hate it!'

'Tess,' he insisted; 'don't speak so! It came to me like a jolly new idea! And you don't believe me? What don't you believe?'

'Your conversion. Your scheme of religion.'

'Why?'

She dropped her voice. 'Because a better man than you does not believe in such.'

'What a woman's reason! Who is this better man?'

'I cannot tell you.'

'Well,' he declared, a resentment beneath his words seeming ready to

269

spring out at a moment's notice. 'God forbid that I should say I am a good man – and you know I don't say any such thing. I am new to goodness, truly; but new comers see furthest sometimes.'

'Yes,' she replied sadly. 'But I cannot believe in your conversion to a new spirit. Such flashes as you feel, Alec, I fear don't last!'

Thus speaking she turned from the stile over which she had been leaning, and faced him; whereupon his eyes, falling casually upon the familiar countenance and form, remained contemplating her. The inferior man was quiet in him now; but it was surely not extracted, nor even entirely subdued.

'Don't look at me like that!' he said abruptly.

Tess, who had been quite unconscious of her action and mien, instantly withdrew the large dark gaze of her eyes, stammering with a flush, 'I beg your pardon!' And there was revived in her the wretched sentiment which had often come to her before, that in inhabiting the fleshly tabernacle with which nature had endowed her she was somehow doing wrong.

'No, no! Don't beg my pardon. But since you wear a veil to hide your good looks, why don't you keep it down?'

She pulled down the veil, saying hastily, 'It was mostly to keep off the wind.'

'It may seem harsh of me to dictate like this,' he went on; 'but it is better that I should not look too often on you. It might be dangerous.'

'Ssh!' said Tess.

'Well, women's faces have had too much power over me already for me not to fear them! An evangelist has nothing to do with such as they; and it reminds me of the old times that I would forget!'

After this their conversation dwindled to a casual remark now and then as they rambled onward, Tess inwardly wondering how far he was going with her, and not liking to send him back by positive mandate. Frequently when they came to a gate or stile they found painted thereon in red or blue letters some text of Scripture, and she asked him if he knew who had been at the pains to blazon these announcements. He told her that the man was employed by himself and others who were working with him in that district, to paint these reminders that no means might be left untried which might move the hearts of a wicked generation.

At length the road touched the spot called 'Cross-in-Hand'. Of all spots on the bleached and desolate upland this was the most forlorn. It was so far removed from the charm which is sought in landscape by artists and view-lovers as to reach a new kind of beauty, a negative beauty of tragic tone. The place took its name from a stone pillar which stood there, a strange rude monolith, from a stratum unknown in any local quarry, on which was roughly carved a human hand. Differing accounts were given of its history and purport. Some authorities stated that a devotional cross had once formed the complete erection thereon, of which the present relic was but the stump; others that the stone as it stood was entire, and that it had been fixed there to mark a boundary or place of meeting. Anyhow, whatever the origin of the relic, there was and is something sinister, or solemn, according to mood, in the scene amid which it stands; something tending to impress the most phlegmatic passer-by.

'I think I must leave you now,' he remarked, as they drew near to this spot. 'I have to preach at Abbot's-Cernel at six this evening, and my way lies across to the right from here. And you upset me somewhat too, Tessy – I cannot, will not, say why. I must go away and get strength . . . How is it that you speak so fluently now? Who has taught you such good English?'

'I have learnt things in my troubles,' she said evasively.

'What troubles have you had?'

She told him of the first one – the only one that related to him.

D'Urberville was struck mute. 'I knew nothing of this till now!' he next murmured. 'Why didn't you write to me when you felt your trouble coming on?'

She did not reply; and he broke the silence by adding: 'Well – you will see me again.'

'No,' she answered. 'Do not again come near me!'

'I will think. But before we part come here.' He stepped up to the pillar. 'This was once a Holy Cross. Relics are not in my creed; but I fear you at moments – far more than you need fear me at present; and to lessen my fear, put your hand upon that stone hand, and swear that you will never tempt me – by your charms or ways.'

'Good God – how can you ask what is so unnecessary! All that is furthest from my thought!'

'Yes – but swear it.'

Tess, half frightened, gave way to his importunity; placed her hand upon the stone and swore.

'I am sorry you are not a believer,' he continued; 'that some unbeliever should have got hold of you and unsettled your mind. But no more now. At home at least I can pray for you; and I will; and who knows what may not happen? I'm off. Good-bye!'

He turned to a hunting-gate in the hedge, and without letting his eyes again rest upon her leapt over, and struck out across the down in the direction of Abbot's-Cemel. As he walked his pace showed perturbation, and by-and-by, as if instigated by a former thought, he drew from his pocket a small book, between the leaves of which was folded a letter, worn and soiled, as from much re-reading. D'Urberville opened the letter. It was dated several months before this time, and was signed by Parson Clare.

The letter began by expressing the writer's unfeigned joy at d'Urberville's conversion, and thanked him for his kindness in communicating with the parson on the subject. It expressed Mr Clare's warm assurance of forgiveness for d'Urberville's former conduct, and his interest in the young man's plans for the future. He, Mr Clare, would much have liked to see d'Urberville in the Church to whose ministry he had devoted so many years of his own life, and would have helped him to enter a theological college to that end; but since his correspondent had possibly not cared to do this on account of the delay it would have entailed, he was not the man to insist upon its paramount importance. Every man must work as he could best work, and in the method towards which he felt impelled by the Spirit.

D'Urberville read and re-read this letter, and seemed to quiz himself cynically. He also read some passages from memoranda as he walked till his face assumed a calm, and apparently the image of Tess no longer troubled his mind.

She meanwhile had kept along the edge of the hill by which lay her nearest way home. Within the distance of a mile she met a solitary shepherd.

'What is the meaning of that old stone I have passed?' she asked of him. 'Was it ever a Holy Cross?'

'Cross – no; 'twer not a cross! 'Tis a thing of ill-omen, Miss. It was put up in wuld times by the relations of a malefactor who was tortured there by nailing his hand to a post and afterwards hung. The bones lie underneath. They say he sold his soul to the devil, and that he walks at times.'

She felt the *petite mort* at this unexpectedly gruesome information, and left the solitary man behind her. It was dusk when she drew near to Flintcomb-Ash, and in the lane at the entrance to the hamlet she approached a girl and her lover without their observing her. They were talking no secrets, and the clear unconcerned voice of the young woman, in response to the warmer accents of the man, spread into the chilly air as the one soothing thing within the dusky horizon, full of a stagnant obscurity upon which nothing else intruded. For a moment the voices cheered the heart of Tess, till she reasoned that this interview had its origin, on one side or the other, in the same attraction which had been the prelude to her own tribulation. When she came close the girl turned serenely and recognized her, the young man walking off in embarrassment. The woman was Izz Huett, whose interest in Tess's excursion immediately superseded her own proceedings. Tess did not explain very clearly its results, and Izz, who was a girl of tact, began to speak of her own little affair, a phase of which Tess had just witnessed.

'He is Amby Seedling, the chap who used to sometimes come and help at Talbothays,' she explained indifferently. 'He actually inquired and found out that I had come here, and has followed me. He says he's been in love wi' me these two years. But I've hardly answered him.'

❧ Chapter Forty-Six ❧

SEVERAL DAYS HAD PASSED since her futile journey, and Tess was afield. The dry winter wind still blew, but a screen of thatched hurdles erected in the eye of the blast kept its force away from her. On the sheltered side was a turnip-slicing machine, whose bright blue hue of new paint seemed almost vocal in the otherwise subdued scene. Opposite its front was a long mound or 'grave', in which the roots had been preserved since early winter. Tess was standing at the uncovered end, chopping off with a bill-hook the fibres and earth from each root, and throwing it after the operation into the slicer. A man was turning the handle of the machine, and from its trough came the newly-cut swedes, the fresh smell of whose yellow chips was accompanied by the sounds of the snuffling wind, the smart swish of the slicing-blades, and the choppings of the hook in Tess's leather-gloved hand.

The wide acreage of blank agricultural brownness, apparent where the swedes had been pulled, was beginning to be striped in wales of darker brown, gradually broadening to ribands. Along the edge of each of these something crept upon ten legs, moving without haste and without rest up and down the whole length of the field; it was two horses and a man, the plough going between them, turning up the cleared ground for a spring sowing.

For hours nothing relieved the joyless monotony of things. Then, far beyond the ploughing-teams, a black speck was seen. It had come from the corner of a fence, where there was a gap, and its tendency was up the incline, towards the swede-cutters. From the proportions of a mere point it advanced to the shape of a ninepin, and was soon perceived to be a man in black, arriving from the direction of Flintcomb-Ash. The man at the slicer, having nothing else to do with his eyes, continually observed the comer, but Tess, who was occupied, did not perceive him till her companion directed her attention to his approach.

It was not her hard taskmaster, Farmer Groby; it was one in a semi-clerical costume, who now represented what had once been the free-and-easy Alec d'Urberville. Not being hot at his preaching there was less enthusiasm about him now, and the presence of the grinder seemed to embarrass him. A pale distress was already on Tess's face, and she pulled her curtained hood further over it.

D'Urberville came up and said quietly –

'I want to speak to you, Tess.'

'You have refused my last request, not to come near me!' said she.

'Yes, but I have a good reason.'

'Well, tell it.'

'It is more serious than you may think.'

He glanced round to see if he were overheard. They were at some distance from the man who turned the slicer, and the movement of the machine, too, sufficiently prevented Alec's words reaching other ears. D'Urberville placed himself so as to screen Tess from the labourer, turning his back to the latter.

'It is this,' he continued, with capricious compunction. 'In thinking of your soul and mine when we last met, I neglected to inquire as to your worldly condition. You were well dressed, and I did not think of it. But I see now that it is hard – harder than it used to be when I – knew you – harder than you deserve. Perhaps a good deal of it is owing to me!'

She did not answer, and he watched her inquiringly, as, with bent head, her face completely screened by the hood, she resumed her trimming of the swedes. By going on with her work she felt better able to keep him outside her emotions.

'Tess,' he added, with a sigh of discontent, – 'yours was the very worst case I ever was concerned in! I had no idea of what had resulted till you told me. Scamp that I was to foul that innocent life! The whole blame was mine – the whole unconventional business of our time at Trantridge. You, too, the real blood of which I am but the base imitation, what a blind young thing you were as to possibilities! I say in all earnestness that it is a shame for parents to bring up their girls in such dangerous ignorance of the gins and nets that the wicked may set for them, whether their motive be a good one or the result of simple indifference.'

Tess still did no more than listen, throwing down one globular root and taking up another with automatic regularity, the pensive contour of the mere fieldwoman alone marking her.

'But it is not that I came to say,' d'Urberville went on. 'My circumstances are these. I have lost my mother since you were at Trantridge, and the place is my own. But I intend to sell it, and devote myself to missionary work in Africa. A devil of a poor hand I shall make at the trade, no doubt. However, what I want to ask you is, will you put it in my power to do my duty – to make the only reparation I can make for the trick played you: that is, will you be my wife, and go with me? ... I have already obtained this precious document. It was my mother's dying wish.'

He drew a piece of parchment from his pocket, with a slight fumbling of embarrassment.

'What is it?' said she.

'A marriage licence.'

'O no, sir – no!' she said quickly, starting back.

'You will not? Why is that?'

And as he asked the question a disappointment which was not entirely the disappointment of thwarted duty crossed d'Urberville's face. It was unmistakably a sympton that something of his old passion for her had been revived; duty and desire ran hand-in-hand.

'Surely,' he began again, in more impetuous tones, and then looked round at the labourer who turned the slicer.

Tess, too, felt that the argument could not be ended there. Informing the man that a gentleman had come to see her, with whom she wished to walk a little way, she moved off with d'Urberville across the zebra-striped field. When they reached the first newly-ploughed section he held out his hand to help her over it; but she stepped forward on the summits of the earth-rolls as if she did not see him.

'You will not marry me, Tess, and make me a self-respecting man?' he repeated, as soon as they were over the furrows.

'I cannot.'

'But why?'

'You know I have no affection for you.'

'But you would get to feel that in time, perhaps – as soon as you really could forgive me?'

'Never!'

'Why so positive?'

'I love somebody else.'

The words seemed to astonish him.

'You do?' he cried. 'Somebody else? But has not a sense of what is morally right and proper any weight with you?'

'No, no, no – don't say that!'

'Anyhow, then, your love for this other man may be only a passing feeling which you will overcome – '

'No – no.'

'Yes, yes! Why not?'

'I cannot tell you.'

'You must in honour!'

'Well then . . . I have married him.'

'Ah!' he exclaimed; and he stopped dead and gazed at her.

'I did not wish to tell – I did not mean to!' she pleaded. 'It is a secret here, or at any rate but dimly known. So will you, *please* will you, keep from questioning me? You must remember that we are now strangers.'

'Strangers – are we? Strangers!'

For a moment a flash of his old irony marked his face; but he determinedly chastened it down.

'Is that man your husband?' he asked mechanically, denoting by a sign the labourer who turned the machine.

'That man!' she said proudly. 'I should think not!'

'Who, then?'

'Do not ask what I do not wish to tell!' she begged, and flashed her appeal to him from her upturned face and lash-shadowed eyes.

D'Urberville was disturbed.

'But I only asked for your sake!' he retorted hotly. 'Angels of heaven! – God forgive me for such an expression – I came here, I swear, as I thought for your good. Tess – don't look at me so – I cannot stand your looks! There never were such eyes, surely, before Christianity or since! There – I won't lose my head; I dare not. I own that the sight of you has waked up my love for you, which, I believed, was extinguished with all such feelings. But I thought that our marriage might be a sanctification for us both. "The unbelieving husband is sanctified by the wife, and the unbelieving wife is sanctified by the husband," I said to myself. But my plan is dashed from me; and I must bear the disappointment!'

He moodily reflected with his eyes on the ground.

'Married. Married! . . . Well, that being so,' he added, quite calmly, tearing the licence slowly into halves and putting them in his pocket; 'that being prevented, I should like to do some good to you and your husband, whoever he may be. There are many questions that I am tempted to ask but I will not do so, of course, in opposition to your wishes. Though, if I could know your husband, I might more easily benefit him and you. Is he on this farm?'

'No,' she murmured. 'He is far away.'

'Far away? From *you*? What sort of husband can he be?'

'O, do not speak against him! It was through you! He found out – '

'Ah, is it so! . . . That's sad, Tess!'

'Yes.'

'But to stay away from you – to leave you to work like this!'

'He does not leave me to work!' she cried, springing to the defence of the absent one with all her fervour. 'He don't know it! It is by my own arrangement.'

'Then, does he write?'

'I – I cannot tell you. There are things which are private to ourselves.'

'Of course that means that he does not. You are a deserted wife, my fair Tess!'

In an impulse he turned suddenly to take her hand; the buff-glove was on it, and he seized only the rough leather fingers which did not express the life or shape of those within.

'You must not – you must not!' she cried fearfully, slipping her hand from the glove as from a pocket, and leaving it in his grasp. 'O, will you go away – for the sake of me and my husband – go, in the name of your own Christianity!'

'Yes, yes; I will,' he said abruptly, and thrusting the glove back to her turned to leave. Facing round, however, he said 'Tess, as God is my judge, I meant no humbug in taking your hand!'

A pattering of hoofs on the soil of the field, which they had not noticed in their pre-occupation, ceased close behind them; and a voice reached her ear:

'What the devil are you doing away from your work at this time o'day?'

Farmer Groby had espied the two figures from the distance, and had inquisitively ridden across, to learn what was their business in his field.

'Don't speak like that to her!' said d'Urberville, his face blackening with something that was not Christianity.

'Indeed, Mister! And what mid Methodist pa'sons have to do with she?'

'Who is the fellow?' asked d'Urberville, turning to Tess.

She went close up to him.

'Go – I do beg you!' she said.

'What! And leave you to that tyrant? I can see in his face what a churl he is.'

'He won't hurt me. *He's* not in love with me. I can leave at Lady-Day.'

'Well, I have no right but to obey, I suppose. But – well, good-bye!'

Her defender, whom she dreaded more than her assailant, having reluctantly disappeared, the farmer continued his reprimand, which Tess took with the greatest coolness, that sort of attack being independent of sex. To have as a master this man of stone, who would have cuffed her if he had dared, was almost a relief after her former experiences. She silently walked back towards the summit of the field that was the scene of her labour, so absorbed in the interview which had just taken place that she was hardly aware that the nose of Groby's horse almost touched her shoulders.

'If so be you make an agreement to work for me till Lady-Day, I'll see

277

that you carry it out,' he growled. "Od rot the women – now 'tis one thing, and then 'tis another. But I'll put up with it no longer!'

Knowing very well that he did not harass the other women of the farm as he harassed her out of spite for the flooring he had once received, she did for one moment picture what might have been the result if she had been free to accept the offer just made her of being the monied Alec's wife. It would have lifted her completely out of subjection, not only to her present oppressive employer, but to a whole world who seemed to despise her. 'But no, no!' she said breathlessly; 'I could not have married him now! He is so unpleasant to me.'

That very night she began an appealing letter to Clare, concealing from him her hardships, and assuring him of her undying affection. Any one who had been in a position to read between the lines would have seen that at the back of her great love was some monstrous fear – almost a desperation – as to some secret contingencies which were not disclosed. But again she did not finish her effusion; he had asked Izz to go with him, and perhaps he did not care for her at all. She put the letter in her box, and wondered if it would ever reach Angel's hands.

After this her daily tasks were gone through heavily enough, and brought on the day which was of great import to agriculturists – the day of the Candlemas Fair. It was at this fair that new engagements were entered into for the twelve months following the ensuing Lady-Day, and those of the farming population who thought of changing their places duly attended at the county-town where the fair was held. Nearly all the labourers on Flintcomb-Ash Farm intended flight, and early in the morning there was a general exodus in the direction of the town, which lay at a distance of from ten to a dozen miles over hilly country. Though Tess also meant to leave at the quarter-day she was one of the few who did not go to the fair, having a vaguely-shaped hope that something would happen to render another outdoor engagement unnecessary.

It was a peaceful February day, of wonderful softness for the time, and one would almost have thought that winter was over. She had hardly finished her dinner when d'Urberville's figure darkened the window of the cottage wherein she was a lodger, which she had all to herself to-day.

Tess jumped up, but her visitor had knocked at the door, and she could hardly in reason run away. D'Urberville's knock, his walk up to the door, had some indescribable quality of difference from his air when she last saw him. They seemed to be acts of which the doer was ashamed. She thought that she would not open the door; but, as there was no sense in that either, she arose, and having lifted the latch stepped back quickly. He came in, saw her, and flung himself down into a chair before speaking.

'Tess – I couldn't help it!' he began desperately, as he wiped his heated face, which had also a superimposed flush of excitement. 'I felt that I must call at least to ask how you are. I assure you I had not been thinking of you at all till I saw you that Sunday; now I cannot get rid of your image, try how I may! It is hard that a good woman should do harm to a bad man; yet so it is. If you would only pray for me, Tess!'

The suppressed discontent of his manner was almost pitiable, and yet Tess did not pity him.

'How can I pray for you,' she said, 'when I am forbidden to believe that the great Power who moves the world would alter His plans on my account?'

'You really think that?'

'Yes. I have been cured of the presumption of thinking otherwise.'

'Cured? By whom?'

'By my husband, if I must tell.'

'Ah – your husband – your husband! How strange it seems! I remember you hinted something of the sort the other day. What do you really believe in these matters, Tess?' he asked. 'You seem to have no religion – perhaps owing to me.'

'But I have. Though I don't believe in anything supernatural.'

D'Urberville looked at her with misgiving.

'Then do you think that the line I take is all wrong?'

'A good deal of it.'

'H'm – and yet I've felt so sure about it,' he said uneasily.

'I believe in the *spirit* of the Sermon on the Mount, and so did my dear husband . . . But I don't believe – '

Here she gave her negations.

'The fact is,' said d'Urberville drily, 'whatever your dear husband believed you accept, and whatever he rejected you reject, without the least inquiry or reasoning on your own part. That's just like you women. Your mind is enslaved to his.'

'Ah, because he knew everything!' said she, with a triumphant simplicity of faith in Angel Clare that the most perfect man could hardly have deserved, much less her husband.

'Yes, but you should not take negative opinions wholesale from another person like that. A pretty fellow he must be to teach you such scepticism!'

'He never forced my judgment! He would never argue on the subject with me! But I looked at it in this way; what he believed, after inquiring deep into doctrines, was much more likely to be right than what I might believe, who hadn't looked into doctrines at all.'

'What used he to say? He must have said something?'

She reflected; and with her acute memory for the letter of Angel Clare's remarks, even when she did not comprehend their spirit, she recalled a

279

merciless polemical syllogism that she had heard him use when, as it occasionally happened, he indulged in a species of thinking aloud with her at his side. In delivering it she gave also Clare's accent and manner with reverential faithfulness.

'Say that again,' asked d'Urberville, who has listened with the greatest attention.

She repeated the argument, and d'Urberville thoughtfully murmured the words after her.

'Anything else?' he presently asked.

'He said at another time something like this'; and she gave another, which might possibly have been paralleled in many a work of the pedigree ranging from the *Dictionnaire Philosophique* to Huxley's *Essays*.

'Ah – ha! How do you remember them?'

'I wanted to believe what he believed, though he didn't wish me to; and I managed to coax him to tell me a few of his thoughts. I can't say I quite understand that one; but I know it is right.'

'H'm. Fancy your being able to teach me what you don't know yourself!'

He fell into thought.

'And so I threw in my spiritual lot with his,' she resumed. 'I didn't wish it to be different. What's good enough for him is good enough for me.'

'Does he know that you are as big an infidel as he?'

'No – I never told him – if I am an infidel.'

'Well – you are better off to-day than I am, Tess, after all! You don't believe that you ought to preach my doctrine, and, therefore, do no despite to your conscience in abstaining. I do believe I ought to preach it, but like the devils I believe and tremble, for I suddenly leave off preaching it, and give way to my passion for you.'

'How?'

'Why,' he said aridly; 'I have come all the way here to see you to-day! But I started from home to go to Casterbridge Fair, where I have undertaken to preach the Word from a waggon at half-past two this afternoon, and where all the brethren are expecting me this minute. Here's the announcement.'

He drew from his breast-pocket a poster whereon was printed the day, hour, and the place of meeting, at which he, d'Urberville, would preach the Gospel as aforesaid.

'But how can you get there?' said Tess, looking at the clock.

'I cannot get there! I have come here.'

'What, you have really arranged to preach, and – '

'I have arranged to preach, and I shall not be there – by reason of my burning desire to see a woman whom I once despised! – No, by my word and truth, I never despised you; if I had I should not love you now! Why I did not despise you was on account of your being unsmirched in spite of all; you withdrew yourself from me so quickly and resolutely when you saw the situation; you did not remain at my pleasure; so there was one petticoat in the world for whom I had no contempt, and you are she. But you may well despise me now! I thought I worshipped on the mountains, but I find I still serve in the groves! Ha! ha!'

'O Alec d'Urberville! what does this mean? What have I done!'

'Done?' he said, with a soulless sneer in the word. 'Nothing intentionally. But you have been the means – the innocent means – of my backsliding, as they call it. I ask myself, am I, indeed, one of those "servants of corruption" who, "after they have escaped the pollutions of the world, are again entangled therein and overcome" – whose latter end is worse than their beginning?' He laid his hand on her shoulder. 'Tess, my girl, I was on the way to, at least, social salvation till I saw you again!' he said freakishly shaking her, as if she were a child. 'And why then have you tempted me? I was firm as a man could be till I saw those eyes and that mouth again – surely there never was such a maddening mouth since Eve's!' His voice sank, and a hot archness shot from his own black eyes. 'You temptress, Tess; you dear damned witch of Babylon – I could not resist you as soon as I met you again!'

'I couldn't help your seeing me again!' said Tess, recoiling.

'I know it – I repeat that I do not blame you. But the fact remains. When I saw you ill-used on the farm that day I was nearly mad to think that I had no legal right to protect you – that I could not have it; whilst he who has it seems to neglect you utterly!'

'Don't speak against him – he is absent!' she cried in much excitement. 'Treat him honourably – he has never wronged you! O leave his wife before any scandal spreads that may do harm to his honest name!'

'I will – I will,' he said, like a man awakening from a luring dream. 'I have broken my engagement to preach to those poor drunken boobies at the fair – it is the first time I have played such a practical joke. A month ago I should have been horrified at such a possibility. I'll go away – to swear – and – ah, can I! to keep away.' Then, suddenly: 'One clasp, Tessy – one! Only for old friendship – '

'I am without defence, Alec! A good man's honour is in my keeping – think – be ashamed!'

'Pooh! Well yes – yes!'

He clenched his lips, mortified with himself for his weakness. His eyes were equally barren of worldly and religious faith. The corpses of those old fitful passions which had lain inanimate amid the lines of his face ever since his reformation seemed to wake and come together as in a resurrection. He went out indeterminately.

Though d'Urberville had declared that this breach of his engagement to-day was the simple backsliding of a believer, Tess's words, as echoed from Angel Clare, had made a deep impression upon him, and continued to do so after he had left her. He moved on in silence, as if his energies were benumbed by the hitherto undreamt-of possibility that his position was untenable. Reason had had nothing to do with his whimsical conversion, which was perhaps the mere freak of a careless man in search of a new sensation, and temporarily impressed by his mother's death.

The drops of logic Tess had let fall into the sea of his enthusiasm served to chill its effervescence to stagnation. He said to himself, as he pondered again and again over the crystallized phrases that she had handed on to him, 'That clever fellow little thought that, by telling her those things, he might be paving my way back to her!'

❧ Chapter Forty-Seven ☙

IT IS THE THRESHING OF THE last wheat-rick at Flintcomb-Ash Farm. The dawn of the March morning is singularly inexpressive, and there is nothing to show where the eastern horizon lies. Against the twilight rises the trapezoidal top of the stack, which has stood forlornly here through the washing and bleaching of the wintry weather.

When Izz Huett and Tess arrived at the scene of operations only a rustling denoted that others had preceded them; to which, as the light increased, there were presently added the silhouettes of two men on the summit. They were busily 'unhaling' the rick, that is, stripping off the thatch before beginning to throw down the sheaves; and while this was in progress Izz and Tess, with the other women-workers, in their whitey-brown pinners, stood waiting and shivering, Farmer Groby having insisted upon their being on the spot thus early to get the job over if possible by the end of the day. Close under the eaves of the stack, and as yet barely visible, was the red tyrant that the women had come to serve – a timber-framed construction, with straps and wheels appertaining – the threshing-machine which, whilst it was going, kept up a despotic demand upon the endurance of their muscles and nerves.

A little way off there was another indistinct figure; this one black, with a sustained hiss that spoke of strength very much in reserve. The long chimney running up beside an ash-tree, and the warmth which radiated from the spot, explained without the necessity of much daylight that here was the engine which was to act as the *primum mobile* of this little world. By the engine stood a dark motionless being, a sooty and grimy embodiment of tallness, in a sort of trance. The isolation of his manner and colour lent him the appearance of a creature from Tophet, who had strayed into the pellucid smokelessness of this region of yellow grain and pale soil, with which he had nothing in common, to amaze and to discompose its aborigines.

What he looked he felt. He was in the agricultural world, but not of it. He served fire and smoke; these denizens of the fields served weather, vegetation, frost, and sun. He travelled with his engine from farm to farm, from county to county, for as yet the steam threshing-machine was itinerant in this part of Wessex. He spoke in a strange northern accent; his thoughts being turned inwards upon himself, his eye on his iron charge, hardly perceiving the scenes around him, and caring for them not at all: holding only strictly necessary intercourse with the natives, as if some ancient doom compelled him to wander here against his will in the service of his Plutonic master. The long strap which ran from the driving-wheel of his engine to the red thresher under the rick was the sole tie-line between agriculture and him.

While they uncovered the sheaves he stood apathetic beside his portable repository of force, round whose hot blackness the morning air quivered. He had nothing to do with preparatory labour. His fire was waiting incandescent, his steam was at high pressure, in a few seconds he could make the long strap move at an invisible velocity. Beyond its extent the environment might be corn, straw, or chaos; it was all the same to him. If any of the autochthonous idlers asked him what he called himself, he replied shortly, 'an engineer'.

The rick was unhaled by full daylight; the men then took their places, the women mounted, and the work began. Farmer Groby – or, as they called him, 'he' – had arrived ere this, and by his orders Tess was placed on the platform of the machine, close to the man who fed it, her business being to untie every sheaf of corn handed on to her by Izz Huett, who stood next, but on the rick; so that the feeder could seize it and spread it over the revolving drum, which whisked out every grain in one moment.

They were soon in full progress, after a preparatory hitch or two, which rejoiced the hearts of those who hated machinery. The work sped on till breakfast-time, when the thresher was stopped for half an hour; and on starting again after the meal the whole supplementary strength of the farm was thrown into the labour of constructing the straw-rick, which began to grow beside the stack of corn. A hasty lunch was eaten as they stood, without leaving their positions, and then another couple of hours brought them near to dinner-time; the inexorable wheels continuing to spin, and the penetrating hum of the thresher to thrill to the very marrow all who were near the revolving wire-cage.

The old men on the rising straw-rick talked of the past days when they had been accustomed to thresh with flails on the oaken barn-floor; when everything, even to winnowing, was effected by hand-labour, which, to their thinking, though slow, produced better results. Those, too, on the corn-rick talked a little; but the perspiring ones at the machine, including Tess, could not lighten their duties by the exchange of many words. It was the ceaselessness of the work which tried her so severely, and began to make her wish that she had never come to Flintcomb-Ash. The women on the corn-rick – Marian, who was one of them, in particular – could stop to drink ale or cold tea from the flagon now and then, or to exchange a few gossiping remarks while they wiped their faces or cleared the fragments of straw and husk from their clothing; but for Tess there was no respite; for, as the drum never stopped, the man who fed it could not stop, and she, who had to supply the man with untied sheaves, could not stop either, unless Marian changed places with her, which she sometimes did for half an hour in spite of Groby's objection that she was too slow-handed for a feeder.

For some probably economical reason it was usually a woman who was chosen for this particular duty, and Groby gave as his motive in selecting Tess that she was one of those who best combined strength with quickness in untying, and both with staying power, and this may have been true. The hum of the thresher, which prevented speech, increased to a raving whenever the supply of corn fell short of the regular quantity. As Tess and the man who fed could never turn their heads she did not know that just before the dinner-hour a person had come silently into the field by the gate, and had been standing under a second rick watching the scene, and Tess in particular. He was dressed in a tweed suit of fashionable pattern, and he twirled a gay walking-cane.

'Who is that?' said Izz Huett to Marian. She had at first addressed the inquiry to Tess, but the latter could not hear it.

'Somebody's fancy-man, I s'pose,' said Marian laconically.

'I'll lay a guinea he's after Tess.'

'O no. 'Tis a ranter pa'son who's been sniffing after her lately; not a dandy like this.'

'Well – this is the same man.'

'The same man as the preacher? But he's quite different!'

'He hev left off his black coat and white neckercher, and hev cut off his whiskers; but he's the same man for all that.'

'D'ye really think so? Then I'll tell her,' said Marian.

'Don't. She'll see him soon enough, good-now.'

'Well, I don't think it at all right for him to join his preaching to courting a married woman, even though her husband mid be abroad, and she, in a sense, a widow.'

'Oh – he can do her no harm,' said Izz drily. 'Her mind can no more be heaved from that one place where it do bide than a stooded waggon from the hole he's in. Lord love 'ee, neither court-paying, nor preaching, nor the seven thunders themselves, can wean a woman when 'twould be better for her that she should be weaned.'

Dinner-time came, and the whirling ceased; whereupon Tess left her post, her knees trembling so wretchedly with the shaking of the machine that she could scarcely walk.

'You ought to het a quart o' drink into 'ee, as I've done,' said Marian. 'You wouldn't look so white then. Why, souls above us, your face is as if you'd been hagrode!'

It occurred to the good-natured Marian that, as Tess was so tired, her discovery of her visitor's presence might have the bad effect of taking away her appetite; and Marian was thinking of inducing Tess to descend by a ladder on the further side of the stack when the gentleman came forward and looked up.

Tess uttered a short little 'Oh!' And a moment after she said, quickly, 'I shall eat my dinner here – right on the rick.'

Sometimes, when they were so far from their cottages, they all did this; but as there was rather a keen wind going to-day, Marian and the rest descended, and sat under the straw-stack.

The new-comer was, indeed, Alec d'Urberville, the late Evangelist, despite his changed attire and aspect. It was obvious at a glance that the original *Weltlust* had come back; that he had restored himself, as nearly as a man could do who had grown three or four years older, to the old jaunty, slap-dash guise under which Tess had first known her admirer, and cousin so-called. Having decided to remain where she was, Tess sat down among the bundles, out of sight of the ground, and began her meal; till, by-and-by, she heard footsteps on the ladder, and immediately after Alec appeared upon the stack – now an oblong and level platform of sheaves. He strode across them, and sat down opposite to her without a word.

Tess continued to eat her modest dinner, a slice of thick pancake which she had brought with her. The other workfolk were by this time all gathered under the rick, where the loose straw formed a comfortable retreat.

'I am here again, as you see,' said d'Urberville.

'Why do you trouble me so!' she cried, reproach flashing from her very finger-ends.

'*I* trouble *you*? I think I may ask, why do you trouble me?'

'Sure, I don't trouble you any-when!'

'You say you don't? But you do! You haunt me. Those very eyes that you turned upon me with such a bitter flash a moment ago, they come to me just as you showed them then, in the night and in the day! Tess, ever since you told me of that child of ours, it is just as if my feelings, which have been flowing in a strong puritanical stream, had suddenly found a way open in the direction of you, and had all at once gushed through. The religious channel is left dry forthwith; and it is you who have done it!'

She gazed in silence.

'What – you have given up your preaching entirely?' she asked.

She had gathered from Angel sufficient of the incredulity of modern thought to despise flash enthusiasms; but, as a woman, she was somewhat appalled.

In affected severity d'Urberville continued –

'Entirely. I have broken every engagement since that afternoon I was to address the drunkards at Casterbridge Fair. The deuce only knows what I am thought of by the brethren. Ah-ha! The brethren! No doubt they pray for me – weep for me; for they are kind people in their way. But what do I care? How could I go on with the thing when I had lost my faith in it? – it would have been hypocrisy of the basest kind! Among them I should have stood like Hymenaeus and Alexander, who were delivered over to Satan that they might learn not to blaspheme. What a grand revenge you have taken! I saw you innocent, and I deceived you. Four years after, you find me a Christian enthusiast; you then work upon me, perhaps to my complete perdition! But Tess, my coz, as I used to call you, this is only my way of talking, and you must not look so horribly concerned. Of course you have done nothing except retain your pretty face and shapely figure. I saw it on the rick before you saw me – that tight pinafore-thing sets it off, and that wing-bonnet – you field-girls should never wear those bonnets if you wish to keep out of danger.' He regarded her silently for a few moments, and with a short cynical laugh resumed: 'I believe that if the bachelor-apostle, whose deputy I thought I was, had been tempted by such a pretty face, he would have let go the plough for her sake as I do!'

Tess attempted to expostulate, but at this juncture all her fluency failed her, and without heeding he added:

'Well, this paradise that you supply is perhaps as good as any other, after all. But to speak seriously, Tess.' D'Urberville rose and came nearer, reclining sideways amid the sheaves, and resting upon his elbow. 'Since I last saw you, I have been thinking of what you said that *he* said. I have come to the conclusion that there does seem rather a want of common-sense in these threadbare old propositions; how I could have been so fired by poor Parson Clare's enthusiasm, and have gone so madly to work, transcending even him, I cannot make out! As for what you said last time, on the strength of your wonderful husband's intelligence – whose name you have never told me – about having what they call an ethical system without any dogma, I don't see my way to that at all.'

'Why, you have the religion of loving-kindness and purity at least, if you can't have – what do you call it – dogma.'

'O no! I'm a different sort of fellow from that! If there's nobody to say, "Do this, and it will be a good thing for you after you are dead; do that, and it will be a bad thing for you". I can't warm up. Hang it, I am not going to feel responsible for my deeds and passions if there's nobody to be responsible to; and if I were you, my dear, I wouldn't either!'

She tried to argue, and tell him that he had mixed in his dull brain two matters, theology and morals, which in the primitive days of mankind had been quite distinct. But owing to Angel Clare's reticence, to her absolute want of training, and to her being a vessel of emotions rather than reasons, she could not get on.

'Well, never mind,' he resumed. 'Here I am, my love, as in the old times!'

'Not as then – never as then – 'tis different!' she entreated. 'And there was never warmth with me! O why didn't you keep your faith, if the loss of it has brought you to speak to me like this!'

'Because you've knocked it out of me; so the evil be upon your sweet head! Your husband little thought how his teaching would recoil upon him! Ha-ha – I'm awfully glad you have made an apostate of me all the same! Tess, I am more taken with you than ever, and I pity you too. For all your closeness, I see you are in a bad way – neglected by one who ought to cherish you.'

She could not get her morsels of food down her throat; her lips were dry, and she was ready to choke. The voices and laughs of the workfolk eating and drinking under the rick came to her as if they were a quarter of a mile off.

'It is cruelty to me!' she said. 'How – how can you treat me to this talk, if you care ever so little for me?'

'True, true,' he said, wincing a little. 'I did not come to reproach you for my deeds. I came, Tess, to say that I don't like you to be working like this, and I have come on purpose for you. You say you have a husband who is not I. Well, perhaps you have; but I've never seen him, and you've not told me his name; and altogether he seems rather a mythological personage. However, even if you have one, I think I am nearer to you than he is. I, at any rate, try to help you out of trouble, but he does not, bless his invisible face! The words of the stern prophet Hosea that I used to read come back to me. Don't you know them, Tess?

287

– "And she shall follow after her lover, but she shall not overtake him; and she shall seek him, but shall not find him; then shall she say, I will go and return to my first husband; for then was it better with me than now!" . . . Tess, my trap is waiting just under the hill, and – darling mine, not his! – you know the rest.'

Her face had been rising to a dull crimson fire while he spoke; but she did not answer.

'You have been the cause of my backsliding,' he continued, stretching his arm towards her waist; 'you should be willing to share it, and leave that mule you call husband for ever.'

One of her leather gloves, which she had taken off to eat her skimmer-cake, lay in her lap, and without the slightest warning she passionately swung the glove by the gauntlet directly in his face. It was heavy and thick as a warrior's, and it struck him flat on the mouth. Fancy might have regarded the act as the recrudescence of a trick in which her armed progenitors were not practised. Alec fiercely started up from his reclining position. A scarlet oozing appeared where her blow had alighted, and in a moment the blood began dropping from his mouth upon the straw. But he soon controlled himself, calmly drew his handkerchief from his pocket, and mopped his bleeding lips.

She too had sprung up, but she sank down again.

'Now, punish me!' she said, turning up her eyes to him with the hopeless defiance of the sparrow's gaze before its captor twists its neck. 'Whip me, crush me; you need not mind those people under the rick! I shall not cry out. Once victim, always victim – that's the law!'

'O no, no, Tess,' he said blandly. 'I can make full allowance for this. Yet you most unjustly forget one thing, that I would have married you if you have not put it out of my power to do so. Did I not ask you flatly to be my wife – hey? Answer me.'

'You did.'

'And you cannot be. But remember one thing!' His voice hardened as his temper got the better of him with the recollection of his sincerity in asking her and her present ingratitude, and he stepped across to her side and held her by the shoulders, so that she shook under his grasp. 'Remember, my lady, I was your master once! I will be your master again. If you are any man's wife you are mine!'

The threshers now began to stir below.

'So much for our quarrel,' he said, letting her go. 'Now I shall leave you, and shall come again for your answer during the afternoon. You don't know me yet! But I know you.'

She had not spoken again, remaining as if stunned. D'Urberville retreated over the sheaves, and descended the ladder, while the workers below rose and stretched their arms, and shook down the beer they had drunk. Then the threshing-machine started afresh; and amid the renewed rustle of the straw Tess resumed her position by the buzzing drum as one in a dream, untying sheaf after sheaf in endless succession.

❧ Chapter Forty-Eight ❧

IN THE AFTERNOON THE FARMER made it known that the rick was to be finished that night, since there was a moon by which they could see to work, and the man with the engine was engaged for another farm on the morrow. Hence the twanging and humming and rustling proceeded with even less intermission than usual.

It was not till 'nammet'-time, about three o'clock, that Tess raised her eyes and gave a momentary glance round. She felt but little surprise at seeing that Alec d'Urberville had come back, and was standing under the hedge by the gate. He had seen her lift her eyes, and waved his hand urbanely to her, while he blew her a kiss. It meant that their quarrel was over. Tess looked down again, and carefully abstained from gazing in that direction.

Thus the afternoon dragged on. The wheat-rick shrank lower, and the strawrick grew higher, and the corn-sacks were carted away. At six o'clock the wheatrick was about shoulder-high from the ground. But the unthreshed sheaves remaining untouched seemed countless still, notwithstanding the enormous numbers that had been gulped down by the insatiable swallower, fed by the man and Tess, through whose two young hands the greater part of them had passed. And the immense stack of straw where in the morning there had been nothing, appeared as the *faeces* of the same buzzing red glutton. From the west sky a wrathful shine – all that wild March could afford in the way of sunset – had burst forth after the cloudy day, flooding the tired and sticky faces of the threshers, and dyeing them with a coppery light, as also the flapping garments of the women, which clung to them like dull flames.

A panting ache ran through the rick. The man who fed was weary, and Tess could see that the red nape of his neck was encrusted with dirt and husks. She still stood at her post, her flushed and perspiring face coated with the corn-dust, and her white bonnet embrowned by it. She was the only woman whose place was upon the machine so as to

289

be shaken bodily by its spinning, and the decrease of the stack now separated her from Marian and Izz, and prevented their changing duties with her as they had done. The incessant quivering, in which every fibre of her frame participated, had thrown her into a stupefied reverie in which her arms worked on independently of her consciousness. She hardly knew where she was, and did not hear Izz Huett tell her from below that her hair was tumbling down.

By degress the freshest among them began to grow cadaverous and saucereyed. Whenever Tess lifted her head she beheld always the great upgrown strawstack, with the men in shirtsleeves upon it, against the gray north sky; in front of it the long red elevator like a Jacob's ladder, on which a perpetual stream of threshed straw ascended, a yellow river running up-hill, and spouting out on the top of the rick.

She knew that Alec d'Urberville was still on the scene, observing her from some point or other, though she could not say where. There was an excuse for his remaining, for when the threshed rick drew near its final sheaves a little ratting was always done, and men unconnected with the threshing sometimes dropped in for that performance – sporting characters of all descriptions, gents with terriers and facetious pipes, roughs with sticks and stones.

But there was another hour's work before the layer of live rats at the base of the stack would be reached; and as the evening light in the direction of the Giant's Hill by Abbot's-Cernel dissolved away, the white-faced moon of the season arose from the horizon that lay towards Middleton Abbey and Shottsford on the other side. For the last hour or two Marian had felt uneasy about Tess, whom she could not get near enough to speak to, the other women having kept up their strength by drinking ale, and Tess having done without it through traditionary dread, owing to its results at her home in childhood. But Tess still kept going: if she could not fill her part she would have to leave; and this contingency, which she would have regarded with equanimity and even with relief a month or two earlier, had become a terror since d'Urberville had begun to hover round her.

The sheaf-pitchers and feeders had now worked the rick so low that people on the ground could talk to them. To Tess's surprise Farmer Groby came up on the machine to her, and said that if she desired to join her friend he did not wish her to keep on any longer, and would send somebody else to take her place. The 'friend' was d'Urberville, she knew, and also that this concession had been granted in obedience to the request of that friend, or enemy. She shook her head and toiled on.

The time for the rat-catching arrived at last, and the hunt began. The creatures had crept downwards with the subsidence of the rick till they were all together at the bottom, and being now uncovered from their last refuge they ran across the open ground in all directions, a loud shriek from the by-this-time half-tipsy Marian informing her companions that one of the rats had invaded her person – a terror which the rest of the women had guarded against by various schemes of skirt-tucking and self-elevation. The rat was at last dislodged, and, amid the barking of dogs, masculine shouts, feminine screams, oaths, stampings, and confusion as of Pandemonium, Tess untied her last sheaf; the drum slowed, the whizzing ceased, and she stepped from the machine to the ground.

Her lover, who had only looked on at the rat-catching, was promptly at her side.

'What – after all – my insulting slap too!' said she in an underbreath. She was so utterly exhausted that she had not strength to speak louder.

'I should indeed be foolish to feel offended at anything you say or do,' he answered, in the seductive voice of the Trantridge time. 'How the little limbs tremble! You are as weak as a bled calf, you know you are; and yet you need have done nothing since I arrived. How could you be so obstinate? However, I have told the farmer that he has no right to employ women at steam-threshing. It is not proper work for them; and on all the better class of farms it has been given up, as he knows very well. I will walk with you as far as your home.'

'O yes,' she answered with a jaded gait. 'Walk wi' me if you will! I do bear in mind that you came to marry me before you knew o' my state. Perhaps – perhaps you are a little better and kinder than I have been thinking you were. Whatever is meant as kindness I am grateful for; whatever is meant in any other way I am angered at. I cannot sense your meaning sometimes.'

'If I cannot legitimize our former relations at least I can assist you. And I will do it with much more regard for your feelings than I formerly showed. My religious mania, or whatever it was, is over. But I retain a little good nature; I hope I do. Now Tess, by all that's tender and strong between man and woman, trust me! I have enough and more than enough to put you out of anxiety, both for yourself and your parents and sisters. I can make them all comfortable if you will only show confidence in me.'

'Have you seen 'em lately?' she quickly inquired.

'Yes. They didn't know where you were. It was only by chance that I found you here.'

The cold moon looked aslant upon Tess's fagged face between the twigs of the garden-hedge as she paused outside the cottage which was her temporary home, d'Urberville pausing beside her.

'Don't mention my little brothers and sisters – don't make me break down quite!' she said. 'If you want to help them – God knows they need it – do it without telling me. But no, no!' she cried. 'I will take nothing from you, either for them or for me!'

He did not accompany her further, since, as she lived with the household, all was public indoors. No sooner had she herself entered, laved herself in a washing-tub, and shared supper with the family than she fell into thought, and withdrawing to the table under the wall, by the light of her own little lamp wrote in a passionate mood –

MY OWN HUSBAND, – Let me call you so – I must – even if it makes you angry to think of such an unworthy wife as I. I must cry to you in my trouble – I have no one else! I am so exposed to temptation, Angel. I fear to say who it is, and I do not like to write about it at all. But I cling to you in a way you cannot think! Can you not come to me now, at once, before anything terrible happens? O, I know you cannot, because you are so far away! I think I must die if you do not come soon, or tell me to come to you. The punishment you have measured out to me is deserved – I do know that – well deserved – and you are right and just to be angry with me. But, Angel, please, please, not to be just – only a little kind to me, even if I do not deserve it, and come to me! If you would come, I could die in your arms! I would be well content to do that if so be you had forgiven me!

Angel, I live entirely for you. I love you too much to blame you for going away, and I know it was necessary you should find a farm. Do not think I shall say a word of sting or bitterness. Only come back to me. I am desolate without you, my darling, O, so desolate! I do not mind having to work: but if you will send me one little line and say, '*I am coming soon*', I will bide on, Angel – O, so cheerfully!

It has been so much my religion ever since we were married to be faithful to you in every thought and look, that even when a man speaks a compliment to me before I am aware, it seems wronging you. Have you never felt one little bit of what you used to feel when we were at the dairy? If you have, how can you keep away from me? I am the same woman, Angel, as you fell in love with; yes, the very same! – not the one you disliked but never saw. What was the past to me as soon as I met you? It was a dead thing altogether. I became another woman, filled full of new life from you. How could I be the early one? Why do you not see this? Dear, if you would only be a little more conceited, and believe in yourself so far as to see that you were strong enough to work this change in me, you would perhaps be in a mind to come to me, your poor wife.

How silly I was in my happiness when I thought I could trust you always to love me! I ought to have known that such as that was not for poor me. But I am sick at heart, not only for old times, but for the present. Think – think how it do hurt my heart not to see you ever – ever! Ah, if I could only make your dear heart ache one little minute of each day as mine does every day and all day long, it might lead you to show pity to your poor lonely one.

People still say that I am rather pretty, Angel (handsome is the word they use, since I wish to be truthful). Perhaps I am what they say. But I do not value my good looks; I only like to have them because they belong to you, my dear, and that there may be at least one thing about me worth your having. So much have I felt this, that when I met with annoyance on account of the same I tied up my face in a bandage as long as people would believe in it. O Angel, I tell you all this not from vanity – you will certainly know I do not – but only that you may come to me!

If you really cannot come to me will you let me come to you! I am, as I say, worried, pressed to do what I will not do. It cannot be that I shall yield one inch, yet I am in terror as to what an accident might lead to, and I so defenceless on account of my first error. I cannot say more about this – it makes me too miserable. But if I break down by falling into some fearful snare, my last state will be worse than my first. O God, I cannot think of it! Let me come at once, or at once come to me!

I would be content, ay, glad, to live with you as your servant, if I may not as your wife; so that I could only be near you, and get glimpses of you, and think of you as mine.

The daylight has nothing to show me, since you are not here, and I don't like to see the rooks and starlings in the fields, because I grieve and grieve to miss you who used to see them with me. I long for only one thing in heaven or earth or under the earth, to meet you, my own dear! Come to me – come to me, and save me from what threatens me! – Your faithful heartbroken

TESS.

❧ Chapter Forty-Nine ❧

THE APPEAL DULY FOUND its way to the breakfast-table of the quiet Vicarage to the westward, in that valley where the air is so soft and the soil so rich that the effort of growth requires but superficial aid by comparison with the tillage at Flintcomb-Ash, and where to Tess the human world seemed so different (though it was much the same). It was purely for security that she had been requested by Angel to send her communications through his father, whom he kept pretty well informed of his changing addresses in the country he had gone to exploit for himself with a heavy heart.

'Now,' said old Mr Clare to his wife, when he had read the envelope, 'if Angel proposes leaving Rio for a visit home at the end of next month, as he told us that he hoped to do, I think this may hasten his plans; for I believe it to be from his wife.' He breathed deeply at the thought of her; and the letter was redirected to be promptly sent on to Angel.

'Dear fellow, I hope he will get home safely.' murmured Mrs Clare. 'To my dying day I shall feel that he has been ill-used. You should have sent him to Cambridge in spite of his want of faith, and given him the same chance as the other boys had. He would have grown out of it under proper influence, and perhaps would have taken Orders after all. Church or no Church, it would have been fairer to him.'

This was the only wail with which Mrs Clare ever disturbed her husband's peace in respect of their sons. And she did not vent this often; for she was as considerate as she was devout, and knew that his mind too was troubled by doubts as to his justice in this matter. Only too often had she heard him lying awake at night, stifling sighs for Angel with prayers. But the uncompromising Evangelical did not even now hold that he would have been justified in giving his son, an unbeliever, the same academic advantages that he had given to the two others, when it was possible, if not probable, that those very advantages might have been used to decry the doctrines which he had made it his life's mission and desire to propagate, and the mission of his ordained sons likewise. To put with one hand a pedestal under the feet of the two faithful ones, and with the other to exalt the unfaithful by the same artificial means, he deemed to be alike inconsistent with his convictions, his position, and his hopes. Nevertheless, he loved his misnamed Angel, and in secret mourned over this treatment of him as Abraham might have mourned over the doomed Isaac while they went up the hill together. His silent self-generated regrets were far bitterer than the reproaches which his wife rendered audible.

They blamed themselves for this unlucky marriage. If Angel had never been destined for a farmer he would never have been thrown with agricultural girls. They did not distinctly know what had separated him and his wife, nor the date on which the separation had taken place. At first they had supposed it must be something of the nature of a serious aversion. But in his later letters he occasionally alluded to the intention of coming home to fetch her; from which expressions they hoped the division might not owe its origin to anything so hopelessly permanent as that. He had told them that she was with her relatives, and in their doubts they had decided not to intrude into a situation which they knew no way of bettering.

The eyes for which Tess's letter was intended were gazing at this time on a limitless expanse of country from the back of a mule which was bearing him from the interior of the South-American Continent towards the coast. His experiences of this strange land had been sad. The severe illness from which he had suffered shortly after his arrival had never wholly left him, and he had by degrees almost decided to relinquish his hope of farming here, though, as long as the bare possibility existed of his remaining, he kept this change of view a secret from his parents.

The crowds of agricultural labourers who had come out to the country in his wake, dazzled by representations of easy independence, had suffered, died, and wasted away. He would see mothers from English farms trudging along with their infants in their arms, when the child would be stricken with fever and would die; the mother would pause to dig a hole in the loose earth with her bare hands, would bury the babe therein with the same natural grave-tools, shed one tear, and again trudge on.

Angel's original intention had not been emigration to Brazil, but a northern or eastern farm in his own country. He had come to this place in a fit of desperation, the Brazil movement among the English agriculturists having by chance coincided with his desire to escape from his past existence.

During this time of absence he had mentally aged a dozen years. What arrested him now as of value in life was less its beauty that its pathos. Having long discredited the old systems of mysticism, he now began to discredit the old appraisements of morality. He thought they wanted readjusting. Who was the moral man? Still more pertinently, who was the moral woman? The beauty or ugliness of a character lay not only in its achievements, but in its aims and impulses; its true history lay, not among things done, but among things willed.

How, then, about Tess?

Viewing her in these lights, a regret for his hasty judgment began to oppress him. Did he reject her eternally, or did he not? He could no longer say that he would always reject her, and not to say that was in spirit to accept her now.

This growing fondness of her memory coincided in point of time with her residence at Flintcomb-Ash, but it was before she had felt herself at liberty to trouble him with a word about her circumstances or her feelings. He was greatly perplexed; and in his perplexity as to her motives in withholding intelligence he did not inquire. Thus her silence of docility was misinterpreted. How much it really said if he had understood! – that she adhered with literal exactness to orders which he had given and forgotten; that despite her natural fearlessness she asserted no rights, admitted his judgment to be in every respect the true one, and bent her head dumbly thereto.

In the before-mentioned journey by mules through the interior of the country, another man rode beside him. Angel's companion was also an Englishman, bent on the same errand, though he came from another part of the island. They were both in a state of mental depression, and they spoke of home affairs. Confidence begat confidence. With that curious tendency evinced by men, more especially when in distant lands, to entrust to strangers details of their lives which they would on no account mention to friends, Angel admitted to this man as they rode along the sorrowful facts of his marriage.

The stranger had sojourned in many more lands and among many more peoples than Angel; to his cosmopolitan mind such deviations from the social norm, so immense to domesticity, were no more than are the irregularities of vale and mountainchain to the whole terrestrial curve. He viewed the matter in quite a different light from Angel; thought that what Tess had been was of no importance beside what she would be, and plainly told Clare that he was wrong in coming away from her.

The next day they were drenched in a thunderstorm. Angel's companion was struck down with fever, and died by the week's end. Clare waited a few hours to bury him, and then went on his way.

The cursory remarks of the large-minded stranger, of whom he knew absolutely nothing beyond a commonplace name, were sublimed by his death, and influenced Clare more than all the reasoned ethics of the philosophers. His own parochialism made him ashamed by its contrast. His inconsistencies rushed upon him in a flood. He had persistently elevated Hellenic Paganism at the expense of Christianity; yet in that civilization an illegal surrender was not certain disesteem. Surely then he might have regarded that abhorrence of the un-intact state, which he had inherited with the creed of mysticism, as at least open to correction when the result was due to treachery. A remorse struck into him. The words of Izz Huett, never quite stilled in his memory, came back to him. He had asked Izz if she loved him, and she had replied in the affirmative.

Did she love him more than Tess did? No, she had replied; Tess would lay down her life for him, and she herself could do no more.

He thought of Tess as she had appeared on the day of the wedding. How her eyes had lingered upon him; how she had hung upon his words as if they were a god's! And during the terrible evening over the hearth, when her simple soul uncovered itself to his, how pitiful her face had looked by the rays of the fire, in her inability to realize that his love and protection could possibly be withdrawn.

Thus from being her critic he grew to be her advocate. Cynical things he had uttered to himself about her; but no man can be always a cynic and live; and he withdrew them. The mistake of expressing them had arisen from his allowing himself to be influenced by general principles to the disregard of the particular instance.

But the reasoning is somewhat musty; lovers and husbands have gone over the ground before to-day. Clare had been harsh towards her; there is no doubt of it. Men are too often harsh with women they love or have loved; women with men. And yet these harshnesses are tenderness itself when compared with the universal harshness out of which they grow; the harshness of the position towards the temperament, of the means towards the aims, of to-day towards yesterday, of hereafter towards to-day.

The historic interest of her family – the masterful line of d'Urbervilles – whom he had despised as a spent force, touched his sentiments now. Why had he not known the difference between the political value and the imaginative value of these things? In the latter aspect her d'Urberville descent was a fact of great dimensions; worthless to economics, it was a most useful ingredient to the dreamer, to the moralizer on declines and falls. It was a fact that would soon be forgotten – that bit of distinction in poor Tess's blood and name, and oblivion would fall upon her hereditary link with the marble monuments and leaded skeletons at Kingsbere. So does Time ruthlessly destroy his own romances. In recalling her face again and again, he thought now that he could see therein a flash of the dignity which must have graced her grand-dames; and the vision sent that *aura* through his veins which he had formerly felt, and which left behind it a sense of sickness.

Despite her not inviolate past, what still abode in such a woman as Tess outvalued the freshness of her fellows. Was not the gleaming of the grapes of Ephraim better than the vintage of Abi-ezer?

So spoke love renascent, preparing the way for Tess's devoted outpouring, which was then just being forwarded to him by his father; though owing to his distance inland it was to be a long time in reaching him.

Meanwhile the writer's expectation that Angel would come in response to the entreaty was alternately great and small. What lessened it was that the facts of her life which had led to the parting had not changed – could never change; and that, if her presence had not attenuated them, her absence could not. Nevertheless she addressed her mind to the tender question of what she could do to please him best if he should arrive. Sighs were expended on the wish that she had taken more notice of the tunes he played on his harp, that she had inquired more curiously of him which were his favourite ballads among those the country-girls sang. She indirectly inquired of Amby Seedling, who had followed Izz from Talbothays, and by chance Amby remembered that, amongst the snatches of melody in which they had indulged at the dairyman's, to include the cows to let down their milk, Clare had seemed to like 'Cupid's Gardens', 'I have parks, I have hounds', and 'The break o' the day'; and had seemed not to care for 'The Tailor's Breeches', and 'Such a beauty I did grow', excellent ditties as they were.

To perfect the ballads was now her whimsical desire. She practised them privately at odd moments, especially 'The break o' the day:'

> Arise, arise, arise!
> And pick your love a posy,
> All o' the sweetest flowers
> That in the garden grow.
> The turtle doves and sma' birds
> In every bough a-building,
> So early in the May-time,
> At the break o' the day!

It would have melted the heart of a stone to hear her singing these ditties, whenever she worked apart from the rest of the girls in this cold dry time; the tears running down her cheeks all the while at the thought that perhaps he would not, after all, come to hear her, and the simple silly words of the songs resounding in painful mockery of the aching heart of the singer.

Tess was so wrapt up in this fanciful dream that she seemed not to know how the season was advancing; that the days had lengthened, that Lady-Day was at hand, and would soon be followed by Old Lady-Day, the end of her term here.

But before the quarter-day had quite come something happened which made Tess think of far different matters. She was at her lodging as usual one evening, sitting in the downstairs room with the rest of the family, when somebody knocked at the door and inquired for Tess. Through the doorway she saw against the declining light a figure with the height of a woman and the breadth of a child, a tall, thin, girlish creature whom she did not recognize in the twilight till the girl said 'Tess!'

'What – is it 'Liza-Lu?' asked Tess, in startled accents. Her sister, whom a little over a year ago she had left at home as a child, had sprung up by a sudden shoot to a form of this presentation, of which as yet Lu seemed herself scarce able to understand the meaning. Her thin legs, visible below her once long frock, now short by her growing, and her uncomfortable hands and arms, revealed her youth and inexperience.

'Yes, I have been traipsing about all day, Tess,' said Lu, with unemotional gravity, 'a-trying to find 'ee; and I'm very tired.'

'What is the matter at home?'

'Mother is took very bad, and the doctor says she's dying, and as father is not very well neither, and says 'tis wrong for a man of such a high family as his to slave and drave at common labouring work, we don't know what to do.'

Tess stood in reverie a long time before she thought of asking 'Liza-Lu to come in and sit down. When she had done so, and 'Liza-Lu was having some tea, she came to a decision. It was imperative that she should go home. Her agreement did not end till Old Lady-Day, the sixth of April, but as the interval thereto was not a long one she resolved to run the risk of starting at once.

To go that night would be a gain of twelve hours; but her sister was too tired to undertake such a distance till the morrow. Tess ran down to where Marian and Izz lived, informed them of what had happened, and begged them to make the best of her case to the farmer. Returning, she got Lu a supper, and after that, having tucked the younger into her own bed, packed up as many of her belongings as would go into a withy basket, and started, directing Lu to follow her next morning.

❧ Chapter Fifty ❧

SHE PLUNGED INTO THE CHILLY equinoctial darkness as the clock struck ten, for her fifteen miles' walk under the steely stars. In lonely districts night is a protection rather than a danger to a noiseless pedestrian, and knowing this Tess pursued the nearest course along by-lanes that she would almost have feared in the day time; but marauders were wanting now, and spectral fears were driven out of her mind by thoughts of her mother. Thus she proceeded mile after mile, ascending and descending till she came to Bulbarrow, and about midnight looked from that height into the abyss of chaotic shade which was all that revealed itself of the vale on whose further side she was born. Having already traversed about five miles on the upland she had now some ten or eleven in the lowland before her journey would be finished. The winding road downwards became just visible to her under the wan starlight as she followed it, and soon she paced a soil so contrasting with that above it that the difference was perceptible to the tread and to the smell. It was the heavy clay land of Blackmoor Vale, and a part of the Vale to which turnpike-roads had never penetrated. Superstitions linger longest on these heavy soils. Having once been forest, at this shadowy time it seemed to assert something of its old character, the far and the near being blended, and every tree and tall hedge making the most of its presence. The harts that had been hunted here, the witches that had been pricked and ducked, the green-spangled fairies that 'whickered' at you as you passed; – the place teemed with beliefs in them still, and they formed an impish multitude now.

At Nuttlebury she passed the village inn, whose sign creaked in response to the greeting of her footsteps, which not a human soul heard but herself. Under the thatched roofs her mind's eye beheld relaxed tendons and flaccid muscles, spread out in the darkness beneath coverlets made of little purple patchwork squares, and undergoing a bracing process at the hands of sleep for renewed labour on the morrow, as soon as a hint of pink nebulosity appeared on Hambledon Hill.

At three she turned the last corner of the maze of lanes she had threaded, and entered Marlott, passing the field in which, as a club-girl, she had first seen Angel Clare, when he had not danced with her; the sense of disappointment remained with her yet. In the direction of her mother's house she saw a light. It came from the bedroom window, and a branch waved in front of it and made it wink at her. As soon as she could discern the outline of the house – newly thatched with her money – it had all its old effect upon Tess's imagination. Part of her body and life it ever seemed to be; the slope of its dormers, the finish of its gables, the broken courses of brick which topped the chimney, all had something in common with her personal character. A stupefaction had come into these features, to her regard; it meant the illness of her mother.

She opened the door so softly as to disturb nobody; the lower room was vacant, but the neighbour who was sitting up with her mother came to the top of the stairs, and whispered that Mrs Durbeyfield was no better, though she was sleeping just then. Tess prepared herself a breakfast, and then took her place as nurse in her mother's chamber.

In the morning, when she contemplated the children, they had all a curiously elongated look; although she had been away little more than a year their growth was astounding; and the necessity of applying herself heart and soul to their needs took her out of her own cares.

Her father's ill-health was of the same indefinite kind, and he sat in his chair as usual. But the day after her arrival he was unusually bright. He had a rational scheme for living, and Tess asked him what it was.

'I'm thinking of sending round to all the old antiqueerians in this part of England,' he said, 'asking them to subscribe to a fund to maintain me. I'm sure they'd see it as a romantical, artistical, and proper thing to do. They spend lots o' money in keeping up old ruins, and finding the bones o' things, and such like; and living remains must be more interesting to 'em still, if they only knowed of me. Would that somebody would go round and tell 'em what there is living among 'em, and they thinking nothing of him! If Pa'son Tringham, who discovered me, had lived, he'd ha' done it, I'm sure.'

Tess postponed her arguments on this high project till she had grappled with pressing matters in hand, which seemed little improved by her remittances. When indoor necessities had been eased she turned her attention to external things. It was now the season for planting and sowing; many gardens and allotments of the villagers had already received their spring tillage; but the garden and the allotment of the Durbeyfields were behindhand. She found, to her dismay, that this was owing to their having eaten all the seed potatoes, – that last lapse of the improvident. At the earliest moment she obtained what others she could procure, and in a few days her father was well enough to see to the garden, under Tess's persuasive efforts: while she herself undertook the allotment-plot which they rented in a field a couple of hundred yards out of the village.

She liked doing it after the confinement of the sick chamber, where she was not now required by reason of her mother's improvement. Violent motion relieved thought. The plot of ground was in a high, dry, open enclosure, where there were forty or fifty such pieces, and where labour was at its briskest when the hired labour of the day had ended. Digging began usually at six o'clock, and extended indefinitely into the dusk or moonlight. Just now heaps of dead weeds and refuse were burning on many of the plots, the dry weather favouring their combustion.

One fine day Tess and 'Liza-Lu worked on here with their neighbours till the last rays of the sun smote flat upon the white pegs that divided the plots. As soon as twilight succeeded to sunset the flare of the couch-grass and cabbage-stalk fires began to light up the allotments fitfully, their outlines appearing and disappearing under the dense smoke as wafted by the wind. When a fire glowed, banks of smoke, blown level along the ground, would themselves become illuminated to an opaque lustre, screening the workpeople from one another; and the meaning of the 'pillar of a cloud', which was a wall by day and a light by night, could be understood.

As evening thickened some of the gardening men and women gave over for the night, but the greater number remained to get their planting done, Tess being among them, though she sent her sister home. It was on one of the couch-burning plots that she laboured with her fork, its four shining prongs resounding against the stones and dry clods in little clicks. Sometimes she was completely involved in the smoke of her fire; then it would leave her figure free, irradiated by the brassy glare from the heap. She was oddly dressed to-night, and presented a somewhat staring aspect, her attire being a gown bleached by many washings, with a short black jacket over it, the effect of the whole being that of a wedding and funeral guest in one. The women further back wore white aprons, which, with their pale faces, were all that could be seen of them in the gloom, except when at moments they caught a flash from the flames.

Westward, the wiry boughs of the bare thorn hedge which formed the boundary of the field rose against the pale opalescence of the lower sky. Above, Jupiter hung like a full-blown jonquil, so bright as almost to throw a shade. A few small nondescript stars were appearing elsewhere. In the distance a dog barked, and wheels occasionally rattled along the dry road.

Still the prongs continued to click assiduously, for it was not late; and though the air was fresh and keen there was a whisper of spring in it that cheered the workers on. Something in the place, the hour, the crackling fires, the fantastic mysteries of light and shade, made others as well as Tess enjoy being there. Nightfall, which in the frost of winter comes as a fiend and in the warmth of summer as a lover, came as a tranquillizer on this March day.

Nobody looked at his or her companions. The eyes of all were on the soil as its turned surface was revealed by the fires. Hence as Tess stirred the clods, and sang her foolish little songs with scarce now a hope that Clare would ever hear them, she did not for a long time notice the person who worked nearest to her – a man in a long smockfrock who, she found, was forking the same plot as herself, and whom she supposed her father had sent there to advance the work. She became more conscious of him when the direction of his digging brought him closer. Sometimes the smoke divided them; then it swerved, and the two were visible to each other but divided from all the rest.

Tess did not speak to her fellow-worker, nor did he speak to her. Nor did she think of him further than to recollect that he had not been there when it was broad daylight, and that she did not know him as any one of the Marlott labourers, which was no wonder, her absences having been so long and frequent of late years. By-and-by he dug so close to her that the fire-beams were reflected as distinctly from the steel prongs of his fork as from her own. On going up to the fire to throw a pitch of dead weeds upon it, she found that he did the same on the other side. The fire flared up, and she beheld the face of d'Urberville.

The unexpectedness of his presence, the grotesqueness of his appearance in a gathered smockfrock, such as was now worn only by the most old-fashioned of the labourers, had a ghastly comicality that chilled her as to its bearing. D'Urberville emitted a low long laugh.

'If I were inclined to joke I should say, How much this seems like Paradise!' he remarked whimsically, looking at her with an inclined head.

'What do you say?' she weakly asked.

'A jester might say this is just like Paradise. You are Eve, and I am the old Other One come to tempt you in the disguise of an inferior animal. I used to be quite up in that scene of Milton's when I was theological. Some of it goes –

> "Empress, the way is ready, and not long,
>   Beyond a row of myrtles . . .
>   . . . If thou accept
> My conduct, I can bring thee thither soon."
>   "Lead then," said Eve.

And so on. My dear, dear Tess, I am only putting this to you as a thing that you might have supposed or said quite untruly, because you think so badly of me.'

'I never said you were Satan, or thought it. I don't think of you in that way at all. My thoughts of you are quite cold, except when you affront me. What, did you come digging here entirely because of me?'

'Entirely. To see you; nothing more. The smockfrock, which I saw hanging for sale as I came along, was an after-thought, that I mightn't be noticed. I come to protest against your working like this.'

'But I like doing it – it is for my father.'

'Your engagement at the other place is ended?'

'Yes.'

'Where are you going to next? To join your dear husband?'

She could not bear the humiliating reminder.

'O – I don't know!' she said bitterly. 'I have no husband!'

'It is quite true – in the sense you mean. But you have a friend, and I have determined that you shall be comfortable in spite of yourself. When you get down to your house you will see what I have sent there for you.'

'O, Alec, I wish you wouldn't give me anything at all! I cannot take it from you! I don't like – it is not right!'

'It is right!' he cried lightly. 'I am not going to see a woman whom I feel so tenderly for as I do for you, in trouble without trying to help her.'

'But I am very well off! I am only in trouble about – about – not about living at all!'

She turned, and desperately resumed her digging, tears dripping upon the fork-handle and upon the clods.

'About the children – your brothers and sisters,' he resumed. 'I've been thinking of them.'

Tess's heart quivered – he was touching her in a weak place. He had divined her chief anxiety. Since returning home her soul had gone out to those children with an affection that was passionate.

'If your mother does not recover, somebody ought to do something for them; since your father will not be able to do much, I suppose?'

'He can with my assistance. He must!'

'And with mine.'

'No, sir!'

'How damned foolish this is!' burst out d'Urberville. 'Why, he thinks we are the same family; and will be quite satisfied!'

'He don't. I've undeceived him.'

'The more fool you!'

D'Urberville in anger retreated from her to the hedge, where he pulled off the long smockfrock which had disguised him; and rolling it up and pushing it into the couch-fire, went away.

Tess could not get on with her digging after this; she felt restless; she wondered if he had gone back to her father's house; and taking the fork in her hand proceeded homewards.

Some twenty yards from the house she was met by one of her sisters.

'O, Tessy – what do you think! 'Liza-Lu is a-crying, and there's a lot of folk in the house, and mother is a good deal better, but they think father is dead!'

The child realized the grandeur of the news; but not as yet its sadness; and stood looking at Tess with round-eyed importance, till, beholding the effect produced upon her, she said –

'What, Tess, shan't we talk to father never no more?'

'But father was only a little bit ill!' exclaimed Tess distractedly.

'Liza-Lu came up.

'He dropped down just now, and the doctor who was there for mother said there was no chance for him, because his heart was growed in.'

Yes; the Durbeyfield couple had changed places; the dying one was out of danger, and the indisposed one was dead. The news meant even more than it sounded. Her father's life had a value apart from his personal achievements, or perhaps it would not have had much. It was the last of the three lives for whose duration the house and premises were held under a lease; and it had long been coveted by the tenant-farmer for his regular labourers, who were stinted in cottage accommodation. Moreover, 'liviers' were disapproved of in villages almost as much as little freeholders, because of their independence of manner, and when a lease determined it was never renewed.

Thus the Durbeyfields, once d'Urbervilles, saw descending upon them the destiny which, no doubt, when they were among the Olympians of the county, they had caused to descend many a time, and severely enough, upon the heads of such landless ones as they themselves were now. So do flux and reflux – the rhythm of change – alternate and persist in everything under the sky.

ê Chapter Fifty-One ê

AT LENGTH IT WAS THE EVE of Old Lady-Day, and the agricultural world was in a fever of mobility such as only occurs at that particular date of the year. It is a day of fulfilment; agreements for outdoor service during the ensuing year, entered into at Candlemas, are to be now carried out. The labourers – or 'work-folk', as they used to call themselves immemorially till the other word was introduced from without – who wish to remain no longer in old places are removing to the new farms.

These annual migrations from farm to farm were on the increase here. When Tess's mother was a child the majority of the field-folk about Marlott had remained all their lives on one farm, which had been the home also of their fathers and grandfathers; but latterly the desire for yearly removal had risen to a high pitch. With the younger families it was a pleasant excitement which might possibly be an advantage. The Egypt of one family was the Land of Promise to the family who saw it from a distance, till by residence there it became in turn their Egypt also; and so they changed and changed.

However, all the mutations so increasingly discernible in village life did not originate entirely in the agricultural unrest. A depopulation was also going on. The village had formerly contained, side by side with the agricultural labourers, an interesting and better-informed class, ranking distinctly above the former – the class to which Tess's father and mother had belonged – and including the carpenter, the smith, the shoemaker, the huckster, together with nondescript workers other than farm-labourers; a set of people who owed a certain stability of aim and conduct to the fact of their being life-holders like Tess's father, or copyholders, or, occasionally, small freeholders. But as the long holdings fell in they were seldom again let to similar tenants, and were mostly pulled down, if not absolutely required by the farmer for his hands. Cottagers who were not directly employed on the land were looked upon with disfavour, and the banishment of some starved the trade of others, who were thus obliged to follow. These families, who had formed the backbone of the village life in the past, who were the depositaries of the village traditions, had to seek refuge in the large centres; the process, humorously designated by statisticians as 'the tendency of the rural population towards the large towns', being really the tendency of water to flow uphill when forced by machinery.

The cottage accommodation at Marlott having been in this manner considerably curtailed by demolitions, every house which remained standing was required by the agriculturist for his work-people. Ever since the occurrence of the event which had cast such a shadow over Tess's life, the Durbeyfield family (whose descent was not credited) had been tacitly looked on as one which would have to go when their lease ended, if only in the interests of morality. It was, indeed, quite true that the household had not been shining examples either of temperance, soberness, or chastity. The father, and even the mother, had got drunk at times, the younger children seldom had gone to church, and the eldest daughter had made queer unions. By some means the village had to be kept pure. So on this, the first Lady-Day on which the Durbeyfields were expellable, the house, being roomy, was required for a carter with a large family; and Widow Joan, her daughters Tess and 'Liza-Lu, the boy Abraham and the younger children, had to go elsewhere.

On the evening preceding their removal it was getting dark betimes by reason of a drizzling rain which blurred the sky. As it was the last night they would spend in the village which had been their home and birthplace, Mrs Durbeyfield, 'Liza-Lu, and Abraham had gone out to bid some friends good-bye, and Tess was keeping house till they should return.

She was kneeling in the window-bench, her face close to the casement, where an outer pane of rain-water was sliding down the inner pane of glass. Her eyes rested on the web of a spider, probably starved long ago, which had been mistakenly placed in a corner where no flies ever came, and shivered in the slight draught through the casement. Tess was reflecting on the position of the household, in which she perceived her own evil influence. Had she not come home her mother and the children might probably have been allowed to stay on as weekly tenants. But she had been observed almost immediately on her return by some people of scrupulous character and great influence: they had seen her idling in the churchyard, restoring as well as she could with a little trowel a baby's obliterated grave. By this means they had found that she was living here again; her mother was scolded for 'harbouring' her; sharp retorts had ensued from Joan who had independently offered to leave at once; she had been taken at her word; and here was the result.

'I ought never to have come home,' said Tess to herself, bitterly.

She was so intent upon these thoughts that she hardly at first took note of a man in a white mackintosh whom she saw riding down the street. Possibly it was owing to her face being near to the pane that he saw her so quickly, and directed his horse so close to the cottage-front that his hoofs were almost upon the narrow border for plants growing under the wall. It was not till he touched the window with his riding-crop that she observed him. The rain had nearly ceased, and she opened the casement in obedience to his gesture.

'Didn't you see me?' asked d'Urberville.

'I was not attending,' she said. 'I heard you, I believe, though I fancied it was a carriage and horses. I was in a sort of dream.'

'Ah! you heard the d'Urberville Coach, perhaps. You know the legend, I suppose?'

'No. My – somebody was going to tell it me once, but didn't.'

'If you are a genuine d'Urberville I ought not to tell you either, I suppose. As for me, I'm a sham one, so it doesn't matter. It is rather dismal. It is that this sound of a non-existent coach can only be heard by one of d'Urberville blood, and it is held to be of ill-omen to the one who hears it. It has to do with a murder, committed by one of the family, centuries ago.'

'Now you have begun it, finish it.'

'Very well. One of the family is said to have abducted some beautiful woman, who tried to escape from the coach in which he was carrying her off, and in the struggle he killed her – or she killed him – I forget which. Such is one version of the tale . . . I see that your tubs and buckets are packed. Going away, aren't you?'

'Yes, to-morrow – Old Lady-Day.'

'I heard you were, but could hardly believe it; it seems so sudden. Why is it?'

'Father's was the last life on the property, and when that dropped we had no further right to stay. Though we might, perhaps, have stayed as weekly tenants – if it had not been for me.'

'What about you?'

'I am not a – proper woman.'

D'Urberville's face flushed.

'What a blasted shame! Miserable snobs! May their dirty souls be burnt to cinders!' he exclaimed in tones of ironic resentment. 'That's why you are going, is it? Turned out?'

'We are not turned out exactly; but as they said we should have to go soon, it was best to go now everybody was moving, because there are better chances.'

'Where are you going to?'

'Kingsbere. We have taken rooms there. Mother is so foolish about father's people that she will go there.'

'But your mother's family are not fit for lodgings, and in a little hole of a town like that. Now why not come to my gardenhouse at Trantridge? There are hardly any poultry now, since my mother's death; but there's the house, as you know it, and the garden. It can be whitewashed in a day, and your mother can live there quite comfortably; and I will put the children to a good school. Really I ought to do something for you!'

'But we have already taken the rooms at Kingsbere!' she declared. 'And we can wait there – '

'Wait – what for? For that nice husband, no doubt. Now look here, Tess, I know what men are, and, bearing in mind the *grounds* of your separation, I am quite positive he will never make it up with you. Now, though I have been your enemy, I am your friend, even if you won't believe it. Come to this cottage of mine. We'll get up a regular colony of fowls, and your mother can attend to them excellently; and the children can go to school.'

Tess breathed more and more quickly, and at length she said –

'How do I know that you would do all this? Your views may change – and then – we should be – my mother would be – homeless again.'

'Oh no – no. I would guarantee you against such as that in writing, if necessary. Think it over.'

Tess shook her head. But d'Urberville persisted; she had seldom seen him so determined; he would not take a negative.

'Please just tell your mother,' he said, in emphatic tones. 'It is her business to judge – not yours. I shall get the house swept out and whitened to-morrow morning, and fires lit; and it will be dry by the evening, so that you can come straight there. Now mind, I shall expect you.'

Tess again shook her head; her throat swelling with complicated emotion. She could not look up at d'Urberville.

'I owe you something for the past, you know,' he resumed. 'And you cured me, too, of that craze; so I am glad – '

'I would rather you had kept the craze, so that you had kept the practice which went with it!'

'I am glad of this opportunity of repaying you a little. Tomorrow I shall expect to hear your mother's goods unloading ... Give me your hand on it now – dear, beautiful Tess!'

With the last sentence he had dropped his voice to a murmur, and put his hand in at the half-open casement. With stormy eyes she pulled the stay-bar quickly, and, in doing so, caught his arm between the casement and the stone mullion.

'Damnation – you are very cruel!' he said, snatching out his arm. 'No, no! – I know you didn't do it on purpose. Well, I shall expect you, or your mother and the children at least.'

'I shall not come – I have plenty of money!' she cried.

'Where?'

'At my father-in-law's, if I ask for it.'

'*If* you ask for it. But you won't, Tess; I know you; you'll never ask for it – you'll starve first!'

With these words he rode off. Just at the corner of the street he met the man with the paint-pot, who asked him if he had deserted the brethren.

'You go to the devil!' said d'Urberville.

Tess remained where she was a long while, till a sudden rebellious sense of injustice caused the region of her eyes to swell with the rush of hot tears thither. Her husband, Angel Clare himself, had, like others, dealt out hard measure to her, surely he had! She had never before admitted such a thought; but he had surely! Never in her life – she could swear it from the bottom of her soul – had she ever intended to do wrong; yet these hard judgments had come. Whatever her sins, they were not sins of intention, but of inadvertence, and why should she have been punished so persistently?

She passionately seized the first piece of paper that came to hand, and scribbled the following lines:

O why have you treated me so monstrously, Angel! I do not deserve it. I have thought it all over carefully, and I can never, never forgive you! You know that I did not intend to wrong you – why have you so wronged me? You are cruel, cruel indeed! I will try to forget you. It is all injustice I have received at your hands!

T.

She watched till the postman passed by, ran out to him with her epistle, and then again took her listless place inside the window-panes.

It was just as well to write like that as to write tenderly. How could he give way to entreaty? The facts had not changed: there was no new event to alter his opinion.

It grew darker, the fire-light shining over the room. The two biggest of the younger children had gone out with their mother; the four smallest, their ages ranging from three-and-a-half years to eleven, all in black frocks, were gathered round the hearth babbling their own little subjects. Tess at length joined them, without lighting a candle.

'This is the last night that we shall sleep here, dears, in the house where we were born,' she said quickly. 'We ought to think of it, oughtn't we?'

They all became silent; with the impressibility of their age they were ready to burst into tears at the picture of finality she had conjured up, though all the day hitherto they had been rejoicing in the idea of a new place. Tess changed the subject.

'Sing to me, dears,' she said.

'What shall we sing?'

'Anything you know; I don't mind.'

There was a momentary pause; it was broken, first, by one little tentative note; then a second voice strengthened it, and a third and a fourth chimed in in unison, with words they had learnt at the Sunday-school –

> Here we suffer grief and pain,
> Here we meet to part again;
> In heaven we part no more.

The four sang on with the phlegmatic passivity of persons who had long ago settled the question, and there being no mistake about it, felt that further thought was not required. With features strained hard to enunciate the syllables they continued to regard the centre of the flickering fire, the notes of the youngest straying over into the pauses of the rest.

Tess turned from them, and went to the window again. Darkness had now fallen without, but she put her face to the pane as though to peer into the gloom. It was really to hide her tears. If she could only believe what the children were singing; if she were only sure, how different all would now be; how confidently she would leave them to Providence and their future kingdom! But, in default of that, it behoved her to do something; to be their Providence; for to Tess, as to not a few millions of others, there was ghastly satire in the poet's lines –

> Not in utter nakedness
> But trailing clouds of glory do we come.

To her and her like, birth itself was an ordeal of degrading personal compulsion, whose gratuitousness nothing in the result seemed to justify, and at best could only palliate.

In the shades of the wet road she soon discerned her mother with tall

'Liza-Lu and Abraham. Mrs Durbeyfield's pattens clicked up to the door, and Tess opened it.

'I see the tracks of a horse outside the window.' said Joan. 'Hev somebody called?'

'No,' said Tess.

The children by the fire looked gravely at her, and one murmured 'Why, Tess, the gentleman a-horseback!'

'He didn't call,' said Tess. 'He spoke to me in passing.'

'Who was the gentleman?' asked her mother. 'Your husband?'

'No. He'll never, never come,' answered Tess in stony hopelessness.

'Then who was it?'

'Oh, you needn't ask. You've seen him before, and so have I.'

'Ah! What did he say?' said Joan curiously.

'I will tell you when we are settled in our lodgings at Kingsbere to-morrow – every word.'

It was not her husband, she had said. Yet a consciousness that in a physical sense this man alone was her husband seemed to weigh on her more and more.

❧ Chapter Fifty-Two ❧

DURING THE SMALL HOURS of the next morning, while it was still dark, dwellers near the highways were conscious of a disturbance of their night's rest by rumbling noises, intermittently continuing till daylight – noises as certain to recur in this particular first week of the month as the voice of the cuckoo in the third week of the same. They were the preliminaries of the general removal, the passing of the empty waggons and teams to fetch the goods of the migrating families; for it was always by the vehicle of the farmer who required his services that the hired man was conveyed to his destination. That this might be accomplished within the day was the explanation of the reverberation occurring so soon after midnight, the aim of the carters being to reach the door of the outgoing households by six o'clock, when the loading of their movables at once began.

But to Tess and her mother's household no such anxious farmer sent his team. They were only women; they were not regular labourers; they were not particularly required anywhere; hence they had to hire a waggon at their own expense, and got nothing sent gratuitously.

It was a relief to Tess, when she looked out of the window that morning, to find that though the weather was windy and louring, it did not rain, and that the waggon had come. A wet Lady-Day was a spectre which removing families never forgot; damp furniture, damp bedding, damp clothing accompanied it, and left a train of ills.

Her mother, 'Liza-Lu, and Abraham were also awake, but the younger children were let sleep on. The four breakfasted by the thin light, and the 'house-ridding' was taken in hand.

It proceeded with some cheerfulness, a friendly neighbour or two assisting. When the large articles of furniture had been packed in position a circular nest was made of the beds and bedding, in which Joan Durbeyfield and the young children were to sit through the journey. After loading there was a long delay before the horses were brought, these having been unharnessed during the ridding; but at length, about two o'clock, the whole was under way, the cooking-pot swinging from the axle of the waggon, Mrs Durbeyfield and family at the top, the matron having in her lap, to prevent injury to its works, the head of the clock, which, at any exceptional lurch of the waggon, struck one, or one-and-a-half, in hurt tones. Tess and the next eldest girl walked alongside till they were out of the village.

They had called on a few neighbours that morning and the previous evening, and some came to see them off, all wishing them well, though, in their secret hearts, hardly expecting welfare possible to such a family, harmless as the Durbeyfields were to all except themselves. Soon the equipage began to ascend to higher ground, and the wind grew keener with the change of level and soil.

The day being the sixth of April, the Durbeyfield waggon met many other waggons with families on the summit of the load, which was built on a wellnigh unvarying principle, as peculiar, probably, to the rural labourer as the hexagon to the bee. The ground work of the arrangement was the family dresser, which, with its shining handles, and finger-marks, and domestic evidences thick upon it, stood importantly in front, over the tails of the shaft-horses, in its erect and natural position, like some Ark of the Covenant that they were bound to carry reverently.

Some of the households were lively, some mournful; some were stopping at the doors of wayside inns; where, in due time, the Durbeyfield menagerie also drew up to bait horses and refresh the travellers.

During the halt Tess's eyes fell upon a three-pint blue mug, which was ascending and descending through the air to and from the feminine section of a household, sitting on the summit of a load that had also drawn up at a little distance from the same inn. She followed one of the mug's journeys upward, and perceived it to be clasped by hands whose owner she well knew. Tess went towards the waggon.

'Marian and Izz!' she cried to the girls, for it was they, sitting with the moving family at whose house they had lodged. 'Are you house-ridding to-day, like everybody else?'

They were, they said. It had been too rough a life for them at Flintcomb-Ash, and they had come away, almost without notice, leaving Groby to prosecute them if he chose. They told Tess their destination, and Tess told them hers.

Marian leant over the load, and lowered her voice. 'Do you know that the gentleman who follows 'ee – you'll guess who I mean – came to ask for 'ee at Flintcomb after you had gone? We didn't tell'n where you was, knowing you wouldn't wish to see him.'

'Ah – but I did see him!' Tess murmured. 'He found me.'

'And do he know where you be going?'

'I think so.'

'Husband come back?'

'No.'

She bade her acquaintance good-bye – for the respective carters had now come out from the inn – and the two waggons resumed their journey in opposite directions; the vehicle whereon sat Marian, Izz, and the ploughman's family with whom they had thrown in their lot, being brightly painted, and drawn by three powerful horses with shining brass ornaments on their harness; while the waggon on which Mrs Durbeyfield and her family rode was a creaking erection that would scarcely bear the weight of the superincumbent load; one which had known no paint since it was made, and drawn by two horses only. The contrast well marked the difference between being fetched by a thriving farmer and conveying oneself whither no hirer waited one's coming.

The distance was great – too great for a day's journey – and it was with the utmost difficulty that the horses performed it. Though they had started so early it was quite late in the afternoon when they turned the flank of an eminence which formed part of the upland called Greenhill. While the horses stood to stale and breathe themselves Tess looked around. Under the hill, and just ahead of them, was the half-dead townlet of their pilgrimage, Kingsbere, where lay those ancestors of whom her father had spoken and sung to painfulness: Kingsbere, the spot of all spots in the world which could be considered the d'Urbervilles' home, since they had resided there for full five hundred years.

A man could be seen advancing from the outskirts towards them, and when he beheld the nature of their waggon-load he quickened his steps.

'You be the woman they call Mrs Durbeyfield, I reckon?' he said to Tess's mother, who had descended to walk the remainder of the way.

She nodded. 'Though widow of the late Sir John d'Urberville, poor nobleman, if I cared for my rights; and returning to the domain of his forefathers.'

'Oh? Well, I know nothing about that; but if you be Mrs Durbeyfield, I am sent to tell 'ee that the rooms you wanted be let. We didn't know you was coming till we got your letter this morning – when 'twas too late. But no doubt you can get other lodgings somewhere.'

The man had noticed the face of Tess, which had become ash-pale at his intelligence. Her mother looked hopelessly at fault. 'What shall we do now, Tess?' she said bitterly. 'Here's a welcome to your ancestors' lands! However, let's try further.'

They moved on into the town, and tried with all their might, Tess remaining with the waggon to take care of the children whilst her mother and 'Liza-Lu made inquiries. At the last return of Joan to the vehicle, an hour later, when her search for accommodation had still been fruitless, the driver of the waggon said the goods must be unloaded, as the horses were half-dead, and he was bound to return part of the way at least that night.

'Very well – unload it here,' said Joan recklessly. 'I'll get shelter somewhere.'

The waggon had drawn up under the churchyard wall, in a spot screened from view, and the driver, nothing loth, soon hauled down the poor heap of household goods. This done she paid him, reducing herself to almost her last shilling thereby, and he moved off and left them, only too glad to get out of further dealings with such a family. It was a dry night, and he guessed that they would come to no harm.

Tess gazed desperately at the pile of furniture. The cold sunlight of this spring evening peered invidiously upon the crocks and kettles, upon the bunches of dried herbs shivering in the breeze, upon the brass handles of the dresser, upon the wickercradle they had all been rocked in, and upon the well-rubbed clock-case, all of which gave out the reproachful gleam of indoor articles abandoned to the vicissitudes of a roofless exposure for which they were never made. Round about were deparked hills and slopes – now cut up into little paddocks – and the green foundations that showed where the d'Urberville mansion once had stood; also an outlying stretch of Egdon Heath that had always belonged to the estate. Hard by, the aisle of the church called the d'Urberville Aisle looked on imperturbably.

'Isn't your family vault your own freehold?' said Tess's mother, as she returned from a reconnoitre of the church and graveyard. 'Why of course 'tis, and that's where we will camp, girls, till the place of your ancestors finds us a roof! Now Tess and 'Liza and Abraham, you help me. We'll make a nest for these children, and then we'll have another look round.'

Tess listlessly lent a hand, and in a quarter of an hour the old four-post bedstead was dissociated from the heap of goods, and erected under the south wall of the church, the part of the building known as the d'Urberville Aisle, beneath which the huge vaults lay. Over the tester of the bedstead was a beautifully traceried window, of many lights, its date being the fifteenth century. It was called the d'Urberville Window, and in the upper part could be discerned heraldic emblems like those on Durbeyfield's old seal and spoon.

Joan drew the curtains round the bed so as to make an excellent tent of it, and put the smaller children inside. 'If it comes to the worst we can sleep there too, for one night,' she said. 'But let us try further on, and get something for the dears to eat! O, Tess, what's the use of your playing at marrying gentlemen, if it leaves us like this!'

Accompanied by 'Liza-Lu and the boy she again ascended the little lane which secluded the church from the townlet. As soon as they got into the street they beheld a man on horseback gazing up and down. 'Ah – I'm looking for you!' he said, riding up to them. 'This is indeed a family gathering on the historic spot!'

It was Alec d'Urberville. 'Where is Tess?' he asked.

Personally Joan had no liking for Alec. She cursorily signified that direction of the church, and went on, d'Urberville saying that he would see them again, in case they should be still unsuccessful in their search for shelter, of which he had just heard. When they had gone d'Urberville rode to the inn, and shortly after came out on foot.

In the interim Tess, left with the children inside the bedstead, remained talking with them awhile, till, seeing that no more could be done to make them comfortable just then, she walked about the churchyard, now beginning to be embrowned by the shades of nightfall. The door of the church was unfastened, and she entered it for the first time in her life.

Within the window under which the bedstead stood were the tombs of the family, covering in their dates several centuries. They were canopied, altarshaped, and plain; their carvings being defaced and broken; their brasses torn from the matrices, the rivet-holes remaining like marten-holes in a sand-cliff. Of all the reminders that she had ever received that her people were socially extinct there was none so forcible as this spoliation.

She drew near to a dark stone on which was inscribed:

Ostium sepulchri antiquae familiae d'Urberville

Tess did not read Church-Latin like a Cardinal, but she knew that this was the door of her ancestral sepulchre, and that the tall knights of whom her father had chanted in his cups lay inside.

She musingly turned to withdraw, passing near an altartomb, the oldest of them all, on which was a recumbent figure. In the dusk she had not noticed it before, and would hardly have noticed it now but for an odd fancy that the effigy moved. As soon as she drew close to it she discovered all in a moment that the figure was a living person; and the shock to her sense of not having been alone was so violent that she was quite overcome, and sank down nigh to fainting, not however till she had recognized Alec d'Urberville in the form.

He leapt off the slab and supported her.

'I saw you come in,' he said smiling 'and got up there not to interrupt your meditations. A family gathering, is it not, with these old fellows under us here? Listen.'

He stamped with his heel heavily on the floor; whereupon there arose a hollow echo from below.

'That shook them a bit, I'll warrant!' he continued. 'And you thought I was the mere stone reproduction of one of them. But no. The old order changeth. The little finger of the sham d'Urberville can do more for you than the whole dynasty of the real underneath . . . Now command me. What shall I do?'

'Go away!' she murmured.

'I will – I'll look for your mother,' said he blandly. But in passing her he whispered: 'Mind this; you'll be civil yet!'

When he was gone she bent down upon the entrance to the vaults, and said –

'Why am I on the wrong side of this door!'

In the meantime Marian and Izz Huett had journeyed onward with the chattels of the ploughman in the direction of their land of Canaan – the Egypt of some other family who had left it only that morning. But the girls did not for a long time think of where they were going. Their talk was of Angel Clare and Tess, and Tess's persistent lover, whose connection with her previous history they had partly heard and partly guessed ere this.

''Tis as though she had never known him afore,' said Marian. 'His having won her once makes all the difference in the world. 'Twould be a thousand pities if he were to tole her away again. Mr Clare can never be anything to us, Izz; and why should we grudge him to her, and not try to mend this quarrel? If he could on'y know what straits she's put to, and what's hovering round, he might come to take care of his own.'

'Could we let him know?'

They thought of this all the way to their destination; but the bustle of re-establishment in their new place took up all their attention then. But when they were settled, a month later, they heard of Clare's approaching return, though they had learnt nothing more of Tess. Upon that, agitated anew by their attachment to him, yet honourably disposed to her, Marian uncorked the penny ink-bottle they shared, and a few lines were concocted between the two girls.

HONOUR'D SIR – Look to your Wife if you do love her as much as she do love you. For she is sore put to by an Enemy in the shape of a Friend. Sir, there is one near her who ought to be Away. A woman should not be try'd beyond her Strength, and continual dropping will wear away a Stone – ay, more – a Diamond.

FROM TWO WELL WISHERS.

This they addressed to Angel Clare at the only place they had ever heard him to be connected with, Emminster Vicarage; after which they continued in a mood of emotional exaltation at their own generosity, which made them sing in hysterical snatches and weep at the same time.

PHASE THE SEVENTH

Fulfilment

❧ Chapter Fifty-Three ❦

IT WAS EVENING AT EMMINSTER Vicarage. The two customary candles were burning under their green shades in the Vicar's study, but he had not been sitting there. Occasionally he came in, stirred the small fire which sufficed for the increasing mildness of the spring, and went out again; sometimes pausing at the front door, going on to the drawing-room, then returning again to the front door.

It faced westward, and though gloom prevailed inside, there was still light enough without to see with distinctness. Mrs Clare, who had been sitting in the drawing-room, followed him hither.

'Plenty of time yet,' said the Vicar. 'He doesn't reach Chalk-Newton till six, even if the train should be punctual, and ten miles of country-road, five of them in Crimmercrock Lane, are not jogged over in a hurry by our old horse.'

'But he has done it in an hour with us, my dear.'

'Years ago.'

Thus they passed the minutes, each well knowing that this was only waste of breath, the one essential being simply to wait.

At length there was a slight noise in the lane, and the old pony-chaise appeared indeed outside the railings. They saw alight therefrom a form which they affected to recognize, but would actually have passed by in the street without identifying had he not got out of their carriage at the particular moment when a particular person was due.

Mrs Clare rushed through the dark passage to the door, and her husband came more slowly after her.

The new arrival, who was just about to enter, saw their anxious faces in the doorway and the gleam of the west in their spectacles because they confronted the last rays of day; but they could only see his shape against the light.

'O, my boy, my boy – home again at last!' cried Mrs Clare, who cared no more at that moment for the stains of heterodoxy which had caused all this separation than for the dust upon his clothes. What woman, indeed, among the most faithful adherents of the truth, believes the promises and threats of the Word in the sense in which she believes in her own children, or would not throw her theology to the wind if weighed against their happiness? As soon as they reached the room where the candles were lighted she looked at his face.

'O, it is not Angel – not my son – the Angel who went away!' she cried in all the irony of sorrow, as she turned herself aside.

His father, too, was shocked to see him, so reduced was that figure from its former contours by worry and the bad season that Clare had experienced, in the climate to which he had so rashly hurried in his first aversion to the mockery of events at home. You could see the skeleton behind the man, and almost the ghost behind the skeleton. He matched Crivelli's dead *Christus*. His sunken eye-pits were of morbid hue, and the light in his eyes had waned. The angular hollows and lines of his aged ancestors had succeeded to their reign in his face twenty years before their time.

'I was ill over there, you know,' he said. 'I am all right now.'

As if, however, to falsify this assertion, his legs seemed to give way, and he suddenly sat down to save himself from falling. It was only a slight attack of faintness, resulting from the tedious day's journey, and the excitement of arrival.

'Has any letter come for me lately?' he asked. 'I received the last you sent on by the merest chance, and after considerable delay through being inland; or I might have come sooner.'

'It was from your wife, we supposed?'

'It was.'

Only one other had recently come. They had not sent it on to him, knowing he would start for home so soon.

He hastily opened the letter produced, and was much disturbed to read in Tess's handwriting the sentiments expressed in her last hurried scrawl to him.

O why have you treated me so monstrously, Angel! I do not deserve it. I have thought it all over carefully, and I can never, never forgive you! You know that I did not intend to wrong you – why have you so wronged me? You are cruel, cruel indeed! I will try to forget you. It is all injustice I have received at your hands! T.

'It is quite true! said Angel, throwing down the letter. 'Perhaps she will never be reconciled to me!'

'Don't, Angel, be so anxious about a mere child of the soil!' said his mother.

'Child of the soil! Well, we all are children of the soil. I wish she were so in the sense you mean; but let me now explain to you what I have never explained before, that her father is a descendant in the male line of one of the oldest Norman houses, like a good many others who lead obscure agricultural lives in our villages, and are dubbed "sons of the soil!".'

He soon retired to bed; and the next morning, feeling exceedingly unwell, he remained in his room pondering. The circumstances amid which he had left Tess were such that though, while on the south of the Equator and just in receipt of her loving epistle, it had seemed the easiest thing in the world to rush back to her arms the moment he chose to forgive her, now that he had arrived it was not so easy as it had seemed. She was passionate, and her present letter, showing that her estimate of him had changed under his delay – too justly changed, he sadly owned, – made him ask himself if it would be wise to confront her unannounced in the presence of her parents. Supposing that her love had indeed turned to dislike during the last weeks of separation, a sudden meeting might lead to bitter words.

Clare therefore thought it would be best to prepare Tess and her family by sending a line to Marlott announcing his return, and his hope that she was still living with them there, as he had arranged for her to do when he left England. He despatched the inquiry that very day, and before the week was out there came a short reply from Mrs Durbeyfield which did not remove his embarrassment, for it bore no address, though to his surprise it was not written from Marlott.

SIR – J write these few lines to say that my Daughter is away from me at present, and J am not sure when she will return, but J will let you know as Soon as she do. J do not feel at liberty to tell you Where she is temperly biding. J should say that me and my Family have left Marlott for some Time. – Yours,

J.D. URBEYFIELD.

It was such a relief to Clare to learn that Tess was at least apparently well that her mother's still reticence as to her whereabouts did not long distress him. They were all angry with him, evidently. He would wait till Mrs Durbeyfield could inform him of Tess's return, which her letter implied to be soon. He deserved no more. His had been a love 'which alters when it alteration finds'. He had undergone some strange experiences in his absence; he had seen the virtual Faustina in the literal Cornelia; a spiritual Lucretia in a corporeal Phryne; he had thought of the women taken and set in the midst as one deserving to be stoned, and the wife of Uriah being made a queen; and he had asked himself why he had not judged Tess constructively rather than biographically, by the will rather than by the deed?

A day or two passed while he waited at his father's house for the promised second note from Joan Durbeyfield, and indirectly to recover a little more strength. The strength showed signs of coming back, but there was no sign of Joan's letter. Then he hunted up the old letter sent to him in Brazil, which Tess had written from Flintcomb-Ash, and re-read it. The sentences touched him now as much as when he had first perused them.

> I must cry to you in my trouble – I have no one else ... I think I must die if you do not come soon, or tell me to come to you ... Please, please not to be just; only a little kind to me! ... If you would come I could die in your arms! I would be well content to do that if so be you had forgiven me! ... If you will send me one little line and say, *I am coming soon,* I will bide on, Angel, I so cheerfully! ... Think how it do hurt my heart not to see you ever, ever! Ah, if I could only make your dear heart ache one little minute of each day as mine does every day and all day long, it might lead you to show pity to your poor lonely one ... I would be content, ay, glad, to live with you as your servant, if I may not as your wife; so that I could only be near you, and get glimpses of you, and think of you as mine ... I long for only one thing in heaven, or earth, or under the earth, to meet you, my own dear! Come to me, come to me, and save me from what threatens me.

Clare determined that he would no longer believe in her more recent and severer regard of him; but would go and find her immediately. He asked his father if she had applied for any money during his absence. His father returned a negative, and then for the first time it occurred to Angel that her pride had stood in her way, and that she had suffered privation. From his remarks his parents now gathered the real reason of the separation; and their Christianity was such that, reprobates being their especial care, the tenderness towards Tess which her blood, her simplicity, even her poverty, had not engendered, was instantly excited by her sin.

Whilst he was hastily packing together a few articles for his journey he glanced over a poor plain missive also lately come to hand – the one from Marian and Izz Huett, beginning –

'HONOUR'D SIR – Look to your wife if you do love her as much as she do you,' and signed, 'FROM TWO WELL-WISHERS.'

♦ Chapter Fifty-Four ♦

IN A QUARTER OF AN HOUR Clare was leaving the house, whence his mother watched his thin figure as it disappeared into the street. He had declined to borrow his father's old mare, well knowing of its necessity to the household. He went to the inn, where he hired a trap, and could hardly wait during the harnessing. In a very few minutes after he was driving up the hill out of the town which, three or four months earlier in the year, Tess had descended with such hopes and ascended with such shattered purposes.

Benvill Lane soon stretched before him, its hedges and trees purple with buds; but he was looking at other things, and only recalled himself to the scene sufficiently to enable him to keep the way. In something less than an hour-and-a-half he had skirted the south of the King's Hintock estates and ascended to the untoward solitude of Cross-in-Hand, the unholy stone whereon Tess had been compelled by Alec d'Urberville, in his whim of reformation, to swear the strange oath that she would never wilfully tempt him again. The pale and blasted nettlestems of the preceding year even now lingered nakedly in the banks, young green nettles of the present spring growing from their roots.

Thence he went along the verge of the upland overhanging the other Hintocks, and, turning to the right, plunged into the bracing calcareous region of Flintcomb-Ash, the address from which she had written to him in one of the letters, and which he supposed to be the place of sojourn referred to by her mother. Here, of course, he did not find her; and what added to his depression was the discovery that no 'Mrs Clare' had ever been heard of by the cottagers or by the farmer himself, though Tess was remembered well enough by her Christian name. His name she had obviously never used during their separation, and her dignified sense of their total severance was shown not much less by this abstention than by the hardships she had chosen to undergo (of which he now learnt for the first time) rather than apply to his father for more funds.

From this place they told him Tess Durbeyfield had gone, without due notice, to the home of her parents on the other side of Blackmoor, and it therefore became necessary to find Mrs Durbeyfield. She had told him she was not now at Marlott, but had been curiously reticent as to her actual address, and the only course was to go to Marlott and inquire for it. The farmer who had been so churlish with Tess was quite smooth-tongued to Clare, and lent him a horse and man to drive him towards Marlott, the gig he had arrived in being sent back to Emminster; for the limit of a day's journey with that horse was reached.

Clare would not accept the loan of the farmer's vehicle for a further distance than to the outskirts of the Vale, and, sending it back with the man who had driven him, he put up at an inn, and next day entered on foot the region wherein was the spot of his dear Tess's birth. It was as yet too early in the year for much colour to appear in the gardens and foliage; the so-called spring was but winter overlaid with a thin coat of greenness. and it was of a parcel with his expectations.

The house in which Tess had passed the years of her childhood was now inhabited by another family who had never known her. The new residents were in the garden, taking as much interest in their own doings as if the homestead had never passed its primal time in conjunction with the histories of others, beside which the histories of these were but as a tale told by an idiot. They walked about the garden paths with thoughts of their own concerns entirely uppermost, bringing their actions at every moment into jarring collision with the dim ghosts behind them, talking as though the time when Tess lived there were not one whit intenser in story than now. Even the spring birds sang over their heads as if they thought there was nobody missing in particular.

On inquiry of these previous innocents, to whom even the name of their predecessors was a failing memory, Clare learned that John Durbeyfield was dead; that his widow and children had left Marlott, declaring that they were going to live at Kingsbere, but instead of doing so had gone on to another place they mentioned. By this time Clare abhorred the house for ceasing to contain Tess, and hastened away from its hated presence without once looking back.

His way was by the field in which he had first beheld her at the dance. It was as bad as the house – even worse. He passed on through the churchyard, where, amongst the new headstones, he saw one of a somewhat superior design to the rest. The inscription ran thus:

In memory of John Durbeyfield, rightly d'Urberville, of the once powerful family of that Name, and Direct Descendant through an Illustrious Line from Sir Pagan d'Urberville, one of the Knights of the Conqueror. Died March 10th, 18 –

How are the Mighty Fallen.

Some man, apparently the sexton, had observed Clare standing there, and drew nigh. 'Ah, sir, now that's a man who didn't want to lie here, but wished to be carried to Kingsbere, where his ancestors be.'

'And why didn't they respect his wish?'

'Oh – no money. Bless your soul, sir, why – there, I wouldn't wish to say it everywhere, but – even this headstone, for all the flourish wrote upon en, is not paid for.'

'Ah, who put it up?'

The man told the name of a mason in the village, and, on leaving the churchyard, Clare called at the mason's house. He found that the statement was true, and paid the bill. This done he turned in the direction of the migrants.

The distance was too long for a walk, but Clare felt such a strong desire for isolation that at first he would neither hire a conveyance nor go to a circuitous line of railway by which he might eventually reach the place. At Shaston, however, he found he must hire; but the way was such that he did not enter Joan's place till about seven o'clock in the evening, having traversed a distance of over twenty miles since leaving Marlott.

The village being small he had little difficulty in finding Mrs Durbeyfield's tenement, which was a house in a walled garden, remote from the main road, where she had stowed away her clumsy old furniture as best she could. It was plain that for some reason or other she had not wished him to visit her, and he felt his call to be somewhat of an intrusion. She came to the door herself, and the light from the evening sky fell upon her face.

This was the first time that Clare had ever met her, but he was too preoccupied to observe more than that she was still a handsome woman, in the garb of a respectable widow. He was obliged to explain that he was Tess's husband, and his object in coming there, and he did it awkwardly enough. 'I want to see her at once,' he added. 'You said you would write to me again, but you have not done so.'

'Because she've not come home,' said Joan.

'Do you know if she is well?'

'I don't. But you ought to, sir,' said she.

'I admit it. Where is she staying?'

From the beginning of the interview Joan had disclosed her embarrassment by keeping her hand to the side of her cheek.

'I – don't know exactly where she is staying,' she answered. 'She was – but – '

'Where was she?'

'Well, she is not there now.'

In her evasiveness she paused again, and the younger children had by this time crept to the door, where, pulling at his mother's skirts, the youngest murmured –

'In this the gentleman who is going to marry Tess?'

'He has married her,' Joan whispered. 'Go inside.'

Clare saw her efforts for reticence, and asked –

'Do you think Tess would wish me to try and find her? If not, of course – '

'I don't think she would.'

'Are you sure?'

'I am sure she wouldn't.'

He was turning away; and then he thought of Tess's tender letter.

'I am sure she would!' he retorted passionately. 'I know her better than you do.'

'That's very likely, sir; for I have never really known her.'

'Please tell me her address, Mrs Durbeyfield, in kindness to a lonely wretched man!'

Tess's mother again restlessly swept her cheek with her vertical hand, and seeing that he suffered, she at last said, in a low voice –

'She is at Sandbourne.'

'Ah – where there? Sandbourne has become a large place, they say.'

'I don't know more particularly than I have said – Sandbourne. For myself, I was never there.'

It was apparent that Joan spoke the truth in this, and he pressed her no further.

'Are you in want of anything?' he said gently.

'No, sir,' she replied. 'We are fairly well provided for.'

Without entering the house Clare turned away. There was a station three miles ahead, and paying off his coachman, he walked thither. The last train to Sandbourne left shortly after, and it bore Clare on its wheels.

◈ Chapter Fifty-Five ◈

AT ELEVEN O'CLOCK THAT night, having secured a bed at one of the hotels and telegraphed his address to his father immediately on his arrival, he walked out into the streets of Sandbourne. It was too late to call on or inquire for any one, and he reluctantly postponed his purpose till the morning. But he could not retire to rest just yet.

This fashionable watering-place, with its eastern and its western stations, its piers, it groves of pines, its promenades, and its covered gardens, was, to Angel Clare, like a fairy place suddenly created by the stroke of a wand, and allowed to get a littly dusty. An outlying eastern tract of the enormous Egdon Waste was close at hand, yet on the very verge of that tawny piece of antiquity such a glittering novelty as this pleasure city had chosen to spring up. Within the space of a mile from its outskirts every irregularity of the soil was prehistoric, every channel an undisturbed British trackway; not a sod having been turned there since the days of the Caesars. Yet the exotic had grown here, suddenly as the prophet's gourd; and had drawn hither Tess.

By the midnight lamps he went up and down the winding ways of this new world in an old one, and could discern between the trees and against the stars the lofty roofs, chimneys, gazebos, and towers of the numerous fanciful residences of which the place was composed. It was a city of detached mansions; a Mediterranean lounging-place on the English Channel; and as seen now by night it seemed even more imposing than it was.

The sea was near at hand, but not intrusive; it murmured, and he thought it was the pines; the pines murmured in precisely the same tones, and he thought they were the sea.

Where could Tess possibly be, a cottage-girl, his young wife, amidst all this wealth and fashion? The more he pondered the more was he puzzled. Were there any cows to milk here? There certainly were no fields to till. She was most probably engaged to do something in one of these large houses; and he sauntered along, looking at the chamber-windows and their lights going out one by one; and wondered which of them might be hers.

Conjecture was useless, and just after twelve o'clock he entered and went to bed. Before putting out his light he re-read Tess's impassioned letter. Sleep, however, he could not, – so near her, yet so far from her – and he continually lifted the window-blind and regarded the backs of the opposite houses, and wondered behind which of the sashes she reposed at that moment.

He might almost as well have sat up all night. In the morning he arose at seven, and shortly after went out, taking the direction of the chief post-office. At the door he met an intelligent postman coming out with letters for the morning delivery.

'Do you know the address of a Mrs Clare?' asked Angel.

The postman shook his head.

Then, remembering that she would have been likely to continue the use of her name, Clare said –

'Or a Miss Durbeyfield?'

'Durbeyfield?'

This also was strange to the postman addressed.

'There's visitors coming and going every day, as you know sir,' he said; 'and without the name of the house 'tis impossible to find 'em.'

One of his comrades hastening out at that moment, the name was repeated to him.

'I know no name of Durbeyfield; but there is the name of d'Urberville at The Herons,' said the second.

'That's it!' cried Clare, pleased to think that she had reverted to the real pronunciation. 'What place is The Herons?'

'A stylish lodging-house. 'Tis all lodging-houses here, bless 'ee.'

Clare received directions how to find the house, and hastened thither, arriving with the milkman. The Herons, though an ordinary villa, stood in its own grounds, and was certainly the last place in which one would have expected to find lodgings so private was its appearance. If poor Tess was a servant here, as he feared, she would go to the back-door to that milkman, and he was inclined to go thither also. However, in his doubts he turned to the front, and rang.

The hour being early the landlady herself opened the door. Clare inquired for Teresa d'Urberville or Durbeyfield.

'Mrs d'Urberville?'

'Yes.'

Tess, then, passed as a married woman, and he felt glad even though she had not adopted his name.

'Will you kindly tell her that a relative is anxious to see her?'

'It is rather early. What name shall I give, sir?'

'Angel.'

'Mr Angel?'

'No; Angel. It is my Christian name. She'll understand.'

'I'll see if she is awake.'

He was shown into the front room – the dining-room – and looked out through the spring curtains at the little lawn, and the rhododendrons and other shrubs upon it. Obviously her position was by no means so bad as he had feared, and it crossed his mind that she must somehow have claimed and sold the jewels to attain it. He did not blame her for one moment. Soon his sharpened ear detected footsteps upon the stairs, at which his heart thumped so painfully that he could hardly stand firm. 'Dear me! what will she think of me, so altered as I am!' he said to himself; and the door opened.

Tess appeared on the threshold – not at all as he had expected to see her – bewilderingly otherwise, indeed. Her great natural beauty was, if not heightened, rendered more obvious by her attire. She was loosely wrapped in a cashmere dressing-gown of gray-white, embroidered in half-mourning tints, and she wore slippers of the same hue. Her neck rose out of a frill of down, and her well-remembered cable of dark-brown hair was partially coiled up in a mass at the back of her head and partly hanging on her shoulder – the evident result of haste.

He had held out his arms, but they had fallen again to his side; for she had not come forward, remaining still in the opening of the doorway.

Mere yellow skeleton that he was now he felt the contrast between them, and thought his appearance distasteful to her.

'Tess!' he said huskily, 'can you forgive me for going away? Can't you – come to me? How do you get to be – like this?'

'It is too late,' said she, her voice sounding hard through the room, her eyes shining unnaturally.

'I did not think rightly of you – I did not see you as you were!' he continued to plead. 'I have learnt to since, dearest Tessy mine!'

'Too late, too late!' she said, waving her hand in the impatience of a person whose tortures cause every instant to seem an hour. 'Don't come close to me, Angel! No – you must not. Keep away.'

'But don't you love me, my dear wife, because I have been so pulled down by illness? You are not so fickle – I am come on purpose for you – my mother and father will welcome you now!'

'Yes – O, yes, yes! But I say, I say it is too late.'

She seemed to feel like a fugitive in a dream, who tries to move away, but cannot. 'Don't you know all – don't you know it? Yet how do you come here if you do not know?'

'I inquired here and there, and I found the way.'

'I waited and waited for you,' she went on, her tones suddenly resuming their old fluty pathos. 'But you did not come! And I wrote to you, and you did not come! He kept on saying you would never come any more, and that I was a foolish woman. He was very kind to me, and to mother, and to all of us after father's death. He – '

'I don't understand.'

'He has won me back to him.'

Clare looked at her keenly, then, gathering her meaning flagged like one plague-stricken, and his glance sank; it fell on her hands, which, once rosy, were now white and more delicate.

She continued –

'He is upstairs. I hate him now, because he told me a lie – that you would not come again; and you *have* come! These clothes are what he's put upon me: I didn't care what he did wi' me! But – will you go away, Angel, please, and never come any more?'

They stood fixed, their baffled hearts looking out of their eyes with a joylessness pitiful to see. Both seemed to implore something to shelter them from reality.

'Ah – it is my fault!' said Clare.

But he could not get on. Speech was as inexpressive as silence. But he had a vague consciousness of one thing, though it was not clear to him till later; that his original Tess had spiritually ceased to recognize the body before him as hers – allowing it to drift, like a corpse upon the current, in a direction dissociated from its living will.

A few instants passed, and he found that Tess was gone. His face grew colder and more shrunken as he stood concentrated on the moment, and a minute or two after he found himself in the street, walking along he did not know whither.

❧ Chapter Fifty-Six ❧

MRS BROOKS, THE LADY WHO was the householder at The Herons, and owner of all the handsome furniture, was not a person of an unusually curious turn of mind. She was too deeply materialized, poor woman, by her long and enforced bondage to that arithmetical demon Profit-and-Loss, to retain much curiosity for its own sake, and apart from possible lodgers' pockets. Nevertheless, the visit of Angel Clare to her well-paying tenants, Mr and Mrs d'Urberville, as she deemed them, was sufficiently exceptional in point of time and manner to reinvigorate the feminine proclivity which had been stifled down as useless save in its bearings on the letting trade.

Tess had spoken to her husband from the doorway, without entering the dining-room, and Mrs Brooks, who stood with the partly-closed door of her own sitting-room at the back of the passage, could hear fragments of the conversation – if conversation it could be called – between those two wretched souls. She heard Tess re-ascend the stairs to the first floor, and the departure of Clare, and the closing of the front door behind him. Then the door of the room above was shut, and Mrs Brooks knew that Tess had re-entered her apartment. As the young lady was not fully dressed Mrs Brooks knew that she would not emerge again for some time.

She accordingly ascended the stairs softly, and stood at the door of the front room – a drawing-room, connected with the room immediately behind it (which was a bedroom) by folding doors in the common manner. This first floor, containing Mrs Brooks's best apartments, had been taken by the week by the d'Urbervilles. The back room was now in silence; but from the drawing-room there came sounds.

All that she could at first distinguish of them was one syllable, continually repeated in a low note of moaning, as if it came from a soul bound to some Ixionian wheel –

'O – O – O!'

Then a silence, then a heavy sigh, and again –

'O – O – O!!'

The landlady looked through the keyhole. Only a small space of the room inside was visible, but within that space came a corner of the breakfast table, which was already spread for the meal, and also a chair beside. Over the seat of the chair Tess's face was bowed, her posture being a kneeling one in front of it; her hands were clasped over her head, the skirts of her dressing-gown and the embroidery of her night-gown flowed upon the floor behind her, and her stockingless feet, from which the slippers had fallen, protruded upon the carpet. It was from her lips that came the murmur of unspeakable despair.

Then a man's voice from the adjoining bedroom –

'What's the matter?'

She did not answer, but went on, in a tone which was a soliloquy rather than an exclamation, and a dirge rather than a soliloquy. Mrs Brooks could only catch a portion:

'And then my dear, dear husband came home to me . . . and I did not know it! . . . And you had used your cruel persuasion upon me . . . you did not stop using it – no – you did not stop! My little sisters and brothers and my mother's needs – they were the things you moved me by . . . and you said my husband would never come back – never; and you taunted me, and said what a simpleton I was to expect him! . . . And at last I believed you and gave way! . . . And then he came back! Now he is gone. Gone a second time, and I have lost him now for ever . . . and he will not love me the littlest bit ever any more – only hate me! . . . O yes, I have lost him now – again because of – you!' In writhing, with her head on the chair, she turned her face towards the door, and Mrs Brooks could see the pain upon it; and that her lips were bleeding from the clench of her teeth upon them, and that the long lashes of her closed eyes stuck in wet tags to her cheeks. She continued: 'And he is dying – he looks as if he is dying! . . . And my sin will kill him and not kill me! . . . O, you have torn my life all to pieces . . . made me be what I prayed you in pity not to make me be again! . . . My own true husband will never, never – O God – I can't bear this! – I cannot!'

There were more and sharper words from the man; then a sudden rustle; she had sprung to her feet. Mrs Brooks, thinking that the speaker was coming to rush out of the door, hastily retreated down the stairs.

She need not have done so, however, for the door of the sitting-room was not opened. But Mrs Brooks felt it unsafe to watch on the landing again, and entered her own parlour below.

She could hear nothing through the floor, although she listened intently, and thereupon went to the kitchen to finish her interrupted breakfast. Coming up presently to the front room on the ground floor she took up some sewing, waiting for her lodgers to ring that she might take away the breakfast, which she meant to do herself, to discover what was the matter if possible. Overhead, as she sat, she could now hear the floorboards slightly creak, as if some one were walking about, and presently the movement was explained by the rustle of garments against the banisters, the opening and the closing of the front door, and the form of Tess passing to the gate on her way into the street. She was fully dressed now in the walking costume of a well-to-do young lady in which she had arrived, with the sole addition that over her hat and black feathers a veil was drawn.

Mrs Brooks had not been able to catch any word of farewell, temporary or otherwise, between her tenants at the door above. They might have quarrelled, or Mr d'Urberville might still be asleep, for he was not an early riser.

She went into the back room which was more especially her own apartment, and continued her sewing there. The lady lodger did not return, nor did the gentleman ring his bell. Mrs Brooks pondered on the delay, and on what probable relation the visitor who had called so early bore to the couple upstairs. In reflecting she leant back in her chair.

As she did so her eyes glanced casually over the ceiling till they were arrested by a spot in the middle of its white surface which she had never noticed there before. It was about the size of a wafer when she first observed it, but it speedily grew as large as the palm of her hand, and then she could perceive that it was red. The oblong white ceiling, with this scarlet blot in the midst, had the appearance of a gigantic ace of hearts.

Mrs Brooks had strange qualms of misgiving. She got upon the table, and touched the spot in the ceiling with her fingers. It was damp, and she fancied that it was a blood stain.

Descending from the table, she left the parlour, and went upstairs, intending to enter the room overhead, which was the bedchamber at the back of the drawing-room. But nerveless woman as she had now become, she could not bring herself to attempt the handle. She listened. The dead silence within was broken only by a regular beat.

Drip, drip, drip.

Mrs Brooks hastened downstairs, opened the front door, and ran into the street. A man she knew, one of the workmen employed at an adjoining villa, was passing by, and she begged him to come in and go upstairs with her; she feared something had happened to one of her lodgers. The workman assented, and followed her to the landing.

She opened the door of the drawing-room, and stood back for him to pass in, entering herself behind him. The room was empty; the breakfast

333

– a substantial repast of coffee, eggs, and a cold ham – lay spread upon the table untouched, as when she had taken it up, excepting that the carving knife was missing. She asked the man to go through the folding-doors into the adjoining room.

He opened the doors, entered a step or two, and came back almost instantly with a rigid face. 'My good God, the gentleman in bed is dead! I think he has been hurt with a knife – a lot of blood has run down upon the floor!'

The alarm was soon given, and the house which had lately been so quiet resounded with the tramp of many footsteps, a surgeon among the rest. The wound was small, but the point of the blade had touched the heart of the victim, who lay on his back, pale, fixed, dead, as if he had scarcely moved after the infliction of the blow. In a quarter of an hour the news that a gentleman who was a temporary visitor to the town had been stabbed in his bed, spread through every street and villa of the popular watering-place.

꘎ Chapter Fifty-Seven ꘎

MEANWHILE ANGEL CLARE HAD walked automatically along the way by which he had come, and, entering his hotel, sat down over the breakfast, staring at nothingness. He went on eating and drinking unconsciously till on a sudden he demanded his bill; having paid which he took his dressing-bag in his hand, the only luggage he had brought with him, and went out.

At the moment of his departure a telegram was handed to him – a few words from his mother, starting that they were glad to know his address, and informing him that his brother Cuthbert had proposed to and been accepted by Mercy Chant.

Clare crumpled up the paper, and followed the route to the station; reaching it, he found that there would be no train leaving for an hour and more. He sat down to wait, and having waited a quarter of an hour felt that he could wait there no longer. Broken in heart and numbed, he had nothing to hurry for; but he wished to get out of a town which had been the scene of such an experience, and turned to walk to the first station onward, and let the train pick him up there.

The highway that he followed was open, and at a little distance dipped into a valley, across which it could be seen running from edge to edge. He had traversed the greater part of this depression, and was climbing the western acclivity, when, pausing for breath, he unconsciously looked back. Why he did so he could not say, but something seemed to impel him to the act. The tape-like surface of the road diminished in his rear as far as he could see, and as he gazed a moving spot intruded on the white vacuity of its perspective.

It was a human figure running. Clare waited with a dim sense that somebody was trying to overtake him.

The form descending the incline was a woman's, yet so entirely was his mind blinded to the idea of his wife's following him that even when she came nearer he did not recognize her under the totally changed attire in which he now beheld her. It was not till she was quite close that he could believe her to be Tess.

'I saw you – turn away from the station – just before I got there – and I have been following you all this way!'

She was so pale, so breathless, so quivering in every muscle, that he did not ask her a single question, but seizing her hand, and pulling it within his arm, he led her along. To avoid meeting any possible wayfarers he left the high road, and took a footpath under some fir-trees. When they were deep among the moaning boughs he stopped and looked at her inquiringly.

'Angel,' she said, as if waiting for this, 'do you know what I have been running after you for? To tell you that I have killed him!' A pitiful white smile lit her face as she spoke.

'What!' said he, thinking from the strangeness of her manner that she was in some delirium.

'I have done it – I don't know how,' she continued. 'Still, I owed it to you, and to myself, Angel. I feared long ago, when I struck him on the mouth with my glove, that I might do it some day for the trap he set for me in my simple youth, and his wrong to you through me. He has come between us and ruined us, and now he can never do it any more. I never loved him at all, Angel, as I loved you. You know it, don't you? You believe it? You didn't come back to me, and I was obliged to go back to him. Why did you go away – why did you – when I loved you so? I can't think why you did it. But I don't blame you; only, Angel, will you forgive me my sin against you, now I have killed him? I thought as I ran along that you would be sure to forgive me now I have done that. It came to me as a shining light that I should get you back that way. I could not bear the loss of you any longer – you don't know how entirely I was unable to bear your not loving me! Say you do now, dear, dear husband; say you do, now I have killed him!'

'I do love you, Tess – O, I do – it is all come back!' he said, tightening his arms round her with fervid pressure. 'But how do you mean – you have killed him?'

'I mean that I have,' she murmured in a reverie.

'What, bodily? Is he dead?'

'Yes. He heard me crying about you, and he bitterly taunted me; and called you by a foul name; and then I did it. My heart could not bear it. He had nagged me about you before. And then I dressed myself and came away to find you.'

By degrees he was inclined to believe that she had faintly attempted, at least, what she said she had done; and his horror at her impulse was mixed with amazement at the strength of her affection for himself, and at the strangeness of its quality, which had apparently extinguished her moral sense altogether. Unable to realize the gravity of her conduct she seemed at last content; and he looked at her as she lay upon his shoulder, weeping with happiness, and wondered what obscure strain in the d'Urberville blood had led to this aberration – if it were an aberration. There momentarily flashed through his mind that the family tradition of the coach and murder might have arisen because the d'Urbervilles had been known to do these things. As well as his confused and excited ideas could reason, he supposed that in the moment of mad grief of which she spoke her mind had lost its balance, and plunged her into this abyss.

It was very terrible if true; if a temporary hallucination, sad. But, anyhow, here was this deserted wife of his, this passionately-fond woman, clinging to him without a suspicion that he would be anything to her but a protector. He saw that for him to be otherwise was not, in her mind, within the region of the possible. Tenderness was absolutely dominant in Clare at last. He kissed her endlessly with his white lips, and held her hand, and said –

'I will not desert you! I will protect you by every means in my power, dearest love, whatever you may have done or not have done!'

They then walked on under the trees, Tess turning her head every now and then to look at him. Worn and unhandsome as he had become, it was plain that she did not discern the least fault in his appearance. To her he was, as of old, all that was perfection, personally and mentally. He was still her Antinous, her Apollo even; his sickly face was beautiful as the morning to her affectionate regard on this day no less than when she first beheld him; for was it not the face of the one man on earth who had loved her purely, and who had believed in her as pure.

With an instinct as to possibilities he did not now, as he had intended, make for the first station beyond the town, but plunged still farther under the firs, which here abounded for miles. Each clasping the other round the waist they promenaded over the dry bed of fir-needles, thrown into a vague intoxicating atmosphere at the consciousness of being together at last, with no living soul between them; ignoring that there was a corpse. Thus they proceeded for several miles till Tess, arousing herself, looked about her, and said, timidly –

'Are we going anywhere in particular?'

'I don't know, dearest. Why?'

'I don't know.'

'Well, we might walk a few miles further, and when it is evening find lodgings somewhere or other – in a lonely cottage, perhaps. Can you walk well, Tessy?'

'O yes! I could walk for ever and ever with your arm round me!'

Upon the whole it seemed a good thing to do. Thereupon they quickened their pace, avoiding high roads, and following obscure paths tending more or less northward. But there was an unpractical vagueness in their movements throughout the day; neither one of them seemed to consider any question of effectual escape, disguise, or long concealment. Their every idea was temporary and unforefending, like the plans of two children.

At mid-day they drew near to a roadside inn, and Tess would have entered it with him to get something to eat, but he persuaded her to remain among the trees and bushes of this half-woodland, half-moorland part of the country, till he should come back. Her clothes were of recent fashion; even the ivory-handled parasol that she carried was of a shape unknown in the retired spot to which they had now wandered; and the cut of such articles would have attracted attention in the settle of a tavern. He soon returned, with food enough for half-a-dozen people and two bottles of wine – enough to last them for a day or more, should any emergency arise.

They sat down upon some dead boughs and shared their meal. Between one and two o'clock they packed up the remainder and went on again.

'I feel strong enough to walk any distance,' said she.

'I think we may as well steer in a general way towards the interior of the country, where we can hide for a time, and are less likely to be looked for than anywhere near the coast,' Clare remarked. 'Later on, when they have forgotten us, we can make for some port.'

She made no reply to this beyond that of grasping him more tightly, and straight inland they went. Though the season was an English May the weather was serenely bright, and during the afternoon it was quite warm. Through the latter miles of their walk their footpath had taken them into the depths of the New Forest, and towards evening, turning the corner of a lane, they perceived behind a brook and bridge a large board on which was painted in white letters, 'This desirable Mansion to be Let Furnished'; particulars following, with directions to apply to some London agents. Passing through the gate they could see the house, an old brick building of regular design and large accommodation.

'I know it,' said Clare. 'It is Bramshurst Court. You can see that it is shut up, and grass is growing on the drive.'

'Some of the windows are open,' said Tess.

'Just to air the rooms, I suppose.'

'All these rooms empty, and we without a roof to our heads!'

'You are getting tired, my Tess!' he said. 'We'll stop soon.' And kissing her sad mouth he again led her onwards.

He was growing weary likewise, for they had wandered a dozen or fifteen miles, and it became necessary to consider what they should do for rest. They looked from afar at isolated cottages and little inns, and were inclined to approach one of the latter, when their hearts failed them, and they sheered off. At length their gait dragged, and they stood still.

'Could we sleep under the trees?' she asked.

He thought the season insufficiently advanced.

'I have been thinking of that empty mansion we passed,' he said. 'Let us go back towards it again.'

They retraced their steps, but it was half an hour before they stood without the entrance-gate as earlier. He then requested her to stay where she was, whilst he went to see who was within.

She sat down among the bushes within the gate, and Clare crept towards the house. His absence lasted some considerable time, and when he returned Tess was wildly anxious, not for herself, but for him. He had found out from a boy that there was only an old woman in charge as caretaker, and she only came there on fine days, from the hamlet near, to open and shut the windows. She would come to shut them at sunset. 'Now, we can get in through one of the lower windows, and rest there,' said he.

Under his escort she went tardily forward to the main front, whose shuttered windows, like sightless eyeballs, excluded the possibility of watchers. The door was reached a few steps further, and one of the windows beside it was open. Clare clambered in, and pulled Tess in after him.

Except the hall the rooms were all in darkness, and they ascended the staircase. Up here also the shutters were tightly closed, the ventilation being perfunctorily done, for this day at least, by opening the hall-window in front and an upper window behind. Clare unlatched the door of a large chamber, felt his way across it, and parted the shutters to the width of two or three inches. A shaft of dazzling sunlight glanced into the room, revealing heavy, old-fashioned furniture, crimson damask hangings, and an enormous four-post bedstead, along the head of which were carved running figures, apparently Atalanta's race.

'Rest at last!' said he, setting down his bag and the parcel of viands.

They remained in great quietness till the caretaker should have come to shut the windows: as a precaution, putting themselves in total darkness by barring the shutters as before, lest the woman should open the door of their chamber for any casual reason. Between six and seven o'clock she came, but did not approach the wing they were in. The heard her close the windows, fasten them, lock the door, and go away. Then Clare again stole a chink of light from the window, and they shared another meal, till by-and-by they were enveloped in the shades of night which they had no candle to disperse.

❧ Chapter Fifty-Eight ❧

THE NIGHT WAS STRANGELY solemn and still. In the small hours she whispered to him the whole story of how he had walked in his sleep with her in his arms across the Froom stream, at the imminent risk of both their lives, and laid her down in the stone coffin at the ruined abbey. He had never known of that till now.

'Why didn't you tell me next day?' he said. 'It might have prevented much misunderstanding and woe.'

'Don't think of what's past!' said she. 'I am not going to think outside of now. Why should we! Who knows what tomorrow has in store?'

But it apparently had no sorrow. The morning was wet and foggy, and Clare, rightly informed that the caretaker only opened the windows on fine days, ventured to creep out of their chamber, and explore the house, leaving Tess asleep. There was no food on the premises, but there was water, and he took advantage of the fog to emerge from the mansion, and fetch tea, bread, and butter from a shop in a little place two miles beyond, as also a small tin kettle and spirit-lamp, that they might get fire without smoke. His re-entry awoke her; and they breakfasted on what he had brought.

They were indisposed to stir abroad, and the day passed, and the night following, and the next, and next; till, almost without their being aware, five days had slipped by in absolute seclusion, not a sight or sound of a human being disturbing their peacefulness, such as it was. The changes of the weather were their only events, the birds of the New Forest their only company. By tacit consent they hardly once spoke of any incident of the past subsequent to their wedding-day. The gloomy intervening time seemed to sink into chaos, over which the present and prior times closed as if it never had been. Whenever he suggested that they should leave their shelter, and go forwards towards Southampton or London, she showed a strange unwillingness to move.

'Why should we put an end to all that's sweet and lovely!' she deprecated. 'What must come will come.' And, looking through the shutter-chink: 'All is trouble outside there; inside here content.'

He peeped out also. It was quite true; within was affection, union, error forgiven; outside was the inexorable.

'And – and,' she said, pressing her cheek against his; 'I fear that what you think of me now may not last. I do not wish to outlive your present feeling for me. I would rather not. I would rather be dead and buried when the times comes for you to despise me, so that it may never be known to me that you despised me.'

'I cannot ever despise you.'

'I also hope that. But considering what my life has been I cannot see why any man should, sooner or later, be able to help despising me ... How wickedly mad I was! Yet formerly I never could bear to hurt a fly or a worm, and the sight of a bird in a cage used often to make me cry.'

They remained yet another day. In the night the dull sky cleared, and the result was that the old caretaker at the cottage awoke early. The brilliant sunrise made her unusually brisk; she decided to open the contiguous mansion immediately, and to air it thoroughly on such a day. Thus it occurred that, having arrived and opened the lower rooms before six o'clock, she ascended to the bechambers, and was about to turn the handle of the one wherein they lay. At that moment she fancied she could hear the breathing of persons within. Her slippers and her antiquity had rendered her progress a noiseless one so far, and she made for instant retreat; then, deeming that her hearing might have deceived her, she turned anew to the door and softly tried the handle. The lock was out of order, but a piece of furniture had been moved forward on the inside, which prevented her opening the door more than an inch or two. A stream of morning light through the shutter-chink fell upon the faces of the pair, wrapped in profound slumber, Tess's lips being parted like a half-opened flower near his cheek. The caretaker was so struck with their innocent appearance, and with the elegance of Tess's gown hanging across a chair, her silk stockings beside it, the pretty parasol, and the other habits in which she had arrived because she had none else, that her first indignation at the effrontery of tramps and vagabonds gave way to a momentary sentimentality over this genteel elopement, as it seemed. She closed the door, and withdrew as softly as she had come, to go and consult with her neighbours on the odd discovery.

Not more than a minute had elapsed after her withdrawal when Tess woke, and then Clare. Both had a sense that something had disturbed them, though they could not say what; and the uneasy feeling which it engendered grew stronger. As soon as he was dressed he narrowly scanned the lawn through the two or three inches of shutter-chink.

'I think we will leave at once,' said he. 'It is a fine day. And I cannot help fancying somebody is about the house. At any rate, the woman will be sure to come to-day.'

She passively assented, and putting the room in order they took up the few articles that belonged to them, and departed noiselessly. When they had got into the Forest she turned to take a last look at the house.

'Ah, happy house – good-bye!' she said. 'My life can only be a question of a few weeks. Why should we not have stayed there?'

'Don't say it, Tess! We shall soon get out of this district altogether. We'll continue our course as we've begun it, and keep straight north. Nobody will think of looking for us there. We shall be looked for at the Wessex ports if we are sought at all. When we are in the north we will get to a port and away.'

Having thus persuaded her the plan was pursued, and they kept a bee line northward. Their long repose at the manor-house lent them walking power now; and towards mid-day they found that they were approaching the steepled city of Melchester, which lay directly in their way. He decided to rest her in a clump of trees during the afternoon, and push onward under cover of darkness. At dusk Clare purchased food as usual, and their night march began, the boundary between Upper and Mid-Wessex being crossed about eight o'clock.

To walk across country without much regard to roads was not new to Tess, and she showed her old agility in the performance. The intercepting city, ancient Melchester, they were obliged to pass through in order to take advantage of the town bridge for crossing a large river that obstructed them. It was about midnight when they went along the deserted streets, lighted fitfully by the few lamps, keeping off the pavement that it might not echo their footsteps. The graceful pile of cathedral architecture rose dimly on their left hand, but it was lost upon them now. Once out of the town they followed the turnpike-road, which after a few miles plunged across an open plain.

Though the sky was dense with cloud a diffused light from some fragment of a moon had hitherto helped them a little. But the moon had now sunk, the clouds seemed to settle almost on their heads, and the night grew as dark as a cave. However, they found their way along, keeping as much on the turf as possible that their tread might not resound, which it was easy to do, there being no hedge or fence of any kind. All around was open loneliness and black solitude, over which a stiff breeze blew.

They had proceeded thus gropingly two or three miles further when on a sudden Clare became conscious of some vast erection close in his front, rising sheer from the grass. They had almost struck themselves against it.

'What monstrous place is this?' said Angel.

'It hums,' said she. 'Hearken!'

He listened. The wind, playing upon the edifice, produced a booming tune, like the note of some gigantic one-stringed harp. No other sound came from it, and lifting his hand and advancing a step or two, Clare felt the vertical surface of the structure. It seemed to be of solid stone, without joint or moulding. Carrying his fingers onward he found that what he had come in contact with was a colossal rectangular pillar; by stretching out his left hand he could feel a similar one adjoining. At an indefinite height overhead something made the black sky blacker, which had the semblance of a vast architrave uniting the pillars horizontally. They carefully entered beneath and between; the surfaces echoed their soft rustle; but they seemed to be still out of doors. The place was roofless. Tess drew her breath fearfully, and Angel, perplexed, said –

'What can it be?'

Feeling sideways they encountered another tower-like pillar, square and uncompromising as the first; beyond it another and another. The place was all doors and pillars, some connected above by continuous architraves.

'A very Temple of the Winds,' he said.

The next pillar was isolated; others composed a trilithon; others were prostrate, their flanks forming a causeway wide enough for a carriage; and it was soon obvious that they made up a forest of monoliths grouped upon the grassy expanse of the plain. The couple advanced further into this pavilion of the night till they stood in its midst.

'It is Stonehenge!' said Clare.

'The heathen temple, you mean?'

'Yes. Older than the centuries; older than the d'Urbervilles! Well, what shall we do, darling? We may find shelter further on.'

But Tess, really tired by this time, flung herself upon an oblong slab that lay close at hand, and was sheltered from the wind by a pillar. Owing to the action of the sun during the preceding day the stone was warm and dry, in comforting contrast to the rough and chill grass around, which had damped her skirts and shoes.

'I don't want to go any further, Angel,' she said stretching out her hand for his. 'Can't we bide here?'

'I fear not. This spot is visible for miles by day, although it does not seem so now.'

'One of my mother's people was a shepherd hereabouts, now I think of it. And you used to say at Talbothays that I was a heathen. So now I am at home.'

He knelt down beside her outstretched form, and put his lips upon hers.

'Sleepy are you, dear? I think you are lying on an altar.'

'I like very much to be here,' she murmured. 'It is so solemn and lonely – after my great happiness – with nothing but the sky above my face. It seems as if there were no folk in the world but we two; and I wish there were not – except 'LizaLu.'

Clare thought she might as well rest here till it should get a little lighter, and he flung his overcoat upon her, and sat down by her side.

'Angel, if anything happens to me, will you watch over 'Liza-Lu for my sake?' she asked, when they had listened a long time to the wind among the pillars.

'I will.'

'She is so good and simple and pure. O, Angel – I wish you would marry her if you lose me, as you will do shortly. O, if you would!'

'If I lose you I lose all! And she is my sister-in-law.'

'That's nothing, dearest. People marry sister-laws continually about Marlott; and 'Liza-Lu is so gentle and sweet, and she is growing so beautiful. O I could share you with her willingly when we are spirits! If you would train her and teach her, Angel, and bring her up for your own self! ... She has all the best of me without the bad of me; and if she were to become yours it would almost seem as if death had not divided us ... Well, I have said it: I won't mention it again.'

She ceased, and he fell into thought. In the far north-east sky he could see between the pillars a level streak of light. The uniform concavity of black cloud was lifting bodily like the lid of a pot, letting in at the earth's edge the coming day, against which the towering monoliths and trilithons began to be blackly defined.

'Did they sacrifice to God here?' asked she.

'No,' said he.

'Who to?'

'I believe to the sun. That lofty stone set away by itself is in the direction of the sun, which will presently rise behind it.'

'This reminds me, dear,' she said. 'You remember you never would interfere with any belief of mine before we were married? But I knew your mind all the same, and I thought as you thought – not from any reasons of my own, but because you thought so. Tell me now, Angel, do you think we shall meet again after we are dead? I want to know.'

He kissed her to avoid a reply at such a time.

'O, Angel – I fear that means no!' said she, with a suppressed sob. 'And I wanted so to see you again – so much, so much! What – not even you and I, Angel, who love each other so well?'

Like a greater than himself, to the critical question at the critical time he did not answer; and they were again silent. In a minute or two her breathing became more regular, her clasp of his hand relaxed, and she fell asleep. The band of silver paleness along the east horizon made even the distant parts of the Great Plain appear dark and near; and the whole enormous landscape bore that impress of reserve, taciturnity, and hesitation which is usual just before day. The eastward pillars and their architraves stood up blackly against the light, and the great flame-shaped Sun-stone beyond them; and the Stone of Sacrifice midway. Presently the night wind died out, and the quivering little pools in the cup-like hollows of the stones lay still. At the same time something seemed to move on the verge of the dip eastward – a mere dot. It was the head of a man approaching them from the hollow beyond the Sun-stone. Clare wished they had gone onward, but in the circumstances decided to remain quiet. The figure came straight towards the circle of pillars in which they were.

He heard something behind him, the brush of feet. Turning, he saw over the prostrate columns another figure; then before he was aware, another was at hand on the right, under a trilithon, and another on the left. The dawn shone full on the front of the man westward, and Clare could discern from this that he was tall, and walked as if trained. They all closed in with evident purpose. Her story then was true! Springing to his feet, he looked around for a weapon, loose stone, means of escape, anything. By this time the nearest man was upon him.

'It is no use, sir,' he said. 'There are sixteen of us on the Plain, and the whole country is reared.'

'Let her finish her sleep!' he implored in a whisper of the men as they gathered round.

When they saw where she lay, which they had not done till then, they showed no objection, and stood watching her, as still as the pillars around. He went to the stone and bent over her, holding one poor little hand; her breathing now was quick and small, like that of a lesser creature than a woman. All waited in the growing light, their faces and hands as if they were silvered, the remainder of their figures dark, the stones glistening green-gray, the Plain still a mass of shade. Soon the light was strong, and a ray shone upon her unconscious form, peering under her eyelids and waking her.

'What is it, Angel?' she said, starting up. 'Have they come for me?'

'Yes, dearest,' he said. 'They have come.'

'It is as it should be,' she murmured. 'Angel, I am almost glad – yes, glad! This happiness could not have lasted. It was too much. I have had enough; and now I shall not live for you to despise me!'

She stood up, shook herself, and went forward, neither of the men having moved.

'I am ready,' she said quietly.

❧ Chapter Fifty-Nine ❧

THE CITY OF WINTONCESTER, that fine old city, aforetime capital of Wessex, lay amidst its convex and concave downlands in all the brightness and warmth of a July morning. The gabled brick, tile, and freestone houses had almost dried off for the season their integument of lichen, the streams in the meadows were low, and in the sloping High Street, from the West Gateway to the mediaeval cross, and from the mediaeval cross to the bridge, that leisurely dusting and sweeping was in progress which usually ushers in an old-fashioned market-day.

From the western gate aforesaid the highway, as every Wintoncestrian knows, ascends a long and regular incline of the exact length of a measured mile, leaving the houses gradually behind. Up this road from the precincts of the city two persons were walking rapidly, as if unconscious of the trying ascent-unconscious through preoccupation and not through buoyancy. They had emerged upon this road through a narrow barred wicket in a high wall a little lower down. They seemed anxious to get out of the sight of the houses and of their kind, and this road appeared to offer the quickest means of doing so. Though they were young they walked with bowed heads, which gait of grief the sun's rays smiled on pitilessly.

One of the pair was Angel Clare, the other a tall budding creature – half girl, half woman – a spiritualized image of Tess, slighter than she, but with the same beautiful eyes – Clare's sister-in-law, 'Liza-Lu. Their pale faces seemed to have shrunk to half their natural size. They moved on hand in hand, and never spoke a word, the drooping of their heads being that of Giotto's 'Two Apostles'.

When they had nearly reached the top of the great West Hill the clocks in the town struck eight. Each gave a start at the notes, and, walking onward yet a few steps, they reached the first milestone, standing whitely on the green margin of the grass, and backed by the down, which here was open to the road. They entered upon the turf, and, impelled by a force that seemed to overrule their will, suddenly stood still, turned, and waited in paralyzed suspense beside the stone.

The prospect from this summit was almost unlimited. In the valley beneath lay the city they had just left, its more prominent buildings showing as in an isometric drawing – among them the broad cathedral tower, with its Norman windows and immense length of aisle and nave, the spires of St Thomas's, the pinnacled tower of the College, and, more to the right, the tower and gables of the ancient hospice, where to this day the pilgrim may receive his dole of bread and ale. Behind the city swept the rotund upland of St Catherine's Hill; further off, landscape beyond landscape, till the horizon was lost in the radiance of the sun hanging above it.

Against these far stretches of country rose, in front of the other city edifices, a large red-brick building, with level gray roofs, and rows of short barred windows bespeaking captivity, the whole contrasting greatly by its formalism with the quaint irregularities of the Gothic erections. It was somewhat disguised from the road in passing it by yews and evergreen oaks, but it was visible enough up here. The wicket from which the pair had lately emerged was in the wall of this structure. From the middle of the building an ugly flat-topped octagonal tower ascended against the east horizon, and viewed from this spot, on its shady side and against the light, it seemed the one blot in the city's beauty. Yet it was with this blot, and not with the beauty, that the two gazers were concerned.

Upon the cornice of the tower a tall staff was fixed. Their eyes were riveted on it. A few minutes after the hour had struck something moved slowly up the staff, and extended itself upon the breeze. It was a black flag.

'Justice' was done, and the President of the Immortals, in Aeschylean phrase, had ended his sport with Tess. And the d'Urberville knights and dames slept on in their tombs unknowing. The two speechless gazers bent themselves down to the earth, as if in prayer, and remained thus a long time, absolutely motionless: the flag continued to wave silently. As soon as they had strength they arose, joined hands again, and went on.

UNDER THE GREENWOOD TREE

OR

THE MELLSTOCK QUIRE

A RURAL PAINTING OF THE DUTCH

SCHOOL

Author's Preface

THIS STORY OF THE MELLSTOCK QUIRE and its old established west-gallery musicians, with some supplementary descriptions of similar officials in *Two on a Tower, A Few Crusted Characters*, and other places, is intended to be a fairly true picture, at first hand, of the personages, ways, and customs which were common among such orchestral bodies in the villages of fifty or sixty years ago.

One is inclined to regret the displacement of these ecclesiastical bandsmen by an isolated organist (often at first a barrel-organist) or harmonium player; and despite certain advantages in point of control and accomplishment which were, no doubt, secured by installing the single artist, the change has tended to stultify the professed aims of the clergy, its direct result being to curtail and extinguish the interest of parishioners in church doings. Under the old plan, from half a dozen to ten full-grown players, in addition to the numerous more or less grown-up singers, were officially occupied with the Sunday routine, and concerned in trying their best to make it an artistic outcome of the combined musical taste of the congregation. With a musical executive limited, as it mostly is limited now, to the parson's wife or daughter and the school-children, or to the school-teacher and the children, an important union of interests has disappeared.

The zest of these bygone instrumentalists must have been keen and staying, to take them, as it did, on foot every Sunday after a toilsome week through all weathers to the church, which often lay at a distance from their homes. They usually received so little in payment for their performances that their efforts were really a labour of love. In the parish I had in my mind when writing the present tale, the gratuities received yearly by the musicians at Christmas were somewhat as follows: From the manor-house ten shillings and a supper; from the vicar ten shillings; from the farmers five shillings each; from each cottage-household one shilling; amounting altogether to not more than ten shillings a head annually – just enough, as an old executant told me, to pay for their fiddlestrings, repairs, rosin, and music-paper (which they mostly ruled themselves). Their music in those days was all in their own manuscript, copied in the evenings after work, and their music-books were home-bound.

It was customary to inscribe a few jigs, reels, hornpipes, and ballads in the same book, by beginning it at the other end, the insertions being continued from front and back till sacred and secular met together in the middle, often with bizarre effect, the words of some of the songs exhibiting that ancient and broad humour which our grandfathers, and possibly grandmothers, took delight in, and is in these days unquotable.

The aforesaid fiddle-strings, rosin, and music-paper were supplied by a pedlar, who travelled exclusively in such wares from parish to parish, coming to each village about every six months. Tales are told of the consternation once caused among the church fiddlers when, on the occasion of their producing a new Christmas anthem, he did not come to time, owing to being snowed up on the downs, and the straits they were in through having to make shift with whipcord and twine for strings. He was generally a musician himself, and sometimes a composer in a small way, bringing his own new tunes, and tempting each choir to adopt them for a consideration. Some of these compositions which now lie before me, with their repetitions of lines, half-lines, and half-words, their fugues and their intermediate symphonies, are good singing still, though they would hardly be admitted into such hymn-books as are popular in the churches of fashionable society at the present time.

August 1896

Under the Greenwood Tree was first brought out in the summer of 1872 in two volumes. The name of the story was originally intended to be, more appropriately, *The Mellstock Quire*, and this has been appended as a sub-title since the early editions, it having been thought unadvisable to displace for it the title by which the book first became known.

In rereading the narrative after a long interval there occurs the inevitable reflection that the realities out of which it was spun were material for another kind of study of this little group of church musicians than is found in the chapters here penned so lightly, even so farcically and flippantly at times. But circumstances would have rendered any aim at a deeper, more essential, more transcendent handling unadvisable at the date of writing; and the exhibition of the Mellstock Quire in the following pages must remain the only extant one, except for the few glimpses of that perished band which I have given in verse elsewhere.

T.H.

April 1912

PART THE FIRST

Winter

ONE

❧ Mellstock-Lane ❧

To DWELLERS IN A WOOD almost every species of tree has its voice as well as its feature. At the passing of the breeze the fir-trees sob and moan no less distinctly than they rock; the holly whistles as it battles with itself; the ash hisses amid its quiverings; the beech rustles while its flat boughs rise and fall. And winter, which modifies the note of such trees as shed their leaves, does not destroy its individuality.

On a cold and starry Christmas-eve within living memory a man was passing up a lane towards Mellstock Cross in the darkness of a plantation that whispered thus distinctively to his intelligence. All the evidences of his nature were those afforded by the spirit of his footsteps, which succeeded each other lightly and quickly, and by the liveliness of his voice as he sang in a rural cadence:

With the rose and the lily
And the daffodowndilly,
The lads and the lasses a-sheep-shearing go.

The lonely lane he was following connected one of the hamlets of Mellstock parish with Upper Mellstock and Lewgate, and to his eyes, casually glancing upward, the silver and blackstemmed birches with their characteristic tufts, the pale grey boughs of beech, the dark-creviced elm, all appeared now as black and flat outlines upon the sky, wherein the white stars twinkled so vehemently that their flickering seemed like the flapping of wings. Within the woody pass, at a level anything lower than the horizon, all was dark as the grave. The copsewood forming the sides of the bower interlaced its branches so densely, even at this season of the year, that the draught from the north-east flew along the channel with scarcely an interruption from lateral breezes.

After passing the plantation and reaching Mellstock Cross the white surface of the lane revealed itself between the dark hedgerows like a ribbon jagged at the edges; the irregularity being caused by temporary accumulations of leaves extending from the ditch on either side.

The song (many times interrupted by flitting thoughts which took the place of several bars, and resumed at a point it would have reached had its continuity been unbroken) now received a more palpable check, in the shape of 'Ho-i-i-i-i-i!' from the crossing lane to Lower Mellstock, on the right of the singer who had just emerged from the trees.

'Ho-i-i-i-i-i!' he answered, stopping and looking round, though with no idea of seeing anything more than imagination pictured.

'Is that thee, young Dick Dewy?' came from the darkness.

'Ay, sure, Michael Mail.'

'Then why not stop for fellow-craters – going to thy own father's house too, as we be, and knowen us so well?'

Dick Dewy faced about and continued his tune in an underwhistle, implying that the business of his mouth could not be checked at a moment's notice by the placid emotion of friendship.

Having come more into the open he could now be seen rising against the sky, his profile appearing on the light background like the portrait of a gentleman in black cardboard. It assumed the form of a low-crowned hat, an ordinary-shaped nose, an ordinary chin, an ordinary neck, and ordinary shoulders. What he consisted of further down was invisible from lack of sky low enough to picture him on.

Shuffing, halting, irregular footsteps of various kinds were now heard coming up the hill, and presently there emerged from the shade severally five men of different ages and gaits, all of them working villagers of the parish of Mellstock. They, too, had lost their rotundity with the daylight, and advanced against the sky in flat outlines, which suggested some processional design on Greek or Etruscan pottery. They represented the chief portion of Mellstock parish choir.

The first was a bowed and bent man, who carried a fiddle under his arm, and walked as if engaged in studying some subject connected with the surface of the road. He was Michael Mail, the man who had hallooed to Dick.

The next was Mr Robert Penny, boot- and shoe-maker; a little man who, though rather round-shouldered, walked as if that fact had not come to his own knowledge, moving on with his back very hollow and his face fixed on the north-east quarter of the heavens before him, so that his lower waistcoat-buttons came first, and then the remainder of his figure. His features were invisible; yet when he occasionally looked round, two faint moons of light gleamed for an instant from the precincts of his eyes, denoting that he wore spectacles of a circular form.

The third was Elias Spinks, who walked perpendicularly and dramatically. The fourth outline was Joseph Bowman's, who had now no distinctive appearance beyond that of a human being. Finally came a weak lath-like form, trotting and stumbling along with one shoulder forward and his head inclined to the left, his arms dangling nervelessly in the wind as if they were empty sleeves. This was Thomas Leaf.

'Where be the boys?' said Dick to this somewhat indifferently-matched assembly.

The eldest of the group, Michael Mail, cleared his throat from a great depth.

'We told them to keep back at home for a time, thinken they wouldn't be wanted yet awhile; and we could choose the tuens, and so on.'

'Father and grandfather William have expected ye a little sooner. I have just been for a run round by Ewelease Stile and Hollow Hill to warm my feet.'

'To be sure father did! To be sure 'a did expect us – to taste the little barrel beyond compare that he's going to tap.'

''Od rabbit it all! Never heard a word of it!' said Mr Penny, gleams of delight appearing upon his spectacle-glasses, Dick meanwhile singing parenthetically –

> The lads and the lasses a-sheep-shearing go.

'Neighbours, there's time enough to drink a sight of drink now afore bedtime?' said Mail.

'True, true – time enough to get as drunk as lords!' replied Bowman cheerfully.

This opinion being taken as convincing they all advanced between the varying hedges and the trees dotting them here and there, kicking their toes occasionally among the crumpled leaves. Soon appeared glimmering indications of the few cottages forming the small hamlet of Upper Mellstock for which they were bound, whilst the faint sound of church-bells ringing a Christmas peal could be heard floating over upon the breeze from the direction of Longpuddle and Weatherbury parishes on the other side of the hills. A little wicket admitted them to the garden, and they proceeded up the path to Dick's house.

TWO

❧ The Tranter's ❧

IT WAS A LONG LOW COTTAGE with a hipped roof of thatch, having dormer windows breaking up into the eaves, a chimney standing in the middle of the ridge and another at each end. The window-shutters were not yet closed, and the fire- and candle-light within radiated forth upon the thick bushes of box and laurestinus growing in clumps outside, and upon the bare boughs of several codlin-trees hanging about in various distorted shapes, the result of early training as espaliers combined with careless climbing into their boughs in later years. The walls of the dwelling were for the most part covered with creepers, though these were rather beaten back from the doorway – a feature which was worn and scratched by much passing in and out, giving it by day the appearance of an old keyhole. Light streamed through the cracks and joints of outbuildings a little way from the cottage, a sight which nourished a fancy that the purpose of the erection must be rather to veil bright attractions than to shelter unsightly necessaries. The noise of a beetle and wedges and the splintering of wood was periodically heard from this direction; and at some little distance further a steady regular munching and the occasional scurr of a rope betokened a stable, and horses feeding within it.

The choir stamped severally on the door-stone to shake from their boots any fragment of earth or leaf adhering thereto, then entered the house and looked around to survey the condition of things. Through the open doorway of a small inner room on the right hand, of a character between pantry and cellar, was Dick Dewy's father Reuben, by vocation a 'tranter', or irregular carrier. He was a stout florid man about forty years of age, who surveyed people up and down when first making their acquaintance, and generally smiled at the horizon or other distant object during conversations with friends, walking about with a steady sway, and turning out his toes very considerably. Being now occupied in bending over a hogshead that stood in the pantry ready horsed for the process of broaching, he did not take the trouble to turn or raise his eyes at the entry of his visitors, well knowing by their footsteps that they were the expected old comrades.

The main room, on the left, was decked with bunches of holly and other evergreens, and from the middle of the beam bisecting the ceiling hung the mistletoe, of a size out of all proportion to the room, and extending so low that it became necessary for a full-grown person to walk round it in passing, or run the risk of entangling his hair. This apartment contained Mrs Dewy the tranter's wife, and the four remaining children, Susan, Jim, Bessy, and Charley, graduating uniformly though at wide stages from the age of sixteen to that of four years – the eldest of the series being separated from Dick the firstborn by a nearly equal interval.

Some circumstance had apparently caused much grief to Charley just previous to the entry of the choir, and he had absently taken down a small looking-glass, holding it before his face to learn how the human countenance appeared when engaged in crying, which survey led him to pause at the various points in each wail that were more than ordinarily striking, for a thorough appreciation of the general effect. Bessy was leaning against a chair, and glancing under the plaits about the waist of the plaid frock she wore, to notice the original unfaded pattern of the material as there preserved, her face bearing an expression of regret that the brightness had passed away from the visible portions. Mrs Dewy sat in a brown settle by the side of the glowing wood fire – so glowing that with a heedful compression of the lips she would now and then rise and put her hand upon the hams and flitches of bacon lining the chimney, to reassure herself that they were not being broiled instead of smoked – a misfortune that had been known to happen now and then at Christmas-time.

'Hullo my sonnies, here you be, then!' said Reuben Dewy at length, standing up and blowing forth a vehement gust of breath. 'How the blood do puff up in anybody's head, to be sure, a-stooping like that! I was just going out to gate to hark for ye.' He then carefully began to wind a strip of brown paper round a brass tap he held in his hand. 'This in the cask here is a drop o' the right sort' (tapping the cask); ''tis a real drop o' cordial from the best picked apples – Sansoms, Stubbards, Five-corners, and such-like – you d'mind the sort, Michael?' (Michael nodded.) 'And there's a sprinkling of they that grow down by the orchard-rails – streaked ones – rail apples we d'call 'em, as 'tis by the rails they grow, and not knowing the right name. The water-cider from 'em is as good as most people's best cider is.'

'Ay, and of the same make too,' said Bowman. ' "It rained when we wrung it out, and the water got into it," folk will say. But 'tis on'y an excuse. Watered cider is too common among us.'

'Yes, yes; too common it is!' said Spinks with an inward sigh, whilst his eyes seemed to be looking at the case in an abstract form rather than at the scene before him. 'Such poor liquor do make a man's throat feel very melancholy – and is a disgrace to the name of stimmilent.'

'Come in, come in, and draw up to the fire; never mind your shoes,' said Mrs Dewy, seeing that all except Dick had paused to wipe them upon the doormat. 'I am glad that you've stepped up-along at last; and, Susan, you run down to Grammer Kaytes's ar.l see if you can borrow some larger candles than these fourteens. Tommy Leaf, don't ye be afeard! Come and sit here in the settle.'

This was addressed to the young man before mentioned, consisting chiefly of a human skeleton and a smock-frock, who was very awkward in his movements, apparently on account of having grown so very fast that before he had had time to get used to his height he was higher.

'Hee – hee – ay!' replied Leaf, letting his mouth continue to smile for some time after his mind had done smiling, so that his teeth remained in view as the most conspicuous members of his body.

'Here, Mr Penny,' resumed Mrs Dewy, 'you sit in this chair. And how's your daughter, Mrs Brownjohn?'

'Well, I suppose I must say pretty fair.' He adjusted his spectacles a quarter of an inch to the right. 'But she'll be worse before she's better, 'a b'lieve.'

'Indeed – poor soul! And how many will that make in all, four or five?'

'Five; they've buried three. Yes, five; and she not much more than a maid yet. She do know the multiplication table onmistakable well. However, 'twas to be, and none can gainsay it.'

Mrs Dewy resigned Mr Penny. 'Wonder where your grandfather James is?' she inquired of one of the children. 'He said he'd drop in tonight.'

'Out in fuel-house with grandfather William,' said Jimmy.

'Now let's see what we can do,' was heard spoken about this time by the tranter in a private voice to the barrel, beside which he had again established himself, and was stooping to cut away the cork.

'Reuben, don't make such a mess o' tapping that barrel as is mostly made in this house,' Mrs Dewy cried from the fireplace. 'I'd tap a hundred without wasting more than you do in one. Such a squizzling and squirting job as 'tis in your hands! There, he always was such a clumsy man indoors.'

'Ay, ay; I know you'd tap a hundred beautiful, Ann – I know you would; two hundred, perhaps. But I can't promise. This is a' old cask, and the wood's rotted away about the tap-hole. The husbird of a feller Sam Lawson – that ever I should call'n such, now he's dead and gone, poor heart! – took me in completely upon the feat of buying this cask. "Reub," says he – 'a always used to call me plain Reub, poor old heart! – "Reub," he said says he, "that there cask, Reub, is as good as new; yes, good as new. 'Tis a wine-hogshead; the best port-wine in the commonwealth have been in that there cask; and you shall have en for ten shillens, Reub," – 'a said says he – "he's worth twenty, ay, five-and-twenty, if he's worth one; and an iron hoop or two put round en among the wood ones will make en worth thirty shillens of any man's money, if – "'

'I think I should have used the eyes that Providence gave me to use afore I paid any ten shillens for a jimcrack wine-barrel; a saint is sinner enough not to be cheated. But 'tis like all your family was, so easy to be deceived.'

'That's as true as gospel of this member,' said Reuben.

Mrs Dewy began a smile at the answer, then altering her lips and refolding them so that it was not a smile, commenced smoothing little

Bessy's hair; the tranter having meanwhile suddenly become oblivious to conversation, occupying himself in a deliberate cutting and arrangement of some more brown paper for the broaching operation.

'Ah, who can believe sellers!' said old Michael Mail in a carefully-cautious voice, by way of tiding-over this critical point of affairs.

'No one at all,' said Joseph Bowman, in the tone of a man fully agreeing with everybody.

'Ay,' said Mail, in the tone of a man who did not agree with everybody as a rule, though he did now; 'I knowed a' auctioneering feller once – a very friendly feller 'a was too. And so one hot day as I was walking down the front street o' Casterbridge, jist below the King's Arms, I passed a' open winder and see him inside, stuck upon his perch, a-selling off. I jist nodded to en in a friendly way as I passed, and went my way, and thought no more about it. Well, next day, as I was oilen my boots by fuel-house door, if a letter didn't come wi' a bill charging me with a feather-bed, bolster, and pillers, that I had bid for at Mr Taylor's sale. The slim-faced martel had knocked 'em down to me because I nodded to en in my friendly way; and I had to pay for 'em too. Now, I hold that that was coming it very close, Reuben?'

''Twas close, there's no denying,' said the general voice.

'Too close, 'twas,' said Reuben, in the rear of the rest. 'And as to Sam Lawson – poor heart! now he's dead and gone too! – I'll warrant, that if so be I've spent one hour in making hoops for that barrel, I've spent fifty, first and last. That's one of my hoops' – touching it with his elbow – 'that's one of mine, and that, and that, and all these.'

'Ah, Sam was a man,' said Mr Penny, contemplatively.

'Sam was!' said Bowman.

'Especially for a drap o' drink,' said the tranter.

'Good, but not religious-good,' suggested Mr Penny.

The tranter nodded. Having at last made the tap and hole quite ready, 'Now then, Suze, bring a mug,' he said. 'Here's luck to us, my sonnies!'

The tap went in, and the cider immediately squirted out in a horizontal shower over Reuben's hands, knees, and leggings, and into the eyes and neck of Charley, who, having temporarily put off his grief under pressure of more interesting proceedings, was squatting down and blinking near his father.

'There 'tis again!' said Mrs Dewy.

'Devil take the hole, the cask, and Sam Lawson too, that good cider should be wasted like this!' exclaimed the tranter. 'Your thumb! Lend me your thumb, Michael! Ram it in here, Michael! I must get a bigger tap, my sonnies.'

'Idd it cold inthide te hole?' inquired Charley of Michael, as he continued in a stooping posture with his thumb in the corkhole.

'What wonderful odds and ends that chiel has in his head to be sure!' Mrs Dewy admiringly exclaimed from the distance. 'I lay a wager that he thinks more about how 'tis inside that barrel than in all the other parts of the world put together.'

All persons present put on a speaking countenance of admiration for the cleverness alluded to, in the midst of which Reuben returned. The operation was then satisfactorily performed; when Michael arose and stretched his head to the extremest fraction of height that his body would allow of, to restraighten his back and shoulders – thrusting out his arms and twisting his features to a mass of wrinkles to emphasize the relief acquired. A quart or two of the beverage was then brought to table, at which all the new arrivals reseated themselves with wide-spread knees, their eyes meditatively seeking out any speck or knot in the board upon which the gaze might precipitate itself.

'Whatever is father a-biding out in fuel-house so long for?' said the tranter. 'Never such a man as father for two things – cleaving up old dead apple-tree wood and playing the bass-viol. "A'd pass his life between the two, that 'a would.' He stepped to the door and opened it.

'Father!'

'Ay!' rang thinly from round the corner.

'Here's the barrel tapped, and we all awaiting!'

A series of dull thuds, that had been heard without for some time past, now ceased; and after the light of a lantern had passed the window and made wheeling rays upon the ceiling inside the eldest of the Dewy family appeared.

THREE

❦ The Assembled Quire ❧

WILLIAM DEWY – OTHERWISE GRANDFATHER WILLIAM – was now about seventy; yet an ardent vitality still preserved a warm and roughened bloom upon his face, which reminded gardeners of the sunny side of a ripe ribstone-pippin: though a narrow strip of forehead, that was protected from the weather by lying above the line of his hat-brim, seemed to belong to some town man, so gentlemanly was its whiteness. His was a humorous and kindly nature, not unmixed with a frequent melancholy; and he had a firm religious faith. But to his neighbours he had no character in particular. If they saw him pass by their windows when they had been bottling off old mead, or when they had just been called long-headed men who might do anything in the world if they chose, they thought concerning him, 'Ah, there's that good-hearted man – open as a child!' If they saw him just after losing a shilling or half-a-crown, or accidentally letting fall a piece of crockery, they thought, 'There's that poor weak-minded man Dewy again! Ah, he's never done much in the world either!' If he passed when fortune neither smiled nor frowned on them, they merely thought him old William Dewy.

'Ah, so's – here you be! – Ah, Michael and Joseph and John – and you too, Leaf! a merry Christmas all! We shall have a rare log-wood fire directly, Reub, to reckon by the toughness of the job I had in cleaving 'em.' As he spoke he threw down an armful of logs which fell in the chimney-corner with a rumble, and looked at them with something of the admiring enmity he would have bestowed on living people who had been very obstinate in holding their own. 'Come in, grandfather James.'

Old James (grandfather on the maternal side) had simply called as a visitor. He lived in a cottage by himself, and many people considered him a miser; some, rather slovenly in his habits. He now came forward from behind grandfather William, and his stooping figure formed a well-illuminated picture as he passed towards the fire-place. Being by trade a mason, he wore a long linen apron reaching almost to his toes, corduroy breeches and gaiters, which, together with his boots, graduated in tints of whitish-brown by constant friction against lime and stone. He also wore a very stiff fustian coat, having folds at the elbows and shoulders as unvarying in their arrangement as those in a pair of bellows: the ridges and the projecting parts of the coat collectively exhibiting a shade different from that of the hollows, which were lined with small ditch-like accumulations of stone and mortar-dust. The extremely large sidepockets, sheltered beneath wide flaps, bulged out convexly whether empty or full; and as he was often engaged to work at buildings far away – his breakfasts and dinners being eaten in a strange chimney-corner, by a garden wall, on a heap of stones, or walking along the road – he carried in these pockets a small tin canister of butter, a small canister of sugar, a small canister of tea, a paper of salt, and a paper of pepper; the bread, cheese, and meat, forming the substance of his meals, hanging up behind him in his basket among the hammers and chisels. If a passer-by looked hard at him when he was drawing forth any of these, 'My buttery,' he said, with a pinched smile.

'Better try over number seventy-eight before we start, I suppose?' said William, pointing to a heap of old Christmas-carol books on a side table.

'Wi' all my heart,' said the choir generally.

'Number seventy-eight was always a teaser – always. I can mind him ever since I was growing up a hard boy-chap.'

'But he's a good tune, and worth a mint o' practice,' said Michael.

'He is; though I've been mad enough wi' that tune at times to seize en and tear en all to linnit. Ay, he's a splendid carrel – there's no denying that.'

'The first line is well enough,' said Mr Spinks; 'but when you come to "O, thou man," you make a mess o't.'

'We'll have another go into en, and see what we can make of the martel. Half-an-hour's hammering at en will conquer the toughness of en; I'll warn it.'

"Od rabbit it all!' said Mr Penny, interrupting with a flash of his spectacles, and at the same time clawing at something in the depths of a large side-pocket. 'If so be I hadn't been as scatter-brained and thirtingill as a chiel I should have called at the schoolhouse wi' a boot as I cam up along. Whatever is coming to me I really can't estimate at all!'

'The brain has its weaknesses,' murmured Mr Spinks, waving his head ominously. Mr Spinks was considered to be a scholar, having once kept a nightschool, and always spoke up to that level.

'Well, I must call with en the first thing tomorrow. And I'll empt my pocket o' this last too, if you don't mind, Mrs Dewy.' He drew forth a last, and placed it on a table at his elbow. The eyes of three or four followed it.

'Well,' said the shoemaker, seeming to perceive that the interest the object had excited was greater than he had anticipated, and warranted the last's being taken up again and exhibited; 'now, whose foot do ye suppose this last was made for? It was made for Geoffrey Day's father, over at Yalbury Wood. Ah, many's the pair o' boots he've had off the last! Well, when 'a died, I used the last for Geoffrey, and have ever since, though a little doctoring was wanted to make it do. Yes, a very queer natured last it is now, 'a b'lieve,' he continued, turning it over caressingly. 'Now, you notice that there' (pointing to a lump of leather bradded to the toe), 'that's a very bad bunion that he've had ever since 'a was a boy. Now, this remarkable large piece' (pointing to a patch nailed to the side), 'shows a' accident he received by the tread of a horse, that squashed his foot a'most to a pomace. The horse-shoe came full-butt on this point, you see. And so I've just been over to Geoffrey's, to know if he wanted his bunion altered or made bigger in the new pair I'm making.'

During the latter part of this speech Mr Penny's left hand wandered towards the cider-cup as if the hand had no connection with the person speaking; and bringing his sentence to an abrupt close all but the extreme margin of the bootmaker's face was eclipsed by the circular brim of the vessel.

'However, I was going to say,' continued Penny, putting down the cup, 'I ought to have called at the school' – here he went groping again in the depths of his pocket – 'to leave this without fail, though I suppose the first thing tomorrow will do.'

He now drew forth and placed upon the table a boot – small, light, and prettily shaped – upon the heel of which he had been operating.

'The new schoolmistress's!'

'Ay, no less, Miss Fancy Day; as neat a little figure of fun as ever I see, and just husband-high.'

'Never Geoffrey's daughter Fancy?' said Bowman, as all glances present converged like wheelspokes upon the boot in the centre of them.

'Yes, sure,' resumed Mr Penny, regarding the boot as if that alone were his auditor; ''tis she that's come here schoolmistress. You knowed his daughter was in training?'

'Strange, isn't it, for her to be here Christmas-night, Master Penny?'

'Yes; but here she is, 'a b'lieve.'

'I know how she comes here – so I do!' chirruped one of the children.

'Why?' Dick inquired with subtle interest.

'Pa'son Maybold was afraid he couldn't manage us all tomorrow at the dinner, and he talked o'getting her just to come over and help him hand about the plates, and see we didn't make pigs of ourselves; and that's what she's come for!'

'And that's the boot, then,' continued its mender imaginatively, 'that she'll walk to church in tomorrow morning. I don't care to mend boots I don't make; but there's no knowing what it may lead to, and her father always comes to me.'

There, between the cider-mug and the candle, stood this interesting receptacle of the little unknown's foot; and a very pretty boot it was. A character, in fact – the flexible bend at the instep, the rounded localities of the small nestling toes, scratches from careless scampers now forgotten – all, as repeated in the tell-tale leather, evidencing a nature and a bias. Dick surveyed it with a delicate feeling that he had no right to do so without having first asked the owner of the foot's permission.

'Now, neighbours, though no common eye can see it,' the shoemaker went on, 'a man in the trade can see the likeness between this boot and that last, although that is so deformed as hardly to recall one of God's creatures, and this is one of as pretty a pair as you'd get for ten-and-sixpence in Casterbridge. To you, nothing; but 'tis father's voot and daughter's voot to me, as plain as houses.'

'I don't doubt there's a likeness, Master Penny – a mild likeness – a fantastical likeness,' said Spinks. 'But *I* han't got imagination enough to see it, perhaps.'

Mr Penny adjusted his spectacles.

'Now, I'll tell ye what happened to me once on this very point. You used to know Johnson the dairyman, William?'

'Ay, sure; I did.'

'Well, 'twasn't opposite his house, but a little lower down – by his paddock, in front o' Parkmaze Pool. I was a-bearing across towards Bloom's End, and lo and behold, there was a man just brought out o' the Pool, dead; he had un'rayed for a dip, but not being able to pitch it just there had gone in flop over his head. Men looked at en; women looked at en; children looked at en; nobody knowed en. He was covered wi' a sheet; but I catched sight of his voot, just showing out as they carried en along. "I don't care what name that man went by," I said, in my way, "but he's John Woodward's brother; I can swear to the family voot." At that very moment up comes John Woodward, weeping and teaving, "I've lost my brother! I've lost my brother!" '

'Only to think of that!' said Mrs Dewy.

''Tis well enough to know this foot and that foot,' said Mr Spinks. ''Tis long-headed, in fact, as far as feet do go. I know little, 'tis true – I say no more; but show *me* a man's foot, and I'll tell you that man's heart.'

'You must be a cleverer feller, then, than mankind in jineral,' said the tranter.

'Well, that's nothing for me to speak of,' returned Mr Spinks. 'A man lives and learns. Maybe I've read a leaf or two in my time. I don't wish to say anything large, mind you; but nevertheless, maybe I have.'

'Yes, I know,' said Michael soothingly, 'and all the parish knows, that ye've read sommat of everything a'most, and have been a great filler of young folks' brains. Learning's a worthy thing, and ye've got it, Master Spinks.'

'I make no boast, though I may have read and thought a little; and I know – it may be from much perusing, but I make no boast – that by the time a man's head is finished 'tis almost time for him to creep underground. I am over forty-five.'

Mr Spinks emitted a look to signify that if his head was not finished, nobody's head ever could be.

'Talk of knowing people by their feet!' said Reuben. 'Rot me, my sonnies, then, if I can tell what a man is from all his members put together, oftentimes.'

'But still, look is a good deal,' observed grandfather William absently, moving and balancing his head till the tip of grandfather James's nose was exactly in a right line with William's eye and the mouth of a miniature cavern he was discerning in the fire. 'By the way,' he continued in a fresher voice, and looking up, 'that young creature, the schoolmis'ess, must be sung to tonight wi' the rest? If her ear is as fine as her face, we shall have enough to do to be up-sides with her.'

'What about her face?' said young Dewy.

'Well, as to that,' Mr Spinks replied, ''tis a face you can hardly gainsay. A very good pink face, as far as that do go. Still, only a face, when all is said and done.'

'Come, come, Elias Spinks, say she's a pretty maid and have done wi' her,' said the tranter, again preparing to visit the cider-barrel.

FOUR

❧ Going the Rounds ❧

SHORTLY AFTER TEN O'CLOCK the singing-boys arrived at the tranter's house, which was invariably the place of meeting, and preparations were made for the start. The older men and musicians wore thick coats, with stiff perpendicular collars, and coloured handkerchiefs wound round and round the neck till the end came to hand, over all which they just showed their ears and noses, like people looking over a wall. The remainder, stalwart ruddy men and boys, were dressed mainly in snowwhite smock-frocks, embroidered upon the shoulders and breasts in ornamental forms of hearts, diamonds, and zigzags. The cider-mug was emptied for the ninth time, the music-books were arranged, and the pieces finally decided upon. The boys in the meantime put the old horn-lanterns in order, cut candles into short lengths to fit the lanterns; and, a thin fleece of snow having fallen since the early part of the evening, those who had no leggings went to the stable and wound wisps of hay round their ankles to keep the insidious flakes from the interior of their boots.

Mellstock was a parish of considerable acreage, the hamlets composing it lying at a much greater distance from each other than is ordinarily the case. Hence several hours were consumed in playing and singing within hearing of every family, even if but a single air were bestowed on each. There was Lower Mellstock, the main village; half a mile from this were the church and vicarage, and a few other houses, the spot being rather lonely now, though in past centuries it had been the most thickly-populated quarter of the parish. A mile north-east lay the hamlet of Upper Mellstock, where the tranter lived; and at other points knots of cottages, besides solitary farmsteads and dairies.

Old William Dewy, with the violoncello, played the bass; his grandson Dick the treble violin; and Reuben and Michael Mail the tenor and second violins respectively. The singers consisted of four men and seven boys, upon whom devolved the task of carrying and attending to the lanterns, and holding the books open for the players. Directly music was the theme old William ever and instinctively came to the front.

'Now mind, neighbours,' he said, as they all went out one by one at the door, he himself holding it ajar and regarding them with a critical face as they passed, like a shepherd counting out his sheep. 'You two counter-boys, keep your ears open to Michael's fingering, and don't ye go straying into the treble part along o'Dick and his set, as ye did last year; and mind this especially when we be in "Arise, and hail." Billy Chimlen, don't you sing quite so raving mad as you fain would; and, all o' ye, whatever ye do, keep from making a great scuffle on the ground when we go in at people's gates; but go quietly, so as to strike up all of a sudden, like spirits.'

'Farmer Ledlow's first?'

'Farmer Ledlow first; the rest as usual.'

'And, Voss,' said the tranter terminatively, 'you keep house here till about half-past two; then heat the metheglin and cider in the warmer you'll find turned up upon the copper; and bring it wi' the victuals to church-hatch, as th'st know.'

Just before the clock struck twelve they lighted the lanterns and started. The moon, in her third quarter, had risen since the snowstorm' but the dense accumulation of snow-cloud weakened her power to a faint twilight which was rather pervasive of the landscape than traceable to the sky. The breeze had gone down, and the rustle of their feet and tones of their speech echoed with an alert rebound from every post, boundary-stone, and ancient wall they passed, even where the distance of the echo's origin was less than a few yards. Beyond their own slight noises nothing was to be heard save the occasional bark of foxes in the direction of Yalbury Wood, or the brush of a rabbit among the grass now and then as it scampered out of their way.

Most of the outlying homesteads and hamlets had been visited by about two o'clock; they then passed across the outskirts of a wooded park toward the main village, nobody being at home at the Manor. Pursuing no recognized track, great care was necessary in walking lest their faces should come in contact with the low-hanging boughs of the old lime-trees, which in many spots formed dense overgrowths of interlaced branches.

'Times have changed from the times they used to be,' said Mail, regarding nobody can tell what interesting old panoramas with an inward eye, and letting his outward glance rest on the ground because it was as convenient a position as any. 'People don't care much about us now!' I've been thinking we must be almost the last left in the county of the old string players? Barrel-organs, and the things next door to 'em that you blow wi' your foot, have come in terribly of late years.'

'Ay!' said Bowman shaking his head; and old William on seeing him did the same thing.

'More's the pity,' replied another. 'Time was – long and merry ago now! – when not one of the varmits was to be heard of; but it served some of the quires right. They should have stuck to strings as we did, and kept out clarinets, and done away with serpents. If you'd thrive in musical religion, stick to strings, says I.'

'Strings be safe soul-lifters, as far as that do go,' said Mr Spinks.

'Yet there's worse things than serpents,' said Mr Penny. 'Old things pass away, 'tis true; but a serpent was a good old note: a deep rich note was the serpent.'

'Clar'nets, however, be bad at all times,' said Michael Mail. 'One Christmas – years agone now, years – I went the rounds wi' the Weatherbury quire. 'Twas a hard frosty night, and the keys of all the clar'nets froze – ah, they did freeze! – so that 'twas like drawing a cork every time a key was opened; and the players o' 'em had to go into a hedger-and-ditcher's chimley-corner, and thaw their clar'nets every now and then. An icicle o' spet hung down from the end of every man's clar'net a span long; and as to fingers – well, there, if ye'll believe me, we had no fingers at all, to our knowing.'

'I can well bring back to my mind,' said Mr Penny, 'what I said to poor Joseph Ryme (who took the treble part in Chalk-Newton Church for two-and-forty year) when they thought of having clar'nets there. "Joseph," I said says I, "depend upon't, if so be you have them tooting clar'nets you'll spoil the whole set-out. Clar'nets were not made for the service of the Lard; you can see it by looking at 'em," I said. And what came o't? Why, souls, the parson set up a barrel-organ on his own account within two years o' the time I spoke, and the old quire went to nothing.'

'As far as look is concerned,' said the tranter, 'I don't for my part see that a fiddle is much nearer heaven than a clar'net. 'Tis further off. There's always a rakish, scampish twist about a fiddle's looks that seems to say the Wicked One had a hand in making o'en; while angels be supposed to play clar'nets in heaven, or som'at like 'em if ye may believe picters.'

'Robert Penny, you was in the right,' broke in the eldest Dewy. 'They should ha' stuck to strings. Your brass-man is a rafting dog – well and good; your reed-man is a dab at stirring ye – well and good; your drum-man is a rare bowel-shaker – good again. But I don't care who hears me say it, nothing will spak to your heart wi' the sweetness o' the man of strings!'

'Strings for ever!' said little Jimmy.

'Strings alone would have held their ground against all the new comers in creation.' ('True, true!' said Bowman.) 'But clarinets was death.' ('Death they was!' said Mr Penny.) 'And harmonions,' William continued in a louder voice, and getting excited by these signs of approval, 'harmonions and barrelorgans' ('Ah!' and groans from Spinks) 'be miserable – what shall I call 'em? – miserable – '

'Sinners,' suggested Jimmy, who made large strides like the men and did not lag behind with the other little boys.

'Miserable dumbledores!'

'Right, William, and so they be – miserable dumbledores!' said the choir with unanimity.

By this time they were crossing to a gate in the direction of the school which, standing on a slight eminence at the junction of three ways, now rose in unvarying and dark flatness against the sky. The instruments were retuned, and all the band entered the school enclosure, enjoined by old William to keep upon the grass.

'Number seventy-eight,' he softly gave out as they formed round in a semicircle, the boys opening the lanterns to get a clearer light, and directing their rays on the books.

Then passed forth into the quiet night an ancient and timeworn hymn, embodying a quaint Christianity in words orally transmitted from father to son through several generations down to the present characters, who sang them out right earnestly:

Remember Adam's fall,
O thou Man:
Remember Adam's fall
From Heaven to Hell.
Remember Adam's fall;
How he hath condemn'd all
In Hell perpetual
There for to dwell.

Remember God's goodnesse
O thou Man:
Remember God's goodnesse,
His promise made.
Remember God's goodnesse;
He sent His Son sinlesse
Our ails for to redress;
Be not afraid!

368

In Bethlehem He was born,
O thou Man:
In Bethlehem He was born,
For mankind's sake.
In Bethlehem He was born,
Christmas-day i' the morn:
Our Saviour thought no scorn
Our faults to take.

Give thanks to God alway,
O thou Man:
Give thanks to God alway
With heart-most joy.
Give thanks to God alway
On this our joyful day:
Let all men sing and say,
Holy, Holy!

Having concluded the last note they listened for a minute or two, but found that no sound issued from the schoolhouse.

'Four breaths, and then, "O, what unbounded goodness!" number fifty-nine,' said William.

This was duly gone through, and no notice whatever seemed to be taken of the performance.

'Good guide us, surely 'tisn't a' empty house, as befell us in the year thirty-nine and forty-three!' said old Dewy.

'Perhaps she's jist come from some musical city, and sneers at our doings?' tranter whispered.

"Od rabbit her!' said Mr Penny, with an annihilating look at a corner of the school chimney, 'I don't quite stomach her, if this is it. Your plain music well done is as worthy as your other sort done bad, a' b'lieve, souls; so say I.'

'Four breaths, and then the last,' said the leader authoritatively. ' "Rejoice, ye Tenants of the Earth," number sixty-four.'

At the close, waiting yet another minute, he said in a clear loud voice, as he had said in the village at that hour and season for the previous forty years –

'A merry Christmas to ye!'

FIVE

❦ The Listeners ❧

WHEN THE EXPECTANT STILLNESS CONSEQUENT upon the exclamation had nearly died out of them all, an increasing light made itself visible in one of the windows of the upper floor. It came so close to the blind that the exact position of the flame could be perceived from the outside. Remaining steady for an instant, the blind went upward from before it, revealing to thirty concentrated eyes a young girl framed as a picture by the window architrave, and unconsciously illuminating her countenance to a vivid brightness by a candle she held in her left hand, close to her face, her right hand being extended to the side of the window. She was wrapped in a white robe of some kind, whilst down her shoulders fell a twining profusion of marvellously rich hair, in a wild disorder which proclaimed it to be only during the invisible hours of the night that such a condition was discoverable. Her bright eyes were looking into the grey world outside with an uncertain expression, oscillating between courage and shyness, which, as she recognized the semicircular group of dark forms gathered before her, transformed itself into pleasant resolution.

Opening the window, she said lightly and warmly –

'Thank you, singers, thank you!'

Together went the window quickly and quietly, and the blind started downward on its return to its place. Her fair forehead and eyes vanished; her little mouth; her neck and shoulders; all of her. Then the spot of candlelight shone nebulously as before; then it moved away.

'How pretty!' exclaimed Dick Dewy.

'If she'd been rale wexwork she couldn't ha' been comelier,' said Michael Mail.

'As near a thing to a spiritual vision as ever *I* wish to see!' said tranter Dewy.

'O, sich I never, never see!' said Leaf fervently.

All the rest, after clearing their throats and adjusting their hats, agreed that such a sight was worth singing for.

'Now to Farmer Shiner's, and then replenish our insides, father?' said the tranter.

'Wi' all my heart,' said old William, shouldering his bass-viol.

Farmer Shiner's was a queer lump of a house, standing at the corner of a lane that ran into the principal thoroughfare. The upper windows

370

were much wider than they were high, and this feature, together with a broad bay-window where the door might have been expected, gave it by day the aspect of a human countenance turned askance, and wearing a sly and wicked leer. Tonight nothing was visible but the outline of the roof upon the sky.

The front of this building was reached, and the preliminaries arranged as usual.

'Four breaths, and number thirty-two, "Behold the Morning Star," ' said old William.

They had reached the end of the second verse, and the fiddlers were doing the up bow-stroke previously to pouring forth the opening chord of the third verse, when, without a light appearing or any signal being given a roaring voice exclaimed –

'Shut up, woll 'ee! Don't make your blaring tow here! A feller wi' a headache enough to split his skull likes a quiet night!'

Slam went the window.

'Hullo, that's a' ugly blow for we!' said the tranter, in a keenly appreciative voice, and turning to his companions.

'Finish the carrel, all who be friends of harmony!' commanded old William; and they continued to the end.

'Four breaths, and number nineteen!' said William firmly. 'Give it him well; the quire can't be insulted in this manner!'

A light now flashed into existence, the window opened, and the farmer stood revealed as one in a terrific passion.

'Drown en! – drown en!' the tranter cried, fiddling frantically. 'Play fortissimy, and drown his spaking!'

'Fortissimy!' said Michael Mail, and the music and singing waxed so loud that it was impossible to know what Mr Shiner had said, was saying, or was about to say; but wildly flinging his arms and body about in the forms of capital Xs and Ys, he appeared to utter enough invectives to consign the whole parish to perdition.

'Very onseemly – very!' said old William, as they retired. 'Never such a dreadful scene in the whole round o' my carrel practice – never! And he a churchwarden!'

'Only a drap o' drink got into his head,' said the tranter. 'Man's well enough when he's in his religious frame. He's in his worldly frame now. Must ask en to our bit of a party tomorrow night, I suppose, and so put en in humour again. We bear no mortal man ill-will.'

They now crossed Mellstock Bridge, and went along an embowered path beside the Froom towards the church and vicarage, meeting Voss with the hot mead and bread-and-cheese as they were approaching the churchyard. This determined them to eat and drink before proceeding further, and they entered the church and ascended to the gallery. The lanterns were opened, and the whole body sat round against the wall on benches and whatever else was available, and made a hearty meal. In the pauses of conversation there could be heard through the floor overhead a little world of undertones and creaks from the halting clockwork, which never spread further than the tower they were born in, and raised in the more meditative minds a fancy that here lay the direct pathway of Time.

Having done eating and drinking they again tuned the instruments, and once more the party emerged into the night air.

'Where's Dick?' said old Dewy.

Every man looked round upon every other man, as if Dick might have been transmuted into one or the other; and then they said they didn't know.

'Well now, that's what I call very nasty of Master Dicky, that I do,' said Michael Mail.

'He've clinked off home-along, depend upon't,' another suggested, though not quite believing that he had.

'Dick!' exclaimed the tranter, and his voice rolled sonorously forth among the yews.

He suspended his muscles rigid as stone whilst listening for an answer, and finding he listened in vain, turned to the assemblage.

'The treble man too! Now if he'd been a tenor or counter chap, we might ha' contrived the rest o't without en, you see. But for a quire to lose the treble, why, my sonnies, you may so well lose your ...' The tranter paused, unable to mention an image vast enough for the occasion.

'Your head at once,' suggested Mr Penny.

The tranter moved a pace as if it were puerile of people to complete sentences when there were more pressing things to be done.

'Was ever heard such a thing as a young man leaving his work half done and turning tail like this!'

'Never,' replied Bowman, in a tone signifying that he was the last man in the world to wish to withhold the formal finish required of him.

'I hope no fatal tragedy has overtook the lad!' said his grandfather.

'O no,' replied tranter Dewy placidly. 'Wonder where he's put that there fiddle of his. Why that fiddle cost thirty shillings, and good words besides. Somewhere in the damp, without doubt; that instrument will be unglued and spoilt in ten minutes – ten! ay, two.'

'What in the name o' righteousness can have happened?' said old William, more uneasily. 'Perhaps he's drownded!'

Leaving their lanterns and instruments in the belfry they retraced their steps along the waterside track. 'A strapping lad like Dick d'know better than let anything happen onawares,' Reuben remarked. 'There's sure to be some poor little scram reason for't staring us in the face all the while.'

He lowered his voice to a mysterious tone: 'Neighbours, have ye noticed any sign of a scornful woman in his head, or suchlike?'

'Not a glimmer of such a body. He's as clear as water yet.'

'And Dicky said he should never marry,' cried Jimmy, 'but live at home always along wi' mother and we!'

'Ay, ay, my sonny; every lad has said that in his time.'

They had now again reached the precincts of Mr Shiner's, but hearing nobody in that direction, one or two went across to the schoolhouse. A light was still burning in the bedroom, and though the blind was down the window had been slightly opened, as if to admit the distant notes of the carollers to the ears of the occupant of the room.

Opposite the window, leaning motionless against a beech tree, was the lost man, his arms folded, his head thrown back, his eyes fixed upon the illuminated lattice.

'Why, Dick, is that thee? What b'st doing here?'

Dick's body instantly flew into a more rational attitude, and his head was seen to turn east and west in the gloom as if endeavouring to discern some proper answer to that question; and at last he said in rather feeble accents –

'Nothing, father.'

'Th'st take long enough time about it then, upon my body,' said the tranter as they all turned anew towards the vicarage.

'I thought you hadn't done having snap in the gallery,' said Dick.

'Why, we've been traypsing and rambling about, looking everywhere, and thinking you'd done fifty deathly things, and here have you been at nothing at all!'

'The stupidity lies in that point of it being nothing at all,' murmured Mr Spinks.

The vicarage front was their next field of operation, and Mr Maybold, the lately-arrived incumbent, duly received his share of the night's harmonies. It was hoped that by reason of his profession he would have been led to open the window, and an extra carol in quick time was added to draw him forth. But Mr Maybold made no stir.

'A bad sign!' said old William, shaking his head.

However, at that same instant a musical voice was heard exclaiming from inner depths of bedclothes –

'Thanks, villagers!'

'What did he say?' asked Bowman, who was rather dull of hearing. Bowman's voice, being therefore loud, had been heard by the vicar within.

'I said, "Thanks, villagers!" ' cried the vicar again.

'Oh, we didn't hear 'ee the first time!' cried Bowman.

'Now don't for heaven's sake spoil the young man's temper by answering like that!' said the tranter.

'You won't do that, my friends!' the vicar shouted.

'Well to be sure, what ears!' said Mr Penny in a whisper. 'Beats any horse or dog in the parish, and depend upon't that's a sign he's a proper clever chap.'

'We shall see that in time,' said the tranter.

Old William, in his gratitude for such thanks from a comparatively new inhabitant, was anxious to play all the tunes over again; but renounced his desire on being reminded by Reuben that it would be best to leave well alone.

'Now putting two and two together,' the tranter continued, as they went their way over the hill, and across to the last remaining houses; 'that is, in the form of that young female vision we zeed just now, and this young tenor-voiced parson, my belief is she'll wind en round her finger, and twist the pore young feller about like the figure of 8 – that she will, my sonnies.'

SIX

❧ Christmas Morning ❧

THE CHOIR AT LAST REACHED their beds, and slept like the rest of the parish. Dick's slumbers, through the three or four hours remaining for rest, were disturbed and slight; an exhaustive variation upon the incidents that had passed that night in connection with the school-window going on in his brain every moment of the time.

In the morning, do what he would – go upstairs, downstairs, out of doors, speak of the wind and weather, or what not – he could not refrain from an unceasing renewal, in imagination, of that interesting enactment. Tilted on the edge of one foot he stood beside the fireplace, watching his mother grilling rashers; but there was nothing in grilling, he thought, unless the Vision grilled. The limp rasher hung down between the bars of the gridiron like a cat in a child's arms; but there was nothing in similes unless She uttered them. He looked at the daylight shadows of a yellow hue, dancing with the firelight shadows in blue on the whitewashed chimney corner, but there was nothing in shadows. 'Perhaps the new young wom – sch – Miss Fancy Day will sing in church with us this morning,' he said.

The tranter looked a long time before he replied, 'I fancy she will; and yet I fancy she won't.'

Dick implied that such a remark was rather to be tolerated than admired; though deliberateness in speech was known to have, as a rule, more to do with the machinery of the tranter's throat than with the matter enunciated.

They made preparations for going to church as usual; Dick with extreme alacrity, though he would not definitely consider why he was so religious. His wonderful nicety in brushing and cleaning his best light boots had features which elevated it to the rank of an art. Every particle and speck of last week's mud was scraped and brushed from toe and heel; new blacking from the packet was carefully mixed and made use of, regardless of expense. A coat was laid on and polished; then another coat for increased blackness; and lastly a third, to give the perfect and mirror-like jet which the hoped-for rencounter demanded.

It being Christmas-day, the tranter prepared himself with Sunday particularity. Loud sousing and snorting noises were heard to proceed from a tub in the back quarters of the dwelling, proclaiming that he was there performing his great Sunday wash, lasting half-an-hour, to which his washings on workingday mornings were mere flashes in the pan. Vanishing into the outhouse with a large brown towel, and the above-named bubblings and snortings being carried on for about twenty minutes, the tranter would appear round the edge of the door, smelling like a summer fog, and looking as if he had just narrowly escaped a watery grave with the loss of much of his clothes, having since been weeping bitterly till his eyes were red; a crystal drop of water hanging ornamentally at the bottom of each ear, one at the tip of his nose, and others in the form of spangles about his hair.

After a great deal of crunching upon the sanded stone floor by the feet of father, son, and grandson as they moved to and fro in these preparations. the bass-viol and fiddles were taken from their nook, and the strings examined and screwed a little above concert-pitch that they might keep their tone when the service began, to obviate the awkward contingency of having to retune them at the back of the gallery during a cough, sneeze, or amen – an inconvenience which had been known to arise in damp wintry weather.

The three left the door and paced down Mellstock-lane and across the ewe-lease, bearing under their arms the instruments in faded green-baize bags, and old brown music-books in their hands; Dick continually finding himself in advance of the other two, and the tranter moving on with toes turned outwards to an enormous angle.

At the foot of an incline the church became visible through the north gate, or 'church hatch', as it was called here. Seven agile figures in a clump were observable beyond, which proved to be the choristers waiting; sitting on an altar-tomb to pass the time, and letting their heels dangle against it. The musicians being now in sight the youthful party scampered off and rattled up the old wooden stairs of the gallery like a regiment of cavalry; the other boys of the parish waiting outside and observing birds, cats, and other creatures till the vicar entered, when they suddenly subsided into sober church-goers, and passed down the aisle with echoing heels.

The gallery of Mellstock Church had a status and sentiment of its own. A stranger there was regarded with a feeling altogether differing from that of the congregation below towards him. Banished from the nave as an intruder whom no originality could make interesting, he was received above as a curiosity that no unfitness could render dull. The gallery, too, looked down upon and knew the habits of the nave to its remotest peculiarity, and had an extensive stock of exclusive information about it; while the nave knew nothing of the gallery folk, as gallery folk, beyond their loud-sounding minims and chest notes. Such topics as that the clerk was always chewing tobacco except at the moment of crying amen; that he had a dust-hole in his pew; that during the sermon certain young daughters of the village had left off caring to read anything so mild as the marriage service for some years, and now regularly studied the one which chronologically follows it, that a pair of lovers touched fingers through a knot-hole between their pews in the manner ordained by their great exemplars, Pyramus and Thisbe; that Mrs Ledlow, the farmer's wife, counted her money and reckoned her week's marketing expenses during the first lesson – all news to those below – were stale subjects here.

Old William sat in the centre of the front row, his violoncello between his knees and two singers on each hand. Behind him, on the left, came the treble singers and Dick; and on the right the tranter and the tenors. Further back was old Mail with the altos and supernumeraries.

But before they had taken their places, and whilst they were standing in a circle at the back of the gallery practising a psalm or two, Dick cast his eyes over his grandfather's shoulder, and saw the vision of the past night enter the porch-door as methodically as if she had never been a vision at all. A new atmosphere seemed suddenly to be puffed into the ancient edifice by her movement, which made Dick's body and soul tingle with novel sensations. Directed by Shiner, the churchwarden, she proceeded to the small aisle on the north side of the chancel, a spot now allotted to a throng of Sunday-school girls, and distinctly visible from the gallery-front by looking under the curve of the furthermost arch on that side.

Before this moment the church had seemed comparatively empty – now it was thronged; and as Miss Fancy rose from her knees and looked around her for a permanent place in which to deposit herself – finally choosing the remotest corner – Dick began to breathe more freely the warm new air she had brought with her; to feel rushings of blood, and to have impressions that there was a tie between her and himself visible to all the congregation.

Ever afterwards the young man could recollect individually each part of the service of that bright Christmas morning, and the trifling occurrences which took place as its minutes slowly drew along; the duties of that day dividing themselves by a complete line from the services of other times. The tunes they that morning essayed remained with him for years, apart from all others; also the text; also the appearance of the layer of dust upon the capitals of the piers; that the holly-bough in the chancel archway was hung a little out of the centre – all the ideas, in short, that creep into the mind when reason is only exercising its lowest activity through the eye.

By chance or by fate, another young man who attended Mellstock Church on that Christmas morning had towards the end of the service the same instinctive perception of an interesting presence, in the shape of the same bright maiden, though his emotion reached a far less developed stage. And there was this difference, too, that the person in question was surprised at his condition, and sedulously endeavoured to reduce himself to his normal state of mind. He was the young vicar, Mr Maybold.

The music on Christmas mornings was frequently below the standard of church-performances at other times. The boys were sleepy from the heavy exertions of the night; the men were slightly wearied; and now, in addition to these constant reasons, there was a dampness in the atmosphere that still further aggravated the evil. Their strings, from the recent long exposure to the night air, rose whole semitones, and snapped with a loud twang at the most silent moment; which necessitated more retiring than ever to the back of the gallery, and made the gallery throats quite husky with the quantity of coughing and hemming required for tuning in. The vicar looked cross.

When the singing was in progress there was suddenly discovered to be a strong and shrill reinforcement from some point, ultimately found to be the school-girls' aisle. At every attempt it grew bolder and more distinct. At the third time of singing, these intrusive feminine voices were as mighty as those of the regular singers; in fact, the flood of sound from this quarter assumed such an individuality, that it had a time, a

377

key, almost a tune of its own, surging upwards when the gallery plunged downwards, and the reverse.

Now this had never happened before within the memory of man. The girls, like the rest of the congregation, had always been humble and respectful followers of the gallery; singing at sixes and sevens if without gallery leaders; never interfering with the ordinances of these practised artists – having no will, union, power, or proclivity except it was given them from the established choir enthroned above them.

A good deal of desperation became noticeable in the gallery throats and strings, which continued throughout the musical portion of the service. Directly the fiddles were laid down, Mr Penny's spectacles put in their sheath, and the text had been given out, an indignant whispering began.

'Did ye hear that, souls?' Mr Penny said, in a groaning breath.

'Brazen-faced hussies!' said Bowman.

'True; why, they were every note as loud as we, fiddles and all, if not louder!'

'Fiddles and all!' echoed Bowman bitterly.

'Shall anything saucier be found than united 'ooman?' Mr Spinks murmured.

'What I want to know is,' said the tranter (as if he knew already, but that civilization required the form of words), 'what business people have to tell maidens to sing like that when they don't sit in a gallery, and never have entered one in their lives? That's the question, my sonnies.'

''Tis the gallery have got to sing, all the world knows,' said Mr Penny. 'Why, souls, what's the use o' the ancients spending scores of pounds to build galleries if people down in the lowest depths of the church sing like that at a moment's notice?'

'Really, I think we useless ones had better march out of church, fiddles and all!' said Mr Spinks, with a laugh which, to a stranger, would have sounded mild and real. Only the initiated body of men he addressed could understand the horrible bitterness of irony that lurked under the quiet words 'useless ones', and the ghastliness of the laughter apparently so natural.

'Never mind! Let 'em sing too – 'twill make it all the louder – hee, hee!' said Leaf.

'Thomas Leaf, Thomas Leaf! Where have you lived all your life?' said grandfather William sternly.

The quailing Leaf tried to look as if he had lived nowhere at all.

'When all's said and done, my sonnies,' Reuben said, 'there'd have been no real harm in their singing if they had let nobody hear 'em, and only jined in now and then.'

'None at all,' said Mr Penny. 'But though I don't wish to accuse people wrongfully, I'd say before my lord judge that I could hear every note o' that last psalm come from 'em as much as from us – every note as if 'twas their own.'

'Know it! ah, I should think I did know it!' Mr Spinks was heard to observe at this moment without reference to his fellow-players – shaking his head at some idea he seemed to see floating before him, and smiling as if he were attending a funeral at the time. 'Ah, do I or don't I know it!'

No one said, 'Know what?' because all were aware from experience that what he knew would declare itself in process of time.

'I could fancy last night that we should have some trouble wi' that young man,' said the tranter, pending the continuance of Spinks's speech, and looking towards the unconscious Mr Maybold in the pulpit.

'I fancy,' said old William, rather severely, 'I fancy there's too much whispering going on to be of any spiritual use to gentle or simple.' Then folding his lips and concentrating his glance on the vicar, he implied that none but the ignorant would speak again; and accordingly there was silence in the gallery, Mr Spinks's telling speech remaining for ever unspoken.

Dick had said nothing, and the tranter little, on this episode of the morning; for Mrs Dewy at breakfast expressed it as her intention to invite the youthful leader of the culprits to the small party it was customary with them to have on Christmas night – a piece of knowledge which had given a particular brightness to Dick's reflections since he had received it. And in the tranter's slightly-cynical nature, party feeling was weaker than in the other members of the choir, though friendliness and faithful partnership still sustained in him a hearty earnestness on their account.

SEVEN

❧ The Tranter's Party ❧

DURING THE AFTERNOON UNUSUAL ACTIVITY was seen to prevail about the precincts of tranter Dewy's house. The flagstone floor was swept of dust, and a sprinkling of the finest yellow sand from the innermost stratum of the adjoining sand-pit lightly scattered thereupon. Then were produced large knives and forks, which had been shrouded in darkness and grease since the last occasion of the kind, and bearing upon their sides, 'Shear-steel, warranted,' in such emphatic letters of assurance, that the warranter's name was not required as further proof, and not given. The key was left in the tap of the cider-barrel instead of being carried in a pocket. And finally the tranter had to stand up in the room and let his wife wheel him round like a turnstile, to see if anything discreditable was visible in his appearance.

'Stand still till I've been for the scissors,' said Mrs Dewy.

The tranter stood as still as a sentinel at the challenge.

The only repairs necessary were a trimming of one or two whiskers that had extended beyond the general contour of the mass; a like trimming of a slightly-frayed edge visible on his shirt-collar; and a final tug at a grey hair – to all of which operations he submitted in resigned silence, except the last, which produced a mild 'Come, come, Ann', by way of expostulation.

'Really, Reuben, 'tis quite a disgrace to see such a man,' said Mrs Dewy, with the severity justifiable in a long-tried companion, giving him another turn round, and picking several of Smiler's hairs from the shoulder of his coat. Reuben's thoughts seemed engaged elsewhere, and he yawned. 'And the collar of your coat is a shame to behold – so plastered with dirt, or dust, or grease, or something. Why, wherever could you have got it?'

''Tis my warm nater in summer-time, I suppose. I always did get in such a heat when I bustle about.'

'Ay, the Dewys always were such a coarse-skinned family. There's your brother Bob just as bad – as fat as a porpoise – wi' his low, mean, "How'st do, Ann?" whenever he meets me. I'd "How'st do" him indeed! If the sun only shines out a minute, there be you all streaming in the face – I never see!'

'If I be hot week-days, I must be hot Sundays.'

'If any of the girls should turn after their father 'twill be a bad look-out for 'em, poor things! None of my family was sich vulgar sweaters, not one of 'em. But, Lord-a-mercy, the Dewys! I don't know how ever I cam' into such a family!'

'Your woman's weakness when I asked ye to jine us. That's how it was, I suppose.' But the tranter appeared to have heard some such words from his wife before, and hence his answer had not the energy it might have shown if the inquiry had possessed the charm of novelty.

'You never did look so well in a pair o' trousers as in them,' she continued in the same unimpassioned voice, so that the unfriendly criticism of the Dewy family seemed to have been more normal than spontaneous. 'Such a cheap pair as 'twas too. As big as any man could wish to have, and lined inside, and double-lined in the lower parts, and an extra piece of stiffening at the bottom. And 'tis a nice high cut that comes up right under your armpits, and there's enough turned down inside the seams to make half a pair more, besides a piece of cloth left that will make an honest waistcoat – all by my contriving in buying the stuff at a bargain, and having it made up under my eye. It only shows what may be done by taking a little trouble, and not going straight to the rascally tailors.'

The discourse was cut short by the sudden appearance of Charley on the scene, with a face and hands of hideous blackness, and a nose like a guttering candle. Why, on that particularly cleanly afternoon, he should have discovered that the chimney-crook and chain from which the hams were suspended should have possessed more merits and general interest as playthings than any other articles in the house, is a question for nursing mothers to decide. However, the humour seemed to lie in the result being, as has been seen, that any given player with these articles was in the long-run daubed with soot. The last that was seen of Charley by daylight after this piece of ingenuity was when in the act of vanishing from his father's presence round the corner of the house – looking back over his shoulder with an expression of great sin on his face, like Cain as the Outcast in Bible pictures.

The guests had all assembled, and the tranter's party had reached that degree of development which accords with ten o'clock p.m. in rural assemblies. At that hour the sound of a fiddle in process of tuning was heard from the inner pantry.

'That's Dick,' said the tranter. 'That lad's crazy for a jig.'

'Dick! Now I cannot – really, I cannot have any dancing at all till Christmas-day is out,' said old William emphatically. 'When the clock ha' done striking twelve, dance as much as ye like.'

'Well, I must say there's reason in that, William,' said Mrs Penny. 'If you do have a party on Christmas-night, 'tis only fair and honourable to the sky-folk to have it a sit-still party. Jigging parties be all very well on the Devil's holidays; but a jigging party looks suspicious now. O yes; stop till the clock strikes, young folk – so say I.'

It happened that some warm mead accidentally got into Mr Spinks's head about this time.

'Dancing,' he said, 'is a most strengthening, livening, and courting movement, 'specially with a little beverage added! And dancing is good. But why disturb what is ordained, Richard and Reuben, and the company zhinerally? Why, I ask, as far as that do go?'

'Then nothing till after twelve,' said William.

Though Reuben and his wife ruled on social points, religious questions were mostly disposed of by the old man, whose firmness on this head quite counterbalanced a certain weakness in his handling of domestic matters. The hopes of the younger members of the household were

381

therefore relegated to a distance of one hour and three-quarters – a result that took visible shape in them by a remote and listless look about the eyes – the singing of songs being permitted in the interim.

At five minutes to twelve the soft tuning was again heard in the back quarters; and when at length the clock had whizzed forth the last stroke, Dick appeared ready primed, and the instruments were boldly handled; old William very readily taking the bass-viol from its accustomed nail, and touching the strings as irreligiously as could be desired.

The country-dance called the 'Triumph, or Follow my Lover', was the figure with which they opened. The tranter took for his partner Mrs Penny, and Mrs Dewy was chosen by Mr Penny, who made so much of his limited height by a judicious carriage of the head, straightening of the back, and important flashes of his spectacle-glasses, that he seemed almost as tall as the tranter. Mr Shiner, age about thirty-five, farmer and church-warden, a character principally composed of a crimson stare, vigorous breath, and a watch-chain, with a mouth hanging on a dark smile but never smiling, had come quite willingly to the party, and showed a wondrous obliviousness of all his antics on the previous night. But the comely, slender, prettily-dressed prize Fancy Day fell to Dick's lot, in spite of some private machinations of the farmer, for the reason that Mr Shiner, as a richer man, had shown too much assurance in asking the favour, whilst Dick had been duly courteous.

We gain a good view of our heroine as she advances to her place in the ladies' line. She belonged to the taller division of middle height. Flexibility was her first characteristic, by which she appeared to enjoy the most easeful rest when she was in gliding motion. Her dark eyes – arched by brows of so keen, slender, and soft a curve that they resembled nothing so much as two slurs in music – showed primarily a bright sparkle each. This was softened by a frequent thoughtfulness, yet not so frequent as to do away, for more than a few minutes at a time, with a certain coquettishness; which in its turn was never so decided as to banish honesty. Her lips imitated her brows in their clearly-cut outline and softness of bend; and her nose was well shaped – which is saying a great deal, when it is remembered that there are a hundred pretty mouths and eyes for one pretty nose. Add to this, plentiful knots of dark-brown hair, a gauzy dress of white with blue facings; and the slightest idea may be gained of the young maiden who showed, amidst the rest of the dancing-ladies, like a flower among vegetables. And so the dance proceeded. Mr Shiner, according to the interesting rule laid down, deserted his own partner and made off down the middle with this fair one of Dick's – the pair appearing from the top of the room like two persons tripping down a lane to be married. Dick trotted behind with what was intended to be a look of composure, but which was, in fact, a rather silly expression of feature – implying, with too much earnestness, that such an elopement could not be tolerated. Then they turned and came back, when Dick grew more rigid around his mouth, and blushed with ingenuous ardour as he joined hands with the rival and formed the arch over his lady's head, which presumably gave the figure its name; relinquishing her again at setting to partners, when Mr Shiner's new chain quivered in every link, and all the loose flesh upon the tranter – who here came into action again – shook like jelly. Mrs Penny, being always rather concerned for her personal safety when she danced with the tranter, fixed her face to a chronic smile of timidity the whole time it lasted – a peculiarity which filled her features with wrinkles, and reduced her eyes to little straight lines like hyphens, as she jigged up and down opposite him; repeating in her own person not only his proper movements, but also the minor flourishes which the richness of the tranter's imagination led him to introduce from time to time – an imitation which had about it something of slavish obedience, not unmixed with fear.

The ear-rings of the ladies now flung themselves wildly about, turning violent summersaults, banging this way and that, and then swinging quietly against the ears sustaining them. Mrs Crumpler – a heavy woman, who, for some reason which nobody ever thought worth inquiry, danced in a clean apron – moved so smoothly through the figure that her feet were never seen; conveying to imaginative minds the idea that she rolled on castors.

Minute after minute glided by, and the party reached the period when ladies' back-hair begins to look forgotten and dissipated; when a perceptible dampness makes itself apparent upon the faces even of delicate girls – a ghastly dew having for some time rained from the features of their masculine partners; when skirts begin to be torn out of their gathers; when elderly people, who have stood up to please their juniors, begin to feel sundry small tremblings in the region of the knees, and to wish the interminable dance was at Jericho; when (at country parties of the thorough sort) waistcoats begin to be unbuttoned, and when the fiddlers' chairs have been wriggled, by the frantic bowing of their occupiers, to a distance of about two feet from where they originally stood.

Fancy was dancing with Mr Shiner. Dick knew that Fancy, by the law of good manners, was bound to dance as pleasantly with one partner as with another; yet he could not help suggesting to himself that she need not have put *quite* so much spirit into her steps, nor smiled *quite* so frequently whilst in the farmer's hands.

'I'm afraid you didn't cast off,' said Dick mildly to Mr Shiner, before the latter man's watch-chain had done vibrating from a recent whirl.

Fancy made a motion of accepting the correction; but her partner took no notice, and proceeded with the next movement with an affectionate bend towards her.

'That Shiner's too fond of her,' the young man said to himself as he watched them. They came to the top again, Fancy smiling warmly towards her partner, and went to their places.

'Mr Shiner, you didn't cast off,' said Dick, for want of something else to demolish him with; casting off himself, and being put out at the farmer's irregularity.

'Perhaps I shan't cast off for any man,' said Mr Shiner.

'I think you ought to, sir.'

Dick's partner, a young lady of the name of Lizzy – called Lizz for short – tried to mollify.

'I can't say that I myself have much feeling for casting off,' she said.

'Nor I,' said Mrs Penny, following up the argument; 'especially if a friend and neighbour is set against it. Not but that 'tis a terrible tasty thing in good hands and well done; yes, indeed, so say I.'

'All I meant was,' said Dick, rather sorry that he had spoken correctingly to a guest, 'that 'tis in the dance; and a man has hardly any right to hack and mangle what was ordained by the regular dance-maker, who, I daresay, got his living by making 'em, and thought of nothing else all his life.'

'I don't like casting off: then very well; I cast off for no dance-maker that ever lived.'

Dick now appeared to be doing mental arithmetic, the act being really an effort to present to himself, in an abstract form, how far an argument with a formidable rival ought to be carried when that rival was his mother's guest. The dead-lock was put an end to by the stamping arrival up the middle of the tranter, who, despising minutiae on principle, started a theme of his own.

'I assure you, neighbours,' he said, 'the heat of my frame no tongue can tell!' He looked around and endeavoured to give, by a forcible gaze of self-sympathy, some faint idea of the truth.

Mrs Dewy formed one of the next couple.

'Yes,' she said in an auxiliary tone, 'Reuben always was such a hot man.'

Mrs Penny implied the species of sympathy that such a class of affliction required by trying to smile and to look grieved at the same time.

'If he only walk round the garden of a Sunday morning his shirt-collar is as limp as no starch at all,' continued Mrs Dewy, her countenance lapsing parenthetically into a housewifely expression of concern at the reminiscence.

'Come, come, you women-folk; 'tis hands-across – come, come!' said the tranter; and the conversation ceased for the present.

EIGHT

❧ They Dance more Wildly ❧

DICK HAD AT LENGTH SECURED Fancy for that most delightful of country-dances, opening with six-hands-round.

'Before we begin,' said the tranter, 'my proposal is, that 'twould be a right and proper plan for every mortal man in the dance to pull off his jacket, considering the heat.'

'Such low notions as you have, Reuben! Nothing but strip will go down with you when you are a-dancing. Such a hot man as he is!'

'Well, now, look here, my sonnies,' he argued to his wife, whom he often addressed in the plural masculine for economy of epithet merely: 'I don't see that. You dance and get hot as fire; therefore you lighten your clothes. Isn't that nature and reason for gentle and simple? If I strip by myself and not necessary, 'tis rather pot-housey I own; but if we stout chaps strip one and all, why, 'tis the native manners of the country, which no man can gainsay? Hey – what did you say, my sonnies?'

'Strip we will!' said the three other heavy men who were in the dance; and their coats were accordingly taken off and hung in the passage, whence the four sufferers from heat soon reappeared marching in close column, with flapping shirt-sleeves, and having as common to them all a general glance of being now a match for any man or dancer in England or Ireland. Dick, fearing to lose ground in Fancy's good opinion, retained his coat like the rest of the thinner men; and Mr Shiner did the same from superior knowledge.

And now a further phase of revelry had disclosed itself. It was the time of night when a guest may write his name in the dust upon the tables and chairs, and a bluish mist pervades the atmosphere, becoming a distinct halo round the candles; when people's nostrils, wrinkles, and crevices in general seem to be getting gradually plastered up; when the very fiddlers as well as the dancers get red in the face, the dancers having advanced further still towards incandescence, and entered the cadaverous phase; the fiddlers no longer sit down, but kick back their chairs and saw madly at the strings with legs firmly spread and eyes closed, regardless of the visible world. Again and again did Dick share his Love's hand with another man, and wheel round; then, more delightfully, promenade in a circle with her all to himself, his arm holding her waist more firmly each time, and his elbow getting further and further behind

her back, till the distance reached was rather noticeable; and, most blissful, swinging to places shoulder to shoulder, her breath curling round
his neck like a summer zephyr that had strayed from its proper date.
Threading the couples one by one they reached the bottom, when there
arose in Dick's mind a minor misery lest the tune should end before they
could work their way to the top again, and have anew the same exciting
run down through. Dick's feelings on actually reaching the top in spite
of his doubts were supplemented by a mortal fear that the fiddling might
even stop at this supreme moment; which prompted him to convey a
stealthy whisper to the far-gone musicians to the effect that they were
not to leave off till he and his partner had reached the bottom of the
dance once more, which remark was replied to by the nearest of those
convulsed and quivering men by a private nod to the anxious young
man between two semiquavers of the tune, and a simultaneous 'All right,
ay, ay', without opening the eyes. Fancy was now held so closely that
Dick and she were practically one person. The room became to Dick like
a picture in a dream; all that he could remember of it afterwards being
the look of the fiddlers going to sleep as humming-tops sleep, by increasing their motion and hum, together with the figures of grandfather James
and Old Simon Crumpler sitting by the chimney-corner talking and
nodding in dumb-show, and beating the air to their emphatic sentences
like people near a threshing machine.

The dance ended. 'Piph-h-h-h!' said tranter Dewy, blowing out his
breath in the very finest stream of vapour that a man's lips could form.
'A regular tightener, that one, sonnies!' He wiped his forehead, and went
to the cider and ale mugs on the table.

'Well!' said Mrs Penny, flopping into a chair, 'my heart haven't been
in such a thumping state of uproar since I used to sit up on old Mid-
summer-eves to see who my husband was going to be.'

'And that's getting on for a good few years ago now, from what I've
heard you tell,' said the tranter without lifting his eyes from the cup
he was filling. Being now engaged in the business of handing round
refreshments he was warranted in keeping his coat off still, though the
other heavy men had resumed theirs.

'And a thing I never expected would come to pass, if you'll believe
me, came to pass then,' continued Mrs Penny. 'Ah, the first spirit ever I
see on a Midsummer-eve was a puzzle to me when he appeared, a hard
puzzle, so say I!'

'So I should have fancied,' said Elias Spinks.

'Yes,' said Mrs Penny, throwing her glance into past times and talking
on in a running tone of complacent abstraction, as if a listener were not
a necessity. 'Yes; never was I in such a taking as on that Midsummer-
eve! I sat up, quite determined to see if John Wildway was going to

marry me or no. I put the bread-and-cheese and beer quite ready, as the witch's book ordered, and I opened the door, and I waited till the clock struck twelve, my nerves all alive and so strained that I could feel every one of 'em twitching like bell-wires. Yes, sure! and when the clock had struck, lo and behold I could see through the door a *little small* man in the lane wi' a shoemaker's apron on.'

Here Mr Penny stealthily enlarged himself half an inch.

'Now, John Wildway,' Mrs Penny continued, 'who courted me at that time, was a shoemaker, you see, but he was a very fair-sized man, and I couldn't believe that any such a little small man had anything to do wi' me, as anybody might. But on he came, and crossed the threshold – not John, but actually the same little man in the shoemaker's apron – '

'You needn't be so mighty particular about little and small!' said her husband.

'In he walks, and down he sits, and O my goodness me, didn't I flee upstairs, body and soul hardly hanging together! Well, to cut a long story short, by-long and by-late John Wildway and I had a miff and parted; and lo and behold, the coming man came! Penny asked me if I'd go snacks with him, and afore I knew what I was about a'most, the thing was done.'

'I've fancied you never knew better in your life; but I mid be mistaken,' said Mr Penny in a murmur.

After Mrs Penny had spoken, there being no new occupation for her eyes she still let them stay idling on the past scenes just related, which were apparently visible to her in the centre of the room. Mr Penny's remark received no reply.

During this discourse the tranter and his wife might have been observed standing in an unobtrusive corner in mysterious closeness to each other, a just perceptible current of intelligence passing from each to each, which had apparently no relation whatever to the conversation of their guests, but much to their sustenance. A conclusion of some kind having at length been drawn, the palpable confederacy of man and wife was once more obliterated, the tranter marching off into the pantry humming a tune that he couldn't quite recollect, and then breaking into the words of a song of which he could remember about one line and a quarter. Mrs Dewy spoke a few words about preparations for a bit of supper.

That elder portion of the company which loved eating and drinking put on a look to signify that till this moment they had quite forgotten that it was customary to expect suppers on these occasions; going even further than this politeness of feature, and starting irrelevant subjects, the exceeding flatness and forced tone of which rather betrayed their object. The younger members said they were quite hungry, and that supper would be delightful though it was so late.

Good luck attended Dick's love-passes during the meal. He sat next Fancy, and had the thrilling pleasure of using permanently a glass which had been taken by Fancy in mistake; of letting the outer edge of the sole of his boot touch the lower verge of her skirt; and to add to these delights the cat, which had lain unobserved in her lap for several minutes, crept across into his own, touching him with fur that had touched her hand a moment before. There were, besides, some little pleasures in the shape of helping her to vegetable she didn't want, and when it had nearly alighted on her plate taking it across for his own use, on the plea of waste not, want not. He also, from time to time, sipped sweet sly glances at her profile; noticing the set of her head, the curve of her throat, and other artistic properties of the lively goddess, who the while kept up a rather free, not to say too free, conversation with Mr Shiner sitting opposite; which, after some uneasy criticism, and much shifting of argument backwards and forwards in Dick's mind, he decided not to consider of alarming significance.

'A new music greets our ears now,' said Miss Fancy, alluding, with the sharpness that her position as village sharpener demanded, to the contrast between the rattle of knives and forks and the late notes of the fiddlers.

'Ay; and I don't know but what 'tis sweeter in tone when you get above forty,' said the tranter; 'except, in faith, as regards father there. Never such a mortal man as he for tunes. They do move his soul; don't 'em, father?'

The eldest Dewy smiled across from his distant chair an assent to Reuben's remark.

'Spaking of being moved in soul,' said Mr Penny, 'I shall never forget the first time I heard the "Dead March". 'Twas at poor Corp'l Nineman's funeral at Casterbridge. It fairly made my hair creep and fidget about like a vlock of sheep – ah, it did, souls! And when they had done, and the last trump had sounded, and the guns was fired over the dead hero's grave, a' icy-cold drop o' moist sweat hung upon my forehead, and another upon my jawbone. Ah, 'tis a very solemn thing!'

'Well, as to father in the corner there,' the tranter said, pointing to old William, who was in the act of filling his mouth; 'he'd starve to death for music's sake now, as much as when he was a boy-chap of fifteen.'

'Truly, now,' said Michael Mail, clearing the corner of his throat in the manner of a man who meant to be convincing; 'there's a friendly tie of some sort between music and eating.' He lifted the cup to his mouth, and drank himself gradually backwards from a perpendicular position to a slanting one, during which time his looks performed a circuit from the wall opposite him to the ceiling overhead. Then clearing the other corner of his throat: 'Once I was a-setting in the little kitchen of the Dree Mariners at Casterbridge, having a bit of dinner, and a brass band struck up in the street. Such a beautiful band as that were! I was setting eating fried liver and lights, I well can mind – ah, I was! and to save my life, I couldn't help chawing to the tune. Band played six-eight time; six-eight chaws I, willynilly. Band plays common; common time went my teeth among the liver and lights as true as a hair. Beautiful 'twere! Ah, I shall never forget that there band!'

'That's as tuneful a thing as ever I heard of,' said grandfather James, with the absent gaze which accompanies profound criticism.

'I don't like Michael's tuneful stories then,' said Mrs Dewy. 'They are quite coarse to a person o' decent taste.'

Old Michael's mouth twitched here and there, as if he wanted to smile but didn't know where to begin, which gradually settled to an expression that it was not displeasing for a nice woman like the tranter's wife to correct him.

'Well, now,' said Reuben, with decisive earnestness, 'that sort o' coarse touch that's so upsetting to Ann's feelings is to my mind a recommendation; for it do always prove a story to be true. And for the same reason, I like a story with a bad moral. My sonnies, all true stories have a coarse touch or a bad moral, depend upon't. If the story-tellers could ha' got decency and good morals from true stories, who'd have troubled to invent parables?' Saying this the tranter arose to fetch a new stock of cider, ale, mead, and home-made wines.

Mrs Dewy sighed and appended a remark (ostensibly behind her husband's back, though that the words should reach his ears distinctly was understood by both): 'Such a man as Dewy is! Nobody do know the trouble I have to keep that man barely respectable. And did you ever hear too – just now at supper-time – talking about "taties" with Michael in such a work-folk way. Well, 'tis what I was never brought up to! With our family 'twas never less than "taters", and very often "pertatoes" outright; mother was so particular and nice with us girls: there was no family in the parish that kept themselves up more than we.'

The hour of parting came. Fancy could not remain for the night because she had engaged a woman to wait up for her. She disappeared temporarily from the flagging party of dancers, and then came downstairs wrapped up and looking altogether a different person from whom she had been hitherto, in fact (to Dick's sadness and disappointment), a woman somewhat reserved and of a phlegmatic temperament – nothing left in her of the romping girl that she had seemed but a short quarter-hour before, who had not minded the weight of Dick's hand upon her waist, nor shirked the purlieus of the mistletoe.

'What a difference!' thought the young man – hoary cynic *pro tem.* 'What a miserable deceiving difference between the manners of a maid's life at dancing times and at others! Look at this lovely Fancy! Through the whole past evening touchable, squeezable – even kissable! For whole half-hours I held her so close to me that not a sheet of paper could have been slipped between us; and I could feel her heart only just outside my own, her life beating on so close to mine, that I was aware of every breath in it. A flit is made upstairs – a hat and a cloak put on – and I no more dare to touch her than – ' Thought failed him, and he returned to realities.

But this was an endurable misery in comparison with what followed. Mr Shiner and his watch-chain, taking the intrusive advantage that ardent bachelors who are going homeward along the same road as a pretty young woman always do take of that circumstance, came forward to assure Fancy – with a total disregard of Dick's emotions, and in tones which were certainly not frigid – that he (Shiner) was not the man to go to bed before seeing his Lady Fair safe within her own door – not he, nobody should say he was that; – and that he would not leave her side an inch till the thing was done – drown him if he would. The proposal was assented to by Miss Day, in Dick's foreboding judgement, with one degree – or at any rate, an appreciable fraction of a degree – of warmth beyond that required by a disinterested desire for protection from the dangers of the night.

All was over; and Dick surveyed the chair she had last occupied, looking now like a setting from which the gem has been torn. There stood her glass, and the romantic teaspoonful of elder wine at the bottom that she couldn't drink by trying ever so hard, in obedience to the mighty arguments of the tranter (his hand coming down upon her shoulder the while like a Nasmyth hammer), but the drinker was there no longer. There were the nine or ten pretty little crumbs she had left on her plate; but the eater was no more seen.

There seemed a disagreeable closeness of relationship between himself and the members of his family now that they were left alone again face to face. His father seemed quite offensive for appearing to be in just as high spirits as when the guests were there; and as for grandfather James (who had not yet left), he was quite fiendish in being rather glad they were gone.

'Really,' said the tranter, in a tone of placid satisfaction, 'I've had so little time to attend to myself all the evenen that I mean to enjoy a quiet meal now! A slice of this here ham – neither too fat nor too lean – so; and then a drop of this vinegar and pickles – there, that's it – and I shall be as fresh as a lark again! And to tell the truth, my sonny, my inside has been as dry as a lime-basket all night.'

'I like a party very well once in a while,' said Mrs Dewy, leaving off the adorned tones she had been bound to use throughout the evening and returning to the natural marriage voice; 'but, Lord; 'tis such a sight of heavy work next day! What with the dirty plates, and knives and forks, and dust and smother, and bits kicked off your furniture, and I don't know what all, why a body could a'most wish there were no such things as Christmases ... Ah'h dear!' she yawned, till the clock in the corner had ticked several beats. She cast her eyes round upon the displaced, dust-laden furniture, and sat down overpowered at the sight.

'Well, I be getting all right by degrees, thank the Lord for't' said the tranter cheerfully through a mangled mass of ham and bread, without lifting his eyes from his plate, and chopping away with his knife and fork as if he were felling trees. 'Ann, you may as well go on to bed at once, and not bide there making such sleepy faces; you look as long-favoured as a fiddle, upon my life, Ann. There, you must be wearied out, 'tis true. I'll do the doors and draw up the clock; and you go on, or you'll be as white as a sheet tomorrow.'

'Ay; I don't know whether I shan't or no.' The matron passed her hand across her eyes to brush away the film of sleep till she got upstairs.

Dick wondered how it was that when people were married they could be so blind to romance; and was quite certain that if he ever took to wife that dear impossible Fancy, he and she would never be so dreadfully practical and undemonstrative of the Passion as his father and mother were. The most extraordinary thing was that all the fathers and mothers he knew were just as undemonstrative as his own.

NINE

❦ Dick calls at the School ❧

THE EARLY DAYS OF THE year drew on, and Fancy, having spent the holiday weeks at home, returned again to Mellstock.

Every spare minute of the week following her return was used by Dick in accidentally passing the schoolhouse in his journeys about the neighbourhood; but not once did she make herself visible. A handkerchief belonging to her had been providentially found by his mother in clearing the rooms the day after that of the dance; and by much contrivance Dick got it handed over to him, to leave with her at any time he should be near the school after her return. But he delayed taking the extreme measure of calling with it lest, had she really no sentiment of interest in him, it might be regarded as a slightly absurd errand, the reason guessed, and the sense of the ludicrous, which was rather keen in her, do his dignity considerable injury in her eyes; and what she thought of him, even apart from the question of her loving, was all the world to him now.

But the hour came when the patience of love at twenty-one could endure no longer. One Saturday he approached the school with a mild air of indifference, and had the satisfaction of seeing the object of his quest at the further end of her garden, trying by the aid of a spade and gloves, to root a bramble that had intruded itself there.

He disguised his feelings from some suspicious-looking cottage-windows opposite by endeavouring to appear like a man in a great hurry of business, who wished to leave the handkerchief and have done with such trifling errands.

This endeavour signally failed; for on approaching the gate he found it locked to keep the children, who were playing 'cross-dadder' in the front, from running into her private grounds.

She did not see him; and he could only think of one thing to be done, which was to shout her name.

'Miss Day!'

The words were uttered with a jerk and a look meant to imply to the cottages opposite that he was now simply one who liked shouting as a pleasant way of passing his time, without any reference to persons in gardens. The name died away, and the unconscious Miss Day continued digging and pulling as before.

He screwed himself up to enduring the cottage-windows yet more stoically, and shouted again. Fancy took no notice whatever.

He shouted the third time, with desperate vehemence, turning suddenly about and retiring a little distance as if it were by no means for his own pleasure that he had come.

This time she heard him, came down the garden, and entered the school at the back. Footsteps echoed across the interior, the door opened, and three-quarters of the blooming young school-mistress's face and figure stood revealed before him; a slice on her left-hand side being cut off by the edge of the door. Having surveyed and recognized him she came to the gate.

At sight of him had the pink of her cheeks increased, lessened, or did it continue to cover its normal area of ground? It was a question meditated several hundreds of times by her visitor in after-hours – the meditation, after wearying involutions, always ending in one way, that it was impossible to say.

'Your handkerchief: Miss Day: I called with.' He held it out spasmodically and awkwardly. 'Mother found it: under a chair.'

'O, thank you very much for bringing it, Mr Dewy. I couldn't think where I had dropped it.'

Now Dick, not being an experienced lover – indeed, never before having been engaged in the practice of love-making at all, except in a small schoolboy way – could not take advantage of the situation; and out came the blunder which afterwards cost him so many bitter moments and a sleepless night: –

'Good-morning, Miss Day.'

'Good-morning, Mr Dewy.'

The gate was closed; she was gone; and Dick was standing outside, unchanged in his condition from what he had been before he called. Of course the Angel was not to blame – a young woman living alone in a house could not ask him indoors unless she had known him better – he should have kept her outside before floundering into that fatal farewell. He wished that before he called he had realized more fully than he did the pleasure of being about to call; and turned away.

Spring

ONE

❦ Passing by the School ❧

IT FOLLOWED THAT AS THE spring advanced Dick walked abroad much more frequently than had hitherto been usual with him, and was continually finding that his nearest way to or from home lay by the road which skirted the garden of the school. The first-fruits of his perseverance were that, on turning the angle on the nineteenth journey by that track, he saw Miss Fancy's figure, clothed in a dark-grey dress, looking from a high open window upon the crown of his hat. The friendly greeting resulting from this rencounter was considered so valuable an elixir that Dick passed still oftener; and by the time he had almost trodden a little path under the fence where never a path was before, he was rewarded with an actual meeting face to face on the open road before her gate. This brought another meeting, and another, Fancy faintly showing by her bearing that it was a pleasure to her of some kind to see him there; but the sort of pleasure she derived, whether exultation at the hope her exceeding fairness inspired, or the true feeling which was alone Dick's concern, he could not anyhow decide, although he meditated on her every little movement for hours after it was made.

❦ A Meeting of the Quire ❧

IT WAS THE EVENING OF a fine spring day. The descending sun appeared as a nebulous blaze of amber light, its outline being lost in cloudy masses hanging round it like wild locks of hair.

The chief members of Mellstock parish choir were standing in a group in front of Mr Penny's workshop in the lower village. They were all brightly illuminated, and each was backed up by a shadow as long as a steeple; the lowness of the source of light rendering the brims of their hats of no use at all as a protection to the eyes.

Mr Penny's was the last house in that part of the parish, and stood in a hollow by the roadside; so that cart-wheels and horses' legs were about level with the sill of his shop-window. This was low and wide, and was open from morning till evening, Mr Penny himself being invariably seen working inside like a framed portrait of a shoemaker by some modern Moroni. He sat facing the road, with a boot on his knees and the awl in his hand, only looking up for a moment as he stretched out his arms and bent forward at the pull, when his spectacles flashed in the passer's face with a shine of flat whiteness, and then returned again to the boot as usual. Rows of lasts, small and large, stout and slender, covered the wall which formed the background, in the extreme shadow of which a kind of dummy was seen sitting, in the shape of an apprentice with a string tied round his hair (probably to keep it out of his eyes). He smiled at remarks that floated in from without, but was never known to answer them in Mr Penny's presence. Outside the window the upper-leather of a Wellington-boot was usually hung, pegged to a board as if to dry. No sign was over his door; in fact – as with old banks and mercantile houses – advertising in any shape was scorned, and it would have been felt as beneath his dignity to paint up, for the benefit of strangers, the name of an establishment whose trade came solely by connection based on personal respect.

His visitors now came and stood on the outside of his window, some-times leaning against the sill, sometimes moving a pace or two backwards and forwards in front of it. They talked with deliberate gesticulations to Mr Penny, enthroned in the shadow of the interior.

'I do like a man to stick to men who be in the same line o'life – o' Sundays, anyway – that I do so.'

''Tis like all the doings of folk who don't know what a day's work is, that's what I say.'

'My belief is the man's not to blame; 'tis *she* – she's the bitter weed!'

'No, not altogether. He's a poor gawk-hammer. Look at his sermon yesterday.'

'His sermon was well enough, a very good guessable sermon, only he couldn't put it into words and speak it. That's all was the matter wi' the sermon. He hadn't been able to get it past his pen.'

'Well – ay, the sermon might have been good; for, 'tis true, the sermon of Old Eccl'iastes himself lay in Eccl'iastes's inkbottle afore he got it out.'

Mr Penny, being in the act of drawing the last stitch tight, could afford time to look up and throw in a word at this point.

'He's no spouter – that must be said, 'a b'lieve.'

''Tis a terrible muddle sometimes with the man, as far as spout do go,' said Spinks.

'Well, we'll say nothing about that,' the tranter answered; 'for I don't believe 'twill make a penneth o' difference to we poor martels here or hereafter whether his sermons be good or bad, my sonnies.'

Mr Penny made another hole with his awl, pushed in the thread, and looked up and spoke again at the extension of arms.

''Tis his goings-on, souls, that's what it is.' He clenched his features for an Herculean addition to the ordinary pull, and continued, 'The first thing he done when he came here was to be hot and strong about church business.'

'True,' said Spinks; 'that was the very first thing he done.'

Mr Penny, having now been offered the ear of the assembly, accepted it, ceased stitching, swallowed an unimportant quantity of air as if it were a pill, and continued:

'The next thing he do do is to think about altering the church, until he found 'twould be a matter o' cost and what not, and then not to think no more about it.'

'True: that was the next thing he done.'

'And the next thing was to tell the young chaps that they were not on no account to put their hats in the christening font during service.'

'True.'

'And then 'twas this, and then 'twas that, and now 'tis – '

Words were not forcible enough to conclude the sentence, and Mr Penny gave a huge pull to signify the concluding word.

'Now 'tis to turn us out of the quire neck and crop,' said the tranter after an interval of half a minute, not by way of explaining the pause and pull, which had been quite understood, but as a means of keeping the subject well before the meeting.

Mrs Penny came to the door at this point in the discussion. Like all good wives, however much she was inclined to play the Tory to her husband's Whiggism, and *vice versâ*, in times of peace, she coalesced with him heartily enough in time of war.

'It must be owned he's not all there,' she replied in a general way to the fragments of talk she had heard from indoors. 'Far below poor Mr Grinham' (the late vicar).

'Ay, there was this to be said for he, that you were quite sure he'd never come mumbudgeting to see ye, just as you were in the middle of your work, and put you out with his fuss and trouble about ye.'

'Never. But as for this new Mr Maybold, though he mid be a very well-intending party in that respect, he's unbearable; for as to sifting your cinders, scrubbing your floors, or emptying your slops, why, you can't do it. I assure you I've not been able to empt them for several days, unless I throw 'em up the chimley or out of winder; for as sure as the sun you meet him at the door, coming to ask how you are, and 'tis such a confusing thing to meet a gentleman at the door when ye are in the mess o' washing.'

''Tis only for want of knowing better, poor gentleman,' said the tranter. 'His meaning's good enough. Ay, your pa'son comes by fate: 'tis heads or tails, like pitch-halfpenny, and no choosing; so we must take en as he is, my sonnies, and thank God he's no worse, I suppose.'

'I fancy I've seen him look across at Miss Day in a warmer way than Christianity asked for,' said Mrs Penny musingly; 'but I don't quite like to say it.'

'O no; there's nothing in that,' said grandfather William.

'If there's nothing, we shall see nothing,' Mrs Penny replied in the tone of a woman who might possibly have private opinions still.

'Ah, Mr Grinham was the man!' said Bowman. 'Why, he never troubled us wi' a visit from year's end to year's end. You might go anywhere, do anything: you'd be sure never to see him.'

'Yes; he was a right sensible pa'son,' said Michael. 'He never entered our door but once in his life, and that was to tell my poor wife – ay, poor soul, dead and gone now, as we all shall! – that as she was such a' old aged person, and lived so far from the church, he didn't at all expect her to come any more to the service.'

'And 'a was a very jinerous gentleman about choosing the psalms and hymns o' Sundays. "Confound ye," says he, "blare and scrape what ye will, but don't bother me!"'

'And he was a very honourable man in not wanting any of us to come and hear him if we were all on-end for a jaunt or spree, or to bring the babies to be christened if they were inclined to squalling. There's good in a man's not putting a parish to unnecessary trouble.'

'And there's this here man never letting us have a bit o' peace; but keeping on about being good and upright till 'tis carried to such a pitch as I never see the like afore nor since!'

'No sooner had he got here than he found the font wouldn't hold water, as it hadn't for years off and on; and when I told him that Mr Grinham never minded it, but used to spet upon his vinger and christen 'em just as well, 'a said, "Good Heavens! Send for a workman immediate. What place have I come to!" Which was no compliment to us, come to that.'

'Still, for my part,' said old William, 'though he's arrayed against us, I like the hearty borus-snorus ways of the new pa'son.'

'You, ready to die for the quire,' said Bowman reproachfully, 'to stick up for the quire's enemy, William!'

'Nobody will feel the loss of our church-work so much as I,' said the old man firmly: 'that you d'all know. I've a-been in the quire man and boy ever since I was a chiel of eleven. But for all that 'tisn't in me to call the man a bad man, because I truly and sincerely believe en to be a good young feller.'

Some of the youthful sparkle that used to reside there animated William's eye as he uttered the words, and a certain nobility of aspect was also imparted to him by the setting sun, which gave him a Titanic shadow at least thirty feet in length, stretching away to the east in outlines of imposing magnitude, his head finally terminating upon the trunk of a grand old oak-tree.

'Mayble's a hearty feller enough,' the tranter replied, 'and will spak to you be you dirty or be you clane. The first time I met en was in a drong, and though 'a didn't know me no more than the dead 'a passed the time of day. "D'ye do!" he said says he, nodding his head. "A fine day." Then the second time I met en was full-buff in town street, when my breeches were tore into a long strent by getting through a copse of thorns and brimbles for a short cut home-along; and not wanting to disgrace the man by spaking in that state, I fixed my eye on the weathercock to let en pass me as a stranger. But no: "How d'ye do, Reuben?" says he, right hearty, and shook my hand. If I'd been dressed in silver spangles from top to toe the man couldn't have been civiller.'

At this moment Dick was seen coming up the village-street, and they turned and watched him.

THREE

❧ A Turn in the Discussion ❧

'I'M AFRAID DICK'S A LOST man,' said the tranter.

'What? – no!' said Mail, implying by his manner that it was a far commoner thing for his ears to report what was not said than that his judgement should be at fault.

'Ay,' said the tranter, still gazing at Dick's unconscious advance. 'I don't at all like what I see! There's too many o' them looks out of the winder without noticing anything; too much shining of boots; too much peeping round corners; too much looking at the clock; telling about clever things *she* did till you be sick of it, and then upon a hint to that effect a horrible silence about her. I've walked the path once in my life and know the country, neighbours; and Dick's a lost man!' The tranter turned a quarter round and smiled a smile of miserable satire at the setting new moon, which happened to catch his eye.

The others became far too serious at this announcement to allow them to speak; and they still regarded Dick in the distance.

''Twas his mother's fault,' the tranter continued, 'in asking the young woman to our party last Christmas. When I eyed the blue frock and light heels o' the maid, I had my thoughts directly. "God bless thee, Dicky my sonny," I said to myself, "there's a delusion for thee!" '

'They seemed to be rather distant in manner last Sunday, I thought?' Mail tentatively observed, as became one who was not a member of the family.

'Ay, that's a part of the zickness. Distance belongs to it, slyness belongs to it, queerest things on earth belongs to it! There, 'tmay as well come early as late s'far as I know. The sooner begun, the sooner over; for come it will.'

'The question I ask is,' said Mr Spinks, connecting into one thread the two subjects of discourse, as became a man learned in rhetoric, and beating with his hand in a way which signified that the manner rather than the matter of his speech was to be observed, 'how did Mr Maybold know she could play the organ? You know we had it from her own lips, as far as lips go, that she has never, first or last, breathed such a thing to him; much less that she ever would play.'

In the midst of this puzzle Dick joined the party, and the news which had caused such a convulsion among the ancient musicians was unfolded to him. 'Well,' he said, blushing at the allusion to Miss Day, 'I know by some words of hers that she has a particular wish not to play, because she is a friend of ours; and how the alteration comes I don't know.'

'Now, this is my plan,' said the tranter, reviving the spirit of the discussion by the infusion of new ideas, as was his custom – 'this is my plan; if you don't like it, no harm's done. We all know one another very well, don't we, neighbours?'

That they knew one another very well was received as a statement which, though familiar, should not be omitted in introductory speeches.

Then I say this' – and the tranter in his emphasis slapped down his hand on Mr Spinks's shoulder with a momentum of several pounds, upon which Mr Spinks tried to look not in the least startled – 'I say that we all move down-along straight as a line to Pa'son Mayble's when the clock has gone six tomorrow night. There we one and all stand in the passage; then one or two of us go in and spak to en, man and man, and say, "Pa'son Mayble, every tradesman d'like to have his own way in his workshop, and Mellstock Church is yours. Instead of turning us out neck and crop, let us stay on till Christmas, and we'll gie way to the young woman, Mr Mayble, and make no more ado about it. And we shall always be quite willing to touch our hats when we meet ye, Mr Mayble, just as before." That sounds very well? Hey?'

'Proper well, in faith, Reuben Dewy.'

'And we won't sit down in his house; 'twould be looking too familiar when only just reconciled?'

'No need at all to sit down. Just do our duty man and man, turn round, and march out – he'll think all the more of us for it.'

'I hardly think Leaf had better go wi' us?' said Michael, turning to Leaf and taking his measure from top to bottom by the eye. 'He's so terrible silly that he might ruin the concern.'

'He don't want to go much; do ye, Thomas Leaf?' said William.

'Hee-hee! no; I don't want to. Only a teeny bit!'

'I be mortal afeard, Leaf, that you'll never be able to tell how many cuts d'take to sharpen a spar,' said Mail.

'I never had no head, never! that's how it happened to happen, hee-hee!'

They all assented to this, not with any sense of humiliating Leaf by disparaging him after an open confession, but because it was an accepted thing that Leaf didn't in the least mind having no head, that deficiency of his being an unimpassioned matter of parish history.

'But I can sing my treble!' continued Thomas Leaf, quite delighted at being called a fool in such a friendly way; 'I can sing my treble well as any maid, or married woman either, and better! And if Jim had lived, I should have had a clever brother! Tomorrow is poor Jim's birthday. He'd ha' been twenty-six if he'd lived till tomorrow.'

'You always seem very sorry for Jim,' said old William musingly.

'Ah! I do. Such a stay to mother as he'd always have been! She'd never have had to work in her old age if he had continued strong, poor Jim!'

'What was his age when 'a died?'

'Four hours and twenty minutes, poor Jim. 'A was born as might be at night; and 'a didn't last as might be till the morning. No, 'a didn't last. Mother called en Jim on the day that would ha' been his christening-day if he had lived; and she's always thinking about en. You see he died so very young.'

'Well, 'twas rather youthful,' said Michael.

'Now to my mind that woman is very romantical on the matter o' children?' said the tranter, his eye sweeping his audience.

'Ah, well she mid be,' said Leaf. 'She had twelve regular one after another, and they all, except myself, died very young; either before they was born or just afterwards.'

'Pore feller, too. I suppose th'st want to come wi' us?' the tranter murmured.

403

'Well, Leaf, you shall come wi' us as yours is such a melancholy family,' said old William rather sadly.

'I never see such a melancholy family as that afore in my life,' said Reuben. 'There's Leaf's mother, poor woman! Every morning I see her eyes mooning out through the panes of glass like a pot-sick winder-flower; and as Leaf sings a very high treble, and we don't know what we should do without en for upper G, we'll let en come as a trate, poor feller.'

'Ay, we'll let en come, 'a b'lieve,' said Mr Penny, looking up, as the pull happened to be at that moment.

'Now,' continued the tranter, dispersing by a new tone of voice these digressions about Leaf; 'as to going to see the pa'son, one of us might call and ask en his meaning, and 'twould be just as well done; but it will add a bit of a flourish to the cause if the quire waits on him as a body. Then the great thing to mind is, not for any of our fellers to be nervous; so before starting we'll one and all come to my house and have a rasher of bacon; then every man-jack het a pint of cider into his inside; then we'll warm up an extra drop wi' some mead and a bit of ginger; every one take a thimbleful – just a glimmer of a drop, mind ye, no more, to finish off his inner man – and march off to Pa'son Mayble. Why, sonnies, a man's not himself till he is fortified wi' a bit and a drop? We shall be able to look any gentleman in the face then without shrink or shame.'

Mail recovered from a deep meditation and downward glance into the earth in time to give a cordial approval to this line of action, and the meeting adjourned.

FOUR

◆ The Interview with the Vicar ◆

At six o'clock next day the whole body of men in the choir emerged from the tranter's door, and advanced with a firm step down the lane. This dignity of march gradually became obliterated as they went on, and by the time they reached the hill behind the vicarage a faint resemblance to a flock of sheep might have been discerned in the venerable party. A word from the tranter, however, set them right again; and as they descended the hill, the regular tramp, tramp, tramp of the united feet was clearly audible from the vicarage garden. At the opening of the gate there was another short interval of irregular shuffling, caused by a rather peculiar habit the gate had, when swung open quickly, of striking against the bank and slamming back into the opener's face.

'Now keep step again, will ye?' said the tranter. 'It looks better, and more becomes the high class of arrant which has brought us here.' Thus they advanced to the door.

At Reuben's ring the more modest of the group turned aside, adjusted their hats, and looked critically at any shrub that happened to lie in the line of vision; endeavouring thus to give a person who chanced to look out of the windows the impression that their request, whatever it was going to be, was rather a casual thought occurring whilst they were inspecting the vicar's shrubbery and grass-plot than a predetermined thing. The tranter who, coming frequently to the vicarage with luggage, coals, firewood, etc., had none of the awe for its precincts that filled the breasts of most of the others, fixed his eyes firmly on the knocker during this interval of waiting. The knocker having no characteristic worthy of notice he relinquished it for a knot in one of the door-panels, and studied the winding lines of the grain.

'O, sir, please, here's Tranter Dewy, and old William Dewy, and young Richard Dewy, O, and all the quire too, sir, except the boys, a-come to see you!' said Mr Maybold's maid-servant to Mr Maybold, the pupils of her eyes dilating like circles in a pond.

'All the choir?' said the astonished vicar (who may be shortly described as a good-looking young man with courageous eyes, timid mouth, and neutral nose), abandoning his writing and looking at his parlourmaid after speaking, like a man who fancied he had seen her face before but couldn't recollect where.

'And they looks very firm, and Tranter Dewy do turn neither to the right hand nor to the left, but stares quite straight and solemn with his mind made up!'

'O, all the choir,' repeated the vicar to himself, trying by that simple device to trot out his thoughts on what the choir could come for.

'Yes; every man-jack of 'em, as I be alive!' (The parlour-maid was rather local in manner, having in fact been raised in the same village.) 'Really, sir, 'tis thoughted by many in town and country that – '

'Town and country! – Heavens, I had no idea that I was public property in this way!' said the vicar, his face acquiring a hue somewhere between that of the rose and the peony. 'Well, "It is thought in town and country that – " '

'It is thought that you be going to get it hot and strong! – excusen my incivility, sir.'

The vicar suddenly recalled to his recollection that he had long ago settled it to be decidedly a mistake to encourage his servant Jane in giving personal opinions. The servant Jane saw by the vicar's face that he recalled this fact to his mind; and removing her forehead from the edge of the door, and rubbing away the indent that edge had made, vanished into the passage as Mr Maybold remarked, 'Show them in, Jane.'

A few minutes later a shuffling and jostling (reduced to as refined a form as was compatible with the nature of shuffles and jostles) was heard in the passage; then an earnest and prolonged wiping of shoes, conveying the notion that volumes of mud had to be removed; but the roads being so clean that not a particle of dirt appeared on the choir's boots (those of all the elder members being newly oiled, and Dick's brightly polished), this wiping might have been set down simply as a desire to show that respectable men had no wish to take a mean advantage of clean roads for curtailing proper ceremonies. Next there came a powerful whisper from the same quarter: –

'Now stand stock-still there, my sonnies, one and all! And don't make no noise; and keep your backs close to the wall, that company may pass in and out easy if they want to without squeezing through ye: and we two are enough to go in.' . . . The voice was the tranter's.

'I wish I could go in too and see the sight!' said a reedy voice – that of Leaf.

''Tis a pity Leaf is so terrible silly, or else he might,' another said.

'I never in my life seed a quire go into a study to have it out about the playing and singing,' pleaded Leaf; 'and I should like to see it just once!'

'Very well; we'll let en come in,' said the tranter. 'You'll be like chips in porridge.* Leaf – neither good nor hurt. All right, my sonny, come along;' and immediately himself, old William, and Leaf appeared in the room.

'We took the liberty to come and see 'ee, sir,' said Reuben, letting his hat hang in his left hand, and touching with his right the brim of an imaginary one on his head. 'We've come to see 'ee, sir, man and man, and no offence, I hope?'

'None at all,' said Mr Maybold.

'This old aged man standing by my side is father; William Dewy by name, sir.'

'Yes; I see it is,' said the vicar, nodding aside to old William, who smiled.

'I thought ye mightn't know en without his bass-viol,' the tranter

* This, a local expression, must be a corruption of something less questionable.

apologized. 'You see, he always wears his best clothes and his bass-viol a-Sundays, and it do make such a difference in a' old man's look.'

'And who's that young man?' the vicar said.

'Tell the pa'son yer name,' said the tranter, turning to Leaf, who stood with his elbows nailed back to a bookcase.

'Please, Thomas Leaf, your holiness!' said Leaf, trembling.

'I hope you'll excuse his looks being so very thin,' continued the tranter deprecatingly, turning to the vicar again. 'But 'tisn't his fault, poor feller. He's rather silly by nature, and could never get fat; though he's a' excellent treble, and so we keep him on.'

'I never had no head, sir,' said Leaf, eagerly grasping at this opportunity for being forgiven his existence.

'Ah, poor young man!' said Mr Maybold.

'Bless you, he don't mind it a bit, if you don't, sir,' said the tranter assuringly. 'Do ye, Leaf?'

'Not I – not a morsel – hee, hee! I was afeard it mightn't please your holiness, sir, that's all.'

The tranter, finding Leaf get on so very well through his negative qualities, was tempted in a fit of generosity to advance him still higher, by giving him credit for positive ones. 'He's very clever for a silly chap, good-now, sir. You never knowed a young feller keep his smock-frocks so clane; very honest too. His ghastly looks is all there is against en, poor feller; but we can't help our looks, you know, sir.'

'True: we cannot. You live with your mother, I think, Leaf?'

The tranter looked at Leaf to express that the most friendly assistant to his tongue could do no more for him now, and that he must be left to his own resources.

'Yes, sir: a widder, sir. Ah, if brother Jim had lived she'd have had a clever son to keep her without work!'

'Indeed! poor woman. Give her this half-crown. I'll call and see your mother.'

'Say, "Thank you, sir," ' the tranter whispered imperatively towards Leaf.

'Thank you, sir!' said Leaf.

'That's it, then; sit down, Leaf,' said Mr Maybold.

'Y-yes, sir!'

The tranter cleared his throat after this accidental parenthesis about Leaf, rectified his bodily position, and began his speech.

'Mr Mayble,' he said, 'I hope you'll excuse my common way, but I always like to look things in the face.'

Reuben made a point of fixing this sentence in the vicar's mind by gazing hard at him at the conclusion of it, and then out of the window.

Mr Maybold and old William looked in the same direction, apparently under the impression that the things' faces alluded to were there visible.

'What I have been thinking' – the tranter implied by this use of the past tense that he was hardly so discourteous as to be positively thinking it then – 'is that the quire ought to be gie'd a little time, and not done away wi' till Christmas, as a fair thing between man and man. And, Mr Mayble, I hope you'll excuse my common way?'

'I will, I will. Till Christmas,' the vicar murmured, stretching the two words to a great length, as if the distance to Christmas might be measured in that way. 'Well, I want you all to understand that I have no personal fault to find, and that I don't wish to change the church music by forcible means, or in a way which should hurt the feelings of any parishioners. Why I have at last spoken definitely on the subject is that a player has been brought under – I may say pressed upon – my notice several times by one of the churchwardens. And as the organ I brought with me is here waiting' (pointing to a cabinet-organ standing in the study), 'there is no reason for longer delay.'

'We made a mistake I suppose then, sir? But we understood the young woman didn't want to play particularly?' The tranter arranged his countenance to signify that he did not want to be inquisitive in the least.

'No, nor did she. Nor did I definitely wish her to just yet; for your playing is very good. But, as I said, one of the churchwardens has been so anxious for a change that, as matters stand, I couldn't consistently refuse my consent.'

Now for some reason or other the vicar at this point seemed to have an idea that he had prevaricated; and as an honest vicar it was a thing he determined not to do. He corrected himself, blushing as he did so, though why he should blush was not known to Reuben.

'Understand me rightly,' he said: 'the churchwarden proposed it to me, but I had thought myself of getting – Miss Day to play.'

'Which churchwarden might that be who proposed her, sir? – excusing my common way.' The tranter intimated by his tone that so far from being inquisitive he did not even wish to ask a single question.

'Mr Shiner, I believe.'

'Clk, my sonny! – beg your pardon, sir, that's only a form of words of mine, and slipped out accidental – he nourishes enmity against us for some reason or another; perhaps because we played rather hard upon en Christmas night. Anyhow 'tis certain sure that Mr Shiner's real love for music of a particular kind isn't his reason. He've no more ear than that chair. But let that be.'

'I don't think you should conclude that, because Mr Shiner wants a different music, he has any ill-feeling for you. I myself, I must own, prefer organ-music to any other. I consider it most proper, and feel justified in endeavouring to introduce it; but then, although other music is better, I don't say yours is not good.'

'Well then, Mr Mayble, since death's to be, we'll die like men any day you name (excusing my common way).'

Mr Maybold bowed his head.

'All we thought was, that for us old ancient singers to be choked off quiet at no time in particular, as now, in the Sundays after Easter, would seem rather mean in the eyes of other parishes, sir. But if we fell glorious with a bit of a flourish at Christmas, we should have a respectable end, and not dwindle away at some nameless paltry second-Sunday-after or Sunday-next-before something, that's got no name of his own.'

'Yes, yes, that's reasonable; I own it's reasonable.'

'You see, Mr Mayble, we've got – do I keep you inconvenient long sir?'

'No, no.'

'We've got our feelings – father there especially.'

The tranter, in his earnestness, had advanced his person to within six inches of the vicar's.

'Certainly, certainly!' said Mr Maybold, retreating a little for convenience of seeing. 'You are all enthusiastic on the subject, and I am all the more gratified to find you so. A Laodicean luke-warmness is worse than wrongheadedness itself.'

'Exactly, sir. In fact now, Mr Mayble,' Reuben continued more impressively, and advancing a little closer still to the vicar, 'father there is a perfect figure o' wonder, in the way of being fond of music!'

The vicar drew back a little further, the tranter suddenly also standing back a foot or two to throw open the view of his father, and pointing to him at the same time.

Old William moved uneasily in the large chair, and with a minute smile on the mere edge of his lips for good-manners, said he was indeed very fond of tunes.

'Now, you see exactly how it is,' Reuben continued, appealing to Mr Maybold's sense of justice by looking sideways into his eyes. The vicar seemed to see how it was so well that the gratified tranter walked up to him again with even vehement eagerness, so that his waistcoat-buttons almost rubbed against the vicar's as he continued: 'As to father, if you or I, or any man or woman of the present generation, at the time music is a-playing, was to shake your fist in father's face, as may be this way, and say, "Don't you be delighted with that music!" ' – the tranter went back to where Leaf was sitting, and held his fist so close to Leaf's face that the latter pressed his head back against the wall: 'All right, Leaf, my sonny, I won't hurt you; 'tis just to show my meaning to Mr Mayble. – As I was saying, if you or I, or any man, was to shake your fist in father's face this way, and say, "William, your life or your music!" he'd say, "My life!" Now that's father's nature all over; and you see, sir, it must hurt the feelings of a man of that kind for him and his bass-viol to be done away wi' neck and crop.'

The tranter went back to the vicar's front and again looked earnestly at his face.

'True, true, Dewy,' Mr Maybold answered, trying to withdraw his head and shoulders without moving his feet; but finding this impracticable edging back another inch. These frequent retreats had at last jammed Mr Maybold between his easy-chair and the edge of the table.

And at the moment of the announcement of the choir Mr Maybold had just re-dipped the pen he was using; at their entry, instead of wiping it, he had laid it on the table with the nib overhanging. At the last retreat his coat-tails came in contact with the pen, and down it rolled, first against the back of the chair, thence turning a summersault into the seat, thence falling to the floor with a rattle.

The vicar stooped for his pen, and the tranter, wishing to show that, however great their ecclesiastical differences, his mind was not so small as to let this affect his social feelings, stooped also.

'And have you anything else you want to explain to me, Dewy?' said Mr Maybold from under the table.

'Nothing, sir. And, Mr Mayble, you be not offended? I hope you see our desire is reason?' said the tranter from under the chair.

'Quite, quite; and I shouldn't think of refusing to listen to such a reasonable request,' the vicar replied. Seeing that Reuben had secured the pen he resumed his vertical position, and added, 'You know, Dewy, it is often said how difficult a matter it is to act up to our convictions and please all parties. It may be said with equal truth, that it is difficult for a man of any appreciativeness to have convictions at all. Now in my case, I see right in you, and right in Shiner. I see that violins are good, and that an organ is good; and when we introduce the organ it will not be that fiddles were bad, but that an organ was better. That you'll clearly understand, Dewy?'

'I will; and thank you very much for such feelings, sir. Piph-h-h-h! How the blood do get into my head, to be sure, whenever I quat down like that!' said Reuben, who having also risen to his feet stuck the pen vertically in the inkstand and almost through the bottom, that it might not roll down again under any circumstances whatever.

Now the ancient body of minstrels in the passage felt their curiosity surging higher and higher as the minutes passed. Dick, not having much affection for this errand, soon grew tired, and went away in the direction of the school. Yet their sense of propriety would probably have restrained them from any attempt to discover what was going on in the study had not the vicar's pen fallen to the floor. The conviction that the movement of chairs, &c., necessitated by the search, could only have been caused by the catastrophe of a bloody fight beginning, overpowered all other considerations; and they advanced to the door, which had only just fallen to. Thus, when Mr Maybold raised his eyes after the stooping he beheld glaring through the door Mr Penny in full-length portraiture, Mail's face and shoulders above Mr Penny's head, Spinks's forehead and eyes over Mail's crown, and a fractional part of Bowman's countenance under Spinks's arm – crescent-shaped portions of other heads and faces being visible behind these – the whole dozen and odd eyes bristling with eager inquiry.

Mr Penny, as is the case with excitable bootmakers and men, seeing the vicar look at him and hearing no word spoken, thought it incumbent upon himself to say something of any kind. Nothing suggested itself till he had looked for about half a minute at the vicar.

'You'll excuse my naming of it, sir,' he said, regarding with much commiseration the mere surface of the vicar's face; 'but perhaps you don't know that your chin have bust out a-bleeding where you cut yourself a-shaving this morning, sir.'

'Now, that was the stooping, depend upon't,' the tranter suggested, also looking with much interest at the vicar's chin. 'Blood always will bust out again if you hang down the member that's been bleeding.'

Old William raised his eyes and watched the vicar's bleeding chin likewise; and Leaf advanced two or three paces from the bookcase, absorbed in the contemplation of the same phenomenon with parted lips and delighted eyes.

'Dear me, dear me!' said Mr Maybold hastily, looking very red and brushing his chin with his hand, then taking out his handkerchief and wiping the place.

'That's it, sir; all right again now, 'a b'lieve – a mere nothing,' said Mr Penny. 'A little bit of fur off your hat will stop it in a minute if it should bust out again.'

'I'll let 'ee have a bit off mine,' said Reuben, to show his good feeling; 'my hat isn't so new as yours, sir, and 'twon't hurt mine a bit.'

'No, no; thank you, thank you,' Mr Maybold again nervously replied.

''Twas rather a deep cut seemingly?' said Reuben, feeling these to be the kindest and best remarks he could make.

'O, no; not particularly.'

'Well, sir, your hand will shake sometimes a-shaving, and just when it comes into your head that you may cut yourself, there's the blood.'

'I have been revolving in my mind that question of the time at which we make the change,' said Mr Maybold, 'and I know you'll meet me half-way. I think Christmas-day as much too late for me as the present time is too early for you. I suggest Michaelmas or thereabout as a convenient time for both parties; for I think your objection to a Sunday which has no name is not one of any real weight.'

'Very good, sir. I suppose mortal men mustn't expect their own way entirely; and I express in all our names that we'll make shift and be satisfied with what you say.' The tranter touched the brim of his imaginary hat again, and all the choir did the same. 'About Michaelmas, then, as far as you are concerned, sir, and then we make room for the next generation.'

'About Michaelmas,' said the vicar.

FIVE

❧ Returning Homeward ❧

''A TOOK IT VERY WELL, THEN?' said Mail, as they all walked up the hill.

'He behaved like a man; 'a did so,' said the tranter. 'And I'm glad we've let en know our minds. And though, beyond that, we ha'n't got much by going, 'twas worth while. He won't forget it. Yes, he took it very well. Supposing this tree here was Pa'son Mayble, and I standing here, and thik gr't stone is father sitting in the easy-chair. "Dewy," says he, "I don't wish to change the church music in a forcible way." '

'That was very nice o' the man, even though words be wind.'

'Proper nice – out and out nice. The fact is,' said Reuben confidentially, ''tis how you take a man. Everybody must be managed. Queens must be managed: kings must be managed; for men want managing almost as much as women, and that's saying a good deal.'

''Tis truly!' murmured the husbands.

'Pa'son Mayble and I were as good friends all through it as if we'd been sworn brothers. Ay, the man's well enough; 'tis what's put in his head that spoils him, and that's why we've got to go.'

'There's really no believing half you hear about people nowadays.'

'Bless ye, my sonnies, 'tisn't the pa'son's move at all. That gentleman over there' (the tranter nodded in the direction of Shiner's farm) 'is at the root of the mischty.'

'What! Shiner?'

'Ay; and I see what the pa'son don't see. Why, Shiner is for putting forward that young woman that only last night I was saying was our

Dick's sweetheart, but I suppose can't be, and making much of her in the sight of the congregation, and thinking he'll win her by showing her off. Well, perhaps 'a woll.'

'Then the music is second to the woman, the other church-warden is second to Shiner, the pa'son is second to the church-wardens, and God A'mighty is nowhere at all.'

'That's true; and you see,' continued Reuben, 'at the very beginning it put me in a stud as to how to quarrel wi' en. In short, to save my soul, I couldn't quarrel wi' such a civil man without belying my conscience. Says he to father there, in a voice as quiet as a lamb's, "William, you are a' old aged man, as all shall be, so sit down in my easy-chair, and rest yourself." And down father zot. I could fain ha' laughed at thee, father; for thou'st take it so unconcerned at first, and then looked so frightened when the chair-bottom sunk in.'

'You see,' said old William, hastening to explain, 'I was scared to find the bottom gie way – what should I know o' spring bottoms? – and thought I had broke it down: and of course as to breaking down a man's chair, I didn't wish any such thing.'

'And, neighbours, when a feller, ever so much up for a miff, d'see his own father sitting in his enemy's easy-chair, and a poor chap like Leaf made the best of, as if he almost had brains – why, it knocks all the wind out of his sail at once: it did out of mine.'

'If that young figure of fun – Fance Day, I mean,' said Bowman, 'hadn't been so mighty forward wi' showing herself off to Shiner and Dick and the rest, 'tis my belief we should never ha' left the gallery.'

''Tis my belief that though Shiner fired the bullets, the parson made 'em,' said Mr Penny. 'My wife sticks to it that he's in love wi' her.'

'That's a thing we shall never know. I can't onriddle her, nohow.'

'Thou'st ought to be able to onriddle such a little chiel as she,' the tranter observed.

'The littler the maid, the bigger the riddle, to my mind. And coming of such a stock, too, she may well be a twister.'

'Yes; Geoffrey Day is a clever man if ever there was one. Never says anything: not he.'

'Never.'

'You might live wi' that man, my sonnies, a hundred years, and never know there was anything in him.'

'Ay; one o' these up-country London ink-bottle chaps would call Geoffrey a fool.'

'Ye never find out what's in that man: never,' said Spinks. 'Close? ah, he is close! He can hold his tongue well. That man's dumbness is wonderful to listen to.'

'There's so much sense in it. Every moment of it is brimmen over wi' sound understanding.'

"A can hold his tongue very clever – very clever truly.' echoed Leaf. "A do look at me if 'a could see my thoughts running round like the works of a clock.'

'Well, all will agree that the man can halt well in his talk, be it a long time or be it a short time. And though we can't expect his daughter to inherit his closeness, she may have a few dribblets from his sense.'

'And his pocket, perhaps.'

'Yes; the nine hundred pound that everybody says he's worth; but I call it four hundred and fifty; for I never believe more than half I hear.'

'Well, he've made a pound or two, and I suppose the maid will have it, since there's nobody else. But 'tis rather sharp upon her, if she's born to fortune, to bring her up as if not born for it, and letting her work so hard.'

"Tis all upon his principle. A long-headed feller!'

'Ah,' murmured Spinks, "twould be sharper upon her if she were born for fortune, and not to it! I suffer from that affliction.'

SIX

❧ Yalbury Wood and the Keeper's ❧ House

A MOOD OF BLITHENESS RARELY experienced even by young men was Dick's on the following Monday morning. It was the week after the Easter holidays, and he was journeying along with Smart the mare and the light spring-cart, watching the damp slopes of the hill-sides as they streamed in the warmth of the sun, which at this unsettled season shone on the grass with the freshness of an occasional inspector rather than as an accustomed proprietor. His errand was to fetch Fancy, and some additional household goods, from her father's house in the neighbouring parish to her dwelling at Mellstock. The distant view was darkly shaded with clouds; but the nearer parts of the landscape were whitely illumined by the visible rays of the sun streaming down across the heavy grey shade behind.

The tranter had not yet told his son of the state of Shiner's heart that had been suggested to him by Shiner's movements. He preferred to let

414

such delicate affairs right themselves; experience having taught him that the uncertain phenomenon of love, as it existed in other people, was not a groundwork upon which a single action of his own life could be founded.

Geoffrey Day lived in the depths of Yalbury Wood, which formed portion of one of the outlying estates of the Earl of Wessex, to whom Day was head gamekeeper, timber-steward, and general overlooker for this district. The wood was intersected by the highway from Casterbridge to London at a place not far from the house, and some trees had of late years been felled between its windows and the ascent of Yalbury Hill, to give the solitary cottager a glimpse of the passers-by.

It was a satisfaction to walk into the keeper's house, even as a stranger, on a fine spring morning like the present. A curl of wood-smoke came from the chimney and drooped over the roof like a blue feather in a lady's hat; and the sun shone obliquely upon the patch of grass in front, which reflected its brightness through the open doorway and up the staircase opposite, lighting up each riser with a shiny green radiance and leaving the top of each step in shade.

The window-sill of the front room was between four and five feet from the floor, dropping inwardly to a broad low bench, over which, as well as over the whole surface of the wall beneath, there always hung a deep shade, which was considered objectionable on every ground save one, namely, that the perpetual sprinkling of seeds and water by the caged canary above was not noticed as an eyesore by visitors. The window was set with thickly-leaded diamond glazing, formed, especially in the lower panes, of knotty glass of various shades of green. Nothing was better known to Fancy than the extravagant manner in which these circular knots or eyes distorted everything seen through them from the outside – lifting hats from heads, shoulders from bodies; scattering the spokes of cart-wheels, and bending the straight fir-trunks into semi-circles. The ceiling was carried by a beam traversing its midst, from the side of which projected a large nail, used solely and constantly as a peg for Geoffrey's hat; the nail was arched by a rainbow-shaped stain, imprinted by the brim of the said hat when it was hung there dripping wet.

The most striking point about the room was the furniture. This was a repetition upon inanimate objects of the old principle introduced by Noah, consisting for the most part of two articles of every sort. The duplicate system of furnishing owed its existence to the forethought of Fancy's mother, exercised from the date of Fancy's birthday onwards. The arrangement spoke for itself: nobody who knew the tone of the household could look at the goods without being aware that the second set was a provision for Fancy when she should marry and have a house of her own. The most noticeable instance was a pair of green-faced eight-day clocks ticking alternately, which were severally two-and-a-half minutes and three minutes striking the hour of twelve, one proclaiming, in Italian flourishes, Thomas Wood as the name of its maker, and the other – arched at the top, and altogether of more cynical appearance – that of Ezekiel Saunders. They were two departed clockmakers of Casterbridge, whose desperate rivalry throughout their lives was nowhere more emphatically perpetuated than here at Geoffrey's. These chief specimens of the marriage provision were supported on the right by a couple of kitchen dressers, each fitted complete with their cups, dishes, and plates, in their turn followed by two dumb-waiters, two family Bibles, two warming-pans, and two intermixed sets of chairs.

But the position last reached – the chimney-corner – was, after all, the most attractive side of the parallelogram. It was large enough to admit, in addition to Geoffrey himself, Geoffrey's wife, her chair, and her work-table, entirely within the line of the mantel, without danger or even inconvenience from the heat of the fire; and was spacious enough over-head to allow of the insertion of wood poles for the hanging of bacon, which were cloaked with long shreds of soot floating on the draught like the tattered banners on the walls of ancient aisles.

These points were common to most chimney-corners of the neighbour-hood; but one feature there was which made Geoffrey's fireside not only an object of interest to casual aristocratic visitors – to whom every cottage fireside was more or less a curiosity – but the admiration of friends who were accustomed to fireplaces of the ordinary hamlet model. This peculiarity was a little window in the chimney-back, almost over the fire, around which the smoke crept caressingly when it left the perpendicular course. The window-board was curiously stamped with black circles, burnt thereon by the heated bottoms of drinking-cups which had rested there after previously standing on the hot ashes of the hearth for the purpose of warming their contents, the result giving to the ledge the look of an envelope which has passed through innumerable post offices.

Fancy was gliding about the room preparing dinner, her head inclining now to the right, now to the left, and singing the tips and ends of tunes that sprang up in her mind like mushrooms. The footsteps of Mrs Day could be heard in the room overhead. Fancy went finally to the door.

'Father! Dinner.'

A tall spare figure was seen advancing by the window with periodical steps, and the keeper entered from the garden. He appeared to be a man who was always looking down as if trying to recollect something he said yesterday. The surface of his face was fissured rather than wrinkled, and over and under his eyes were folds which seemed as a kind of exterior eyelids. His nose had been thrown backwards by a blow in a poaching fray, so that when the sun was low and shining in his face people could see far into his head. There was in him a quiet grimness which would in his moments of displeasure have become surliness, had it not been tempered by honesty of soul, and which was often wrongheadedness because not allied with subtlety.

Although not an extraordinarily taciturn man among friends slightly richer than himself, he never wasted words upon outsiders, and to his trapper Enoch his ideas were seldom conveyed by any other means than nods and shakes of the head. Their long acquaintance with each other's ways, and the nature of their labours, rendered words between them almost superfluous as vehicles of thought, whilst the coincidence of their horizons, and the astonishing equality of their social views, by startling the keeper from time to time as very damaging to the theory of master and man, strictly forbade any indulgence in words as courtesies.

Behind the keeper came Enoch (who had been assisting in the garden) at the well-considered chronological distance of three minutes – an interval of non-appearance on the trapper's part not arrived at without some reflection. Four minutes had been found to express indifference to indoor arrangements, and simultaneousness had implied too great an anxiety about meals.

'A little earlier than usual, Fancy,' the keeper said, as he sat down and looked at the clocks. 'That Ezekiel Saunders o' thine is tearing on afore Thomas Wood again.'

'I kept in the middle between them,' said Fancy, also looking at the two clocks.

'Better stick to Thomas,' said her father. 'There's a healthy beat in Thomas that would lead a man to swear by en offhand. He is as true as the town time. How is it your stap-mother isn't here?'

As Fancy was about to reply the rattle of wheels was heard, and 'Wehhey, Smart!' in Mr Richard Dewy's voice rolled into the cottage from round the corner of the house.

'Hullo! there's Dewy's cart come for thee, Fancy – Dick driving – afore time, too. Well, ask the lad to have pot-luck with us.'

Dick on entering made a point of implying by his general bearing that he took an interest in Fancy simply as in one of the same race and country as himself; and they all sat down. Dick could have wished her manner had not been so entirely free from all apparent consciousness of those accidental meetings of theirs; but he let the thought pass. Enoch sat diagonally at a table afar off under the corner cupboard, and drank his cider from a long perpendicular pint cup having tall fir-trees done in brown on its sides. He threw occasional remarks into the general tide of conversation, and with this advantage to himself, that he participated in the pleasures of a talk (slight as it was) at meal-times, without saddling himself with the responsibility of sustaining it.

'Why don't your stap-mother come down, Fancy?' said Geoffrey. 'You'll excuse her, Mister Dick, she's a little queer sometimes.'

'O yes, – quite,' said Richard, as if he were in the habit of excusing people every day.

'She d'belong to that class of womankind that become second wives: a rum class rather.'

'Indeed,' said Dick, with sympathy for an indefinite something.

'Yes; and 'tis trying to a female, especially if you've been a first wife, as she have.'

'Very trying it must be.'

'Yes: you see her first husband was a young man who let her go too far; in fact, she used to kick up Bob's-a-dying at the least thing in the world. And when I'd married her and found it out, I thought, thinks I, '"Tis too late now to being to cure 'ee;" and so I let her bide. But she's queer, – very queer, at times!'

'I'm sorry to hear that.'

'Yes: there; wives be such a provoking class of society because, though they be never right, they be never more than half wrong.'

Fancy seemed uneasy under the infliction of this household moralizing, which might tend to damage the airy-fairy nature that Dick, as maiden shrewdness told her, had accredited her with. Her dead silence impressed Geoffrey with the notion that something in his words did not agree with her educated ideas, and he changed the conversation.

'Did Fred Shiner send the cask 'o drink, Fancy?'

'I think he did: O yes, he did.'

'Nice solid feller, Fred Shiner!' said Geoffrey to Dick as he helped himself to gravy, bringing the spoon round to his plate by way of the potato-dish, to obviate a stain on the cloth in the event of a spill.

Now Geoffrey's eyes had been fixed upon his plate for the previous four or five minutes, and in removing them he had only carried them to the spoon, which, from its fulness and the distance of its transit, necessitated a steady watching through the whole of the route. Just as intently as the keeper's eyes had been fixed on the spoon Fancy's had been fixed on her father's, without premeditation or the slightest phase of furtiveness; but there they were fastened. This was the reason why:

Dick was sitting next to her on the right side, and on the side of the table opposite to her father. Fancy had laid her right hand lightly down upon the tablecloth for an instant, and to her alarm Dick, after dropping his fork and brushing his forehead as a reason, flung down his own left hand, overlapping a third of Fancy's with it, and keeping it there. So the innocent Fancy, instead of pulling her hand from the trap, settled her eyes on her father's, to guard against his discovery of this perilous game of Dick's. Dick finished his mouthful; Fancy finished her crumb, and nothing was done beyond watching Geoffrey's eyes. Then the hands slid apart; Fancy's going over six inches of cloth, Dick's over one. Geoffrey's eye had risen.

'I said Fred Shiner is a nice solid feller,' he repeated more emphatically.

'He is; yes, he is,' stammered Dick; 'but to me he is little more than a stranger.'

'O, sure. Now I know en as well as any man can be known. And you know en very well too, don't ye, Fancy?'

Geoffrey put on a tone expressing that these words signified at present about one hundred times the amount of meaning they conveyed literally.

Dick looked anxious.

'Will you pass me some bread?' said Fancy in a flurry, the red of her face becoming slightly disordered, and looking as solicitous as a human being could look about a piece of bread.

'Ay, that I will,' replied the unconscious Geoffrey. 'Ay,' he continued, returning to the displaced idea, 'we are likely to remain friendly wi' Mr Shiner if the wheels d'run smooth.'

'An excellent thing – a very capital thing, as I should say,' the youth answered with exceeding relevance, considering that his thoughts, instead of following Geoffrey's remark, were nestling at a distance of about two feet on his left the whole time.

'A young woman's face will turn the north wind, Master Richard: my heart if 'twon't.' Dick looked more anxious and was attentive in earnest at these words. 'Yes; turn the north wind,' added Geoffrey after an impressive pause. 'And though she's one of my own flesh and blood . . .'

'Will you fetch down a bit of raw-mil' cheese from pantry-shelf?' Fancy interrupted as if she were famishing.

'Ay, that I will, chiel; chiel, says I, and Mr Shiner only asking last Saturday night . . . cheese you said, Fancy?'

Dick controlled his emotion at these mysterious allusions to Mr Shiner – the better enabled to do so by perceiving that Fancy's heart went not with her father's – and spoke like a stranger to the affairs of the neighbourhood. 'Yes, there's a great deal to be said upon the power of maiden faces in settling your courses,' he ventured, as the keeper retreated for the cheese.

'The conversation is taking a very strange turn: nothing that I have ever done warrants such things being said!' murmured Fancy with emphasis just loud enough to reach Dick's ears.

'You think to yourself, 'twas to be,' cried Enoch from his distant corner, by way of filling up the vacancy caused by Geoffrey's momentary absence. 'And so you marry her, Master Dewy, and there's an end o't.'

'Pray don't say such things, Enoch,' came from Fancy severely, upon which Enoch relapsed into servitude.

'If we be doomed to marry, we marry; if we be doomed to remain single, we do,' replied Dick.

Geoffrey had by this time sat down again, and he now made his lips thin by severely straining them across his gums, and looked out of the window along the vista to the distant highway up Yalbury Hill. 'That's not the case with some folk,' he said at length, as if he read the words on a board at the further end of the vista.

Fancy looked interested, and Dick said, 'No?'

'There's that wife o' mine. It was her doom to be nobody's wife at all in the wide universe. But she made up her mind that she would, and did it twice over. Doom? Doom is nothing beside a elderly woman – quite a chiel in her hands!'

A movement was now heard along the upstairs passage, and footsteps descending. The door at the foot of the stairs opened and the second Mrs Day appeared in view, looking fixedly at the table as she advanced towards it, with apparent obliviousness of the presence of any other human being than herself. In short, if the table had been the personage, and the persons the table, her glance would have been the most natural imaginable.

She showed herself to possess an ordinary woman's face, iron-grey hair, hardly any hips, and a great deal of cleanliness in a broad white apron-string as it appeared upon the waist of her dark stuff dress.

'People will run away with a story now, I suppose,' she began saying, 'that Jane Day's tablecloths are as poor and ragged as any union beggar's!'

Dick now perceived that the tablecloth was a little the worse for wear, and reflecting for a moment concluded that 'people' in step-mother language probably meant himself. On lifting his eyes he found that Mrs Day had vanished again upstairs, and presently returned with an armful of new damask-linen tablecloths folded square and hard as boards by long compression. These she flounced down into a chair; then took one, shook it out from its folds, and spread it on the table by instalments, transferring the plates and dishes one by one from the old to the new cloth.

'And I suppose they'll say, too, that she ha'n't a decent knife and fork in her house!'

'I shouldn't say any such ill-natured thing, I am sure – ' began Dick. But Mrs Day had vanished into the next room. Fancy appeared distressed.

'Very strange woman, isn't she?' said Geoffrey, quietly going on with his dinner. 'But 'tis too late to attempt curing. My heart! 'tis so growed

into her that 'twould kill her to take it out. Ay, she's very queer: you'd
be amazed to see what valuable goods we've got stowed away upstairs.'

Back again came Mrs Day with a box of bright steel horn-handled
knives, silver-plated forks, carver, and all complete. These were wiped
of the preservative oil which coated them, and then a knife and fork
were laid down to each individual with a bang, the carving knife and
fork thrust into the meat dish, and the old ones they had hitherto used
tossed away.

Geoffrey placidly cut a slice with the new knife and fork, and asked
Dick if he wanted any more.

The table had been spread for the mixed midday meal of dinner and
tea which was common among frugal countryfolk. 'The parishioners
about here,' continued Mrs Day, not looking at any living being, but
snatching up the brown delf tea-things, 'are the laziest, gossipest,
poachest, jailest set of any ever I came among. And they'll talk about my
teapot and tea-things next, I suppose!' She vanished with the teapot,
cups, and saucers, and reappeared with a tea-service in white china, and
a packet wrapped in brown paper. This was removed, together with
folds of tissue-paper underneath; and a brilliant silver teapot appeared.

'I'll help to put the things right,' said Fancy soothingly, and rising
from her seat. 'I ought to have laid out better things, I suppose. But'
(here she enlarged her looks so as to include Dick) 'I have been away
from home a good deal, and I make shocking blunders in my housekeep-
ing.' Smiles and suavity were then dispensed all around by this bright
little bird.

After a little more preparation and modification Mrs Day took her seat
at the head of the table, and during the latter or tea division of the meal
presided with much composure. It may cause some surprise to learn
that, now her vagary was over, she showed herself to be an excellent
person with much common sense, and even a religious seriousness of
tone on matters pertaining to her afflictions.

SEVEN

❧ Dick makes himself Useful ❧

THE EFFECT OF GEOFFREY'S incidental allusions to Mr Shiner was to
restrain a considerable flow of spontaneous chat that would otherwise

have burst from young Dewy along the drive homeward. And a certain remark he had hazarded to her, in rather too blunt and eager a manner, kept the young lady herself even more silent than Dick. On both sides there was an unwillingness to talk on any but the most trivial subjects, and their sentences rarely took a larger form than could be expressed in two or three words.

Owing to Fancy being later in the day than she had promised the charwoman had given up expecting her; whereupon Dick could do no less than stay and see her comfortably tided over the disagreeable time of entering and establishing herself in an empty house after an absence of a week. The additional furniture and utensils that had been brought (a canary and cage among the rest) were taken out of the vehicle, and the horse was unharnessed and put in the plot opposite, where there was some tender grass. Dick lighted the fire already laid; and activity began to loosen their tongues a little.

'There!' said Fancy, 'we forgot to bring the fire-irons!'

She had originally found in her sitting-room, to bear out the expression 'nearly furnished' which the school-manager had used in his letter to her, a table, three chairs, a fender, and a piece of carpet. This 'nearly' had been supplemented hitherto by a kind friend, who had lent her fire-irons and crockery until she should fetch some from home.

Dick attended to the young lady's fire, using his whip-handle for a poker till it was spoilt, and then flourishing a hurdle stick for the remainder of the time.

'The kettle boils; now you shall have a cup of tea,' said Fancy, diving into the hamper she had brought.

'Thank you,' said Dick, whose drive had made him ready for some, especially in her company.

'Well, here's only one cup-and-saucer, as I breathe! Whatever could mother be thinking about? Do you mind making shift, Mr Dewy?'

'Not at all, Miss Day,' said that civil person.

' – And only having a cup by itself? or a saucer by itself?'

'Don't mind in the least.'

'Which do you mean by that?'

'I mean the cup if you like the saucer.'

'And the saucer if I like the cup?'

'Exactly, Miss Day.'

'Thank you, Mr Dewy, for I like the cup decidedly. Stop a minute; there are no spoons now!' She dived into the hamper again, and at the end of two or three minutes looked up and said, 'I suppose you don't mind if I can't find a spoon?'

'Not at all,' said the agreeable Richard.

'The fact is the spoons have slipped down somewhere; right under the other things. O yes, here's one, and only one. You would rather have one than not I suppose, Mr Dewy?'

'Rather not. I never did care much about spoons.'

'Then I'll have it. I do care about them. You must stir up your tea with a knife. Would you mind lifting the kettle off, that it may not boil dry?'

Dick leapt to the fireplace, and earnestly removed the kettle.

'There! you did it so wildly that you have made your hand black. We always use kettle-holders; didn't you learn housewifery as far as that, Mr Dewy? Well, never mind the soot on your hand. Come here. I am going to rinse mine, too.'

They went to a basin she had placed in the back room. 'This is the only basin I have,' she said. 'Turn up your sleeves, and by that time my hands will be washed, and you can come.'

Her hands were in the water now. 'O, how vexing!' she exclaimed. 'There's not a drop of water left for you unless you draw it, and the well is I don't know how many furlongs deep; all that was in the pitcher I used for the kettle and this basin. Do you mind dipping the tips of your fingers in the same?'

'Not at all. And to save time I won't wait till you have done, if you have no objection?'

Thereupon he plunged in his hands, and they paddled together. It being the first time in his life that he had touched female fingers under water, Dick duly registered the sensation as rather a nice one.

'Really, I hardly know which are my own hands and which are yours, they have got so mixed up together,' she said, withdrawing her own very suddenly.

'It doesn't matter at all,' said Dick, 'at least as far as I am concerned.'

'There! no towel! Whoever thinks of a towel till the hands are wet?'

'Nobody.'

' "Nobody." How very dull it is when people are so friendly! Come here, Mr Dewy. Now do you think you could lift the lid of that box with your elbow, and then, with something or other, take out a towel you will find under the clean clothes? Be *sure* don't touch any of them with your wet hands, for the things at the top are all Starched and Ironed.'

Dick managed by the aid of a knife and fork to extract a towel from under a muslin dress without wetting the latter; and for a moment he ventured to assume a tone of criticism.

'I fear for that dress,' he said, as they wiped their hands together.

'What?' said Miss Day, looking into the box at the dress alluded to. 'O, I know what you mean – that the vicar will never let me wear muslin?'

'Yes.'

'Well, I know it is condemned by all orders in the church as flaunting,

423

and unfit for common wear for girls who've their living to get; but we'll see.'

'In the interest of the church I hope you don't speak seriously.'

'Yes, I do; but we'll see.' There was a comely determination on her lip, very pleasant to a beholder who was neither bishop, priest, nor deacon. 'I think I can manage any vicar's views about me if he's under forty.'

Dick rather wished she had never thought of managing vicars.

'I certainly shall be glad to get some of your delicious tea,' he said in rather a free way, yet modestly, as became one in a position between that of visitor and inmate, and looking wistfully at his lonely saucer.

'So shall I. Now is there anything else we want, Mr Dewy?'

'I really think there's nothing else, Miss Day.'

She prepared to sit down, looking musingly out of the window at Smart's enjoyment of the rich grass. 'Nobody seems to care about me,' she murmured, with large lost eyes fixed upon the sky beyond Smart.

'Perhaps Mr Shiner does,' said Dick, in the tone of a slightly injured man.

'Yes, I forgot – he does, I know.' Dick precipitately regretted that he had suggested Shiner since it had produced such a miserable result as this.

'I'll warrant you'll care for somebody very much indeed another day, won't you, Mr Dewy?' she continued, looking very feelingly into the mathematical centre of his eyes.

'Ah, I'll warrant I shall,' said Dick, feelingly too, and looking back into her dark pupils, whereupon they were turned aside.

'I meant,' she went on, preventing him from speaking just as he was going to narrate a forcible story about his feelings; 'I meant that nobody comes to see if I have returned – not even the vicar.'

'If you want to see him, I'll call at the vicarage directly we have had some tea.'

'No, no! Don't let him come down here, whatever you do, whilst I am in such a state of disarrangement. Parsons look so miserable and awkward when one's house is in a muddle; walking about and making impossible suggestions in quaint academic phrases till your flesh creeps and you wish them dead. Do you take sugar?'

Mr Maybold was at this instant seen coming up the path.

'There! That's he coming! How I wish you were not here! – that is, how awkward – dear, dear!' she exclaimed, with a quick ascent of blood to her face, and irritated with Dick rather than the vicar, as it seemed.

'Pray don't be alarmed on my account, Miss Day – good-afternoon!' said Dick in a huff, putting on his hat and leaving the room hastily by the back-door.

The horse was caught and put in, and on mounting the shafts to start he saw through the window the vicar, standing upon some books piled in a chair, and driving a nail into the wall; Fancy, with a demure glance, holding the canary-cage up to him as if she had never in her life thought of anything but vicars and canaries.

EIGHT

❧ Dick meets his Father ❧

FOR SEVERAL MINUTES DICK DROVE along homeward, with the inner eye of reflection so anxiously set on his passages at arms with Fancy that the road and scenery were as a thin mist over the real pictures of his mind. Was she a coquette? The balance between the evidence that she did love him and that she did not was so nicely struck that his opinion had no stability. She had let him put his hand upon hers; she had allowed her gaze to drop plumb into the depths of his – his into hers – three or four times; her manner had been very free with regard to the basin and towel; she had appeared vexed at the mention of Shiner. On the other hand, she had driven him about the house like a quiet dog or cat, said Shiner cared for her, and seemed anxious that Mr Maybold should do the same.

Thinking thus as he neared the handpost at Mellstock Cross, sitting on the front board of the spring cart – his legs on the outside, and his whole frame jigging up and down like a candle-flame to the time of Smart's trotting – who should he see coming down the hill but his father in the light wagon, quivering up and down on a smaller scale of shakes, those merely caused by the stones in the road. They were soon crossing each other's front.

'Weh-hey!' said the tranter to Smiler.

'Weh-hey!' said Dick to Smart, in an echo of the same voice.

'Th'st hauled her back, I suppose?' Reuben inquired peaceably.

'Yes,' said Dick, with such a clinching period at the end that it seemed he was never going to add another word. Smiler, thinking this the close of the conversation, prepared to move on.

'Weh-hey!' said the tranter. 'I tell thee what it is, Dick. That there maid is taking up thy thoughts more than's good for thee, my sonny. Thou'rt never happy now unless th'rt making thyself miserable about her in one way or another.'

'I don't know about that, father,' said Dick rather stupidly.

'But I do – Wey, Smiler! – 'Od rot the women, 'tis nothing else wi' 'em nowadays but getting young men and leading 'em astray.'

'Pooh, father! you just repeat what all the common world says; that's all you do.'

'The world's a very sensible feller on things in jineral, Dick; very sensible indeed.'

Dick looked into the distance at a vast expanse of mortgaged estate. 'I wish I was as rich as a squire when he's as poor as a crow,' he murmured; 'I'd soon ask Fancy something.'

'I wish so too, wi' all my heart, sonny; that I do. Well, mind what beest about, that's all.'

Smart moved on a step or two. 'Supposing now, father, – We-hey, Smart! – I did think a little about her, and I had a chance, which I ha'n't; don't you think she's a very good sort of – of – one?'

'Ay, good; she's good enough. When you've made up your mind to marry, take the first respectable body that comes to hand – she's as good as any other; they be all alike in the groundwork; 'tis only in the flourishes there's a difference. She's good enough; but I can't see what the nation a young feller like you – wi' a comfortable house and home, and father and mother to take care o' thee, and who sent 'ee to a school so good that 'twas hardly fair to the other children – should want to go hollering after a young woman for, when she's quietly making a husband in her pocket, and not troubled by chick nor chiel, to make a poverty-stric' wife and family of her, and neither hat, cap, wig, nor waistcoat to set 'em up with: be drowned if I can see it, and that's the long and short o't, my sonny!'

Dick looked at Smart's ears, then up the hill; but no reason was suggested by any object that met his gaze.

'For about the same reason that you did, father, I suppose.'

'Dang it, my sonny, thou'st got me there!' And the tranter gave vent to a grim admiration, with the mien of a man who was too magnanimous not to appreciate artistically a slight rap on the knuckles, even if they were his own.

'Whether or no,' said Dick, 'I asked her a thing going along the road.'

'Come to that, is it? Turk! won't thy mother be in a taking! Well, she's ready, I don't doubt?'

'I didn't ask her anything about having me; and if you'll let me speak, I'll tell 'ee what I want to know. I just said, Did she care about me?'

'Piph-ph-ph!'

'And then she said nothing for a quarter of a mile, and then she said she didn't know. Now, what I want to know is, what was the meaning of that speech?' The latter words were spoken resolutely, as if he didn't care for the ridicule of all the fathers in creation.

'The meaning of that speech is,' the tranter replied deliberately, 'that the meaning is meant to be rather hid at present. Well, Dick, as an honest father to thee, I don't pretend to deny what you d'know well enough; that is, that her father being rather better in the pocket than we, I should welcome her ready enough if it must be somebody.'

'But what d'ye think she really did mean?' said the unsatisfied Dick.

'I'm afeard I am not o' much account in guessing, especially as I was not there when she said it, and seeing that your mother was the only 'ooman I ever cam' into such close quarters as that with.'

'And what did mother say to you when you asked her?' said Dick musingly.

'I don't see that that will help 'ee.'

'The principle is the same.'

'Well – ay: what did she say? Let's see. I was oiling my working-day boots without taking 'em off, and wi' my head hanging down, when she just brushed on by the garden hatch like a flittering leaf. "Ann," I said says I, and then, – but, Dick, I'm afeard 'twill be no help to thee; for we were such a rum couple, your mother and I, leastways one half was, that is myself – and your mother's charms was more in the manner than the material.'

'Never mind! "Ann," said you.'

' "Ann," said I, as I was saying . . . "Ann," I said to her when I was oiling my working-day boots wi' my head hanging down, "Woot hae me?" . . . What came next I can't quite call up at this distance o' time. Perhaps your mother would know, – she's got a better memory for her little triumphs than I. However, the long and the short o' the story is that we were married somehow, as I found afterwards. 'Twas on White Tuesday, – Mellstock Club walked the same day, every man two and two, and a fine day 'twas, – hot as fire; how the sun did strike down upon my back going to church! I well can mind what a bath o' sweating I was in, body and soul! But Fance will ha' thee, Dick – she won't walk with another chap – no such good luck.'

'I don't know about that,' said Dick, whipping at Smart's flank in a fanciful way which, as Smart knew, meant nothing in connection with going on. 'There's Pa'son Maybold, too – that's all against me.'

'What about he? She's never been stuffing into thy innocent heart that he's in love with her? Lord, the vanity o' maidens!'

'No, no. But he called, and she looked at him in such a way, and at me in such a way – quite different the ways were, – and as I was coming off there was he hanging up her birdcage.'

'Well, why shouldn't the man hang up her birdcage? Turk seize it all, what's that got to do wi' it? Dick, that thou beest a white-lyvered chap

427

I don't say, but if thou beestn't as mad as a cappel-faced bull let me
smile no more.'

'O, ay.'

'And what's think now, Dick?'

'I don't know.'

'Here's another pretty kettle o' fish for thee. Who d'ye think's the bitter
weed in our being turned out? Did our party tell 'ee?'

'No. Why, Pa'son Maybold, I suppose.'

'Shiner, – because he's in love with thy young woman, and d'want to
see her young figure sitting up at that queer instrument, and young
fingers rum-strumming upon the keys.'

A sharp ado of sweet and bitter was going on in Dick during this
communication from his father. 'Shiner's a fool! – no, that's not it; I don't
believe any such thing, father. Why, Shiner would never take a bold step
like that unless she'd been a little made up to, and had taken it kindly.
Pooh!'

'Who's to say she didn't?'

'I do.'

'The more fool you.'

'Why, father of me?'

'Has she ever done more to thee?'

'No.'

'Then she has done as much to he -rot 'em! Now, Dick, this is how a
maid is. She'll swear she's dying for thee; and she is dying for thee, and
she will die for thee; but she'll fling a look over t'other shoulder at
another young feller, though never leaving off dying for thee just the
same.'

'She's not dying for me, and so she didn't fling a look at him.'

'But she may be dying for him, for she looked at thee.'

'I don't know what to make of it at all,' said Dick gloomily.

'All I can make of it is,' the tranter said, raising his whip, arranging
his different joints and muscles, and motioning to the horse to move on,
'that if you can't read a maid's mind by her motions, nature d'seem to
say thou'st ought to be a bachelor. Clk, clk! Smiler!' And the tranter
moved on.

Dick held Smart's rein firmly, and the whole concern of horse, cart,
and man remained rooted in the lane. How long this condition would
have lasted is unknown, had not Dick's thoughts, after adding up numerous items of misery, gradually wandered round to the fact that as something must be done it could not be done by staying there all night.

Reaching home he went up to his bedroom, shut the door as if he
were going to be seen no more in this life, and taking a sheet of paper
and uncorking the ink-bottle he began a letter. The dignity of the writer's

mind was so powerfully apparent in every line of this effusion that it obscured the logical sequence of facts and intentions to an appreciable degree; and it was not at all clear to a reader whether he there and then left off loving Miss Fancy Day; whether he had never loved her seriously and never meant to; whether he had been dying up to the present moment and now intended to get well again; or whether he had hitherto been in good health and intended to die for her forthwith.

He put this letter in an envelope, sealed it up, directed it in a stern handwriting of straight dashes – easy flourishes being rigorously excluded. He walked with it in his pocket down the lane in strides not an inch less than three feet long. Reaching her gate he put on a resolute expression – then put it off again, turned back homeward, tore up his letter, and sat down.

That letter was altogether in a wrong tone – that he must own. A heartless man-of-the-world tone was what the juncture required. That he rather wanted her, and rather did not want her – the latter for choice; but that as a member of society he didn't mind making a query in jaunty terms, which could only be answered in the same way: did she mean anything by her bearing towards him, or did she not?

This letter was considered so satisfactory in every way that, being put into the hands of a little boy and the order given that he was to run with it to the school, he was told in addition not to look behind him if Dick called after him to bring it back, but to run along with it just the same. Having taken this precaution against vacillation Dick watched his messenger down the road, and turned into the house whistling an air in such ghastly jerks and starts that whistling seemed to be the act the very furthest removed from that which was instinctive in such a youth.

The letter was left as ordered: the next morning came and passed – and no answer. The next. The next. Friday night came. Dick resolved that if no answer or sign were given by her the next day, on Sunday he would meet her face to face, and have it all out by word of mouth.

'Dick,' said his father, coming in from the garden at that moment – in each hand a hive of bees tied in a cloth to prevent their egress – 'I think you'd better take these two swarms of bees to Mrs Maybold's tomorrow, instead o' me, and I'll go wi' Smiler and the wagon.'

It was a relief; for Mrs Maybold, the vicar's mother, who had just taken into her head a fancy for keeping bees (pleasantly disguised under the pretence of its being an economical wish to produce her own honey), lived near the watering-place of Budmouth Regis, ten miles off, and the business of transporting the hives thither would occupy the whole day, and to some extent annihilate the vacant time between this evening and the coming Sunday. The best spring-cart was washed throughout, the axles oiled, and the bees placed therein for the journey.

PART THE THIRD

Summer

ONE

❧ Driving out of Budmouth ❧

AN EASY BEND OF NECK AND graceful set of head; full and wavy bundles
of dark-brown hair; light fall of little feet; pretty devices on the skirt of
the dress; clear deep eyes; in short, a bunch of sweets: it was Fancy!
Dick's heart went round to her with a rush.

The scene was the corner of Mary Street in Budmouth-Regis, near the
King's statue, at which point the white angle of the last house in the row
cut perpendicularly an embayed and nearly motionless expanse of salt
water projected from the outer ocean – today lit in bright tones of green
and opal. Dick and Smart had just emerged from the street, and there
on the right, against the brilliant sheet of liquid colour, stood Fancy Day;
and she turned and recognized him.

Dick suspended his thoughts of the letter and wonder at how she
came there by driving close to the chains of the Esplanade – incontinently
displacing two chairmen, who had just come to life for the summer in
new clean shirts and revivified clothes, and being almost displaced
in turn by a rigid boy rattling along with a baker's cart and looking
neither to the right nor the left. He asked if she were going to Mellstock
that night.

'Yes, I'm waiting for the carrier,' she replied, seeming, too, to suspend
thoughts of the letter.

'Now I can drive you home nicely, and you save half an hour. Will ye
come with me?'

As Fancy's power to will anything seemed to have departed in some
mysterious manner at that moment, Dick settled the matter by getting
out and assisting her into the vehicle without another word.

The temporary flush upon her cheek changed to a lesser hue which
was permanent, and at length their eyes met; there was present between
them a certain feeling of embarrassment, which arises at such moments
when all the instinctive acts dictated by the position have been performed. Dick, being engaged with the reins, thought less of this awkwardness than did Fancy, who had nothing to do but to feel his presence,
and to be more and more conscious of the fact that by accepting a seat
beside him in this way she succumbed to the tone of his note. Smart

jogged along, and Dick jogged, and the helpless Fancy necessarily jogged too; and she felt that she was in a measure captured and made a prisoner.

'I am so much obliged to you for your company, Miss Day,' he observed, as they drove past the two semicircular bays of the Old Royal Hotel, where His Majesty King George the Third had many a time attended the balls of the burgesses.

To Miss Day, crediting him with the same consciousness of mastery – a consciousness of which he was perfectly innocent – this remark sounded like a magnanimous intention to soothe her, the captive.

'I didn't come for the pleasure of obliging you with my company,' she said.

The answer had an unexpected manner of incivility in it that must have been rather surprising to young Dewy. At the same time it may be observed that when a young woman returns a rude answer to a young man's civil remark her heart is in a state which argues rather hopefully for his case than otherwise.

There was silence between them till they had left the seafront and passed about twenty of the trees that ornamented the road leading up out of the town towards Casterbridge and Mellstock.

'Though I didn't come for that purpose either, I would have done it,' said Dick at the twenty-first tree.

'Now, Mr Dewy, no flirtation, because it's wrong, and I don't wish it.'

Dick seated himself afresh just as he had been sitting before, arranged his looks very emphatically, and cleared his throat.

'Really, anybody would think you had met me on business and were just going to commence,' said the lady intractably.

'Yes, they would.'

'Why, you never have, to be sure!'

This was a shaky beginning. He chopped round and said cheerily, as a man who had resolved never to spoil his jollity by loving one of womankind –

'Well, how are you getting on Miss Day at the present time? Gaily, I don't doubt for a moment.'

'I am not gay, Dick; you know that.'

'Gaily doesn't mean decked in gay dresses.'

'I didn't suppose gaily was gaily dressed. Mighty me, what a scholar you've grown!'

'Lots of things have happened to you this spring, I see.'

'What have you seen?'

'O, nothing; I've heard, I mean!'

'What have you heard?'

'The name of a pretty man with brass studs, and a copper ring, and a tin watch-chain, a little mixed up with your own. That's all.'

'That's a very unkind picture of Mr Shiner, for that's who you mean! The studs are gold as you know, and its a real silver chain; the ring I can't conscientiously defend, and he only wore it once.'

'He might have worn it a hundred times without showing it half so much.'

'Well, he's nothing to me,' she serenely observed.

'Not any more than I am?'

'Now, Mr Dewy,' said Fancy severely, 'certainly he isn't any more to me than you are!'

'Not so much?'

She looked aside to consider the precise compass of that question. 'That I can't exactly answer,' she replied with soft archness.

As they were going rather slowly another spring-cart, containing a farmer, farmer's wife, and farmer's man, jogged past them; and the farmer's wife and farmer's man eyed the couple very curiously. The farmer never looked up from the horse's tail.

'Why can't you exactly answer?' said Dick, quickening Smart a little, and jogging on just behind the farmer and farmer's wife and man.

As no answer came, and as their eyes had nothing else to do, they both contemplated the picture presented in front, and noticed how the farmer's wife sat flattened between the two men, who bulged over each end of the seat to give her room till they almost sat upon their respective wheels; and they looked too at the farmer's wife's silk mantle inflating itself between her shoulders like a balloon and sinking flat again at each jog of the horse. The farmer's wife, feeling their eyes sticking into her back, looked over her shoulder. Dick dropped ten yards further behind.

'Fancy, why can't you answer?' he repeated.

'Because how much you are to me depends upon how much I am to you,' said she in low tones.

'Everything,' said Dick, putting his hand towards hers and casting emphatic eyes upon the upper curve of her cheek.

'Now, Richard Dewy, no touching me! I didn't say in what way your thinking of me affected the question – perhaps inversely, don't you see? No touching, sir! Look; goodness me, don't, Dick!'

The cause of her sudden start was the unpleasant appearance over Dick's right shoulder of an empty timber-wagon and four journeymen-carpenters reclining in lazy postures inside it, their eyes directed upwards at various oblique angles into the surrounding world, the chief object of their existence being apparently to criticize to the very backbone and marrow every animate object that came within the compass of their vision. This difficulty of Dick's was overcome by trotting on till the wagon and carpenters were beginning to look rather misty by reason of a film of dust that accompanied their wagon-wheels and rose around their heads like a fog.

'Say you love me, Fancy.'

'No, Dick, certainly not; 'tisn't time to do that yet.'

'Why, Fancy?'

' "Miss Day" is better at present – don't mind my saying so; and I ought not to have called you Dick.'

'Nonsense! when you know that I would do anything on earth for your love. Why, you make any one think that loving is a thing that can be done and undone, and put on and put off at a mere whim.'

'No, no, I don't,' she said gently; 'but there are things which tell me I ought not to give way to much thinking about you, even if – '

'But you want to, don't you? Yes, say you do; it is best to be truthful. Whatever they may say about a woman's right to conceal where her love lies, and pretend it doesn't exist, and things like that, it is not best; I do know it, Fancy. And an honest woman in that, as well as in all her daily concerns, shines most brightly, and is thought most of in the long-run.'

'Well then, perhaps, Dick, I do love you a little,' she whispered tenderly; 'but I wish you wouldn't say any more now.'

'I won't say any more now, then, if you don't like it, dear. But you do love me a little, don't you?'

'Now you ought not to want me to keep saying things twice; I can't say any more now, and you must content with what you have.'

'I may at any rate call you Fancy? There's no harm in that.'

'Yes, you may.'

'And you'll not call me Mr Dewy any more?'

'Very well.'

TWO

❧ Further along the Road ❧

DICK'S SPIRITS HAVING RISEN in the course of these admissions of his sweetheart he now touched Smart with the whip; and on Smart's neck, not far behind his ears. Smart, who had been lost in thought for some time, never dreaming that Dick could reach so far with a whip which, on this particular journey, had never been extended further than his flank, tossed his head and scampered along with exceeding briskness, which was very pleasant to the young couple behind him till, turning a bend in the road, they came instantly upon the farmer, farmer's man, and farmer's wife with the flapping mantle, all jogging on just the same as ever.

'Bother those people! Here we are upon them again.'

'Well, of course. They have as much right to the road as we.'

'Yes, but it is provoking to be overlooked so. I like a road all to myself. Look what a lumbering affair theirs is!' The wheels of the farmer's cart just at that moment jogged into a depression running across the road, giving the cart a twist, whereupon all three nodded to the left, and on coming out of it all three nodded to the right, and went on jerking their backs in and out as usual. 'We'll pass them when the road gets wider.'

When an opportunity seemed to offer itself for carrying this intention into effect they heard light flying wheels behind, and on their quartering there whizzed along past them a brand-new gig, so brightly polished that the spokes of the wheels sent forth a continual quivering light at one point in their circle, and all the panels glared like mirrors in Dick and Fancy's eyes. The driver, and owner as it appeared, was really a handsome man; his companion was Shiner. Both turned round as they passed Dick and Fancy and stared with bold admiration in her face till they were obliged to attend to the operation of passing the farmer. Dick glanced for an instant at Fancy while she was undergoing their scrutiny; then returned to his driving with rather a sad countenance.

'Why are you so silent?' she said after a while, with real concern.

'Nothing.'

'Yes, it is, Dick. I couldn't help those people passing.'

'I know that.'

'You look offended with me. What have I done?'

'I can't tell without offending you.'

'Better out.'

'Well,' said Dick, who seemed longing to tell even at the risk of offending her, 'I was thinking how different you in love are from me in love. Whilst those men were staring you dismissed me from your thoughts altogether and – '

'You can't offend me further now; tell all!'

'And showed upon your face a pleased sense of being attractive to 'em.'

'Don't be silly, Dick! You know very well I didn't.'

Dick shook his head sceptically and smiled.

'Dick, I always believe flattery *if possible* – and it was possible then. Now there's an open confession of weakness. But I showed no consciousness of it.'

Dick, perceiving by her look that she would adhere to her statement, charitably forbore saying anything that could make her prevaricate. The sight of Shiner, too, had recalled another branch of the subject to his mind; that which had been his greatest trouble till her company and words had obscured its probability.

'By the way, Fancy, do you know why our quire is to be dismissed?'

'No: except that it is Mr Maybold's wish for me to play the organ.'

'Do you know how it came to be his wish?'

'That I don't.'

'Mr Shiner, being churchwarden, has persuaded the vicar; who, however, was willing enough before. Shiner, I know, is crazy to see you playing every Sunday; I suppose he'll turn over your music, for the organ will be close to his pew. But – I know you have never encouraged him?'

'Never once!' said Fancy emphatically, and with eyes full of earnest truth. 'I don't like him indeed, and I never heard of his doing this before! I have always felt that I should like to play in a church, but I never wished to turn you and your choir out; and I never even said that I could play till I was asked. You don't think for a moment that I did, surely, do you?'

'I know you didn't, dear.'

'Or that I care the least morsel of a bit for him?'

'I know you don't.'

The distance between Budmouth and Mellstock was ten or eleven miles, and there being a good inn, 'The Ship', four miles out of Budmouth, with a mast and cross-trees in front, Dick's custom in driving thither was to divide his journey into three stages by resting at this inn going and coming, and not troubling the Budmouth stables at all, whenever his visit to the town was a mere call and deposit, as today.

Fancy was ushered into a little tea-room and Dick went to the stables to see to the feeding of Smart. In face of the significant twitches of feature that were visible in the ostler and labouring men idling around, Dick endeavoured to look unconscious of the fact that there was any sentiment between him and Fancy beyond a tranter's desire to carry a passenger home. He presently entered the inn and opened the door of Fancy's room.

'Dick, do you know, it has struck me that it is rather awkward my being here alone with you like this. I don't think you had better come in with me.'

'That's rather unpleasant, dear.'

'Yes, it is, and I wanted you to have some tea as well as myself too, because you must be tired.'

'Well, let me have some with you, then. I was denied once before, if you recollect, Fancy.'

'Yes, yes, never mind! And it seems unfriendly of me now, but I don't know what to do.'

'It shall be as you say, then.' Dick began to retreat with a dissatisfied wrinkling of face, and a farewell glance at the cosy tea-tray.

'But you don't see how it is, Dick, when you speak like that,' she said with more earnestness than she had ever shown before. 'You do know that even if I care very much for you I must remember that I have a difficult position to maintain. The vicar would not like me, as his schoolmistress, to indulge in a *tête-à-tête* anywhere with anybody.'

'But I am not *any* body!' exclaimed Dick.

'No, no, I mean with a young man;' and she added softly, 'unless I were really engaged to be married to him.'

'Is that all? Then, dearest, dearest, why we'll be engaged at once, to be sure we will, and down I sit! There it is, as easy as a glove!'

'Ah! but suppose I won't! And, goodness me, what have I done!' she faltered, getting very red. 'Positively, it seems as if I meant you to say that!'

'Let's do it! I mean get engaged,' said Dick. 'Now, Fancy, will you be my wife?'

'Do you know, Dick, it was rather unkind of you to say what you did coming along the road,' she remarked as if she had not heard the latter part of his speech; though an acute observer might have noticed about her breast as the word 'wife' fell from Dick's lips a soft silent escape of breaths, with very short rests between each.

'What did I say?'

'About my trying to look attractive to those men in the gig.'

'You couldn't help looking so, whether you tried or no. And, Fancy, you do care for me?'

'Yes.'

'Very much?'

'Yes.'

'And you'll be my own wife?'

Her heart quickened, adding to and withdrawing from her cheek varying tones of red to match each varying thought. Dick looked expectantly at the ripe tint of her delicate mouth, waiting for what was coming forth.

'Yes – if father will let me.'

Dick drew himself close to her, compressing his lips and pouting them out as if he were about to whistle the softest melody known.

'O no!' said Fancy solemnly.

The modest Dick drew back a little.

'Dick, Dick, kiss me and let me go instantly! – here's somebody coming!' she whisperingly exclaimed.

*

Half an hour afterwards Dick emerged from the inn, and if Fancy's lips had been real cherries probably Dick's would have appeared deeply stained. The landlord was standing in the yard.

'Heu-heu! hay-hay, Master Dewy? Ho-ho!' he laughed, letting the laugh slip out gently and by degrees that it might make little noise in its exit, and smiting Dick under the fifth rib at the same time. 'This will never do, upon my life, Master Dewy! calling for tay for a feymel passenger, and then going in and sitting down and having some too, and biding such a fine long time!'

'But surely you know?' said Dick, with great apparent surprise. 'Yes, yes! Ha-ha!' smiting the landlord under the ribs in return.

'Why, what? Yes, yes; ha-ha!'

'You know, of course!'

'Yes, of course! But – that is – I don't.'

'Why about – between that young lady and me?' nodding to the window of the room that Fancy occupied.

'No; not I!' said the innkeeper, bringing his eyes into circles.

'And you don't!'

'Not a word, I'll take my oath!'

'But you laughed when I laughed.'

'Ay, that was me sympathy; so did you when I laughed!'

'Really, you don't know? Goodness – not knowing that!'

'I'll take my oath I don't!'

'O yes,' said Dick, with frigid rhetoric of pitying astonishment, 'we're engaged to be married, you see, and I naturally look after her.'

'Of course, of course! I didn't know that, and I hope ye'll excuse any little freedom of mine, Mr Dewy. But it is a very odd thing; I was talking to your father very intimate about family matters only last Friday in the world, and who should come in but Keeper Day, and we all then fell a-talking o' family matters; but neither one o' them said a mortal word about it; knowen me too so many years, and I at your father's own wedding. 'Tisn't what I should have expected from an old neighbour!'

'Well, to say the truth, we hadn't told father of the engagement at that time; in fact, 'twasn't settled.'

'Ah! the business was done Sunday. Yes, yes, Sunday's the courting day. Heu-heu!'

'No, 'twasn't done Sunday in particular.'

'After school-hours this week? Well, a very good time, a very proper good time.'

'O no, 'twasn't done then.'

'Coming along the road today then, I suppose?'

'Not at all; I wouldn't think of getting engaged in a dog-cart.'

'Dammy – might as well have said at once the *when* be blowed! Anyhow, 'tis a fine day, and I hope next time you'll come as one.'

Fancy was duly brought out and assisted into the vehicle, and the newly affianced youth and maiden passed up the steep hill to the Ridgeway, and vanished in the direction of Mellstock.

THREE

❧ A Confession ❦

IT WAS A MORNING OF the latter summer-time; a morning of lingering dews, when the grass is never dry in the shade. Fuchsias and dahlias were laden till eleven o'clock with small drops and dashes of water, changing the colour of their sparkle at every movement of the air; and elsewhere hanging on twigs like small silver fruit. The threads of garden-spiders appeared thick and polished. In the dry and sunny places dozens of longlegged crane-flies whizzed off the grass at every step the passer took.

Fancy Day and her friend Susan Dewy the tranter's daughter were in such a spot as this, pulling down a bough laden with early apples. Three months had elapsed since Dick and Fancy had journeyed together from Budmouth, and the course of their love had run on vigorously during the whole time. There had been just enough difficulty attending its development, and just enough finesse required in keeping it private, to lend the passion an ever-increasing freshness on Fancy's part, whilst, whether from these accessories or not, Dick's heart had been at all times as fond as could be desired. But there was a cloud on Fancy's horizon now.

'She is so well off – better than any of us,' Susan Dewy was saying. 'Her father farms five hundred acres, and she might marry a doctor or curate or anything of that kind if she contrived a little.'

'I don't think Dick ought to have gone to that gipsy-party at all when he knew I couldn't go,' replied Fancy uneasily.

'He didn't know that you would not be there till it was too late to refuse the invitation,' said Susan.

'And what was she like? Tell me.'

'Well, she was rather pretty, I must own.'

'Tell straight on about her, can't you! Come, do, Susan. How many times did you say he danced with her?'

'Once.'

'Twice, I think you said?'

'Indeed I'm sure I didn't.'

'Well, and he wanted to again, I expect.'

'No; I don't think he did. She wanted to dance with him again bad enough, I know. Everybody does with Dick, because he's so handsome and such a clever courter.'

'O, I wish! – How did you say she wore her hair?'

'In long curls, – and her hair is light, and it curls without being put in paper: that's how it is she's so attractive.'

'She's trying to get him away! yes, yes, she is! And through keeping this miserable school I mustn't wear my hair in curls! But I will; I don't care if I leave the school and go home, I will wear my curls! Look, Susan, do! is her hair as soft and long as this?' Fancy pulled from its coil under her hat a twine of her own hair and stretched it down her shoulder to show its length, looking at Susan to catch her opinion from her eyes.

'It is about the same length as that, I think,' said Miss Dewy.

Fancy paused hopelessly. 'I wish mine was lighter, like hers!' she continued mournfully. 'But hers isn't so soft, is it? Tell me, now.'

'I don't know.'

Fancy abstractedly extended her vision to survey a yellow butterfly and a red-and-black butterfly that were flitting along in company, and then became aware that Dick was advancing up the garden.

'Susan, here's Dick coming; I suppose that's because we've been talking about him.'

'Well, then, I shall go indoors now – you won't want me;' and Susan turned practically and walked off.

Enter the single-minded Dick, whose only fault at the gipsying, or picnic, had been that of loving Fancy too exclusively and depriving himself of the innocent pleasure the gathering might have afforded him, by sighing regretfully at her absence, – who had danced with the rival in sheer despair of ever being able to get through that stale, flat, and unprofitable afternoon in any other way; but this she would not believe.

Fancy had settled her plan of emotion. To reproach Dick? O no, no. 'I am in great trouble,' said she, taking what was intended to be a hopelessly melancholy survey of a few small apples lying under the tree; yet a critical ear might have noticed in her voice a tentative tone as to the effect of the words upon Dick when she uttered them.

'What are you in trouble about? Tell me of it,' said Dick earnestly. 'Darling, I will share it with 'ee and help 'ee.'

'No, no: you can't! Nobody can!'

'Why not? You don't deserve it, whatever it is. Tell me, dear.'

'O, it isn't what you think! It is dreadful: my own sin!'

'Sin, Fancy! as if you could sin! I know it can't be.'

''Tis, 'tis!' said the young lady, in a pretty little frenzy of sorrow. 'I have done wrong, and I don't like to tell it! Nobody will forgive me, nobody! and you above all will not! . . . I have allowed myself to – to – fl – '

'What, – not flirt!' he said, controlling his emotion as it were by a sudden pressure inward from his surface. 'And you said only the day before yesterday that you hadn't flirted in your life!'

'Yes, I did: and that was a wicked story! I have let another love me, and – '

'Good G – ! Well, I'll forgive you, – yes, if you couldn't help it, – yes, I will!' said the now dismal Dick. 'Did you encourage him?'

'O, – I don't know, – yes – no. O, I think so!'

'What was it?'

A pause.

'Tell me!'

'Mr Shiner.'

After a silence that was only disturbed by the fall of an apple, a long-checked sigh from Dick, and a sob from Fancy, he said with real austerity –

'Tell it all; – every word!'

'He looked at me, and I looked at him, and he said, "Will you let me show you how to catch bullfinches down here by the stream?" And I – wanted to know very much – I did so long to have a bullfinch! I couldn't help that! – and I said, "Yes!" and then he said, "Come here." And I went with him down to the lovely river, and then he said to me, "Look and see how I do it, and then you'll know: I put this birdlime round this twig, and then I go here," he said, "and hide away under a bush; and presently clever Mister Bird comes and perches upon the twig, and flaps his wings, and you've got him before you can say Jack" – something; O, O, O, I forget what!'

'Jack Sprat,' mournfully suggested Dick through the cloud of his misery.

'No, not Jack Sprat,' she sobbed.

'Then 'twas Jack Robinson!' he said with the emphasis of a man who had resolved to discover every iota of the truth or die.

'Yes, that was it! And then I put my hand upon the rail of the bridge to get across, and – That's all.'

'Well, that isn't much, either,' said Dick critically and more cheerfully. 'Not that I see what business Shiner has to take upon himself to teach

443

you anything. But it seems – it do seem there must have been more than that to set you up in such a dreadful taking?'

He looked into Fancy's eyes. Misery of miseries! – guilt was written there still.

'Now, Fancy, you've not told me all!' said Dick, rather sternly for a quiet young man.

'O, don't speak so cruelly! I am afraid to tell now! If you hadn't been harsh I was going on to tell all; now I can't!'

'Come, dear Fancy, tell: come. I'll forgive; I must, – by heaven and earth, I must, whether I will or no; I love you so!'

'Well, when I put my hand on the bridge, he touched it – '

'A scamp!' said Dick, grinding an imaginary human frame to powder.

'And then he looked at me, and at last he said, "Are you in love with Dick Dewy?" And I said, "Perhaps I am!" and then he said, "I wish you weren't then, for I want to marry you, with all my soul." '

'There's a villain now! Want to marry you!' And Dick quivered with the bitterness of satirical laughter. Then suddenly remembering that he might be reckoning without his host: 'Unless, to be sure, you are willing to have him, – perhaps you are,' he said, with the wretched indifference of a castaway.

'No, indeed I am not!' she said, her sobs just beginning to take a favourable turn towards cure.

'Well, then,' said Dick, coming a little to his senses, 'you've been stretching it very much in giving such a dreadful beginning to such a mere nothing. And I know what you've done it for, – just because of that gipsy-party!' He turned away from her and took five paces decisively, as if he were tired of an ungrateful country, including herself. 'You did it to make me jealous, and I won't stand it!' He flung the words to her over his shoulder and then stalked on, apparently very anxious to walk to the remotest of the Colonies that very minute.

'O, O, O, Dick – Dick!' she cried, trotting after him like a pet lamb and really seriously alarmed at last, 'you'll kill me! My impulses are bad – miserably wicked, – and I can't help it; forgive me, Dick! And I love you always; and those times when you look silly and don't seem quite good enough for me, – just the same, I do, Dick! And there is something more serious, though not concerning that walk with him.'

'Well, what is it?' said Dick, altering his mind about walking to the Colonies; in fact, passing to the other extreme, and standing so rooted to the road that he was apparently not even going home.

'Why this,' she said, drying the beginning of a new flood of tears she had been going to shed, 'this is the serious part. Father has told Mr Shiner that he would like him for a son-in-law if he could get me; – that he has his right hearty consent to come courting me!'

FOUR

❧ An Arrangement ❧

'THAT IS SERIOUS,' SAID DICK, more intellectually than he had spoken for a long time.

The truth was that Geoffrey knew nothing about his daughter's continued walks and meetings with Dick. When a hint that there were symptoms of an attachment between them had first reached Geoffrey's ears he stated so emphatically that he must think the matter over before any such thing could be allowed that, rather unwisely on Dick's part, whatever it might have been on the lady's, the lovers were careful to be seen together no more in public; and Geoffrey, forgetting the report, did not think over the matter at all. So Mr Shiner resumed his old position in Geoffrey's brain by mere flux of time. Even Shiner began to believe that Dick existed for Fancy no more, – though that remarkably easy-going man had taken no active steps on his own account as yet.

'And father has not only told Mr Shiner that,' continued Fancy, 'but he has written me a letter to say he should wish me to encourage Mr Shiner if 'twas convenient!'

'I must start off and see your father at once!' said Dick, taking two or three vehement steps to the south, recollecting that Mr Day lived to the north, and coming back again.

'I think we had better see him together. Not tell him what you come for, or anything of the kind, until he likes you, and so win his brain through his heart, which is always the way to manage people. I mean in this way: I am going home on Saturday week to help them in the honey-taking. You might come there to me, have something to eat and drink, and let him guess what your coming signifies, without saying it in so many words.'

'We'll do it, dearest. But I shall ask him for you, flat and plain; not wait for his guessing.' And the lover then stepped close to her, and attempted to give her one little kiss on the cheek, his lips alighting, however, on an outlying tract of her back hair by reason of an impulse that had caused her to turn her head with a jerk. 'Yes, and I'll put on my second-best suit and a clean shirt and collar, and black my boots as if 'twas a Sunday. 'Twill have a good appearance, you see, and that's a great deal to start with.'

'You won't wear that old waistcoat, will you, Dick?'

'Bless you, no! Why I – '

'I didn't mean to be personal, dear Dick,' she said, fearing she had hurt his feelings. ''Tis a very nice waistcoat, but what I meant was, that though it is an excellent waistcoat for a settled-down man, it is not quite one for' (she waited, and a blush expanded over her face, and then she went on again) – 'for going courting in.'

'No, I'll wear my best winter one, with the leather lining, that mother made. It is a beautiful, handsome waistcoat inside, yes, as ever anybody saw. In fact, only the other day, I unbuttoned it to show a chap that very lining, and he said it was the strongest handsomest lining you could wish to see on the king's waistcoat himself.'

'I don't quite know what to wear,' she said, as if her habitual indifference alone to dress had kept back so important a subject till now.

'Why, that blue frock you wore last week.'

'Doesn't set well round the neck. I couldn't wear that.'

'But I shan't care.'

'No, you won't mind.'

'Well, then it's all right. Because you only care how you look to me, do you, dear? I only dress for you, that's certain.'

'Yes, but you see I couldn't appear in it again very well.'

'Any strange gentleman you mid meet in your journey might notice the set of it, I suppose. Fancy, men in love don't think so much about how they look to other women.' It is difficult to say whether a tone of playful banter or of gentle reproach prevailed in the speech.

'Well then, Dick,' she said, with good-humoured frankness, 'I'll own it. I shouldn't like a stranger to see me dressed badly even though I am in love. 'Tis our nature, I suppose.'

'You perfect woman!'

'Yes; if you lay the stress on "woman",' she murmured, looking at a group of hollyhocks in flower, round which a crowd of butterflies had gathered like female idlers round a bonnet-shop.

'But about the dress. Why not wear the one you wore at our party?'

'That sets well, but a girl of the name of Bet Tallor, who lives near our house, has had one made almost like it (only in pattern, though of miserably cheap stuff), and I couldn't wear it on that account. Dear me, I am afraid I can't go now.'

'O yes, you must; I know you will!' said Dick, with dismay. 'Why not wear what you've got on?'

'What! this old one! After all, I think that by wearing my grey one Saturday, I can make the blue one do for Sunday. Yes, I will. A hat or a bonnet, which shall it be? Which do I look best in?'

'Well, I think the bonnet is nicest, more quiet and matronly.'

'What's the objection to the hat? Does it make me look old?'

'O no; the hat is well enough; but it makes you look rather too – you won't mind me saying it, dear?'

'Not at all, for I shall wear the bonnet.'

' – Rather too coquettish and flirty for an engaged young woman.'

She reflected a minute. 'Yes; yes. Still, after all, the hat would do best; hats *are* best, you see. Yes, I must wear the hat, dear Dicky, because I ought to wear a hat, you know.'

PART THE FOURTH

Autumn

ONE

❧ Going Nutting ❧

DICK, DRESSED IN HIS SECOND-BEST suit, burst into Fancy's sitting-room with a glow of pleasure on his face.

It was two o'clock on Friday, the day before her contemplated visit to her father, and for some reason connected with cleaning the school the children had been given this Friday afternoon for pastime, in addition to the usual Saturday.

'Fancy! it happens just right that it is a leisure half day with you. Smart is lame in his near-foot-afore, and so, as I can't do anything, I've made a holiday afternoon of it, and am come for you to go nutting with me!'

She was sitting by the parlour window with a blue frock lying across her lap and scissors in her hand.

'Go nutting! Yes. But I'm afraid I can't go for an hour or so.'

'Why not? 'Tis the only spare afternoon we may both have together for weeks.'

'This dress of mine, that I am going to wear on Sunday at Yalbury; – I find it fits so badly that I must alter it a little, after all. I told the dressmaker to make it by a pattern I gave her at the time; instead of that, she did it her own way, and made me look a perfect fright.'

'How long will you be?' he inquired, looking rather disappointed.

'Not long. Do wait and talk to me; come, do, dear.'

Dick sat down. The talking progressed very favourably amid the snipping and sewing till about half-past two, at which time his conversation began to be varied by a slight tapping upon his toe with a walking-stick he had cut from the hedge as he came along. Fancy talked and answered him, but sometimes the answers were so negligently given that it was evident her thoughts lay for the greater part in her lap with the blue dress.

The clock struck three. Dick arose from his seat, walked round the room with his hands behind him, examined all the furniture, then sounded a few notes on the harmonium, then looked inside all the books he could find, then smoothed Fancy's head with his hand. Still the snipping and sewing went on.

The clock struck four. Dick fidgeted about, yawned privately; counted the knots in the table, yawned publicly; counted the flies on the ceiling, yawned horribly; went into the kitchen and scullery and so thoroughly studied the principle upon which the pump was constructed that he could have delivered a lecture on the subject. Stepping back to Fancy, and finding still that she had not done, he went into her garden and looked at her cabbages and potatoes, and reminded himself that they seemed to him to wear a decidedly feminine aspect; then pulled up several weeds and came in again. The clock struck five, and still the snipping and sewing went on.

Dick attempted to kill a fly, peeled all the rind off his walking-stick, then threw the stick into the scullery because it was spoilt, produced hideous discords from the harmonium, and accidentally overturned a vase of flowers, the water from which ran in a rill across the table and dribbled to the floor, where it formed a lake, the shape of which, after the lapse of a few minutes, he began to modify considerably with his foot till it was like a map of England and Wales.

'Well, Dick, you needn't have made quite such a mess.'

'Well, I needn't, I suppose.' He walked up to the blue dress, and looked at it with a rigid gaze. Then an idea seemed to cross his brain.

'Fancy.'

'Yes.'

'I thought you said you were going to wear your grey gown all day tomorrow on your trip to Yalbury, and in the evening too, when I shall be with you, and ask your father for you?'

'So I am.'

'And the blue one only on Sunday?'

'And the blue one Sunday.'

'Well, dear, I shan't be at Yalbury Sunday to see it.'

'No, but I shall walk to Longpuddle church in the afternoon with father, and such lots of people will be looking at me there, you know; and it did set so badly round the neck.'

'I never noticed it, and 'tis like nobody else would.'

'They might.'

'Then why not wear the grey one on Sunday as well? 'Tis as pretty as the blue one.'

'I might make the grey one do, certainly. But it isn't so good; it didn't cost half so much as this one, and besides, it would be the same I wore Saturday.'

'Then wear the striped one, dear.'

'I might.'

'Or the dark one.'

'Yes, I might; but I want to wear a fresh one they haven't seen.'

'I see, I see,' said Dick, in a voice in which the tones of love were decidedly inconvenienced by a considerable emphasis, his thoughts meanwhile running as follows: 'I, the man she loves best in the world, as she says, am to understand that my poor half-holiday is to be lost, because she wants to wear on Sunday a gown there is not the slightest necessity for wearing, simply, in fact, to appear more striking than usual in the eyes of the Longpuddle young men; and I not there, either.'

'Then there are three dresses good enough for my eyes, but neither is good enough for the youths of Longpuddle,' he said.

'No, not that exactly, Dick. Still, you see, I do want – to look pretty to them – there, that's honest! But I shan't be much longer.'

'How much?'

'A quarter of an hour.'

'Very well; I'll come in in a quarter of an hour.'

'Why go away?'

'I mid as well.'

He went out, walked down the road, and sat upon a gate. Here he meditated and meditated, and the more he meditated the more decidedly did he begin to fume, and the more positive was he that his time had been scandalously trifled with by Miss Fancy Day – that, so far from being the simple girl who had never had a sweetheart before, as she had solemnly assured him time after time, she was, if not a flirt, a woman who had had no end of admirers; a girl most certainly too anxious about her frocks; a girl, whose feelings, though warm, were not deep; a girl who cared a great deal too much how she appeared in the eyes of other men. 'What she loves best in the world,' he thought, with an incipient spice of his father's grimness, 'is her hair and complexion. What she loves next best, her gowns and hats; what she loves next best, myself, perhaps!'

Suffering great anguish at this disloyalty in himself and harshness to his darling, yet disposed to persevere in it, a horribly cruel thought crossed his mind. He would not call for her, as he had promised, at the end of a quarter of an hour! Yes, it would be a punishment she well deserved. Although the best part of the afternoon had been wasted he would go nutting as he had intended, and go by himself.

He leaped over the gate, and pushed up the lane for nearly two miles, till a winding path called Snail-Creep sloped up a hill and entered a hazel copse by a hole like a rabbit's burrow. In he plunged, vanished among the bushes, and in a short time there was no sign of his existence upon earth save an occasional rustling of boughs and snapping of twigs in divers points of Grey's Wood.

Never man nutted as Dick nutted that afternoon. He worked like a galley slave. Half-hour after half-hour passed away, and still he gathered without ceasing. At last, when the sun had set, and bunches of nuts could not be distinguished from the leaves which nourished them, he shouldered his bag, containing quite two pecks of the finest produce of the wood, about as much use to him as two pecks of stones from the road, strolled down the woodland track, crossed the highway and entered the homeward lane, whistling as he went.

Probably, Miss Fancy Day never before or after stood so low in Mr Dewy's opinion as on that afternoon. In fact, it is just possible that a few more blue dresses on the Longpuddle young men's account would have clarified Dick's brain entirely, and made him once more a free man.

But Venus had planned other developments, at any rate for the present. Cuckoo-Lane, the way he pursued, passed over a ridge which rose keenly against the sky about fifty yards in his van. Here, upon the bright after-glow about the horizon, was now visible an irregular shape, which at first he conceived to be a bough standing a little beyond the line of its neighbours. Then it seemed to move, and, as he advanced still further, there was no doubt that it was a living being sitting in the bank, head bowed on hand. The grassy margin entirely prevented his footsteps from being heard, and it was not till he was close that the figure recognized him. Up it sprang, and he was face to face with Fancy.

'Dick, Dick! O, is it you, Dick!'

'Yes, Fancy,' said Dick, in a rather repentant tone, and lowering his nuts.

She ran up to him, flung her parasol on the grass, put her little head against his breast, and then there began a narrative disjointed by such a hysterical weeping as was never surpassed for intensity in the whole history of love.

'O Dick,' she sobbed out, 'where have you been away from me? O, I have suffered agony, and thought you would never come any more! 'Tis cruel, Dick; no 'tisn't, it is justice! I've been walking miles and miles up and down Grey's Wood, trying to find you, till I was wearied and worn out, and I could walk no further, and had come back this far! O Dick, directly you were gone I thought I had offended you and I put down the dress; 'tisn't finished now, and I never will finish it, and I'll wear an old one Sunday! Yes, Dick, I will, because I don't care what I wear when you are not by my side – ha, you think I do, but I don't! – and I ran after you, and I saw you go up Snail-Creep and not look back once, and then you plunged in, and I after you; but I was too far behind. O, I did wish the horrid bushes had been cut down so that I could see your dear shape again! And then I called out to you and nobody answered, and I was afraid to call very loud lest anybody else should hear me. Then I kept wandering and wandering about, and it was dreadful misery, Dick. And then I shut my eyes and fell to picturing you looking at some other woman, very pretty and nice, but with no affection or truth in her at all, and then imagined you saying to yourself. "Ah, she's as good as Fancy, for Fancy told me a story, and was a flirt, and cared for herself more than me, so now I'll have this one for my sweetheart." O, you won't, will you, Dick, for I do love you so!'

It is scarcely necessary to add that Dick renounced his freedom there and then, and kissed her ten times over, and promised that no pretty woman of the kind alluded to should ever engross his thoughts; in short, that though he had been vexed with her all such vexation was past, and that henceforth and for ever it was simply Fancy or death for him. And then they set about proceeding homewards, very slowly on account of Fancy's weariness, she leaning upon his shoulder and in addition receiving support from his arm round her waist; though she had sufficiently recovered from her desperate condition to sing to him, 'Why are you wandering here, I pray?' during the latter part of their walk. Nor is it necessary to describe in detail how the bag of nuts was quite forgotten until three days later, when it was found among the brambles and restored empty to Mrs Dewy, her initials being marked thereon in red cotton; and how she puzzled herself till her head ached upon the question of how on earth her meal-bag could have got into Cuckoo-Lane.

TWO

❧ Honey-taking, and Afterwards ❧

SATURDAY EVENING SAW DICK DEWY journeying on foot to Yalbury Wood, according to the arrangement with Fancy.

The landscape being concave, at the going down of the sun everything suddenly assumed a uniform robe of shade. The evening advanced from sunset to dusk long before Dick's arrival, and his progress during the latter portion of his walk through the trees was indicated by the flutter of terrified birds that had been roosting over the path. And in crossing the glades, masses of hot dry air that had been formed on the hills during the day greeted his cheeks alternately with clouds of damp night air from the valleys. He reached the keepersteward's house, where the grass-plot and the garden in front appeared light and pale against the unbroken darkness of the grove from which he had emerged, and paused at the garden gate.

He had scarcely been there a minute when he beheld a sort of procession advancing from the door in his front. It consisted first of Enoch the trapper, carrying a spade on his shoulder and a lantern dangling in his hand; then came Mrs Day, the light of the lantern revealing that she bore in her arms curious objects about a foot long in the form of Latin crosses (made of lath and brown paper dipped in brimstone – called matches by beemasters); next came Miss Day with a shawl thrown over her head; and behind all, in the gloom, Mr Frederic Shiner.

Dick in his consternation at finding Shiner present was at a loss how to proceed, and retired under a tree to collect his thoughts.

'Here I be, Enoch,' said a voice; and the procession advancing further, the lantern's rays illuminated the figure of Geoffrey awaiting their arrival beside a row of bee-hives in front of the path. Taking the spade from Enoch he proceeded to dig two holes in the earth beside the hives, the others standing round in a circle except Mrs Day, who deposited her matches in the fork of an apple-tree and returned to the house. The party remaining were now lit up in front by the lantern in their midst, their shadows radiating each way upon the garden-plot like the spokes of a wheel. An apparent embarrassment of Fancy at the presence of Shiner caused a silence in the assembly, during which the preliminaries of execution were arranged, the matches fixed, the stake kindled, the two hives placed over the two holes, and the earth stopped round the edges. Geoffrey then stood erect, and rather more, to straighten his backbone after the digging.

'They were a peculiar family,' said Mr Shiner, regarding the hives reflectively.

Geoffrey nodded.

'Those holes will be the grave of thousands!' said Fancy. 'I think 'tis rather a cruel thing to do.'

Her father shook his head. 'No,' he said, tapping the hives to shake the dead bees from their cells, 'if you suffocate 'em this way, they only die once: if you fumigate 'em in the new way, they come to life again, and die o' starvation; so the pangs o' death be twice upon 'em.'

'I incline to Fancy's notion,' said Mr Shiner, laughing lightly.

'The proper way to take honey, so that the bees be neither starved nor murdered, is a puzzling matter,' said the keeper steadily.

'I should like never to take it from them,' said Fancy.

'But 'tis the money,' said Enoch musingly. 'For without money man is a shadder!'

The lantern-light had disturbed many bees that had escaped from hives destroyed some days earlier, and, demoralized by affliction, were now getting a living as marauders about the doors of other hives. Several flew round the head and neck of Geoffrey; then darted upon him with an irritated bizz.

Enoch threw down the lantern and ran off and pushed his head into a currant bush; Fancy scudded up the path; and Mr Shiner floundered away helter-skelter among the cabbages. Geoffrey stood his ground, unmoved and firm as a rock. Fancy was the first to return, followed by Enoch picking up the lantern. Mr Shiner still remained invisible.

'Have the craters stung ye?' said Enoch to Geoffrey.

'No, not much – on'y a little here and there,' he said with leisurely solemnity, shaking one bee out of his shirt sleeve, pulling another from among his hair, and two or three more from his neck. The rest looked on during this proceeding with a complacent sense of being out of it, – much as a European nation in a state of internal commotion is watched by its neighbours.

'Are those all of them, father?' said Fancy, when Geoffrey had pulled away five.

'Almost all, – though I feel one or two more sticking into my shoulder and side. Ah! there's another just begun again upon my backbone. You lively young mortals, how did you get inside there? However, they can't sting me many times more, poor things, for they must be getting weak. They mid as well stay in me till bedtime now, I suppose.'

As he himself was the only person affected by this arrangement it seemed satisfactory enough; and after a noise of feet kicking against cabbages in a blundering progress among them the voice of Mr Shiner was heard from the darkness in that direction.

'Is all quite safe again?'

No answer being returned to this query he apparently assumed that he might venture forth, and gradually drew near the lantern again. The hives were now removed from their position over the holes, one being handed to Enoch to carry indoors, and one being taken by Geoffrey himself.

'Bring hither the lantern, Fancy: the spade can bide.'

Geoffrey and Enoch then went towards the house, leaving Shiner and Fancy standing side by side on the garden-plot.

'Allow me,' said Shiner. stooping for the lantern and seizing it at the same time with Fancy.

'I can carry it,' said Fancy, religiously repressing all inclination to trifle. She had thoroughly considered that subject after the tearful explanation of the bird-catching adventure to Dick, and had decided that it would be dishonest in her as an engaged young woman to trifle with men's eyes and hands any more. Finding that Shiner still retained his hold of the lantern she relinquished it, and he, having found her retaining it, also let go. The lantern fell and was extinguished. Fancy moved on.

'Where is the path?' said Mr Shiner.

'Here,' said Fancy. 'Your eyes will get used to the dark in a minute or two.'

'Till that time will ye lend me your hand?'

Fancy gave him the extreme tips of her fingers and they stepped from the plot into the path.

'You don't accept attentions very freely.'

'It depends upon who offers them.'

'A fellow like me, for instance.'

A dead silence.

'Well, what do you say, Missie?'

'It then depends upon how they are offered.'

'Not wildly, and yet not careless-like; not purposely, and yet not by chance; not too quick nor yet too slow.'

'How then?' said Fancy.

'Coolly and practically,' he said. 'How would that kind of love be taken?'

'Not anxiously, and yet not indifferently; neither blushing nor pale; nor religiously not yet quite wickedly.'

'Well, how?'

'Not at all.'

Geoffrey Day's storehouse at the back of his dwelling was hung with bunches of dried horehound, mint, and sage; brownpaper bags of thyme and lavender; and long ropes of clean onions. On shelves were spread large red and yellow apples, and choice selections of early potatoes for seed next year; – vulgar crowds of commoner kind lying beneath in heaps. A few empty beehives were clustered around a nail in one corner, under which stood two or three barrels of new cider of the first crop, each bubbling and squirting forth from the yet open bunghole.

Fancy was now kneeling beside the two inverted hives, one of which rested against her lap for convenience in operating upon the contents. She thrust her sleeves above her elbows, and inserted her small pink hand edgewise between each white lobe of honeycomb, performing the act so adroitly and gently as not to unseal a single cell. Then cracking the piece off at the crown of the hive by a slight backward and forward movement she lifted each portion as it was loosened into a large blue platter placed on a bench at her side.

'Bother these little mortals!' said Geoffrey, who was holding the light to her and giving his back an uneasy twist. 'I really think I may as well go indoors and take 'em out, poor things! for they won't let me alone. There's two a stinging wi' all their might now. I'm sure I wonder their strength can last so long.'

'All right, friend; I'll hold the candle whilst you are gone,' said Mr

Shiner, leisurely taking the light and allowing Geoffrey to depart, which he did with his usual long paces.

He could hardly have gone round to the housedoor when other foot-steps were heard approaching the outbuilding; the tip of a finger appeared in the hole through which the wood latch was lifted, and Dick Dewy came in, having been all this time walking up and down the wood vainly waiting for Shiner's departure.

Fancy looked up and welcomed him rather confusedly. Shiner grasped the candlestick more firmly, and, lest doing this in silence should not imply to Dick with sufficient force that he was quite at home and cool, he sang invincibly –

> 'King Arthur he had three sons.'

'Father here?' said Dick.

'Indoors, I think,' said Fancy, looking pleasantly at him.

Dick surveyed the scene and did not seem inclined to hurry off just at that moment. Shiner went on singing –

> 'The miller was drown'd in his pond,
> The weaver was hung in his yarn,
> And the d – ran away with the little tail-or,
> With the broadcloth under his arm.'

'That's a terrible crippled rhyme, if that's your rhyme!' said Dick, with a grain of superciliousness in his tone.

'It's no use your complaining to me about the rhyme!' said Mr Shiner. 'You must go to the man that made it.'

Fancy by this time had acquired confidence.

'Taste a bit, Mr Dewy,' she said, holding up to him a small circular piece of honeycomb that had been the last in the row of layers, remaining still on her knees and flinging back her head to look in his face: 'and then I'll taste a bit too.'

'And I, if you please,' said Mr Shiner. Nevertheless the farmer looked superior, as if he could even now hardly join the trifling from very importance of station; and after receiving the honeycomb from Fancy he turned it over in his hand till the cells began to be crushed, and the liquid honey ran down from his fingers in a thin string.

Suddenly a faint cry from Fancy caused them to gaze at her.

'What's the matter, dear?' said Dick.

'It is nothing, but – O-ol – a bee has stung the inside of my lip! He was in one of the cells I was eating!'

'We must keep down the swelling or it may be serious!' said Shiner, stepping up and kneeling beside her. 'Let me see it.'

'No, no!'

'Just let *me* see it,' said Dick kneeling on the other side; and after some hesitation she pressed down her lip with one finger to show the place. 'O, I hope 'twill soon be better! I don't mind a sting in ordinary places, but it is so bad upon your lip,' she added with tears in her eyes, and writhing a little from the pain.

Shiner held the light above his head and pushed his face close to Fancy's, as if the lip had been shown exclusively to himself, upon which Dick pushed closer, as if Shiner were not there at all.

'It is swelling,' said Dick to her right aspect.

'It isn't swelling,' said Shiner to her left aspect.

'Is it dangerous on the lip?' cried Fancy. 'I know it is dangerous on the tongue.'

'O no, not dangerous,' answered Dick.

'Rather dangerous,' had answered Shiner simultaneously.

'I must try to bear it!' said Fancy, turning again to the hives.

'Hartshorn-and-oil is a good thing to put to it, Miss Day,' said Shiner with great concern.

'Sweet-oil-and-hartshorn I've found to be a good thing to cure stings, Miss Day,' said Dick with greater concern.

'We have some mixed indoors; would you kindly run and get it for me?' she said.

Now whether by inadvertence or whether by mischievous intention, the individuality of the *you* was so carelessly denoted that both Dick and Shiner sprang to their feet like twin acrobats, and marched abreast to the door; both seized the latch and lifted it, and continued marching on shoulder to shoulder in the same manner to the dwelling-house. Not only so but, entering the room, they marched as before straight up to Mrs Day's chair, letting the door in the oak partition slam so forcibly that the rows of pewter on the dresser rang like a bell.

'Mrs Day, Fancy has stung her lip and wants you to give me the hartshorn, please,' said Mr Shiner, very close to Mrs Day's face.

'O, Mrs Day, Fancy has asked me to bring out the hartshorn, please, because she has stung her lip!' said Dick, a little closer to Mrs Day's face.

'Well, men alive! that's no reason why you should eat me, I suppose!' said Mrs Day, drawing back.

She searched in the corner-cupboard, produced the bottle, and began to dust the cork, the rim, and every other part very carefully, Dick's hand and Shiner's hand waiting side by side.

'Which is head man?' said Mrs Day. 'Now, don't come mumbudgeting so close again. Which is head man?'

460

Neither spoke; and the bottle was inclined towards Shiner. Shiner, as a high-class man, would not look in the least triumphant, and turned to go off with it as Geoffrey came downstairs after the search in his linen for concealed bees.

'O – that you, Master Dewy?'

Dick assured the keeper that it was; and the young man then determined upon a bold stroke for the attainment of his end, forgetting that the worst of bold strokes is the disastrous consequences they involve if they fail.

'I've come on purpose to speak to you very particular, Mr Day,' he said, with a crushing emphasis intended for the ears of Mr Shiner, who was vanishing round the door-post at that moment.

'Well, I've been forced to go upstairs and unrind myself, and shake some bees out o' me,' said Geoffrey, walking slowly towards the open door and standing on the threshold. 'The young rascals got into my shirt and wouldn't be quiet nohow.'

Dick followed him to the door.

'I've come to speak a word to you,' he repeated, looking out at the pale mist creeping up from the gloom of the valley. 'You may perhaps guess what it is about.'

The keeper lowered his hands into the depths of his pockets, twirled his eyes, balanced himself on his toes, looked as perpendicularly downward as if his glance were a plumb-line, then horizontally, collecting together the cracks that lay about his face till they were all in the neighbourhood of his eyes.

'Maybe I don't know,' he replied.

Dick said nothing; and the stillness was disturbed only by some small bird that was being killed by an owl in the adjoining wood, whose cry passed into the silence without mingling with it.

'I've left my hat up in chammer,' said Geoffrey; 'wait while I step up and get en.'

'I'll be in the garden,' said Dick.

He went round by a side wicket into the garden, and Geoffrey went upstairs. It was the custom in Mellstock and its vicinity to discuss matters of pleasure and ordinary business inside the house, and to reserve the garden for very important affairs, a custom which, as is supposed, originated in the desirability of getting away at such times from the other members of the family when there was only one room for living in, though it was now quite as frequently practised by those who suffered from no such limitation to the size of their domiciles.

The head-keeper's form appeared in the dusky garden, and Dick walked towards him. The elder paused and leant over the rail of a piggery that stood on the left of the path, upon which Dick did the same;

and they both contemplated a whitish shadowy shape that was moving about and grunting among the straw of the interior.

'I've come to ask for Fancy,' said Dick.

'I'd as lief you hadn't.'

'Why should that be, Mr Day?'

'Because it makes me say that you've come to ask what ye be'n't likely to have. Have ye come for anything else?'

'Nothing.'

'Then I'll just tell 'ee you've come on a very foolish errand. D'ye know what her mother was?'

'No.'

'A teacher in a landed family's nursery, who was foolish enough to marry the keeper of the same establishment; for I was only a keeper then, though now I've a dozen other irons in the fire as steward here for my lord, what with the timber sales and the yearly fellings, and the gravel and sand sales, and one thing and t'other. However, d'ye think Fancy picked up her good manners, the smooth turn of her tongue, her musical notes, and her knowledge of books, in a homely hole like this?'

'No.'

'D'ye know where?'

'No.'

'Well, when I went a-wandering after her mother's death she lived with her aunt, who kept a boarding-school, till her aunt married Lawyer Green – a man as sharp as a needle – and the school was broke up. Did ye know that then she went to the training-school, and that her name stood first among the Queen's scholars of her year?'

'I've heard so.'

'And that when she sat for her certificate as Government teacher, she had the highest of the first class?'

'Yes.'

'Well, and do ye know what I live in such a miserly way for when I've got enough to do without it, and why I make her work as a schoolmistress instead of living here?'

'No.'

'That if any gentleman, who sees her to be his equal in polish, should want to marry her, and she want to marry him, he shan't be superior to her in pocket. Now do ye think after this that you be good enough for her?'

'No.'

'Then good-night t'ee, Master Dewy.'

'Good-night, Mr Day.'

Modest Dick's reply had faltered upon his tongue, and he turned away wondering at his presumption in asking for a woman whom he had seen from the beginning to be so superior to him.

THREE

❦ Fancy in the Rain ❦

THE NEXT SCENE IS A tempestuous afternoon in the following month, and Fancy Day is discovered walking from her father's home towards Mellstock.

A single vast grey cloud covered the country, from which the small rain and mist had just begun to blow down in wavy sheets, alternately thick and thin. The trees of the fields and plantations writhed like miserable men as the air wound its way swiftly among them: the lowest portions of their trunks, that had hardly ever been known to move, were visibly rocked by the fiercer gusts, distressing the mind by its painful unwontedness, as when a strong man is seen to shed tears. Lowhanging boughs went up and down; high and erect boughs went to and fro; the blasts being so irregular, and divided into so many cross-currents, that neighbouring branches of the same tree swept the skies in independent motions, crossed each other, or became entangled. Across the open spaces flew flocks of green and yellowish leaves which, after travelling a long distance from their parent trees, reached the ground and lay there with their under-sides upward.

As the rain and wind increased, and Fancy's bonnet-ribbons leapt more and more snappishly against her chin, she paused on entering Mellstock Lane to consider her latitude, and the distance to a place of shelter. The nearest house was Elizabeth Endorfield's in Higher Mellstock, whose cottage and garden stood not far from the junction of that hamlet with the road she followed. Fancy hastened onward, and in five minutes entered a gate which shed upon her toes a flood of water-drops as she opened it.

'Come in, chiel!' a voice exclaimed before Fancy had knocked: a promptness that would have surprised her had she not known that Mrs Endorfield was an exceedingly and exceptionally sharp woman in the use of her eyes and ears.

Fancy went in and sat down. Elizabeth was paring potatoes for her husband's supper.

Scrape, scrape, scrape; then a toss, and splash went a potato into a bucket of water.

Now as Fancy listlessly noted these proceedings of the dame she began to reconsider an old subject that lay uppermost in her heart. Since the interview between her father and Dick the days had been melancholy days for her. Geoffrey's firm opposition to the notion of Dick as a son-in-law was more than she had expected. She had frequently seen her lover since that time, it is true, and had loved him more for the opposition than she would have otherwise dreamt of doing – which was a happiness of a certain kind. Yet, though love is thus an end in itself it must be believed to be the means to another end if it is to assume the rosy hues of an unalloyed pleasure. And such a belief Fancy and Dick were emphatically denied just now.

Elizabeth Endorfield had a repute among women which was in its nature something between distinction and notoriety. It was founded on the following items of character. She was shrewd and penetrating; her house stood in a lonely place; she never went to church; she wore a red cloak; she always retained her bonnet indoors; and she had a pointed chin. Thus far her attributes were distinctly Satanic; and those who looked no further called her, in plain terms, a witch. But she was not gaunt, nor ugly in the upper part of her face, nor particularly strange in manner; so that, when her more intimate acquaintances spoke of her the term was softened, and she became simply a Deep Body, who was as long-headed as she was high. It may be stated that Elizabeth belonged to a class of suspects who were gradually losing their mysterious characteristics under the administration of the young vicar; though during the long reign of Mr Grinham the parish of Mellstock had proved extremely favourable to the growth of witches.

While Fancy was revolving all this in her mind, and putting it to herself whether it was worth while to tell her troubles to Elizabeth, and ask her advice in getting out of them, the witch spoke.

'You be down – proper down,' she said suddenly, dropping another potato into the bucket.

Fancy took no notice.

'About your young man.'

Fancy reddened. Elizabeth seemed to be watching her thoughts. Really one would almost think she must have the powers people ascribed to her.

'Father not in the humour for't hey?' Another potato was finished and flung in. 'Ah, I know about it. Little birds tell me things that people don't dream of my knowing.'

Fancy was desperate about Dick, and here was a chance – O, such a wicked chance! – of getting help; and what was goodness beside love!

'I wish you'd tell me how to put him in the humour for it?' she said.

'That I could soon do,' said the witch quietly.

'Really? O, do; anyhow – I don't care – so that it is done! How could I do it, Mrs Endorfield?'

'Nothing so mighty wonderful in it.'

'Well, but how?'

'By witchery, of course!' said Elizabeth.

'No!' said Fancy.

''Tis, I assure ye. Didn't you ever hear I was a witch?'

'Well,' hesitated Fancy, 'I have heard you called so.'

'And you believed it?'

'I can't say that I did exactly believe it, for 'tis very horrible and wicked; but, O, how I do wish it was possible for you to be one!'

'So I am. And I'll tell you how to bewitch your father to let you marry Dick Dewy.'

'Will it hurt him, poor thing?'

'Hurt who?'

'Father.'

'No; the charm is worked by common sense, and the spell can only be broke by your acting stupidly.'

Fancy looked rather perplexed, and Elizabeth went on:

'This fear of Lizz – whatever 'tis –
By great and small,
She makes pretence to common sense
And that's all.

You must do it like this.' The witch laid down her knife and potato, and then poured into Fancy's ear a long and detailed list of directions, glancing up from the corner of her eye into Fancy's face with an expression of sinister humour. Fancy's face brightened, clouded, rose and sank, as the narrative proceeded. 'There,' said Elizabeth at length, stooping for the knife and another potato, 'do that, and you'll have him by-long and by-late, my dear.'

'And do it I will!' said Fancy.

She then turned her attention to the external world once more. The rain continued as usual, but the wind had abated considerably during the discourse. Judging that it was now possible to keep an umbrella erect she pulled her hood again over her bonnet, bade the witch good-bye, and went her way.

FOUR

❧ The Spell ❧

Mrs Endorfield's advice was duly followed.

'I be proper sorry that your daughter isn't so well as she might be,' said a Mellstock man to Geoffrey one morning.

'But is there anything in it?' said Geoffrey uneasily, as he shifted his hat to the right. 'I can't understand the report. She didn't complain to me a bit when I saw her.'

'No appetite at all, they say.'

Geoffrey crossed to Mellstock and called at the school that afternoon. Fancy welcomed him as usual, and asked him to stay and take tea with her.

'I be'n't much for tea this time o' day,' he said, but stayed.

During the meal he watched her narrowly. And to his great consternation discovered the following unprecedented change in the healthy girl – that she cut herself only a diaphanous slice of bread-and-butter, and, laying it on her plate, passed the meal-time in breaking it into pieces, but eating no more than about one-tenth of the slice. Geoffrey hoped she would say something about Dick and finish up by weeping, as she had done after the decision against him a few days subsequent to the interview in the garden. But nothing was said, and in due time Geoffrey departed again for Yalbury Wood.

''Tis to be hoped poor Miss Fancy will be able to keep on her school,' said Geoffrey's man Enoch to Geoffrey the following week, as they were shovelling up ant-hills in the wood.

Geoffrey stuck in the shovel, swept seven or eight ants from his sleeve, and killed another that was prowling round his ear, then looked perpendicularly into the earth, as usual, waiting for Enoch to say more. 'Well, why shouldn't she?' said the keeper at last.

'The baker told me yesterday,' continued Enoch, shaking out another emmet that had run merrily up his thigh, 'that the bread he've left at that there school-house this last month would starve any mouse in the three creations; that 'twould so! And afterwards I had a pint o' small down at Morris's, and there I heard more.'

'What might that ha' been?'

'That she used to have a pound o' the best rolled butter a week, regular as clockwork, from Dairyman Viney's for herself, as well as just so much salted for the helping girl, and the 'ooman she calls in; but now the same quantity d'last her three weeks, and then 'tis thoughted she throws it away sour.'

'Finish doing the emmets, and carry the bag home-along.' The keeper resumed his gun, tucked it under his arm, and went on without whistling to the dogs, who however followed with a bearing meant to imply that they did not expect any such attentions when their master was reflecting.

On Saturday morning a note came from Fancy. He was not to trouble about sending her the couple of rabbits as was intended, because she feared she should not want them. Later in the day Geoffrey went to Casterbridge and called upon the butcher who served Fancy with fresh meat, which was put down to her father's account.

'I've called to pay up our little bill, Neighbour Haylock, and you can gie me the chiel's account at the same time.'

Mr Haylock turned round three-quarters of a circle in the midst of a heap of joints, altered the expression of his face from meat to money, went into a little office consisting only of a door and a window, looked very vigorously into a book which possessed length but no breadth; and then, seizing a piece of paper and scribbling thereupon, handed the bill.

Probably it was the first time in the history of commercial transactions that the quality of shortness in a butcher's bill was a cause of tribulation to the debtor. 'Why, this isn't all she've had in a whole month!' said Geoffrey.

'Every mossel,' said the butcher – '(now, Dan, take that leg and shoulder to Mrs White's, and this eleven pound here to Mr Martin's) – you've been treating her to smaller joints lately, to my thinking, Mr Day?'

'Only two or three little scram rabbits this last week, as I am alive – I wish I had!'

'Well, my wife said to me – (Dan! not too much, not too much on that tray at a time; better go twice) – my wife said to me as she posted up the books: "Haylock," she says, "Miss Day must have been affronted this summer during that hot muggy weather that spoilt so much for us; for depend upon't," she says, "she've been trying John Grimmett unknown to us: see her account else." 'Tis little, of course, at the best of times, being only for one, but now 'tis next kin to nothing.'

'I'll inquire,' said Geoffrey despondingly.

He returned by way of Mellstock, and called upon Fancy in fulfilment of a promise. It being Saturday the children were enjoying a holiday, and on entering the residence Fancy was nowhere to be seen. Nan the charwoman was sweeping the kitchen.

'Where's my da'ter?' said the keeper.

'Well, you see she was tired with the week's teaching, and this morning she said, "Nan, I shan't get up till the evening." You see, Mr Day, if people don't eat they can't work; and as she've gie'd up eating she must gie up working.'

'Have ye carried up any dinner to her?'

'No; she don't want any. There, we all know that such things don't come without good reason – not that I wish to say anything about a broken heart, or anything of the kind.'

Geoffrey's own heart felt inconveniently large just then. He went to the staircase and ascended to his daughter's door.

'Fancy!'

'Come in, father.'

To see a person in bed from any cause whatever on a fine afternoon is depressing enough; and here was his only child Fancy not only in bed, but looking very pale. Geoffrey was visibly disturbed.

'Fancy, I didn't expect to see thee here, chiel,' he said. 'What's the matter?'

'I'm not well, father.'

'How's that?'

'Because I think of things.'

'What things can you have to think o' so mortal much?'

'You know, father.'

'You think I've been cruel to thee in saying that that penniless Dick o' thine shan't marry thee, I suppose?'

No answer.

'Well, you know, Fancy, I do it for the best, and he isn't good enough for thee. You know that well enough.' Here he again looked at her as she lay. 'Well, Fancy, I can't let my only chiel die; and if you can't live without en, you must ha' en, I suppose.'

'O, I don't want him like that; all against your will, and everything so disobedient!' sighed the invalid.

'No, no, 'tisn't against my will. My wish is, now I d'see how 'tis hurten thee to live without en, that he shall marry thee as soon as we've considered a little. That's my wish flat and plain, Fancy. There, never cry, my little maid! You ought to have cried afore; no need o'crying now 'tis all over. Well, howsoever, try to step over and see me and mother-law tomorrow, and ha' a bit of dinner wi' us.'

'And – Dick too?'

'Ay, Dick too, 'far's I know.'

'And *when* do you think you'll have considered, father, and he may marry me?' she coaxed.

'Well, there, say next Midsummer; that's not a day too long to wait.'

On leaving the school Geoffrey went to the tranter's. Old William opened the door.

'Is your grandson Dick in 'ithin, William?'

'No, not just now, Mr Day. Though he've been at home a good deal lately.'

'O, how's that?'

'What wi' one thing, and what wi' t'other, he's all in a mope, as might be said. Don't seem the feller he used to. Ay, 'a will sit studding and thinking as if 'a were going to turn chapel-member, and then do nothing but traypse and wamble about. Used to be such a chatty boy, too, Dick did; and now 'a don't speak at all. But won't ye step inside? Reuben will be home soon, 'a b'lieve.'

'No, thank you, I can't stay now. Will ye just ask Dick if he'll do me the kindness to step over to Yalbury tomorrow with my da'ter Fancy, if she's well enough? I don't like her to come by herself, now she's not so terrible topping in health.'

'So I've heard. Ay, sure, I'll tell him without fail.'

FIVE

❧ After gaining her Point ❧

THE VISIT TO GEOFFREY PASSED off as delightfully as a visit might have been expected to pass off when it was the first day of smooth experience in a hitherto obstructed love-course. And then came a series of several happy days of the same undisturbed serenity. Dick could court her when he chose; stay away when he chose, – which was never; walk with her by winding streams and waterfalls and autumn scenery till dews and twilight sent them home. And thus they drew near the day of the Harvest Thanksgiving, which was also the time chosen for opening the organ in Mellstock Church.

It chanced that Dick on that very day was called away from Mellstock. A young acquaintance had died of consumption at Charmley. a neighbouring village, on the previous Monday, and Dick in fulfilment of a long-standing promise was to assist in carrying him to the grave. When on Tuesday Dick went towards the school to acquaint Fancy with the fact it is difficult to say whether his own disappointment at being denied the sight of her triumphant *début* as organist, was greater than his vexation that his pet should on this great occasion be deprived of the pleasure of his presence. However, the intelligence was communicated.

She bore it as she best could, not without many expressions of regret and convictions that her performance would be nothing to her now.

Just before eleven o'clock on Sunday he set out upon his sad errand. The funeral was to be immediately after the morning service, and as there were four good miles to walk, driving being inconvenient, it became necessary to start comparatively early. Half an hour later would certainly have answered his purpose quite as well, yet at the last moment nothing would content his ardent mind but that he must go a mile out of his way in the direction of the school, in the hope of getting a glimpse of his Love as she started for church.

Striking therefore into the lane towards the school, instead of across the eweleaze direct to Charmley, he arrived opposite her door as his goddess emerged.

If ever a woman looked a divinity Fancy Day appeared one that morning as she floated down those school steps, in the form of a nebulous collection of colours inclining to blue. With an audacity unparalleled in the whole history of village-schoolmistresses at this date – partly owing, no doubt, to papa's respectable accumulation of cash, which rendered her profession not altogether one of necessity – she had actually donned a hat and feather and lowered her hitherto plainly looped-up hair, which now fell about her shoulders in a profusion of curls. Poor Dick was astonished: he had never seen her look so distractingly beautiful before save on Christmas-eve, when her hair was in the same luxuriant condition of freedom. But his first burst of delighted surprise was followed by less comfortable feelings as soon as his brain recovered its power to think.

Fancy had blushed; – was it with confusion? She had also involuntarily pressed back her curls. She had not expected him.

'Fancy, you didn't know me for a moment in my funeral clothes, did you?'

'Good-morning, Dick – no, really, I didn't know you for an instant in such a sad suit.'

He looked again at the gay tresses and hat. 'You've never dressed so charming before, dearest.'

'I like to hear you praise me in that way, Dick,' she said, smiling archly. 'It is meat and drink to a woman. Do I look nice really?'

'Fie! you know it. Did you remember, – I mean didn't you remember about my going away today?'

'Well, yes, I did, Dick; but, you know, I wanted to look well; – forgive me.'

'Yes, darling; yes, of course, – there's nothing to forgive. No, I was only thinking that when we talked on Tuesday and Wednesday and Thursday and Friday about my absence today, and I was so sorry for it, you said, Fancy, so were you sorry, and almost cried, and said it would be no pleasure to you to be the attraction of the church today since I could not be there.'

'My dear one, neither will it be so much pleasure to me ... But I do take a little delight in my life, I suppose,' she pouted.

'Apart from mine?'

She looked at him with perplexed eyes. 'I know you are vexed with me, Dick, and it is because the first Sunday I have curls and a hat and feather since I have been here happens to be the very day you are away and won't be with me. Yes, say it is, for that is it! And you think that all this week I ought to have remembered you wouldn't be here today, and not have cared to be better dressed than usual. Yes, you do, Dick, and it is rather unkind!'

'No, no,' said Dick earnestly and simply, 'I didn't think so badly of you as that. I only thought that – if *you* had been going away, I shouldn't have tried new attractions for the eyes of other people. But then of course you and I are different, naturally.'

'Well, perhaps we are.'

'Whatever will the vicar say, Fancy?'

'I don't fear what he says in the least!' she answered proudly. 'But he won't say anything of the sort you think. No, no.'

'He can hardly have conscience to, indeed.'

'Now come, you say, Dick, that you quite forgive me, for I must go,' she said with sudden gaiety, and skipped backwards into the porch. 'Come here, sir; – say you forgive me, and then you shall kiss me; – you never have yet when I have worn curls, you know. Yes, just where you want to so much, – yes, you may!'

Dick followed her into the inner corner, where he was probably not slow in availing himself of the privilege offered.

'Now that's a treat for you, isn't it?' she continued. 'Goodbye, or I shall be late. Come and see me tomorrow: you'll be tired tonight.'

Thus they parted, and Fancy proceeded to the church. The organ stood on one side of the chancel, close to and under the immediate eye of the vicar when he was in the pulpit and also in full view of the congregation. Here she sat down, for the first time in such a conspicuous position, her seat having previously been in a remote spot in the aisle.

'Good heavens – disgraceful! Curls and a hat and feather!' said the daughters of the small gentry, who had either only curly hair without a hat and feather, or a hat and feather without curly hair. 'A bonnet for church always!' said sober matrons.

That Mr Maybold was conscious of her presence close beside him during his sermon; that he was not at all angry at her development of costume; that he admired her, she perceived. But she did not see that he loved her during that sermon-time as he had never loved a woman before; that her proximity was a strange delight to him; and that he gloried in her musical success that morning in a spirit quite beyond a mere cleric's glory at the inauguration of a new order of things.

The old choir, with humbled hearts, no longer took their seats in the gallery as heretofore (which was now given up to the school-children who were not singers, and a pupil-teacher), but were scattered about with their wives in different parts of the church. Having nothing to do with conducting the service for almost the first time in their lives they all felt awkward, out of place, abashed, and inconvenienced by their hands. The tranter had proposed that they should stay away today and go nutting, but grandfather William would not hear of such a thing for a moment. 'No,' he replied reproachfully, and quoted a verse: ' "Though this has come upon us let not our hearts be turned back, or our steps go out of the way." '

So they stood and watched the curls of hair trailing down the back of the successful rival, and the waving of her feather as she swayed her head. After a few timid notes and uncertain touches her playing became markedly correct, and towards the end full and free. But, whether from prejudice or unbiased judgement, the venerable body of musicians could not help thinking that the simpler notes they had been wont to bring forth were more in keeping with the simplicity of their old church than the crowded chords and interludes it was her pleasure to produce.

SIX

Into Temptation

THE DAY WAS DONE, AND Fancy was again in the school-house. About five o'clock it began to rain, and in rather a dull frame of mind she wandered into the schoolroom for want of something better to do. She was thinking – of her lover Dick Dewy? Not precisely. Of how weary she was of living alone; how unbearable it would be to return to Yalbury under the rule of her strange-tempered step-mother; that it was far better to be married to anybody than do that; that eight or nine long months had yet to be lived through ere the wedding could take place.

At the side of the room were high windows of Ham-hill stone, upon either sill of which she could sit by first mounting a desk and using it as a footstool. As the evening advanced here she perched herself, as was her custom on such wet and gloomy occasions, put on a light shawl and bonnet, opened the window, and looked out at the rain.

The window overlooked a field called the Grove, and it was the position from which she used to survey the crown of Dick's passing hat in the early days of their acquaintance and meetings. Not a living soul was now visible anywhere; the rain kept all people indoors who were not forced abroad by necessity, and necessity was less importunate on Sundays than during the week.

Sitting here and thinking again – of her lover, or of the sensation she had created at church that day? – well, it is unknown – thinking and thinking she saw a dark masculine figure arising into distinctness at the further end of the Grove – a man without an umbrella. Nearer and nearer he came, and she perceived that he was in deep mourning, and then that it was Dick. Yes, in the fondness and foolishness of his young heart, after walking four miles in a drizzling rain without overcoat or umbrella and in face of a remark from his love that he was not to come because he would be tired, he had made it his business to wander this mile out of his way again from sheer wish of spending ten minutes in her presence.

'O Dick, how wet you are!' she said, as he drew up under the window. 'Why, your coat shines as if it had been varnished, and your hat – my goodness, there's a streaming hat!'

'O, I don't mind, darling!' said Dick cheerfully. 'Wet never hurts me, though I am rather sorry for my best clothes. However, it couldn't be helped; we lent all the umbrellas to the women. I don't know when I shall get mine back.'

'And look, there's a nasty patch of something just on your shoulder.'

'Ah, that's japanning; it rubbed off the clamps of poor Jack's coffin when we lowered him from our shoulders upon the bier! I don't care about that, for 'twas the last deed I could do for him; and 'tis hard if you can't afford a coat for an old friend.'

Fancy put her hand to her mouth for half a minute. Underneath the palm of that little hand there existed for that half-minute a little yawn.

'Dick, I don't like you to stand there in the wet. And you mustn't sit down. Go home and change your things. Don't stay another minute.'

'One kiss after coming so far,' he pleaded.

'If I can reach, then.'

He looked rather disappointed at not being invited round to the door. She twisted from her seated position and bent herself downwards, but not even by standing on the plinth was it possible for Dick to get his lips into contact with hers as she held them. By great exertion she might have reached a little lower; but then she would have exposed her head to the rain.

'Never mind, Dick; kiss my hand,' she said, flinging it down to him. 'Now, good-bye.'

'Good-bye.'

He walked slowly away, turning and turning again to look at her till he was out of sight. During the retreat she said to herself, almost involuntarily, and still conscious of that morning's triumph –

'I like Dick, and I love him; but how plain and sorry a man looks in the rain, with no umbrella, and wet through!'

As he vanished she made as if to descend from her seat; but glancing in the other direction she saw another form coming along the same track. It was also that of a man. He, too, was in black from top to toe; but he carried an umbrella.

He drew nearer, and the direction of the rain caused him so to slant his umbrella that from her height above the ground his head was invisible, as she was also to him. He passed in due time directly beneath her, and in looking down upon the exterior of his umbrella her feminine eyes perceived it to be of superior silk – less common at that date than since – and of elegant make. He reached the entrance to the building, and Fancy suddenly lost sight of him. Instead of pursuing the roadway as Dick had done he had turned sharply round into her own porch.

She jumped to the floor, hastily flung off her shawl and bonnet, smoothed and patted her hair till the curls hung in passable condition, and listened. No knock. Nearly a minute passed, and still there was no knock. Then there arose a soft series of raps no louder than the tapping of a distant woodpecker, and barely distinct enough to reach her ears. She composed herself and flung open the door.

In the porch stood Mr Maybold.

There was a warm flush upon his face and a bright flash in his eyes which made him look handsomer than she had ever seen him before.

'Good-evening, Miss Day.'

'Good-evening, Mr Maybold,' she said, in a strange state of mind. She had noticed, beyond the ardent hue of his face, that his voice had a singular tremor in it, and that his hand shook like an aspen leaf when he laid his umbrella in the corner of the porch. Without another word being spoken by either he came into the schoolroom, shut the door, and moved close to her. Once inside the expression of his face was no more discernible by reason of the increasing dusk of evening.

'I want to speak to you,' he then said; 'seriously – on a perhaps unexpected subject, but one which is all the world to me – I don't know what it may be to you, Miss Day.'

No reply.

'Fancy, I have come to ask you if you will be my wife?'

As a person who has been idly amusing himself with rolling a snowball might start at finding he had set in motion an avalanche, so did Fancy start at these words from the young vicar. And in the dead silence which followed them the breathings of the man and of the woman could be distinctly and separately heard; and there was this difference between them – his respirations gradually grew quieter and less rapid after the enunciation; hers, from having been low and regular, increased in quickness and force till she almost panted.

'I cannot, I cannot, Mr Maybold – I cannot! Don't ask me!' she said.

'Don't answer in a hurry!' he entreated. 'And do listen to me. This is no sudden feeling on my part. I have loved you for more than six months! Perhaps my late interest in teaching the children here has not been so single-minded as it seemed. You will understand my motive – like me better, perhaps, for honestly telling you that I have struggled against my emotion continually, because I have thought that it was not well for me to love you! But I resolved to struggle no longer; I have examined the feeling; and the love I bear you is as genuine as that I could bear any woman! I see your great charm; I respect your natural talents, and the refinement they have brought into your nature – they are quite enough, and more than enough for me! They are equal to anything ever required of the mistress of a quiet parsonage-house – the place in which I shall pass my days, wherever it may be situated. O Fancy, I have watched you, criticized you even severely, brought my feelings to the light of judgement, and still have found them rational, and such as any man might have expected to be inspired with by a woman like you! So there is nothing hurried, secret, or untoward in my desire to do this. Fancy, will you marry me?'

No answer was returned.

'Don't refuse; don't,' he implored. 'It would be foolish of you – I mean cruel! Of course we would not live here, Fancy. I have had for a long time the offer of an exchange of livings with a friend in Yorkshire, but I have hitherto refused on account of my mother. There we would go. Your musical powers shall be still further developed; you shall have whatever pianoforte you like; you shall have anything. Fancy, anything to make you happy – pony-carriage, flowers, birds, pleasant society; yes, you have enough in you for any society, after a few months of travel with me! Will you, Fancy, marry me?'

Another pause ensued, varied only by the surging of the rain against the window-panes, and then Fancy spoke, in a faint and broken voice.

'Yes, I will,' she said.

'God bless you, my own!' He advanced quickly, and put his arm out to embrace her. She drew back hastily. 'No no, not now!' she said in an agitated whisper. 'There are things; – but the temptation is, O, too strong, and I can't resist it; I can't tell you now, but I must tell you! Don't, please,

475

don't come near me now! I want to think. I can scarcely get myself used to the idea of what I have promised yet.' The next minute she turned to a desk, buried her face in her hands, and burst into a hysterical fit of weeping. 'O, leave me to myself!' she sobbed; 'leave me! O, leave me!'

'Don't be distressed; don't, dearest!' It was with visible difficulty that he restrained himself from approaching her. 'You shall tell me at your leisure what it is that grieves you so; I am happy – beyond all measure happy! – at having your simple promise.'

'And do go and leave me now!'

'But I must not, in justice to you, leave for a minute, until you are yourself again.'

'There then,' she said, controlling her emotion, and standing up; 'I am not disturbed now.'

He reluctantly moved towards the door. 'Good-bye!' he murmured tenderly. 'I'll come tomorrow about this time.'

SEVEN

❧ Second Thoughts ❧

THE NEXT MORNING THE VICAR rose early. The first thing he did was to write a long and careful letter to his friend in Yorkshire. Then, eating a little breakfast, he crossed the meadows in the direction of Casterbridge, bearing his letter in his pocket, that he might post it at the town office, and obviate the loss of one day in its transmission that would have resulted had he left it for the foot-post through the village.

It was a foggy morning, and the trees shed in noisy waterdrops the moisture they had collected from the thick air, an acorn occasionally falling from its cup to the ground in company with the drippings. In the meads sheets of spiders'-web, almost opaque with wet, hung in folds over the fences, and the falling leaves appeared in every variety of brown, green, and yellow hue.

A low and merry whistling was heard on the highway he was approaching, then the light footsteps of a man going in the same direction as himself. On reaching the junction of his path with the road the vicar beheld Dick Dewy's open and cheerful face. Dick lifted his hat, and the vicar came out into the highway that Dick was pursuing.

'Good-morning, Dewy. How well you are looking!' said Mr Maybold.

'Yes, sir, I am well – quite well! I am going to Casterbridge now, to get Smart's collar; we left it there Saturday to be repaired.'

'I am going to Casterbridge, so we'll walk together,' the vicar said. Dick gave a hop with one foot to put himself in step with Mr Maybold, who proceeded: 'I fancy I didn't see you at church yesterday, Dewy. Or were you behind the pier?'

'No; I went to Charmley. Poor John Dunford chose me to be one of his bearers a long time before he died, and yesterday was the funeral. Of course I couldn't refuse, though I should have liked particularly to have been at home as 'twas the day of the new music.'

'Yes, you should have been. The musical portion of the service was successful – very successful indeed; and what is more to the purpose no ill-feeling whatever was evinced by any of the members of the old choir. They joined in the singing with the greatest good-will.'

''Twas natural enough that I should want to be there, I suppose,' said Dick, smiling a private smile; 'considering who the organ-player was.'

At this the vicar reddened a little, and said, 'Yes, yes,' though not at all comprehending Dick's true meaning, who, as he received no further reply, continued hesitatingly, and with another smile denoting his pride as a lover –

'I suppose you know what I mean, sir? You've heard about me and – Miss Day?'

The red in Maybold's countenance went away: he turned and looked Dick in the face.

'No,' he said constrainedly, 'I've heard nothing whatever about you and Miss Day.'

'Why, she's my sweetheart, and we are going to be married next Midsummer. We are keeping it rather close just at present, because 'tis a good many months to wait; but it is her father's wish that we don't marry before, and of course we must submit. But the time 'ill soon slip along.'

'Yes, the time will soon slip along – Time glides away every day – yes.'

Maybold said these words, but he had no idea of what they were. He was conscious of a cold and sickly thrill throughout him; and all he reasoned was this that the young creature whose graces had intoxicated him into making the most imprudent resolution of his life was less an angel than a woman.

'You see, sir,' continued the ingenuous Dick, ''twill be better in one sense. I shall by that time be the regular manager of a branch o' father's business which we think of starting elsewhere. It has very much increased lately, and we expect next year to keep a' extra couple of horses. We've already our eye on one – brown as a berry, neck like a rainbow, fifteen

hands, and not a grey hair in her – offered us at twenty-five want a
crown. And to kip pace with the times I have had some cards prented,
and I beg leave to hand you one, sir.'

'Certainly,' said the vicar, mechanically taking the card that Dick
offered him.

'I turn in here by Grey's Bridge,' said Dick. 'I suppose you go straight
on and up town?'

'Yes.'

'Good-morning, sir.'

'Good-morning, Dewy.'

Maybold stood still upon the bridge, holding the card as it had been
put into his hand, and Dick's footsteps died away towards Durnover
Mill. The vicar's first voluntary action was to read the card: –

DEWY AND SON,

TRANTERS AND HAULIERS,

MELLSTOCK.

N.B. – *Furniture, Coals, Potatoes, Live and Dead Stock, removed to any distance
on the shortest notice.*

Mr Maybold leant over the parapet of the bridge and looked into the
river. He saw – without heeding – how the water came rapidly from
beneath the arches, glided down a little steep, then spread itself over a
pool in which dace, trout, and minnows sported at ease among the long
green locks of weed that lay heaving and sinking with their roots towards
the current. At the end of ten minutes spent leaning thus he drew from
his pocket the letter to his friend, tore it deliberately into such minute
fragments that scarcely two syllables remained in juxtaposition, and sent
the whole handful of shreds fluttering into the water. Here he watched
them eddy, dart, and turn, as they were carried downwards towards the
ocean and gradually disappeared from his view. Finally he moved off,
and pursued his way at a rapid pace back again to Mellstock Vicarage.

Nerving himself by a long and intense effort he sat down in his study
and wrote as follows:

DEAR MISS DAY, – The meaning of your words, 'the temptation is too
strong,' of your sadness and your tears, has been brought home to me
by an accident. I know today what I did not know yesterday – that
you are not a free woman.

Why did you not tell me – why didn't you? Did you suppose I
knew? No. Had I known, my conduct in coming to you as I did would
have been reprehensible.

But I don't chide you! Perhaps no blame attaches to you – I can't tell. Fancy, though my opinion of you is assailed and disturbed in a way which cannot be expressed, I love you still, and my word to you holds good yet. But will you, in justice to an honest man who relies upon your word to him, consider whether, under the circumstances, you can honourably forsake him? – yours ever sincerely,

ARTHUR MAYBOLD.

He rang the bell. 'Tell Charles to take these copybooks and this note to the school at once.'

The maid took the parcel and the letter, and in a few minutes a boy was seen to leave the vicarage gate with the one under his arm and the other in his hand. The vicar sat with his hand to his brow, watching the lad as he descended Church Lane and entered the waterside path which intervened between that spot and the school.

Here he was met by another boy, and after a free salutation and pugilistic frisk had passed between the two the second boy came on his way to the vicarage, and the other vanished out of sight.

The boy came to the door, and a note for Mr Maybold was brought in.

He knew the writing. Opening the envelope with an unsteady hand he read the subjoined words:

DEAR MR MAYBOLD, – I have been thinking seriously and sadly through the whole of the night of the question you put to me last evening; and of my answer. That answer, as an honest woman, I had no right to give.

It is my nature – perhaps all women's – to love refinement of mind and manners; but even more than this, to be ever fascinated with the idea of surroundings more elegant and pleasing than those which have been customary. And you praised me, and praise is life to me. It was alone my sensations at these things which prompted my reply. Ambition and vanity they would be called; perhaps they are so.

After this explanation I hope you will generously allow me to withdraw the answer I too hastily gave.

And one more request. To keep the meeting of last night, and all that passed between us there, for ever a secret. Were it to become known it would utterly blight the happiness of a trusting and generous man, whom I love still, and shall love always. – yours sincerely,

FANCY DAY

The last written communication that ever passed from the vicar to Fancy was a note containing these words only:

Tell him everything; it is best. He will forgive you.

479

PART THE FIFTH

Conclusion

❦ 'The Knot there's no Untying' ❧

THE LAST DAY OF THE story is dated just subsequent to that point in the development of the seasons when country people go to bed among nearly naked trees, are lulled to sleep by a fall of rain, and awake next morning among green ones; when the landscape appears embarrassed with the sudden weight and brilliancy of its leaves; when the night-jar comes and strikes up for the summer his tune of one note; when the apple-trees have bloomed, and the roads and orchard-grass become spotted with fallen petals; when the faces of the delicate flowers are darkened and their heads weighed down by the throng of honey-bees, which increase their humming till humming is too mild a term for the all-pervading sound; and when cuckoos, blackbirds, and sparrows, that have hitherto been merry and respectful neighbours, become noisy and persistent intimates.

The exterior of Geoffrey Day's house in Yalbury Wood appeared exactly as was usual at that season, but a frantic barking of the dogs at the back told of unwonted movements somewhere within. Inside the door the eyes beheld a gathering which was a rarity indeed for the dwelling of the solitary woodsteward and keeper.

About the room were sitting and standing, in various gnarled attitudes, our old acquaintance grandfathers James and William, the tranter, Mr Penny, two or three children, including Jimmy and Charley, besides three or four country ladies and gentlemen from a greater distance who do not require any distinction by name. Geoffrey was seen and heard stamping about the outhouse and among the bushes of the garden, attending to details of daily routine before the proper time arrived for their performance, in order that they might be off his hands for the day. He appeared with his shirt-sleeves rolled up; his best new nether garments, in which he had arrayed himself that morning, being temporarily disguised under a week-day apron whilst these proceedings were in operation. He occasionally glanced at the hives in passing to see if his wife's bees were swarming, ultimately rolling down his shirt-sleeves and going indoors, talking to tranter Dewy whilst buttoning the wristbands, to save time; next going upstairs for his best waistcoat, and coming down again to make another remark whilst buttoning that, during the time looking fixedly in the tranter's face as if he were a looking-glass.

The furniture had undergone attenuation to an alarming extent, every duplicate piece having been removed, including the clock by Thomas Wood; Ezekiel Saunders being at last left sole referee in matters of time.

Fancy was stationary upstairs, receiving her layers of clothes and adornments and answering by short fragments of laughter which had more fidgetiness than mirth in them, remarks that were made from time to time by Mrs Dewy and Mrs Penny, who were assisting her at the toilet, Mrs Day having pleaded a queerness in her head as a reason for shutting herself up in an inner bedroom for the whole morning. Mrs Penny appeared with nine corkscrew curls on each side of her temples, and a back comb stuck upon her crown like a castle on a steep.

The conversation just now going on was concerning the banns, the last publication of which had been on the Sunday previous.

'And how did they sound?' Fancy subtly inquired.

'Very beautiful indeed,' said Mrs Penny. 'I never heard any sound better.'

'But *how*?'

'O, *so* natural and elegant, didn't they, Reuben!' she cried through the chinks of the unceiled floor to the tranter downstairs.

'What's that?' said the tranter, looking up inquiringly at the floor above him for an answer.

'Didn't Dick and Fancy sound well when they were called home in church last Sunday?' came downwards again in Mrs Penny's voice.

'Ay, that they did, my sonnies! – especially the first time. There was a terrible whispering piece of work in the congregation, wasn't there, neighbour Penny?' said the tranter, taking up the thread of conversation on his own account and, in order to be heard in the room above, speaking very loud to Mr Penny, who sat at the distance of three feet from him, or rather less.

'I never can mind seeing such a whispering as there was,' said Mr Penny, also loudly, to the room above. 'And such sorrowful envy on the maidens' faces; really, I never did see such envy as there was!'

Fancy's lineaments varied in innumerable little flushes and her heart palpitated innumerable little tremors of pleasure. 'But perhaps,' she said, with assumed indifference, 'it was only because no religion was going on just then?'

'O, no; nothing to do with that. 'Twas because of your high standing in the parish. It was just as if they had one and all caught Dick kissing and coling ye to death, wasn't it, Mrs Dewy?'

'Ay; that 'twas.'

'How people will talk about one's doings!' Fancy exclaimed.

'Well, if you make songs about yourself, my dear, you can't blame other people for singing 'em.'

'Mercy me! how shall I go through it?' said the young lady again, but merely to those in the bedroom, with a breathing of a kind between a sigh and a pant, round shining eyes, and warm face.

'O, you'll get through it well enough, child,' said Mrs Dewy placidly. 'The edge of the performance is took off at the calling home; and when once you get up to the chancel end o' the church you feel as saucy as you please. I'm sure I felt as brave as a sodger all through the deed – though of course I dropped my face and looked modest, as was becoming to a maid. Mind you do that, Fancy.'

'And I walked into the church as quiet as a lamb, I'm sure,' subjoined Mrs Penny. 'There, you see Penny is such a little small man. But certainly I was flurried in the inside o' me. Well, thinks I, 'tis to be, and here goes! And do you do the same: say, "'Tis to be, and here goes!"'

'Is there such wonderful virtue in "'Tis to be, and here goes!"' inquired Fancy.

'Wonderful! 'Twill carry a body through it all from wedding to church-ing, if you only let it out with spirit enough.'

'Very well, then,' said Fancy, blushing. "'Tis to be, and here goes!'

'That's a girl for a husband!' said Mrs Dewy.

'I do hope he'll come in time!' continued the bride-elect, inventing a new cause of affright now that the other was demolished.

"'Twould be a thousand pities if he didn't come, now you be so brave,' said Mrs Penny.

Grandfather James, having overheard some of these remarks, said downstairs with mischievous loudness –

'I've known some would-be weddings when the men didn't come.'

'They've happened not to come, before now, certainly,' said Mr Penny, cleaning one of the glasses of his spectacles.

'O, do hear what they are saying downstairs,' whispered Fancy. 'Hush, hush!'

She listened.

'They have, haven't they, Geoffrey?' continued grim grandfather James, as Geoffrey entered.

'Have what?' said Geoffrey.

'The men have been known not to come.'

'That they have,' said the keeper.

'Ay; I've knowed times when the wedding had to be put off through his not appearing, being tired of the woman. And another case I knowed was when the man was catched in a man-trap crossing Oaker's Wood, and the three months had run out before he got well, and the banns had to be published over again.'

'How horrible!' said Fancy.

'They only say it on purpose to tease 'ee, my dear,' said Mrs Dewy.

''Tis quite sad to think what wretched shifts poor maids have been put to,' came again from downstairs. 'Ye should hear Clerk Wilkins, my brother-law, tell his experiences in marrying couples these last thirty year: sometimes one thing, sometimes another – 'tis quite heart-rending – enough to make your hair stand on end.'

'Those things don't happen very often, I know,' said Fancy with smouldering uneasiness.

'Well, really 'tis time Dick was here,' said the tranter.

'Don't keep on at me so, grandfather James and Mr Dewy, and all you down there!' Fancy broke out, unable to endure any longer. 'I am sure I shall die, or do something, if you do!'

'Never you hearken to these old chaps, Miss Day!' cried Nat Callcome the best man, who had just entered, and threw his voice upward through the chinks of the floor as the others had done. ''Tis all right; Dick's coming on like a wild feller; he'll be here in a minute. The hive o' bees his mother gie'd en for his new garden swarmed jist as he was starting, and he said, "I can't afford to lose a stock o' bees; no, that I can't, though I fain would; and Fancy wouldn't wish it on any account." So he jist stopped to ting to 'em and shake 'em.'

'A genuine wise man,' said Geoffrey.

'To be sure what a day's work we had yesterday!' Mr Callcome continued, lowering his voice as if it were not necessary any longer to include those in the room above among his audience, and selecting a remote corner of his best clean handkerchief for wiping his face. 'To be sure!'

'Things so heavy, I suppose,' said Geoffrey, as if reading through the chimney-window from the far end of the vista.

'Ay,' said Nat, looking round the room at points from which furniture had been removed. 'And so awkward to carry, too. 'Twas ath'art and across Dick's garden; in and out Dick's door: up and down Dick's stairs; round and round Dick's chammers till legs were worn to stumps: and Dick is so particular, too. And the stores of victuals and drink that lad has laid in: why, 'tis enough for Noah's ark! I'm sure I never wish to see a choicer half-dozen of hams than he's got there in his chimley; and the cider I tasted was a very pretty drop, indeed; – none could desire a prettier cider.'

'They be for the love and the stalled ox both. Ah, the greedy martels!' said grandfather James.

'Well, may-be they be. "Surely." says I, "that couple between 'em have heaped up so much furniture and victuals that anybody would think they were going to take hold the big end of married life first, and begin wi' a grown-up family." Ah, what a bath of heat we two chaps were in, to be sure, a-getting that furniture in order!'

'I do so wish the room below was ceiled,' said Fancy as the dressing went on; 'we can hear all they say and do down there.'

'Hark! Who's that?' exclaimed a small pupil-teacher, who also assisted this morning to her great delight. She ran half-way down the stairs and peeped round the banister. 'O, you should, you should, you should!' she exclaimed, scrambling up to the room again.

'What?' said Fancy.

'See the bridesmaids! They've just a-come! 'Tis wonderful, really! 'tis wonderful how muslin can be brought to it. There, they don't look a bit like themselves, but like some very rich sisters o' theirs that nobody knew they had!'

'Make them come up to me, make them come up!' cried Fancy ecstatically; and the four damsels appointed, namely, Miss Susan Dewy, Miss Bessie Dewy, Miss Vashti Sniff, and Miss Mercy Onmey surged upstairs and floated along the passage.

'I wish Dick would come!' was again the burden of Fancy.

The same instant a small twig and flower from the creeper outside the door flew in at the open window, and a masculine voice said, 'Ready, Fancy dearest?'

'There he is, he is!' cried Fancy, tittering spasmodically and breathing as it were for the first time that morning.

The bridesmaids crowded to the window and turned their heads in the direction pointed out, at which motion eight earrings all swung as one: – not looking at Dick because they particularly wanted to see him, but with an important sense of their duty as obedient minister of the will of that apotheosised being – the Bride.

'He looks very taking!' said Miss Vashti Sniff, a young lady who blushed cream-colour and wore yellow bonnet-ribbons.

Dick was advancing to the door in a painfully new coat of shining cloth, primrose-coloured waistcoat, hat of the same painful style of newness, and with an extra quantity of whiskers shaved off his face and hair cut to an unwonted shortness in honour of the occasion.

'Now I'll run down,' said Fancy, looking at herself over her shoulder in the glass, and flitting off.

'O Dick!' she exclaimed, 'I am so glad you are come! I knew you would, of course, but I thought, O, if you shouldn't!'

'Not come, Fancy! Het or wet, blow or snow, here come I today! Why, what's possessing your little soul? You never used to mind such things a bit.'

'Ah, Mr Dick, I hadn't hoisted my colours and committed myself then!' said Fancy.

''Tis a pity I can't marry the whole five of ye!' said Dick, surveying them all round.

'Heh-heh-heh!' laughed the four bridesmaids, and Fancy privately touched Dick and smoothed him down behind his shoulder as if to assure herself that he was there in flesh and blood as her own property.

'Well, whoever would have thought such a thing?' said Dick, taking off his hat, sinking into a chair, and turning to the elder members of the company.

The latter arranged their eyes and lips to signify that in their opinion nobody could have thought such a thing, whatever it was.

'That my bees should ha' swarmed just then, of all times and seasons!' continued Dick, throwing a comprehensive glance like a net over the whole auditory. 'And 'tis a fine swarm, too: I haven't seen such a fine swarm for these ten years.'

'A' excellent sign,' said Mrs Penny, from the depths of experience. 'A' excellent sign.'

'I am glad everything seems so right,' said Fancy with a breath of relief.

'And so am I,' said the four bridesmaids with much sympathy.

'Well, bees can't be put off,' observed the inharmonious grandfather James. 'Marrying a woman is a thing you can do at any moment; but a swarm o' bees won't come for the asking.'

Dick fanned himself with his hat. 'I can't think,' he said thoughtfully, 'whatever 'twas I did to offend Mr Maybold, – a man I like so much, too. He rather took to me when he came first, and used to say he should like to see me married, and that he'd marry me, whether the young woman I chose lived in his parish or no. I just hinted to him of it when I put in the banns, but he didn't seem to take kindly to the notion now, and so I said no more. I wonder how it was.'

'I wonder!' said Fancy, looking into vacancy with those beautiful eyes of hers – too refined and beautiful for a tranter's wife; but, perhaps, not too good.

'Altered his mind, as folks will, I suppose,' said the tranter. 'Well, my sonnies, there'll be a good strong party looking at us today as we go along.'

'And the body of the church,' said Geoffrey, 'will be lined with females, and a row of young fellers' heads, as far down as the eyes, will be noticed just above the sills of the chancel-winders.'

'Ay, you've been through it twice,' said Reuben, 'and well mid know.'

'I can put up with it for once,' said Dick, 'or twice either, or a dozen times.'

'O Dick!' said Fancy reproachfully.

'Why, dear, that's nothing, – only just a bit of a flourish. You be as nervous as a cat today.'

'And then, of course, when 'tis all over,' continued the tranter, 'we shall march two and two round the parish.'

'Yes, sure,' said Mr Penny: 'two and two: every man hitched up to his woman, 'a b'lieve.'

'I never can make a show of myself in that way!' said Fancy, looking at Dick to ascertain if he could.

'I'm agreed to anything you and the company like, my dear!' said Mr Richard Dewy heartily.

'Why, we did when we were married, didn't we, Ann?' said the tranter; 'and so do everybody, my sonnies.'

'And so did we,' said Fancy's father.

'And so did Penny and I,' said Mrs Penny: 'I wore my best Bath clogs, I remember, and Penny was cross because it made me look so tall.'

'And so did father and mother,' said Miss Mercy Onmey.

'And I mean to, come next Christmas!' said Nat the groomsman vigorously, and looking towards the person of Miss Vashti Sniff.

'Respectable people don't nowadays,' said Fancy. 'Still, since poor mother did, I will.'

'Ay,' resumed the tranter, ''twas on a White Tuesday when I committed it. Mellstock Club walked the same day, and we new-married folk went a-gaying round the parish behind 'em. Everybody used to wear something white at Whitsuntide in them days. My sonnies, I've got the very white trousers that I wore, at home in box now. Ha'n't I, Ann?'

'You had till I cut 'em up for Jimmy,' said Mrs Dewy.

'And we ought, by rights, after doing this parish, to go round Higher and Lower Mellstock, and call at Viney's, and so work our way hither again across He'th,' said Mr Penny, recovering scent of the matter in hand. 'Dairyman Viney is a very respectable man, and so is Farmer Kex, and we ought to show ourselves to them.'

'True,' said the tranter, 'we ought to go round Mellstock to do the thing well. We shall form a very striking object walking along in rotation, good-now, neighbours?'

'That we shall: a proper pretty sight for the nation,' said Mrs Penny.

'Hullo!' said the tranter, suddenly catching sight of a singular human figure standing in the doorway, and wearing a long smock-frock of pillow-case cut and of snowy whiteness. 'Why, Leaf! whatever dost thou do here?'

'I've come to know if so be I can come to the wedding – hee-hee!' said Leaf in a voice of timidity.

'Now, Leaf,' said the tranter reproachfully, 'you know we don't want 'ee here today: we've got no room for 'ee, Leaf.'

'Thomas Leaf, Thomas Leaf, fie upon 'ee for prying!' said old William.

'I know I've got no head, but I thought, if I washed and put on a clane shirt and smock-frock, I might just call,' said Leaf, turning away disappointed and trembling.

'Poor feller!' said the tranter, turning to Geoffrey. 'Suppose we must let en come? His looks are rather against en, and he is terrible silly: but 'a have never been in jail, and 'a won't do no harm.'

Leaf looked with gratitude at the tranter for these praises, and then anxiously at Geoffrey, to see what effect they would have in helping his cause.

'Ay, let en come,' said Geoffrey decisively. 'Leaf, th'rt welcome, 'st know'; and Leaf accordingly remained.

They were now all ready for leaving the house, and began to form a procession in the following order: Fancy and her father, Dick and Susan Dewy, Nat Callcome and Vashti Sniff, Ted Waywood and Mercy Onmey, and Jimmy and Bessie Dewy. These formed the executive, and all appeared in strict wedding attire. Then came the tranter and Mrs Dewy, and last of all Mr and Mrs Penny; – the tranter conspicuous by his enormous gloves, size eleven and threequarter, which appeared at a distance like boxing gloves bleached and sat rather awkwardly upon his brown hands; this hall-mark of respectability having been set upon himself today (by Fancy's special request) for the first time in his life.

'The proper way is for the bridesmaids to walk together,' suggested Fancy.

'What? 'Twas always young man and young woman, arm in crook, in my time!' said Geoffrey, astounded.

'And in mine!' said the tranter.

'And in ours!' said Mr and Mrs Penny.

'Never heard o' such a thing as woman and woman!' said old William; who, with grandfather James and Mrs Day, was to stay at home.

'Whichever way you and the company like, my dear!' said Dick, who, being on the point of securing his right to Fancy, seemed willing to renounce all other rights in the world with the greatest pleasure. The decision was left to Fancy.

'Well, I think I'd rather have it the way mother had it,' she said, and the couples moved along under the trees, every man to his maid.

'Ah!' said grandfather James to grandfather William as they retired, 'I wonder which she thinks most about, Dick or her wedding raiment!'

'Well, 'tis their nature,' said grandfather William. 'Remember the words of the prophet Jeremiah: "Can a maid forget her ornaments, or a bride her attire?" '

Now among dark perpendicular firs, like the shafted columns of a cathedral; now through a hazel copse, matted with primroses and wild

490

hyacinths; now under broad beeches in bright young leaves they threaded their way into the high road over Yalbury Hill, which dipped at that point directly into the village of Geoffrey Day's parish; and in the space of a quarter of an hour Fancy found herself to be Mrs Richard Dewy, though, much to her surprise, feeling no other than Fancy Day still.

On the circuitous return walk through the lanes and fields, amid much chattering and laughter, especially when they came to stiles, Dick discerned a brown spot far up a turnip field.

'Why, tis' Enoch!' he said to Fancy. 'I thought I missed him at the house this morning. How is it he's left you?'

'He drank too much cider, and it got into his head, and they put him in Weatherbury stocks for it. Father was obliged to get somebody else for a day or two, and Enoch hasn't had anything to do with the woods since.'

'We might ask him to call down tonight. Stocks are nothing for once, considering 'tis our wedding day.' The bridal party was ordered to halt.

'Eno-o-o-o-ch!' cried Dick at the top of his voice.

'Y-a-a-a-a-as!' said Enoch from the distance.

'D'ye know who I be-e-e-e-e-e?'

'No-o-o-o-o-o-o!'

'Dick Dew-w-w-w-wy!'

'O-h-h-h-h-h!'

'Just a-ma-a-a-a-a-arried!'

'O-h-h-h-h-h!'

'This is my wife, Fa-a-a-a-a-ancy!' (holding her up to Enoch's view as if she had been a nosegay).

'O-h-h-h-h-h!'

'Will ye come across to the party to-ni-i-i-i-i-i-ight!'

'Ca-a-a-a-a-an't!'

'Why n-o-o-o-o-ot?'

'Don't work for the family no-o-o-o-ow!'

'Not nice of Master Enoch,' said Dick as they resumed their walk.

'You mustn't blame en,' said Geoffrey; 'the man's not hisself now; he's in his morning frame of mind. When he's had a gallon o' cider or ale, or a pint or two of mead, the man's well enough, and his manners be as good as anybody's in the kingdom.'

TWO

❧ Under the Greenwood Tree ❦

THE POINT IN YALBURY WOOD which abutted on the end of Geoffrey Day's premises was closed with an ancient tree, horizontally of enormous extent, though having no great pretensions to height. Many hundreds of birds had been born amidst the boughs of this single tree; tribes of rabbits and hares had nibbled at its bark from year to year; quaint tufts of fungi had sprung from the cavities of its forks; and countless families of moles and earthworms had crept about its roots. Beneath and beyond its shade spread a carefully-tended grass-plot, its purpose being to supply a healthy exercise-ground for young chickens and pheasants: the hens, their mothers, being enclosed in coops placed upon the same green flooring.

All these encumbrances were now removed, and as the afternoon advanced the guests gathered on the spot, where music, dancing, and the singing of songs went forward with great spirit throughout the evening. The propriety of every one was intense, by reason of the influence of Fancy, who, as an additional precaution in this direction had strictly charged her father and the tranter to carefully avoid saying 'thee' and 'thou' in their conversation, on the plea that those ancient words sounded so very humiliating to persons of newer taste; also that they were never to be seen drawing the back of the hand across the mouth after drinking – a local English custom of extraordinary antiquity, but stated by Fancy to be decidedly dying out among the better classes of society.

In addition to the local musicians present a man who had a thorough knowledge of the tambourine was invited from the village of Tantrum Clangley, – a place long celebrated for the skill of its inhabitants as performers on instruments of percussion. These important members of the assembly were relegated to a height of two or three feet from the ground, upon a temporary erection of planks supported by barrels. Whilst the dancing progressed the older persons sat in a group under the trunk of the tree, – the space being allotted to them somewhat grudgingly by the young ones, who were greedy of pirouetting room, – and fortified by a table against the heels of the dancers. Here the gaffers and gammers whose dancing days were over told stories of great impressiveness, and at intervals surveyed the advancing and retiring

492

couples from the same retreat, as people on shore might be supposed to survey a naval engagement in the bay beyond; returning again to their tales when the pause was over. Those of the whirling throng who, during the rests between each figure, turned their eyes in the direction of these seated ones, were only to discover, on account of the music and bustle, that a very striking circumstance was in course of narration – denoted by an emphatic sweep of the hand, snapping of the fingers, close of the lips, and fixed look into the centre of the listener's eye for the space of a quarter of a minute, which raised in that listener such a reciprocating working of face as to sometimes make the distant dancers half wish to know what such an interesting tale could refer to.

Fancy caused her looks to wear as much matronly expression as was obtainable out of six hours' experience as a wife, in order that the contrast between her own state of life and that of the unmarried young women present might be duly impressed upon the company: occasionally stealing glances of admiration at her left hand, but this quite privately; for her ostensible bearing concerning the matter was intended to show that, though she undoubtedly occupied the most wondrous position in the eyes of the world that had ever been attained, she was almost unconscious of the circumstances, and that the somewhat prominent position in which that wonderfully-emblazoned left hand was continually found to be placed when handing cups and saucers, knives, forks, and glasses, was quite the result of accident. As to wishing to excite envy in the bosoms of her maiden companions by the exhibition of the shining ring, every one was to know it was quite foreign to the dignity of such an experienced married woman. Dick's imagination in the meantime was far less capable of drawing so much wontedness from his new condition. He had been for two or three hours trying to feel himself merely a newly-married man, but had been able to get no further in the attempt than to realize that he was Dick Dewy, the tranter's son, at a party given by Lord Wessex's head man-in-charge, on the outlying Yalbury estate, dancing and chatting with Fancy Day.

Five country dances, including 'Haste to the Wedding', two reels, and three fragments of hornpipes, brought them to the time for supper which, on account of the dampness of the grass from the immaturity of the summer season, was spread indoors. At the conclusion of the meal Dick went out to put the horse in; and Fancy, with the elder half of the four bridesmaids, retired upstairs to dress for the journey to Dick's new cottage near Mellstock.

'How long will you be putting on your bonnet, Fancy?' Dick inquired at the foot of the staircase. Being now a man of business and married he was strong on the importance of time, and doubled the emphasis of his words in conversing, and added vigour to his nods.

'Only a minute.'

'How long is that?'

'Well, dear, five.'

'Ah, sonnies!' said the tranter, as Dick retired, ''tis a talent of the female race that low numbers should stand for high, more especially in matters of waiting, matters of age, and matters of money.'

'True, true, upon my body,' said Geoffrey.

'Ye spak with feeling, Geoffrey, seemingly.'

'Anybody that d'know my experience might guess that.'

'What's she doing now, Geoffrey?'

'Claning out all the upstairs drawers and cupboards, and dusting the second-best chainey – a thing that's only done once a year. "If there's work to be done I must do it," says she, "wedding or no." '

''Tis my belief she's a very good woman at bottom.'

'She's terrible deep, then.'

Mrs Penny turned round. 'Well, 'tis humps and hollers with the best of us; but still and for all that, Dick and Fancy stand as fair a chance of having a bit of sunsheen as any married pair in the land.'

'Ay, there's no gainsaying it.'

Mrs Dewy came up, talking to one person and looking at another. 'Happy, yes,' she said. ''Tis always so when a couple is so exactly in tune with one another as Dick and she.'

'When they be'n't too poor to have time to sing,' said grandfather James.

'I tell ye, neighbours, when the pinch comes,' said the tranter: 'when the oldest daughter's boots be only a size less than her mother's, and the rest o' the flock close behind her. A sharp time for a man that, my sonnies; a very sharp time! Chanticleer's comb is a-cut then, 'a believe.'

'That's about the form o't,' said Mr Penny. 'That'll put the stuns upon a man, when you must measure mother and daughters' lasts to tell 'em apart.'

'You've no cause to complain, Reuben, of such a close-coming flock,' said Mrs Dewy; 'for ours was a straggling lot enough, God knows!'

'I d'know it, I d'know it,' said the tranter. 'You be a well-enough woman, Ann.'

Mrs Dewy put her mouth in the form of a smile and put it back again without smiling.

'And if they come together, they go together,' said Mrs Penny, whose family had been the reverse of the tranter's; 'and a little money will make either fate tolerable. And money can be made by our young couple, I know.'

'Yes, that it can!' said the impulsive voice of Leaf, who had hitherto humbly admired the proceedings from a corner. 'It can be done – all that's wanted is a few pounds to begin with. That's all! I know a story about it!'

'Let's hear thy story, Leaf,' said the tranter. 'I never knew you were clever enough to tell a story. Silence, all of ye! Mr Leaf will tell a story.'

'Tell your story, Thomas Leaf,' said grandfather William in the tone of a schoolmaster.

'Once,' said the delighted Leaf, in an uncertain voice, 'there was a man who lived in a house! Well, this man went thinking and thinking night and day. At last, he said to himself, as I might. "If I had only ten pound, I'd make a fortune." At last by hook or by crook, behold he got the ten pounds!'

'Only think of that!' said Nat Callcome satirically.

'Silence!' said the tranter.

'Well, now comes the interesting part of the story! In a little time he made that ten pounds twenty. Then a little time after that he doubled it, and made it forty. Well, he went on, and a good while after that he made it eighty, and on to a hundred. Well, by-and-by he made it two hundred! Well, you'd never believe it, but – he went on and made it four hundred! He went on, and what did he do? Why, he made it eight hundred! Yes, he did,' continued Leaf in the highest pitch of excitement, bringing down his fist upon his knee with such force that he quivered with the pain; 'yes, and he went on and made it A THOUSAND!'

'Hear, hear!' said the tranter. 'Better than the history of England, my sonnies!'

'Thank you for your story, Thomas Leaf,' said grandfather William; and then Leaf gradually sank into nothingness again.

Amid a medley of laughter, old shoes, and elderwine, Dick and his bride took their departure side by side in the excellent new spring-cart which the young tranter now possessed. The moon was just over the full, rendering any light from lamps or their own beauties quite unnecessary to the pair. They drove slowly along Yalbury Bottom, where the road passed between two copses. Dick was talking to his companion.

'Fancy,' he said, 'why we are so happy is because there is such full confidence between us. Ever since that time you confessed to that little flirtation with Shiner by the river (which was really no flirtation at all), I have thought how artless and good you must be to tell me o' such a trifling thing, and to be so frightened about it as you were. It has won me to tell you my every deed and word since then. We'll have no secrets from each other, darling, will we ever? – no secret at all.'

'None from today,' said Fancy. 'Hark! what's that?'

From a neighbouring thicket was suddenly heard to issue in a loud, musical, and liquid voice –

'Tippiwit! swe-e-et! ki-ki-ki! Come hither, come hither, come hither!'

'O, 'tis the nightingale,' murmured she, and thought of a secret she would never tell.

THE WELL-BELOVED

A SKETCH OF A TEMPERAMENT

'One shape of many names.' – P. B. SHELLEY.

Preface

THE PENINSULA CARVED BY TIME out of a single stone, whereon most of the following scenes are laid, was for centuries immemorial the home of a curious and well-nigh distinct people, cherishing strange beliefs and singular customs, now for the most part obsolescent. Fancies, like certain soft-wooded plants which cannot bear the silent inland frosts, but thrive by the sea in the roughest of weather, seem to grow up naturally here, in particular amongst those natives who have no active concern in the labours of the 'Isle.' Hence it is a spot apt to generate a type of personage like the character imperfectly sketched in these pages – a native of natives – whom some may choose to call a fantast (if they honour him with their consideration so far), but whom others may see only as one that gave objective continuity and a name to a delicate dream which in a vaguer form is more or less common to all men, and is by no means new to Platonic philosophers.

To those who know the rocky coign of England here depicted – overlooking the great Channel Highway with all its suggestiveness, and standing out so far into mid-sea that touches of the Gulf Stream soften the air till February – it is matter of surprise that the place has not been more frequently chosen as the retreat of artists and poets in search of inspiration – for at least a month or two in the year, the tempestuous rather than the fine seasons by preference. To be sure, one nook therein is the retreat, at their country's expense, of other geniuses from a distance; but their presence is hardly discoverable. Yet perhaps it is as well that the artistic visitors do not come, or no more would be heard of little freehold houses being bought and sold there for a couple of hundred pounds – built of solid stone, and dating from the sixteenth century and earlier, with mullions, copings, and corbels complete. These transactions, by the way, are carried out and covenanted, or were till lately, in the parish church, in the face of the congregation, such being the ancient custom of the Isle.

As for the story itself, it may be worth while to remark that, differing from all or most others of the series in that the interest aimed at is of an ideal or subjective nature, and frankly imaginative, verisimilitude in the sequence of events has been subordinated to the said aim.

The first publication of this tale in an independent form was in 1897; but it had appeared in the periodical press in 1892, under the title of 'The Pursuit of the Well-Beloved.' A few chapters of that experimental issue were rewritten for the present and final form of the narrative.

T. H.

August 1912.

PART FIRST

A Young man of Twenty

– 'Now, if Time knows
That Her, whose radiant brows
Weave them a garland of my vows;

Her that dares be
What these lines wish to see:
I seek no further, it is She.'

R. CRASHAW.

❧ A Supposititious Presentment ❧ of her

A PERSON WHO DIFFERED FROM the local wayfarers was climbing the steep road which leads through the sea-skirted townlet definable as the Street of Wells, and forms a pass into that Gibraltar of Wessex, the singular peninsula once an island, and still called such, that stretches out like the head of a bird into the English Channel. It is connected with the mainland by a long thin neck of pebbles 'cast up by rages of the se,' and unparalleled in its kind in Europe.

The pedestrian was what he looked like – a young man from London and the cities of the Continent. Nobody could see at present that his urbanism sat upon him only as a garment. He was just recollecting with something of self-reproach that a whole three years and eight months had flown since he paid his last visit to his father at this lonely rock of his birthplace, the intervening time having been spent amid many contrasting societies, peoples, manners, and scenes.

What had seemed usual in the isle when he lived there always looked quaint and odd after his later impressions. More than ever the spot seemed what it was said once to have been, the ancient Vindilia Island, and the Home of the Slingers. The towering rock, the houses above houses, one man's doorstep rising behind his neighbour's chimney, the gardens hung up by one edge to the sky, the vegetables growing on apparently almost vertical planes, the unity of the whole island as a solid and single block of limestone four miles long, were no longer familiar and commonplace ideas. All now stood dazzlingly unique and white against the tinted sea, and the sun flashed on infinitely stratified walls of oolite,

The melancholy ruins
Of cancelled cycles, . . .

with a distinctiveness that called the eyes to it as strongly as any spectacle he had beheld afar.

After a laborious clamber he reached the top, and walked along the plateau towards the eastern village. The time being about two o'clock, in the middle of the summer season, the road was glaring and dusty, and drawing near to his father's house he sat down in the sun.

He stretched out his hand upon the rock beside him. It felt warm. That was the island's personal temperature when in its afternoon sleep as now. He listened, and heard sounds: whirr-whirr, saw-saw-saw. Those were the island's snores – the noises of the quarrymen and stone-sawyers.

Opposite to the spot on which he sat was a roomy cottage or home-stead. Like the island it was all of stone, not only in walls but in window-frames, roof, chimneys, fence, stile, pigsty and stable, almost door.

He remembered who had used to live there – and probably lived there now – the Caro family; the 'roan-mare' Caros, as they were called to distinguish them from other branches of the same pedigree, there being but half-a-dozen christian and surnames in the whole island. He crossed the road and looked in at the open doorway. Yes, there they were still.

Mrs Caro, who had seen him from the window, met him in the entry, and an old-fashioned greeting took place between them. A moment after a door leading from the back rooms was thrown open, and a young girl about seventeen or eighteen came bounding in.

'Why, 'tis dear Joce!' she burst out joyfully. And running up to the young man she kissed him.

The demonstration was sweet enough from the owner of such an affectionate pair of bright hazel eyes and brown tresses of hair. But it was so sudden, so unexpected by a man fresh from towns, that he winced for a moment quite involuntarily; and there was some constraint in the manner in which he returned her kiss, and said, 'My pretty little Avice, how do you do after so long?'

For a few seconds her impulsive innocence hardly noticed his start of surprise; but Mrs Caro, the girl's mother, had observed it instantly. With a pained flush she turned to her daughter.

'Avice – my dear Avice! Why – what are you doing? Don't you know that you've grown up to be a woman since Jocelyn – Mr Pierston – was last down here? Of course you mustn't do now as you used to do three or four years ago!'

The awkwardness which had arisen was hardly removed by Pierston's assurance that he quite expected her to keep up the practice of her childhood, followed by several minutes of conversation on general sub-jects. He was vexed from his soul that his unaware movement should so have betrayed him. At his leaving he repeated that if Avice regarded him otherwise than as she used to do he would never forgive her; but though they parted good friends her regret at the incident was visible in her face. Jocelyn passed out into the road and onward to his father's house hard by. The mother and daughter were left alone.

'I was quite amazed at 'ee, my child!' exclaimed the elder. 'A young man from London and foreign cities, used now to the strictest company manners, and ladies who almost think it vulgar to smile broad! How could ye do it, Avice?'

'I – I didn't think about how I was altered!' said the conscience-stricken girl. 'I used to kiss him, and he used to kiss me before he went away.'

'But that was years ago, my dear!'

'O yes, and for the moment I forgot! He seemed just the same to me as he used to be.'

'Well, it can't be helped now. You must be careful in the future. He's got lots of young women, I'll warrant, and has few thoughts left for you. He's what they call a sculptor, and he means to be a great genius in that line some day, they do say.'

'Well, I've done it; and it can't be mended!' moaned the girl.

Meanwhile Jocelyn Pierston, the sculptor of budding fame, had gone onward to the house of his father, an inartistic man of trade and commerce merely, from whom, nevertheless, Jocelyn condescended to accept a yearly allowance pending the famous days to come. But the elder, having received no warning of his son's intended visit, was not at home to welcome him. Jocelyn looked round the familiar premises, glanced across the Common at the great yards within which eternal saws were going to and fro upon eternal blocks of stone – the very same saws and the very same blocks that he had seen there when last in the island, so it seemed to him – and then passed through the dwelling into the back garden.

Like all the gardens in the isle it was surrounded by a wall of dry-jointed spawls, and at its further extremity it ran out into a corner, which adjoined the garden of the Caros. He had no sooner reached this spot than he became aware of a murmuring and sobbing on the other side of the wall. The voice he recognized in a moment as Avice's, and she seemed to be confiding her trouble to some young friend of her own sex.

'O, what shall I *do*! what *shall* I do!' she was saying bitterly. 'So bold as it was – so shameless! How could I think of such a thing! He will never forgive me – never. Never like me again. He'll think me a forward hussy, and yet – and yet I quite forgot how much I had grown. But that he'll never believe!' The accents were those of one who had for the first time become conscious of her womanhood, as an unwonted possession which shamed and frightened her.

'Did he seem angry at it?' inquired the friend.

'O no – not angry! Worse. Cold and haughty. O, he's such a fashionable person now – not at all an island man. But there's no use in talking of it. I wish I was dead!'

Pierston retreated as quickly as he could. He grieved at the incident which had brought such pain to this innocent soul; and yet it was beginning to be a source of vague pleasure to him. He returned to the house, and when his father had come back and welcomed him, and they had shared a meal together, Jocelyn again when out, full of an earnest desire to soothe his young neighbour's sorrow in a way she little expected; though, to tell the truth, his affection for her was rather that of a friend than of a lover, and he felt by no means sure that the migratory, elusive idealization he called his Love who, ever since his boyhood, had flitted from human shell to human shell an indefinite number of times, was going to take up her abode in the body of Avice Caro.

TWO

❧ The Incarnation is Assumed ☙
to be True

IT WAS DIFFICULT TO MEET her again, even though on this lump of rock the difficulty lay as a rule rather in avoidance than in meeting. But Avice had been transformed into a very different kind of young woman by the self-consciousness engendered of her impulsive greeting, and, notwithstanding their near neighbourhood, he could not encounter her, try as he would. No sooner did he appear an inch beyond his father's door than she was to earth like a fox; she bolted upstairs to her room.

Anxious to soothe her after his unintentional slight he could not stand these evasions long. The manners of the isle were primitive and straightforward, even among the well-to-do, and noting her disappearance one day he followed her into the house and onward to the foot of the stairs.

'Avice!' he called.

'Yes, Mr Pierston.'

'Why do you run upstairs like that?'

'O – only because I wanted to come up for something.'

'Well, if you've got it, can't you come down again?'

'No, I can't very well.'

'Come, *dear* Avice. That's what you are, you know.'

There was no response.

'Well, if you won't, you won't!' he continued. 'I don't want to bother you.' And Pierston went away.

He was stopping to look at the old-fashioned flowers under the garden walls when he heard a voice behind him.

'Mr Pierston – I wasn't angry with you. When you were gone I thought – you might mistake me, and I felt I could do no less than come and assure you of my friendship still.'

Turning he saw the blushing Avice immediately behind him.

'You are a good, dear girl!' said he, and, seizing her hand, set upon her cheek the kind of kiss that should have been the response to hers on the day of his coming.

'Darling Avice, forgive me for the slight that day! Say you do. Come, now! And then I'll say to you what I have never said to any other woman, living or dead: "Will you have me as your husband?" '

'Ah! – mother says I am only one of many!'

'You are not, dear. You knew me when I was young, and others didn't.'

Somehow or other her objections were got over, and though she did not give an immediate assent, she agreed to meet him later in the afternoon, when she walked with him to the southern point of the island called the Beal, or, by strangers, the Bill, pausing over the treacherous cavern known as Cave Hole, into which the sea roared and splashed now as it had done when they visited it together as children. To steady herself while looking in he offered her his arm, and she took it, for the first time as a woman, for the hundredth time as his companion.

They rambled on to the lighthouse, where they would have lingered longer if Avice had not suddenly remembered an engagement to recite poetry from a platform that very evening at the Street of Wells, the village commanding the entrance to the island – the village that has now advanced to be a town.

'Recite!' said he. 'Who'd have thought anybody or anything could recite down here except the reciter we hear away there – the never speechless sea.'

'O but we are quite intellectual now. In the winter particularly. But, Jocelyn – don't come to the recitation, will you? It would spoil my performance if you were there, and I want to be as good as the rest.'

'I won't if you really wish me not to. But I shall meet you at the door and bring you home.'

'Yes!' she said, looking up into his face. Avice was perfectly happy now; she could never have believed on that mortifying day of his coming that she would be so happy with him. When they reached the east side of the isle they parted, that she might be soon enough to take her place on the platform. Pierston went home, and after dark, when it was about the hour for accompanying her back, he went along the middle road northward to the Street of Wells.

He was full of misgiving. He had known Avice Caro so well of old that his feeling for her now was rather comradeship than love; and what he had said to her in a moment of impulse that morning rather appalled him in its consequences. Not that any of the more sophisticated and accomplished women who had attracted him successively would be likely to rise inconveniently between them. For he had quite disabused his mind of the assumption that the idol of his fancy was an integral part of the personality in which it had sojourned for a long or a short while.

To his Well-Beloved he had always been faithful; but she had had many embodiments. Each individuality known as Lucy, Jane, Flora, Evangeline, or whatnot, had been merely a transient condition of her. He did not recognize this as an excuse or as a defence, but as a fact simply. Essentially she was perhaps of no tangible substance; a spirit, a dream, a frenzy, a conception, an aroma, an epitomized sex, a light of the eye, a parting of the lips. God only knew what she really was; Pierston did not. She was indescribable.

Never much considering that she was a subjective phenomenon vivified by the weird influences of his descent and birthplace, the discovery of her ghostliness, of her independence of physical laws and failings, had occasionally given him a sense of fear. He never knew where she next would be, whither she would lead him, having herself instant access to all ranks and classes, to every abode of men. Sometimes at night he dreamt that she was 'the wile-weaving Daughter of high Zeus' in person, bent on tormenting him for his sins against her beauty in his art – the implacable Aphrodite herself indeed. He knew that he loved the masquerading creature wherever he found her, whether with blue eyes, black eyes, or brown; whether presenting herself as tall, fragile, or plump. She was never in two places at once; but hitherto she had never been in one place long.

By making this clear to his mind some time before today, he had escaped a good deal of ugly self-reproach. It was simply that she who always attracted him, and led him whither she would as by a silken thread, had not remained the occupant of the same fleshly tabernacle in her career so far. Whether she would ultimately settle down to one he could not say.

Had he felt that she was becoming manifest in Avice, he would have tried to believe that this was the terminal spot of her migrations, and have been content to abide by his words. But did he see the Well-Beloved in Avice at all? The question was somewhat disturbing.

He had reached the brow of the hill, and descended towards the village, where in the long straight Roman street he soon found the lighted hall. The performance was not yet over; and by going round to the side of the building and standing on a mound he could see the interior as far down as the platform level. Avice's turn, or second turn, came on almost immediately. Her pretty embarrassment on facing the audience rather won him away from his doubts. She was, in truth, what is called a 'nice' girl; attractive, certainly, but above all things nice – one of the class with whom the risks of matrimony approximate most nearly to zero. Her intelligent eyes, her broad forehead, her thoughtful carriage, ensured one thing, that of all the girls he had known he had never met one with more charming and solid qualities than Avice Caro's. This was not a mere conjecture – he had known her long and thoroughly; her every mood and temper.

A heavy wagon passing without drowned her small soft voice for him; but the audience were pleased, and she blushed at their applause. He now took his station at the door, and when the people had done pouring out he found her within awaiting him.

They climbed homeward slowly by the Old Road, Pierston dragging himself up the steep by the wayside hand-rail and pulling Avice after him upon his arm. At the top they turned and stood still. To the left of them the sky was streaked like a fan with the lighthouse rays, and under their front, at periods of a quarter of a minute, there arose a deep, hollow stroke like the single beat of a drum, the intervals being filled with a long-drawn rattling, as of bones between huge canine jaws. It came from the vast concave of Deadman's Bay, rising and falling against the pebble dyke.

The evening and night winds here were, to Pierston's mind, charged with a something that did not burden them elsewhere. They brought it up from that sinister Bay to the west, whose movement she and he were hearing now. It was a presence – an imaginary shape or essence from the human multitude lying below: those who had gone down in vessels of war, East Indiamen, barges, brigs, and ships of the Armada – select people, common, and debased, whose interests and hopes had been as wide asunder as the poles, but who had rolled each other to oneness on that restless sea-bed. There could almost be felt the brush of their huge composite ghost as it ran a shapeless figure over the isle, shrieking for some good god who would disunite it again.

The twain wandered a long way that night amid these influences – so far as to the old Hope Churchyard, which lay in a ravine formed by a landslip ages ago. The church had slipped down with the rest of the cliff, and had long been a ruin. It seemed to say that in this last local stronghold of the Pagan divinities, where Pagan customs lingered yet, Christianity had established itself precariously at best. In that solemn spot Pierston kissed her.

The kiss was by no means on Avice's initiative this time. Her former demonstrativeness seemed to have increased her present reserve.

That day was the beginning of a pleasant month passed mainly in each other's society. He found that she could not only recite poetry at intellectual gatherings, but play the piano fairly, and sing to her own accompaniment.

He observed that every aim of those who had brought her up had been to get her away mentally as far as possible from her natural and individual life as an inhabitant of a peculiar island: to make her an exact copy of tens of thousands of other people, in whose circumstances there was nothing special, distinctive, or picturesque; to teach her to forget all the experiences of her ancestors; to drown the local ballads by songs purchased at the Budmouth fashionable music-sellers', and the local vocabulary by a governess-tongue of no country at all. She lived in a house that would have been the fortune of an artist, and learnt to draw London suburban villas from printed copies.

Avice had seen all this before he pointed it out, but, with a girl's tractability, had acquiesced. By constitution she was local to the bone, but she could not escape the tendency of the age.

The time for Jocelyn's departure drew near, and she looked forward to it sadly, but serenely, their engagement being now a settled thing. Pierston thought of the native custom on such occasions, which had prevailed in his and her family for centuries, both being of the old stock of the isle. The influx of 'kimberlins,' or 'foreigners' (as strangers from the mainland of Wessex were called), had led in a large measure to its discontinuance; but underneath the veneer of Avice's education many an old-fashioned idea lay slumbering, and he wondered if, in her natural melancholy at his leaving, she regretted the changing manners which made unpopular the formal ratification of a betrothal, according to the precedent of their sires and grandsires.

THREE

The Appointment

'WELL,' SAID HE, 'HERE WE are, arrived at the fag-end of my holiday. What a pleasant surprise my old home, which I have not thought worth coming to see for three or four years, had in store for me!'

'You must go to-morrow?' she asked uneasily.

'Yes.'

Something seemed to overweigh them; something more than the natural sadness of a parting which was not to be long; and he decided that instead of leaving in the daytime as he had intended, he would defer his departure till night, and go by the mail-train from Budmouth. This would give him time to look into his father's quarries, and enable her, if she chose, to walk with him along the beach as far as to Henry the Eighth's Castle above the sands, where they could linger and watch the moon rise over the sea. She said she thought she could come.

So after spending the next day with his father in the quarries Jocelyn prepared to leave, and at the time appointed set out from the stone house of his birth in this stone isle to walk to Budmouth-Regis by the path along the beach, Avice having some time earlier gone down to see some friends in the Street of Wells, which was halfway towards the spot of their tryst. The descent soon brought him to the pebble bank, and leaving behind him the last houses of the isle, and the ruins of the village destroyed by the November gale of 1824, he struck out along the narrow thread of land. When he had walked a hundred yards he stopped, turned aside to the pebble ridge which walled out the sea, and sat down to wait for her.

Between him and the lights of the ships riding at anchor in the roadstead two men passed slowly in the direction he intended to pursue. One of them recognized Jocelyn, and bade him good-night, adding, 'Wish you joy, sir, of your choice, and hope the wedden will be soon?'

'Thank you, Seaborn. Well – we shall see what Christmas will do towards bringing it about.'

'My wife opened upon it this mornen: "Please God, I'll up and see that there wedden," says she, "knowing 'em both from their crawling days." '

The men moved on, and when they were out of Pierston's hearing the one who had not spoken said to his friend, 'Who was that young kimberlin? He don't seem one o' we.'

'O, he is, though, every inch o' en. He's Mr Jocelyn Pierston, the stwone-merchant's only son up at East Quarriers. He's to be married to a stylish young body; her mother, a widow woman, carries on the same business as well as she can; but their trade is not a twentieth part of Pierston's. He's worth thousands and thousands, they say, though 'a do live on in the same wold way up in the same wold house. This son is doen great things in London as a' image-carver; and I can mind when, as a boy, 'a first took to carving soldiers out o' bits o' stwone from the softbed of his father's quarries; and then 'a made a set o' stwonen chessmen, and so 'a got on. He's quite the gent in London, they tell me; and the wonder is that 'a cared to come back here and pick up little Avice Caro – nice maid as she is notwithstanding ... Hullo! there's to be a change in the weather soon.'

Meanwhile the subject of their remarks waited at the appointed place till seven o'clock, the hour named between himself and his affianced, had struck. Almost at the moment he saw a figure coming forward from the last lamp at the bottom of the hill. But the figure speedily resolved itself into that of a boy, who, advancing to Jocelyn, inquired if he were Mr Pierston, and handed him a note.

FOUR

❦ A Lonely Pedestrian ❧

WHEN THE BOY HAD GONE Jocelyn retraced his steps to the last lamp, and read, in Avice's hand:

MY DEAREST – I shall be sorry if I grieve you at all in what I am going to say about our arrangement to meet tonight in the Sandsfoot ruin. But I have fancied that my seeing you again and again lately is inclining your father to insist, and you as his heir to feel, that we ought to carry out Island Custom in our courting – your people being such old inhabitants in an unbroken line. Truth to say, mother supposes that your father, for natural reasons, may have hinted to you that we ought. Now, the thing is contrary to my feelings: it is nearly left off; and I do not think it good, even where there is property, as in your case, to justify it, in a measure. I would rather trust in Providence.

On the whole, therefore, it is best that I should not come – if only for appearances – and meet you at a time and place suggesting the custom, to others than ourselves, at least, if known.

I am sure that this decision will not disturb you much; that you will understand my modern feelings, and think no worse of me for them. And dear, if it were to be done, and we were unfortunate in the result, we might both have enough old family feeling to think, like our forefathers, and possibly your father, that we could not marry honourably; and hence we might be made unhappy.

However, you will come again shortly, will you not, dear Jocelyn? –

512

and then the time will soon draw on when no more good-byes will be required. – Always and ever yours,

AVICE

Jocelyn, having read the letter, was surprised at the naïveté it showed, and at Avice and her mother's antiquated simplicity in supposing that to be still a grave and operating principle which was a bygone barbarism to himself and other absentees from the island. His father, as a money-maker, might have practical wishes on the matter of descendants which lent plausibility to the conjecture of Avice and her mother; but to Jocelyn he had never expressed himself in favour of the ancient ways, old-fashioned as he was.

Amused therefore at her regard of herself as modern, Jocelyn was disappointed, and a little vexed, that such an unforeseen reason should have deprived him of her company. How the old ideas survived under the new education!

The reader is asked to remember that the date, though recent in the history of the Isle of Slingers, was more than forty years ago.

Finding that the evening seemed louring, yet indisposed to go back and hire a vehicle, he went on quickly alone. In such an exposed spot the night wind was gusty, and the sea behind the pebble barrier kicked and flounced in complex rhythms, which could be translated equally well as shocks of battle or shouts of thanksgiving.

Presently on the pale road before him he discerned a figure, the figure of a woman. He remembered that a woman passed him while he was reading Avice's letter by the last lamp, and now he was overtaking her.

He did hope for a moment that it might be Avice, with a changed mind. But it was not she, nor anybody like her. It was a taller, squarer form than that of his betrothed, and although the season was only autumn she was wrapped in furs, or in thick and heavy clothing of some kind.

He soon advanced abreast of her, and could get glimpses of her profile against the roadstead lights. It was dignified, arresting, that of a very Juno. Nothing more classical had he ever seen. She walked at a swinging pace, yet with such ease and power that there was but little difference in their rate of speed for several minutes; and during this time he regarded and conjectured. However, he was about to pass her by when she suddenly turned and addressed him.

'Mr Pierston, I think, of East Quarriers?'

He assented, and could just discern what a handsome, commanding, imperious face it was – quite of a piece with the proud tones of her

513

voice. She was a new type altogether in his experience; and her accent was not so local as Avice's.

'Can you tell me the time, please?'

He looked at his watch by the aid of a light, and in telling her that it was a quarter past seven observed, by the momentary gleam of his match, that her eyes looked a little red and chafed, as if with weeping.

'Mr Pierston, will you forgive what will appear very strange to you, I dare say? That is, may I ask you to lend me some money for a day or two? I have been so foolish as to leave my purse on the dressing-table.'

It did appear strange: and yet there were features in the young lady's personality which assured him in a moment that she was not an impostor. He yielded to her request, and put his hand in his pocket. Here it remained for a moment. How much did she mean by the words 'some money'? The Junonian quality of her form and manner made him throw himself by an impulse into harmony with her, and he responded regally. He scented a romance. He handed her five pounds.

His munificence caused her no apparent surprise. 'It is quite enough, thank you,' she remarked quietly, as he announced the sum, lest she should be unable to see it for herself.

While overtaking and conversing with her he had not observed that the rising wind, which had proceeded from puffing to growling, and from growling to screeching, with the accustomed suddenness of its changes here, had at length brought what it promised by these vagaries – rain. The drops, which had at first hit their left cheeks like the pellets of a popgun, soon assumed the character of a raking fusillade from the bank adjoining, one shot of which was sufficiently smart to go through Jocelyn's sleeve. The tall girl turned, and seemed to be some-what concerned at an onset which she had plainly not foreseen before her starting.

'We must take shelter,' said Jocelyn.

'But where?' said she.

To windward was the long, monotonous bank, too obtusely piled to afford a screen, over which they could hear the canine crunching of pebbles by the sea without; on their right stretched the inner bay or roadstead, the distant riding-lights of the ships now dim and glimmer-ing; behind them a faint spark here and there in the lower sky showed where the island rose; before there was nothing definite, and could be nothing, till they reached a precarious wood bridge, a mile further on, Henry the Eighth's Castle being a little further still.

But just within the summit of the bank, whither it had apparently been hauled to be out of the way of the waves, was one of the local boats called lerrets, bottom upwards. As soon as they saw it the pair ran up the pebbly slope towards it by a simultaneous impulse. They then perceived that it had lain there a long time, and were comforted to find it capable of affording more protection than anybody would have expected from a distant view. It formed a shelter or store for the fishermen, the bottom of the lerret being tarred as a roof. By creeping under the bows, which overhung the bank on props to leeward, they made their way within, where, upon some thwarts, oars, and other fragmentary woodwork, lay a mass of dry netting – a whole seine. Upon this they scrambled and sat down, through inability to stand upright.

FIVE

♣ A Charge ♣

THE RAIN FELL UPON THE keel of the old lerret like corn thrown in handfuls by some colossal sower, and darkness set in to its full shade.

They crouched so close to each other that he could feel her furs against him. Neither had spoken since they left the roadway till she said, with attempted unconcern: 'This is unfortunate.'

He admitted that it was, and found, after a few further remarks had passed, that she certainly had been weeping, there being a suppressed gasp of passionateness in her utterance now and then.

'It is more unfortunate for you, perhaps, than for me,' he said, 'and I am very sorry that it should be so.'

She replied nothing to this, and he added that it was rather a desolate place for a woman, alone and afoot ... He hoped nothing serious had happened to drag her out at such an untoward time.

At first she seemed not at all disposed to show any candour on her own affairs, and he was left to conjecture as to her history and name, and how she could possibly have known him. But, as the rain gave not the least sign of cessation, he observed: 'I think we shall have to go back.'

'Never!' said she, and the firmness with which she closed her lips was audible in the word.

'Why not?' he inquired.

'There are good reasons.'

515

'I cannot understand how you should know me, while I have no knowledge of you.'

'O but you know me – about me, at least.'

'Indeed I don't. How should I? You are a kimberlin.'

'I am not. I am a real islander – or was, rather ... Haven't you heard of the Best-Bed Stone Company?'

'I should think so! They tried to ruin my father by getting away his trade – or, at least, the founder of the company did – old Bencomb.'

'He's my father!'

'Indeed. I am sorry I should have spoken so disrespectfully of him, for I never knew him personally. After making over his large business to the company, he retired, I believe, to London?'

'Yes. Our house, or rather his, not mine, is at South Kensington. We have lived there for years. But we have been tenants of Sylvania Castle, on the island here, this season. We took it for a month or two of the owner, who is away.'

'Then I have been staying quite near you, Miss Bencomb. My father's is a comparatively humble residence hard by.'

'But he could afford a much bigger one if he chose.'

'You have heard so? I don't know. He doesn't tell me much of his affairs.'

'My father,' she burst out suddenly, 'is always scolding me for my extravagance! And he has been doing it to-day more than ever. He said I go shopping in town to simply a diabolical extent, and exceed my allowance!'

'Was that this evening?'

'Yes. And then it reached such a storm of passion between us that I pretended to retire to my room for the rest of the evening, but I slipped out; and I am never going back home again.'

'What will you do?'

'I shall go first to my aunt in London; and if she won't have me, I'll work for a living. I have left my father for ever! What I should have done if I had not met you I cannot tell – I must have walked all the way to London, I suppose. Now I shall take the train as soon as I reach the mainland.'

'If you ever do in this hurricane.'

'I must sit here till it stops.'

And there on the nets they sat. Pierston knew of old Bencomb as his father's bitterest enemy, who had made a great fortune by swallowing up the small stone-merchants, but had found Jocelyn's sire a trifle too big to digest – the latter being, in fact, the chief rival of the Best-Bed Company to that day. Jocelyn thought it strange that he should be thrown by fate into a position to play the son of the Montagues to this daughter of the Capulets.

As they talked there was a mutual instinct to drop their voices, and on this account the roar of the storm necessitated their drawing quite close together. Something tender came into their tones as quarter-hour after quarter-hour went on, and they forgot the lapse of time. It was quite late when she started up, alarmed at her position.

'Rain or no rain, I can stay no longer,' she said.

'Do come back,' said he, taking her hand. 'I'll return with you. My train has gone.'

'No; I shall go on, and get a lodging in Budmouth town, if ever I reach it.'

'It is so late that there will be no house open, except a little place near the station where you won't care to stay. However, if you are determined I will show you the way. I cannot leave you. It would be too awkward for you to go there alone.'

She persisted, and they started through the twanging and spinning storm. The sea rolled and rose so high on their left, and was so near them on their right, that it seemed as if they were traversing its bottom like the Children of Israel. Nothing but the frail bank of pebbles divided them from the raging gulf without, and at every bang of the tide against it the ground shook, the shingle clashed, the spray rose vertically, and was blown over their heads. Quantities of sea-water trickled through the pebble wall, and ran in rivulets across their path to join the sea within. The 'Island' was an island still.

They had not realized the force of the elements till now. Pedestrians had often been blown into the sea hereabout, and drowned, owing to a sudden breach in the bank; which, however, had something of a supernatural power in being able to close up and join itself together again after such disruption, like Satan's form when, cut in two by the sword of Michael,

'The ethereal substance closed,
Not long divisible.'

Her clothing offered more resistance to the wind than his, and she was consequently in the greater danger. It was impossible to refuse his proffered aid. First he gave his arm, but the wind tore them apart as easily as coupled cherries. He steadied her bodily by encircling her waist with his arm; and she made no objection.

Somewhere about this time – it might have been sooner, it might have been later – he became conscious of a sensation which, in its incipient and unrecognized form, had lurked within him from some unnoticed moment when he was sitting close to his new friend under the lerret. Though a young man, he was too old a hand not to know what this was, and felt alarmed – even dismayed. It meant a possible migration of the Well-Beloved. The thing had not, however, taken place; and he went on thinking how soft and warm the lady was in her fur covering, as he held her so tightly; the only dry spots in the clothing of either being her left side and his right, where they excluded the rain by their mutual pressure.

As soon as they had crossed the ferry-bridge there was a little more shelter, but he did not relinquish his hold till she requested him. They passed the ruined castle, and having left the island far behind them trod mile after mile till they drew near to the outskirts of the neighbouring watering-place. Into it they plodded without pause, crossing the harbour bridge about midnight, wet to the skin.

He pitied her, and, while he wondered at it, admired her determination. The houses facing the bay now sheltered them completely, and they reached the vicinity of the new railway terminus (which the station was at this date) without difficulty. As he had said, there was only one house open hereabout, a little temperance inn, where the people stayed up for the arrival of the morning mail and passengers from the Channel boats. Their application for admission led to the withdrawal of a bolt, and they stood within the gaslight of the passage.

He could see now that though she was such a fine figure, quite as tall as himself, she was but in the bloom of young womanhood. Her face was certainly striking, though rather by its imperiousness than its beauty; and the beating of the wind and rain and spray had inflamed her cheeks to peony hues.

She persisted in the determination to go on to London by an early morning train, and he therefore offered advice on lesser matters only. 'In that case,' he said, 'you must go up to your room and send down your things, that they may be dried by the fire immediately, or they will not be ready. I will tell the servant to do this, and send you up something to eat.'

She assented to his proposal, without, however, showing any marks of gratitude; and when she had gone Pierston despatched her the light supper promised by the sleepy girl who was 'night porter' at this establishment. He felt ravenously hungry himself, and set about drying his clothes as well as he could, and eating at the same time.

At first he was in doubt what to do, but soon decided to stay where he was till the morrow. By the aid of some temporary wraps, and some slippers from the cupboard, he was contriving to make himself comfortable when the maid-servant came downstairs with a damp armful of woman's raiment.

Pierston withdrew from the fire. The maid-servant knelt down before the blaze and held up with extended arms one of the habiliments of the Juno upstairs, from which a cloud of steam began to rise. As she knelt, the girl nodded forward, recovered herself, and nodded again.

'You are sleepy, my girl,' said Pierston.

'Yes, sir; I have been up a long time. When nobody comes I lie down on the couch in the other room.'

'Then I'll relieve you of that; go and lie down in the other room, just as if we were not here. I'll dry the clothing and put the articles here in a heap, which you can take up to the young lady in the morning.'

The 'night porter' thanked him and left the room, and he soon heard her snoring from the adjoining apartment. Then Jocelyn opened proceedings, overhauling the robes and extending them one by one. As the steam went up he fell into a reverie. He again became conscious of the change which had been initiated during the walk. The Well-Beloved was moving house – had gone over to the wearer of this attire.

In the course of ten minutes he adored her.

And how about little Avice Caro? He did not think of her as before.

He was not sure that he had ever seen the real Beloved in that friend of his youth, solicitous as he was for her welfare. But, loving her or not, he perceived that the spirit, emanation, idealism, which called itself his Love was flitting stealthily from some remoter figure to the near one in the chamber overhead.

Avice had not kept her engagement to meet him in the lonely ruin, fearing her own imaginings. But he, in fact, more than she, had been educated out of the island innocence that had upheld old manners; and this was the strange consequence of Avice's misapprehension.

SIX

❧ On The Brink ❧

MISS BENCOMB WAS LEAVING THE hotel for the railway, which was quite near at hand, and had only recently been opened, as if on purpose for this event. At Jocelyn's suggestion she wrote a message to inform her father that she had gone to her aunt's, with a view to allaying anxiety and deterring pursuit. They walked together to the platform and bade each other goodbye; each obtained a ticket independently, and Jocelyn got his luggage from the cloakroom.

On the platform they encountered each other again, and there was a light in their glances at each other which said, as by a flash-telegraph: 'We are bound for the same town, why not enter the same compartment?'

They did.

She took a corner seat, with her back to the engine; he sat opposite. The guard looked in, thought they were lovers, and did not show other travellers into that compartment. They talked on strictly ordinary matters; what she thought he did not know, but at every stopping station he dreaded intrusion. Before they were halfway to London the event he had just begun to realize was a patent fact. The Beloved was again embodied; she filled every fibre and curve of this woman's form.

Drawing near the great London station was like drawing near Doomsday. How should he leave her in the turmoil of a crowded city street? She seemed quite unprepared for the rattle of the scene. He asked her where her aunt lived.

'Bayswater,' said Miss Bencomb.

He called a cab, and proposed that she should share it till they arrived at her aunt's, whose residence lay not much out of the way to his own. Try as he would he could not ascertain if she understood his feelings, but she assented to his offer and entered the vehicle.

'We are old friends,' he said, as they drove onward.

'Indeed, we are,' she answered, without smiling.

'But hereditarily we are mortal enemies, dear Juliet.'

'Yes – What did you say?'

'I said Juliet.'

She laughed in a half-proud way, and murmured: 'Your father is my father's enemy, and my father is mine. Yes, it is so.' And then their eyes caught each other's glance. 'My queenly darling!' he burst out; 'instead of going to your aunt's, will you come and marry me?'

A flush covered her over, which seemed akin to a flush of rage. It was not exactly that, but she was excited. She did not answer, and he feared he had mortally offended her dignity. Perhaps she had only made use of him as a convenient aid to her intentions. However, he went on –

'Your father would not be able to reclaim you, then? After all, this is not so precipitate as it seems. You know all about me, my history, my prospects. I know all about you. Our families have been neighbours on that isle for hundreds of years, though you are now such a London product.'

'Will you ever be a Royal Academician?' she asked musingly, her excitement having calmed down.

'I hope to be – I *will* be, if you will be my wife.'

His companion looked at him long.

'Think what a short way out of your difficulty this would be,' he continued. 'No bother about aunts, no fetching home by an angry father.'

It seemed to decide her. She yielded to his embrace.

'How long will it take to marry?' Miss Bencomb asked by-and-by, with obvious self-repression.

'We could do it to-morrow. I could get to Doctors' Commons by noon to-day, and the licence would be ready by to-morrow morning.'

'I won't go to my aunt's: I will be an independent woman! I have been reprimanded as if I were a child of six, I'll be your wife if it is as easy as you say.'

They stopped the cab while they held a consultation. Pierston had rooms and a studio in the neighbourhood of Campden Hill; but it would be hardly desirable to take her thither till they were married. They decided to go to an hotel.

Changing their direction, therefore, they went back to the Strand, and soon ensconced themselves in one of the venerable old taverns of Covent Garden, a precinct which in those days was frequented by West-country people. Jocelyn then left her and proceeded on his errand eastward.

It was about three o'clock when, having arranged all preliminaries necessitated by this sudden change of front, he began strolling slowly back; he felt bewildered, and to walk was a relief. Gazing occasionally into this shop window and that, he called a hansom as by an inspiration, and directed the driver to 'Mellstock Gardens.' Arrived here he rang the bell of a studio, and in a minute or two it was answered by a young man in shirt-sleeves, about his own age, with a great smeared palette on his left thumb.

'O, you, Pierston! I thought you were in the country. Come in. I'm awfully glad of this. I am here in town finishing off a painting for an American, who wants to take it back with him.'

Pierston followed his friend into the painting-room, where a pretty young woman was sitting sewing. At a signal from the painter she disappeared without speaking.

'I can see from your face you have something to say; so we'll have it all to ourselves. You are in some trouble? What'll you drink?'

'O! it doesn't matter what, so that it is alcohol in some shape or form . . . Now, Somers, you must just listen to me, for I *have* something to tell.'

Pierston had sat down in an arm-chair, and Somers had resumed his painting. When a servant had brought in brandy to soothe Pierston's nerves, and soda to take off the injurious effects of the brandy, and milk to take off the depleting effects of the soda, Jocelyn began his narrative, addressing it rather to Somers's Gothic chimney-piece, and Somers's

Gothic clock, and Somers's Gothic rugs, than to Somers himself, who stood at his picture a little behind his friend.

'Before I tell you what has happened to me,' Pierston said, 'I want to let you know the manner of man I am.'

'Lord – I know already.'

'No, you don't. It is a sort of thing one doesn't like to talk of. I lie awake at night thinking about it.'

'No!' said Somers, with more sympathy, seeing that his friend was really troubled.

'I am under a curious curse, or influence. I am posed, puzzled and perplexed by the legerdemain of a creature – a deity rather; by Aphrodite, as a poet would put it, as I should put it myself in marble ... But I forget – this is not to be a deprecatory wail, but a defence – a sort of *Apologia pro vitâ meâ*.'

'That's better. Fire away!'

SEVEN

❧ Her Earlier Incarnations ❧

'YOU, SOMERS, ARE NOT, I know, one of those who continue to indulge in the world-wide, fond superstition that the Beloved One of any man always, or even usually, cares to remain in one corporeal nook or shell for any great length of time, however much he may wish her to do so. If I am wrong, and you do still hold to that ancient error – well, my story will seem rather queer.'

'Suppose you say the Beloved of some men, not of any man.'

'All right – I'll say one man, this man only, if you are so particular. We are a strange, visionary race down where I come from, and perhaps that accounts for it. The Beloved of this one man, then, has had many incarnations – too many to describe in detail. Each shape, or embodiment, has been a temporary residence only, which she has entered, lived in awhile, and made her exit from, leaving the substance, so far as I have been concerned, a corpse, worse luck! Now, there is no spiritualistic nonsense in this – it is simple fact, put in the plain form that the conventional public are afraid of. So much for the principle.'

'Good. Go on.'

'Well; the first embodiment of her occurred, so nearly as I can recollect, when I was about the age of nine. Her vehicle was a little blue-eyed girl of eight or so, one of a family of eleven, with flaxen hair about her shoulders, which attempted to curl, but ignominiously failed, hanging like chimney-crooks only. This defect used rather to trouble me; and was, I believe, one of the main reasons of my Beloved's departure from that tenement. I cannot remember with any exactness when the departure occurred. I know it was after I had kissed my little friend in a garden-seat on a hot noontide, under a blue gingham umbrella, which we had opened over us as we sat, that passers through East Quarriers might not observe our marks of affection, forgetting that our screen must attract more attention than our persons.

'When the whole dream came to an end through her father leaving the island, I thought my Well-Beloved had gone for ever (being then in the unpractised condition of Adam at sight of the first sunset). But she had not. Laura had gone for ever, but not my Beloved.

'For some months after I had done crying for the flaxen-haired edition of her, my Love did not reappear. Then she came suddenly, unexpectedly, in a situation I should never have predicted. I was standing on the kerbstone of the pavement in Budmouth-Regis, outside the Preparatory School, looking across towards the sea, when a middle-aged gentleman on horseback, and beside him a young lady, also mounted, passed down the street. The girl turned her head, and – possibly because I was gaping at her in awkward admiration, or smiling myself – smiled at me. Having ridden a few paces, she looked round again and smiled.

'It was enough, more than enough, to set me on fire. I understood in a moment the information conveyed to me by my emotion – the Well-Beloved had reappeared. This second form in which it had pleased her to take up her abode was quite a grown young woman's, darker in complexion than the first. Her hair, also worn in a knot, was of an ordinary brown, and so, I think, were her eyes, but the niceties of her features were not to be gathered so cursorily. However, there sat my coveted one, re-embodied; and, bidding my schoolmates a hasty farewell as soon as I could do so without suspicion, I hurried along the Esplanade in the direction she and her father had ridden. But they had put their horses to a canter, and I could not see which way they had gone. In the greatest misery I turned down a side street, but was soon elevated to a state of excitement by seeing the same pair galloping towards me. Flushing up to my hair, I stopped and heroically faced her as she passed. She smiled again, but, alas! upon my Love's cheek there was no blush of passion for me.'

Pierston paused, and drank from his glass, as he lived for a brief moment in the scene he had conjured up. Somers reserved his comments, and Jocelyn continued –

'That afternoon I idled about the streets, looking for her in vain. When I next saw one of the boys who had been with me at her first passing I stealthily reminded him of the incident, and asked if he knew the riders.

' "O yes," he said. "That was Colonel Targe and his daughter Elsie."

' "How old do you think she is?" said I, a sense of disparity in our ages disturbing my mind.

' "O – nineteen, I think they say. She's going to be married the day after to-morrow to Captain Popp, of the 501st, and they are ordered off to India at once."

'The grief which I experienced at this intelligence was such that at dusk I went away to the edge of the harbour, intending to put an end to myself there and then. But I had been told that crabs had been found clinging to the dead faces of persons who had fallen in thereabout, leisurely eating them, and the idea of such an unpleasant contingency deterred me. I should state that the marriage of my Beloved concerned me little; it was her departure that broke my heart. I never saw her again.

'Though I had already learnt that the absence of the corporeal matter did not involve the absence of the informing spirit, I could scarce bring myself to believe that in this case it was possible for her to return to my view without the form she had last inhabited.

'But she did.

'It was not, however, till after a good space of time, during which I passed through that bearish age in boys, their middle teens, when girls are their especial contempt. I was about seventeen, and was sitting one evening over a cup of tea in a confectioner's at the very same watering-place, when opposite me a lady took her seat with a little girl. We looked at each other awhile, the child made advances, till I said: "She's a good little thing."

'The lady assented, and made a further remark.

' "She has the soft fine eyes of her mother," said I.

' "Do you think her eyes are good?" asks the lady, as if she had not heard what she had heard most – the last three words of my opinion.

' "Yes – for copies," said I, regarding her.

'After this we got on very well. She informed me that her husband had gone out in a yacht, and I said it was a pity he didn't take her with him for the airing. She gradually disclosed herself in the character of a deserted young wife, and later on I met her in the street without the child. She was going to the landing-stage to meet her husband, so she told me; but she did not know the way.

'I offered to show her, and did so. I will not go into particulars, but I afterwards saw her several times, and soon discovered that the Beloved (as to whose whereabouts I had been at fault so long) lurked here. Though why she had chosen this tantalizing situation of an inaccessible matron's form when so many others offered, it was beyond me to dis-cover. The whole affair ended innocently enough, when the lady left the town with her husband and child: she seemed to regard our acquaintance as a flirtation; yet it was anything but a flirtation for me!

'Why should I tell the rest of the tantalizing tale! After this, the Well-Beloved put herself in evidence with greater and greater frequency, and it would be impossible for me to give you details of her various incar-nations. She came nine times in the course of the two or three ensuing years. Four times she masqueraded as a brunette, twice as a pale-haired creature, and two or three times under a complexion neither light nor dark. Sometimes she was a tall, fine girl, but more often, I think, she preferred to slip into the skin of a lithe airy being, of no great stature. I grew so accustomed to these exits and entrances that I resigned myself to them quite passively, talked to her, kissed her, corresponded with her, ached for her, in each of her several guises. So it went on until a month ago. And then for the first time I was puzzled. She either had, or she had not, entered the person of Avice Caro, a young girl I had known from infancy. Upon the whole, I have decided that, after all, she did not enter the form of Avice Caro, because I retain so great a respect for her still.'

Pierston here gave in brief the history of his revived comradeship with Avice, the verge of the engagement to which they had reached, and its unexpected rupture by him, merely through this meeting with a woman into whom the Well-Beloved unmistakably moved under his very eyes – by name Miss Marcia Bencomb. He described their spontaneous decision to marry off-hand; and then he put it to Somers whether he ought to marry or not – her or anybody else – in such circumstances.

'Certainly not,' said Somers. 'Though, if anybody, little Avice. But not even her. You are like other men, only rather worse. Essentially, all men are fickle, like you; but not with such perceptiveness.'

'Surely fickle is not the word? Fickleness means getting weary of a thing while the thing remains the same. But I have always been faithful to the elusive creature whom I have never been able to get a firm hold of, unless I have done so now. And let me tell you that her flitting from each to each individual has been anything but a pleasure for me – certainly not a wanton game of my instigation. To see the creature who has hitherto been perfect, divine, lose under your very gaze the divinity which has informed her, grow commonplace, turn from flame to ashes, from a radiant vitality to a relic, is anything but a pleasure for any man, and has been nothing less than a racking spectacle to my sight. Each mournful emptied shape stands ever after like the nest of some beautiful bird from which the inhabitant has departed and left it to fill with snow.

I have been absolutely miserable when I have looked in a face for her I used to see there, and could see her there no more.'

'You ought not to marry,' repeated Somers.

'Perhaps I oughtn't to! Though poor Marcia will be compromised, I'm afraid, if I don't . . . Was I not right in saying I am accursed in this thing? Fortunately nobody but myself has suffered on account of it till now. Knowing what to expect, I have seldom ventured on a close acquaintance with any woman, in fear of prematurely driving away the dear one in her; who, however, has in time gone off just the same.'

Pierston soon after took his leave. A friend's advice on such a subject weighs little. He quickly returned to Miss Bencomb.

She was different now. Anxiety had visibly brought her down a notch or two, undone a few degrees of that haughty curl which her lip could occasionally assume. 'How long you have been away!' she said with a show of impatience.

'Never mind, darling. It is all arranged,' said he. 'We shall be able to marry in a few days.'

'Not to-morrow?'

'We can't to-morrow. We have not been here quite long enough.'

'But how did the people at Doctors' Commons know that?'

'Well – I forgot that residence, real or assumed, was necessary, and unfortunately admitted that we had only just arrived.'

'O how stupid! But it can't be helped now. I think, dear, I should have known better, however!'

EIGHT

❦ 'Too Like The Lightning' ❧

THEY LIVED ON AT THE hotel some days longer, eyed curiously by the chambermaids, and burst in upon every now and then by the waiters as if accidentally. When they were walking together, mostly in back streets for fear of being recognized, Marcia was often silent, and her imperious face looked gloomy.

'Dummy!' he said playfully, on one of these occasions.

'I am vexed that by your admissions at Doctors' Commons you prevented them giving you the licence at once! It is not nice, my living on with you like this!'

'But we are going to marry, dear!'

'Yes,' she murmured, and fell into reverie again. 'What a sudden resolve it was of ours!' she continued. 'I wish I could get my father and mother's consent to our marriage . . . As we can't complete it for another day or two, a letter might be sent to them and their answer received? I have a mind to write.'

Pierston expressed his doubts of the wisdom of this course, which seemed to make her desire it the more, and the result was a tiff between them. 'Since we are obliged to delay it, I won't marry without their consent!' she cried at last passionately.

'Very well then, dear. Write,' he said.

When they were again indoors she sat down to a note, but after a while threw aside her pen despairingly. 'No: I cannot do it!' she said. 'I can't bend my pride to such a job. Will *you* write for me, Jocelyn?'

'I? I don't see why I should be the one, particularly as I think it premature.'

'But you have not quarrelled with my father as I have done.'

'Well no. But there is a long-standing antagonism, which would make it odd in me to be the writer. Wait till we are married, and then I will write. Not till then.'

'Then I suppose I must. You don't know my father. He might forgive me marrying into any other family without his knowledge, but he thinks yours such a mean one, and so resents the trade rivalry, that he would never pardon till the day of his death my becoming a Pierston secretly. I didn't see it at first.'

This remark caused an unpleasant jar on the mind of Pierston. Despite his independent artistic position in London, he was staunch to the simple old parent who had stubbornly held out for so many years against Bencomb's encroaching trade, and whose money had educated and maintained Jocelyn as an art-student in the best schools. So he begged her to say no more about his mean family, and she silently resumed her letter, giving an address at a post-office that their quarters might not be discovered, at least just yet.

No reply came by return of post; but, rather ominously, some letters for Marcia that had arrived at her father's since her departure were sent on in silence to the address given. She opened them one by one, till on reading the last, she exclaimed, 'Good gracious!' and burst into laughter.

'What is it?' asked Pierston.

Marcia began to read the letter aloud. It came from a faithful lover of hers, a youthful Jersey gentleman, who stated that he was soon going to start for England to claim his darling, according to her plighted word.

She was half risible, half concerned. 'What shall I do?' she said.

'Do? My dear girl, it seems to me that there is only one thing to do, and that a very obvious thing. Tell him as soon as possible that you are just on the point of marriage.'

Marcia thereupon wrote out a reply to that effect, Jocelyn helping her to shape the phrases as gently as possible.

'I repeat' (her letter concluded) 'that I had quite forgotten! I am deeply sorry; but that is the truth. I have told my intended husband everything, and he is looking over my shoulder as I write.'

Said Jocelyn when he saw this set down: 'You might leave out the last few words. They are rather an extra stab for the poor boy.'

'Stab? It is not that, dear. Why does he want to come bothering me? Jocelyn, you ought to be very proud that I have put you in my letter at all. You said yesterday that I was conceited in declaring I might have married that science-man I told you of. But now you see there was yet another available.'

He, gloomily: 'Well, I don't care to hear about that. To my mind this sort of thing is decidedly unpleasant, though you treat it so lightly.'

'Well,' she pouted, 'I have only done half what you have done!'

'What's that?'

'I have only proved false through forgetfulness, but you have while remembering!'

'O yes; of course you can use Avice Caro as a retort. But don't vex me about her, and make me do such an unexpected thing as regret the falseness.'

She shut her mouth tight, and her face flushed.

The next morning there did come an answer to the letter asking her parents' consent to her union with him; but to Marcia's amazement her father took a line quite other than the one she had expected him to take. Whether she had compromised herself or whether she had not seemed a question for the future rather than the present with him, a native islander, born when old island marriage views prevailed in families; he was fixed in his disapproval of her marriage with a hated Pierston. He did not consent; he would not say more till he could see her: if she had any sense at all she would, if still unmarried, return to the home from which she had evidently been enticed. He would then see what he could do for her in the desperate circumstances she had made for herself; otherwise he would do nothing.

Pierston could not help being sarcastic at her father's evidently low estimate of him and his belongings; and Marcia took umbrage at his sarcasms.

'I am the one deserving of satire if anybody!' she said. 'I begin to feel I was a foolish girl to run away from a father for such a trumpery reason as a little scolding because I had exceeded my allowance.'

'I advised you to go back, Marcie.'

'In a sort of way: not in the right tone. You spoke most contemptuously of my father's honesty as a merchant.'

'I couldn't speak otherwise of him than I did, I'm afraid, knowing what – '

'What have you to say against him?'

'Nothing – to you, Marcie, beyond what is matter of common notoriety. Everybody knows that at one time he made it the business of his life to ruin my father; and the way he alludes to me in that letter shows that his enmity still continues.'

'That miser ruined by an open-handed man like my father!' said she. 'It is like your people's misrepresentations to say that!'

Marcia's eyes flashed, and her face burnt with an angry heat, the enhanced beauty which this warmth might have brought being killed by the rectilinear sternness of countenance that came therewith.

'Marcia – this temper is too exasperating! I could give you every step of the proceeding in detail – anybody could – the getting the quarries one by one, and everything, my father only holding his own by the most desperate courage. There is no blinking facts. Our parents' relations are an ugly fact in the circumstances of us two people who want to marry, and we are just beginning to perceive it; and how we are going to get over it I cannot tell.'

She said steadily: 'I don't think we shall get over it at all!'

'We may not – we may not – altogether,' Pierston murmured, as he gazed at the fine picture of scorn presented by his Juno's classical face and dark eyes.

'Unless you beg my pardon for having behaved so!'

Pierston could not quite bring himself to see that he had behaved badly to his too imperious lady, and declined to ask forgiveness for what he had not done.

She thereupon left the room. Later in the day she re-entered and broke a silence by saying bitterly: 'I showed temper just now, as you told me. But things have causes, and it is perhaps a mistake that you should have deserted Avice for me. Instead of wedding Rosaline, Romeo must needs go eloping with Juliet. It was a fortunate thing for the affections of those two Veronese lovers that they died when they did. In a short time the enmity of their families would have proved a fruitful source of dissension; Juliet would have gone back to her people, he to his; the subject would have split them as much as it splits us.'

Pierston laughed a little. But Marcia was painfully serious, as he found at tea-time, when she said that since his refusal to beg her pardon she had been thinking over the matter, and had resolved to go to her aunt's after all – at any rate till her father could be induced to agree to their union. Pierston was as chilled by this resolve of hers as he was surprised at her independence in circumstances which usually make women the reverse. But he put no obstacles in her way, and, with a kiss strangely cold after their recent ardour, the Romeo of the freestone Montagues went out of the hotel, to avoid even the appearance of coercing his Juliet of the rival house. When he returned she was gone.

A correspondence began between these too-hastily pledged ones; and it was carried on in terms of serious reasoning upon their awkward situation on account of the family feud. They saw their recent love as what it was:

'Too rash, too unadvised, too sudden;
Too like the lightning . . .

They saw it with an eye whose calmness, coldness, and, it must be added, wisdom, did not promise well for their reunion.

Their debates were clinched by a final letter from Marcia, sent from no other place than her recently left home in the Isle. She informed him that her father had appeared suddenly at her aunt's, and had induced her to go home with him. She had told her father all the circumstances of their elopement, and what mere accidents had caused it: he had persuaded her on what she had almost been convinced of by their disagreement; that all thought of their marriage should be at least postponed for the present; any awkwardness and even scandal being better than that they should immediately unite themselves for life on the strength of a two or three days' resultless passion, and be the wretched victims of a situation they could never change.

Pierston saw plainly enough that he owed it to her father being a born islander, with all the ancient island notions of matrimony lying underneath his acquired conventions, that the stone-merchant did not immediately insist upon the usual remedy for a daughter's precipitancy in such cases, but preferred to await issues.

But the young man still thought that Marcia herself, when her temper had quite cooled, and she was more conscious of her real position, would return to him, in spite of the family hostility. There was no social reason against such a step. In birth the pair were about on one plane; and though Marcia's family had gained a start in the accumulation of wealth, and in the beginnings of social distinction, which lent colour to the feeling that the advantages of the match would be mainly on one side, Pierston was a sculptor who might rise to fame; so that potentially their marriage could not be considered inauspicious for a woman who, beyond being the probable heiress to a considerable fortune, had no exceptional opportunities.

Thus, though disillusioned, he felt bound in honour to remain on call at his London address as long as there was the slightest chance of Marcia's reappearance, or of the arrival of some message requesting him to join her, that they might, after all, go to the altar together. Yet in the night he seemed to hear sardonic voices, and laughter in the wind at this development of his little romance, and during the slow and colourless days he had to sit and behold the mournful departure of his Well-Beloved from the form he had lately cherished, till she had almost vanished away. The exact moment of her complete withdrawal Pierston knew not, but not many lines of her were longer discernible in Marcia's remembered contours, nor many sounds of her in Marcia's recalled accents. Their acquaintance, though so fervid, had been too brief for such lingering.

There came a time when he learnt, through a trustworthy channel, two pieces of news affecting himself. One was the marriage of Avice Caro with her cousin, the other that the Bencombs had started on a tour round the world, which was to include a visit to a relation of Mr Bencomb's who was a banker in San Francisco. Since retiring from his former large business the stone-merchant had not known what to do with his leisure, and finding that travel benefited his health he had decided to indulge himself thus. Although he was not so informed, Pierston concluded that Marcia had discovered that nothing was likely to happen as a consequence of their elopement, and that she had accompanied her parents. He was more than ever struck with what this signified – her father's obstinate antagonism to her union with one of his blood and name.

NINE

❧ Familiar Phenomena In The ❧ Distance

BY DEGREES PIERSTON BEGAN TO trace again the customary lines of his existence; and his profession occupied him much as of old. The next year or two only once brought him tidings, through some residents at his former home, of the movements of the Bencombs. The extended voyage of Marcia's parents had given them quite a zest for other scenes and countries; and it was said that her father, a man still in vigorous health except at brief intervals, was utilizing the outlook which his cosmopolitanism afforded him by investing capital in foreign undertakings. What he had supposed turned out to be true; Marcia was with them; no necessity for joining him had arisen; and thus the separation of himself and his nearly married wife by common consent was likely to be a permanent one.

It seemed as if he would scarce ever again discover the carnate dwelling-place of the haunting minion of his imagination. Having gone so near to matrimony with Marcia as to apply for a licence, he had felt for a long while morally bound to her by the incipient contract, and would not intentionally look about him in search of the vanished Ideality. Thus during the first year of Miss Bencomb's absence, when absolutely bound to keep faith with the elusive one's late incarnation if she should return to claim him, this man of the odd fancy would sometimes tremble at the thought of what would become of his solemn intention if the Phantom were suddenly to disclose herself in an unexpected quarter, and seduce him before he was aware. Once or twice he imagined that he saw her in the distance – at the end of a street, on the far sands of a shore, in a window, in a meadow, at the opposite side of a railway station; but he determinedly turned on his heel, and walked the other way.

During the many uneventful seasons that followed Marcia's stroke of independence (for which he was not without a secret admiration at times), Jocelyn threw into plastic creations that ever-bubbling spring of emotion which, without some conduit into space, will surge upwards and ruin all but the greatest men. It was probably owing to this, certainly not on account of any care or anxiety for such a result, that he was successful in his art, successful by a seemingly sudden spurt, which carried him at one bound over the hindrances of years.

He prospered without effort. He was A.R.A.

But recognitions of this sort, social distinctions, which he had once coveted so keenly, seemed to have no utility for him now. By the accident of being a bachelor, he was floating in society without any soul-anchorage or shrine that he could call his own; and, for want of a domestic centre round which honours might crystallize, they dispersed impalpably without accumulating and adding weight to his material wellbeing.

He would have gone on working with his chisel with just as much zest if his creations had been doomed to meet no mortal eye but his own. This indifference to the popular reception of his dream-figures lent him a curious artistic *aplomb* that carried him through the gusts of opinion without suffering them to disturb his inherent bias.

The study of beauty was his only joy for years onward. In the streets he would observe a face, or a fraction of a face, which seemed to express to a hair's breadth in mutable flesh what he was at that moment wishing to express in durable shape. He would dodge and follow the owner like a detective; in omnibus, in cab, in steam-boat, through crowds, into shops, churches, theatres, public-houses, and slums – mostly, when at close quarters, to be disappointed for his pains.

In these professional beauty-chases he sometimes cast his eye across the Thames to the wharves on the south side, and to that particular one whereat his father's tons of freestone were daily landed from the ketches of the south coast. He could occasionally discern the white blocks lying there, vast cubes so persistently nibbled by his parent from his island rock in the English Channel that it seemed as if in time it would be nibbled all away.

One thing it passed him to understand: on what field of observation the poets and philosophers based their assumption that the passion of love was intensest in youth and burnt lower as maturity advanced. It was possibly because of his utter domestic loneliness that, during the productive interval which followed the first years of Marcia's departure, when he was drifting along from five-and-twenty to eight-and-thirty, Pierston occasionally loved with an ardour – though, it is true, also with a self-control – unknown to him when he was green in judgment.

His whimsical isle-bred fancy had grown to be such an emotion that the Well-Beloved – now again visible – was always existing somewhere near him. For months he would find her on the stage of a theatre: then she would flit away, leaving the poor, empty carcase that had lodged her to mumm on as best it could without her – a sorry lay figure to his eyes, heaped with imperfections and sullied with commonplace. She would reappear, it might be, in an at first unnoticed lady, met at some fashion-able evening-party, exhibition, bazaar, or dinner; to flit from her, in turn, after a few months, and stand as a graceful shop-girl at some large drapery warehouse into which he had strayed on an unaccustomed errand. Then she would forsake this figure and redisclose herself in the guise of some popular authoress, piano-player, or fiddleress, at whose shrine he would worship for perhaps a twelvemonth. Once she was a dancing-girl at the Royal Moorish Palace of Varieties, though during her whole continuance at that establishment he never once exchanged a word with her, nor did she first or last ever dream of his existence. He knew that a ten-minutes' conversation in the wings with the substance would send the elusive haunter scurrying fearfully away into some other even less accessible mask–figure.

She was a blonde, a brunette, tall, *petite*, *svelte*, straight-featured, full, curvilinear. Only one quality remained unalterable: her instability of tenure. In Börne's phrase, nothing was permanent in her but change.

'It is odd,' he said to himself, 'that this experience of mine, or idiosyncrasy, or whatever it is, which would be sheer waste of time for other men, creates sober business for me.' For all these dreams he translated into plaster, and found that by them he was hitting a public taste he had never deliberately aimed at, and mostly despised. He was, in short, in danger of drifting away from a solid artistic reputation to a popularity which might possibly be as brief as it would be brilliant and exciting.

'You will be caught some day, my friend,' Somers would occasionally observe to him. 'I don't mean to say entangled in anything discreditable, for I admit that you are in practice as ideal as in theory. I mean the process will be reversed. Some woman, whose Well-Beloved flits about as yours does now, will catch your eye, and you'll stick to her like a limpet, while she follows her Phantom and leaves you to ache as you will.'

'You may be right; but I think you are wrong,' said Pierston. 'As flesh she dies daily, like the Apostle's corporeal self; because when I grapple with the reality she's no longer in it, so that I cannot stick to one incarnation if I would.'

'Wait till you are older,' said Somers.

PART SECOND

A Young man of Forty

'Since Love will needs that I shall love,
Of very force I must agree:
And since no chance may it remove,
In wealth and in adversity
I shall alway myself apply
To serve and suffer patiently.'
                    SIR T. WYATT.

❧ The Old Phantom Becomes ❧ Distinct

IN THE COURSE OF THESE long years Pierston's artistic emotions were abruptly suspended by the news of his father's sudden death at Sandbourne, whither the stone-merchant had gone for a change of air by the advice of his physician.

Mr Pierston, senior, it must be admitted, had been something miserly in his home life, as Marcia had so rashly reminded his son. But he had never stinted Jocelyn. He had been rather a hard taskmaster, though as a paymaster trustworthy; a ready-money man, just and ungenerous. To everyone's surprise, the capital he had accumulated in the stone trade was of large amount for a business so unostentatiously carried on – much larger than Jocelyn had ever regarded as possible. While the son had been modelling and chipping his ephemeral fancies into perennial shapes, the father had been persistently chiselling for half a century at the crude original matter of those shapes, the stern, isolated rock in the Channel; and by the aid of his cranes and pulleys, his trolleys and his boats, had sent off his spoil to all parts of Great Britain. When Jocelyn had wound up everything and disposed of the business, as recommended by his father's will, he found himself enabled to add about eighty thousand pounds to the twelve thousand which he already possessed from professional and other sources.

After arranging for the sale of some freehold properties in the island other than quarries – for he did not intend to reside there – he returned to town. He often wondered what had become of Marcia. He had promised never to trouble her; nor for a whole twenty years had he done so; though he had often sighed for her as a friend of sterling common sense in practical difficulties.

Her parents were, he believed, dead; and she, he knew, had never gone back to the isle. Possibly she had formed some new tie abroad, and had made it next to impossible to discover her by her old name.

A reposeful time ensued. Almost his first entry into society after his father's death occurred one evening, when, for want of knowing what better to do, he responded to an invitation sent by one of the few ladies of rank whom he numbered among his friends, and set out in a cab for the square wherein she lived during three or four months of the year.

The hansom turned the corner, and he obtained a raking view of the houses along the north side, of which hers was one, with the familiar linkman at the door. There were Chinese lanterns, too, on the balcony. He perceived in a moment that the customary 'small and early' reception had resolved itself on this occasion into something very like great and late. He remembered that there had just been a political crisis, which accounted for the enlargement of the Countess of Channelcliffe's assembly; for hers was one of the neutral or non-political houses at which party politics are more freely agitated than at the professedly party gatherings.

There was such a string of carriages that Pierston did not wait to take his turn at the door, but unobtrusively alighted some yards off and walked forward. He had to pause a moment behind the wall of spectators which barred his way, and as he paused some ladies in white cloaks crossed from their carriages to the door on the carpet laid for the purpose. He had not seen their faces, nothing of them but vague forms, and yet he was suddenly seized with a presentiment. Its gist was that he might be going to re-encounter the Well-Beloved that night: after her recent long hiding she meant to reappear and intoxicate him. That liquid sparkle of her eye, that lingual music, that turn of the head, how well he knew it all, despite the many superficial changes, and how instantly he would recognize it under whatever complexion, contour, accent, height, or carriage that it might choose to masquerade!

Pierston's other conjecture, that the night was to be a lively political one, received confirmation as soon as he reached the hall, where a simmer of excitement was perceptible as surplus or overflow from above down the staircase – a feature which he had always noticed to be present when any climax or sensation had been reached in the world of party and faction.

'And where have you been keeping yourself so long, young man?' said his hostess archly, when he had shaken hands with her. (Pierston was always regarded as a young man, though he was now about forty.) 'O yes, of course, I remember,' she added, looking serious in a moment at thought of his loss. The Countess was a woman with a good-natured manner verging on that oft-claimed feminine quality, humour, and was quickly sympathetic.

She then began to tell him of a scandal in the political side to which she nominally belonged, one that had come out of the present crisis; and that, as for herself, she had sworn to abjure politics for ever on account of it, so that he was to regard her forthwith as a more neutral householder than ever. By this time some more people had surged upstairs, and Pierston prepared to move on.

'You are looking for somebody – I can see that,' said she.

'Yes – a lady,' said Pierston.

'Tell me her name, and I'll try to think if she's here.'

'I cannot; I don't know it,' he said.

'Indeed! What is she like!'

'I cannot describe her, not even her complexion or dress.'

Lady Channelcliffe looked a pout, as if she thought he were teasing her, and he moved on in the current. The fact was that, for a moment, Pierston fancied he had made the sensational discovery that the One he was in search of lurked in the person of the very hostess he had conversed with, who was charming always, and particularly charming to-night; he was just feeling an incipient consternation at the possibility of such a jade's trick in his Beloved, who had once before chosen to embody herself as a married woman, though, happily, at that time with no serious results. However, he felt that he had been mistaken, and that the fancy had been solely owing to the highly charged electric condition in which he had arrived by reason of his recent isolation.

The whole set of rooms formed one great utterance of the opinions of the hour. The gods of party were present with their embattled seraphim, but the brilliancy of manner and form in the handling of public questions was only less conspicuous than the paucity of original ideas. No principles of wise government had place in any mind, a blunt and jolly personalism as to the Ins and Outs animating all. But Jocelyn's interest did not run in this stream: he was like a stone in a purling brook, waiting for some peculiar floating object to be brought towards him and to stick upon his mental surface.

Thus looking for the next new version of the fair figure, he did not consider at the moment, though he had done so at other times, that this presentiment of meeting her was, of all presentiments, just the sort of one to work out its own fulfilment.

He looked for her in the knot of persons gathered round a past Prime Minister who was standing in the middle of the largest room discoursing in the genial, almost jovial, manner natural to him at these times. The two or three ladies forming his audience had been joined by another in black and white, and it was on her that Pierston's attention was directed, as well as the great statesman's, whose first sheer gaze at her, expressing 'Who are you?' almost audibly, changed into an interested, listening look as the few words she spoke were uttered – for the Minister differed from many of his standing in being extremely careful not to interrupt a timid speaker, giving way in an instant if anybody else began with him. Nobody knew better than himself that all may learn, and his manner was that of an unconceited man who could catch an idea readily, even if he could not undertake to create one.

The lady told her little story – whatever it was Jocelyn could not hear it – the statesman laughed: 'Haugh-haugh-haugh!'

The lady blushed. Jocelyn, wrought up to a high tension by the aforesaid presentiment that his Shelleyan 'One-shape-of-many-names' was about to reappear, paid little heed to the others, watching for a full view of the lady who had won his attention.

That lady remained for the present partially screened by her neighbours. A diversion was caused by Lady Channelcliffe bringing up somebody to present to the ex-Minister; the ladies got mixed, and Jocelyn lost sight of the one whom he was beginning to suspect as the stealthily returned absentee.

He looked for her in a kindly young lady of the house, his hostess's relation, who appeared to more advantage that night than she had ever done before – in a sky-blue dress, which had nothing between it and the fair skin of her neck, lending her an unusually soft and sylph-like aspect. She saw him, and they converged. Her look of 'What do you think of me *now*?' was suggested, he knew, by the thought that the last time they met she had appeared under the disadvantage of mourning clothes, on a wet day in a country-house, where everybody was cross.

'I have some new photographs, and I want you to tell me whether they are good,' she said. 'Mind you are to tell me truly, and no favour.'

She produced the pictures from an adjoining drawer, and they sat down together upon an ottoman for the purpose of examination. The portraits, taken by the last fashionable photographer, were very good, and he told her so; but as he spoke and compared them his mind was fixed on something else than the mere judgment. He wondered whether the elusive one were indeed in the frame of this girl.

He looked up at her. To his surprise, her mind, too, was on other things bent than on the pictures. Her eyes were glancing away to distant people, she was apparently considering the effect she was producing upon them by this cosy tête-à-tête with Pierston, and upon one in particular, a man of thirty, of military appearance, whom Pierston did not know. Quite convinced now that no phantom belonging to him was contained in the outlines of the present young lady, he could coolly survey her as he responded. They were both doing the same thing – each was pretending to be deeply interested in what the other was talking about, the attention of the two alike flitting away to other corners of the room even when the very point of their discourse was pending.

No, he had not seen Her yet. He was not going to see her, apparently, to-night; she was scared away by the twanging political atmosphere. But he still moved on searchingly, hardly heeding certain spectral imps other than Aphroditean, who always haunted these places, and jeeringly pointed out that under the white hair of this or that ribanded old man, with a forehead grown wrinkled over treaties which had swayed the fortunes of Europe, with a voice which had numbered sovereigns among its respectful listeners, might be a heart that would go inside a nut-shell; that beneath this or that white rope of pearl and pink bosom, might lie the half-lung which had, by hook or by crook, to sustain its possessor above-ground till the wedding-day.

At that moment he encountered his amiable host, and almost simultaneously caught sight of the lady who had at first attracted him and then had disappeared. Their eyes met, far off as they were from each other. Pierston laughed inwardly: it was only in ticklish excitement as to whether this was to prove a true *trouvaille*, and with no instinct to mirth; for when under the eyes of his Jill-o'-the-Wisp he was more inclined to palpitate like a sheep in a fair.

However, for the minute he had to converse with his host, Lord Channelcliffe, and almost the first thing that friend said to him was: 'Who is that pretty woman in the black dress with the white fluff about it and the pearl necklace?'

'I don't know,' said Jocelyn, with incipient jealousy: 'I was just going to ask the same thing.'

'O, we shall find out presently, I suppose. I daresay my wife knows.' They had parted, when a hand came upon his shoulder. Lord Channelcliffe had turned back for an instant: 'I find she is the granddaughter of my father's old friend, the last Lord Hengistbury. Her name is Mrs— Mrs Pine-Avon; she lost her husband two or three years ago, very shortly after their marriage.'

Lord Channelcliffe became absorbed into some adjoining dignitary of the Church, and Pierston was left to pursue his quest alone. A young friend of his – the Lady Mabella Buttermead, who appeared in a cloud of muslin and was going on to a ball – had been brought against him by the tide. A warm-hearted, emotional girl was Lady Mabella, who laughed at the humorousness of being alive. She asked him whither he was bent, and he told her.

'O yes, I know her very well!' said Lady Mabella eagerly. 'She told me one day that she particularly wished to meet you. Poor thing – so sad – she lost her husband. Well, it was a long time ago now, certainly. Women ought not to marry and lay themselves open to such catastrophes, ought they, Mr Pierston? *I* never shall. I am determined never to run such a risk! Now, do you think I shall?'

'Marry? O no; never,' said Pierston drily.

'That's very satisfying.' But Mabella was scarcely comfortable under his answer, even though jestingly returned, and she added: 'But sometimes I think I may, just for the fun of it. . . . Now we'll steer across to her, and catch her, and I'll introduce you. But we shall never get to her at this rate!'

'Never, unless we adopt "the ugly rush," like the citizens who follow the Lord Mayor's Show.'

They talked, and inched towards the desired one, who, as she discoursed with a neighbour, seemed to be of those –

'Female forms, whose gestures beam with mind,'

seen by the poet in his Vision of the Golden City of Islam.

Their progress was continually checked. Pierston was as he had sometimes seemed to be in a dream, unable to advance towards the object of pursuit unless he could have gathered up his feet into the air. After ten minutes given to a preoccupied regard of shoulderblades, back hair, glittering headgear, neck-napes, moles, hairpins, pearl-powder, pimples, minerals cut into facets of many-coloured rays, necklace-clasps, fans, stays, the seven styles of elbow and arm, the thirteen varieties of ear; and by using the toes of his dress-boots as coulters with which he ploughed his way and that of Lady Mabella in the direction they were aiming at, he drew near to Mrs Pine-Avon, who was drinking a cup of tea in the back drawing-room.

'My dear Nichola, we thought we should never get to you, because it is worse to-night, owing to these dreadful politics! But we've done it.' And she proceeded to tell her friend of Pierston's existence hard by.

It seemed that the widow really did wish to know him, and that Lady Mabella Buttermead had not indulged in one of the too frequent inventions in that kind. When the youngest of the trio had made the pair acquainted with each other she left them to talk to a younger man than the sculptor.

Mrs Pine-Avon's black velvets and silks, with their white accompaniments, finely set off the exceeding fairness of her neck and shoulders, which, though unwhitened artificially, were without a speck or blemish of the least degree. The gentle, thoughtful creature she had looked from a distance she now proved herself to be; she held also sound rather than current opinions on the plastic arts, and was the first intellectual woman he had seen there that night, except one or two as aforesaid.

They soon became well acquainted, and at a pause in their conversation noticed the fresh excitement caused by the arrival of some late comers with more news. The latter had been brought by a rippling, bright-eyed lady in black, who made the men listen to her, whether they would or no.

'I am glad I am an outsider,' said Jocelyn's acquaintance, now seated on a sofa beside which he was standing. 'I wouldn't be like my cousin, over there, for the world. She thinks her husband will be turned out at the next election, and she's quite wild.'

'Yes; it is mostly the women who are the gamesters; the men only the cards. The pity is that politics are looked on as being a game for politicians, just as cricket is a game for cricketers; not as the serious duties of political trustees.'

'How few of us ever think or feel that "the nation of every country dwells in the cottage," as somebody says!'

'Yes. Though I wonder to hear you quote that.'

'O – I am of no party, though my relations are. There can be only one best course at all times, and the wisdom of the nation should be directed to finding it, instead of zigzagging in two courses, according to the will of the party which happens to have the upper hand.'

Having started thus, they found no difficulty in agreeing on many points. When Pierston went downstairs from that assembly at a quarter to one, and passed under the steaming nostrils of an ambassador's horses to a hansom which waited for him against the railing of the square, he had an impression that the Beloved had re-emerged from the shadows, without any hint or initiative from him – to whom, indeed, such re-emergence was an unquestionably awkward thing.

In this he was aware, however, that though it might be now, as heretofore, the Loved who danced before him, it was the Goddess behind her who pulled the string of that Jumping Jill. He had lately been trying his artist hand again on the Dea's form in every conceivable phase and mood. He had become a one-part man – a presenter of her only. But his efforts had resulted in failures. In her implacable vanity she might be punishing him anew for presenting her so deplorably.

TWO

❧ She Draws Close And Satisfies ❧

HE COULD NOT FORGET MRS Pine-Avon's eyes, though he remembered nothing of her other facial details. They were round, inquiring, luminous. How that chestnut hair of hers had shone: it required no tiara to set it off, like that of the dowager he had seen there, who had put ten thousand pounds upon her head to make herself look worse than she would have appeared with the ninepenny muslin cap of a servant woman.

Now the question was, ought he to see her again? He had his doubts. But, unfortunately for discretion, just when he was coming out of the rooms he had encountered an old lady of seventy, his friend Mrs Brightwalton – the Honourable Mrs Brightwalton – and she had hastily asked him to dinner for the day after the morrow, stating in the honest way he knew so well that she had heard he was out of town, or she would have asked him two or three weeks ago. Now, of all social things that Pierston liked it was to be asked to dinner off-hand, as a stopgap in place of some bishop, earl, or Under-Secretary who couldn't come, and when the invitation was supplemented by the tidings that the lady who had so impressed him was to be one of the guests, he had promised instantly.

At the dinner he took down Mrs Pine-Avon upon his arm, and talked to nobody else during the meal. Afterwards they kept apart awhile in the drawing-room for form's sake; but eventually gravitated together again, and finished the evening in each other's company. When, shortly after eleven, he came away, he felt almost certain that within those luminous grey eyes the One of his eternal fidelity had verily taken lodgings – and for a long lease. But this was not all. At parting, he had, almost involuntarily, given her hand a pressure of a peculiar and indescribable kind; a little response from her, like a mere pulsation, of the same sort, told him that the impression she had made upon him was reciprocated. She was, in a word, willing to go on.

But was he able?

There had not been much harm in the flirtation thus far; but did she know his history, the curse upon his nature? – that he was the Wandering Jew of the love-world, how restlessly ideal his fancies were, how the artist in him had consumed the wooer, how he was in constant dread lest he should wrong some woman twice as good as himself by seeming to mean what he fain would mean but could not, how useless he was likely to be for practical steps towards householding, though he was all the while pining for domestic life. He was now over forty, she was probably thirty; and he dared not make unmeaning love with the careless selfishness of a younger man. It was unfair to go further without telling her, even though, hitherto, such explicitness had not been absolutely demanded.

He determined to call immediately on the New Incarnation.

She lived not far from the long, fashionable Hamptonshire Square, and he went thither with expectations of having a highly emotional time, at least. But somehow the very bell-pull seemed cold, although she had so earnestly asked him to come.

As the house spoke, so spoke the occupant, much to the astonishment of the sculptor. The doors he passed through seemed as if they had not been opened for a month; and, entering the large drawing-room, he beheld, in an armchair, in the far distance, a lady whom he journeyed across the carpet to reach, and ultimately did reach. To be sure it was Mrs Nichola Pine-Avon, but frosted over indescribably. Raising her eyes in a slightly inquiring manner from the book she was reading, she leant back in the chair, as if soaking herself in luxurious sensations which had nothing to do with him, and replied to his greeting with a few common-place words.

The unfortunate Jocelyn, though recuperative to a degree, was at first terribly upset by this reception. He had distinctly begun to love Nichola, and he felt sick and almost resentful. But happily his affection was incipient as yet, and a sudden sense of the ridiculous in his own position carried him to the verge of risibility during the scene. She signified a chair, and began the critical study of some rings she wore.

They talked over the day's news, and then an organ began to grind outside. The tune was a rollicking air he had heard at some music-hall; and, by way of a diversion, he asked her if she knew the composition.

'No, I don't!' she replied.

'Now, I'll tell you all about it,' said he gravely. 'It is based on a sound old melody called "The Jilt's Hornpipe." Just as they turn Madeira into port in the space of a single night, so this old air has been taken and doctored, and twisted about, and brought out as a new popular ditty.'

'Indeed!'

'If you are in the habit of going much to the music-halls or the bur-lesque theatres – '

'Yes?'

'You would find this is often done, with excellent effect.'

She thawed a little, and then they went on to talk about her house, which had been newly painted, and decorated with greenish-blue satin up to the height of a person's head – an arrangement that somewhat improved her slightly faded, though still pretty, face, and was helped by the awnings over the windows.

'Yes; I have had my house some years,' she observed complacently, 'and I like it better every year.'

'Don't you feel lonely in it sometimes?'

'O never!'

However, before he rose she grew friendly to some degree, and when he left, just after the arrival of three opportune young ladies, she seemed regretful. She asked him to come again; and he thought he would tell the truth. 'No: I shall not care to come again,' he answered, in a tone inaudible to the young ladies.

She followed him to the door. 'What an uncivil thing to say!' she murmured in surprise.

'It is rather uncivil. Good-bye,' said Pierston.

As a punishment she did not ring the bell, but left him to find his way out as he could. 'Now what the devil this means I cannot tell,' he said to himself, reflecting stock-still for a moment on the stairs. And yet the meaning was staring him in the face.

Meanwhile one of the three young ladies had said, 'What interesting man was that, with his lovely head of hair? I saw him at Lady Channel-cliffe's the other night.'

'Jocelyn Pierston.'

'O, Nichola, that *is* too bad! To let him go in that shabby way, when I would have given anything to know him! I have wanted to know him ever since I found out how much his experiences had dictated his statuary, and I discovered them by seeing in a Jersey paper of the marriage of a person supposed to be his wife, who ran off with him many years ago, don't you know, and then wouldn't marry him, in obedience to some novel social principles she had invented for herself.'

'O! didn't he marry her?' said Mrs Pine-Avon, with a start. 'Why, I heard only yesterday that he did, though they have lived apart ever since.'

'Quite a mistake,' said the young lady. 'How I wish I could run after him!'

But Jocelyn was receding from the pretty widow's house with long strides. He went out very little during the next few days, but about a week later he kept an engagement to dine with Lady Iris Speedwell, whom he never neglected, because she was the brightest hostess in London.

By some accident he arrived rather early. Lady Iris had left the drawing-room for a moment to see that all was right in the dining-room, and when he was shown in there stood alone in the lamplight Nichola Pine-Avon. She had been the first arrival. He had not in the least expected to meet her there, further than that, in a general sense, at Lady Iris's you expected to meet everybody.

She had just come out of the cloak-room, and was so tender and even apologetic that he had not the heart to be other than friendly. As the other guests dropped in, the pair retreated into a shady corner, and she talked beside him till all moved off for the eating and drinking.

He had not been appointed to take her across to the dining-room, but at the table found her exactly opposite. She looked very charming between the candles, and then suddenly it dawned upon him that her previous manner must have originated in some false report about Marcia, of whose existence he had not heard for years. Anyhow, he was not disposed to resent an inexplicability in womankind, having found that it usually arose independently of fact, reason, probability, or his own deserts.

So he dined on, catching her eyes and the few pretty words she made opportunity to project across the table to him now and then. He was courteously responsive only, but Mrs Pine-Avon herself distinctly made advances. He re-admired her, while at the same time her conduct in her own house had been enough to check his confidence – enough even to make him doubt if the Well-Beloved really resided within those contours, or had ever been more than the most transitory passenger through that interesting and accomplished soul.

He was pondering this question, yet growing decidedly moved by the playful pathos of her attitude when, by chance, searching his pocket for his handkerchief, something crackled, and he felt there an unopened letter, which had arrived at the moment he was leaving his house, and he had slipped into his coat to read in the cab as he drove along. Pierston drew it sufficiently forth to observe by the post-mark that it came from his natal isle. Having hardly a correspondent in that part of the world now he began to conjecture on the possible sender.

The lady on his right, whom he had brought in, was a leading actress of the town – indeed, of the United Kingdom and America, for that matter – a creature in airy clothing, translucent, like a balsam or sea-anemone, without shadows, and in movement as responsive as some highly lubricated, many-wired machine, which, if one presses a particular spring, flies open and reveals its works. The spring in the present case was the artistic commendation she deserved – and craved. At this particular moment she was engaged with the man on her own right, a representative of Family, who talked positively and hollowly, as if shouting down a vista of five hundred years from the Feudal past. The lady on Jocelyn's left, wife of a Lord Justice of Appeal, was in like manner talking to her companion on the outer side; so that, for the time, he was left to himself. He took advantage of the opportunity, drew out his letter, and read it as it lay upon his napkin, nobody observing him, so far as he was aware.

It came from the wife of one of his father's former workmen, and was concerning his son, whom she begged Jocelyn to recommend as candidate for some post in town that she wished him to fill. But the end of the letter was what arrested him –

You will be sorry to hear, Sir, that dear little Avice Caro, as we used to call her in her maiden days, is dead. She married her cousin, if you do mind, and went away from here for a good-few years, but was left a widow, and came back a twelvemonth ago; since when she faltered and faltered, and now she is gone.

547

THREE

❧ She Becomes an Inaccessible ☙ Ghost

BY IMPERCEPTIBLE AND SLOW DEGREES the scene at the dinner-table receded into the background, behind the vivid presentment of Avice Caro, and the old, old scenes on Isle Vindilia which were inseparable from her personality. The dining-room was real no more, dissolving under the bold stony promontory and the incoming West Sea. The handsome marchioness in geranium-red and diamonds, who was visible to him on his host's right hand opposite, became one of the glowing vermilion sunsets that he had watched so many times over Deadman's Bay, with the form of Avice in the foreground. Between his eyes and the judge who sat next to Nichola, with a chin so raw that he must have shaved every quarter of an hour during the day, intruded the face of Avice, as she had glanced at him in their last parting. The crannied features of the evergreen society lady, who, if she had been a few years older, would have been as old-fashioned as her daughter, shaped themselves to the dusty quarries of his and Avice's parents, down which he had clambered with Avice hundreds of times. The ivy trailing about the table-cloth, the lights in the tall candlesticks, and the bunches of flowers, were transmuted into the ivies of the cliff-built Castle, the tufts of seaweed, and the lighthouses on the isle. The salt airs of the ocean killed the smell of the viands, and instead of the clatter of voices came the monologue of the tide off the Beal.

More than all, Nichola Pine-Avon lost the blooming radiance which she had latterly acquired; she became a woman of his acquaintance with no distinctive traits; she seemed to grow material, a superficies of flesh and bone merely, a person of lines and surfaces; she was a language in living cipher no more.

When the ladies had withdrawn it was just the same. The soul of Avice – the only woman he had *never* loved of those who had loved him – surrounded him like a firmament. Art drew near to him in the person of one of the most distinguished of portrait painters; but there was only one painter for Jocelyn – his own memory. All that was eminent in European surgery addressed him in the person of that harmless and unassuming fogey whose hands had been inside the bodies of hundreds of living men; but the lily-white corpse of an obscure country-girl chilled the interest of discourse with such a king of operators.

Reaching the drawing-room he talked to his hostess. Though she had entertained three-and-twenty guests at her table that night she had known not only what every one of them was saying and doing throughout the repast, but what every one was thinking. So, being an old friend, she said quietly, 'What has been troubling you? Something has, I know. I have been travelling over your face and have seen it there.'

Nothing could less express the meaning his recent news had for him than a statement of its facts. He told of the opening of the letter and the discovery of the death of an old acquaintance.

The only woman whom I never rightly valued, I may almost say!' he added; 'and therefore the only one I shall ever regret!'

Whether she considered it a sufficient explanation or not the woman of experiences accepted it as such. She was the single lady of his circle whom nothing erratic in his doings could surprise, and he often gave her stray ends of his confidence thus with perfect safety.

He did not go near Mrs Pine-Avon again; he could not: and on leaving the house walked abstractedly along the streets till he found himself at his own door. In his room he sat down, and placing his hands behind his head thought his thoughts anew.

At one side of the room stood an escritoire, and from a lower drawer therein he took out a small box tightly nailed down. He forced the cover with the poker. The box contained a variety of odds and ends, which Pierston had thrown into it from time to time in past years for future sorting – an intention that he had never carried out. From the melancholy mass of papers, faded photographs, seals, diaries, withered flowers, and such like, Jocelyn drew a little portrait, one taken on glass in the primitive days of photography, and framed with tinsel in the commonest way.

It was Avice Caro, as she had appeared during the summer month or two which he had spent with her on the island twenty years before this time, her young lips pursed up, her hands meekly folded. The effect of the glass was to lend to the picture much of the softness characteristic of the original. He remembered when it was taken – during one afternoon they had spent together at a neighbouring watering-place, when he had suggested her sitting to a touting artist on the sands, there being nothing else for them to do. A long contemplation of the likeness completed in his emotions what the letter had begun. He loved the woman dead and inaccessible as he had never loved her in life. He had thought of her but at distant intervals during the twenty years since that parting occurred, and only as somebody he could have wedded. Yet now the times of youthful friendship with her, in which he had learnt every note of her innocent nature, flamed up into a yearning and passionate attachment, embittered by regret beyond words.

That kiss which had offended his dignity, which she had so childishly given him before her consciousness of womanhood had been awakened; what he would have offered to have a quarter of it now!

Pierston was almost angry with himself for his feelings of this night, so unreasonably, motivelessly strong were they towards the lost young playmate. 'How senseless of me!' he said, as he lay in his lonely bed. She had been another man's wife almost the whole time since he was estranged from her, and now she was a corpse. Yet the absurdity did not make his grief the less: and the consciousness of the intrinsic, almost radiant, purity of this new-sprung affection for a flown spirit forbade him to check it. The flesh was absent altogether; it was love rarefied and refined to its highest attar. He had felt nothing like it before.

The next afternoon he went down to the club; not his large club, where the men hardly spoke to each other, but the homely one where they told stories of an afternoon, and were not ashamed to confess among themselves to personal weaknesses and follies, knowing well that such secrets would go no further. But he could not tell this. So volatile and intangible was the story that to convey it in words would have been as hard as to cage a perfume.

They observed his altered manner, and said he was in love. Pierston admitted that he was; and there it ended. When he reached home he looked out of his bedroom window, and began to consider in what direction from where he stood that darling little figure lay. It was straight across there, under the young pale moon. The symbol signified well. The divinity of the silver bow was not more excellently pure than she, the lost, had been. Under that moon was the island of Ancient Slingers, and on the island a house, framed from mullions to chimney-top like the isle itself, of stone. Inside the window, the moonlight irradiating her winding-sheet, lay Avice, reached only by the faint noises inherent in the isle; the tink-tink of the chisels in the quarries, the surging of the tides in the Bay, and the muffled grumbling of the currents in the never-pacified Race.

He began to divine the truth. Avice, the departed one, though she had come short of inspiring a passion, had yet possessed a ground-quality absent from her rivals, without which it seemed that a fixed and full-rounded constancy to a woman could not flourish in him. Like his own, her family had been islanders for centuries – from Norman, Anglian, Roman, Balearic-British times. Hence in her nature, as in his, was some mysterious ingredient sucked from the isle; otherwise a racial instinct necessary to the absolute unison of a pair. Thus, though he might never love a woman of the island race, for lack in her of the desired refinement, he could not love long a kimberlin – a woman other than of the island race, for her lack of this groundwork of character.

Such was Pierston's view of things. Another fancy of his, an artist's superstition merely, may be mentioned. The Caros, like some other local families, suggested a Roman lineage, more or less grafted on the stock of the Slingers. Their features recalled those of the Italian peasantry to any one as familiar as he was with them; and there were evidences that the Roman colonists had been populous and long-abiding in and near this corner of Britain. Tradition urged that a temple to Venus once stood at the top of the Roman road leading up into the isle; and possibly one to the love-goddess of the Slingers antedated this. What so natural as that the true star of his soul would be found nowhere but in one of the old island breed?

After dinner his old friend Somers came in to smoke, and when they had talked a little while Somers alluded casually to some place at which they would meet on the morrow.

'I shan't be there,' said Pierston.

'But you promised?'

'Yes. But I shall be at the island – looking at a dead woman's grave.' As he spoke his eyes turned, and remained fixed on a table near. Somers followed the direction of his glance to a photograph on a stand.

'Is that she?' he asked.

'Yes.'

'Rather a bygone affair, then?'

Pierston acknowledged it. 'She's the only sweetheart I ever slighted, Alfred,' he said. 'Because she's the only one I ought to have cared for. That's just the fool I have always been.'

'But if she's dead and buried, you can go to her grave at any time as well as now, to keep up the sentiment.'

'I don't know that she's buried.'

'But to-morrow – the Academy night! Of all days why go then?'

'I don't care about the Academy.'

'Pierston – you are our only inspired sculptor. You are our Praxiteles, or rather our Lysippus. You are almost the only man of this generation who has been able to mould and chisel forms living enough to draw the idle public away from the popular paintings into the usually deserted Lecture-room, and people who have seen your last pieces of stuff say there has been nothing like them since sixteen hundred and – since the sculptors "of the great race" lived and died – whenever that was. Well, then, for the sake of others you ought not to rush off to that God-forgotten searock just when you are wanted in town, all for a woman you last a saw a hundred years ago.'

'No – it was only nineteen and three quarters,' replied his friend, with abstracted literalness. He went the next morning.

Since the days of his youth a railway had been constructed along the pebble bank, so that, except when the rails were washed away by the tides, which was rather often, the peninsula was quickly accessible. At two o'clock in the afternoon he was rattled along by this new means of locomotion, under the familiar monotonous line of bran-coloured stones, and he soon emerged from the station, which stood as a strange exotic among the black lerrets, the ruins of the washed–away village, and the white cubes of oolite, just come to view after burial through unreckonable geologic years.

In entering upon the pebble beach the train had passed close to the ruins of Henry the Eighth's or Sandsfoot Castle, whither Avice was to have accompanied him on the night of his departure. Had she appeared the primitive betrothal, with its natural result, would probably have taken place; and, as no islander had ever been known to break that compact, she would have become his wife.

Ascending the steep incline to where the quarrymen were chipping just as they had formerly done, and within sound of the great stone saws, he looked southward towards the Beal.

The level line of the sea horizon rose above the surface of the isle, a ruffled patch in mid-distance as usual marking the Race, whence many a Lycidas had gone

Visiting the bottom of the monstrous world';

but had not been blest with a poet as a friend. Against the stretch of water, where a school of mackerel twinkled in the afternoon light, was defined, in addition to the distant lighthouse, a church with its tower, standing about a quarter of a mile off, near the edge of the cliff. The churchyard gravestones could be seen in profile against the same vast spread of watery babble and unrest.

Among the graves moved the form of a man clothed in a white sheet, which the wind blew and flapped coldly every now and then. Near him moved six men bearing a long box, and two or three persons in black followed. The coffin, with its twelve legs, crawled across the isle, while around and beneath it the flashing lights from the sea and the school of mackerel were reflected; a fishing-boat, far out in the Channel, being momentarily discernible under the coffin also.

The procession wandered round to a particular corner, and halted, and paused there a long while in the wind, the sea behind them, the surplice of the priest still blowing. Jocelyn stood with his hat off: he was present, though he was a quarter of a mile off; and he seemed to hear the words that were being said, though nothing but the wind was audible.

He instinctively knew that it was none other than Avice whom he was seeing interred; *his* Avice, as he now began presumptuously to call her. Presently the little group withdrew from before the sea-shine, and disappeared.

He felt himself unable to go further in that direction, and turning aside went aimlessly across the open land, visiting the various spots that he had formerly visited with her. But, as if tethered to the churchyard by a cord, he was still conscious of being at the end of a radius whose pivot was the grave of Avice Caro; and as the dusk thickened he closed upon his centre and entered the churchyard gate.

Not a soul was now within the precincts. The grave, newly shaped, was easily discoverable behind the church, and when the same young moon arose which he had observed the previous evening from his window in London he could see the yet fresh footmarks of the mourners and bearers. The breeze had fallen to a calm with the setting of the sun: the lighthouse had opened its glaring eye, and, disinclined to leave a spot sublimed both by early association and present regret, he moved back to the church-wall, warm from the afternoon sun, and sat down upon a window-sill facing the grave.

FOUR

❧ She Threatens to Resume ❧ Corporeal Substance

THE LISPINGS OF THE SEA beneath the cliffs were all the sounds that reached him, for the quarries were silent now. How long he sat here lonely and thinking he did not know. Neither did he know, though he felt drowsy, whether inexpectant sadness – that gentle soporific – lulled him into a short sleep, so that he lost count of time and consciousness of incident. But during some minute or minutes he seemed to see Avice Caro herself, bending over and then withdrawing from her grave in the light of the moon.

She seemed not a year older, not a digit less slender, not a line more angular than when he had parted from her twenty years earlier, in the lane hard by. A renascent reasoning on the impossibility of such a phenomenon as this being more than a dream-fancy roused him with a start from his heaviness.

'I must have been asleep,' he said.

Yet she had seemed so real. Pierston however dismissed the strange impression, arguing that even if the information sent him of Avice's death should be false – a thing incredible – that sweet friend of his youth, despite the transfiguring effects of moonlight, would not now look the same as she had appeared nineteen or twenty years ago. Were what he saw substantial flesh, it must have been some other person than Avice Caro.

Having satisfied his sentiment by coming to the graveside there was nothing more for him to do in the island, and he decided to return to London that night. But some time remaining still on his hands Jocelyn by a natural instinct turned his feet in the direction of East Quarriers, the village of his birth and of hers. Passing the market-square he pursued the arm of road to 'Sylvania Castle,' a private mansion of comparativley modern date, in whose grounds stood the single plantation of trees of which the isle could boast. The cottages extended close to the walls of the enclosure, and one of the last of these dwellings had been Avice's, in which, as it was her freehold, she possibly had died.

To reach it he passed the gates of 'Sylvania,' and observed above the lawn wall a board announcing that the house was to be let furnished. A few steps further revealed the cottage which, with its quaint and massive stone features of two or three centuries' antiquity, was capable even now of longer resistance to the rasp of Time than ordinary new erections. His attention was drawn to the window, still unblinded, though a lamp lit the room. He stepped back against the wall opposite, and gazed in.

At a table covered with a white cloth a young woman stood putting tea-things away into a corner-cupboard. She was in all respects the Avice he had lost, the girl he had seen in the churchyard and had fancied to be the illusion of a dream. And though there was this time no doubt about her reality, the isolation of her position in the silent house lent her a curiously startling aspect. Divining the explanation he waited for footsteps, and in a few moments a quarryman passed him on his journey home. Pierston inquired of the man concerning the spectacle.

'O yes, sir; that's poor Mrs Caro's only daughter, and it must be lonely for her there to-night, poor maid! Yes, good-now; she's the very daps of her mother – that's what everybody says.'

'But how does she come to be so lonely?'

'One of her brothers went to sea and was drowned, and t'other is in America.'

'They were quarryowners at one time?'

The quarryman 'pitched his nitch,' and explained to the seeming stranger that there had been three families thereabouts in the stone trade, who had got much involved with each other in the last generation. They were the Bencombs, the Pierstons, and the Caros. The Bencombs strained their utmost to out-lift the other two, and partially succeeded. They grew enormously rich, sold out, and disappeared altogether from the island which had been their making. The Pierstons kept a dogged middle course, throve without show or noise, and also retired in their turn. The Caros were pulled completely down in the competition with the other two, and when Widow Caro's daughter married her cousin Jim Caro, he tried to regain for the family its original place in the three-cornered struggle. He took contracts at less than he could profit by, speculated more and more, till at last the crash came; he was sold up, went away, and later on came back to live in this little cottage, which was his wife's by inheritance. There he remained till his death; and now his widow was gone. Hardships had helped on her end.

The quarryman proceeded on his way, and Pierston, deeply remorseful, knocked at the door of the minute freehold. The girl herself opened it, lamp in hand.

'Avice!' he said tenderly; 'Avice Caro!' even now unable to get over the strange feeling that he was twenty years younger, addressing Avice the forsaken.

'Ann, sir,' said she.

'Ah, your name is not the same as your mother's!'

'My second name is. And my surname. Poor mother married her cousin.'

'As everybody does here . . . Well, Ann or otherwise, you are Avice to me. And you have lost her now?'

'I have, sir.'

She spoke in the very same sweet voice that he had listened to a score of years before, and bent eyes of the same familiar hazel inquiringly upon him.

'I knew your mother at one time,' he said; 'and learning of her death and burial I took the liberty of calling upon you. You will forgive a stranger doing that?'

'Yes,' she said dispassionately, and glancing round the room. 'This was mother's own house, and now it is mine. I am sorry not to be in mourning on the night of her funeral, but I have just been to put some flowers on her grave, and I took it off afore going that the damp mid not spoil the crape. You see, she was bad a long time, and I have to be careful, and do washing and ironing for a living. She hurt herside with wringing up the large sheets she had to wash for the Castle folks here.'

'I hope you won't hurt yourself doing it, my dear.'

'O no, that I shan't! There's Charl Woollat, and Sammy Scribben, and

Ted Gibsey, and lots o' young chaps; they'll wring anything for me if they happen to come along. But I can hardly trust 'em. Sam Scribben t'other day twisted a linen tablecloth into two pieces, for all the world as if it had been a pipe-light. They never know when to stop in their wringing.'

The voice truly was his Avice's; but Avice the Second was clearly more matter-of-fact, unreflecting, less cultivated than her mother had been. This Avice would never recite poetry from any platform, local or other, with enthusiastic appreciation of its fire. There was a disappointment in his recognition of this; yet she touched him as few had done: he could not bear to go away. 'How old are you?' he asked.

'Going in nineteen.'

It was about the age of her double, Avice the First, when he and she had strolled together over the cliffs during the engagement. But he was now forty, if a day. She before him was a uneducated laundress, and he was a sculptor and a Royal Academician, with a fortune and a reputation. Yet why was it an unpleasant sensation to him just then to recollect that he was two score?

He could find no further excuse for remaining, and having still half-an-hour to spare he went round by the road to the other or west side of the last-century 'Sylvania Castle,' and came to the furthest house out there on the cliff. It was his early home. Used in the summer as a lodging-house for visitors, it now stood empty and silent, the evening wind swaying the euonymus and tamarisk boughs in the front – the only evergreen shrubs that could weather the whipping salt gales which sped past the walls. Opposite the house, far out at sea, the familiar light-ship winked from the sandbank, and all at once there came to him a wild wish – that, instead of having an artist's reputation, he could be living here an illiterate and unknown man, wooing, and in a fair way of winning, the pretty laundress in the cottage hard by.

FIVE

❧ The Resumption Takes Place ❧

HAVING RETURNED TO LONDON HE mechanically resumed his customary life; but he was not really living there. The phantom of Avice, now grown to be warm flesh and blood, held his mind afar. He thought of nothing but the isle, and Avice the Second dwelling therein – inhaling its salt breath, stroked by its singing rains and by the haunted atmosphere of Roman Venus about and around the site of her perished temple there. The very defects in the country girl became charms as viewed from town.

Nothing now pleased him so much as to spend that portion of the afternoon which he devoted to out-door exercise, in haunting the purlieus of the wharves along the Thames, where the stone of his native rock was unshipped from the coasting-craft that had brought it thither. He would pass inside the great gates of these landing-places on the right or left bank, contemplate the white cubes and oblongs, imbibe their associations, call up the *genius loci* whence they came, and almost forget that he was in London.

One afternoon he was walking away from the mudsplashed entrance to one of the wharves, when his attention was drawn to a female form on the opposite side of the way, going towards the spot he had just left. She was somewhat small, slight, and graceful; her attire alone would have been enough to attract him, being simple and countrified to pictur-esqueness; but he was more than attracted by her strong resemblance to Avice Caro the younger – Ann Avice, as she had said she was called.

Before she had receded a hundred yards he felt certain that it was Avice indeed; and his unifying mood of the afternoon was now so intense that the lost and the found Avice seemed essentially the same person. Their external likeness to each other – probably owing to the cousinship between the elder and her husband – went far to nourish the fantasy. He hastily turned, and rediscovered the girl among the pedestrians. She kept on her way to the wharf, where, looking inquiringly around her for a few seconds, with the manner of one unaccustomed to the locality, she opened the gate and disappeared.

Pierston also went up to the gate and entered. She had crossed to the landing-place, beyond which a lumpy craft lay moored. Drawing nearer, he discovered her to be engaged in conversation with the skipper and an elderly woman – both come straight from the oolitic isle, as was apparent in a moment from their accent. Pierston felt no hesitation in making himself known as a native, the ruptured engagement between Avice's mother and himself twenty years before having been known to few or none now living.

The present embodiment of Avice recognized him, and with the artless candour of her race and years explained the situation, though that was rather his duty as an intruder than hers.

'This is Cap'n Kibbs, sir, a distant relation of father's,' she said. 'And this is Mrs Kibbs. We've come up from the island wi'en just for a trip, and are going to sail back wi'en Wednesday.'

'O, I see. And where are you staying?'

'Here – on board.'

'What, you live on board entirely?'

'Yes.'

'Lord, sir,' broke in Mrs Kibbs, 'I should be afeard o' my life to tine my eyes among these here kimberlins at night-time; and even by day, if so be I venture into the streets, I nowhen forget how many turnings to the right and to the left 'tis to get back to Job's vessel – do I, Job?'

The skipper nodded confirmation.

'You are safer ashore than afloat,' said Pierston, 'especially in the Channel, with these winds and those heavy blocks of stone.'

'Well,' said Cap'n Kibbs, after privately clearing something from his mouth, 'as to the winds, there idden much danger in them at this time o' year. 'Tis the oceanbound steamers that make the risk to craft like ours. If you happen to be in their course, under you go – cut clane in two pieces, and they never lying-to to haul in your carcases, and nobody to tell the tale.'

Pierston turned to Avice, wanting to say much to her, yet not knowing what to say. He lamely remarked at last: 'You go back the same way, Avice?'

'Yes, sir.'

'Well, take care of yourself afloat.'

'O yes.'

'I hope – I may see you again soon – and talk to you.'

'I hope so, sir.'

He could not get further, and after a while Pierston left them, and went away thinking of Avice more than ever.

The next day he mentally timed them down the river, allowing for the pause to take in ballast, and on the Wednesday pictured the sail down the open sea. That night he thought of the little craft under the bows of the huge steam-vessels, powerless to make itself seen or heard, and Avice, now growing inexpressibly dear, sleeping in her little berth at the mercy of a thousand chance catastrophes.

Honest perception had told him that this Avice, fairer than her mother in face and form, was her inferior in soul and understanding. Yet the fervour which the first could never kindle in him was, almost to his alarm, burning up now. He began to have misgivings as to some queer trick that his migratory Beloved was about to play him, or rather the capricious Divinity behind that ideal lady.

A gigantic satire upon the mutations of his nymph during the past twenty years seemed looming in the distance. A forsaking of the accomplished and well-connected Mrs Pine-Avon for the little laundress, under the traction of some mystic magnet which had nothing to do with reason – surely that was the form of the satire.

But it was recklessly pleasant to leave the suspicion unrecognized as yet, and follow the lead.

In thinking how best to do this Pierston recollected that, as was customary when the summer-time approached, Sylvania Castle had been advertised for letting furnished. A solitary dreamer like himself, whose wants all lay in an artistic and ideal direction, did not require such gaunt accommodation as the aforesaid residence offered; but the spot was all, and the expenses of a few months of tenancy therein he could well afford. A letter to the agent was dispatched that night, and in a few days Jocelyn found himself the temporary possessor of a place which he had never seen the inside of since his childhood, and had then deemed the abode of unpleasant ghosts.

SIX

❧ The Past Shines In The Present ❧

IT WAS THE EVENING OF Pierston's arrival at Sylvania Castle, a dignified manor-house in a nook by the cliffs, with modern castellations and battlements; and he had walked through the rooms, about the lawn, and into the surrounding plantation of elms, which on this island of treeless rock lent a unique character to the enclosure. In name, nature, and accessories the property within the girdling wall formed a complete antithesis to everything in its precincts. To find other trees between Pebble-bank and Beal, it was necessary to recede a little in time – to dig down to a loose stratum of the underlying stone-beds, where a forest of conifers lay as petrifactions, their heads all in one direction, as blown down by a gale in the Secondary geologic epoch.

Dusk had closed in, and he now proceeded with what was, after all, the real business of his sojourn. The two servants who had been left to take care of the house were in their own quarters, and he went out unobserved. Crossing a hollow overhung by the budding boughs he approached an empty garden-house of Elizabethan design, which stood on the outer wall of the grounds, and commanded by a window the fronts of the nearest cottages. Among them was the home of the resuscitated Avice.

He had chosen this moment for his outlook through knowing that the villagers were in no hurry to pull down their blinds at nightfall. And, as he had divined, the inside of the young woman's living-room was visible to him as formerly, illuminated by the rays of its own lamp.

A subdued thumping came every now and then from the apartment. She was ironing linen on a flannel table-cloth, a row of such apparel hanging on a clothes-horse by the fire. Her face had been pale when he encountered her, but now it was warm and pink with her exertions and the heat of the stove. Yet it was in perfect and passionless repose, which imparted a Minerva cast to the profile. When she glanced up, her lineaments seemed to have all the soul and heart that had characterized her mother's, and had been with her a true index of the spirit within. Could it be possible that in this case the manifestation was fictitious? He had met with many such examples of hereditary persistence without the qualities signified by the traits. He unconsciously hoped that it was at least not entirely so here.

The room was less furnished than when he had last beheld it. The 'bofet,' or double corner-cupboard, where the china was formerly kept, had disappeared, its place being taken by a plain board. The tall old clock, with its ancient oak carcase, arched brow, and humorous mouth, was also not to be seen, a cheap, white-dialled specimen doing its work. What these displacements might betoken saddened his humanity less than it cheered his primitive instinct in pointing out how her necessities might bring them together.

Having fixed his residence near her for some lengthy time he felt in no hurry to obtrude his presence just now, and went indoors. That this girl's frame was doomed to be a real embodiment of that olden seductive one – that Protean dream-creature, who had never seen fit to irradiate the mother's image till it became a mere memory after dissolution – he doubted less every moment.

There was an uneasiness in recognizing such. There was something abnormal in his present proclivity. A certain sanity had, after all, accompanied his former idealizing passions: the Beloved had seldom informed a personality which, while enrapturing his soul, simultaneously shocked his intellect. A change, perhaps, had come.

It was a fine morning on the morrow. Walking in the grounds towards the gate he saw Avice entering his hired castle with a broad oval wicker-basket covered with a white cloth, which burden she bore round to the back door. Of course, she washed for his own household: he had not thought of that. In the morning sunlight she appeared rather as a sylph than as a washerwoman; and he could not but think that the slightness of her figure was as ill adapted to this occupation as her mother's had been.

But, after all, it was not the washerwoman that he saw now. In front of her, on the surface of her, was shining out that more real, more inter-penetrating being whom he knew so well! The occupation of the subserving minion, the blemishes of the temporary creature who formed the background, were of the same account in the presentation of the indispensable one as the supporting posts and framework in a pyrotechnic display.

She left the house and went homeward by a path of which he was not aware, having probably changed her course because she had seen him standing there. It meant nothing, for she had hardly become acquainted with him; yet that she should have avoided him was a new experience. He had no opportunity for a further study of her by distant observation, and hit upon a pretext for bringing her face to face with him. He found fault with his linen, and directed that the laundress should be sent for.

'She is rather young, poor little thing,' said the housemaid apologetically. 'But since her mother's death she has enough to do to keep above water, and we make shift with her. But I'll tell her, sir.'

'I will see her myself. Send her in when she comes,' said Pierston.

One morning, accordingly, when he was answering a spiteful criticism of a late work of his, he was told that she waited his pleasure in the hall. He went out.

'About the washing,' said the sculptor stiffly. 'I am a very particular person, and I wish no preparation of lime to be used.'

'I didn't know folks used it,' replied the maiden, in a scared and reserved tone, without looking at him.

'That's all right. And then, the mangling smashes the buttons.'

'I haven't got a mangle, sir,' she murmured.

'Ah! that's satisfactory. And I object to so much borax in the starch.'

'I don't put any,' Avice returned in the same close way; 'never heard the name o't afore!'

'O I see.'

All this time Pierston was thinking of the girl – or as the scientific might say, Nature was working her plans for the next generation under the cloak of a dialogue on linen. He could not read her individual character, owing to the confusing effect of her likeness to a woman whom he had valued too late. He could not help seeing in her all that he knew of another, and veiling in her all that did not harmonize with his sense of metempsychosis.

The girl seemed to think of nothing but the business in hand. She had answered to the point, and was hardly aware of his sex or of his shape.

'I knew your mother, Avice,' he said. 'You remember my telling you so?'

'Yes.'

'Well – I have taken this house for two or three months, and you will be very useful to me. You still live just outside the wall?'

'Yes, sir,' said the self-contained girl.

Demurely and dispassionately she turned to leave – this pretty creature with features so still. There was something strange in seeing move off thus that form which he knew passing well, she who was once so throbbingly alive to his presence that, not many yards from this spot, she had flung her arms round him and given him a kiss which, despised in its freshness, had revived in him latterly as the dearest kiss of all his life. And now this 'daps' of her mother (as they called her in the dialect here), this perfect copy, why did she turn away?

'Your mother was a refined and well-informed woman, I think I remember?'

'She was, sir; everybody said so.'

'I hope you resemble her.'

She archly shook her head, and drew warily away.

'O! one thing more, Avice. I have not brought much linen, so you must come to the house every day.'

'Very good, sir.'

'You won't forget that?'

'O no.'

Then he let her go. He was a town man and she an artless islander, yet he had opened himself out like a sea-anemone, without disturbing the epiderm of her nature. It was monstrous that a maiden who had assumed the personality of her of his tenderest memory should be so impervious. Perhaps it was he who was wanting. Avice might be Passion masking as Indifference, because he was so many years older in outward show.

This brought him to the root of it. In his heart he was not a day older than when he had wooed the mother at the daughter's present age. His record moved on with the years, his sentiments stood still.

When he beheld those of his fellows who were defined as buffers and fogeys – imperturbable, matter-of-fact, slightly ridiculous beings, past masters in the art of populating homes, schools, and colleges, and present adepts in the science of giving away brides – how he envied them, assuming them to feel as they appeared to feel, with their commerce and their politics, their glasses and their pipes. They had got past the distracting currents of passionateness, and were in the calm waters of middle-aged philosophy. But he, their contemporary, was tossed like a cork hither and thither upon the crest of every fancy, precisely as he had been tossed when he was half his present age, with the burden now of double pain to himself in his growing vision of all as vanity.

Avice had gone, and he saw her no more that day. Since he could not again call upon her, she was as inaccessible as if she had entered the military citadel on the hill-top beyond them.

In the evening he went out and paced down the lane to the Red King's castle overhanging the cliff, beside whose age the castle he occupied was but a thing of yesterday. Below the castle precipice lay enormous blocks, which had fallen from it, and several of them were carved over with names and initials. He knew the spot and the old trick well and by searching in the faint moon-rays he found a pair of names which, as a boy, he himself had cut. They were 'AVICE' and 'JOCELYN' – Avice Caro's and his own. The letters were now nearly worn away by the weather and the brine. But close by, in quite fresh letters, stood 'ANN AVICE,' coupled with the name 'ISAAC.' They could not have been there more than two or three years, and the 'Ann Avice' was probably Avice the Second. Who was Isaac? Some boy admirer of her child-time doubtless.

He retraced his steps, and passed the Caros' house towards his own. The revivified Avice animated the dwelling, and the light within the room fell upon the window. She was just inside that blind.

Whenever she unexpectedly came to the castle he started, and lost placidity. It was not at her presence as such, but at the new condition, which seemed to have something sinister in it. On the other hand, the most abrupt encounter with him moved her to no emotion as it had moved her prototype in the old days. She was indifferent to, almost unconscious of, his propinquity. He was no more than a statue to her; she was a growing fire to him.

A sudden Sapphic terror of love would ever and anon come upon the sculptor, when his matured reflecting powers would insist upon informing him of the fearful lapse from reasonableness that lay in this infatuation. It threw him into a sweat. What if now, at last, he were doomed to do penance for his past emotional wanderings (in a material sense) by being chained in fatal fidelity to an object that his intellect despised? One night he dreamt that he saw dimly masking behind that young countenance 'the Weaver of Wiles' herself, 'with all her subtle face laughing aloud.'

However, the Well-Beloved was alive again; had been lost and was found. He was amazed at the change of front in himself. She had worn the guise of strange women; she had been a woman of every class, from the dignified daughter of some ecclesiastic or peer to a Nubian Almeh with her handkerchief, undulating to the beats of the tom-tom; but all these embodiments had been endowed with a certain smartness, either of the flesh or spirit: some with wit, a few with talent, and even genius. But the new impersonation had apparently nothing beyond sex and prettiness. She knew not how to sport a fan or handkerchief, hardly how to pull on a glove.

But her limited life was innocent, and that went far. Poor little Avice!

her mother's image: there it all lay. After all, her parentage was as good as his own; it was misfortune that had sent her down to this. Odd as it seemed to him, her limitations were largely what he loved her for. Her rejuvenating power over him had ineffable charm. He felt as he had felt when standing beside her predecessor; but, alas! he was twenty years further on towards the shade.

SEVEN

⬥ The New Becomes Established ⬥

A FEW MORNINGS LATER HE was looking through an upper back window over a screened part of the garden. The door beneath him opened, and a figure appeared tripping forth. She went round out of sight to where the gardener was at work, and presently returned with a bunch of green stuff fluttering in each hand. It was Avice, her dark hair now braided up snugly under a cap. She sailed on with a rapt and unconscious face, her thoughts a thousand removes from him.

How she had suddenly come to be an inmate of his own house he could not understand, till he recalled the fact that he had given the castle servants a whole holiday to attend a review of the yeomanry in the watering-place over the bay, on their stating that they could provide a temporary substitute to stay in the house. They had evidently called in Avice. To his great pleasure he discovered their opinion of his requirements to be such a mean one that they had called in no one else.

The Spirit, as she seemed to him, brought his lunch into the room where he was writing, and he beheld her uncover it. She went to the window to adjust a blind which had slipped, and he had a good view of her profile. It was not unlike that of one of the three goddesses in Rubens's 'Judgment of Paris,' and in contour was nigh perfection. But it was in her full face that the vision of her mother was most apparent.

'Did you cook all this, Avice?' he asked, arousing himself.

She turned and half-smiled, merely murmuring, 'Yes, sir.'

Well he knew the arrangement of those white teeth. In the junction of two of the upper ones there was a slight irregularity; no stranger would have noticed it, nor would he, but that he knew of the same mark in her mother's mouth, and looked for it here. Till Avice the Second had revealed it this moment by her smile, he had never beheld that mark since the parting from Avice the First, when she had smiled under his kiss as the copy had done now.

Next morning, when dressing, he heard her through the ricketty floor of the building engaged in conversation with the other servants. Having by this time regularly installed herself as the exponent of the Long-pursued – as one who, by no initiative of his own, had been chosen by some superior Power as the vehicle of her next début, she attracted him by the cadences of her voice; she would suddenly drop it to a rich whisper of roguishness, when the slight rural monotony of its narrative speech disappeared, and soul and heart – or what seemed soul and heart – resounded. The charm lay in the intervals, using that word in its musical sense. She would say a few syllables in one note, and end her sentence in a soft modulation upwards, then downwards, then into her own note again. The curve of sound was as artistic as any line of beauty ever struck by his pencil – as satisfying as the curves of her who was the World's Desire.

The subject of her discourse he cared nothing about – it was no more his interest than his concern. He took special pains that in catching her voice he might not comprehend her words. To the tones he had a right, none to the articulations. By degrees he could not exist long without this sound.

On Sunday evening he found that she went to church. He followed behind her over the open road, keeping his eye on the little hat with its bunch of cock's feathers as on a star. When she had passed in Pierston observed her position and took a seat behind her.

Engaged in the study of her ear and the nape of her white neck, he suddenly became aware of the presence of a lady still further ahead in the aisle, whose attire, though of black materials in the quietest form, was of a cut which rather suggested London than this *Ultima Thule*. For the minute he forgot, in his curiosity, that Avice intervened. The lady turned her head somewhat, and, though she was veiled with unusual thickness for the season, he seemed to recognize Nichola Pine-Avon in the form.

Why should Mrs Pine-Avon be there? Pierston asked himself, if it should, indeed, be she.

The end of the service saw his attention again concentrated on Avice to such a degree that at the critical moment of moving out he forgot the mysterious lady in front of her, and found that she had left the church by the side-door. Supposing it to have been Mrs Pine-Avon, she would probably be discovered staying at one of the hotels at the watering-place over the bay, and to have come along the Pebble-bank to the island as so many did, for an evening drive. For the present, however, the explanation was not forthcoming; and he did not seek it.

When he emerged from the church the great placid eye of the light-house at the Beal Point was open, and he moved thitherward a few steps to escape Nichola, or her double, and the rest of the congregation. Turning at length, he hastened homeward along the now deserted trackway, intending to overtake the revitalized Avice. But he could see nothing of her and concluded that she had walked too fast for him. Arrived at his own gate he paused a moment, and perceived that Avice's little freehold was still in darkness. She had not come.

He retraced his steps, but could not find her, the only persons on the road being a man and his wife, as he knew them to be though he could not see them, from the words of the man –

'If you had not a'ready married me, you'd cut my acquaintance! That's a pretty thing for a wife to say!'

The remark struck his ear unpleasantly, and by-and-by he went back again. Avice's cottage was now lighted: she must have come round by the other road. Satisfied that she was safely domiciled for the night he opened the gate of Sylvania Castle and retired to his room also.

Eastward from the grounds the cliffs were rugged and the view of the opposite coast picturesque in the extreme. A little door from the lawn gave him immediate access to the rocks and shore on this side. Without the door was a dip-well of pure water, which possibly had supplied the inmates of the adjoining and now ruinous Red King's castle at the time of its erection. On a sunny morning he was meditating here when he discerned a figure on the shore below spreading white linen upon the pebbly strand.

Jocelyn descended. Avice, as he had supposed, had now returned to her own occupation. Her shapely pink arms, though slight, were plump enough to show dimples at the elbows, and were set off by her purple cotton print, which the shore-breeze licked and tantalized. He stood near, without speaking. The wind dragged a shirt-sleeve from the 'popple' or pebble which held it down. Pierston stooped and put a heavier one in its place.

'Thank you,' she said quietly. She turned up her hazel eyes, and seemed gratified to perceive that her assistant was Pierston. She had plainly been so wrapped in her own thoughts – gloomy thoughts, by their signs – that she had not considered him till then.

The young girl continued to converse with him in friendly frankness, showing neither ardour nor shyness. As for love – it was evidently further from her mind than even death and dissolution.

When one of the sheets became intractable Jocelyn said, 'Do you hold it down, and I'll put the popples.'

She acquiesced, and in placing a pebble his hand touched hers.

It was a young hand, rather long and thin, a little damp and coddled from her slopping. In setting down the last stone he laid it, by a pure accident, rather heavily on her fingers.

'I am very, very sorry!' Jocelyn exclaimed. 'O, I have bruised the skin, Avice!' He seized her fingers to examine the damage done.

'No, sir, you haven't!' she cried luminously, allowing him to retain her hand without the least objection. 'Why – that's where I scratched it this morning with a pin. You didn't hurt me a bit with the popple-stone!'

Although her gown was purple, there was a little black crape bow upon each arm. He knew what it meant, and it saddened him. 'Do you ever visit your mother's grave?' he asked.

'Yes, sir, sometimes. I am going there to-night to water the daisies.'

She had now finished here, and they parted. That evening, when the sky was red, he emerged by the garden-door and passed her house. The blinds were not down, and he could see her sewing within. While he paused she sprang up as if she had forgotten the hour, and tossed on her hat. Jocelyn strode ahead and round the corner, and was halfway up the straggling street before he discerned her little figure behind him.

He hastened past the lads and young women with clinking buckets who were drawing water from the fountains by the wayside, and took the direction of the church. With the disappearance of the sun the light-house had again set up its flame against the sky, the dark church rising in the foreground. Here he allowed her to overtake him.

'You loved your mother much?' said Jocelyn.

'I did, sir; of course I did,' said the girl, who tripped so lightly that it seemed he might have carried her on his hand.

Pierston wished to say, 'So did I,' but did not like to disclose events which she, apparently, never guessed. Avice fell into thought, and continued –

'Mother had a very sad life for some time when she was about as old as I. I should not like mine to be as hers. Her young man proved false to her because she wouldn't agree to meet him one night, and it grieved mother almost all her life. I wouldn't ha' fretted about him, if I'd been she. She would never name his name, but I know he was a wicked, cruel man; and I hate to think of him.'

After this he could not go into the churchyard with her, and walked onward alone to the south of the isle. He was wretched for hours. Yet he would not have stood where he did stand in the ranks of an imaginative profession if he had not been at the mercy of every haunting of the fancy that can beset man. It was in his weaknesses as a citizen and a national-unit that his strength lay as an artist, and he felt it childish to complain of susceptibilities not only innate but cultivated.

But he was paying dearly enough for his Liliths. He saw a terrible vengeance ahead. What had he done to be tormented like this? The Beloved, after flitting from Nichola Pine-Avon to the phantom of a dead woman whom he never adored in her lifetime, had taken up her abode in the living representative of the dead, with a permanence of hold which the absolute indifference of that little brown-eyed representative only seemed to intensify.

Did he really wish to proceed to marriage with this chit of a girl? He did: the wish had come at last. It was true that as he studied her he saw defects in addition to her social insufficiencies. Judgment, hoodwinked as it was, told him that she was colder in nature, commoner in character, than that well-read, bright little woman Avice the First. But twenty years make a difference in ideals, and the added demands of middle-age in physical form are more than balanced by its concessions as to the spiritual content. He looked at himself in the glass, and felt glad at those inner deficiencies in Avice which formerly would have impelled him to reject her.

There was a strange difference in his regard of his present folly and of his love in his youthful time. Now he could be mad with method, knowing it to be madness: then he was compelled to make believe his madness wisdom. In those days any flash of reason upon his loved one's imperfections was blurred over hastily and with fear. Such penetrative vision now did not cool him. He knew he was the creature of a tendency; and passively acquiesced.

To use a practical eye, it appeared that, as he had once thought, this Caro family – though it might not for centuries, or ever, furbish up an individual nature which would exactly, ideally, supplement his own imperfect one and round with it the perfect whole – was yet the only family he had ever met, or was likely to meet, which possessed the materials for her making. It was as if the Caros had found the clay but not the potter, while other families whose daughters might attract him had found the potter but not the clay.

EIGHT

◆ His Own Soul Confronts Him ◆

FROM HIS ROOMY CASTLE AND its grounds and the cliffs hard by he could command every move and aspect of her who was the rejuvenated Spirit of the Past to him – in the effulgence of whom all sordid details were disregarded.

Among other things he observed that she was often anxious when it rained. If, after a wet day, a golden streak appeared in the sky over Deadman's Bay, under a lid of cloud, her manner was joyous and her tread light.

This puzzled him; and he found that if he endeavoured to encounter her at these times she shunned him – stealthily and subtly, but unmistakably. One evening, when she had left her cottage and tripped off in the direction of the under-hill townlet, he set out by the same route, resolved to await her return along the high roadway which stretched between that place and East Quarriers.

He reached the top of the old road where it makes a sudden descent to the townlet, but she did not appear. Turning back, he sauntered along till he had nearly reached his own house again. Then he retraced his steps, and in the dim night he walked backwards and forwards on the bare and lofty convex of the isle; the stars above and around him, the lighthouse on duty at the distant point, the lightship winking from the sandbank, the combing of the pebble-beach by the tide beneath, the church away south-westward, where the island fathers lay.

He walked the wild summit till his legs ached, and his heart ached – till he seemed to hear on the upper wind the stones of the slingers whizzing past, and the voices of the invaders who annihilated them, and married their wives and daughters, and produced Avice as the ultimate flower of the combined stocks. Still she did not come. It was more than foolish to wait, yet he could not help waiting. At length he discerned a dot of a figure, which he knew to be hers rather by its motion than by its shape.

How incomparably the immaterial dream dwarfed the grandest of substantial things, when here, between those three sublimities – the sky, the rock, and the ocean – the minute personality of this washer-girl filled his consciousness to its extremest boundary, and the stupendous inanimate scene shrank to a corner therein.

But all at once the approaching figure had disappeared. He looked about; she had certainly vanished. At one side of the road was a low wall, but she could not have gone behind that without considerable trouble and singular conduct. He looked behind him; she had reappeared further on the road.

Jocelyn Pierston hurried after; and, discerning his movement, Avice stood still. When he came up, she was slily shaking with restrained laughter.

'Well, what does this mean, my dear girl?' he asked.

Her inner mirth escaping in spite of her she turned askance and said:

'When you was following me to Street o' Wells, two hours ago, I looked round and saw you, and huddied behind a stone! You passed and brushed my frock without seeing me. And when, on my way backalong, I saw you waiting hereabout again, I slipped over the wall, and ran past you! If I had not stopped and looked round at 'ee, you would never have catched me!'

'What did you do that for, you elf!'

'That you shouldn't find me.'

'That's not exactly a reason. Give another, dear Avice,' he said, as he turned and walked beside her homeward.

She hesitated. 'Come!' he urged again.

''Twas because I thought you wanted to be my young man,' she answered.

'What a wild thought of yours! Supposing I did, wouldn't you have me?'

'Not now . . . And not for long, even if it had been sooner than now.'

'Why?'

'If I tell you, you won't laugh at me or let anybody else know?'

'Never.'

'Then I will tell you,' she said quite seriously. ''Tis because I get tired of my lovers as soon as I get to know them well. What I see in one young man for a while soon leaves him and goes into another yonder, and I follow, and then what I admire fades out of him and springs up somewhere else; and so I follow on, and never fix to one. I have loved *fifteen* a'ready! Yes, fifteen, I am almost ashamed to say,' she repeated, laughing. 'I can't help it, sir, I assure you. Of course it is really, to *me*, the same one all through, only I can't catch him!' She added anxiously, 'You won't tell anybody o' this in me, will you, sir? Because if it were known I am afraid no man would like me.'

Pierston was surprised into stillness. Here was this obscure and almost illiterate girl engaged in the pursuit of the impossible ideal, just as he had been himself doing for the last twenty years. She was doing it quite involuntarily, by sheer necessity of her organization, puzzled all the while at her own instinct. He suddenly thought of its bearing upon himself, and said, with a sinking heart –

'Am I – one of them?'

She pondered critically.

'You was – for a week; when I first saw you.'

'Only a week?'

'About that.'

'What made the being of your fancy forsake my form and go elsewhere?'

'Well – though you seemed handsome and gentlemanly at first – '

'Yes?'

'I found you too old soon after.'

'You are a candid young person.'

'But you asked me, sir!' she expostulated.

'I did; and, having been answered, I won't intrude upon you longer. So cut along home as fast as you can. It is getting late.'

When she had passed out of earshot he also followed homewards. This seeking of the Well-Beloved was, then, of the nature of a knife which could cut two ways. To be the seeker was one thing: to be one of the corpses from which the ideal inhabitant had departed was another; and this was what he had become now, in the mockery of new days.

The startling parallel in the idiosyncrasies of Avice and himself – evinced by the elusiveness of the Beloved with her as with him – meant probably that there had been some remote ancestor common to both families, from whom the trait had latently descended and recrudesced. But the result was none the less disconcerting.

Drawing near his own gate he smelt tobacco, and could discern two figures in the side lane leading past Avice's door. They did not, however, enter her house, but strolled onward to the narrow pass conducting to Red-King Castle and the sea. He was in momentary heaviness at the thought that they might be Avice with a worthless lover, but a faintly argumentative tone from the man informed him that they were the same married couple going homeward whom he had encountered on a previous occasion.

The next day he gave the servants a half-holiday to get the pretty Avice into the castle again for a few hours, the better to observe her. While she was pulling down the blinds at sunset a whistle of peculiar quality came from some point on the cliffs outside the lawn. He observed that her colour rose slightly, though she bustled about as if she had noticed nothing.

Pierston suddenly suspected that she had not only fifteen past admirers but a current one. Still, he might be mistaken. Stimulated now by ancient memories and present tenderness to use every effort to make her his wife, despite her conventional unfitness, he strung himself up to sift this mystery. If he could only win her – and how could a country girl refuse such an opportunity? – he could pack her off to school for two or three years, marry her, enlarge her mind by a little travel, and take his chance of the rest. As to her want of ardour for him – so sadly in contrast with her sainted mother's affection – a man twenty years older than his bride could expect no better, and he would be well content to put up with it in the pleasure of possessing one in whom seemed to linger as an aroma all the charm of his youth and his early home.

NINE

❧ Juxtapositions ❧

IT WAS A SAD AND leaden afternoon, and Pierston paced up the long, steep pass or Street of the Wells. On either side of the road young girls stood with pitchers at the fountains which bubbled there, and behind the houses forming the propylaea of the rock rose the massive forehead of the Isle – crested at this part with its enormous ramparts as with a mural crown.

As you approach the upper end of the street all progress seems about to be checked by the almost vertical face of the escarpment. Into it your track apparently runs point-blank: a confronting mass which, if it were to slip down, would overwhelm the whole town. But in a moment you find that the road, the old Roman highway into the peninsula, turns at a sharp angle when it reaches the base of the scarp, and ascends in the stiffest of inclines to the right. To the left there is also another ascending road, modern, almost as steep as the first, and perfectly straight. This is the road to the forts.

Pierston arrived at the forking of the ways, and paused for breath. Before turning to the right, his proper and picturesque course, he looked up the uninteresting left road to the fortifications. It was new, long, white, regular, tapering to a vanishing point, like a lesson in perspective. About a quarter of the way up a girl was resting beside a basket of white linen: and by the shape of her hat and the nature of her burden he recognized her.

She did not see him, and abandoning the right-hand course he slowly ascended the incline she had taken. He observed that her attention was absorbed by something aloft. He followed the direction of her gaze. Above them towered the green-grey mountain of grassy stone, here levelled at the top by military art. The skyline was broken every now and then by a little peg-like object – a sentry-box; and near one of these a small red spot kept creeping backwards and forwards monotonously against the heavy sky.

Then he divined that she had a soldier-lover.

She turned her head, saw him, and took up her clothes-basket to continue the ascent. The steepness was such that to climb it unencumbered was a breathless business; the linen made her task a cruelty to her. 'You'll never get to the forts with that weight,' he said. 'Give it to me.'

But she would not, and he stood still, watching her as she panted up the way; for the moment an irradiated being, the epitome of a whole sex: by the beams of his own infatuation

'... robed in such exceeding glory
That he beheld her not';

beheld her not as she really was, as she was even to himself sometimes. But to the soldier what was she? Smaller and smaller she waned up the rigid mathematical road, still gazing at the soldier aloft, as Pierston gazed at her. He could just discern sentinels springing up at the different coigns of vantage that she passed, but seeing who she was they did not intercept her; and presently she crossed the drawbridge over the enormous chasm surrounding the forts, passed the sentries there also, and disappeared through the arch into the interior. Pierston could not see the sentry now, and there occurred to him the hateful idea that this scarlet rival was meeting and talking freely to her, the unprotected orphan girl of his sweet original Avice; perhaps, relieved of duty, escorting her across the interior, carrying her basket, her tender body encircled by his arm.

'What the devil are you staring at, as if you were in a trance?'

Pierston turned his head: and there stood his old friend Somers – still looking the long-leased bachelor that he was.

'I might say what the devil do you do here? if I weren't so glad to see you.'

Somers said that he had come to see what was detaining his friend in such an out-of-the-way place at that time of year, and incidentally to get some fresh air into his own lungs. Pierston made him welcome, and they went towards Sylvania Castle.

'You were staring, as far as I could see, at a pretty little washerwoman with a basket of clothes?' resumed the painter.

'Yes; it was that to you, but not to me. Behind the mere pretty island-girl (to the world) is, in my eye, the Idea, in Platonic phraseology – the essence and epitome of all that is desirable in this existence ... I am under a doom, Somers. Yes, I am under a doom. To have been always following a phantom whom I saw in woman after woman while she was at a distance, but vanishing away on close approach, was bad enough; but now the terrible thing is that the phantom does *not* vanish, but stays to tantalize me even when I am near enough to see what it is! That girl holds me, *though* my eyes are open, and *though* I see that I am a fool!'

Somers regarded the visionary look of his friend, which rather intensified than decreased as his years wore on, but made no further remark. When they reached the castle Somers gazed round upon the scenery, and

Pierston, signifying the quaint little Elizabethan cottage, said: 'That's where she lives.'

'What a romantic place! – and this island altogether. A man might love a scarecrow or turnip-lantern here.'

'But a woman mightn't. Scenery doesn't impress them, though they pretend it does. This girl is as fickle as –'

'You once were.'

'Exactly – from your point of view. She has told me so – candidly. And it hits me hard.'

Somers stood still in sudden thought. 'Well – that *is* a strange turning of the tables!' he said. 'But you wouldn't really marry her, Pierston?'

'I would – to-morrow. Why shouldn't I? What are fame and name and society to me – a descendant of wreckers and smugglers, like her. Besides, I know what she's made of, my boy, to her innermost fibre; I know the perfect and pure quarry she was dug from: and that gives a man confidence.'

'Then you'll win.'

While they were sitting after dinner that evening their quiet discourse was interrupted by the long low whistle from the cliffs without. Somers took no notice, but Pierston marked it. That whistle always occurred at the same time in the evening when Avice was helping in the house. He excused himself for a moment to his visitor and went out upon the dark lawn. A crunching of feet upon the gravel mixed in with the articulation of the sea – steps light as if they were winged. And he supposed, two minutes later, that the mouth of some hulking fellow was upon hers, which he himself hardly ventured to look at, so touching was its young beauty.

Hearing people about – among others the beforementioned married couple quarrelling, the woman's tones having a kinship to Avice's own – he returned to the house. Next day Somers roamed abroad to look for scenery for a marine painting, and, going out to seek him, Pierston met Avice.

'So you have a lover, my lady!' he said severely. She admitted that it was the fact. 'You won't stick to him,' he continued.

'I think I may to *this* one,' said she, in a meaning tone that he failed to fathom then. 'He deserted me once, but he won't again.'

'I suppose he's a wonderful sort of fellow?'

'He's good enough for me.'

'So handsome, no doubt.'

'Handsome enough for me.'

'So refined and respectable.'

'Refined and respectable enough for me.'

He could not disturb her equanimity, and let her pass. The next day was Sunday, and Somers having chosen his view at the other end of the island, Pierston determined in the afternoon to see Avice's lover. He found that she had left her cottage stronghold, and went on towards the lighthouses at the Beal. Turning back when he had reached the nearest, he saw on the lonely road between the quarries a young man evidently connected with the stone trade, with Avice the Second upon his arm.

She looked prettily guilty and blushed a little under his glance. The man's was one of the typical island physiognomies – his features energetic and wary in their expression, and half covered with a close, crisp black beard. Pierston fancied that out of his keen dark eyes there glimmered a dry sense of humour at the situation.

If so, Avice must have told him of Pierston's symptoms of tenderness. This girl, whom, for her dear mother's sake more than for her own unquestionable attractiveness, he would have guarded as the apple of his eye, how could she estimate him so flippantly!

The mortification of having brought himself to this position with the antitype, by his early slight of the type, blinded him for the moment to what struck him a short time after. The man upon whose arm she hung was not a soldier. What, then, became of her entranced gaze at the sentinel? She could hardly have transferred her affections so promptly; or, to give her the benefit of his own theory, her Beloved could scarcely have flitted from frame to frame in so very brief an interval. And which of them had been he who whistled softly in the dusk to her?

Without further attempt to find Alfred Somers Pierston walked homeward, moodily thinking that the desire to make reparation to the original woman by wedding and enriching the copy – which lent such an unprecedented permanence to his new love – was thwarted, as if by set intention of his destiny.

At the door of the grounds about the castle there stood a carriage. He observed that it was not one of the homely flys from the under-hill town, but apparently from the popular resort across the bay. Wondering why the visitor had not driven in he entered, to find in the drawing-room Nichola Pine-Avon.

At his first glance upon her, fashionably dressed and graceful in movement, she seemed beautiful; at the second, when he observed that her face was pale and agitated, she seemed pathetic likewise. Altogether, she was now a very different figure from her who, sitting in her chair with such finished composure, had snubbed him in her drawing-room in Hamptonshire Square.

'You are surprised at this? Of course you are!' she said, in a low, pleading voice, languidly lifting her heavy eyelids, while he was holding her hand. 'But I couldn't help it! I know I have done something to offend you – have I not? O! what can it be, that you have come away to this outlandish rock, to live with barbarians in the midst of the London season?'

'You have not offended me, dear Mrs Pine-Avon,' he said. 'How sorry I am that you should have supposed it! Yet I am glad, too, that your fancy should have done me the good turn of bringing you here to see me.'

'I am staying at Budmouth-Regis,' she explained.

'Then I did see you at a church-service here a little while back?'

She blushed faintly upon her pallor, and she sighed. Their eyes met. 'Well,' she said at last, 'I don't know why I shouldn't show the virtue of candour. You know what it means. I was the stronger once; now I am the weaker. Whatever pain I may have given you in the ups and downs of our acquaintance I am sorry for, and would willingly repair all errors of the past of – being amenable to reason in the future.'

It was impossible that Jocelyn should not feel a tender impulsion towards this attractive and once independent woman, who from every worldly point of view was an excellent match for him – a superior match, indeed, except in money. He took her hand again and held it awhile, and a faint wave a gladness seemed to flow through her. But no – he could go no further. That island girl, in her coquettish Sunday frock and little hat with its bunch of cock's feathers held him as by strands of Manila rope. He dropped Nichola's hand.

'I am leaving Budmouth to-morrow,' she said. 'That was why I felt I must call. You did not know I had been there all through the Whitsun holidays?'

'I did not, indeed; or I should have come to see you.'

'I didn't like to write. I wish I had, now!'

'I wish you had, too, dear Mrs Pine-Avon.'

But it was 'Nichola' that she wanted to be. As they reached the landau he told her that he should be back in town himself again soon, and would call immediately. At the moment of his words Avice Caro, now alone, passed close along by the carriage on the other side, towards her house hard at hand. She did not turn head or eye to the pair: they seemed to be in her view objects of indifference.

Pierston became cold as a stone. The chill towards Nichola that the presence of the girl, – sprite, witch, troll that she was – brought with it came like a doom. He knew what a fool he was, as he had said. But he was powerless in the grasp of the idealizing passion. He cared more for Avice's finger-tips than for Mrs Pine-Avon's whole personality.

Perhaps Nichola saw it, for she said mournfully: 'Now I have done all I could! I felt that the only counterpoise to my cruelty to you in my drawing-room would be to come as a suppliant to yours.'

'It is most handsome and noble of you, my very dear friend!' said he, with an emotion of courtesy rather than of enthusiasm.

Then adieux were spoken, and she drove away. But Pierston saw only the retreating Avice, and knew that he was helpless in her hands. The church of the island had risen near the foundations of the Pagan temple, and a Christian emanation from the former might be wrathfully torturing him through the very false gods to whom he had devoted himself both in his craft, like Demetrius of Ephesus, and in his heart. Perhaps Divine punishment for his idolatries had come.

TEN

❧ She Fails to Vanish Still ❧

PIERSTON HAD NOT TURNED FAR back towards the castle when he was overtaken by Somers and the man who carried his painting lumber. They paced together to the door; the man deposited the articles and went away, and the two walked up and down before entering.

'I met an extremely interesting woman in the road out there,' said the painter.

'Ah, she is! A sprite, a sylph; Psyche indeed!'

'I was struck with her.'

'It shows how beauty will out through the homeliest guise.'

'Yes, it will; though not always. And this case doesn't prove it, for the lady's attire was in the latest and most approved taste.'

'O, you mean the lady who was driving?'

'Of course. What, were you thinking of the pretty little cottage-girl outside here? I did meet her, but what's she? Very well for one's picture, though hardly for one's fireside. This lady – '

'Is Mrs Pine-Avon. A kind, proud woman, who'll do what people with no pride would not condescend to think of. She is leaving Budmouth to-morrow, and she drove across to see me. You know how things seemed to be going with us at one time? But I am no good to any woman. She's been very generous towards me, which I've not been to her . . . She'll ultimately throw herself away upon some wretch unworthy of her, no doubt.'

'Do you think so?' murmured Somers. After a while he said abruptly, 'I'll marry her myself, if she'll have me. I like the look of her.'

577

'I wish you would, Alfred, or rather could! She has long had an idea of slipping out of the world of fashion into the world of art. She is a woman of individuality and earnest instincts. I am in real trouble about her. I won't say she can be won – it would be ungenerous of me to say that. But try. I can bring you together easily.'

'I'll marry her, if she's willing!' With the phlegmatic dogmatism that was part of him, Somers added: 'When you have decided to marry, take the first nice woman you meet. They are all alike.'

'Well – you don't know her yet,' replied Jocelyn, who could give praise where he could not give love.

'But you do, and I'll take her on the strength of your judgment. Is she really handsome? – I had but the merest glance. But I know she is, or she wouldn't have caught your discriminating eye.'

'You may take my word for it; she looks as well at hand as afar.'

'What colour are her eyes?'

'Her eyes? I don't go much in for colour, being professionally sworn to form. But, let me see – grey; and her hair rather light than dark brown.'

'I wanted something darker,' said Somers airily. 'There are so many fair models among native Englishwomen. Still, blondes are useful property! . . . Well, well; this is flippancy. But I liked the look of her.'

Somers had gone back to town. It was a wet day on the little peninsula: but Pierston walked out as far as the garden-house of his hired castle, where he sat down and smoked. This erection being on the boundary-wall of his property his ear could now and then catch the tones of Avice's voice from her open-doored cottage in the lane which skirted his fence; and he noticed that there were no modulations in it. He knew why that was. She wished to go out, and could not. He had observed before that when she was planning an outing a particular note would come into her voice during the preceding hours: a dove's roundness of sound; no doubt the effect upon her voice of her thoughts of her lover, or lovers. Yet the latter it could not be. She was pure and single-hearted: half an eye could see that. Whence, then, the two men? Possibly the quarrier was a relation.

There seemed reason in this when, going out into the lane he encountered one of the red-jackets he had been thinking of. Soldiers were seldom seen in this outer part of the isle: their beat from the forts, when on pleasure, was in the opposite direction, and this man must have had a special reason for coming hither. Pierston surveyed him. He was a round-faced, good-humoured fellow to look at, having two little pieces of moustache on his upper lip, like a pair of minnows rampant, and small black eyes, over which the Glengarry cap straddled flat. It was a hateful idea that her tender cheek should be kissed by the lips of this heavy young man who had never been sublimed by a single battle, even with defenceless savages.

The soldier went before her house, looked at the door, and moved on down the crooked way to the cliffs, where there was a path back to the forts. But he did not adopt it, returning by the way he had come. This showed his wish to pass the house again. She gave no sign, however, and the soldier disappeared.

Pierston could not be satisfied that Avice was in the house, and he crossed over to the front of her little freehold and tapped at the door, which stood ajar.

Nobody came: hearing a slight movement within he crossed the threshold. Avice was there alone, sitting on a low stool in a dark corner, as though she wished to be unobserved by any casual passer-by. She looked up at him without emotion or apparent surprise; but he could then see that she was crying. The view, for the first time, of distress in an unprotected young girl towards whom he felt drawn by ties of extraordinary delicacy and tenderness, moved Pierston beyond measure. He entered without ceremony.

'Avice, my dear girl!' he said. 'Something is the matter!'

She looked assent, and he went on: 'Now tell me all about it. Perhaps I can help you. Come, tell me.'

'I can't!' she murmured. 'Grammer Stockwool is upstairs, and she'll hear!' Mrs Stockwool was the old woman who had come to live with the girl for company since her mother's death.

'Then come into my garden opposite. There we shall be quite private.'

She rose, put on her hat, and accompanied him to the door. Here she asked him if the lane were empty, and on his assuring her that it was she crossed over and entered with him through the garden-wall.

The place was a shady and secluded one, though through the boughs the sea could be seen quite near at hand, its moanings being distinctly audible. A water-drop from a tree fell here and there, but the rain was not enough to hurt them.

'Now let me hear it,' he said soothingly. 'You may tell me with the greatest freedom. I was a friend of your mother's, you know. That is, I knew her; and I'll be a friend of yours.'

The statement was risky, if he wished her not to suspect him of being her mother's false one. But that lover's name appeared to be unknown to the present Avice.

'I can't tell you, sir,' she replied unwillingly; 'except that it has to do with my own changeableness. The rest is the secret of somebody else.'

'I am sorry for that,' said he.

'I am getting to care for one I ought not to think of, and it means ruin. I ought to get away!'

'You mean from the island?'

'Yes.'

Pierston reflected. His presence in London had been desired for some time; yet he had delayed going because of his new solicitudes here. But to go and take her with him would afford him opportunity of watching over her, tending her mind, and developing it; while it might remove her from some looming danger. It was a somewhat awkward guardianship for him, as a lonely man, to carry out; still, it could be done. He asked her abruptly if she would really like to go away for a while.

'I like best to stay here,' she answered. 'Still, I should not mind going somewhere, because I think I ought to.'

'Would you like London?'

Avice's face lost its weeping shape. 'How could that be?' she said.

'I have been thinking that you could come to my house and make yourself useful in some way. I rent just now one of those new places called flats, which you may have heard of; and I have a studio at the back.'

'I haven't heard of 'em,' she said without interest.

'Well, I have two servants there, and as my man has a holiday you can help them for a month or two.'

'Would polishing furniture be any good? I can do that.'

'I haven't much furniture that requires polishing. But you can clear away plaster and clay messes in the studio, and chippings of stone, and help me in modelling, and dust all my Venus failures, and hands and heads and feet and bones, and other objects.'

She was startled, yet attracted by the novelty of the proposal.

'Only for a time?' she said.

'Only for a time. As short as you like, and as long.'

The deliberate manner in which, after the first surprise, Avice discussed the arrangements that he suggested, might have told him how far was any feeling for himself beyond friendship, and possibly gratitude, from agitating her breast. Yet there was nothing extravagant in the discrepancy between their ages, and he hoped, after shaping her to himself, to win her. What had grieved her to tears she would not more particularly tell.

She had naturally not much need of preparation, but she made even less preparation than he would have expected her to require. She seemed eager to be off immediately, and not a soul was to know of her departure. Why, if she were in love and at first averse to leave the island, she should be so precipitate now he failed to understand.

But he took great care to compromise in no way a girl in whom his interest was as protective as it was passionate. He accordingly left her to get out of the island alone, awaiting her at a station a few miles up the railway, where, discovering himself to her through the carriage-window, he entered the next compartment, his frame pervaded by a glow which was almost joy at having for the first time in his charge one who inherited the flesh and bore the name so early associated with his own, and at the prospect of putting things right which had been wrong through many years.

ELEVEN

❦ The Image Persists ❧

IT WAS DARK WHEN THE four-wheeled cab wherein he had brought Avice from the station stood at the entrance to the pile of flats of which Pierston occupied one floor – rarer then as residences in London than they are now. Leaving Avice to alight and get the luggage taken in by the porter Pierston went upstairs. To his surprise his floor was silent, and on entering with a latchkey the rooms were all in darkness. He descended to the hall, where Avice was standing helpless beside the luggage, while the porter was outside with the cabman.

'Do you know what has become of my servants?' asked Jocelyn.

'What – and ain't they there, saur? Ah, then my belief is that what I suspected is thrue! You didn't leave your winecellar unlocked, did you, saur, by no mistake?'

Pierston considered. He thought he might have left the key with his elder servant, whom he had believed he could trust, especially as the cellar was not well stocked.

'Ah, then it was so! She's been very queer, saur, this last week or two. O yes, sending messages down the spakin'-tube which were like madness itself, and ordering us this and that, till we would take no notice at all. I see them both go out last night, and possibly they went for a holiday not expecting ye, or maybe for good! Shure, if ye'd written, saur, I'd ha' got the place ready, ye being out of a man, too, though it's not me duty at all!'

When Pierston got to his floor again he found that the cellar door was open; some bottles were standing empty that had been full, and many abstracted altogether. All other articles in the house, however, appeared to be intact. His letter to his housekeeper lay in the box as the postman had left it.

By this time the luggage had been sent up in the lift; and Avice, like so much more luggage, stood at the door, the hall-porter behind offering his assistance.

'Come here, Avice,' said the sculptor. 'What shall we do now? Here's a pretty state of affairs!'

Avice could suggest nothing, till she was struck with the bright thought that she should light a fire.

'Light a fire? – ah, yes . . . I wonder if we could manage. This is an odd coincidence – and awkward!' he murmured. 'Very well, light a fire.'

'Is this the kitchen, sir, all mixed up with the parlours?'

'Yes.'

'Then I think I can do all that's wanted here for a bit; at any rate, till you can get help, sir. At least, I could if I could find the fuel-house. 'Tis no such big place as I thought!'

'That's right: take courage!' said he with a tender smile. 'Now, I'll dine out this evening, and leave the place for you to arrange as best you can with the help of the porter's wife downstairs.'

This Pierston accordingly did, and so their common residence began. Feeling more and more strongly that some danger awaited her in her native island he determined not to send her back till the lover or lovers who seemed to trouble her should have cooled off. He was quite willing to take the risk of his action thus far in his solicitous regard for her.

It was a dual solitude, indeed; for, though Pierston and Avice were the only two people in the flat, they did not keep each other company, the former being as scrupulously fearful of going near her now that he had the opportunity as he had been prompt to seek her when he had none. They lived in silence, his messages to her being frequently written on scraps of paper deposited where she could see them. It was not without a pang that he noted her unconsciousness of their isolated position – a position to which, had she experienced any reciprocity of sentiment, she would readily have been alive.

Considering that, though not profound, she was hardly a matter-of-fact girl as that phrase is commonly understood, she was exasperating in the matter-of-fact quality of her responses to the friendly remarks which would escape him in spite of himself, as well as in her general conduct. Whenever he formed some culinary excuse for walking across the few yards of tessellated hall which separated his room from the kitchen, and spoke through the doorway to her, she answered, 'Yes, sir,' or 'No, sir,' without turning her eyes from the particular work that she was engaged in.

In the usual course he would have obtained a couple of properly qualified servants immediately; but he lived on with the one, or rather the less than one, that this cottage–girl afforded. It had been his almost invariable custom to dine at one of his clubs. Now he sat at home over the miserable chop or steak to which he limited himself in dread lest she should complain of there being too much work for one person, and demand to be sent home. A charwoman came every two or three days, effecting an extraordinary consumption of food and alcoholic liquids: yet it was not for this that Pierston dreaded her presence, but lest, in conversing with Avice, she should open the girl's eyes to the oddity of her situation. Avice could see for herself that there must have been two or three servants in the flat during his former residence there: but his reasons for doing without them seemed never to strike her.

His intention had been to keep her occupied exclusively at the studio, but accident had modified this. However, he sent her round one morning, and entering himself shortly after found her engaged in wiping the layers of dust from the casts and models.

The colour of the dust never ceased to amaze her. 'It is like the hold of a Budmouth collier,' she said, 'and the beautiful faces of these clay people are quite spoilt by it.'

'I suppose you'll marry some day, Avice?' remarked Pierston, as he regarded her thoughtfully.

'Some do and some don't,' she said, with a reserved smile, still attending to the casts.

'You are very off-hand,' said he.

She archly weighed that remark without further speech. It was tantalizing conduct in the face of his instinct to cherish her; especially when he regarded the charm of her bending profile; the well-characterized though softly lined nose, the round chin with, as it were, a second leap in its curve to the throat, and the sweep of the eye-lashes over the rosy cheek during the sedulously lowered glance. How futilely he had laboured to express the character of that face in clay, and, while catching it in substance, had yet lost something that was essential!

That evening after dusk, in the stress of writing letters, he sent her out for stamps. She had been absent some quarter of an hour when, suddenly drawing himself up from over his writing-table, it flashed upon him that he had absolutely forgotten her total ignorance of London.

The head post-office, to which he had sent her because it was late, was two or three streets off, and he had made his request in the most general manner, which she had acceded to with alacrity enough. How could he have done such an unreflecting thing?

Pierston went to the window. It was half-past nine o'clock, and owing to her absence the blinds were not down. He opened the casement and stepped out upon the balcony. The green shade of his lamp screened its rays from the gloom without. Over the opposite square the moon hung, and to the right there stretched a long street, filled with a diminishing array of lamps, some single, some in clusters, among them an occasional blue or red one. From a corner came the notes of a piano-organ strumming out a stirring march of Rossini's. The shadowy black figures of pedestrians moved up, down, and across the embrowned roadway. Above the roofs was a bank of livid mist, and higher a greenish-blue sky, in which stars were visible, though its lower part was still pale with daylight, against which rose chimney-pots in the form of elbows, prongs, and fists.

From the whole scene proceeded a ground rumble, miles in extent, upon which individual rattles, voices, a tin whistle, the bark of a dog, rode like bubbles on a sea. The whole noise impressed him with the sense that no one in its enormous mass ever required rest.

In this illimitable ocean of humanity there was a unit of existence, his Avice, wandering alone.

Pierston looked at his watch. She had been gone half an hour. It was impossible to distinguish her at this distance, even if she approached. He came inside, and putting on his hat determined to go out and seek her. He reached the end of the street, and there was nothing of her to be seen. She had the option of two or three routes from this point to the post-office; yet he plunged at random into one, till he reached the office to find it quite deserted. Almost distracted now by his anxiety for her he retreated as rapidly as he had come, regaining home only to find that she had not returned.

He recollected telling her that if she should ever lose her way she must call a cab and drive home. It occurred to him that this was what she would do now. He again went out upon the balcony; the dignified street in which he lived was almost vacant, and the lamps stood like placed sentinels awaiting some procession which tarried long. At a point under him where the road was torn up there stood a red light, and at the corner two men were talking in leisurely repose, as if sunning themselves at noonday. Lovers of a feline disposition, who were never seen by daylight, joked and darted at each other in and out of area gates.

His attention was fixed on the cabs, and he held his breath as the hollow clap of each horse's hoofs drew near the front of the house, only to go onward into the square. The two lamps of each vehicle afar dilated with its near approach, and seemed to swerve towards him. It was Avice surely? No, it passed by.

Almost frantic he again descended and let himself out of the house, moving towards a more central part, where the roar still continued. Before emerging into the noisy thoroughfare he observed a small figure approaching leisurely along the opposite side, and hastened across to find it was she.

❧ A Grille Descends Between ❧

'O AVICE!' HE CRIED, WITH the tenderly subdued scolding of a mother. 'What is this you have done to alarm me so!'

She seemed unconscious of having done anything, and was altogether surprised at his anxiety. In his relief he did not speak further till he asked her suddenly if she would take his arm since she must be tired.

'O no, sir!' she assured him, 'I am not a bit tired, and I don't require any help at all, thank you.'

They went upstairs without using the lift, and he let her and himself in with his latchkey. She entered the kitchen, and he, following, sat down in a chair there.

'Where have you been?' he said, with almost angered concern on his face. 'You ought not to have been absent more than ten minutes.'

'I knew there was nothing for me to do, and thought I should like to see a little of London,' she replied naïvely. 'So when I had got the stamps I went on into the fashionable streets, where ladies are all walking about just as if it were daytime! 'Twas for all the world like coming home by night from Martinmas Fair at the Street o' Wells, only more genteel.'

'O Avice, Avice, you must not go out like this! Don't you know that I am responsible for your safety? I am your – well, guardian, in fact, and am bound by law and morals, and I don't know what-all, to deliver you up to your native island without a scratch or blemish. And yet you indulge in such a midnight vagary as this!'

'But I am sure, sir, the gentlemen in the street were more respectable than they are anywhere at home! They were dressed in the latest fashion, and would have scorned to do me any harm; and as to their love-making, I never heard anything so polite before.'

'Well, you must not do it again. I'll tell you some day why. What's that you have in your hand?'

'A mouse-trap. There are lots of mice in this kitchen – sooty mice, not clean like ours – and I thought I'd try to catch them. That was what I went so far to buy, as there were no shops open just about here. I'll set it now.'

She proceeded at once to do so, and Pierston remained in his seat regarding the operation, which seemed entirely to engross her. It was extraordinary, indeed, to observe how she wilfully limited her interests;

585

with what content she received the ordinary things that life offered, and persistently refused to behold what an infinitely extended life lay open to her through him. If she had only said the word he would have got a licence and married her the next morning. Was it possible that she did not perceive this tendency in him? She could hardly be a woman if she did not; and in her airy, elusive, off-hand demeanour she was very much of a woman indeed.

'It only holds one mouse,' he said absently.

'But I shall hear it throw in the night, and set it again.'

He sighed, and left her to her own resources and retired to rest, though he felt no tendency to sleep. At some small hour of the darkness, owing, possibly, to some intervening door being left open, he heard the mouse-trap click. Another light sleeper must have heard it too, for almost immediately after the pit-pat of naked feet, accompanied by the brushing of drapery, was audible along the passage towards the kitchen. After her absence in that apartment long enough to reset the trap, he was startled by a scream from the same quarter. Pierston sprang out of bed, jumped into his dressing-gown, and hastened in the direction of the cry.

Avice, barefooted and wrapped in a shawl, was standing in a chair; the mouse-trap lay on the floor, the mouse running round and round in its neighbourhood.

'I was trying to take en out,' said she excitedly, 'and he got away from me!'

Pierston secured the mouse while she remained standing on the chair. Then, having set the trap anew, his feeling burst out petulantly –

'A girl like you to throw yourself away upon such a commonplace fellow as that quarryman! Why do you do it?'

Her mind was so intently fixed upon the matter in hand that it was some moments before she caught his irrelevant subject. 'Because I am a foolish girl,' she said quietly.

'What! Don't you love him?' said Jocelyn, with a surprised stare up at her as she stood, in her concern appearing the very Avice who had kissed him twenty years earlier.

'It is not much use to talk about that,' said she.

'Then, is it the soldier?'

'Yes, though I have never spoken to him.'

'Never spoken to the soldier?'

'Never.'

'Has either one treated you badly – deceived you?'

'No. Certainly not.'

'Well, I can't make you out; and I don't wish to know more than you choose to tell me. Come, Avice, why not tell me exactly how things are?'

'Not now, sir!' she said, her pretty pink face and brown eyes turned in simple appeal to him from her pedestal. 'I will tell you all to-morrow; an that I will!'

He retreated to his own room and lay down meditating. Some quarter of an hour after she had retreated to hers the mouse-trap clicked again, and Pierston raised himself on his elbow to listen. The place was so still and the jerry-built door-panels so thin that he could hear the mouse jumping about inside the wires of the trap. But he heard no footstep this time. As he was wakeful and restless he again arose, proceeded to the kichen with a light, and removing the mouse reset the trap. Returning he listened once more. He could see in the far distance the door of Avice's room; but that thoughtful housewife had not heard the second capture. From the room came a soft breathing like that of an infant.

He entered his own chamber and reclined himself gloomily enough. Her lack of all consciousness of him, the aspect of the deserted kitchen, the cold grate, impressed him with a deeper sense of loneliness than he had ever felt before.

Foolish he was, indeed, to be so devoted to this young woman. Her defencelessness, her freedom from the least thought that there lurked a danger in their propinquity, were in fact secondary safeguards, not much less strong than that of her being her mother's image, against risk to her from him. Yet it was out of this that his depression came.

At sight of her the next morning Pierston felt that he must put an end to such a state of things. He sent Avice off to the studio, wrote to an agent for a couple of servants, and then went round to his work. Avice was busy righting all that she was allowed to touch. It was the girl's delight to be occupied among the models and casts, which for the first time she regarded with the wistful interest of a soul struggling to receive ideas of beauty vaguely discerned yet ever eluding her. That brightness in her mother's mind which might have descended to the second Avice with the maternal face and form, had been dimmed by admixture with the mediocrity of her father's, and by one who remembered like Pierston the dual organization the opposites could be often seen wrestling internally.

They were alone in the studio, and his feelings found vent. Putting his arms round her he said, 'My darling, sweet little Avice! I want to ask you something – surely you guess what? I want to know this: will you be married to me, and live here with me always and ever?'

'O, Mr Pierston, what nonsense!'

'Nonsense?' said he, shrinking somewhat.

'Yes, sir.'

'Well, why? Am I too old? Surely there's no serious difference?'

'O no – I should not mind that if it came to marrying. The difference is

587

not much for husband and wife, though it is rather much for keeping company.'

She struggled to get free, and when in the movement she knocked down the Empress Faustina's head he did not try to retain her. He saw that she was not only surprised but a little alarmed.

'You haven't said why it is nonsense!' he remarked tartly.

'Why, I didn't know you was thinking of me like that. I hadn't any thought of it! And all alone here! What shall I do?'

'Say yes, my pretty Avice! We'll then go out and be married at once, and nobody be any the wiser.'

She shook her head. 'I couldn't, sir.'

'It would be well for you. You don't like me, perhaps?'

'Yes I do – very much. But not in that sort of way – quite. Still, I might have got to love you in time, if –'

'Well, then, try,' he said warmly. 'Your mother did!'

No sooner had the words slipped out than Pierston would have recalled them. He had felt in a moment that they jeopardized his cause.

'Mother loved you?' said Avice, incredulously gazing at him.

'Yes,' he murmured.

'You were not her false young man, surely? That one who –'

'Yes, yes! Say no more about it.'

'Who ran away from her?'

'Almost.'

'Then I can *never, never* like you again! I didn't know it was a gentleman – I – I thought –'

'It wasn't a gentleman, then.'

'O, sir, please go away! I can't bear the sight of 'ee at this moment! Perhaps I shall get to – to like you as I did; but –'

'No; I'm d – d if I'll go away!' said Pierston, thoroughly irritated. 'I have been candid with you; you ought to be the same with me!'

'What do you want me to tell?'

'Enough to make it clear to me why you don't accept this offer. Everything you have said yet is a reason for the reverse. Now, my dear, I am not angry.'

'Yes you are.'

'No I'm not. Now what is your reason?'

'The name of it is Isaac Pierston, down home.'

'How?'

'I mean he courted me, and led me on to island custom, and then I went to chapel one morning and married him in secret, because mother didn't care about him; and I didn't either by that time. And then he quarrelled with me; and just before you and I came to London he went away to Guernsey. Then I saw a soldier; I never knew his name, but I fell in love with him because I am so quick at that! Still, as it was wrong, I tried not to think of him, and wouldn't look at him when he passed. But it made me cry very much that I mustn't. I was then very miserable, and you asked me to come to London. I didn't care what I did with myself, and I came.'

'Heaven above us!' said Pierston, his pale and distressed face showing with what a shock this announcement had come. 'Why have you done such extraordinary things? Or, rather, why didn't you tell me of this before? Then, at the present moment you are the wife of a man who is in Guernsey, whom you do not love at all; but instead of him love a soldier whom you have never spoken to; while I have nearly brought scandal upon us both by your letting me love you. Really, you are a very wicked woman!'

'No, I am not!' she pouted.

Still, Avice looked pale and rather frightened, and did not lift her eyes from the floor. 'I said it was nonsense in you to want to have me!' she went on, 'and, even if I hadn't been married to that horrid Isaac Pierston, I couldn't have married you after you told me that you was the man who ran away from my mother.'

'I have paid the penalty!' he said sadly. 'Men of my sort always get the worst of it somehow. Though I never did your mother any harm. Now, Avice – I'll call you dear Avice for your mother's sake and not for your own – I must see what I can do to help you out of the difficulty that unquestionably you are in. Why can't you love your husband now you have married him?'

Avice looked aside at the statuary as if the subtleties of her organization were not very easy to define.

'Was he that black-bearded typical local character I saw you walking with one Sunday? The same surname as mine; though, of course, you don't notice that in a place where there are only half-a-dozen surnames?'

'Yes, that was Ike. It was that evening we disagreed. He scolded me, and I answered him (you must have heard us); and the next day he went away.'

'Well, as I say, I must consider what it will be best to do for you in this. This first thing, it seems to me, will be to get your husband home.'

She impatiently shrugged her shoulders. 'I don't like him!'

'Then why did you marry him?'

'I was obliged to, after we'd proved each other by island custom.'

'You shouldn't have thought of such a thing. It is ridiculous and out of date nowadays.'

'Ah, he's so old-fashioned in his notions that he doesn't think like that. However, he's gone.'

'Ah – it is only a tiff between you, I dare say. I'll start him in business if he'll come. . . . Is the cottage at home still in your hands?'

'Yes, it is my freehold. Grammer Stockwool is taking care o' it for me.'

'Good. And back there you go straightway, my pretty madam, and wait till your husband comes to make it up with you.'

'I won't go! – I don't want him to come!' she sobbed. 'I want to stay here with you, or anywhere, except where he can come!'

'You will get over that. Now, go back to the flat, there's a dear Avice, and be ready in one hour, waiting in the hall for me.'

'I don't want to!'

'But I say you shall!'

She found it was no use to disobey. Precisely at the moment appointed he met her there himself, burdened only with a valise and umbrella, she with a box and other things. Directing the porter to put Avice and her belongings into a four-wheeled cab for the railway-station, he walked onward from the door, and kept looking behind till he saw the cab approaching. He then entered beside the astonished girl, and onward they went together.

They sat opposite each other in an empty compartment, and the tedious railway journey began. Regarding her closely now by the light of her revelation he wondered at himself for never divining her secret. Whenever he looked at her the girl's eyes grew rebellious, and at last she wept.

'I don't want to go to him!' she sobbed in a miserable voice.

Pierston was almost as much distressed as she. 'Why did you put yourself and me in such a position?' he said bitterly. 'It is no use to regret it now! And I can't say that I do. It affords me a way out of a trying position. Even if you had not been married to him you would not have married me!'

'Yes, I would, sir.'

'What! You would? You said you wouldn't not long ago.'

'I like you better now! I like you more and more!'

Pierston sighed, for emotionally he was not much older than she. That hitch in his development, rendering him the most lopsided of God's creatures, was his standing misfortune. A proposal to her which crossed his mind was dismissed as disloyalty, particularly to an inexperienced fellow-islander and one who was by race and traditions almost a kinswoman.

Little more passed between the twain on that wretched, never-to-be-forgotten day. Aphrodite, Ashtaroth, Freyja, or whoever the love-queen of his isle might have been, was punishing him sharply, as she knew but too well how to punish her votaries when they reverted from the ephemeral to the stable mood. When was it to end – this curse of his heart not ageing while his frame moved naturally onward? Perhaps only with life.

His first act the day after depositing her in her own house was to go to the chapel where, by her statement, the marriage had been solemnized, and make sure of the fact. Perhaps he felt an illogical hope that she might be free, even then, in the tarnished condition which such freedom would have involved. However, there stood the words distinctly: Isaac Pierston, Ann Avice Caro, son and daughter of So-and-so, married on such a day, signed by the contracting parties, the officiating minister, and the two witnesses.

THIRTEEN

◆ She is Enshrouded From Sight ◆

ONE EVENING IN EARLY WINTER, when the air was dry and gusty, the dark little lane which divided the grounds of Sylvania Castle from the cottage of Avice, and led down to the adjoining ruin of Red-King Castle, was paced by a solitary man. The cottage was the centre of his beat; its western limit being the gates of the former residence, its eastern the drawbridge of the ruin. The few other cottages thereabout – all as if carved from the solid rock – were in darkness, but from the upper window of Avice's tiny freehold glimmered a light. Its rays were repeated from the far-distant sea by the lightship lying moored over the mysterious Shambles quicksand, which brought tamelessness and domesticity into due position as balanced opposites.

The sea moaned – more than moaned – among the boulders below the ruins, a throe of its tide being timed to regular intervals. These sounds were accompanied by an equally periodic moan from the interior of the cottage chamber; so that the articulate heave of water and the articulate heave of life seemed but differing utterances of the selfsame troubled terrestrial Being – which in one sense they were.

Pierston – for the man in the lane was he – would look from lightship to cottage window; then back again, as he waited there between the travail of the sea without, and the travail of the woman within. Soon an infant's wail of the very feeblest was also audible in the house. He started from his easy pacing, and went again westward, standing at the elbow of the lane a long time. Then the peace of the sleeping village which lay that way was broken by light wheels and the trot of a horse. Pierston went back to the cottage gate and awaited the arrival of the vehicle.

591

It was a light cart, and a man jumped down as it stopped. He was in a broad-brimmed hat, under which no more of him could be perceived than that he wore a black beard clipped like a yew fence – a typical aspect in the island.

'You are Avice's husband?' asked the sculptor quickly.

The man replied that he was, in the local accent. 'I've just come in by to-day's boat,' he added. 'I couldn't git here avore. I had contracted for the job at Peter-Port, and had to see to't to the end.'

'Well,' said Pierston, 'your coming means that you are willing to make it up with her?'

'Ay, I don't know but I be,' said the man. 'Mid so well do that as anything else!'

'If you do, thoroughly, a good business in your old line awaits you here in the island.'

'Wi' all my heart, then,' said the man. His voice was energetic, and, though slightly touchy, it showed, on the whole, a disposition to set things right.

The driver of the trap was paid off, and Jocelyn and Isaac Pierston – undoubtedly scions of a common stock in this isle of intermarriages, though they had no proof of it – entered the house. Nobody was in the ground-floor room, in the centre of which stood a square table, in the centre of the table a little wool mat, and in the centre of the mat a lamp, the apartment having the appearance of being rigidly swept and set in order for an event of interest.

The woman who lived in the house with Avice now came downstairs, and to the inquiry of the comers she replied that matters were progressing favourably, but that nobody could be allowed to go upstairs just then. After placing chairs and viands for them she retreated, and they sat down, the lamp between them – the lover of the sufferer above, who had no right to her, and the man who had every right to her, but did not love her. Engaging in desultory and fragmentary conversation they listened to the trampling of feet on the floor-boards overhead – Pierston full of anxiety and attentiveness, Ike awaiting the course of nature calmly.

Soon they heard the feeble bleats repeated, and then the local practitioner descended and entered the room.

'How is she now?' said Pierston, the more taciturn Ike looking up with him for the answer that he felt would serve for two as well as for one.

'Doing well, remarkably well,' replied the professional gentleman, with a manner of having said it in other places; and his vehicle not being at the door he sat down and shared some refreshment with the others. When he had departed Mrs Stockwool again stepped down, and informed them that Ike's presence had been made known to his wife.

The truant quarrier seemed rather inclined to stay where he was and finish the mug of ale, but Pierston quickened him, and he ascended the staircase. As soon as the lower room was empty Pierston leant with his elbows on the table, and covered his face with his hands.

Ike was absent no great time. Descending with a proprietary mien that had been lacking before, he invited Jocelyn to ascend likewise, since she had stated that she would like to see him. Jocelyn went up the crooked old steps, the husband remaining below.

Avice, though white as the sheets, looked brighter and happier than he had expected to find her, and was apparently very much fortified by the pink little lump at her side. She held out her hand to him.

'I just wanted to tell 'ee,' she said, striving against her feebleness, 'I thought it would be no harm to see you, though 'tis rather soon – to tell 'ee how very much I thank you for getting me settled again with Ike. He is very glad to come home again, too, he says. Yes, you've done a good many kind things for me, sir.'

Whether she were really glad, or whether the words were expressed as a matter of duty, Pierston did not attempt to learn.

He merely said that he valued her thanks. 'Now, Avice,' he added tenderly, 'I resign my guardianship of you. I hope to see your husband in a sound little business here in a very short time.'

'I hope so – for baby's sake,' she said, with a bright sigh. 'Would you – like to see her, sir?'

'The baby? O yes . . . your baby! You must christen her Avice.'

'Yes – so I will!' she murmured readily, and disclosed the infant with some timidity. 'I hope you forgive me, sir, for concealing my thoughtless marriage!'

'If you forgive me for making love to you.'

'Yes. How were you to know! I wish –'

Pierston bade her good-bye, kissing her hand; turned from her and the incipient being whom he was to meet again under very altered conditions, and left the bed-chamber with a tear in his eye.

'Here endeth that dream!' said he.

Hymen, in secret or overt guise, seemed to haunt Pierston just at this time with undignified mockery which savoured rather of Harlequin than of the torch-bearer. Two days after parting in a lone island from the girl he had so disinterestedly loved he met in Piccadilly his friend Somers, wonderfully spruced up, and hastening along with a preoccupied face.

'My dear fellow,' said Somers, 'what do you think! I was charged not to tell you, but, hang it! I may just as well make a clean breast of it now as later.'

'What – you are not going to . . .' began Pierston, with divination.

'Yes. What I said on impulse six months back I am about to carry out in cold blood. Nichola and I began in jest and ended in earnest. We are going to take one another next month for good and all.'

PART THIRD

A Young man of Sixty

'In me thou seest the glowing of such fire,
That on the ashes of his youth doth lie
As the death-bed whereon it must expire,
Consumed with that which it was nourished by.'

W. SHAKESPEARE.

ONE

❧ She Returns For The New Season ❧

TWENTY YEARS HAD SPREAD THEIR films over the events which wound up with the reunion of the second Avice and her husband; and the hoary peninsula called an island looked just the same as before; though many who had formerly projected their daily shadows upon its unrelieved summer whiteness ceased now to disturb the colourless sunlight there.

The general change, nevertheless, was small. The silent ships came and went from the wharf, the chisels clinked in the quarries; file after file of whitey-brown horses, in strings of eight or ten, painfully dragged down the hill the square blocks of stone on the antediluvian wooden wheels just as usual. The lightship winked every night from the quicksands to the Beal Lantern, and the Beal Lantern glared through its eyeglass on the ship. The canine gnawing audible on the Pebble-bank had been repeated ever since at each tide, but the pebbles remained undevoured.

Men drank, smoked, and spat in the inns with only a little more adulteration in their refreshments and a trifle less dialect in their speech than of yore. But one figure had never been seen on the Channel rock in the interval, the form of Pierston the sculptor, whose first use of the chisel that rock had instigated.

He had lived abroad a great deal, and, in fact, at this very date he was staying at an hotel in Rome. Though he had not once set eyes on Avice since parting from her in the room with her firstborn, he had managed to obtain tidings of her from time to time during the interval. In this way Pierston learnt that, shortly after their resumption of a common life in her house, Ike had ill-used her, till fortunately, the business to which Jocelyn had assisted him chancing to prosper, he became immersed in its details, and allowed Avice to pursue her household courses without interference, initiating that kind of domestic reconciliation which is so calm and durable, having as its chief ingredient neither hate nor love, but an all-embracing indifference.

At first Pierston had sent her sums of money privately, fearing lest her husband should deny her material comforts; but he soon found, to his great relief, that such help was unnecessary, social ambition prompting

Ike to set up as quite a gentleman-islander, and to allow Avice a scope for show which he would never have allowed in mere kindness.

Being in Rome, as aforesaid, Pierston returned one evening to his hotel to dine, after spending the afternoon among the busts in the long gallery of the Vatican. The unconscious habit, common to so many people, of tracing likes in unlikes had often led him to discern, or to fancy he discerned, in the Roman atmosphere, in its lights and shades, and particularly in its reflected or secondary lights, something resembling the atmosphere of his native promontory. Perhaps it was that in each case the eye was mostly resting on stone – that the quarries of ruins in the Eternal City reminded him of the quarries of maiden rock at home.

This being in his mind when he sat down to dinner at the common table, he was surprised to hear an American gentleman, who sat opposite, mention the name of Pierston's birthplace. The American was talking to a friend about a lady – an English widow, whose acquaintance they had renewed somewhere in the Channel Islands during a recent tour, after having known her as a young woman who came to San Francisco with her father and mother many years before. Her father was then a rich man just retired from the business of a stone-merchant in the Isle of Slingers; but he had engaged in large speculations, and had lost nearly all his fortune. Jocelyn further gathered that the widowed daughter's name was Mrs Leverre; that she had a step-son, her husband having been a Jersey gentleman, a widower; and that the step-son seemed to be a promising and interesting young man.

Pierston was instantly struck with the perception that these and other allusions, though general, were in accord with the history of his long-lost Marcia. He hardly felt any desire to hunt her up after nearly two score years of separation, but he was impressed enough to resolve to exchange a word with the strangers as soon as he could get opportunity.

He could not well attract their attention through the plants upon the wide table, and even if he had been able he was disinclined to ask questions in public. He waited on till dinner was over, and when the strangers withdrew Pierston withdrew in their rear.

They were not in the drawing-room, and he found that they had gone out. There was no chance of overtaking them, but Pierston, waked to restlessness by their remarks, wandered up and down the adjoining Piazza di Spagna, thinking they might return. The streets below were immersed in shade, the front of the church of the Trinità de' Monti at the top was flooded with orange light, the gloom of evening gradually intensifying upon the broad, long flight of steps, which foot-passengers incessantly ascended and descended with the insignificance of ants; the dusk wrapped up the house to the left, in which Shelley had lived, and that to the right, in which Keats had died.

Getting back to the hotel he learnt that the Americans had only dropped in to dine, and were staying elsewhere. He saw no more of them; and on reflection he was not deeply concerned, for what earthly woman, going off in a freak as Marcia had done, and keeping silence so long, would care for a belated friendship with him now in the sere, even if he were to take the trouble to discover her.

Thus much Marcia. The other thread of his connection with the ancient Isle of Slingers was stirred by a letter he received from Avice a little after this date, in which she stated that her husband Ike had been killed in his own quarry by an accident within the past year; that she herself had been ill, and though well again, and left amply provided for, she would like to see him if he ever came that way.

As she had not communicated for several long years, her expressed wish to see him now was likely to be prompted by something more, something newer, than memories of him. Yet the manner of her writing precluded all suspicion that she was thinking of him as an old lover whose suit events had now made practicable. He told her he was sorry to hear that she had been ill, and that he would certainly take an early opportunity of going down to her home on his next visit to England.

He did more. Her request had revived thoughts of his old home and its associations, and instead of awaiting other reasons for a return he made her the operating one. About a week later he stood once again at the foot of the familiar steep whereon the houses at the entrance to the Isle were perched like grey pigeons on a roof-side.

At Top-o'-Hill – as the summit of the rock was mostly called – he stood looking at the busy doings in the quarries beyond, where the numerous black hoisting-cranes scattered over the central plateau had the appearance of a swarm of crane-flies resting there. He went a little further, made some general inquiries about the accident which had carried off Avice's husband in the previous year, and learnt that though now a widow, she had plenty of friends and sympathizers about her, which rendered any immediate attention to her on his part unnecessary. Considering, therefore, that there was no great reason why he should call on her so soon, and without warning, he turned back. Perhaps after all her request had been dictated by a momentary feeling only, and a considerable strangeness to each other must naturally be the result of a score of dividing years. Descending to the bottom he took his seat in the train on the shore, which soon carried him along the Bank, and round to the watering-place five miles off, at which he had taken up his quarters for a few days.

Here, as he stayed on, his local interests revived. Whenever he went out he could see the island that was once his home lying like a great snail upon the sea across the bay. It was the spring of the year; local steamers had begun to run, and he was never tired of standing on the thinly occupied deck of one of these as it skirted the island and revealed to him on the cliffs far up its height the ruins of Red-King Castle, behind which the little village of East Quarriers lay.

Thus matters went on, if they did not rather stand still, for several days before Pierston redeemed his vague promise to seek Avice out. And in the meantime he was surprised by the arrival of another letter from her by a roundabout route. She had heard, she said, that he had been on the island, and imagined him therefore to be staying somewhere near. Why did he not call as he had told her he would do? She was always thinking of him, and wishing to see him.

Her tone was anxious, and there was no doubt that she really had something to say which she did not want to write. He wondered what it could be, and started the same afternoon.

Avice, who had been little in his mind of late years, began to renew for herself a distinct position therein. He was fully aware that since his earlier manhood a change had come over his regard of womankind. Once the individual had been nothing more to him than the temporary abiding-place of the typical or ideal; now his heart showed its bent to be a growing fidelity to the specimen, with all her pathetic flaws of detail; which flaws, so far from sending him further, increased his tenderness. This maturer feeling, if finer and higher, was less convenient than the old. Ardours of passion could be felt as in youth without the recuperative intervals which had accompanied evanescence.

The first sensation was to find that she had long ceased to live in the little freehold cottage she had occupied of old. In answer to his inquiries he was directed along the road to the west of the modern castle, past the entrance on that side, and onward to the very house that had once been his own home. There it stood as of yore, facing up the Channel, a comfortable roomy structure, euonymus and other shrubs, which alone would stand in the teeth of the salt wind, living on at about the same stature in front of it; but the paint-work much renewed. A thriving man had resided there of late, evidently.

The widow in mourning who received him in the front parlour was, alas! but the sorry shadow of Avice the Second. How could he have fancied otherwise after twenty years? Yet he had been led to fancy otherwise, almost without knowing it, by feeling himself unaltered. Indeed, curiously enough, nearly the first words she said to him were: 'Why – you are just the same!'

'Just the same. Yes, I am, Avice,' he answered sadly; for this inability to ossify with the rest of his generation threw him out of proportion with the time. Moreover, while wearing the aspect of comedy, it was of the nature of tragedy.

'It is well to be you, sir,' she went on. 'I have had troubles to take the bloom off me!'

'Yes; I have been sorry for you.'

She continued to regard him curiously, with humorous interest; and he knew what was passing in her mind: that this man, to whom she had formerly looked up as to a person far in advance of her along the lane of life, seemed now to be a well-adjusted contemporary, the pair of them observing the world with fairly level eyes.

He had come to her with warmth for a vision which, on reaching her, he found to have departed; and, though fairly weaned by the natural reality, he was so far staunch as to linger hankeringly. They talked of past days, his old attachment, which she had then despised, being now far more absorbing and present to her than to himself.

She unmistakably won upon him as he sat on. A curious closeness between them had been produced in his imagination by the discovery that she was passing her life within the house of his own childhood. Her similar surname meant little here; but it was also his, and, added to the identity of domicile, lent a strong suggestiveness to the accident.

'This is where I used to sit when my parents occupied the house,' he said, placing himself beside that corner of the fireplace which commanded a view through the window. 'I could see a bough of tamarisk wave outside at that time, and, beyond the bough, the same abrupt grassy waste towards the sea, and at night the same old lightship blinking far out there. Place yourself on the spot to please me.'

She set her chair where he indicated, and Pierston stood close beside her, directing her gaze to the familiar objects he had regarded thence as a boy. Her head and face – the latter thoughtful and worn enough, poor thing, to suggest a married life none too comfortable – were close to his breast, and, with a few inches further incline, would have touched it.

'And now you are the inhabitant; I the visitor,' he said. 'I am glad to see you here – so glad, Avice! You are fairly well provided for – I think I may assume that?' He looked round the room at the solid mahogany furniture, and at the modern piano and show bookcase.

'Yes, Ike left me comfortable. 'Twas he who thought of moving from my cottage to this larger house. He bought it, and I can live here as long as I choose to.'

Apart from the decline of his adoration to friendship, there seemed to be a general convergence of positions which suggested that he might make amends for the desertion of Avice the First by proposing to this Avice when a meet time should arrive. If he did not love her as he had done when she was a slim thing catching mice in his rooms in London, he could surely be content at his age with comradeship. After all she was only forty to his sixty. The feeling that he really could be thus content was so convincing that he almost believed the luxury of getting old and reposeful was coming to his restless, wandering heart at last.

'Well, you have come at last, sir,' she went on; 'and I am grateful to you. I did not like writing, and yet I wanted to be straightforward. Have you guessed at all why I wished to see you so much that I could not help sending twice to you?'

'I have tried, but cannot.'

'Try again. It is a pretty reason, which I hope you'll forgive.'

'I am sure I shan't unriddle it. But I'll say this on my own account before you tell me. I have always taken a lingering interest in you, which you must value for what it is worth. It originated, so far as it concerns you personally, with the sight of you in that cottage round the corner, nineteen or twenty years ago, when I became tenant of the castle opposite. But that was not the very beginning. The very beginning was a score of years before that, when I, a young fellow of one-and-twenty, coming home here, from London, to see my father, encountered a tender woman as like you as your double; was much attracted by her as I saw her day after day flit past this window; till I made it my business to accompany her in her walks awhile. I, as you know, was not a staunch fellow, and it all ended badly. But, at any rate you, her daughter, and I are friends.'

'Ah! there she is!' suddenly exclaimed Avice, whose attention had wanderd somewhat from his retrospective discourse. She was looking from the window towards the cliffs, where, upon the open ground quite near at hand, a slender female form was seen rambling along. 'She is out for a walk,' Avice continued. 'I wonder if she is going to call here this afternoon? She is living at the castle opposite as governess.'

'O, she's –'

'Yes. Her education was very thorough – better even than her grandmother's. I was the neglected one, and her father and myself both vowed that there should be no complaint on that score about her. We christened her Avice, to keep up the name, as you requested. I wish you could speak to her – I am sure you would like her.'

'Is that the baby?' faltered Jocelyn.

'Yes, the baby.'

The person signified, now much nearer, was a still more modernized, up-to-date edition of the two Avices of that blood with whom he had been involved more or less for the last forty years. A ladylike creature was she – almost elegant. She was altogether finer in figure than her mother or grandmother had ever been, which made her more of a woman in appearance than in years. She wore a large-disked sun-hat, with a brim like a wheel whose spokes were radiating folds of muslin lining the brim, a black margin beyond the muslin being the felloe. Beneath this brim her hair was massed low upon her brow, the colour of the thick tresses being probably, from her complexion, repeated in the irises of her large, deep eyes. Her rather nervous lips were thin and closed, so that they only appeared as a delicate red line. A changeable temperament was shown by that mouth – quick transitions from affection to aversion, from a pout to a smile.

It was Avice the Third.

Jocelyn and the second Avice continued to gaze ardently at her.

'Ah! she is not coming in now; she hasn't time,' murmured the mother, with some disappointment. 'Perhaps she means to run across in the evening.'

The tall girl, in fact, went past and on till she was out of sight. Pierston stood as in a dream. It was the very she, in all essential particulars, and with an intensification of general charm, who had kissed him forty years before. When he turned his head from the window his eyes fell again upon the intermediate Avice at his side. Before but the relic of the Well-Beloved, she had now become its empty shrine. Warm friendship, indeed, he felt for her; but whatever that might have done towards the instauration of a former dream was now hopelessly barred by the rivalry of the thing itself in the guise of a lineal successor.

TWO

❧ Misgivings On The ☙ Re-embodiment

PIERSTON HAD BEEN ABOUT TO leave, but he sat down again on being asked if he would stay and have a cup of tea. He hardly knew for a moment what he did; a dim thought that Avice – the renewed Avice – might come into the house made his reseating himself an act of spontaneity.

He forgot that twenty years earlier he had called the now Mrs Pierston an elf, a witch; and that lapse of time had probably not diminished the subtleties implied by those epithets. He did not know that she had noted every impression that her daughter had made upon him.

How he contrived to attenuate and disperse the rather tender personalities he had opened up with the new Avice's mother, Pierston

never exactly defined. Perhaps she saw more than he thought she saw –
read something in his face – knew that about his nature which he gave
her no credit for knowing. Anyhow, the conversation took the form of a
friendly gossip from that minute, his remarks being often given while
his mind was turned elsewhere.

But a chill passed through Jocelyn when there had been time for
reflection. The renewed study of his art in Rome without any counter-
balancing practical pursuit had nourished and developed his natural
responsiveness to impressions; he now felt that his old trouble, his doom
– his curse, indeed, he had sometimes called it – was come back again.
His divinity was not yet propitiated for that original sin against her
image in the person of Avice the First, and now, at the age of one-and-
sixty, he was urged on and on like the Jew Ahasuerus – or, in the phrase
of the islanders themselves, like a blind ram.

The Goddess, an abstraction to the general, was a fairly real personage
to Pierston. He had watched the marble images of her which stood in
his working-room, under all changes of light and shade – in the brighten-
ing of morning, in the blackening of eve, in moonlight, in lamplight.
Every line and curve of her body none, naturally, knew better than he;
and, though not a belief, it was, as has been stated, a formula, a superstition, that the three Avices were interpenetrated with her essence.

'And the next Avice – your daughter,' he said stumblingly; 'she is, you
say, a governess at the castle opposite?'

Mrs Pierston reaffirmed the fact, adding that the girl often slept at
home because she, her mother, was so lonely. She often thought she
would like to keep her daughter at home altogether.

'She plays that instrument, I suppose?' said Pierston, regarding the
piano.

'Yes, she plays beautifully; she had the best instruction that masters
could give her. She was educated at Sandbourne.'

'Which room does she call hers when at home?' he asked curiously.

'The little one over this.'

It had been his own. 'Strange,' he murmured.

He finished tea, and sat after tea, but the youthful Avice did not arrive.
With the Avice present he conversed as the old friend – no more. At last
it grew dusk, and Pierston could not find an excuse for staying longer.

'I hope to make the acquaintance – of your daughter,' he said in
leaving, knowing that he might have added with predestinate truth, 'of
my new tenderly-beloved.'

'I hope you will,' she answered. 'This evening she evidently has gone
for a walk instead of coming here.'

'And, by-the-bye, you have not told me what you specially wanted to
see me for?'

'Ah, no. I will put it off.'

'Very well. I don't pretend to guess.'

'I must tell you another time.'

'If it is any little business in connection with your late husband's affairs, do command me. I'll do anything I can.'

'Thank you. And I shall see you again soon?'

'Certainly. Quite soon.'

When he was gone she looked reflectively at the spot where he had been standing, and said: 'Best hold my tongue. It will work of itself, without my telling.'

Jocelyn went from the house, but as the white road passed under his feet he felt in no mood to get back to his lodgings in the town on the mainland. He lingered about upon the rugged ground for a long while, thinking of the extraordinary reproduction of the original girl in this new form he had seen, and of himself as of a foolish dreamer in being so suddenly fascinated by the renewed image in a personality not one-third of his age. As a physical fact, no doubt, the preservation of the likeness was no uncommon thing here, but it helped the dream.

Passing round the walls of the new castle he deviated from his homeward track by turning down the familiar little lane which led to the ruined castle of the Red King. It took him past the cottage in which the new Avice was born, from whose precincts he had heard her first infantine cry. Pausing he saw near the west behind him the new moon growing distinct upon the glow.

He was subject to gigantic fantasies still. In spite of himself, the sight of the new moon, as representing one who, by her so-called inconstancy, acted up to his own idea of a migratory Well-Beloved, made him feel as if his wraith in a changed sex had suddenly looked over the horizon at him. In a crowd secretly, or in solitude boldly, he had often bowed the knee three times to this sisterly divinity on her first appearance monthly, and directed a kiss towards her shining shape. The curse of his qualities (if it were not a blessing) was far from having spent itself yet.

In the other direction the castle ruins rose square and dusky against the sea. He went on towards these, around which he had played as a boy, and stood by the walls at the edge of the cliff pondering. There was no wind and but little tide, and he thought he could hear from years ago a voice that he knew. It certainly was a voice, but it came from the rocks beneath the castle ruin.

'Mrs Atway!'

A silence followed, and nobody came. The voice spoke again; 'John Stoney!'

Neither was this summons attended to. The cry continued, with more entreaty: 'William Scribben!'

The voice was that of a Pierston – there could be no doubt of it – young Avice's, surely? Something or other seemed to be detaining her down there against her will. A sloping path beneath the beetling cliff and the castle walls rising sheer from its summit, led down to the lower level whence the voice proceeded. Pierston followed the pathway, and soon beheld a girl in light clothing – the same he had seen through the window – standing upon one of the rocks, apparently unable to move. Pierston hastened across to her.

'O, thank you for coming!' she murmured with some timidity. 'I have met with an awkward mishap. I live near here, and am not frightened really. My foot has become jammed in a crevice of the rock, and I cannot get it out, try how I will. What *shall* I do?'

Jocelyn stooped and examined the cause of discomfiture. 'I think if you can take your boot off,' he said, 'your foot might slip out, leaving the boot behind.'

She tried to act upon this advice, but could not do so effectually. Pierston then experimented by slipping his hand into the crevice till he could just reach the buttons of her boot, which, however, he could not unfasten any more than she. Taking his penknife from his pocket he tried again, and cut off the buttons one by one. The boot unfastened, and out slipped the foot.

'O, how glad I am!' she cried joyfully. 'I was fearing I should have to stay here all night. How can I thank you enough?'

He was tugging to withdraw the boot, but no skill that he could exercise would move it without tearing. At last she said: 'Don't try any longer. It is not far to the house. I can walk in my stocking.'

'I'll assist you in,' he said.

She said she did not want help, nevertheless allowed him to help her on the unshod side. As they moved on she explained that she had come out through the garden door; had been standing on the boulders to look at something out at sea just discernible in the evening light as assisted by the moon, and, in jumping down, had wedged her foot as he had found it.

Whatever Pierston's years might have made him look by day, in the dusk of evening he was fairly presentable as a pleasing man of no marked antiquity, his outline differing but little from what it had been when he was half his years. He was well preserved, still upright, trimly shaven, agile in movement; wore a tightly buttoned suit which set off a naturally slight figure; in brief, he might have been of any age as he appeared to her at this moment. She talked to him with the co-equality of one who assumed him to be not far ahead of her own generation; and, as the growing darkness obscured him more and more, he adopted her assumption of his age with increasing boldness of tone.

The flippant, harmless freedom of the watering-place Miss, which Avice had plainly acquired during her sojourn at the Sandbourne school, helped Pierston greatly in this rôle of *jeune premier* which he was not unready to play. Not a word did he say about being a native of the island; still more carefully did he conceal the fact of his having courted her grandmother, and engaged himself to marry that attractive lady.

He found that she had come out upon the rocks through the same little private door from the lawn of the modern castle which had frequently afforded him egress to the same spot in years long past. Pierston accompanied her across the grounds almost to the entrance of the mansion – the place being now far better kept and planted than when he had rented it as a lonely tenant; almost, indeed, restored to the order and neatness which had characterized it when he was a boy.

Like her granny she was too inexperienced to be reserved, and during this little climb, leaning upon his arm, there was time for a great deal of confidence. When he had bidden her farewell, and she had entered, leaving him in the dark, a rush of sadness through Pierston's soul swept down all the temporary pleasure he had found in the charming girl's company. Had Mephistopheles sprung from the ground there and then with an offer to Jocelyn of restoration to youth on the usual terms of his firm, the sculptor might have consented to sell a part of himself which he felt less immediate need of than of a ruddy lip and cheek and of an unploughed brow.

But what could have been treated as a folly by outsiders was almost a sorrow for him. Why was he born with such a temperament? And this concatenated interest could hardly have arisen, even with Pierston, but for a conflux of circumstances only possible here. The three Avices, the second something like the first, the third a glorification of the first, at all events externally, were the outcome of the immemorial island customs of intermarriage and of prenuptial union, under which conditions the type of feature was almost uniform from parent to child through generations: so that, till quite latterly, to have seen one native man and woman was to have seen the whole population of that isolated rock, so nearly cut off from the mainland. His own predisposition and the sense of his early faithlessness did all the rest.

He turned gloomily away, and let himself out of the precincts. Before walking along the couple of miles of road which would conduct him to the little station on the shore, he redescended to the rocks whereon he had found her, and searched about for the fissure which had made a prisoner of this terribly belated edition of the Beloved. Kneeling down beside the spot he inserted his hand, and ultimately, by much wriggling, withdrew the pretty boot. He mused over it for a moment, put it in his pocket, and followed the stony route to the Street of Wells.

THREE

❧ The Renewed Image Burns ❧ Itself In

THERE WAS NOTHING TO HINDER Pierston in calling upon the new Avice's mother as often as he should choose, beyond the five miles of intervening railway and additional mile or two of clambering over the heights of the island. Two days later, therefore, he repeated his journey and knocked about tea-time at the widow's door.

As he had feared, the daughter was not at home. He sat down beside the old sweetheart who, having eclipsed her mother in past days, had now eclipsed herself in her child. Jocelyn produced the girl's boot from his pocket.

'Then, 'tis *you* who helped Avice out of her predicament?' said Mrs Pierston, with surprise.

'Yes, my dear friènd; and perhaps I shall ask you to help me out of mine before I have done. But never mind that now. What did she tell you about the adventure?'

Mrs Pierston was looking thoughtfully upon him. 'Well, 'tis rather strange it should have been you, sir,' she replied. She seemed to be a good deal interested. 'I thought it might have been a younger man – a much younger man.'

'It might have been as far as feelings were concerned ... Now, Avice, I'll to the point at once. Virtually I have known your daughter any number of years. When I talk to her I can anticipate every turn of her thought, every sentiment, every act, so long did I study those things in your mother and in you. Therefore I do not require to learn her; she was learnt by me in her previous existences. Now, don't be shocked: I am willing to marry her – I should be overjoyed to do it, if there would be nothing preposterous about it, or that would seem like a man making himself too much of a fool, and so degrading her in consenting. I can make her comparatively rich, as you know, and I would indulge her every whim. There is the idea, bluntly put. It would set right something in my mind that has been wrong for forty years. After my death she would have plenty of freedom and plenty of means to enjoy it.'

Mrs Isaac Pierston seemed only a little surprised; certainly not shocked.

'Well, if I didn't think you might be a bit taken with her!' she said with an arch simplicity which could hardly be called unaffected. 'Knowing the set of your mind, from my little time with you years ago, nothing you could do in this way would astonish me.'

'But you don't think badly of me for it?'

'Not at all.... By-the-bye, did you ever guess why I asked you to come? ... But never mind it now: the matter is past.... Of course, it would depend upon what Avice felt.... Perhaps she would rather marry a younger man.'

'And suppose a satisfactory younger man should not appear?'

Mrs Pierston showed in her face that she fully recognized the difference between a rich bird in hand and a young bird in the bush. She looked him curiously up and down.

'I know you would make anybody a very nice husband,' she said. 'I know that you would be nicer than many men half your age; and, though there is a great deal of difference between you and her, there have been more unequal marriages, that's true. Speaking as her mother, I can say that I shouldn't object to you, sir, for her, provided she liked you. That is where the difficulty will lie.'

'I wish you would help me to get over that difficulty,' he said gently. 'Remember, I brought back a truant husband to you twenty years ago.'

'Yes, you did,' she assented; 'and, though I may say no great things as to happiness came of it, I've always seen that your intentions towards me were none the less noble on that account. I would do for you what I would do for no other man, and there is one reason in particular which inclines me to help you with Avice – that I should feel absolutely certain I was helping her to a kind husband.'

'Well, that would remain to be seen. I would, at any rate, try to be worthy of your opinion. Come, Avice, for old times' sake, you must help me. You never felt anything but friendship in those days, you know, and that makes it easy and proper for you to do me a good turn now.'

After a little more conversation his old friend promised that she really would do everything that lay in her power. She did not say how simple she thought him not to perceive that she had already, by writing to him, been doing everything that lay in her power; had created the feeling which prompted his entreaty. And to show her good faith in this promise she asked him to wait till later in the evening, when Avice might possibly run across to see her.

Pierston, who fancied he had won the younger Avice's interest, at least, by the part he had played upon the rocks the week before, had a dread of encountering her in full light till he should have advanced a little further in her regard. He accordingly was perplexed at this proposal, and, seeing his hesitation, Mrs Pierston suggested that they should walk together in the direction whence Avice would come, if she came at all.

He welcomed the idea, and in a few minutes they started, strolling along under the now strong moonlight, and when they reached the gates of Sylvania Castle turning back again towards the house. After two or three such walks up and down the gate of the castle grounds clicked, and a form came forth which proved to be the expected one.

As soon as they met the girl recognized in her mother's companion the gentleman who had helped her on the shore; and she seemed really glad to find that her chivalrous assistant was claimed by her parent as an old friend. She remembered hearing at divers times about this worthy London man of talent and position, whose ancestry were people of her own isle, and possibly, from the name, of a common stock with her own.

'And you have actually lived in Sylvania Castle yourself, Mr Pierston?' asked Avice the daughter, with her innocent young voice. 'Was it long ago?'

'Yes, it was some time ago,' replied the sculptor, with a sinking at his heart lest she should ask how long.

'It must have been when I was away – or when I was very little?'

'I don't think you were away.'

'But I don't think I could have been here?'

'No, perhaps you couldn't have been here.'

'I think she was hiding herself in the parsley-bed,' said Avice's mother blandly.

They talked in this general way till they reached Mrs Pierston's house; but Jocelyn resisted both the widow's invitation and the desire of his own heart, and went away without entering. To risk, by visibly confronting her, the advantage that he had already gained, or fancied he had gained, with the re-incarnate Avice required more courage than he could claim in his present mood.

Such evening promenades as these were frequent during the waxing of that summer moon. On one occasion, as they were all good walkers, it was arranged that they should meet halfway between the island and the town in which Pierston had lodgings. It was impossible that by this time the pretty young governess should not have guessed the ultimate reason of these rambles to be a matrimonial intention; but she inclined to the belief that the widow rather than herself was the object of Pierston's regard; though why this educated and apparently wealthy man should be attracted by her mother – whose homeliness was apparent enough to the girl's more modern training – she could not comprehend.

They met accordingly in the middle of the Pebble-bank, Pierston coming from the mainland, and the women from the peninsular rock. Crossing the wooden bridge which connected the bank with the shore proper they moved in the direction of Henry the Eighth's Castle, on the verge of the rag-stone cliff. Like the Red King's Castle on the island, the interior was open to the sky, and when they entered and the full moon streamed down upon them over the edge of the enclosing masonry, the whole present reality faded from Jocelyn's mind under the press of memories. Neither of his companions guessed what Pierston was thinking of. It was in this very spot that he was to have met the grandmother of the girl at his side, and in which he would have met her had she chosen to keep the appointment, a meeting which might – nay, must – have changed the whole current of his life.

Instead of that, forty years had passed – forty years of severance from Avice, till a secondly renewed copy of his sweetheart had arisen to fill her place. But he, alas, was not renewed. And of all this the pretty young thing at his side knew nothing.

Taking advantage of the younger woman's retreat to view the sea through an opening of the walls, Pierston appealed to her mother in a whisper: 'Have you ever given her a hint of what my meaning is? No? Then I think you might, if you really have no objection.'

Mrs Pierston, as the widow, was far from being so coldly disposed in her own person towards her friend as in the days when he wanted to marry her. Had she now been the object of his wishes he would not have needed to ask her twice. But like a good mother she stifled all this, and said she would sound Avice there and then.

'Avice, my dear,' she said, advancing to where the girl mused in the window-gap, 'what do you think of Mr Pierston paying his addresses to you – coming courting, as I call it in my old-fashioned way. Supposing he were to, would you encourage him?'

'To me, mother?' said Avice, with an inquiring laugh. 'I thought – he meant you!'

'O no, he doesn't mean me,' said her mother hastily. 'He is nothing more than my friend.'

'I don't want any addresses,' said the daughter.

'He is a man in society, and would take you to an elegant house in London suited to your education, instead of leaving you to mope here.'

'I should like that well enough,' replied Avice carelessly.

'Then give him some encouragement.'

'I don't care enough about him to do any encouraging. It is his business, I should think, to do all.'

She spoke in her lightest vein; but the result was that when Pierston, who had discreetly withdrawn, returned to them, she walked docilely, though perhaps gloomily, beside him, her mother dropping to the rear. They came to a rugged descent, and Pierston took her hand to help her. She allowed him to retain it when they arrived on level ground.

Altogether it was not an unsuccessful evening for the man with the unanchored heart, though possibly initial success meant worse for him in the long run than initial failure. There was nothing marvellous in the fact of her tractability thus far. In his modern dress and style, under the rays of the moon, he looked a very presentable gentleman indeed, while his knowledge of art and his travelled manners were not without their attractions for a girl who with one hand touched the educated middle-class and with the other the rude and simple inhabitants of the isle. Her intensely modern sympathies were quickened by her peculiar outlook.

Pierston would have regarded his interest in her as over-much selfish if there had not existed a redeeming quality in the substratum of old pathetic memory by which such love had been created – which still permeated it, rendering it the tenderest, most anxious, most protective instinct he had ever known. It may have had in its composition too much of the boyish fervour that had characterized such affection when he was cherry-cheeked, and light in the foot as a girl; but, if it was all this feeling of youth, it was more.

Mrs Pierston, in fearing to be frank, lest she might seem to be angling for his fortune, did not fully divine his cheerful readiness to offer it, if by so doing he could make amends for his infidelity to her family forty years back in the past. Time had not made him mercenary, and it had quenched his ambitions; and though his wish to wed Avice was not entirely a wish to enrich her, the knowledge that she would be enriched beyond anything that she could have anticipated was what allowed him to indulge his love.

He was not exactly old he said to himself the next morning as he beheld his face in the glass. And he looked considerably younger than he was. But there was history in his face – distinct chapters of it; his brow was not that blank page it once had been. He knew the origin of that line in his forehead; it had been traced in the course of a month or two by past troubles. He remembered the coming of this pale wiry hair; it had been brought by the illness in Rome, when he had wished each night that he might never wake again. This wrinkled corner, that drawn bit of skin, they had resulted from those months of despondency when all seemed going against his art, his strength, his happiness. 'You cannot live your life and keep it, Jocelyn,' he said. Time was against him and love, and time would probably win.

'When I went away from the first Avice,' he continued with whimsical misery, 'I had a presentiment that I should ache for it some day. And I am aching – have ached ever since this jade of an Ideal learnt the unconscionable trick of inhabiting one image only.'

Upon the whole he was not without a bodement that it would be folly to press on.

FOUR

❦ A Dash For The Last Incarnation ❧

THIS DESULTORY COURTSHIP OF A young girl which had been brought
about by her mother's contrivance was interrupted by the appearance of
Somers and his wife and family on the Budmouth Esplanade. Alfred
Somers, once the youthful, picturesque as his own paintings, was now a
middle-aged family man with spectacles – spectacles worn, too, with the
single object of seeing through them – and a row of daughters tailing off
to infancy, who at present added appreciably to the income of the bath-
ing-machine women established along the sands.

Mrs Somers – once the intellectual, emancipated Mrs Pine-Avon – had
now retrograded to the petty and timid mental position of her mother
and grandmother, giving sharp, strict regard to the current literature and
art that reached the innocent presence of her long perspective of girls,
with the view of hiding every skull and skeleton of life from their dear
eyes. She was another illustration of the rule that succeeding generations
of women are seldom marked by cumulative progress, their advance as
girls being lost in their recession as matrons; so that they move up and
down the stream of intellectual development like flotsam in a tidal estu-
ary. And this perhaps not by reason of their faults as individuals, but of
their misfortune as child-rearers.

The landscape-painter, now an Academician like Pierston himself –
rather popular than distinguished – had given up that peculiar and
personal taste in subjects which had marked him in times past, executing
instead many pleasing aspects of nature addressed to the furnishing
householder through the middling critic, and really very good of their
kind. In this way he received many large cheques from persons of wealth
in England and America, out of which he built himself a sumptuous
studio and an awkward house around it, and paid for the education of
the growing maidens.

The vision of Somers's humble position as jackal to this lion of a family
and house and studio and social reputation – Somers, to whom strange
conceits and wild imaginings were departed joys never to return – led
Pierston, as the painter's contemporary, to feel that he ought to be one
of the bygones likewise, and to put on an air of unromantic bufferism.
He refrained from entering Avice's peninsula for the whole fortnight of
Somers's stay in the neighbouring town, although its grey poetical outline

– 'throned along the sea' – greeted his eyes every morn and eve across the roadstead.

When the painter and his family had gone back from their bathing holiday, he thought that he, too, would leave the neighbourhood. To do so, however, without wishing at least the elder Avice good-bye would be unfriendly, considering the extent of their acquaintance. One evening, knowing this time of day to suit her best, he took the few-minutes' journey to the rock along the thin connecting string of junction, and arrived at Mrs Pierston's door just after dark.

A light shone from an upper chamber. On asking for his widowed acquaintance he was informed that she was ill, seriously, though not dangerously. While learning that her daughter was with her, and further particulars, and doubting if he should go in, a message was sent down to ask him to enter. His voice had been heard, and Mrs Pierston would like to see him.

He could not with any humanity refuse, but there flashed across his mind the recollection that Avice the youngest had never yet really seen him, had seen nothing more of him than an outline, which might have appertained as easily to a man thirty years his junior as to himself, and a countenance so renovated by faint moonlight as fairly to correspond. It was with misgiving, therefore, that the sculptor ascended the staircase and entered the little upper sitting-room now arranged as a sick-chamber.

Mrs Pierston reclined on a sofa, her face emaciated to a surprising thinness for the comparatively short interval since her attack. 'Come in, sir,' she said, as soon as she saw him, holding out her hand. 'Don't let me frighten you.'

Avice was seated beside her, reading. The girl jumped up, hardly seeming to recognize him. 'O! it's Mr Pierston,' she said in a moment, adding quickly, with evident surprise and off her guard: 'I thought Mr Pierston was – '

What she had thought he was did not pass her lips, and it remained a riddle for Jocelyn until a new departure in her manner towards him showed that the words 'much younger' would have accurately ended the sentence. Had Pierston not now confronted her anew, he might have endured philosophically her changed opinion of him. But he was seeing her again, and a rooted feeling was revived.

Pierston now learnt for the first time that the widow had been visited by sudden attacks of this sort not infrequently of late years. They were said to be due to angina pectoris, the latter paroxysms having been the most severe. She was at the present moment out of pain, though weak, exhausted, and nervous. She would not, however, converse about herself, but took advantage of her daughter's absence from the room to broach the subject most in her thoughts.

No compunctions had stirred her as they had her visitor on the expediency of his suit in view of his years. Her fever of anxiety lest after all he should not come to see Avice again had been not without an effect upon her health; and it made her more candid than she had intended to be.

'Troubles and sickness raise all sorts of fears, Mr Pierston,' she said. 'What I felt only a wish for, when you first named it, I have hoped for a good deal since; and I have been so anxious that – that it should come to something! I am glad indeed that you are come.'

'My wanting to marry Avice, you mean, dear Mrs Pierston?'

'Yes – that's it. I wonder if you are still in the same mind? You are? Then I wish something could be done – to make her agree to it – so as to get it settled. I dread otherwise what will become of her. She is not a practical girl as I was – she would hardly like now to settle down as an islander's wife; and to leave her living here alone would trouble me.'

'Nothing will happen to you yet, I hope, my dear old friend.'

'Well, it is a risky complaint; and the attacks, when they come, are so agonizing that to endure them I ought to get rid of all outside anxieties, folk say. Now – do you want her, sir?'

'With all my soul! But she doesn't want me.'

'I don't think she is so against you as you imagine. I fancy if it were put to her plainly, now I am in this state, it might be done.'

They lapsed into conversation on the early days of their acquaintance, until Mrs Pierston's daughter re-entered the room.

'Avice,' said her mother, when the girl had been with them a few minutes. 'About this matter that I have talked over with you so many times since my attack. Here is Mr Pierston, and he wishes to be your husband. He is much older than you; but, in spite of it, that you will ever get a better husband I don't believe. Now, will you take him, seeing the state I am in, and how naturally anxious I am to see you settled before I die?'

'But you won't die, mother! You are getting better!'

'Just for the present only. Come, he is a good man and a clever man, and a rich man. I want you, O so much, to be his wife! I can say no more.'

Avice looked appealingly at the sculptor, and then on the floor. 'Does he really wish me to?' she asked almost inaudibly, turning as she spoke to Pierston. 'He has never quite said so to me.'

'My dear one, how can you doubt it?' said Jocelyn quickly. 'But I won't press you to marry me as a favour, against your feelings.'

'I thought Mr Pierston was younger!' she murmured to her mother.

'That counts for little, when you think how much there is on the other side. Think of our position, and of his – a sculptor, with a mansion, and a studio full of busts and statues that I have dusted in my time, and of the beautiful studies you would be able to take up. Surely the life would just suit you? Your expensive education is wasted down here!'

Avice did not care to argue. She was outwardly gentle as her grandmother had been, and it seemed just a question with her of whether she must or must not. 'Very well – I feel I ought to agree to marry him, since you tell me to,' she answered quietly, after some thought. 'I see that it would be a wise thing to do, and that you wish it, and that Mr Pierston really does – like me. So – so that – '

Pierston was not backward at this critical juncture, despite unpleasant sensations. But it was the historic ingredient in this genealogical passion – if its continuity through three generations may be so described – which appealed to his perseverance at the expense of his wisdom. The mother was holding the daughter's hand; she took Pierston's, and laid Avice's in it.

No more was said in argument, and the thing was regarded as determined. Afterwards a noise was heard upon the window-panes, as of fine sand thrown; and, lifting the blind, Pierston saw that the distant lightship winked with a bleared and indistinct eye. A drizzling rain had come on with the dark, and it was striking the window in handfuls. He had intended to walk the two miles back to the station, but it meant a drenching to do it now. He waited and had supper; and, finding the weather no better, accepted Mrs Pierston's invitation to stay over the night.

Thus it fell out that again he lodged in the house he had been accustomed to live in as a boy, before his father had made his fortune, and before his own name had been heard of outside the boundaries of the isle.

He slept but little, and in the first movement of the dawn sat up in bed. Why should he ever live in London or any other fashionable city if this plan of marriage could be carried out? Surely, with this young wife, the island would be the best place for him. It might be possible to rent Sylvania Castle as he had formerly done – better still to buy it. If life could offer him anything worth having it would be a home with Avice there on his native cliffs to the end of his days.

As he sat thus thinking, and the daylight increased, he discerned, a short distance before him, a movement of something ghostly. His position was facing the window, and he found that by chance the looking-glass had swung itself vertical, so that what he saw was his own shape. The recognition startled him. The person he appeared was too grievously far, chronologically, in advance of the person he felt himself to be. Pierston did not care to regard the figure confronting him so mockingly. Its voice seemed to say 'There's tragedy hanging on to this!' But the question of age being pertinent he could not give the spectre up, and ultimately got

616

out of bed under the weird fascination of the reflection. Whether he had overwalked himself lately, or what he had done, he knew not; but never had he seemed so aged by a score of years as he was represented in the glass in that cold grey morning light. While his soul was what it was, why should he have been encumbered with that withering carcase, without the ability to shift it off for another, as his ideal Beloved had so frequently done?

By reason of her mother's illness Avice was now living in the house, and, on going downstairs, he found that they were to breakfast *en tête-à-tête.* She was not then in the room, but she entered in the course of a few minutes. Pierston had already heard that the widow felt better this morning, and elated by the prospect of sitting with Avice at this meal he went forward to her joyously. As soon as she saw him in the full stroke of day from the window she started; and he then remembered that it was their first meeting under the solar rays.

She was so overcome that she turned and left the room as if she had forgotten something; when she re-entered she was visibly pale. She recovered herself, and apologized. She had been sitting up the night before the last, she said, and was not quite so well as usual.

There may have been some truth in this; but Pierston could not get over that first scared look of hers. It was enough to give daytime stability to his night views of a possible tragedy lurking in this wedding project. He determined that, at any cost to his heart, there should be no misapprehension about him from this moment.

'Miss Pierston,' he said as they sat down, 'since it is well you should know all the truth before we go any further, that there may be no awkward discoveries afterwards, I am going to tell you something about myself – if you are not too distressed to hear it?'

'No – let me hear it.'

'I was once the lover of your mother, and wanted to marry her; only she wouldn't, or rather couldn't, marry me.'

'O how strange!' said the girl, looking from him to the breakfast things, and from the breakfast things to him. 'Mother has never told me that. Yet of course, you might have been. I mean, you are old enough.'

He took the remark as a satire she had not intended. 'O yes – quite old enough,' he said grimly. 'Almost too old.'

'Too old for mother? How's that?'

'Because I belonged to your grandmother.'

'No? How can that be?'

'I was her lover likewise. I should have married her if I had gone straight on instead of round the corner.'

'But you couldn't have been, Mr Pierston! You are not old enough? Why, how old are you? – you have never told me.'

'I am very old.'

'My mother's, and my grandmother's,' said she, looking at him no longer as at a possible husband, but as a strange fossilized relic in human form. Pierston saw it, but meaning to give up the game he did not care to spare himself.

'Your mother's and your grandmother's young man,' he repeated.

'And were you my great-grandmother's too?' she asked, with an expectant interest in his case as a drama that overcame her personal considerations for a moment.

'No – not your great-grandmother's. Your imagination beats even my confessions! . . . But I am *very* old, as you see.'

'I did not know it!' said she in an appalled murmur. 'You do not look so; and I thought that what you looked you were.'

'And you – you are very young,' he continued.

A stillness followed, during which she sat in a troubled constraint, regarding him now and then with something in her open eyes and large pupils that might have been sympathy or nervousness. Pierston ate scarce any breakfast, and rising abruptly from the table said he would take a walk on the cliffs as the morning was fine.

He did so, proceeding along the north-east heights for nearly a mile. He had virtually given Avice up, but not formally. His intention had been to go back to the house in half-an-hour and pay a morning visit to the invalid; but by not returning the plans of the previous evening might be allowed to lapse silently, as mere *pourparlers* that had come to nothing in the face of Avice's want of love for him. Pierston accordingly went straight along, and in the course of an hour was at his Budmouth lodgings.

Nothing occurred till the evening to inform him how his absence had been taken. Then a note arrived from Mrs Pierston; it was written in pencil, evidently as she lay.

'I am alarmed,' she said, 'at your going so suddenly. Avice seems to think she has offended you. She did not mean to do that. I am sure. It makes me dreadfully anxious! Will you send a line? Surely you will not desert us now – my heart is so set on my child's welfare!'

'Desert you I won't,' said Jocelyn. 'It is too much like the original case. But I must let her desert me!'

On his return, with no other object than that of wishing Mrs Pierston good-bye, he found her painfully agitated. She clasped his hand and wetted it with her tears.

'O don't be offended with her!' she cried. 'She's young. We are one people – don't marry a kimberlin! It will break my heart if you forsake her now! Avice!'

The girl came. 'My manner was hasty and thoughtless this morning,'

618

she said in a low voice. 'Please pardon me. I wish to abide by my promise.'

Her mother, still tearful, again joined their hands; and the engagement stood as before.

Pierston went back to Budmouth, but dimly seeing how curiously, through his being a rich suitor, ideas of beneficence and reparation were retaining him in the course arranged by her mother, and urged by his own desire in the face of his understanding.

FIVE

❦ On The Verge Of Possession ❧

IN ANTICIPATION OF HIS MARRIAGE Pierston had taken a new red house of the approved Kensington pattern, with a new studio at the back as large as a mediæval barn. Hither, in collusion with the elder Avice – whose health had mended somewhat – he invited mother and daughter to spend a week or two with him, thinking thereby to exercise on the latter's imagination an influence which was not practicable while he was a guest at their house; and by interesting his betrothed in the fitting and furnishing of this residence to create in her an ambition to be its mistress.

It was a pleasant, reposeful time to be in town. There was nobody to interrupt them in their proceedings, and, it being out of the season, the largest tradesmen were as attentive to their wants as if those firms had never before been honoured with a single customer whom they really liked. Pierston and his guests, almost equally inexperienced – for the sculptor had nearly forgotten what knowledge of householding he had acquired earlier in life – could consider and practise thoroughly a species of skeleton-drill in receiving visitors when the pair should announce themselves as married and at home in the coming winter season.

Avice was charming, even if a little cold. He congratulated himself yet again that time should have reserved for him this final chance for one of the line. She was somewhat like her mother, whom he had loved in the flesh, but she had the soul of her grandmother, whom he had loved in the spirit – and, for that matter, loved now. Only one criticism had he to pass upon his choice: though in outward semblance her grandam idealized, she had not the first Avice's candour, but rather her mother's closeness. He never knew exactly what she was thinking and feeling. Yet he seemed to have such prescriptive rights in women of her blood that her occasional want of confidence did not deeply trouble him.

It was one of those ripe and mellow afternoons that sometimes colour London with their golden light at this time of the year, and produce those marvellous sunset effects which, if they were not known to be made up of kitchen coal-smoke and animal exhalations, would be rapturously applauded. Behind the perpendicular, oblique, zigzagged, and curved zinc 'tall-boys,' that formed a grey pattern not unlike early Gothic numerals against the sky, the men and women on the tops of the omnibuses saw an irradiation of topaz hues, darkened here and there into richest russet.

There had been a sharp shower during the afternoon, and Pierston – who had to take care of himself – had worn a pair of goloshes on his short walk in the street. He noiselessly entered the studio, inside which some gleams of the same mellow light had managed to creep, and where he guessed he should find his prospective wife and mother-in-law awaiting him with tea. But only Avice was there, seated beside the teapot of brown delf, which, as artists, they affected, her back being toward him. She was holding her handkerchief to her eyes, and he saw that she was weeping silently.

In another moment he perceived that she was weeping over a book. By this time she had heard him, and came forward. He made it appear that he had not noticed her distress, and they discussed some arrangements of furniture. When he had taken a cup of tea she went away, leaving the book behind her.

Pierston took it up. The volume was an old schoolbook; Stièvenard's 'Lectures Françaises,' with her name in it as a pupil at Sandbourne High School, and datemarkings denoting lessons taken at a comparatively recent time, for Avice had been but a novice as governess when he discovered her.

For a school-girl – which she virtually was – to weep over a schoolbook was strange. Could she have been affected by some subject in the readings? Impossible. Pierston fell to thinking, and zest died for the process of furnishing, which he had undertaken so gaily. Somehow, the bloom was again disappearing from his approaching marriage. Yet he loved Avice more and more tenderly; he feared sometimes that in the solicitousness of his affection he was spoiling her by indulging her every whim.

He looked round the large and ambitious apartment, now becoming clouded with shades, out of which the white and cadaverous countenances of his studies, casts, and other lumber peered meditatively at him, as if they were saying, 'What are you going to do now, old boy?' They had never looked like that while standing in his past homely workshop, where all the real labours of his life had been carried out. What should a man of his age, who had not for years done anything to speak of – certainly not to add to his reputation as an artist – want with a new place like this? It was all because of the elect lady, and she apparently did not want him.

Pierston did not observe anything further in Avice to cause him misgiving till one dinner-time, a week later, towards the end of the visit. Then, as he sat himself between her and her mother at their limited table, he was struck with her nervousness, and was tempted to say, 'Why are you troubled, my little dearest?' in tones which disclosed that he was as troubled as she.

'Am I troubled?' she said with a start, turning her gentle hazel eyes upon him. 'Yes, I suppose I am. It is because I have received a letter – from an old friend.'

'You didn't show it to me,' said her mother.

'No – I tore it up.'

'Why?'

'It was not necessary to keep it, so I destroyed it.'

Mrs Pierston did not press her further on the subject, and Avice showed no disposition to continue it. They retired rather early, as they always did, but Pierston remained pacing about his studio a long while, musing on many things, not the least being the perception that to wed a woman may be by no means the same thing as to be united with her. The 'old friend' of Avice's remark had sounded very much like 'lover.' Otherwise why should the letter have so greatly disturbed her?

There seemed to be something uncanny, after all, about London, in its relation to his contemplated marriage. When she had first come up she was easier with him than now. And yet his bringing her there had helped his cause; the house had decidedly impressed her – almost overawed her, and though he owned that by no law of nature or reason had her mother or himself any right to urge on Avice partnership with him against her inclination, he resolved to make the most of having her under his influence by getting the wedding details settled before she and her mother left.

The next morning he proceeded to do this. When he encountered Avice there was a trace of apprehension on her face; but he set that down to a fear that she had offended him the night before by her taciturnity. Directly he requested her mother, in Avice's presence, to get her to fix the day quite early, Mrs Pierston became brighter and brisker. She, too, plainly had doubts about the wisdom of delay, and turning to her daughter said, 'Now, my dear, do you hear?'

It was ultimately agreed that the widow and her daughter should go back in a day or two, to await Pierston's arrival on the wedding-eve, immediately after their return.

In pursuance of the arrangement Pierston found himself on the south shore of England in the gloom of the aforesaid evening, the isle, as he looked across at it with his approach, being just discernible as a moping countenance, a creature sullen with a sense that he was about to withdraw from its keeping the rarest object it had ever owned. He had come alone, not to embarrass them, and had intended to halt a couple of hours in the neighbouring seaport to give some orders relating to the wedding, but the little railway train being in waiting to take him on, he proceeded with a natural impatience, resolving to do his business here by messenger from the isle.

He passed the ruins of the Tudor castle and the long featureless rib of grinding pebbles that screened off the outer sea, which could be heard lifting and dipping rhythmically in the wide vagueness of the Bay. At the under-hill island townlet of the Wells there were no flys, and leaving his things to be brought on, as he often did, he climbed the eminence on foot.

Half-way up the steepest part of the pass he saw in the dusk a figure pausing – the single person on the incline. Though it was too dark to identify faces, Pierston gathered from the way in which the halting stranger was supporting himself by the handrail, which here bordered the road to assist climbers, that the person was exhausted.

'Anything the matter?' he said.

'O no – not much,' was returned by the other. 'But it is steep just here.'

The accent was not quite that of an Englishman, and struck him as hailing from one of the Channel Islands. 'Can't I help you up to the top?' he said, for the voice, though that of a young man, seemed faint and shaken.

'No, thank you. I have been ill; but I thought I was all right again; and as the night was fine I walked into the island by the road. It turned out to be rather too much for me, as there is some weakness left still; and this stiff incline brought it out.'

'Naturally. You'd better take hold of my arm – at any rate to the brow here.'

Thus pressed the stranger did so, and they went on towards the ridge, till, reaching the lime-kiln standing there the stranger abandoned his hold, saying: 'Thank you for your assistance, sir. Good-night.'

'I don't think I recognize your voice as a native's?'

'No, it is not. I am a Jersey man. Good-night, sir.'

'Good-night, if you are sure you can get on. Here, take this stick – it is no use to me.' Saying which, Pierston put his walking-stick into the young man's hand.

'Thank you again. I shall be quite recovered when I have rested a minute or two. Don't let me detain you, please.'

The stranger as he spoke turned his face towards the south, where the Beal light had just come into view, and stood regarding it with an obstinate fixity. As he evidently wished to be left to himself Jocelyn went on, and troubled no more about him, though the desire of the young man to be rid of his company, after accepting his walking-stick and his arm, had come with a suddenness that was almost emotional; and impressionable as Jocelyn was, no less now than in youth, he was saddened for a minute by the sense that there were people in the world who did not like even his sympathy.

However, a pleasure which obliterated all this arose when Pierston drew near to the house that was likely to be his dear home on all future visits to the isle, perhaps even his permanent home as he grew older and the associations of his youth re-asserted themselves. It had been, too, his father's house, the house in which he was born, and he amused his fancy with plans for its enlargement under the supervision of Avice and himself. It was a still greater pleasure to behold a tall and shapely figure standing against the light of the open door and presumably awaiting him.

Avice, who it was, gave a little jump when she recognized him, but dutifully allowed him to kiss her when he reached her side; though her nervousness was only too apparent, and was like a child's towards a parent who may prove stern.

'How dear of you to guess that I might come on at once instead of later!' says Jocelyn. 'Well, if I had stayed in the town to go to the shops and so on, I could not have got here till the last train. How is mother? – our mother, as I shall call her soon.'

Avice said that her mother had not been so well – she feared not nearly so well since her return from London, so that she was obliged to keep her room. The visit had perhaps been too much for her. 'But she will not acknowledge that she is much weaker, because she will not disturb my happiness.'

Jocelyn was in a mood to let trifles of manner pass, and he took no notice of the effort which had accompanied the last word. They went upstairs to Mrs Pierston, whose obvious relief and thankfulness at sight of him was grateful to her visitor.

'I am so, O so glad you are come!' she said huskily, as she held out her thin hand and stifled a sob. 'I have been so – '

She could get no further for a moment, and Avice turned away weeping, and abruptly left the room.

'I have so set my heart on this,' Mrs Pierston went on, 'that I have not been able to sleep of late, for I have feared I might drop off suddenly before she is yours, and lose the comfort of seeing you actually united. Your being so kind to me in old times has made me so sure that she will find a good husband in you, that I am over anxious, I know. Indeed, I have not liked to let her know quite how anxious I am.'

Thus they talked till Jocelyn bade her good-night, it being noticeable that Mrs Pierston, chastened by her illnesses, maintained no longer any reserve on her gladness to acquire him as her son-in-law; and her feelings destroyed any remaining scruples he might have had from perceiving that Avice's consent was rather an obedience than a desire. As he went downstairs, and found Avice awaiting his descent, he wondered if anything had occurred here during his absence to give Mrs Pierston new uneasiness about the marriage, but it was an inquiry he could not address to a girl whose actions could alone be the cause of such uneasiness.

He looked round for her as he supped, but though she had come into the room with him she was not there now. He remembered her telling him that she had had supper with her mother, and Jocelyn sat on quietly musing and sipping his wine for something near half-an-hour. Wondering then for the first time what had become of her, he rose and went to the door. Avice was quite near him after all – only standing at the front door as she had been doing when he came, looking into the light of the full moon, which had risen since his arrival. His sudden opening of the dining-room door seemed to agitate her.

'What is it, dear?' he asked.

'As mother is much better and doesn't want me, I ought to go and see somebody I promised to take a parcel to – I feel I ought. And yet, as you have just come to see me – I suppose you don't approve of my going out while you are here?'

'Who is the person?'

'Somebody down that way,' she said indefinitely. 'It is not very far off. I am not afraid – I go out often by myself at night hereabout.'

He reassured her good-humouredly. 'If you really wish to go, my dear, of course I don't object. I have no authority to do that till to-morrow, and you know that if I had it I shouldn't use it.'

'O but you have! Mother being an invalid, you are in her place, apart from – to-morrow.'

'Nonsense, darling. Run across to your friend's house by all means if you want to.'

'And you'll be here when I come in?'

'No, I am going down to the inn to see if my things are brought up.'

'But hasn't mother asked you to stay here? The spare room was got ready for you. . . . Dear me, I am afraid I ought to have told you.'

'She did ask me. But I have some things coming, directed to the inn, and I had better be there. So I'll wish you goodnight, though it is not late. I will come in quite early tomorrow, to inquire how your mother is going on, and to wish you good-morning. You will be back again quickly this evening?'

'O yes.'

'And I needn't go with you for company?'

'O no, thank you. It is no distance.'

Pierston then departed, thinking how entirely her manner was that of one to whom a question of doing anything was a question of permission and not of judgment. He had no sooner gone than Avice took a parcel from a cupboard, put on her hat and cloak, and following by the way he had taken till she reached the entrance to Sylvania Castle, there stood still. She could hear Pierston's footsteps passing down East Quarriers to the inn; but she went no further in that direction. Turning into the lane on the right, of which mention has so often been made, she went quickly past the last cottage, and having entered the gorge beyond she clambered into the ruin of the Red King's or Bow-and-Arrow Castle, standing as a square black mass against the moonlit, indefinite sea.

SIX

❦ The Well-Beloved Is – Where? ❧

MRS PIERSTON PASSED A RESTLESS night, but this she let nobody know; nor, what was painfully evident to herself, that her prostration was increased by anxiety and suspense about the wedding on which she had too much set her heart.

During the very brief space in which she dozed Avice came into her room. As it was not infrequent for her daughter to look in upon her thus she took little notice, merely saying to assure the girl: 'I am better, dear. Don't come in again. Get to sleep yourself.'

The mother, however, went thinking anew. She had no apprehensions about this marriage. She felt perfectly sure that it was the best thing she could do for her girl. Not a young woman on the island but was envying Avice at that moment; for Jocelyn was absurdly young for three score, a good-looking man, one whose history was generally know here; as also were the exact figures of the fortune he had inherited from his father, and the social standing he could claim – a standing, however, which that fortune would not have been large enough to procure unassisted by his reputation in his art.

But Avice had been weak enough, as her mother knew, to indulge in fancies for local youths from time to time, and Mrs Pierston could not help congratulating herself that her daughter had been so docile in the circumstances. Yet to every one except, perhaps, Avice herself, Jocelyn was the most romantic of lovers. Indeed was there ever such a romance as that man embodied in his relations to her house? Rejecting the first Avice, the second had rejected him, and to rally to the third with final achievement was an artistic and tender finish to which it was ungrateful in anybody to be blind.

The widow thought that the second Avice might probably not have rejected Pierston on that occasion in the London studio so many years ago if destiny had not arranged that she should have been secretly united to another when the proposing moment came.

But what had come was best. 'My God,' she said at times that night, 'to think my aim in writing to him should be fulfilling itself like this!'

When all was right and done, what a success upon the whole her life would have been. She who had begun her career as a cottage-girl, a small quarry-owner's daughter, had sunk so low as to the position of laundress, had engaged in various menial occupations, had made an unhappy marriage for love which had, however, in the long run, thanks to Jocelyn's management, much improved her position, was at last to see her daughter secure what she herself had just missed securing, and established in a home of affluence and refinement.

Thus the sick woman excited herself as the hours went on. At last, in her tenseness it seemed to her that the time had already come at which the household was stirring, and she fancied she heard conversation in her daughter's room. But she found that it was only five o'clock, and not yet daylight. Her state was such that she could see the hangings of the bed tremble with her tremors. She had declared overnight that she did not require any one to sit up with her, but she now rang a little hand-bell, and in a few minutes a nurse appeared; Ruth Stockwool, an island woman and neighbour, whom Mrs Pierston knew well, and who knew all Mrs Pierston's history.

'I am so nervous that I can't stay by myself,' said the widow. 'And I thought I heard Becky dressing Miss Avice in her wedding things.'

'O no – not yet, ma'am. There's nobody up. But I'll get you something.'

When Mrs Pierston had taken a little nourishment she went on: 'I can't help frightening myself with thoughts that she won't marry him. You see he is older than Avice.'

'Yes, he is,' said her neighbour. 'But I don't see how anything can hender the wedden now.'

'Avice, you know, had fancies; at least one fancy for another man; a young fellow of five-and-twenty. And she's been very secret and odd about it. I wish she had raved and cried and had it out; but she's been quite the other way. I know she's fond of him still.'

'What – that young Frenchman, Mr Leverre o' Sandbourne? I've heard a little of it. But I should say there wadden much between 'em.'

'I don't think there was. But I've a sort of conviction that she saw him last night. I believe it was only to bid him good-bye, and return him some books he had given her; but I wish she had never known him; he is rather an excitable, impulsive young man, and he might make mischief. He isn't a Frenchman, though he has lived in France. His father was a Jersey gentleman, and on his becoming a widower he married as his second wife a native of this very island. That's mainly why the young man is so at home in these parts.'

'Ah – now I follow 'ee. She was a Bencomb, his stepmother: I heard something about her years ago.'

'Yes; her father had the biggest stone-trade on the island at one time; but the name is forgotten here now. He retired years before I was born. However, mother used to tell me that she was a handsome young woman, who tried to catch Mr Pierston when he was a young man, and scandalized herself a bit with him. She went off abroad with her father, who had made a fortune here; but when he got over there he lost it nearly all in some way. Years after she married this Jerseyman, Mr Leverre, who had been fond of her as a girl, and she brought up his child as her own.'

Mrs Pierston paused, but as Ruth did not ask any question she presently resumed her self-relieving murmur:

'How Miss Avice got to know the young man was in this way. When Mrs Leverre's husband died she came from Jersey to live at Sandbourne; and made it her business one day to cross over to this place to make inquiries about Mr Jocelyn Pierston. As my name was Pierston she called upon me with her son, and so Avice and he got acquainted. When Avice went back to Sandbourne to the finishing school they kept up the acquaintance in secret. He taught French somewhere there, and does still, I believe.'

'Well, I hope she'll forget en. He idden good enough.'

'I hope so – I hope so. . . . Now I'll try to get a little nap.'

Ruth Stockwool went back to her room, where, finding it would not be necessary to get up for another hour, she lay down again and soon slept. Her bed was close to the staircase, from which it was divided by a lath partition only, and her consciousness either was or seemed to be aroused by light brushing touches on the outside of the partition, as of fingers feeling the way downstairs in the dark. The slight noise passed, and in a few seconds she dreamt or fancied she could hear the unfastening of the back door.

She had nearly sunk into another sound sleep when precisely the same phenomena were repeated; fingers brushing along the wall close to her head, down, downward, the soft opening of the door, its close, and silence again.

She now became clearly awake. The repetition of the process had made the whole matter a singular one. Early as it was the first sounds might have been those of the housemaid descending, though why she should have come down so stealthily and in the dark did not make itself clear. But the second performance was inexplicable. Ruth got out of bed and lifted her blind. The dawn was hardly yet pink, and the light from the sandbank was not yet extinguished. But the bushes of euonymus against the white palings of the front garden could be seen, also the light surface of the road winding away like a riband to the north entrance of Sylvania Castle, thence round to the village, the cliffs, and the Cove behind. Upon the road two dark figures could just be discerned, one a little way behind the other, but overtaking and joining the foremost as Ruth looked. After all they might be quarriers or lighthouse-keepers from the south of the island, or fishermen just landed from a night's work. There being nothing to connect them with the noises she had heard indoors she dismissed the whole subject, and went to bed again.

Jocelyn had promised to pay an early visit to ascertain the state of Mrs Pierston's health after her night's rest, her precarious condition being more obvious to him than to Avice, and making him a little anxious. Subsequent events caused him to remember that while he was dressing he casually observed two or three boatmen standing near the cliff beyond the village, and apparently watching with deep interest what seemed to be a boat far away towards the opposite shore of South Wessex. At half-past eight he came from the door of the inn and went straight to Mrs Pierston's. On approaching he discovered that a strange expression which seemed to hang about the house-front that morning was more than a fancy, the gate, door, and two windows being open, though the blinds of other windows were not drawn up, the whole lending a vacant, dazed look to the domicile, as of a person gaping in sudden stultification. Nobody answered his knock, and walking into the dining-room he found that no breakfast had been laid. His flashing thought was, 'Mrs Pierston is dead.'

While standing in the room somebody came downstairs, and Jocelyn encountered Ruth Stockwool, an open letter fluttering in her hand.

'O Mr Pierston, Mr Pierston! The Lord-a-Lord!'

'What? Mrs Pierston – '

'No, no! Miss Avice! She is gone! – yes – gone! Read ye this, sir. It was left in her bedroom, and we be fairly gallied out of our senses!'

He took the letter and confusedly beheld that it was in two hand-writings, the first section being in Avice's:

MY DEAR MOTHER, – How ever will you forgive me for what I have done! So deceitful as it seems. And yet till this night I had no idea of deceiving either you or Mr Pierston.

Last night at ten o'clock I went out, as you may have guessed, to see Mr Leverre for the last time, and to give him back his books, letters, and little presents to me. I went only a few steps – to Bow-and-Arrow Castle, where we met as we had agreed to do, since he could not call. When I reached the place I found him there waiting, but quite ill. He had been unwell at his mother's house for some days, and had been obliged to stay in bed, but he had got up on purpose to come and bid me good-bye. The over-exertion of the journey upset him, and though we stayed and stayed till twelve o'clock he felt quite unable to go back home – unable, indeed, to move more than a few yards. I had tried so hard not to love him any longer, but I loved him so now that I could not desert him and leave him out there to catch his death. So I helped him – nearly carrying him – on and on to our door, and then round to the back. Here he got a little better, and as he could not stay there, and everybody was now asleep, I helped him upstairs into the room we had prepared for Mr Pierston if he should have wanted one. I got him into bed, and then fetched some brandy and a little of your tonic. Did you see me come into your room for it, or were you asleep?

I sat by him all night. He improved slowly, and we talked over what we had better do. I felt that, though I had intended to give him up, I could not now becomingly marry any other man, and that I ought to marry him. We decided to do it at once, before anybody could hinder us. So we came down before it was light, and have gone away to get the ceremony solemnized.

Tell Mr Pierston it was not premeditated, but the result of an accident. I am sincerely sorry to have treated him with what he will think unfairness, but though I did not love him I meant to obey you and marry him. But God sent this necessity of my having to give shelter to my Love, to prevent, I think, my doing what I am now convinced would have been wrong. – Ever your loving daughter,

AVICE.

The second was in a man's hand:

DEAR MOTHER (as you will soon be to me), – Avice has clearly explained above how it happened that I have not been able to give her up to Mr Pierston. I think I should have died if I had not accepted the hospitality of a room in your house this night, and your daughter's tender nursing through the dark dreary hours. We love each other beyond expression, and it is obvious that, if we are human, we cannot resist marrying now, in spite of friends' wishes. Will you please send the note lying beside this to my mother. It is merely to explain what I have done. – Yours with warmest regard,

HENRI LEVERRE.

Jocelyn turned away and looked out of the window.

'Mrs Pierston thought she heard some talking in the night, but of course she put it down to fancy. And she remembers Miss Avice coming into her room at one o'clock in the morning, and going to the table where the medicine was standing. A sly girl – all the time her young man within a yard or two, in the very room, and a using the very clean sheets that you, sir, were to have used! They are our best linen ones, got up beautiful, and a kept wi' rosemary. Really, sir, one would say you stayed out o' your chammer o' purpose to oblige the young man with a bed!'

'Don't blame them, don't blame them!' said Jocelyn in an even and characterless voice. 'Don't blame her, particularly. She didn't make the circumstances. I did. . . . It was how I served her grandmother. . . . Well, she's gone! You needn't make a mystery of it. Tell it to all the island: say that a man came to marry a wife, and didn't find her at home. Tell everybody that she's run away. It must be known sooner or later.'

One of the servants said, after waiting a few moments: 'We shan't do that, sir.'

'O – why won't you?'

'We liked her too well, with all her faults.'

'Ah – did you,' said he; and he sighed. He perceived that the younger maids were secretly on Avice's side.

'How does her mother bear it?' Jocelyn asked. 'Is she awake?'

Mrs Pierston had hardly slept, and, having learnt the tidings inadvertently, became so distracted and incoherent as to be like a person in a delirium; till, a few moments before he arrived, all her excitement ceased, and she lay in a weak, quiet silence.

'Let me go up,' Pierston said. 'And send for the doctor.'

Passing Avice's chamber he perceived that the little bed had not been slept on. At the door of the spare room he looked in. In one corner stood a walking-stick – his own.

'Where did that come from?'

'We found it there, sir.'

'Ah yes – I gave it to him. 'Tis like me to play another's game!'

It was the last spurt of bitterness that Jocelyn let escape him. He went on towards Mrs Pierston's room, preceded by the servant.

'Mr Pierston has come, ma'am,' he heard her say to the invalid. But as the latter took no notice the woman rushed forward to the bed, 'What has happened to her, Mr Pierston? O what do it mean?'

Avice the Second was lying placidly in the position in which the nurse had left her; but no breath came from her lips, and a rigidity of feature was accompanied by the precise expression which had characterized her face when Pierston had her as a girl in his studio. He saw that it was death, though she appeared to have breathed her last only a few moments before.

Ruth Stockwool's composure deserted her. ''Tis the shock of finding Miss Avice gone that has done it!' she cried. 'She has killed her mother!'

'Don't say such a terrible thing!' exclaimed Jocelyn.

'But she ought to have obeyed her mother – a good mother as she was! How she had set her heart upon the wedding, poor soul; and we couldn't help her knowing what had happened! O how ungrateful young folk be! That girl will rue this morning's work!'

'We must get the doctor,' said Pierston, mechanically, hastening from the room.

When the local practitioner came he merely confirmed their own verdict, and thought her death had undoubtedly been hastened by the shock of the ill news upon a feeble heart, following a long strain of anxiety about the wedding. He did not consider that an inquest would be necessary.

The two shadowy figures seen through the grey gauzes of the morning by Ruth, five hours before this time, had gone on to the open place by the north entrance of Sylvania Castle, where the lane to the ruins of the old castle branched off. A listener would not have gathered that a single word passed between them. The man walked with difficulty, supported by the woman. At this spot they stopped and kissed each other a long while.

'We ought to walk all the way to Budmouth, if we wish not to be discovered,' he said sadly. 'And I can't even get across the island, even by your help, darling. It is two miles to the foot of the hill.'

She, who was trembling, tried to speak consolingly:

'If you could walk we should have to go down the Street of Wells, where perhaps somebody would know me. Now if we get below here to the Cove, can't we push off one of the little boats I saw there last night, and paddle along close to the shore till we get to the north side? Then we can walk across to the station very well. It is quite calm, and as the tide sets in that direction, it will take us along of itself, without much rowing. I've often got round in a boat that way.'

This seemed to be the only plan that offered, and abandoning the straight road they wound down the defile spanned further on by the old castle arch, and forming the original fosse of the fortress.

The stroke of their own footsteps, lightly as these fell, was flapped back to them with impertinent gratuitousness by the vertical faces of the rock, so still was everything around. A little further, and they emerged upon the open ledge of the lower tier of cliffs, to the right being the sloping pathway leading down to the secluded creek at their base – the single practicable spot of exit from or entrance to the isle on this side by a seagoing craft; once an active wharf, whence many a fine public building had sailed – including Saint Paul's Cathedral.

The timorous shadowy shapes descended the foot-way, one at least of them knowing the place so well that she found it scarcely necessary to guide herself down by touching the natural wall of stone on her right hand, as her companion did. Thus, with quick suspensive breathings they arrived at the bottom, and trod the few yards of shingle which, on the forbidding shore hereabout, could be found at this spot alone. It was so solitary as to be unvisited often for four-and-twenty hours by a living soul. Upon the confined beach were drawn up two or three fishing-lerrets, and a couple of smaller ones, beside them being a rough slipway for launching, and a boathouse of tarred boards. The two lovers united their strength to push the smallest of the boats down the slope, and floating it they scrambled in.

The girl broke the silence by asking, 'Where are the oars?'

He felt about the boat, but could find none. 'I forgot to look for the oars!' he said.

They are locked in the boathouse, I suppose. Now we can only steer and trust to the current!'

The currents here were of a complicated kind. It was true, as the girl had said, that the tide ran round to the north, but at a special moment in every flood there set in along the shore a narrow reflux contrary to the general outer flow, called 'The Southern' by the local sailors. It was produced by the peculiar curves of coast lying east and west of the Beal; these bent southward in two back streams the up-Channel flow on each side of the peninsula, which two streams united outside the Beal, and there met the direct tidal flow, the confluence of the three currents making the surface of the sea at this point to boil like a pot, even in calmest weather. The disturbed area, as is well known, is called the Race.

Thus although the outer sea was now running northward to the roadstead and the mainland of Wessex, 'The Southern' ran in full force towards the Beal and the Race beyond. It caught the lovers' hapless boat in a few moments, and, unable to row across it – mere river's width that it was – they beheld the grey rocks near them, and the grim wrinkled forehead of the isle above, sliding away northwards.

They gazed helplessly at each other, though, in the long-living faith of youth, without distinct fear. The undulations increased in magnitude, and swung them higher and lower. The boat rocked, received a smart slap of the waves now and then, and wheeled round, so that the lightship which stolidly winked at them from the quicksand, the single object which told them of their bearings, was sometimes on their right hand and sometimes on their left. Nevertheless they could always discern from it that their course, whether stemwards or sternwards, was steadily south.

A bright idea occurred to the young man. He pulled out his handkerchief and, striking a light, set it on fire. She gave him hers, and he made that flare up also. The only available fuel left was the small umbrella the girl had brought; this was also kindled in an opened state, and he held it up by the stem till it was consumed.

The lightship had loomed quite large by this time, and a few minutes after they had burnt the handkerchiefs and umbrella a coloured flame replied to them from the vessel. They flung their arms round each other.

'I knew we shouldn't be drowned!' said Avice hysterically.

'I thought we shouldn't too,' said he.

With the appearance of day a boat put off to their assistance, and they were towed towards the heavy red hulk with the large white letters on its side.

SEVEN

An Old Tabernacle In A New Aspect

THE OCTOBER DAY THICKENED INTO dusk, and Jocelyn sat musing beside the corpse of Mrs Pierston. Avice having gone away nobody knew whither, he had acted as the nearest friend of the family, and attended as well as he could to the sombre duties necessitated by her mother's decease. It was doubtful, indeed, if anybody else were in a position to do so. Of Avice the Second's two brothers, one had been drowned at sea, and the other had emigrated, while her only child besides the present Avice had died in infancy. As for her friends, she had become so absorbed in her ambitious and nearly accomplished design of marrying her daughter to Jocelyn, that she had gradually completed that estrangement between herself and the other islanders which had been begun so long ago as when, a young woman, she had herself been asked by Pierston to marry him. On her tantalizing inability to accept the honour offered, she and her husband had been set up in a matter-of-fact business in the stone trade by her patron, but that unforgettable request in the London studio had made her feel ever since a refined kinship with sculpture, and a proportionate aloofness from mere quarrying, which was, perhaps, no more than a venial weakness in Avice the Second. Her daughter's objection to Jocelyn she could never understand. To her own eye he was no older than when he had proposed to her.

As he sat darkling here the ghostly outlines of former shapes taken by his Love came round their sister the unconscious corpse, confronting him from the wall in sad array, like the pictured Trojan women beheld by Æneas on the walls of Carthage. Many of them he had idealized in bust and in figure from time to time, but it was not as such that he remembered and reanimated them now; rather was it in all their natural circumstances, weaknesses, and stains. And then as he came to himself their voices grew fainter; they had all gone off on their different careers, and he was left here alone.

The probable ridicule that would result to him from the events of the day he did not mind in itself at all. But he would fain have removed the misapprehensions on which it would be based. That, however, was impossible. Nobody would ever know the truth about him; *what* it was he had sought that had so eluded, tantalized, and escaped him; what it was that had led him such a dance, and had at last, as he believed just now in the freshness of his loss, been discovered in the girl who had left him. It was not the flesh; he had never knelt low to that. Not a woman in the world had been wrecked by him, though he had been impassioned by so many. Nobody would guess the further sentiment – the cordial loving-kindness – which had lain behind what had seemed to him the enraptured fulfilment of a pleasing destiny postponed for forty years. His attraction to the third Avice would be regarded by the world as the selfish designs of an elderly man on a maid.

His life seemed no longer a professional man's experience, but a ghost story; and he would fain have vanished from his haunts on this critical afternoon, as the rest had done. He desired to sleep away his tendencies, to make something happen which would put an end to his bondage to beauty in the ideal.

So he sat on till it was quite dark, and a light was brought. There was a chilly wind blowing outside, and the lightship on the quicksand afar looked harassed and forlorn. The haggard solitude was broken by a ring at the door.

Pierston heard a voice below, the accents of a woman. They had a ground quality of familiarity, a superficial articulation of strangeness. Only one person in all his experience had ever possessed precisely those tones; rich, as if they had once been powerful. Explanations seemed to be asked for and given, and in a minute he was informed that a lady was downstairs whom perhaps he would like to see.

'Who is the lady?' Jocelyn asked.

The servant hesitated a little. 'Mrs Leverre – the mother of the – young gentleman Miss Avice has run off with.'

'Yes – I'll see her,' said Pierston.

He covered the face of the dead Avice, and descended. 'Leverre,' he said to himself. His ears had known that name before to-day. It was the name those travelling Americans he had met in Rome gave the woman he supposed might be Marcia Bencomb.

A sudden adjusting light burst upon many familiar things at that moment. He found the visitor in the drawing-room, standing up veiled, the carriage which had brought her being in waiting at the door. By the dim light he could see nothing of her features in such circumstances.

'Mr Pierston?'

'I am Mr Pierston.'

'You represent the late Mrs Pierston?'

'I do – though I am not one of the family.'

'I know it. . . . I am Marcia – after forty years.'

'I was divining as much, Marcia. May the lines have fallen to you in pleasant places since we last met! But, of all moments of my life, why do you choose to hunt me up now?'

'Why – I am the step-mother and only relation of the young man your bride eloped with this morning.'

'I was just guessing that, too, as I came downstairs. But – '

'And I am naturally making inquiries.'

'Yes. Let us take it quietly, and shut the door.'

Marcia sat down. And he learnt that the conjunction of old things and new was no accident. What Mrs Pierston had discussed with her nurse and neighbour as vague intelligence, was now revealed to Jocelyn at first hand by Marcia herself; how, many years after their separation, and when she was left poor by the death of her impoverished father, she had become the wife of that bygone Jersey lover of hers, who wanted a tender nurse and mother for the infant left him by his first wife recently deceased; how he had died a few years later, leaving her with the boy, whom she had brought up at St Heliers and in Paris, educating him as well as she could with her limited means, till he became the French master at a school in Sandbourne; and how, a year ago, she and her son had got to know Mrs Pierston and her daughter on their visit to the island, 'to ascertain,' she added, more deliberately, 'not entirely for sentimental reasons, what had become of the man with whom I eloped in the first flush of my young womanhood, and only missed marrying by my own will.'

Pierston bowed.

'Well, that was how the acquaintance between the children began, and their passionate attachment to each other.' She detailed how Avice had induced her mother to let her take lessons in French of young Leverre, rendering their meetings easy. Marcia had never thought of hindering their intimacy, for in her recent years of affliction she had acquired a new interest in the name she had refused to take in her purse-proud young womanhood; and it was not until she knew how determined Mrs Pierston was to make her daughter Jocelyn's wife that she had objected to her son's acquaintance with Avice. But it was too late to hinder what had been begun. He had lately been ill, and she had been frightened by his not returning home the night before. The note she had received from him that day had only informed her that Avice and himself had gone to be married immediately – whither she did not know.

'What do you mean to do?' she asked.

'I do nothing: there is nothing to be done. . . . It is how I served her grandmother – one of Time's revenges.'

'Served her so for me.'

'Yes. Now she me for your son.'

Marcia paused a long while thinking that over, till arousing herself she resumed: 'But can't we inquire which way they went out of the island, or gather some particulars about them?'

'Aye – yes. We will.'

And Pierston found himself as in a dream walking beside Marcia along the road in their common quest. He discovered that almost every one of the neighbouring inhabitants knew more about the lovers than he did himself.

At the corner some men were engaged in conversation on the occurrence. It was allusive only, but knowing the dialect, Pierston and Marcia gathered its import easily. As soon as it had got light that morning one of the boats was discovered missing from the creek below, and when the flight of the lovers was made known it was inferred that they were the culprits.

Unconsciously Pierston turned in the direction of the creek, without regarding whether Marcia followed him, and though it was darker than when Avice and Leverre had descended in the morning he pursued his way down the incline till he reached the water-side.

'Is that you, Jocelyn?'

The inquiry came from Marcia. She was behind him, about half-way down.

'Yes,' he said, noticing that it was the first time she had called him by his Christian name.

'I can't see where you are, and I am afraid to follow.'

Afraid to follow. How strangely that altered his conception of her. Till this moment she had stood in his mind as the imperious, invincible Marcia of old. There was a strange pathos in this revelation. He went back and felt for her hand. 'I'll lead you down,' he said. And he did so.

They looked out upon the sea, and the lightship shining as if it had quite forgotten all about the fugitives. 'I am so uneasy,' said Marcia. 'Do you think they got safely to land?'

'Yes,' replied some one other than Jocelyn. It was a boatman smoking in the shadow of the boathouse. He informed her that they were picked up by the lightship men, and afterwards, at their request, taken across to the opposite shore, where they landed, proceeding thence on foot to the nearest railway station and entering the train for London. This intelligence had reached the island about an hour before.

'They'll be married to-morrow morning!' said Marcia.

'So much the better. Don't regret it, Marcia. He shall not lose by it. I have no relation in the world except some twentieth cousins in this isle, of whom her father was one, and I'll take steps at once to make her a good match for him. As for me . . . I have lived a day too long.'

EIGHT

◆ 'Alas For This Grey Shadow, ◆ Once A Man!'

IN THE MONTH OF NOVEMBER which followed, Pierston was lying dangerously ill of a fever at his house in London.

The funeral of the second Avice had happened to be on one of those drenching afternoons of the autumn, when the raw rain flies level as the missiles of the ancient inhabitants across the beaked promontory which has formed the scene of this narrative, scarcely alighting except against the upright sides of things sturdy enough to stand erect. One person only followed the corpse into the church as chief mourner, Jocelyn Pierston –

fickle lover in the brief, faithful friend in the long run. No means had been found of communicating with Avice before the interment, though the death had been advertised in the local and other papers in the hope that it might catch her eye.

So, when the pathetic procession came out of the church and moved round into the graveyard, a hired vehicle from Budmouth was seen coming at great speed along the open road from Top-o'-Hill. It stopped at the churchyard gate, and a young man and woman alighted and entered, the vehicle waiting. They glided along the path and reached Pierston's side just as the body was deposited by the grave.

He did not turn his head. He knew it was Avice, with Henri Leverre – by this time, he supposed, her husband. Her remorseful grief, though silent, seemed to impregnate the atmosphere with its heaviness. Perceiving that they had not expected him to be there Pierston edged back; and when the service was over he kept still further aloof, an act of considerateness which she seemed to appreciate.

Thus, by his own contrivance, neither Avice nor the young man held communication with Jocelyn by word or by sign. After the burial they returned as they had come.

It was supposed that his exposure that day in the bleakest churchyard in Wessex, telling upon a distracted mental and bodily condition, had thrown Pierston into the chill and fever which held him swaying for weeks between life and death shortly after his return to town. When he had passed the crisis, and began to know again that there was such a state as mental equilibrium and physical calm, he heard a whispered conversation going on around him, and the touch of footsteps on the carpet. The light in the chamber was so subdued that nothing around him could be seen with any distinctness. Two living figures were present, a nurse moving about softly, and a visitor. He discerned that the latter was feminine, and for the time this was all.

He was recalled to his surroundings by a voice murmuring the inquiry: 'Does the light try your eyes?'

The tones seemed familiar; they were spoken by the woman who was visiting him. He recollected them to be Marcia's, and everything that had happened before he fell ill came back to his mind.

'Are you helping to nurse me, Marcia?' he asked.

'Yes. I have come up to stay here till you are better, as you seem to have no other woman friend who cares whether you are dead or alive. I am living quite near. I am glad you have got round the corner. We have been very anxious.'

'How good you are! ... And – have you heard of the others?'

'They are married. They have been here to see you, and are very sorry. She sat by you, but you did not know her. She was broken down when she discovered her mother's death, which had never once occurred to her as being imminent. They have gone away again. I thought it best she should leave, now that you are out of danger. Now you must be quiet till I come and talk again.'

Pierston was conscious of a singular change in himself, which had been revealed by this slight discourse. He was no longer the same man that he had hitherto been. The malignant fever, or his experiences, or both, had taken away something from him, and put something else in its place.

During the next days, with further intellectual expansion, he became clearly aware of what this was. The artistic sense had left him, and he could no longer attach a definite sentiment to images of beauty recalled from the past. His appreciativeness was capable of exercising itself only on utilitarian matters, and recollection of Avice's good qualities alone had any effect on his mind; of her appearance none at all.

At first he was appalled; and then he said 'Thank God!'

Marcia, who, with something of her old absolutism, came to his house continually to inquire and give orders, and to his room to see him every afternoon, found out for herself in the course of his convalescence this strange death of the sensuous side of Jocelyn's nature. She had said that Avice was getting extraordinarily handsome, and that she did not wonder her stepson lost his heart to her – an inadvertent remark which she immediately regretted, in fear lest it should agitate him. He merely answered, however, 'Yes; I suppose she is handsome. She's more – a wise girl who will make a good housewife in time.... I wish you were not handsome, Marcia.'

'Why?'

'I don't quite know why. Well – it seems a stupid quality to me. I can't understand what it is good for any more.'

'O – I as a woman think there's good in it.'

'Is there? Then I have lost all conception of it. I don't know what has happened to me. I only know I don't regret it. Robinson Crusoe lost a day in his illness; I have lost a faculty, for which loss Heaven be praised!'

There was something pathetic in this announcement, and Marcia sighed as she said, 'Perhaps when you get strong it will come back to you.'

Pierston shook his head. It then occurred to him that never since the reappearance of Marcia had he seen her in full daylight, or without a bonnet and thick veil, which she always retained on these frequent visits, and that he had been unconsciously regarding her as the Marcia of their early time, a fancy which the small change in her voice well sustained. The stately figure, the good colour, the classical profile, the rather large handsome nose and somewhat prominent, regular teeth, the full dark eye, formed still the Marcia of his imagination; the queenly creature who had infatuated him when the first Avice was despised and her successors unknown. It was this old idea which, in his revolt from beauty, had led to his regret at her assumed handsomeness. He began wondering now how much remained of that presentation after forty years.

'Why don't you ever let me see you, Marcia?' he asked.

'O, I don't know. You mean without my bonnet? You have never asked me to, and I am obliged to wrap up my face with this wool veil because I suffer so from aches in these cold winter winds, though a thick veil is awkward for any one whose sight is not so good as it was.'

The impregnable Marcia's sight not so good as it was, and her face in the aching stage of life: these simple things came as sermons to Jocelyn.

'But certainly I will gratify your curiosity,' she resumed good-naturedly. 'It is really a compliment that you should still take that sort of interest in me.'

She had moved round from the dark side of the room to the lamp – for the daylight had gone – and she now suddenly took off the bonnet, veil and all. She stood revealed to his eyes as remarkably good-looking, considering the lapse of years.

'I am – vexed!' he said, turning his head aside impatiently. 'You are fair and five-and-thirty – not a day more. You still suggest beauty. You won't do as a chastisement, Marcia!'

'Ah, but I may! To think that you know woman no better after all this time!'

'How?'

'To be so easily deceived. Think: it is lamplight; and your sight is weak at present; and ... Well, I have no reason for being anything but candid now, God knows! So I will tell you. ... My husband was younger than myself; and he had an absurd wish to make people think he had married a young and fresh-looking woman. To fall in with his vanity I tried to look it. We were often in Paris, and I became as skilled in beautifying artifices as any *passée* wife of the Faubourg St Germain. Since his death I have kept up the practice, partly because the vice is almost ineradicable, and partly because I found that it helped me with men in bringing up his boy on small means. At this moment I am frightfully made up. But I can cure that. I'll come in to-morrow morning, if it is bright, just as I really am; you'll find that Time has not disappointed you. Remember I am as old as yourself; and I look it.'

The morrow came and with it Marcia, quite early, as she had promised. It happened to be sunny, and shutting the bedroom door she went round to the window, where she uncovered immediately, in his full view, and said, 'See if I am satisfactory now – to you who think beauty vain. The rest of me – and it is a good deal – lies on my dressing-table at home. I shall never put it on again – never!'

But she was a woman; and her lips quivered, and there was a tear in her eye, as she exposed the ruthless treatment to which she had subjected herself. The cruel morning rays – as with Jocelyn under Avice's scrutiny – showed in their full bareness, unenriched by addition, undisguised by the arts of colour and shade, the thin remains of what had once been Marcia's majestic bloom. She stood the image and superscription of Age – an old woman, pale and shrivelled, her forehead ploughed, her cheek hollow, her hair white as snow. To this the face he once kissed had been brought by the raspings, chisellings, scourgings, bakings, freezings of forty invidious years – by the thinkings of more than half a lifetime.

'I am sorry if I shock you,' she went on huskily but firmly, as he did not speak. 'But the moth frets the garment somewhat in such an interval.'

'Yes – yes! . . . Marcia, you are a brave woman. You have the courage of the great women of history. I can no longer love; but I admire you from my soul!'

'Don't say I am great. Say I have begun to be passably honest. It is more than enough.'

'Well – I'll say nothing then, more than how wonderful it is that a woman should have been able to put back the clock of Time thirty years!'

'It shames me now, Jocelyn. I shall never do it any more!'

As soon as he was strong enough he got her to take him round to his studio in a carriage. The place had been kept aired, but the shutters were shut, and they opened them themselves. He looked round upon the familiar objects – some complete and matured, the main of them seedlings, grafts, and scions of beauty, waiting for a mind to grow to perfection in.

'No – I don't like them!' he said, turning away. 'They are as ugliness to me! I don't feel a single touch of kin with or interest in any one of them whatever.'

'Jocelyn – this is sad.'

'No – not at all.' He went again towards the door. 'Now let me look round.' He looked back, Marcia remaining silent. 'The Aphrodites – how I insulted her fair form by those failures! – the Freyjas, the Nymphs and Fauns, Eves, Avices, and other innumerable Well-Beloveds – I want to see them never any more! . . . "Instead of sweet smell there shall be stink, and there shall be burning instead of beauty," said the prophet.'

And they came away. On another afternoon they went to the National Gallery, to test his taste in paintings, which had formerly been good. As she had expected, it was just the same with him there. He saw no more to move him, he declared, in the time-defying presentations of Perugino,

Titian, Sebastiano, and other statuesque creators than in the work of the pavement artist they had passed on their way.

'It is strange!' said she.

'I don't regret it. That fever has killed a faculty which has, after all, brought me my greatest sorrows, if a few little pleasures. Let us be gone.'

He was now so well advanced in convalescence that it was deemed a most desirable thing to take him down into his native air. Marcia agreed to accompany him. 'I don't see why I shouldn't,' said she. 'An old friendless woman like me, and and you an old friendless man.'

'Yes. Thank Heaven I am old at last. The curse is removed.'

It may be shortly stated here that after his departure for the isle Pierston never again saw his studio or its contents. He had been down there but a brief while when, finding his sense of beauty in art and nature absolutely extinct, he directed his agent in town to disperse the whole collection; which was done. His lease of the building was sold, and in the course of time another sculptor won admiration there from those who knew not Joseph. The next year his name figured on the retired list of Academicians.

As time went on he grew as well as one of his age could expect to be after such a blasting illness, but remained on the isle, in the only house he now possessed, a comparatively small one at the top of the Street of Wells. A growing sense of friendship which it would be foolish to interrupt led him to take a somewhat similar house for Marcia quite near, and remove her furniture thither from Sandbourne. Whenever the afternoon was fine he would call for her, and they would take a stroll together towards the Beal, or the ancient Castle, seldom going the whole way, his sciatica and her rheumatism effectually preventing them, except in the driest atmospheres. He had now changed his style of dress entirely, appearing always in a homely suit of local make, and of the fashion of thirty years before, the achievement of a tailoress at East Quarriers. He also let his iron-grey beard grow as it would, and what little hair he had left from the baldness which had followed the fever. And thus, numbering in years but two-and-sixty, he might have passed for seventy-five.

Though their early adventure as lovers had happened so long ago, its history had become known in the isle with mysterious rapidity and fulness of detail. The gossip to which its bearings on their present friendship gave rise was the subject of their conversation on one of these walks along the cliffs.

'It is extraordinary what an interest our neighbours take in our affairs,' he observed. 'They say "Those old folk ought to marry; better late than never." That's how people are – wanting to round off other people's histories in the best machine-made conventional manner.'

'Yes. They keep on about it to me, too, indirectly.'

'Do they! I believe a deputation will wait upon us some morning, requesting in the interests of match-making that we will please to get married as soon as possible.... How near we were to doing it forty years ago, only you were so independent! I thought you would have come back, and was much surprised that you didn't.'

'My independent ideas were not blameworthy in me, as an islander, though as a kimberlin young lady perhaps they would have been. There was simply no reason from an islander's point of view why I should come back, since no result threatened from our union; and I didn't. My father kept that view before me, and I bowed to his judgment.'

'And so the island ruled our destinies, though we were not on it. Yes – we are in hands not our own.... Did you ever tell your husband?'

'No.'

'Did he ever hear anything?'

'Not that I am aware.'

Calling upon her one day, he found her in a state of great discomfort. In certain gusty winds the chimneys of the little house she had taken here smoked intolerably, and one of these winds was blowing then. Her drawing-room fire could not be kept burning, and rather than let a woman who suffered from rheumatism shiver fireless he asked her to come round and lunch with him as she had often done before. As they went he thought, not for the first time, how needless it was that she should be put to this inconvenience by their occupying two houses, when one would better suit their now constant companionship, and disembarrass her of the objectionable chimneys. Moreover, by marrying Marcia, and establishing a parental relation with the young people, the rather delicate business of his making them a regular allowance would become a natural proceeding.

And so the zealous wishes of the neighbours to give a geometrical shape to their story were fulfilled almost in spite of the chief parties themselves. When he put the question to her distinctly, Marcia admitted that she had always regretted the imperious decision of her youth; and she made no ado about accepting him.

'I have no love to give, you know, Marcia,' he said. 'But such friendship as I am capable of is yours till the end.'

'It is nearly the same with me – perhaps not quite. But, like the other people, I have somehow felt, and you will understand why, that I ought to be your wife before I die.'

It chanced that a day or two before the ceremony, which was fixed to take place very shortly after the foregoing conversation, Marcia's rheumatism suddenly became acute. The attack promised, however, to be only temporary, owing to some accidental exposure of herself in making preparations for removal, and as they thought it undesirable to postpone their union for such a reason, Marcia, after being well wrapped up, was wheeled into the church in a chair.

A month thereafter, when they were sitting at breakfast one morning, Marcia exclaimed 'Well – good heavens!' while reading a letter she had just received from Avice, who was living with her husband in a house Pierston had bought for them at Sandbourne.

Jocelyn looked up.

'Why – Avice says she wants to be separated from Henri! Did you ever hear of such a thing! She's coming here about it to-day.'

'Separated? What does the child mean!' Pierston read the letter. 'Ridiculous nonsense!' he continued. 'She doesn't know what she wants. I say she shan't be separated! Tell her so, and there's an end of it. Why – how long have they been married? Not twelve months. What will she say when they have been married twenty years!'

Marcia remained reflecting. 'I think that remorseful feeling she unluckily has at times, of having disobeyed her mother, and caused her death, makes her irritable,' she murmured. 'Poor child!'

Lunch-time had hardly come when Avice arrived, looking very tearful and excited. Marcia took her into an inner room, had a conversation with her, and they came out together.

'O it's nothing,' said Marcia. 'I tell her she must go back directly she has had some luncheon.'

'Ah, that's all very well!' sobbed Avice. 'B-b-but if you had been m-married so long as I have, y-you wouldn't say go back like that.'

'What is it all about?' inquired Pierston.

'He said that if he were to die I – I – should be looking out for somebody with fair hair and grey eyes, just – just to spite him in his grave, because he's dark, and he's quite sure I don't like dark people! And then he said – But I won't be so treacherous as to tell any more about him! I wish – '

'Avice, your mother did this very thing. And she went back to her husband. Now you are to do the same. Let me see; there is a train – '

'She must have something to eat first. Sit down, dear.'

The question was settled by the arrival of Henri himself at the end of luncheon, with a very anxious and pale face. Pierston went off to a business meeting, and left the young couple to adjust their differences in their own way.

His business was, among kindred undertakings which followed the extinction of the Well-Beloved and other ideals, to advance a scheme for the closing of the old natural fountains in the Street of Wells, because of their possible contamination, and supplying the townlet with water from pipes, a scheme that was carried out at his expense, as is well known. He was also engaged in acquiring some old moss-grown, mullioned Elizabethan cottages, for the purpose of pulling them down because they were damp; which he afterwards did, and built new ones with hollow walls, and full of ventilators.

At present he is sometimes mentioned as 'the late Mr Pierston' by gourd-like young art-critics and journalists; and his productions are alluded to as those of a man not without genius, whose powers were insufficiently recognized in his lifetime.